P9-DEF-303

Dear Reader,

Welcome to my kingdom—my fictional kingdom, that is—in this special three-in-one volume containing the stories of *Cordina's Royal Family,* which were originally published in the Silhouette Intimate Moments line.

The first story in the collection, *Affaire Royale,* is a classic amnesia tale—with a twist. Because the woman who has forgotten her past is none other than Princess Gabriella of Cordina. Fortunately for the princess, she has sexy Reeve MacGee by her side to guide her through the dangers that await her.

In *Command Performance,* Eve Hamilton, friend of the royal family, returns to Cordina and finds herself sparring with the irritating, irresistible Prince Alexander. But when she learns the royal family is in danger, she must lay down her arms and join forces with Alex in order to see the family through to safety.

The Playboy Prince is just what Lady Hannah Rothchild must avoid when she goes undercover at the palace. But when Prince Bennett discovers her true identity, he realizes the lady he has fallen in love with is a force to be reckoned with.

I hope you enjoy these stories of royal romance and palace intrigue. Look for *Cordina's Crown Jewel,* featuring Princess Camilla de Cordina, a brand-new story available from Silhouette Special Edition.

All the best,

Nora Roberts

NORA ROBERTS

Cordina's Royal Family

Published by Silhouette Books

America's Publisher of Contemporary Romance

SILHOUETTE BOOKS

CORDINA'S ROYAL FAMILY

Copyright © 2002 by Harlequin Books S.A.

ISBN 0-373-48483-6

The publisher acknowledges the copyright holder of the individual works as follows:

AFFAIRE ROYALE
Copyright © 1986 by Nora Roberts

COMMAND PERFORMANCE
Copyright © 1987 by Nora Roberts

THE PLAYBOY PRINCE
Copyright © 1987 Nora Roberts

CONTENTS

CORDINA'S ROYAL FAMILY
~House of Bisset~

Armand de Cordina
m.
Elizabeth Bruebeck

Gabriella de Cordina
m.
Reeve MacGee
(AFFAIRE ROYALE)

Alexander de Cordina
m.
Eve Hamilton
(COMMAND PERFORMANCE)

Bennett de Cordina
m.
Hannah Rothchild
(THE PLAYBOY PRINCE)

AFFAIRE ROYALE

To Marianne Willman,
because she understands fairy tales

Prologue

She'd forgotten why she was running. All she knew was that she couldn't stop. If she stopped, she'd lose. It was a race where there were only two places. First and last.

Distance. Every instinct told her to keep running, keep going so that there was distance between her and…where she'd been.

She was wet, for the rain was pounding down, but she no longer jumped at the boom of thunder. Flashes of lightning didn't make her tremble. The dark wasn't what frightened her. She was long past fear of such simple things as the spread of darkness or the violence of the storm. What she feared wasn't clear any longer, only the fear itself. Fear, the only emotion she understood, crawled inside her, settling there as if she'd known nothing else. It was enough to keep her stumbling along the side of the road when her body screamed to lie down in a warm, dry place.

She didn't know where she was. She didn't know where she'd been. There was no memory of the tall, wind-whipped trees. The crash and power of the sea close by meant nothing, nor did the scent of the rain-drenched flowers she crushed underfoot as she fled along the side of a road she didn't know.

She was weeping, but unaware of it. Sobs wracked her, clawing at the fear, doubling it so that it sprinted through her in the absence of everything else. Her mind was so clouded, her legs so unsteady. It would be easy to simply curl up under one of those trees and

give up. Something pushed her on. Not just fear, not just confusion. Strength—though one wouldn't guess it to look at her,
though she herself didn't recognize it—drove her beyond endur-
ance. She wouldn't go back to where she'd been, so there was no
place to go but on.

How long she'd been running wasn't important. She'd no idea
whether it'd been one mile or ten. Rain and tears blinded her. The
lights were nearly on her before she saw them.

Panicked, like a rabbit caught in the beams, she froze. They'd
found her. They'd come after her. They. The horn blasted, tires
squealed. Submitting at last, she crumpled onto the road, unconscious.

Chapter 1

"She's coming out of it."

"Thank God."

"Sir, you must step back for a moment and let me examine her. She may just be drifting again."

Over the mists she was swimming in, she heard the voices. Hollow, distant. Fear scrambled through her. Even in her half-conscious state her breath began to catch. She hadn't escaped. But the fear wouldn't show. She promised herself that. As she came closer to the surface, she closed her hands into tight fists. The feel of her fingers against her palms gave her some sense of self and control.

Slowly she opened her eyes. Her vision ebbed, clouded, then gradually cleared. So, as she stared into the face bending over her, did the fear.

The face wasn't familiar. It wasn't one of them. She'd know, wouldn't she? Her confidence wavered a moment, but she remained still. This face was round and pleasant, with a trim, curling white beard that contrasted with the smooth, bald head. The eyes were shrewd, tired, but kind. When he took her hand in his, she didn't struggle.

"My dear," he said in a charming, low-key voice. Gently he ran a finger over her knuckles until her fingers relaxed. "You're quite safe."

She felt him take her pulse, but continued to stare into his eyes. Safe. Still cautious, she let her gaze wander away from his. Hospital. Though the room was almost elegant and quite large, she knew she was in a hospital. The room smelled strongly of flowers and antiseptics. Then she saw the man standing just to the side.

His bearing was militarily straight and he was impeccably dressed. His hair was flecked with gray, but it was still very dark and full. His face was lean, aristocratic, handsome. It was stern, she thought, but pale, very pale compared to the shadows under his eyes. Despite his stance and dress, he looked as though he hadn't slept in days.

"Darling." His voice shook as he reached down to take her free hand. There were tears under the words as he pressed her fingers to his lips. She thought she felt the hand, which was strong and firm, tremble lightly. "We have you back now, my love. We have you back."

She didn't pull away. Compassion forbade it. With her hand lying limply in his, she studied his face a second time. "Who are you?"

The man's head jerked up. His damp eyes stared into hers. "Who—"

"You're very weak." Gently the doctor cut him off and drew her attention away. She saw him put a hand on the man's arm, in restraint or comfort, she couldn't tell. "You've been through a great deal. Confusion's natural at first."

Lying flat on her back, she watched the doctor send signals to the other man. A raw sickness began to roll inside her stomach. She was warm and dry, she realized. Warm and dry and empty. She had a body, and it was tired. But inside the body was a void. Her voice was surprisingly strong when she spoke again. Both men responded to it.

"I don't know where I am." Beneath the doctor's hand her pulse jerked once, then settled. "I don't know who I am."

"You've been through a great deal, my dear." The doctor spoke soothingly while his brain raced ahead. Specialists, he thought. If she didn't regain her memory in twenty-four hours, he'd need the best.

"You remember nothing?" The other man had straightened at

her words. Now, with his ramrod stance, his sleep-starved eyes direct, he looked down at her.

Confused and fighting back fear, she started to push herself up, and the doctor murmured and settled her back against the pillows. She remembered…running, the storm, the dark. Lights coming up in front of her. Closing her eyes tight, she struggled for composure without knowing why it was so important to retain it. Her voice was still strong, but achingly hollow when she opened them again. "I don't know who I am. Tell me."

"After you've rested a bit more," the doctor began. The other man cut him off with no more than a look. And the look, she saw at a glance, was both arrogant and commanding.

"You're my daughter," he said. Taking her hand again, he held it firmly. Even the light trembling had stopped. "You are Her Serene Highness Gabriella de Cordina."

Nightmare or fairy tale? she wondered as she stared up at him. Her father? Her Serene Highness? Cordina… She thought she recognized the name and clung to it, but what was this talk of royalty? Even as she began to dismiss it, she watched his face. This man wouldn't lie. His face was passive, but his eyes were so full of emotion she was drawn to them even without memory.

"If I'm a princess," she began, and the dry reserve in her voice caused a flicker of emotion to pass over his face briefly. Amusement? she wondered. "Does that make you a king?"

He nearly smiled. Perhaps the trauma had confused her memory, but she was still his Brie. "Cordina is a principality. I am Prince Armand. You're my eldest child. You have two brothers, Alexander and Bennett."

Father and brothers. Family, roots. Nothing stirred. "And my mother?"

This time she read the expression easily: pain. "She died when you were twenty. Since then you've been my official hostess, taking on her duties along with your own. Brie." His tone softened from the formal and dispassionate. "We call you 'Brie.'" He turned her hand up so that the cluster of sapphires and diamonds on her right hand glimmered toward her. "I gave you this on your twenty-first birthday, nearly four years ago."

She looked at it, and at the strong, beautiful hand that held hers. She remembered nothing. But she felt—trust. When she lifted her eyes again, she managed a half smile. "You have excellent taste, Your Highness."

He smiled, but she thought he was perilously close to weeping. As close as she. "Please," she began for both their sakes. "I'm very tired."

"Yes, indeed." The doctor patted her hand as he had, though she didn't know it, since the day she'd been born. "For now, rest is the very best medicine."

Reluctantly Prince Armand released his daughter's hand. "I'll be close."

Her strength was already beginning to ebb. "Thank you." She heard the door close, but sensed the doctor hovering. "Am I who he says I am?"

"No one knows better than I." He touched her cheek, more from affection than the need to check her temperature. "I delivered you. Twenty-five years ago in July. Rest now, Your Highness. Just rest."

Prince Armand strode down the corridor in his quick, trained gait, as a member of the Royal Guard followed two paces behind. He wanted to be alone. God, how he wanted five minutes to himself in some closed-off room. There he could let go of some of the tension, some of the emotion that pulled at him. His daughter, his treasure, had nearly been lost to him. Now that he had her back, she looked at him as though he were a stranger.

When he found who—Armand dismissed the thought. It was for later. He promised himself that.

In the spacious, sun-splashed waiting room were three more Royal Guards and several members of Cordina's police department. Pacing, smoking, was his son and heir, Alexander. He had his father's dark, clean-lined looks and military bearing. He did not, as yet, have his father's meticulous control.

Like a volcano, Armand thought, looking at the twenty-three-year-old prince, that simmers and bubbles, but doesn't quite erupt.

Sprawled across a plush, rose-colored sofa was Bennett. At twenty he threatened to become the newest playboy prince. Though he, too, was dark, his looks reflected the heartbreaking beauty of his mother. Though he was often reckless, too often indiscreet, he had an unflagging compassion and kindness that endeared him to his subjects and the press. As well as the female population of Europe, Armand thought wryly.

Beside Bennett was the American who was there at Armand's request. Both princes were too wrapped in their own thoughts to notice their father's presence. The American missed nothing. That's why Armand had sent for him.

Reeve MacGee sat silently for a moment, watching the prince take in the scene. He was holding up well, Reeve thought, but, then, he'd expected no less. He'd only met Cordina's ruler a handful of times, but Reeve's father had been at Oxford with him, where a friendship and mutual respect had been established that had lasted through the years and over the distances.

Armand had gone on to become the ruler of a small, charming country snuggled on the Mediterranean. Reeve's father had become a diplomat. Though he'd grown up with politics and protocol, Reeve had chosen a more behind-the-scenes career for himself. Undercover.

After ten years of dealing with the less elite portion of the nation's capital, Reeve had turned in his badge and started his own private business. There'd come a time in his life when he'd grown tired of following other people's rules. His own were often even more strict, more unbending, but they were his own. The experience he'd gained in Homicide, and then in Special Services had taught him to trust his own instincts first.

He'd been born wealthy. He'd added to his wealth through his own skill. Once he'd looked at his profession as a means of income and a means of excitement. Reeve no longer worked for money. He took few jobs, a select few. If, and only if, something intrigued him, he accepted the client and the responsibility. To the outside world, and often to himself, he was only a farmer, a novice at that. Less than a year before, he'd bought a farm with thoughts, dreams, perhaps, of retiring there. It was, for him, an answer. Ten years of dealing with good and bad, law and disorder on a daily basis had been enough.

Telling himself he'd paid his dues, he'd dropped out of public service. A private detective could pick and choose his clients. He could work at his own pace, name his own fee. If a job led him into danger, he could deal with it in his own fashion. Still, during this past year he'd taken on fewer and fewer of his private cases.

He was easing himself out. If he'd had qualms, no one knew of them but himself. The farm was a chance for a different kind of life. One day, he'd promised himself, it would be his whole life. He'd postponed his first shot at spring planting to answer Armand's request.

He looked more like a soldier than a farmer. When he rose at Armand's entrance, his long, rangy body moved subtly, muscle by muscle. The neat linen jacket was worn over a plain T-shirt and trim slacks, but he could give them the air of formality or casualness as he chose. He was the kind of man whose clothes, no matter how attractive, were noticed only after he was. His face drew the attention first, perhaps because of the smooth good looks he'd inherited from his Scotch-Irish ancestors. His skin would have been pale if he hadn't spent so much time out of doors. His dark hair was cut well, but insisted on falling over his brow. His mouth was wide and tended to look serious.

His bone structure was excellent and his eyes were the charming, sizzling blue of the Black Irish. He'd used them to charm when it suited him, just as he'd used them to intimidate.

His stance was less rigid than the prince's, but no less watchful. "Your Highness."

At Reeve's words, both Alexander and Bennett sprang to attention. "Brie?" they asked together, but while Bennett was already beside his father, Alexander stood where he was. He crushed out his cigarette in an ashtray. Reeve watched it snap in two.

"She was conscious," Armand said briefly. "I was able to speak with her."

"How does she feel?" Bennett looked at his father with dark, concerned eyes. "When can we see her?"

"She's very tired," Armand said, touching his son's arm only lightly. "Perhaps tomorrow."

Still at the window, Alexander smoldered. "Does she know who—"

"That's for later," his father cut him off.

Alexander might have said more, but his upbringing had been too formal. He knew the rules and the restrictions that went with his title. "We'll take her home soon," he said quietly, coming very close to challenging his father. He cast a quick look around at the guards and police. Gabriella might be protected here, but he wanted her home.

"As soon as possible."

"She may be tired," Bennett began, "but she'll want to see a familiar face later on. Alex and I can wait."

A familiar face. Armand looked beyond his son to the window. There were no familiar faces for his Brie. He'd explain to them, but later, in private. For now, he could only be the prince. "You may go." His words took in both his sons. "Tomorrow she'll be more rested. Now I need a word with Reeve." He dismissed his sons without a gesture. When they hesitated, he lifted a brow. It was not, as it could have been, done with heat.

"Is she in pain?" Alexander blurted out.

Armand's look softened. Only someone who knew him well would have seen it. "No. I promise you. Soon," he added when Alexander remained unsatisfied, "you'll see for yourself. Gabriella is strong." It was said with a simplicity that was filled with pride.

With a nod, Alexander accepted. What else he had to say would have to wait for a private moment. He walked out with his brother, flanked by guards.

Armand watched his sons, then turned to Reeve. "Please," he began, and gestured. "We'll use Dr. Franco's office for a moment." He moved across the corridor and down as though he didn't notice the guards. Reeve did. He felt them close and tense. A royal kidnapping, he mused, tended to make people nervous. Armand opened a door, waited until Reeve was inside, then closed it again.

"Sit, please," he invited. "I can't just yet." Reaching into his pocket, he drew out a dark-brown cigarette, one of the ten he permitted himself daily. Before he could do so himself, Reeve lit it and waited. "I'm grateful you came, Reeve. I haven't had the opportunity to tell you how I appreciate it."

"There's no need to thank me, Your Highness. I haven't done anything yet."

Armand blew out smoke. He could relax, just a little, in front of the son of his friend. "You think I'm too hard on my sons."

"I think you know your sons better than I."

Armand gave a half laugh and sat. "You have your father's diplomatic tongue."

"Sometimes."

"You have, also, if I see clearly, his clear and clever mind."

Reeve wondered if his father would appreciate the comparison, and smiled. "Thank you, Your Highness."

"Please, in private, it must be Armand." For the first time since his daughter had awoken, his emotions slipped. With one hand he kneaded the skin just above his eyebrows. The band of tension there could be ignored for only so long. "I think I'm about to impose on your father's friendship through you, Reeve. I think, because of my love for my daughter, I have no other choice."

Reeve measured the man who sat across from him. Now he saw more than the royalty. He saw a father desperately hanging on to control. In silence, Reeve took out a cigarette of his own, lit it and gave Armand just a few more minutes. "Tell me."

"She remembers nothing."

"She doesn't remember who kidnapped her?" With a faint scowl Reeve studied the toe of his shoe. "Did she see them at all?"

"She remembers nothing," Armand repeated, and lifted his head. "Not even her own name."

Reeve took in all the implications, and their consequences. He merely nodded, showing none of the thoughts that formed and raced through his mind. "Temporary amnesia would be common enough after what she's been through, I imagine. What does the doctor say?"

"I will speak to him shortly." The strain, having gone on for six days, wore on him, but he didn't allow it to come through in his voice. "You came, Reeve, because I asked you. Yet you never asked me why."

"No."

"As an American citizen, you're under no obligation to me."

Reeve blew out a thin stream of Virginia tobacco to mix with the French of Armand's. "No."

Armand's lips curved. Like his father, the prince thought. And like his father, Reeve MacGee could be trusted. He was about to trust him with his most prized possession. "In my position, there is always a certain element of danger. You understand this."

"Any leader lives with it."

"Yes. And, by birth and proximity, a leader's children." For a moment he looked down at his hands, at the ornate gold ring of his office. He was, by birth, a prince. He was also a father. Still, he'd never had a choice about which came first. He'd been born, educated and molded to rule. Armand had always known his first obligation was to his people.

"Naturally, my children have their own personal security." With a kind of controlled violence, he crushed out his cigarette. "It seems that it is inadequate. Brie—Gabriella—is often impatient with the need for guards. She's stubborn about her privacy. Perhaps I've spoiled her. We're a peaceful country, Reeve. The Royal Family of Cordina is loved by its citizens. If my daughter slipped away from her guards from time to time, I made little of it."

"Is that what happened this time?"

"She wanted to drive in the country. It's something she does from time to time. The responsibilities of her title are many. Gabriella needs an escape valve. Until six days ago, it seemed like a very harmless one, which was why I permitted it."

The very tone told Reeve that Armand ruled his family as he did his country, with a just, but cool hand. He absorbed the feeling as easily as he did the information. "Until six days ago," Reeve repeated. "When your daughter was abducted."

Armand nodded calmly. There were facts to be dealt with; emotion only clouded them. "Now, until we're certain who abducted her and why, she can't be allowed something so harmless. I would trust the Royal Guards with my life. I can't trust them with my daughter's."

Reeve tapped out his cigarette gently. The drift was coming across loud and clear. "I'm not on the force any longer, Armand. And you don't want a cop."

"You have your own business. I understand you're something of an expert on terrorism."

"In my own country," Reeve pointed out. "I certainly have no credentials in Cordina." He felt his curiosity pick up another notch. Impatient with himself, he frowned at Armand. "I've had the opportunity to make contacts over the years. I could give you the names of some good men. If you're looking for a royal bodyguard—"

"I'm looking for a man I can trust with my daughter's life," Armand interrupted. He said it quietly, but the thread of power lay just beneath. "A man I can trust to remain as objective as I myself must remain. A man who has had experience dealing with a potentially explosive situation with…finesse. I've followed your career." He gave another quick smile at Reeve's bland look. "I have a few connections in Washington. Your record was exemplary, Reeve. Your father can be proud of you."

Reeve shifted uncomfortably at the mention of his father. The connection was too damn personal, he thought. It would make it more difficult for him to accept and be objective, or to refuse graciously—guiltlessly. "I appreciate that. But I'm not a cop. I'm not a bodyguard. I'm a farmer."

Armand's expression remained grave, but Reeve caught the quick light of humor in his eyes. "Yes, so I've been told. If you prefer, we can leave it at that. However, I have a need. A great need. I won't press you now." Armand knew when to advance and when to retreat. "Give some thought to what I've said. Tomorrow, perhaps we can talk again, and you can speak with Gabriella yourself. In the meantime, you are our guest." He rose, signaling an end to the interview. "My car will take you back to the palace. I will remain here a bit longer."

The late-morning sunlight filtered into the room. Vaguely wanting a cigarette, Reeve watched its patterns on the floor. He'd spoken with Armand again, over a private breakfast in the prince's suite. If there was one thing Reeve understood, it was quiet determination and cold power. He'd grown up with it.

Swearing lightly, Reeve looked through the window at the mountains that cupped Cordina so beautifully.

Why the hell was he here? His land was thousands of miles away and waiting for his plow. Instead he was in this little fairy-tale country where the air was seductively soft and the sea was blue and close. He should never have come, Reeve told himself ruthlessly. When Armand had contacted him, he should simply have made his excuses. When his father had called to add weight to the prince's request, Reeve should have told him he had fields to till and hay to plant.

He hadn't. With a sigh, Reeve admitted why. His father had asked so little of him and had given so much. The friendship that bound Ambassador Francis MacGee to His Royal Highness Armand of Cordina was strong and real. Armand had flown to the States for his mother's funeral. It wasn't possible to forget how much that support had meant to his father.

And he hadn't forgotten the princess. He continued to stare out of the window. The woman slept behind him in the hospital bed, pale, vulnerable, fragile. Reeve remembered her ten years before, when he'd joined his parents for a trip to Cordina.

It had been her sixteenth birthday, Reeve remembered. He'd been in his twenties, already working his way up on the force. He hadn't been a man with illusions. Certainly not one to believe in fairy tales. But that had been exactly what Her Serene Highness Gabriella had been.

Her dress—he could still remember it—had been a pale, mint-colored silk nipped into an impossibly small waist, billowing out like clouds. Against it, her skin had been glowing with life and youth. She'd worn a little ring of diamonds in her hair, glittering, winking, sizzling, against that deep, rich chestnut. It was hair a man wanted to run his fingers through, possessively. Her face had been all roses and cream and delicacy, with a mouth that was full and promising. And her eyes… Reeve remembered them most of all. Her eyes, under dark, arched brows, surrounded by lush, lush lashes, had been like topaz.

Almost reluctantly, he turned to look at her now.

Her face was still delicate, perhaps more so since she'd grown from girl to woman. The sweep of her cheekbones gave her dignity. Her skin was pale, as though the life and youth had been washed out of it. Her hair was still rich, but it was brushed straight back, leaving her face vulnerable. The beauty was still there, but it was so fragile a man would be afraid to touch.

One arm was thrown across her body, and he could see the sparkle of diamonds and sapphire. Yet her nails were short and uneven, as though they'd been bitten or broken off. The IV still fed into her wrist. He remembered when she was sixteen she'd worn a bracelet of pearls there.

It was that memory that caused the anger to roll through him. It had been a week since her abduction, two days since the young couple had found her collapsed on the side of the road, yet no one knew what she'd been through. He could remember the scent of her perfume from ten years before. She couldn't remember her own name.

Some puzzles could be left on the shelf and easily ignored; some could be speculated on and left to others. Then there were those that intrigued and tempted. They called to the part of him that was seduced by questions, riddles and the often violent way of solving them that, he'd nearly convinced himself, had been overcome.

Armand had been clever, Reeve thought grimly, very clever, to insist that he see Princess Gabriella for himself. What was he going to do about her? he asked himself. What in hell was he going to do? He had his own life to start, the new one he'd chosen for himself. A man trying for a second beginning didn't have time to mix himself up in other people's problems. Hadn't that been just what he'd wanted to get away from?

His brow was furrowed in the midst of his contemplations; that was how she saw him when she opened her eyes. Brie stared into the grim, furious face, saw the smoldering blue irises, the tight mouth, and froze. What was dream and what was real? she asked herself as she braced herself. The hospital. She allowed her gaze to leave his only long enough to assure herself she was still there. Her fingers tightened on the sheets until they were white, but her voice came calmly.

"Who are you?"

Whatever else had changed about her over the years or over the past week, the eyes were the same. Tawny, deep. Fascinating. Reeve kept his hands in his pockets. "I'm Reeve MacGee, a friend of your father's."

Brie relaxed a little. She remembered the man with the tired eyes and military stance who'd told her he was her father. No one knew how restless and frustrated a night she'd spent trying to find some glimmer of memory. "Do you know me?"

"We met several years ago, Your Highness." The eyes that had fascinated him in the girl, and now in the woman, seemed to devour him. She needs something, he thought. She's groping for any handhold. "It was your sixteenth birthday. You were exquisite."

"You're American, Reeve MacGee?"

He hesitated a moment, his eyes narrowing. "Yes. How do you know?"

"Your voice." Confusion came and went in her eyes. He could

almost see her grab on to that one thin thread. "I hear it in your voice. I've been there... Have I been there?"

"Yes, Your Highness."

He knew, she thought. He knew, but she could only guess. "Nothing." Tears welled up and were vanquished. She was too much her father's daughter. "Can you imagine," she began very steadily, "what it is to wake up with nothing? My life is blank pages. I have to wait for others to fill it for me. What happened to me?"

"Your Highness—"

"Must you call me that?" she demanded.

The flash of impatient spirit took him back a pace. He tried not to smile. He tried not to admire it. "No," he said simply, and made himself comfortable on the edge of her bed. "What would you like to be called?"

"By my name." Brie looked down in annoyance at the bandage on her wrist. That would be done away with soon, she decided, then managed to shift herself up. "I'm told it's Gabriella."

"You're more often known as Brie."

She was silent a moment as she struggled to find the familiarity. The blank pages remained blank. "Very well, then. Now tell me what happened to me."

"We don't have the details."

"You must," she corrected, watching him. "If not all, you have some. I want them."

He studied her. Fragile, yes, but under the fragility was a core of strength. She'd have to build on it again. "Last Sunday afternoon you went out for a drive in the country. The next day, your car was found abandoned. There were calls. Ransom calls. Allegedly you'd been abducted and were being held." He didn't add what the threats had been or what would have been done to her if the ransom demands weren't met. Nor did he add that the ransom demands had ranged from exorbitant amounts of money to the release of certain prisoners.

"Kidnapped." Brie's fingers reached out and gripped his. She saw images, shadows. A small, dark room. The smell of...kerosene and must. She remembered the nausea, the headaches. The terror came back, but little else. "It won't come clear," she murmured.

"Somehow I know it's true, but there's a film I can't brush away."

"I'm no doctor." Reeve spoke in brisk tones because her fight to find herself affected him too strongly. "But I'd say not to push it. You'll remember when you're ready to remember."

"Easy to say." She released his hand. "Someone's stolen my life from me, Mr. MacGee... What's your place in this?" she demanded suddenly. "Were we lovers?"

His brow lifted. She certainly didn't beat around the bush, he mused. Nor, he thought, only half-amused, did she sound too thrilled by the prospect. "No. As I said, you were sixteen the one and only time we met. Our fathers are old friends. They'd have been a bit annoyed if I'd seduced you."

"I see. Then why are you here?"

"Your father asked me to come. He's concerned about your security."

She glanced down at the ring on her finger. Exquisite, she thought. Then she saw her nails and frowned. That was wrong, wasn't it? she wondered. Why would she wear such a ring and not take care of her hands? Another flicker of memory taunted her. Brie closed her hands into fists as it hovered, then faded. "If my father is concerned about my security," she continued, unaware that Reeve watched her every expression, "what is that to you?"

"I've had some experience with security. Prince Armand has asked me to look out for you."

She frowned again, in a quiet, thoughtful way she had no idea was habit. "A bodyguard?" She said it in the same impatient way he had. "I don't think I'd like that."

The simple dismissal had him doing a complete reversal. He'd given up his free time, come thousands of miles, and she didn't think she'd like it. "You'll find, Your Highness, that even a princess has to do things she doesn't like. Might as well get used to it."

She studied him blandly, the way she did when her temper threatened her good sense. "I think not, Mr. MacGee. I find myself certain that I wouldn't tolerate having someone hover around me. When I get home—" She stopped, because home was another blank. "When I get home," she repeated, "I'll find another way of dealing with it. You may tell my father that I declined your kind offer.''

"The offer isn't to you, but to your father." Reeve rose. This time Brie was able to see that for sheer size he was impressive. His leanness didn't matter, nor did his casually expensive clothes. If he meant to block your way, you'd be blocked. Of that much she was sure.

He made her uneasy. She didn't know why, or, annoyingly, if she should know. Yet he did, and because of this she wanted nothing to do with him on a day-to-day basis. Her life was jumbled enough at the moment without a man like Reeve MacGee in her way.

She asked if they'd been lovers because the idea both stirred and frightened. When he'd said no, she hadn't felt relief but the same blank flatness she'd been dealing with for two days. Perhaps she was a woman of little emotion, Brie considered. Perhaps life was simpler that way.

"I've been told I'm nearly twenty-five, Mr. MacGee."

"Must you call me that?" he countered, deliberately using the same tone she had. He saw her smile quickly. The light came on and switched off.

"I am an adult," she went on. "I make my own decisions about my life."

"Since you're a member of the Royal Family of Cordina, some of those decisions aren't just yours to make." He walked to the door and, opening it, stood with his hand on the knob. "I've got better things to do, Gabriella, than princess-sit." His smile came quickly, also, and was wry. "But even commoners don't always have a choice."

She waited until the door was closed again, then sat up. Dizziness swept over her. For a moment, just a moment, she wanted to lie back until someone came to help, to tend. But she wouldn't tolerate being tied down any longer. Swinging out of bed, she waited for the weakness to fade. It was something she had to accept for now. Then carefully, slowly, she walked toward the mirror on the far wall.

She'd avoided this. Remembering nothing of her looks, a thousand possibilities had formed in her mind. Who was she? How could she begin to know when she didn't know the color of her eyes. Taking a steadying breath, she stood in front of the mirror and looked.

Too thin, she thought quickly. Too pale. But not, she added with foolish relief, hideous. Perhaps her eyes were an odd color, but they weren't crossed or beady. Lifting a hand to her face, she traced it. Thin, she thought again. Delicate, frightened. There was nothing in the reflection that resembled the man who was her father. She'd seen strength in his face. In her own she saw frailty—too much of it.

Who are you? Brie demanded as she pressed her palm against the glass. What are you?

Then, despising herself, she gave in to her despair and wept.

Chapter 2

It wasn't something she'd do again, Brie told herself as she stepped out of a hot, soothing shower. She wouldn't bury her face in her hands and cry because things were piling up on her. What she would do, what she would begin to do right now, was to shift them, one at a time. If there were answers to be found, that was the way to find them.

First things first. Brie slipped into the robe she'd found hanging in the closet. It was thick and plush and emerald green. It was also frayed a bit around the cuffs. An old favorite, she decided, accepting the comfort she felt with the robe around her. But the closet had offered her nothing else. Decisively Brie pushed the button and waited for the nurse.

"I want my clothes," Brie said immediately.

"Your Highness, you shouldn't be—"

"I'll speak to the doctor if necessary. I need a hairbrush, cosmetics and suitable clothes." She folded her hands in a gesture that looked commanding, but had more to do with nerves. "I'm going home this morning."

One didn't argue with royalty. The nurse curtsied her way out of the room and went directly for the doctor.

"Now what's all this?" He came bustling into the room, all warmth, all good cheer and patience. She thought of a short, stout brick wall cleverly concealed behind ivy and moss. "Your Highness, you have no business getting up."

"Dr. Franco." It was time, Brie decided, to test herself. "I appreciate your skill and your kindness. I'm going home today."

"Home." His eyes sharpened as he stepped forward. "My dear Gabriella."

"No." She shook her head, denying his unspoken question. "I don't remember."

Franco nodded. "I've spoken to Dr. Kijinsky, Your Highness. He's much more knowledgeable about this condition than I. This afternoon—"

"I'll see your Kijinsky, Dr. Franco, but not this afternoon." She dipped her hands into the deep pockets of the robe and touched something small and slim. Bringing it out, Brie found herself holding a hairpin. She closed her hand tightly over it, as if it might bring something rushing back. "I need to try to figure this out my way. Perhaps if I'm back where things are familiar to me, I'll remember. You assured me yesterday after my...father left, that this memory loss is temporary and that other than fatigue and shock, I have no major injuries. If that's the case, I can rest and recuperate just as well at home."

"Your rest and recuperation can be monitored more efficiently here."

She gave him a quiet, very stubborn smile. "I don't choose to be monitored, Dr. Franco. I choose to go home."

"Perhaps neither of you remembers Gabriella said the same thing only hours after her tonsils were removed." Armand stood in the doorway, watching his delicately built daughter face down the tanklike Franco. Coming in, he held out his hand. Though her hesitation to accept it hurt, he curled his fingers gently over hers. "Her Highness will come home," he said without looking at the doctor. Before Brie could smile, he went on, "You'll give me a list of instructions for her care. If she doesn't follow them, she'll be sent back."

The urge to protest came and went. Something inherent quelled it. Instead she inclined her head. What should have been a subservient movement was offset by the arrogant lift of brow. Armand's fingers tightened on hers as he saw the familiar gesture.

She'd given him that look countless times when she'd bargained for and received what she wanted.

"I'll send for your things."

"Thank you."

But she didn't add "father." Both of them knew it.

Within an hour, she was walking out. She liked the cheerful, spring dress splashed with pastels that she was wearing. She had felt both relief and satisfaction when she'd discovered she had a clever hand with cosmetics.

As Brie stepped into the sunlight there was a faint blush of color in her cheeks, and the shadows under her eyes had been blotted out. Her hair was loose, swinging down to brush her shoulders. The scent she'd dabbed on had been unapologetically French and teasing. She found, like the robe, that she was comfortable in it.

She recognized the car as a limo and knew the interior would be roomy and smell rich. She couldn't remember riding in it before, or the face of the driver who smiled and bowed as he ushered her inside. She sat in silence a moment as her father settled in the seat across from her.

"You look stronger, Brie."

There was so much to say, yet she had so little. Details eluded her. Instead there were feelings. She didn't feel odd in the plush quiet of the limo. The weight of the glittery ring she wore was comfortable on her hand. She knew her shoes were Italian, but only the scuffs on the soles showed her that they'd been worn before. By her, certainly. The fit was perfect.

The scent her father wore soothed her nerves. She looked at him again, searching. "I know I speak French as easily as English, because some of my thoughts come in that language," she began. "I know what roses smell like. I know which direction I should look to see the sun rise over the water and what it looks like at dawn. I don't know if I'm a kind person or a selfish one. I don't know the color of the walls of my own room. I don't know if I've done well with my life or if I've wasted it."

It tore at him to watch her sitting calmly across from him, trying to explain why she couldn't give him the love he was entitled to. "I could give you the answers."

She nodded, as controlled as he. "But you won't."

"I think if you find them yourself, you'll find more."

"Perhaps." Looking down, she smoothed her fingers over the white snakeskin bag she carried. "I've already discovered I'm impatient."

Quick, dashing, he grinned. Brie found herself drawn to him, smiling back. "Then you've begun."

"And I have to be satisfied with a beginning."

"My dear Gabriella, I have no illusions that you'll be satisfied with that for long."

Brie glanced at the window as they climbed up, steadily up, a long, winding road. There were many trees, with palms among them, their fronds fluttering. There was rock, gray, craggy rock thrusting out, but wildflowers shoved their way through the cracks. The sea was below, deep, paintbrush blue and serene.

If she looked up, following the direction of the road, she could see the town with its pink and white buildings stacked like pretty toys on the jutting, uneven promontory.

A fairy tale, she thought again, yet it didn't surprise her. As they approached, Brie felt again a sense of quiet comfort. The town lost nothing of its charm on closer contact. The houses and buildings seemed content to push their way out of the side of rock, balanced with one another and the lay of the land. There was an overall tidiness and a sense of age.

No skyscrapers, no frantic rush. Something inside her recognized this, but, she thought, she'd been to cities where the pace was fast and the buildings soared up and up. Yet this was home. She felt no urge to argue. This was home.

"You won't tell me about myself." She looked at Armand again and her eyes were direct, her voice strong. "Tell me about Cordina."

She'd pleased him. Brie could see it in the way his lips curved just slightly. "We are old," he said, and she heard the pride. "The Bissets—that's our family name—have lived and ruled here since the seventeenth century. Before, Cordina was under many governments, Spanish, Moorish, Spanish again, then French. We are a port, you see, and our position on the Mediterranean is valuable.

"In 1657, another Armand Bisset was granted the principality of Cordina. It has remained in Bisset hands, and will remain so as long as there is a male heir. The title cannot pass to a daughter."

"I see." After a moment's thought Brie tilted her head. "Personally I can be grateful for that, but as a policy, it's archaic."

"So you've said before," he murmured.

"I see." And she saw children playing in a green leafy park where a fountain gushed. She saw a store with glittery dresses in the front, and a bakery window filled with pink and white confections. There was a house where the lawn flamed with azaleas. "And have the Bissets ruled well?"

It was like her to ask, he thought. While she didn't remember, the questing mind remained, and the compassion. "Cordina is at peace," he said simply. "We are a member of the United Nations. I govern, assisted by Loubet, Minister of State. There is the Council of the Crown, which meets three times a year. On international treaties, I must consult them. All laws must be approved by the National Council, which is elected."

"Are there women in the government?"

He lifted a finger to lightly rub his chin. "You haven't lost your taste for politics. There are women," he told her. "Though you wouldn't be satisfied by the percentages, Cordina is a progressive country."

"Perhaps 'progressive' is a relative term."

"Perhaps." He smiled, because this particular debate was an old one. "Shipping is, naturally, our biggest industry, but tourism is not far behind. We have beauty, culture and an enviable climate. We are just," he said with simplicity. "Our country is small, but it is not insignificant. We rule well."

This she accepted without any questions, but if she'd had them, they would have flown from her mind by the sight of the palace.

It stood, as was fitting, on the highest point of Cordina's rocky jut of land. It faced the sea, with huge rocks and sheer cliffs tumbling down to the water.

It was a place King Arthur might have visited, and would recognize if his time came again. The recognition came to Brie the same way everything else had, a vague feeling, as if she were seeing something in a dream.

It was made of white stone and the structure spread out in a jumble of battlements, parapets and towers. It had been built for both royalty and defense, and remained unchanged. It hovered over the capital like a protection and a blessing.

There were guards at the gate, but the gates weren't closed. In their tidy red uniforms they looked efficient, yet fanciful. Brie thought of Reeve MacGee.

"Your friend spoke to me—Mr. MacGee." Brie tore her gaze away from the palace. Business first, she reflected. It seemed to be her way. "He tells me you've asked for his assistance. While I appreciate your concern, I find the idea of yet another stranger in my life uncomfortable."

"Reeve is the son of my oldest and closest friend. He isn't a stranger." Nor am I, he thought, and willed himself to be patient.

"To me he is. By his own account he tells me we've met only once, almost ten years ago. Even if I could remember him, he'd be a stranger."

He'd always admired the way she could use such clean logic when it suited her. And willfulness when it didn't. Admiration, however, didn't overshadow necessity. "He was a member of the police force in America and handled the sort of security we require now."

She thought of the neat red uniforms at the gate, and the men who sat in the car following the limo. "Aren't there enough guards?"

Armand waited until the driver stopped in front of the entrance. "If there were, none of this would be necessary." He stepped from the car first and turned to assist his daughter himself. "Welcome home, Gabriella."

Her hand remained in his and the light breeze ruffled between them. She wasn't ready to go in. Armand felt it, and waited.

She could smell the flowers now. Jasmine, vanilla, spice, and the roses that grew in the courtyard. The grass was so green, the stone so white it was almost blinding. There had to have been a drawbridge once, she was sure of it. Now there was an arched mahogany door at the top of curved stone steps. Glass, sometimes clear, sometimes tinted, glistened as it should in palaces. At the topmost tower a flag whipped in the wind. Snowy white with an arrogant diagonal slash of red.

Slowly she looked over the building. It tugged at her, welcoming her. The sense of peace wasn't something she imagined. It was as real as the fear she'd felt not long before. Yet she couldn't say which of those sparkling windows were hers. She'd come to find out, Brie reminded herself, and stepped forward.

Even as she did, the wide door was flung open. A young man with dark, thick hair and a dancer's build dashed out. "Brie!" Then he was on her, embracing her with all the strength and enthusiasm of youth. He smelled comfortably of horses. "I'd just come in from the stables when Alex told me you were on your way."

Brie felt the waves of love coming from him, and looked helplessly over his shoulder to her father.

"Your sister needs rest, Bennett."

"Of course. She'll rest better here." Grinning, he drew back, keeping her hands tight in his. He looked so young, she thought, so beautiful, so happy. When he saw her face, his eyes sobered quickly. "You don't remember? Still?"

She wanted to reach out to him. He seemed to need it so. All she could do was return the squeeze of hand to hand. "I'm sorry."

He opened his mouth, then shut it again, slipping an arm around her waist. "Nonsense." His voice was cheerful, but he kept her carefully between himself and their father. "You'll remember soon enough now that you're home. Alex and I thought we'd have to wait until this afternoon to see you in the hospital. This is so much better."

As he spoke he was easing her gently in the front door, talking quickly, she was sure, to put both her and himself at ease. She saw the hall, wide and stunning with its frescoed ceiling and polished floor, the gracious sweep of stairs leading up and up, to what she didn't yet know. Because her heart was pounding, she concentrated on the scents that soothed her. Fresh flowers and lemon wax. She heard the sound of her heels striking the wood and echoing.

There was a tall, glossy urn on a stand. She knew it was Ming, just as she knew the stand was Louis XIV. Things, Brie thought. She could identify them, catalog them, but she couldn't relate herself to them. Sunlight poured through two high arched windows but didn't warm her skin.

Escape. The need for it rolled around inside her. She wanted to turn around and walk out, go back to the safe, impersonal hospital room. There weren't so many demands there, so many of these unspoken questions that hung on the air. She wouldn't feel such an outpouring of love, or the need from those around for her to return it. Had she ever? she wondered. When she remembered who she was, would she find a cold, unfeeling woman?

Bennett felt her tense, and tightened his arm around her. "Everything's going to be all right now, Brie."

From somewhere she found the strength to smile. "Yes, of course."

Several paces down the hall a door opened. Brie knew the man to be her brother only because of the strong resemblance between him and the man at her side. She tried to empty herself so that any emotions she might feel would have room.

He wasn't as smoothly handsome as Bennett. His good looks were more intense and less comfortable than his younger brother's. Though he was young, she sensed the same immovable dignity in him as she did in their father. But of course, she reminded herself. He was the heir. Such things were both a gift and a burden.

"Gabriella." Alex didn't rush to her as Bennett did, but came forward steadily, watching her. When he stood in front of her, he lifted his hands and framed her face. The gesture seemed natural, as if he'd done so time and again in the past. The past, she thought as his fingers were warm and firm on her skin, she didn't have. "We've missed you. No one's shouted at me in a week."

"I..." Floundering, she said nothing. What should she say? What should she feel? She knew only that this was too much and she hadn't been as prepared as she'd thought. Then, over Alexander's shoulder, she saw Reeve.

Obviously he'd been closeted with her brother but had stood back to watch the reunion. Another time she might resent it, but now she found she needed his calm impartiality. Hanging on to control, she touched her brother's hand. "I'm sorry, I'm very tired."

She saw something flicker in Alexander's eyes, but then he stepped back. "Of course you are. You should rest. I'll take you up."

"No." Brie struggled not to let the refusal sound as blunt as it was. "Forgive me, I need some time. Perhaps Mr. MacGee wouldn't mind taking me to my room."

"Brie—"

Bennett's protest was immediately quelled by Armand. "Reeve, you know Gabriella's rooms."

"Of course." He stepped forward and took her arm, but the touch was impersonal. He thought he felt her sigh in relief. "Your Highness?"

He led her away, up the curving stairs, where she paused once to look back down on the three men who watched. She seemed so distant from them, so separated. The pull and tug of emotion came and went, so that she climbed the rest of the stairs in silence.

She recognized nothing in the wide, gleaming corridors, nothing in the exquisite wall hangings or draping curtains. Once they passed a servant whose eyes filled as she stopped and curtsied.

"How is it I'm loved like this?" Brie murmured.

Reeve walked on, his hand barely touching her arm as he guided her. "People generally want to be loved."

"Don't people generally wonder if they deserve it?" With an impatient shake of her head, she went on. "It's as if I've stepped into a body. The body has a past, but I don't. Inside this woman, I look out and see other's reactions to her."

"You could use it to your advantage."

She sent him a quick, interested look. "In what way?"

"You have the advantage of seeing the people around you without having your own emotions color what you see. Observation without prejudice. It might be an interesting way to understand yourself."

She didn't relax so much as accept. "You see now why I asked you to bring me up."

He stopped in front of a beautifully carved door. "Do I?"

"I thought only moments ago that I wanted no more strangers in my life. And yet... You haven't any strong feelings for me and you don't expect them in return. It's easy for you to look at me and be practical."

He studied her now in the misty light of the corridor. It wasn't possible for a man to look at her and think practical thoughts, but it wasn't the time to mention that. "You were frightened downstairs."

She tilted her chin and met his eyes. "Yes."

"So you've decided to trust me."

"No." She smiled then, beautifully. Something of the girl he'd met with diamonds in her hair came through. Too much of the attraction he'd felt crept along with it. "Trust isn't something I can give so quickly under the circumstances."

Perhaps more than the smile, the strength attracted him. "What have you decided, then?"

Perhaps more than his looks, his confidence attracted her. "I don't want your services as a policeman, Reeve, but I think your services as a stranger might be invaluable. My father is determined to have you in any case, so perhaps we might come to an agreement between us."

"Of what kind?"

"I don't want to be hovered over. I think I can be certain that's the one thing that was always true. I'd like to consider you as more of a buffer between me and..."

"Your family?" he finished.

Her lashes swept down and her fingers tightened on her bag. "Don't make it sound so cold."

Touching her would be a mistake. He had to remind himself of that. "You've a right to the time and distance you need, Gabriella."

"They have needs, as well. I'm not unaware of that." Her head came up again, but she looked beyond him to the door. "This is my room?"

For a moment she'd looked so lost, so totally lost. He wanted to offer comfort, but knew it was the last thing she wanted or needed. "Yes."

"Would you think I was a coward if I said I didn't want to go in alone?"

For an answer, he opened the door and walked in just ahead of her.

So, she preferred pastels. As Brie looked around the small, charming sitting room she saw the pale, sun-washed colors. No frills, she noted, rather pleased. Even without them, the room was essentially feminine. She felt a sense of relief that she accepted her womanhood without needing elaborate trappings to prove it. Maybe, just maybe, she'd find she liked Gabriella.

The room wasn't cluttered, nor was any space wasted. There were fresh flowers in a bowl on a Queen Anne desk. On the dresser was a collection of tiny bottles in pretty shapes and colors that could have no use at all. They, too, pleased her.

She stepped onto a rug in muted shades of rose and touched the curved back of a chair.

"I'm told you redecorated your room about three years ago," Reeve said casually. "It must be a comfort to know you have good taste."

Had she chosen the material for the soft, cushioned love seat herself? Brie ran her finger over it as if the feel would trigger some hint. Anything. From the window she could look down on Cordina as she must have done countless times before.

There were gardens, a roll of lawn, a jut of rock, the sea. Farther out was the city, houses and hills and green. Though she couldn't see, she was sure children were still playing in the park near the fountain.

"Why am I blocking this out?" Brie demanded suddenly. When she turned around Reeve saw that the calm, reserved woman he'd brought upstairs had turned into an impassioned and desperate one. "Why do I block out what I want so badly to remember?"

"Maybe there are other things you're not ready to remember."

"I can't believe this." She flung down her purse on the love seat and began to pace, rubbing her hands against each other. "I can't bear having this wall between me and myself."

Fragility aside, he thought, there was a great deal of passion here. A man could find it difficult to overlook the combination and go about his business. "You'll have to be patient." And as he said it, he wondered if he was cautioning her or himself.

"Patient?" With a laugh she dragged a hand through her hair. "Why am I so sure that's something I'm not? I feel if I could push one brick, just one brick out of the wall, the rest would crumble away. But how?" She continued to move, quickly, with the kind of grace she'd been born with. "You could help me."

"Your family's here for that."

"No." The toss of her head was regal, and though her voice was soft, it held command. "They know me, of course, but their feelings—and mine—will keep the wall up longer than I can stand. They look at me and hurt because I don't know them."

"But I don't know you."

"Exactly." She swept her hair away from her face with a gesture that seemed less impatient than habitual. "You'll be objective. Because you won't constantly try to protect my feelings you won't pull at them. Since you've already agreed to my father's request—haven't you?"

Reeve thought of his land. As he dipped his hands into his pockets, he frowned. "Yes."

"You've put yourself in the position of breathing over my shoulder," she continued smoothly, "and since you'll be there, you may as well be of some use to me."

He gave a half laugh. "My pleasure, Your Highness."

"Now I've annoyed you." With a shrug, she walked to him. "Well, I suppose we'll annoy each other a great deal before it's over. I'll be honest with you, not because I want your pity, but because I have to say it to someone. I feel so alone." Her voice wavered only slightly. The sun rushing through the windows betrayed her by revealing her pallor. "I have nothing I can see or touch that I know is mine. It isn't possible for me to look back a year and remember something funny or sad or sweet. I don't even know my full name."

He touched her. Perhaps he shouldn't have, but he couldn't stop. His fingers lifted to her face and just skimmed her cheek. "Her Serene Highness Gabriella Madeline Justine Bisset of Cordina."

"So much." She managed a smile, but her hand reached up to grip his tightly. The contact seemed a bit too natural for both of them, but neither broke it. "Brie seems easier. I can relax with Brie. Tell me, do you care for my family?"

"Yes."

"Then help me give them back the woman they need. Help me find her. In one week I've lost twenty-five years. I need to know why. You must understand that."

"I understand." But he told himself he shouldn't be touching her. "It doesn't mean I can help."

"But you can. You can because you have no need. Don't be patient with me, be harsh. Don't be kind, be hard."

He continued to hold her hand. "It might not be healthy for an American ex-cop to give a princess a hard time."

She laughed. It was the first time he'd heard it in ten years, yet he remembered. And he remembered, as she didn't, the swirl of the waltz they'd shared, the magic of moonlight. Staying wasn't wise, he knew. But he couldn't leave. Not quite yet.

Her fingers relaxed in his. "Do we still behead in Cordina? Surely we have more civilized methods of dealing with rabble. Immunity." Suddenly she looked young and at ease. "I'll grant you immunity, Reeve MacGee. Hereby you have my permission to shout, probe, prod and be a general nuisance without fear of reprisal."

"You willing to put the royal seal on it?"

"After someone tells me where it is."

The intensity was gone. Pale and weary she might be, but her smile was lovely. He felt something else from her now. Hope and determination. He'd help her, Reeve thought. Later, perhaps, he'd ask himself why. "Your word's good enough."

"And yours. Thank you."

He brought the hand he still held to his lips. It was a gesture, he knew, she should be as accustomed to as breathing. Yet just as his lips brushed her knuckles he saw something flicker in her eyes. Princess or not, she was a woman. Reeve knew arousal when he saw it. Just as he knew it when he felt it. Cautious, he released her hand. The step back was for both of them.

"I'll leave you to rest. Your maid's name is Bernadette. Unless you want her sooner, she'll be in an hour before dinner."

Brie let her hand fall to her side as if it weren't part of her. "I appreciate what you're doing."

"You won't always." When he reached the door, he judged the distance to be enough. Then he looked back, and she was still in front of the window. Light rioted in, flowing across her hair, shimmering over her skin. "Let it rest for today, Brie," he told her quietly. "Tomorrow we can start knocking at that brick."

Chapter 3

She hadn't meant to sleep but to think. Still, she felt herself drifting awake as groggy and disoriented as she'd been that first time in the hospital.

Gabriella, she told herself. Her name was Gabriella and she was lying in her room, on the soft blue-and-rose colored quilt that spread over her big carved oak bed. There was a breeze fluttering over her because she'd opened the windows herself when she'd explored her bedroom.

Her name was Gabriella and there was no reason to wake up afraid. Safe, she repeated over and over in her head until her muscles believed it and relaxed.

"So."

At the one indignant syllable, Brie sat up abruptly, panicked. An old woman was seated neatly in a straight-backed chair across from the bed. Her hair was pulled back into a knot so tight that not a single wisp escaped. It was gray, stone gray, without a hint of softening white. Her face was like parchment, thin skinned, a bit yellowed and generously lined. Two small dark eyes peered out, and though her mouth was withered with age, it looked strong. She wore a dignified, no-nonsense black dress, sturdy black shoes and, quaintly, a cameo on a velvet ribbon around her neck.

Since Brie had no memory to rely on, she used instincts. Reeve had told her to observe without prejudice. It was advice she saw the wisdom in. There was no fear as she stared back at the old woman. Relaxing again, she remained sitting. "Hello."

"Fine thing," the old woman said in what rang to Brie as a Slavic accent. "You come home after giving me a week of worry and don't bother to see me."

"I'm sorry." The apology came out so naturally she smiled.

"They gave me this nonsense about your not remembering. Bah!" She lifted a hand and slapped it against the arm of the chair. "My Gabriella not remembering her own Nanny."

Brie studied the woman but knew no sense of connection would come. It just wasn't time. "I don't remember," she said quietly. "I don't remember anything."

Nanny hadn't lived for seventy-three years, raised a nurseryful of children and buried one of her own without being prepared for any shock. After a moment's silence, she rose. Her face might be lined, her hands curled slightly with arthritis, but she pulled herself from the chair with the grace and ease of youth. As she stood over Brie's bed, the princess saw a small, birdlike woman in black with a stern face and rosary beads hanging from her belt.

"I am Carlotta Baryshnova, nanny to the Lady Honoria Bruebeck, your aunt, and Lady Elizabeth Bruebeck, your mother. When she became Princess Elizabeth of Cordina I came with her to be nanny to her children. I have diapered you, bandaged your knees and blown your nose. When you marry, I will do the same for your children."

"I see." Because the woman seemed more annoyed than upset, Brie smiled again. It occurred to her she had yet to see herself smile. She'd have to go back to the mirror again. "And was I a good child?"

"Hmph." The sound could have meant anything, but Brie caught a tiny hint of pleasure in it. "Sometimes worse, sometimes better than your brothers. And they were always a trial." Coming closer, she peered down at Brie with the intensity of the nearsighted. "Not sleeping well," she said briskly. "No wonder. Tonight I'll bring you hot milk."

Brie angled her head. "Do I like it?"

"No. But you'll drink it. Now I'll run your bath. Too much excitement and too many doctors, that's what's wrong with you. I told that silly Bernadette I would see to your needs this evening.

What have you done to your hands?'' she demanded abruptly, and snatched one up. She began mumbling over it like an old hen over a backward chick. ''Only a week away and you ruin your nails. Worse than a kitchen maid's. Chipped and broken, and with all the money you spend on manicures.''

Brie sat still while Nanny fussed and complained. There was something, something in the feel of that dry, warm hand and scolding voice. Even as she tried to hold it, it faded. ''I have manicures often?''

''Once a week.'' Nanny sniffed, but continued to grip Brie's fingers.

''It appears I need another one.''

''You can have that stiff-lipped secretary of yours make an appointment. Your hair, too,'' Nanny said, scowling at it. ''A fine thing for a princess to run around with chipped nails and flyaway hair. Fine thing,'' she continued, as she walked into an adjoining room. ''Fine thing, indeed.''

Brie rose and stripped. She felt no invasion of privacy at having the woman fuss and hover around during her bath. Even as she drew off her hose, the woman was there, bundling her into a short silk robe.

''Pin up your hair,'' Nanny said grumpily. ''We'll do what we can with it after your bath.'' When she saw Brie's hesitation, she went to the dresser herself and opened a small enameled box. Hairpins were jumbled inside. ''Here now.'' And her voice was more gentle. ''Your hair is thick like your mother's. You need a lot of pins.'' She was nudging her along, clucking, into the room where water ran. Stopping a moment, Brie just looked.

There was a skylight, strategically placed so that the sun or rain or moonlight would be visible while looking up from the tub. The floor and walls were all tiled in white with flowering plants hanging everywhere in a room already steamy. Even with them, the tub dominated the room with its splash of rich, deep green. Its clover shape would accommodate three, she mused, and wondered if it ever had. Bemused, she watched the water pour out of a wide glistening faucet that turned it into a miniature waterfall.

She saw both the pristine and the passionate, and wondered if it reflected her. The scent rising out of the tub was the same that had been in the little glass bottle the prince had sent for that morning. Gabriella's scent, Brie reminded herself.

Letting the robe slip away, she lowered herself into the bath. It was easy to give herself to it as Nanny disappeared, muttering about laying out her clothes.

The water flowed hot around her. This was something she'd need, Brie discovered, if she were to make it through the evening ahead. She must have relaxed here countless times, looking up at the sky while thinking through what had to be done.

There would be dinner. In her mind she could imagine a complex, formal place setting. The silver, linen, crystal and china. It wasn't difficult for her to conjure up a menu and choose which wines with which course. That all seemed basic somehow, a knowledge that remained like knowing which articles of clothing to put on first. But she had no idea what pattern the china would have any more than she'd known what she'd find behind the wall of closets in her bedroom.

Struggling with impatience, she slipped lower in the water. Impatience, she'd discovered, was very much a part of her. Memory would come, Brie assured herself. And if it didn't come soon, naturally she'd find another way.

Reeve MacGee. Brie reached for the soap and a soft, oversized sponge. He might be her access to another way. Who was he? It was a relief to think of him rather than herself for a while. A former policeman, she remembered, and a friend of the family. Though not a close enough friend, Brie remembered, that he knew her well. He had his own life in America. Had she been there? He'd said she had.

She lay there, willing her mind to open. Only impressions came to her. Stately marble buildings and long formal dinners. And a river, a river with lush green grass on its banks and much boat traffic. It tired her, she discovered, to push herself to remember something even so unimportant. Still, she thought she'd been to Reeve's country.

Concentrate on him, Brie told herself. If he were to be any help to her she had to understand him. Good-looking, she thought, and very smooth on the outside. She wasn't so sure about what lay within. He seemed to her a man who would be ruthless and solitary, a man who did things in his own style. Good, she thought. That was precisely what she needed.

He had no reason, as her family did, to want to shield her. Nor did he have a reason, she added with a frown, to give her the help she wanted. Perhaps he'd agreed only to keep close to her so that he could do the job her father had commissioned him for. Bodyguard, she thought with annoyance. She wanted no one's shadow falling over hers.

And yet, Brie continued as she dipped the sponge into the water, isn't that what she'd asked for herself when she'd spoken to him? Because she'd felt…what, when she'd seen him standing in the hall? Relief. It shamed her to admit it. Her family had been there, concerned and loving, and yet she'd felt an overwhelming sense of relief seeing a stranger standing behind them.

Perhaps it was better that she'd forgotten herself. Brie threw down the sponge so that water splashed up and hit the side of the porcelain. How was she to know if she would like the woman she was? She might easily find herself to be someone cold, unfeeling, selfish. All she had discovered was that she was a woman who liked beautiful clothes and manicures. Perhaps she was just that shallow.

But they loved her. Brie picked up the sponge again to press it against her face. The water was hot and smelled like an expensive woman. The love she'd seen in her family's eyes had been real. Would they love her if she didn't deserve it? How long would it take to discover what depths there were in her?

Passions. She remembered the flare she'd felt when Reeve had kissed her hand. It had been sharp and raw and stunning. Didn't that mean she had normal feminine needs? But had she ever acted on them? With a half laugh, Brie lay her head back and closed her eyes. How many woman could honestly say they didn't know if they were innocent or not?

Would he know? Would a man like Reeve sense such things about a woman? Sometimes when he looked at her Brie felt him reaching inside and finding nerves no stranger had a right to find. Now when she thought of him, she wondered what it would be like to have him touch her—really touch her. Fingertips against the skin, palm against flesh. She felt the arousal start deep, and let it work through her.

Was this a new experience? Brie wondered as she pressed a hand to her stomach. Had other men made her feel so…hungry? Were there other men who had sent her mind to wandering, imagining, dreaming? Perhaps she was a careless sort of woman who desired a man just because he was a man. Was she a woman a man would desire?

Rising from the tub, she let the water cascade from her. Reeve had been right about the possible advantages of her situation. She could watch and observe what reactions she brought to others. Tonight she would.

On the arm of her father, Brie walked down the long stairway. There'd be cocktails in the *petit salon*, he'd told her, but hadn't added he'd come for her because she wouldn't know the way. He did pause at the base of the stairs to kiss her hand. It was a gesture much like Reeve's, but brought her a smile rather than excitement.

"You look lovely, Brie."

"Thank you. But it would be difficult not to with the collection of clothes in my room."

He laughed and looked young. "You've often said clothes were your only vice."

"And are they?"

He heard the need behind the light question and kissed her hand again. "I've never been anything but proud of you." Tucking her hand through his arm again, he led her down the corridor.

Reeve noticed a certain tension between Alexander and Loubet, Armand's minister of state. It came out in politeness, the rigid sort. When Alexander takes the throne, Reeve thought dispassionately, Loubet would not be at his side.

Alexander interested Reeve. The young prince was so internal. Control didn't sit on him as easily as it did his father; he worked for it. Whatever simmered beneath was kept there, never permitted to boil—at least not in public. Unlike Bennett, Reeve thought, shifting his gaze to the other prince.

Bennett was relaxed in his chair, only half listening to the conversation around him. He didn't seem to be compelled to analyze words and meanings as his brother did. His willingness to enjoy what came interested Reeve, as well.

As Gabriella did. Reeve had no way of knowing if the girl he'd met once had become an intense woman like her first brother, or a cheerful one like her second. Perhaps she was nothing like either. After two short conversations, he was as curious to find out as Brie herself.

Who was she? He asked of her the same question Brie had asked of him. Beautiful, yes. Classic looks and elegance hadn't been lost along with her memory. He sensed a steel will beneath them. She'd need it, he decided, if she was to discover herself.

Attraction. He certainly felt it for her. It wasn't anything like the dazzle he'd experienced ten years before. Now he saw her as a woman who struggled every moment not to lose control of a situation she couldn't even understand. If she could hang on while her world turned upside down around her, she wasn't a woman to underestimate.

Desire. He'd felt that, as well, each time he saw her. She had a way of looking at a man with those topaz eyes. Had she always? he wondered. Or was it simply now, when she was groping? A man had to be careful. She might look like a woman who could be touched, seduced, bedded, but she was and would always be a princess. Not the frothy fairy-tale sort, he thought, but flesh and blood.

When he turned and saw her, she seemed to be both.

Her head was lifted, as if she were walking into an arena rather than a salon. Clusters of pearls gleamed at her ears, at her throat, in her hair where it was swept back from her face. Her dress was the color of grapes just before they ripen. The silk and pearls suited her skin. Her stance suited her title. She didn't cling to her father, though Reeve thought she might have liked to cling to something. She was braced and ready. And, he thought with approval, she was watching.

"Your Highness."

Brie waited calmly while Loubet crossed the room and bowed. She saw a man, older than Reeve, younger than her father. His blond hair was just touched with gray, his face just touched with lines. He smelled distinguished, she thought, then smiled at how her mind worked. He walked with a slight stiffness of the left side, but his bow was very elegant and his smile charming.

"It's good to see you home."

She felt nothing when their hands touched, nothing when their eyes met. "Thank you."

"Monsieur Loubet and I had some business to attend to this evening." Her father gave her the cue smoothly. "Unfortunately he won't be able to join us for dinner."

"Business and no pleasure, Monsieur Loubet," Brie said just as smoothly.

"It's a pleasure just to see you home safely, Your Highness."

Brie saw the quick glance that passed between the minister and her father. "Since the business pertained to me, perhaps you'll elaborate over drinks."

As she crossed the room, she caught Reeve's small nod of approval. Some of the knots in her stomach loosened. "Please, gentlemen, be comfortable." She indicated for everyone to sit. Everyone, she noted with a smile, but Bennett, who was already at his ease. "Do I have a favorite?" she asked him with a gesture toward the bar.

"Artesian water and lime," he said with a grin. "You've always said there's enough wine served at dinner without fuzzing your mind beforehand."

"Very sensible of me."

Reeve walked to the bar to see to her drink while Brie took a seat on one of the sofas. The men settled around her. Was her life so dominated by men? she wondered briefly, then took the glass and sipped. "Well, shall I tell you what I see?" Without waiting for a reply, she set down her glass and began. "I see Alexander is annoyed, and that my father is picking his way carefully, as a man through a minefield. I'm at the core of this."

"She should be left alone," Alexander stated suddenly. "It's family business."

"Your family's business remains Cordina's business, Your Highness." Loubet spoke gently but without, Brie thought, any affection. "Princess Gabriella's condition is a matter of concern both personally and for the government. I'm very much afraid that the matter of the temporary amnesia would be exploited by the world press if news of it leaks. We're just now settling our people down after the kidnapping. I wish only to give them and Her Serene Highness an opportunity to rest."

"Loubet is quite correct, Alexander." Armand spoke without gentleness, but Brie heard the affection.

"In theory." As he drank, Alexander shot Reeve a quietly resentful look. "But we already have outsiders involved. Gabriella needs rest and therapy. Whoever did this…" His fingers tightened on the facets of his glass. "Whoever did this will pay dearly."

"Alexander." Brie laid a hand on his in a gesture he recognized, but she didn't. "I have to remember what happened before anyone can pay."

"When you're ready, you will. In the meantime—"

"In the meantime," his father interrupted, "Brie must be protected in every possible way. And after consideration, I agree with Loubet that part of this protection should come from concealing the amnesia publicly. If the kidnappers knew you hadn't told us anything, they might feel compelled to silence you before you regained your memory."

Brie picked up her glass again, and though she sipped calmly, Reeve saw her eyes were anything but. "How can we conceal it?"

"If I may, Your Highness," Loubet began with a glance at Armand before he turned to Brie. "Until you're well, Your Highness, we think it best that you remain home, among those who can be trusted. It's a simple matter to postpone or cancel your outside commitments. The kidnapping, the strain and shock of it alone, will suffice without going further. The doctor who cared for you is your father's man. There's no fear that he'll leak any news of your condition except what we wish him to."

Brie set down her glass again. "No."

"I beg your—"

"No," she repeated very gently to Loubet, though her gaze shifted to her father. "I will not remain here like a prisoner. I believe I've been a prisoner quite long enough. If I have commitments, I'll meet them." She saw Bennett grin and lift his glass in salute.

"Your Highness, you must see how complicated and how dangerous this would be. If for no other reason than the police have yet to apprehend whoever kidnapped you."

"So, the solution is for me to remain closed up and closed in?" She shook her head. "I refuse."

"Gabriella, our duty is not always comfortable for us." Her father tapped the cigarette he'd lit during the conversation.

"Perhaps not. I can't speak from experience at the moment." She looked down at her hands, to the ring that was becoming familiar. "Whoever kidnapped me is still free. I mean to see they're not comfortable with that. Monsieur Loubet, you know me?"

"Your Highness, since you were a baby."

"Would you say I am a reasonably intelligent woman?"

Humor touched his eyes. "Far more than reasonably."

"I think then, with a bit of coaching, I could have my way, and you yours. The amnesia can be kept quiet if you feel that's best, but I won't hide in my rooms."

Armand started to speak, then sat back. A slight smile played on his lips. His daughter, he mused with approval, hadn't changed.

"Your Highness, I would personally be pleased to help you in any way, but—"

"Thank you, Loubet, but Mr. MacGee has already agreed to do so." Her voice was gracious and final. "Whatever I need to know in order to be Princess Gabriella, he'll tell me."

There was quick resentment again from Alexander, speculation from Armand and barely controlled annoyance from Loubet. Reeve felt them all. "The princess and I have an arrangement of sorts." He sat comfortably, watching the reactions around him. "She feels that the company of a stranger might have certain advantages for her."

"We'll discuss this later." Armand rose, and though the words weren't abrupt, they were as final as his daughter's had been. "I regret your schedule doesn't permit you to dine, Loubet. We'll finish our business tomorrow morning."

"Yes, Your Highness."

Polite goodbyes, a distinguished exit. Brie looked after him thoughtfully. "He seems very sincere and dedicated. Do I like him?"

Her father smiled as he reached for her hand. "You never said specifically. He does his job well."

"And he's a dead bore," Bennett announced ungraciously as he rose. "Let's eat." He pulled Brie close by linking arms.

"We're having the best of the best tonight in celebration. You can have a half-dozen raw oysters if you like."

"Raw? Do I like them?"

"Love them," he said blithely, and led her into dinner.

"It was...amusing to find Bennett enjoys a joke," Brie said some two hours later as she stepped onto a terrace with Reeve.

"Was it enlightening to learn you can take one?" He paused to cup his hand around his lighter. Smoke caught the breeze and billowed into the dark.

"Actually, yes. I've also learned I detest oysters and that I have a character that demands restitution. I'll get him back for tricking me into swallowing one of those things. In the meantime..." Turning, she leaned back against the strong stone banister. "I can see I've put you in a bit of an awkward position, Reeve. I didn't intend to, but now that I have, I'm afraid I don't intend to let you out."

"I can handle that for myself, when and if I choose."

"Yes." She smiled again. Then the smile became a laugh as she tossed her head back. Fear seemed so far away. Tension was so much simpler to deal with. "You could at that. Perhaps that's why I feel easy around you. Tonight I took your advice."

"Which was?"

"To observe. I have a good father. His position doesn't weigh lightly on him, nor does the strain of this past week. I see the servants treat him with great respect, but no fear, so I think he's just. Would you agree?"

The moonlight played tricks with her hair, making the pearls look like teardrops. "I would."

"Alexander is...what's the word I want?" With a shake of her head, she looked overhead to the sky. The long, pale line of her throat was exposed. "Driven, I suppose. He has the intensity of a much older man. I suppose he needs it. He hasn't decided to like you." When she shifted her head again, he found his eyes were on line with her lips.

"No."

"It doesn't bother you?"

"Not everyone's required to like me."

"I wish I had your confidence," she murmured. "In any case, I've added to whatever resentment he might feel toward you. Tonight when I said I wanted to walk outside and asked you to come with me, it annoyed him. His sense of family is very strong and very exclusive.''

"You're his responsibility—in his opinion," Reeve added when she started to protest.

"His opinion will have to change. Bennett's different. He seems so carefree. Perhaps it's his age, or the fact that he's the younger son. Still, he watched me as though I might trip at any moment and need him to catch me. Loubet, what do you think of him?''

"I don't know him.''

"Neither do I," she said wryly. "An opinion?''

"His position doesn't sit lightly on him, either.''

It wasn't an evasion, Brie decided, any more than it was an answer. "You're a very elemental man, aren't you? Is it an American trait?''

"It's a matter of pushing away frills that just get in the way. You seem to be a very elemental woman.''

"Do I?'' She pursed her lips in thought. "It might be true, or it might be true now only out of necessity. I can't afford frills, can I?''

The strain of the evening had been more than she'd admit, Reeve observed as she turned again to rest her palms against the stone. She was tired, but he understood her reluctance to go in where she'd have nothing but her own questions for company.

"Brie, have you thought about taking a few days and going away?'' She lifted her head. Sensing the anger in her, he laid a hand on her shoulder. "Not running away, getting away. It's human.''

"I can't afford to be human until I know who I am.''

"Your doctor said the amnesia's temporary.''

"What's temporary?'' she demanded. "A week, month, year? Not good enough, Reeve. I won't just sit and wait for things to come to me. In the hospital I had dreams.'' She closed her eyes a moment, breathed deep and continued. "In the dreams I was awake, but not awake. I couldn't move. It was dark and I couldn't make myself move. Voices. I could hear voices, and I'd struggle and struggle to understand them, recognize them, but I'm afraid. In the dream I'm terrified, and when I wake, I'm terrified.''

He drew in sharply on his cigarette. She said it without any emotion, and the lack of feeling said a great deal. "You were drugged."

Very slowly, she turned toward him again. In the shadowed light her eyes were very clear. "How do you know?"

"The doctors had to pump you. It's the opinion from the state you were in that you were kept drugged. Even when your memory comes back, Brie, you may not be able to pinpoint anything that happened during the week you were held. That's something you'd better face now."

"Yes, I will." She pressed her lips together until she was certain her voice would be strong. "I will remember. How much more do you know?"

"Not a great deal."

"Out with it."

He flipped his cigarette over the banister and into the void. "All right, then. You were abducted sometime Sunday. No one knows the exact time, as you were out driving alone. Sunday evening a call came in to Alexander."

"Alex?"

"Yes, he usually works on Sunday evenings in his office. He has a separate line there as all of you do in your own quarters. The call was brief. It said simply that you'd been taken and would be held until the ransom demands were met. No demands were made at that time."

And where had she been held? Dark. All she could be certain of was dark. "What did Alex do?"

"He went directly to your father. You were searched for. Monday morning your car was found on a lane about forty miles from town. There's a plot of land out there you own. It seems you have a habit of driving out there just to be alone and poke around. Monday afternoon, the first ransom demand was made. That was for money. There was no question about it being paid, of course, but before the arrangement could be made, another call came. This one demanded the release of four prisoners in exchange for you."

"And that complicated things."

"Two of them are set for execution. Espionage," he added when she remained silent. "It took the matter out of your father's hands. Money was one thing, releasing prisoners another. Negotiations were well under way when you were found on the side of the road.''

"I'll go back there,'' Brie mused. "To the place my car was found and to the place I was found.''

"Not right away. I agreed to help you, Brie, but in my way.''

Her eyes narrowed ever so slightly. "Which is?''

"My way,'' he said simply. "When I think you're strong enough, I'll take you. Until then, we move slow.''

"If I don't agree?''

"Your father might just take Loubet's plan more seriously.''

"And I'd go nowhere.''

"That's right.''

"I knew you wouldn't be an easy man, Reeve.'' She walked a few feet away, into a stream of moonlight. "I haven't much choice. I don't like that. Choice seems to me to be the most essential freedom. I keep wondering when I'll have mine back. Tomorrow, after I meet with my secretary…''

"Smithers,'' Reeve supplied. "Janet Smithers.''

"What a prim name,'' Brie observed. "I'll go over my schedule with Janet Smithers in the morning. Then I'd like to go over it with you. Whatever it is I'm committed to do, I want to do. Even if it's spending hours shopping or sitting in a beauty parlor.''

"Is that how you think you spend your time?''

"It's a possibility. I'm rich, aren't I?''

"Yes.''

"Well, then…'' With a shrug, she trailed off. "Tonight, before dinner, I lay in the bath and wondered. Actually, I thought of you and wondered.''

Very slowly he dipped his hands in his pockets. "Did you?''

"I tried to analyze you. In some ways I could and others not. If I had a great deal of experience with men, it's forgotten along with everything else, you see.'' She felt no embarrassment as she walked to him again. "I wondered if I were to kiss you, be held by you, if I'd see that part of me.''

Rocking back on his heels, he studied her blandly. "Just part of the job, Your Highness?''

Annoyance flickered in her eyes. "I don't care how you look at it.''

"Maybe I do.''

"Do you find me unattractive?"

He saw the way her lip thrust forward so slightly in a pout as she asked. She seemed a woman accustomed to flowery, imaginative compliments. She wouldn't get them from him. "Not unattractive."

She wondered why it sounded almost like an insult. "Well, then, do you have a woman you're committed to? Would you feel dishonest if you kissed me?"

He made no move toward her, and the bland smile remained. "I've no commitments, Your Highness."

"Why are you calling me that now?" she demanded. "Is it only to annoy me?"

"Yes."

She started to become angry, then ended up laughing. "It works."

"It's late." He took her hand in a friendly manner. "Let me take you up."

"You don't find me unattractive." She strolled along with him, but at her own pace. "You have no allegiances. Why won't you kiss me then and help? You did agree to help."

He stopped and looked down at her. The top of her head came to his chin. With her chin tilted back, she looked eye to eye with him. "I told your father I'd keep you out of trouble."

"You told me you'd help me find out who I am. But perhaps your word means nothing," she said lightly. "Or perhaps you're a man who doesn't enjoy kissing a woman."

She'd taken only two steps, when he caught her arm. "You don't pull any punches, do you?"

She smiled. "Apparently."

He nodded, then held her close in his arms. "Neither do I."

He touched his lips to hers with every intention of keeping the kiss dispassionate, neutral. Though he understood her reasons, her needs, he also understood she'd goaded him into doing something he was better off avoiding. Hadn't he wondered what that soft, curving mouth would taste like? Hadn't he imagined how that slim, fragile body would feel in his arms? But he'd agreed to do a job. He'd never taken any job lightly.

So he touched his lips to hers, intending on keeping the kiss neutral. Neutrality lasted no more than an instant.

She was soft, frail, sweet. He had to protect her. She was warm, tempting, arousing. He had to take her. Her eyes were open, just. He could see the glimmer of gold through the thick lashes as he slid his hand up to cup her neck. And he could feel, as the kiss deepened beyond intention, her unhesitating, unapologetic response.

Their tongues met, skimmed, then lingered, drawing out flavors. She wound her arms invitingly around him so that her body pressed without restriction to his. The scent she wore was darker then the sky, deeper than the mixed fragrance of night blossoms that rose from the gardens below. Moonlight splashed over him and onto her. He could almost believe in fairy tales again.

She thought she'd known what to expect. Somewhere inside her was the memory of what a kiss was, just as she knew what food, what drink were. And yet, with his mouth on hers, her mind, her emotions were a clean slate. He wrote on them what he chose.

If her blood had run hot before, she didn't remember it. If her head had swum, she had no recollection. Everything was fresh, new, exciting. And yet...and yet there was a depth here, a primitive need that came without surprise.

Yearning, dreaming, longing. She may have done so before. Aching, needing, wanting. She might not remember, but she understood. It was him, holding her close—him, rushing kisses over her face—him, breathing her name onto her lips, that brought these things all home again.

But had there been others? Who? How many? Had she stood in the moonlight wrapped in strong arms before? Had she given herself so unhesitatingly to passion before? Had it meant nothing to her, or everything? Shaken, she drew away. What kind of woman gave a man her soul before she knew him? Or even herself?

"Reeve." She stepped back carefully. Doubts dragged at her. "I'm not sure I understand any better."

He'd felt it from her. Complete, unrestricted passion. Even as he wanted to reach out for it again, the same reasoning came to him. How many others? Unreasonably he wanted that heat, that desire to be his alone. He offered his hand but kept his distance. It wasn't a feeling he welcomed.

"We'd both better sleep on it."

Chapter 4

She felt like an imposter. Brie was in her tidy no-frills all-elegance office only because Reeve had taken her there. She'd been grateful when he'd knocked on her sitting room door at eight with a simple, "Are you ready?" and nothing else. The prospect of having to ask one of the palace staff to show her the way hadn't appealed. On her first full day back, Brie didn't want to have to start off dealing with expectations and curiosity. With him, she didn't have to apologize, fumble or explain.

Reeve was here, Brie told herself, to do exactly what he was doing: guide her discreetly along. As long as she remembered that, and not the moments they'd spent on the terrace the night before, she'd be fine. She'd have felt better if she hadn't woken up thinking of them.

After a short, nearly silent walk through the corridors, where Brie had felt all the strain on her side and none on Reeve's, he'd shown her to the third-floor corner room in the east wing.

Once there, she toured it slowly. The room wasn't large, but it was all business. Good light, a practical set-up, privacy. The furniture might have been exquisite, but it wasn't frivolous. That relieved her.

The capable mahogany desk that stood in the center was orderly. The colors were subdued, pastels again, she noted, brushing past the two chairs with their intricate Oriental upholstery and ebony wood. Again, flowers were fresh and plentiful—pink roses bursting up in a Sevres vase, white carnations delicate in Wedgwood. She pulled out a bud and twirled it by its stem as she turned back to Reeve.

"So I work here." She saw the thick leather book on the desk, but only touched it. Would she open it to find her days filled with lunches, teas, fittings, shopping? And if she did, could she face it? "What work do I do?"

It was a challenge. It was a plea. Both were directed to him.

He'd done his homework. While Brie had slept the afternoon before, Reeve had gone through her files, her appointment book, even her diary. There was little of Her Serene Highness Gabriella de Cordina he didn't know. But Brie Bisset was a bit more internal.

He'd spent an hour with her secretary and another with the palace manager. There had been a brief, cautious interview with her former nanny in which he'd had to gradually chip away at a protective instinct that spanned generations. The picture he gained made Princess Gabriella more complex, and Brie Bisset more intriguing than ever.

He'd decided to help her because she needed help, but nothing was ever that simple. The puzzle of her kidnapping nagged at him, prodded, taunted. On the surface, it seemed as though her father was leaving the investigation to the police and going about his business. Reeve rarely believed what was on the surface. If Armand was playing a chess game with him as queen's knight, he'd play along, and make some moves of his own. It hadn't taken Reeve long to discover that royalty was insular, private and close-mouthed. So much better the challenge. He wanted to put the pieces of the kidnapping together, but to do so, he had to put the pieces of Gabriella together first.

From her description of her family the day before, Reeve had thought her perceptive. Her impression of herself, however, was far from accurate. Or perhaps it was the fear of herself, Reeve reflected. For a moment, he speculated on what it would be like to wake up one morning with no past, no ties, no sense of self. Paralyzing. Then he quickly dismissed the idea. The more sympathetic he was toward her, the more difficult his job.

"You're involved in a number of projects," he said simply, and stepped forward to the desk. ''Some you'd term day-to-day duties, and others official.''

It came back to her then, hard, just what had passed between them the night before. Being moved, being driven. Had any other man made her feel like that before? She didn't step back, but she braced herself. Emotions, whatever they might be, couldn't be allowed to interfere with what she had to do.

''Projects?'' she repeated smoothly. ''Other than having my nails painted?''

''You're a bit hard on Gabriella, aren't you?'' Reeve murmured. He dropped his hand on hers, on the leather book. For five humming seconds they stood just so.

''Perhaps. But I have to know her to understand her. At this point, she's more a stranger to me than you are.''

Sympathy rose up again. Whatever his wish, he couldn't deny it completely. The hand under his was firm; her voice was strong, but in her eyes he saw the self-doubt, the confusion and the need. ''Sit down, Brie.''

The gentleness of his voice had her hesitating. When a man could speak like that, what woman was safe? Slowly she withdrew her hand from his and chose one of the trim upholstered chairs. ''Very well. This is to be lesson one?''

''If you like.'' He sat on the edge of the desk so that there was a comfortable distance between them, and so that he could look fully into her face. ''Tell me what you think of when you think of a princess.''

''Are you playing analyst?''

He crossed his ankles. ''It's a simple question. You can make the answer as simple as you like.''

She smiled and seemed to relax with it. ''Prince Charming, fairy godmothers, glass slippers.'' She brushed the rose petals idly against her cheek and looked beyond him to a sunbeam that shot onto the floor. ''Footmen in dashing uniforms, carriages with white satin seats, pretty silver crowns, floaty dresses. Crowds of people.... Crowds of people,'' she repeated, and her eyes focused on the stream of sunlight, ''cheering below the window. The sun's in your eyes so that it's difficult to see, but you hear. You wave. There's the smell of roses, strong. A sea of people with their voices rising up and up so that they wash over you. Lovely, sweet, demanding.'' She fell silent, then dropped the rose in her lap.

Her hand had trembled; he'd seen it the instant before she'd dropped the flower. ''Is that your imagination, or do you remember that?''

''I...'' How could she explain? She could still smell the roses, hear the cheers, but she couldn't remember. She could feel the way the sun made her eyes sting, but she couldn't put herself at the window. ''Impressions only,'' she told him after a moment. ''They come and go. They never stay.''

''Don't push it.''

Her head whipped around. ''I want—''

''I know what you want.'' His voice was calm, even careless. Annoyance flashed in her eyes. It was something he knew how to deal with. He picked up the appointment book but didn't open it. ''I'll give you an average day in the life of Her Serene Highness Gabriella de Cordina.''

''And how do you know?''

Reeve tested the weight of the book as he watched her. ''It's my job to know. You rise at seven-thirty and breakfast in your room. From eight-thirty to nine you meet with the palace manager.''

''*Régisseur.*'' She blinked, then her brows knit. ''That's the French. He would be called *régisseur*, not manager.''

Reeve made no comment while she continued to frown, struggling to remember why the term was so familiar to her. ''You decide on the day's menus. If there's no official dinner, you normally plan the main meal for midday. This was a duty you assumed when your mother died.''

''I see.'' She waited for the grief. Longed for it. She felt nothing. ''Go on.''

''From nine to ten-thirty you're here in your office with your secretary, handling official correspondence. Generally, you'll dictate to her how to answer, then sign the letters yourself once they're in order.''

''How long has she been with me?'' Brie asked abruptly. ''This Janet Smithers?''

''A little under a year. Your former secretary had her first child and retired.''

"Am I..." Groping for the word, she wiggled her fingers. "Do I have a satisfactory relationship with her?"

Reeve tilted his head. "No one told me of any complaint."

Frustrated, Brie shook her head. How could she explain to a man that she wanted to know how she and her secretary were woman to woman? How could she explain that she wondered if she had any close female friends, any woman that would break the circle of men she seemed to be surrounded with? Perhaps this was one more thing she'd have to determine for herself. "Please, continue."

"If there's time, you take care of any personal correspondence, as well, during the morning session. Otherwise, you leave that for the evening."

It seemed tedious, she mused, then thought that obligations often were. "What is 'official correspondence'?"

"You're the president for the Aid to Handicapped Children Organization. The AHC is Cordina's largest charity. You're also a spokesperson for the International Red Cross. In addition you're deeply involved with the Fine Arts Center, which was built in your mother's name. It falls to you to handle correspondence from the wives of heads of state, to head or serve on various committees, to accept or decline invitations and to entertain during state functions. Politics and government are your father's province, and to some extent, Alexander's."

"So I confine myself to more—feminine duties?"

She saw the grin, fast, appealing, easy. "I wouldn't put a label on it after looking at your schedule, Brie."

"Which so far," she pointed out, "consists of answering letters."

"Three days a week you go to the headquarters of the AHC. Personally, I wouldn't want to handle the influx of paperwork. You've been bucking the National Council for eighteen months on an increase in budget for the Fine Arts Center. Last year you toured fifteen countries for the Red Cross and spent ten days in Ethiopia. There was a ten-page spread in *World* magazine. I'll see that you get a copy."

She picked up the rose again, running her finger over the petals as she rose to pace. "But am I clever at it?" she demanded. "Do

I know what I'm doing, or am I simply there as some kind of figurehead?''

Reeve drew out a cigarette. "Both. A beautiful young princess draws attention, press, funds and interest. A clever young woman uses that and her brain to get what she's after. According to your diary—''

"You've read my diary?''

He lifted a brow, studying the combination of outrage and embarrassment on her face. She'd have no idea, he mused, if there was any need for the embarrassment. "You've asked me to help you," he reminded her. "I can't help you unless I know you. But relax—'' Reeve lit the cigarette with a careless flick of his lighter "—you're very discreet, Gabriella, even in what you write in your personal papers.''

There was no use squirming, she told herself. He'd very probably enjoy it. "You were saying?''

"According to your diary, the traveling is wearing. You've never been particularly fond of it, but you do it, year in and year out, because it's necessary. Funds must be raised, functions attended. You work, Gabriella. I promise you.''

"I'll have to take your word for it.'' She slipped the rose back into the vase. "And I want to begin. First, if I'm to keep the loss of memory discreet, I need the names of people I should know.'' Skirting around the desk, she took her seat and picked up a pen. "You'll give me what you know. Then I'll call Janet Smithers. Do I have appointments today?''

"One o'clock at the AHC Center.''

"Very well. I've a lot to learn before one.''

By the time Reeve left her with her secretary, he'd given Brie more than fifty names, with descriptions and explanations. He'd consider it a minor miracle if she retained half of them.

If he'd had a choice, Reeve would have gotten in his car and driven. Toward the sea, toward the mountains—it didn't matter. Palaces, no matter how spacious, how beautiful, how historically fascinating, were still walls and ceilings and floors. He wanted the sky around him.

Only briefly, Reeve paused at a window to look out before he climbed to the fourth floor and Prince Armand's office. A cop's work, he thought with some impatience. Legwork and paperwork. He was still a long way from escaping it.

He was admitted immediately, to find the prince pouring coffee. The room was twice the size of Brie's, much more ornate and rigidly masculine. The molding on the lofted ceiling might have been intricately carved and gilded, but the chairs were wide, the desk oak and solid. Armand had the windows open, so that the light spilled across the huge red carpet.

"Loubet has just left," Armand said without preliminary. "You've seen the paper?"

"Yes." Reeve accepted the coffee but didn't sit, as the prince remained standing. He knew when to reject protocol and when to bow to it. "It appears there's relief that Her Highness is back safely and a lot of speculation on the kidnapping itself. It's to be expected."

"And a great deal of criticism of Cordina's police department," Armand added, then shrugged. "That, too, is to be expected. I feel so myself, but, then, they have next to nothing to go on."

Reeve inclined his head, coolly. "Don't they?"

Their look held, each measuring the other. "The police have their duty, I mine and you yours. You've been with Gabriella this morning?"

"Yes."

"Sit." With an impatient gesture he motioned toward a chair. Protocol be damned, he wasn't ready to sit himself. "How is she?"

Reeve took a seat and watched the prince walk around the room with the same nervous grace his daughter had. "Physically, I'd say she's bouncing back fast. Emotionally, she's holding on because she's determined to. Her secretary's briefing her on names and faces at the moment. She intends to keep her schedule, starting today."

Armand drank half his coffee, then set the cup down. He'd already had too much that morning. "And you'll go with her?"

Reeve sipped his coffee. It was dark and rich and hot. "I'll go with her."

"It's difficult—" Armand broke off, struggling with some emotion. Anger, sorrow, frustration? Reeve couldn't be quite sure. "It's difficult," he repeated, but with perfect calm, "to stand back and do little, give little. You came at my request. You stayed at my request. And now I find myself jealous that you have my daughter's trust.''

'''Trust' might be a bit premature. She considers me useful at the moment.'' He heard the annoyance in his voice and carefully smoothed it over. "I can give her information about herself without drawing on her emotions.''

"Like her mother, she has many of them. When she loves, she loves completely. That in itself is a treasure.''

Armand let his coffee cool as he walked around to sit at his desk. It was an official move, of that Reeve was certain. Imperceptibly he came to attention. "Last evening Bennett pointed out to me that I may have put you in an awkward position.''

Reeve sipped his coffee, outwardly relaxed, inwardly waiting. "In what way?''

"You'll be at Gabriella's side, privately and publicly. Being who she is, Brie is photographed often. Her life is a subject for discussion.'' The prince picked up a smooth white rock that sat on his desk. It just fitted in the palm of his hand; it was a rock his wife had found years before on a rocky beach. "With my thoughts centered around Gabriella's safety and her recovery, I hadn't considered the implications of your presence.''

"As to my...place in Gabriella's life?''

Armand's lips curved. "It's a relief not to have to explain everything with delicacy. Bennett's young, and his own affairs are lovingly described in the international press.'' There seemed to be a mixture of pride and annoyance. A parent's fate, Reeve thought with some amusement. He'd seen it in his father often enough. "Perhaps that's why this occurred to him first.''

"I'm here for Her Highness's security,'' Reeve commented. "It seems simple enough.''

"For the ruler of Cordina to have asked a former policeman, an American policeman, to guard his daughter, is not simple. It would, perhaps rightly, be considered an insult. We're a small country, Reeve, but pride is no small thing.''

Reeve sat silently a moment, weighing, considering. "Do you want me to leave?''

"No.''

Relief. It shouldn't be what he was feeling, certainly not so intensely. But his hand on the cup relaxed. "I can't change my nationality, Armand."

"No." His answer was just as brief. He passed the rock into his other hand. "It would be possible, however, to change your position in such a way that would allow you to remain close to Gabriella without causing the wrong kind of speculation."

This time it was Reeve who smiled. "As a suitor?"

"Again you make it easy for me." Armand sat back, studying the son of his friend. Under less complicated circumstances, he might have approved of a match between Reeve and his daughter. He couldn't deny he had hoped Brie would marry before this, and that he'd purposely tossed her together with members of British royalty and gentry, eligible men of the French aristocracy. Still, the MacGees had an impressive lineage and a flawless reputation. He wouldn't have been displeased if what he was now proposing hypothetically were fact.

"I would, however, take it one step closer than a suitor. If you have no objections, I'd like to announce your engagement to Gabriella." He waited for some sign, some gesture or expression. Reeve gave him nothing more than what seemed to be polite interest. Armand rubbed a thumb over the rock. He could respect a man who could keep his thoughts to himself.

"As her fiancé," he continued, "you can be by her side without raising any questions."

"The question might arise as to how I became Her Highness's fiancé after being in Cordina only a few days."

Armand nodded, liking the clean, emotionless response. "My long association with your father makes this more than plausible. Brie was in your country only last year. It could be said that you developed your relationship then."

Reeve drew out a cigarette. He found he needed one. "Engagements have a habit of leading to marriage."

"Proper ones, yes." Armand set the stone back on his desk and folded his hands. "This, of course, is only one for our convenience. When the need is over, we'll announce that you and Gabriella have had a change of heart. The engagement will be broken and you'll each go your own way. The press will enjoy the melodrama and no harm will be done."

The princess and the farmer, Reeve thought, and grinned. It

might be an interesting game at that. Before it was over, there might be a few moments to remember. "Even if I agree, there's another player involved."

"Gabriella will do what's best for herself and her country." He spoke simply, as a man who knows his own power. "The choice is yours, not hers."

A lack of choice. Hadn't she said that was what she resented most? There was more to being royal than the pretty silver crown and glass slipper. Reeve blew out a stream of smoke. He might sympathize, but it wouldn't stop him from making this choice for her. "I can understand your reasons. We'll play it your way, Armand."

The prince rose. "I'll speak to Gabriella."

Reeve hadn't thought she'd be pleased. When it came down to it, he didn't want her to be. It was easier on him when she was a bit prickly, a little icy. It was the lost, vulnerable look that undid him.

When Brie swept out of the palace a few minutes before one, he wasn't disappointed. She'd thrown on a jacket, the same dark, rich suede as her skirt. Her hair fell free down the back and caught every color of the sun. Her eyes, when she tossed her head back and aimed them at him, were gold, glorious and molten. A creature of the light, he thought as he lounged against the car. She didn't belong behind castle walls, but under the sky.

Reeve gave her a small bow as he opened the door for her. Brie sent him one long smoldering look. "You stabbed me in the back." She dropped into the front seat and stared straight ahead.

Reeve jingled the keys in his pocket as he crossed over to the driver's side. He could handle it delicately...or he could handle it as he chose. "Something wrong, darling?" he asked her when he settled beside her.

"You're joking?" She looked at him again, hard and full. "You dare?"

He took her hand, holding it though she gave it a good, hard jerk. "Gabriella, some things are best taken lightly."

"This farce. This deceit!" Abruptly, and with finesse, she went off in a stream of rapid, indignant French he could only partially follow. The tone, however, was crystal clear. "First I have to accept you as a bodyguard," she continued, reverting to English without a pause. "So that whenever I turn you'll be there, hovering. Now this pretense that we're to be married. And for what?" she demanded. "So that it won't be known that my father has engaged a bodyguard who isn't Cordinian or French. So that I may be seen constantly with a man without damaging my reputation. Hah!" In a bad tempered and undeniably regal gesture, she flung out a hand. "It's *my* reputation."

"There's always mine," he said coolly.

With that she turned to him, giving him a haughty stare, first down, then up. "I believe it's safe to say you have one already. And it doesn't concern me," she added before he could speak.

"As my fiancée, it certainly should." Reeve started the engine and began the leisurely drive down.

"It's a ridiculous charade."

"Agreed."

That stopped her. She had opened her mouth to continue to rage, then closed it again with a nearly audible snap. "You find it ridiculous to be engaged to me?"

"Absolutely."

She discovered something else about herself. She had a healthy supply of vanity. "Why?"

"I generally don't get engaged to women I barely know. Then, too, I'd think twice about hooking up with someone who was willful, selfish and bad tempered."

Her chin came up. From out of her bag she grabbed a pair of tinted glasses and stuck them on her nose. "Then you're fortunate it's only a pretense, aren't you?"

"Yes."

She snapped her bag closed. "And of short duration."

He didn't grin. A man only takes a certain amount of risks in one day. "The shorter the better."

"I'll do my best to accommodate you." She took the rest of the journey in simmering silence.

It was a short one, but she wasn't grateful for it. Having something, someone, specific to direct her anger at helped ease the fear of facing people who were only names to her. She would have liked more time to prepare.

The building that housed the headquarters for the Aid to Handicapped Children Organization was old and distinguished. It had once been the home of her great-grandmother, the thin, efficient Janet Smithers had told her.

Brie stepped from the car with practiced ease. Her stomach muscles were jumping. As she walked to the entrance, she went over the floor plan in her mind. She wouldn't have reached for Reeve's hand, but when his closed over hers, she didn't pull away. Sometimes it was necessary, even preferable, to hold hands with the devil.

She stepped inside, into a cool white hall. Immediately a woman who sat at a desk just beyond the entrance rose and curtsied. "Your Highness. It's so good to see you safe."

"Thank you, Claudia." The hesitation on the name was so brief Reeve hardly noticed it himself.

"We didn't expect you, Your Highness. After what—what happened." Her voice faltered. Her eyes filled.

Compassion moved Brie, before instinct, before politics. She held out both hands. "I'm fine, Claudia. Anxious to get to work." There was a warmth here, a bond she hadn't felt with her personal secretary. Still, there could be no pursuing it until she understood it. "This is Mr. MacGee. He's…staying with us. Claudia's been with AHC for nearly ten years, Reeve." Brie gave him the information he'd given her only that morning. "I believe she could run the organization single-handed. Tell me, Claudia, have you left anything for me to do?"

"There's the ball, Your Highness. As usual, there are complications."

The Annual Charity Ball, Brie recited to herself. A tradition in Cordina and the biggest fund-raiser for the AHC. She, as president, would organize. As princess she would hostess. It drew the rich, the famous and the important to Cordina every spring. "It wouldn't be the ball without complications. I'll get to work, then. Come on, Reeve, we'll see how useful you can be."

Past the first hurdle, she went up the stairs, down the hall and into the second room on the right.

"Well done," Reeve told her as she closed the door.

"I keep hoping…" With a shrug, she let the thought go. She kept hoping that someone would trigger something, would trip the first lock on her memory so that remembrances would come through. Briskly she moved over and drew the curtains.

The room wasn't as elegant as her personal office. There was a row of file cabinets along one wall, metal and businesslike. Though the desk was ornate, made of beautiful cherry, it was covered with files and notes and papers. Going over, she sat down and picked one up. It was a note concerning a donation to the pediatric ward of the hospital in her handwriting.

Odd to see it, she mused. Earlier she'd tested herself by simply picking up a pen and writing out her name, just to see her signature. The writing was big, looping, just bordering on the undisciplined, and very distinctive. Brie set down the note and wondered where to begin.

"I'll see about some coffee," Reeve suggested.

"And some cakes or cookies," Brie said absently as she began to sort through the papers on her desk. "I missed lunch." Looking up, she lifted a brow. "I was too angry to eat, but it appears I'm going to need something before this is done."

"Hamburger?"

"Cheeseburger, no onions." Then she grinned because it had come out so naturally. "I like them well done." She could almost, almost picture herself sitting at that desk with a harried, impromptu lunch while she made calls and signed papers. With a burst of enthusiasm, she began to organize.

She was good at it. It was thrilling to discover she had a talent. Within two hours she'd assessed the situation in her office and had begun, slowly, systematically to cope with details, problems and decisions. It came naturally, as dressing, eating, walking came. She had only to think of the angles, consider them and work her way through. At the end of her two hours, her confidence was strong and her mood high. When she left the office her desk was still cluttered. But it was her clutter now—she understood it.

"It felt good," she said to Reeve when she settled in the car again. "So good. You'll think I'm foolish."

"Not at all." He sat beside her but didn't reach for the key just yet. "You accomplished a hell of a lot in a couple of hours, Brie. As a cop, I know just how frustrating and boring paperwork can be."

"But when it does something, it's worth the headache, isn't it? AHC is a good organization. It doesn't just preach. It helps. All that equipment in the pediatric ward, the new wing. The wheelchairs, walkers, hearing aids, tutors. They cost money, and we get the money.'' She glanced down at the glitter of diamonds and sapphires on her finger. ''It makes me feel justified.''

''Do you need to be?''

''Yes. Just because I was born to something doesn't mean I don't have to earn the right to it. Especially now when...''

''You can't remember being born to it.''

''I don't know how I felt before,'' she murmured, staring down at the elegant little leather purse she carried. ''I only know how I feel now. I've been given a title, but it doesn't come without a price, that I know.''

He started the car. ''You learn fast.''

''I have to.'' Weariness was there, but she didn't relax. She couldn't. ''Reeve, I don't want to go back just yet. Can we drive? Anywhere, it doesn't matter. I just need to be out.''

''All right.'' He understood the need to be away from walls, from restrictions. He'd grown up with them, as well. He'd rebelled against them, as well. Without thinking, he headed toward the sea.

There were places just outside the capital where the road stretched and curved along the seawall. There were places before Cordina's port, Lebarre, where the land was wild and free and open. Reeve pulled up beside a clump of pitted rocks where the trees grew slanted, leaning away from the wind.

Brie got out of the car and drank the scene in. Somehow she knew the scent and taste of the sea. She couldn't be certain she'd been to this spot before, yet it soothed her. Letting the need to know slip away, she walked toward the old, sturdy seawall.

Tiny springy purple flowers crowded their way up through the cracks, determined to have the sun. She reached to touch one but didn't pick it. It would die too quickly. Unmindful of her skirt, she sat on the wall and looked down.

The sea was single-mindedly blue. If it had had its way, it would have consumed the land. The wall prevented that, but didn't tame it. Farther out she could see ships, big freighters that were on their way to or from the port, sleek sailing boats with their canvas taut. She thought her hands had known the feel of rope, her body the sway of the sea. Perhaps soon she'd test it.

''Some things are comfortable right away. Familiar, I mean. This is one of them.''

"You couldn't grow up near the sea and not find spots like this." The wind whipped her hair back, tossing it up and away from her face. Its color was nearly gold in this light, with small flames licking through it. He sat beside her, but not too close.

"I think I'd come to a place like this, just to breathe when the protocol became too tedious to stand." She sighed, closing her eyes as she lifted her face to the wind. "I wonder if I always felt that way."

"You could ask your father."

She lowered her head. When their eyes met, he saw the weariness she'd been so careful to hide. She wasn't back on full power yet, he reflected. And he wasn't immune to vulnerability.

"It's difficult." Anger and annoyance, strain and tension were forgotten as she felt herself drawn to him again. She could talk to him, say whatever was on her mind, without consequences. "I don't want to hurt him. I feel such intense love, such fierce protection from him it disturbs me. I know he's waiting for me to remember everything."

"Aren't you?"

She looked back out to sea, silent.

"Brie, don't you want to remember?"

It was the sea she continued to look at, not him. "Part of me does—desperately. And then another part pushes away, as if it's all just too much. If I remember the good, won't I remember the bad?"

"You're not a coward."

"I wonder. Reeve, I remember running. The rain, the wind. I remember running until I thought I'd die from it. Most of all, I remember the fear, a fear so great that I would have preferred dying to stopping. I'm not sure that part of me will allow the memory to come back."

He understood what she described. The knowledge ate at him, something he couldn't allow. Something he couldn't prevent. "When you're strong enough, you won't give yourself a choice."

"Something inside of me is afraid of that, too. At a time like this—" she shook her hair back and enjoyed the feel of it lifting off her neck "—it would be so easy to relax and let it go, to just allow things to happen. If I weren't what I am I could do that. No one would care."

"You are what you are."

"You don't dream?" she asked with a half smile. "You don't ever ask yourself, what if? I could sit here now and pretend I had a cottage in the hills and a garden. Perhaps my husband's a farmer and I'm carrying our first child. Life is simple and very sweet."

"And the woman in the cottage could pretend she was a princess who lived in a palace." He touched a strand of her hair that danced in the wind. "Life's full of dreams, Brie. It's never simple, but it can be sweet."

"What do you dream?"

He curled her hair around the tip of his finger, then set it free. "Of tilling my own land, watching my crops grow. Being away from the streets."

"You have land in America? A farm?"

"Yeah." He thought of it waiting for him. Next year, he promised himself. He'd waited this long.

"But I thought you were a policeman—no, a detective now, working for yourself. A kind of adventurer."

He laughed at the term, not bitter, just amused. "People outside the business tend to think of dark alleys and forget the paperwork."

"But you've seen the dark alleys."

He gave her a look, one hard and calm enough to make her swallow. "I've seen them, maybe too many of them."

She thought she understood. She knew, without knowing, that she'd traveled a dark alley herself. For a moment she looked at the sea and sky. It wasn't the time to think of the dark. "What will you grow on your farm?"

He thought of it. At times like this he almost believed it would happen. "Corn, hay, some apples."

"And you have a house." Caught up, she twisted around to face him more directly. "A farmhouse?"

"It needs some work."

"It has a front porch? A big front porch?"

He laughed, pleasing her. "It's big enough. After I've replaced a few boards it might even be safe."

"On warm nights you'd sit out on a rocker and listen to the wind."

He tugged her hair. "The grass is always greener."

"So they say. Still, I think I could deal with fifty weeks of demands, of being on display, if only I had two weeks to sit on a rocker and listen to the wind. So you have land, a farmhouse, but no wife. Why?"

"An odd question from one's fiancée."

"You only say that to annoy me and evade answering."

"You're perceptive, Brie." He dropped off the wall and held out his hand. "We should be getting back."

"It only seems fair that I know more of your life when you know so much of mine." But she gave him her hand. "Have you ever been in love?"

"No."

"I wonder sometimes if I have." Her voice was wistful as she looked back out to sea. "That's why I goaded you into kissing me last night. I thought perhaps it might remind me."

He saw the humor in her statement, but he wasn't amused. "And did it?"

"No. It wasn't as though I'd never been kissed before, but it didn't bring anyone to mind."

Was she deliberately challenging him again, or was she just that artless? It didn't seem to matter. His hand slipped to her wrist. "No one?"

She heard the change, that gentle, dangerous tone. It was a tone a woman would be wise to be wary of. But she wasn't just a woman, Brie reminded herself as she lifted her head. She was a princess. "No one. It makes me think no man's been important to me before."

"You responded like a woman who knows what it is to want."

She didn't back away, though he was closer now. His face, she thought, wasn't one a woman would be comfortable with on long, rainy evenings. It would excite continually. His hands, large, elegant, strong, wouldn't make a woman dream softly. They'd make her pulse, even in sleep. She already knew it.

"Perhaps I am. After all, I'm not a child."

"No." He closed the gap. The wind whipped between them as he stepped forward. "Neither of us is."

Her mouth was soft, but it wasn't hesitant. It answered his, as it had the night before. No, life was never simple, he thought as he drew her closer. But God, it could be sweet.

She gave herself to him. Somehow she needed to just then with the sea thrashing below and the wind moaning. They were so alone it seemed right that they come together, body to body, mouth to mouth. She felt his hand slide up to her hair, firm, strong. As his fingers tangled in it, she let her head fall back. It wasn't surrender, but temptation.

His heartbeat was as hard and quick as hers. She could feel it pound against her. The sun was strong, so she kept her eyes closed until the light was red and warm. He tasted…enticing. Male, dark, not quite safe. She felt as if she were walking along the top of a wall, above the rock and water. It was frightening. Wonderful. She ran her hands up over his back. There was muscle there. Security. Danger. She wanted both. Just for a moment, this moment, she could be any woman. Even royalty bows to passion.

She was soft, but she wasn't safe. He knew it. He'd known it before he'd let himself be driven to touch her. Just as he knew he'd be driven to touch again and again what he was beginning to crave. The scent she wore seemed to swim around him, lighter than the air, darker than the sea.

Did she know? Even as he submerged himself deeper in her, he wondered if she knew what she did. The eyes of a sorceress, the face of an angel. What man wouldn't be on his knees to her? Yet her sigh, quiet, low, was that of a woman. Flesh and blood or fairy tale, she was bound to tempt him. She wasn't meant to be resisted.

But he had no choice.

He drew her away much as he had the night before—slowly, reluctantly, but inevitably. Her eyes remained closed for just a moment longer, as if she were savoring the moment. But when they opened, her look was direct and level. Perhaps both of them knew they had to step back from the edge.

"Your family will wonder where you are."

She nodded, taking the final step back. "Yes. Obligations come first, don't they?"

He didn't answer, but they walked back to the car together.

Chapter 5

"Brie! Brie, wait a minute."

Turning, Brie shielded her eyes from the sun and watched Bennett step into the gardens with two Russian wolfhounds fretting at his heels.

His Royal Highness Prince Bennett de Cordina was dressed like a stablehand—worn jeans tucked into the tops of grimy boots, a shirt with a streak of dirt down one sleeve. As he drew closer, she caught the earthy smell of horses and hay on him. Like the dogs that fretted around his legs, he seemed to hold great stores of energy just under control.

"You're alone." He gave her a quick grin as he put one hand on the head of one dog and slipped another under the collar of the second. "Easy, Boris," he said offhandedly as the dog tried to slobber over Brie's shoes.

Boris and…Natasha, she thought, flipping back in her mental files for the names Reeve had given her. Even dogs couldn't be ignored. They'd been a present to Bennett from the Russian ambassador, and with his penchant for irony, Bennett had named them after characters in an American cartoon show—inept Russian spies who found it difficult to outwit a squirrel and a moose.

Bennett controlled his dogs—barely. "It's the first morning I've seen you out."

"It's the first morning this week I haven't had meetings." She smiled, not certain if she was guilty or pleased. "Have you been riding?"

Did she ride? Her mind worked at the quick double pace that was becoming familiar. She thought she knew how to sit a horse, how to groom one. Brie struggled for the sensation even while she smiled easily at her brother.

"Early. There was some work to do in the stables." They stood awkwardly a moment as they both wondered what should be said. "You don't have your American shadow," Bennett blurted out, then grinned a little sheepishly when Brie only lifted a brow. "Alex's nickname for Reeve," he said, and shrugged off any embarrassment. He generally found it a waste of time. "I like him, actually. I think Alex does, too, or he'd be more frigidly polite and pompous. It's just harder for him to accept an outsider right now."

"None of us were consulted about it, were we?"

"Well, he seems okay." Bennett let Boris rub up against him, not noticing or caring about the transfer of dog hair. "Not stuffy, anyway. I've been meaning to ask him where he gets his clothes."

She felt both tolerance and amusement, and wondered if this was habitual. "So the man might not be easily accepted, but his clothes are?"

"He certainly has an eye for them," Bennett commented as he pushed one of the dog's heads aside. "Does it bother you to have him around?"

Did it? Brie plucked a blossom from a creamy white azalea. It had been a week since she'd returned to the palace. A week since she'd returned to the life that wasn't yet her life. Feelings were something she had to reexplore every day.

She supposed she was nearly used to having Reeve there, at her side almost every waking moment. Yet she felt no less a stranger to him, to her family. To herself.

"No, but there are times when…" She looked out over the lush, blooming garden. Looked beyond. "Bennett, did I always have this need to get away? Everyone's so kind, so attentive, but I feel that if I could just go somewhere where I could breathe. Somewhere where I could lie on my back in the grass and leave everything behind."

"That's why you bought the little farm."

She turned back, brows knit. "Little farm?"

"We called it that, though it's really just a few acres of ground no one's ever done anything with. You threaten to build a house there from time to time."

A farmhouse, she mused. Perhaps that was why she'd felt so in tune with Reeve when they'd talked of his. "Is that where I was going when I..."

"Yes." The dogs were restless, so he let them go sniff around the bases of bushes and beat each other with their tails. "I wasn't here. I was at school. If father has his way, I'll be back at Oxford next week." Suddenly he looked as he was—a boy on the edge of manhood who had to bow to his father's wishes even as he strained against them. From somewhere inside Brie rose up an understanding and an affection. On impulse she linked her arm through his, and they began to walk.

"Bennett, do we like each other?"

"That's a silly—" He cut himself off and nudged at the dog that trotted alongside him. It wasn't as easy for him to control his emotions as it was for his father, for his brother. He had to concentrate on it, and as often as not, he still lost. But this was Brie; that made all the difference. "Yes, we like each other. It isn't easy to have friends, you know, who aren't somehow tied to our position. We're friends. You've always been my liaison to Father."

"Have I? In what way?"

"Whenever I'd get into trouble—"

"You have a habit of it?"

"Apparently." But he didn't sound displeased.

"And I don't?"

"You're more discreet." He gave her another of those quick, dashing smiles. "I've always admired the way you could do almost anything you wanted without making waves. I don't seem to be able to keep a low profile. I'm still dealing with the French singer fiasco."

"Oh?" Interested, she tilted her head up to look at him. God, she realized all at once. He was beautiful. There simply wasn't another word for it. If a woman drew an image of Prince Charming in her head, it would be Bennett. "A female singer, I take it."

"Lily." This time his smile didn't look young, but infinitely experienced. No, she realized, he wasn't really a boy, after all.

"She was...talented," he decided with a flash of irony that was as mature as the smile. "And unsuitable. She sang in this little club in Paris. I spent a few weeks there last summer and we...we met."

"And had a blistering affair."

"It seemed like a good idea at the time. The press licked their chops, rubbed their hands together and went to it. Lily's career skyrocketed." He smiled again, quick and crooked. "She got a recording contract and was—let's say she was very, very grateful."

"And you, of course, modestly accepted her gratitude."

"Of course. On the other hand, Father was furious. I'm sure he would have yanked me back to Cordina and put me in solitary confinement if you hadn't calmed him down."

She lifted both brows, impressed with herself. The man with the straight back and intense eyes wouldn't be easy to soothe. "Just how did I manage that?"

"If I knew how you get around him, Brie, I'd do my best to make it my own art."

She considered this, pleased and curious. "I must be good at it."

"The best. Father's fond of saying that of all his children, you're the only one with basic common sense."

"Oh, dear." She wrinkled her nose. "And you still like me?"

He did something so sweet, so natural, it brought tears to her eyes. He ruffled her hair. She blinked the tears away. "I'd just as soon you had the common sense. It would get in my way."

"And Alexander? How do I—you," she amended, "feel about him?"

"Oh, Alex is okay." He spoke with the tolerance of a brother for a brother. "He has the hardest road, after all, with the press forever hounding him and linking him with every woman he looks twice at. Discretion's an art with Alex. He has to be twice as good at everything, you know, because it's expected. And he has this roaring temper that he has to pull back. The heir isn't permitted to make public scenes. Even private ones can leak out. Remember when that overweight French count drank too much champagne at dinner and—" Smile fading, he broke off. "I'm sorry."

"No, don't be." She let out a sigh because the tension was back. "All this must be frustrating for you."

"For once I'm not thinking of myself." Then he stopped and took her hands. "Brie, when father called me at school and told me you'd been abducted—nothing's ever scared me like that. I hope nothing ever will again. It was as though someone drained the blood out of me—out of all of us. It's enough just to have you back."

She held his hands firmly. "I want to remember. When I do, we can walk in the gardens again and laugh over the French count who drank too much at dinner."

"Maybe you could let your memory be selective," he suggested. "I wouldn't mind you forgetting the time I put worms in your bed."

Brie's eyes widened as he continued to look at her. He was bland, innocent and attractive. "Neither would I."

"You didn't take it very well," he told her, thinking back. "Nanny gave me a tongue-lashing that left me raw for a week."

"Children have to be taught respect."

"Children?" This time he grinned and pinched her chin. "It was only last year." When she laughed he hesitated a moment, then gave in to the need and pressed his cheek against hers. "I miss you, Brie. Hurry back."

She rested there a moment, drawing in his scents, making him familiar. "I'll try."

He, more than anyone, understood that love had its own pressure. When he released her, his voice was light again, undemanding. "I've got to take the dogs back before they dig up the jasmine. Would you like me to walk you back?"

"No, I'll stay awhile. I have a fitting this afternoon for my dress for the AHC ball. I don't think I'll enjoy it."

"You detest it," Bennett said cheerfully. "I'll be done with Oxford and back for the ball." Done with Oxford, he thought again. The idea was nearly too good to be true. "I can dance with you while I look over the girls and decide which one I'm going to devastate."

She laughed. "I believe you have all the makings of a rake."

"I'm doing my best. Boris, Natasha." He called for the dogs and strolled out of the gardens with them scrambling at his heels.

She liked him. It relieved her to know it, to feel it. She might not remember the twenty years they'd shared together as brother and sister, but she liked the man he was today.

Sticking her hands in the pockets of her comfortable baggy slacks, Brie walked a little farther. The scents from the garden were mixed and heady, but not overpowering. The colors weren't a rainbow, but a kaleidoscope. As she walked, she tested herself. Without effort, she could identify each plant. The same way, she mused, she'd been able to identify the artists of the dozens of paintings in the Long Gallery in the west wing.

The artists, yes. But not the subjects. Her own mother's face would have been that of a stranger if Brie's resemblance to her hadn't been so strong. Looking at the portrait, Brie had seen where she'd inherited the color of her eyes, her hair, the shape of her face, her mouth. There was no doubt that Princess Elizabeth de Cordina had been more beautiful than her daughter. Brie could look at the painting and at the big, sweeping portrait of herself objectively and see this.

Princess Gabriella had been younger, twenty, twenty-one, Brie had decided. And she'd been rather spectacular in the deep violet dress she'd worn, its vivid pink sash a slash of heat. Looking at herself, Brie had wondered how she'd had the nerve to choose those shades for the sittings. And how she'd known they would be so effective.

But the face in her mother's portrait had been breathtaking. Heartbreaking. She'd worn creamy white, and had held soft pink roses that had given her a dreamy, poetic sort of beauty. Bennett had her look, as well as the spark of mischief Brie was certain she detected in the painting.

Alex was like their father—the military bearing, the intensity. She'd seen those qualities both in the flesh and in the official portraits. She wondered if Alex enjoyed the role of prince and heir or merely accepted it. More, she wondered if she and Alex had been close enough that she'd known his feelings, his hopes. She wondered when she'd know her own.

There was an arbor draped with wisteria and under it a pair of padded chairs and a marble table. Like the spot by the seawall, Brie felt a sense of comfort there.

It was easier to admit when she was alone that she still tired quickly. Sitting, Brie stretched out her legs, while the shade and muted light dappled over her. The blossoms had a sweet, undemanding scent. The drone of bees had a lazy sound. There didn't seem to be anything else. She closed her eyes and drifted.

Drowsy. She felt almost foolishly drowsy. It wasn't the comfortable, relaxed feeling she had come out to the country for. Whenever she drove out to the little farm it was to steal a little time away from Princess Gabriella for Brie Bisset. Time was precious. If she'd wanted a nap, she could have spent Sunday afternoon in her room.

Brie drank more of the coffee from her thermos. It was strong, the way she preferred it. The sun was warm, the bees humming. Yet she didn't seem to have the energy to walk as she'd planned. Perhaps she'd just close her eyes for a little while.... She couldn't seem to hold the coffee steadily in any case. Perhaps she'd just lean back against the rock and close her eyes....

Then the sun wasn't warm and strong any longer. There was a chill, as though the clouds had covered the sky and threatened rain. She couldn't smell the sweet grass, the sun-warmed flowers, but mustiness and damp. She hurt—ached all over, yet she hardly seemed to feel at all. Someone was talking, but she couldn't really hear. Mumbling, droning, but not bees. Men.

They'll make the exchange for the princess. They won't have a choice. Whispers, just whispers.

Tracks are covered. She'll sleep until morning. Deal with her again.

And she was afraid, terribly, paralyzingly afraid. She had to wake up. She had to wake up and—

"Brie."

With a muffled scream, she jolted in the chair, half springing up before hands closed over her arms. "No, don't! Don't touch me!"

"Easy." Reeve kept his hands firm as he lowered her back in her chair. She was cold, her eyes glazed. Thinking quickly, he decided that if she didn't calm within moments, he'd take her back to the palace and call Franco. "Just take it easy."

"I thought—" She glanced around quickly, the garden, the sun, the bees. When she discovered her heart was pounding, she made herself sit back and just breathe. "I must have been dreaming."

He studied her, searching for signs of shock. Apparently she wouldn't allow herself the luxury. "I wouldn't have woken you, but you looked like you were having a bad dream."

He released her only to sit in the chair beside her. He'd been there, beneath the wisteria, watching her sleep for five minutes, perhaps ten. She'd appeared so content, and he could look at her knowing the reserve she normally held herself in wasn't there.

He'd wanted to look at her, just look. There was no use denying it to himself. When he watched her, he could remember her as she'd been years before, a young girl, pleased with herself, confident, innocently sensual. He could remember her as she'd been in his arms—a woman, arousing, bold, giving. He knew, as he looked at her, that he wanted her there again. And more.

Beyond that, he was aware that desire for her interfered with his objectivity. And a cop was nothing without objectivity, he knew. But he wasn't a cop any longer. Wasn't one of the reasons he'd turned in his badge that the constant struggle to be uninvolved and distant had become distasteful to him? He'd wanted something different in his life. He just hadn't counted on it being a princess.

He sat back, waiting until Brie's breathing steadied. For her sake, he'd better remember the rules he'd lived with during his years on the force. "Tell me," he said simply.

"There's not that much. It's confusing."

He took out a cigarette. "Tell me, anyway."

She sent him a look that he interpreted, correctly, as half resentment, half exasperation. It was better than neutrality. "I thought you were here as bodyguard, not analyst."

"I'm flexible." He lit the cigarette, watching her over the flame. "Are you?"

"Not very, I think." She rose. He'd already learned she rarely sat still when she was nervous. After she plucked off a spray of wisteria, she ran it lightly down her cheek. Another habit he'd noted. "I wasn't here, but someplace quiet. There was grass. I could smell it, very strong and sweet. It seemed I was sleepy, but I didn't want to be. It was annoying, because I was alone and wanted to enjoy the solitude."

This was accompanied by a look of pure defiance. Reeve merely nodded and leaned back. There was very little satisfaction in insulting him, Brie observed, and tucked the spray of wisteria in her hair.

"I was drinking coffee to try to stay awake."

His look sharpened, but she didn't notice. "Where did you get the coffee?"

"Where?" She frowned, finding it a foolish question when they were discussing a dream. "I had a thermos. A big, red thermos with the handle gone from the top. The coffee didn't seem to help and I dozed off. I remember the sun was very warm and I could hear the bees, just like now. Then..." He saw her fingers tense before she stuck them in her pockets. "I wasn't there any longer. It was dark and a bit damp. It smelled musty. There were voices."

He tensed, as well, but his voice was calm. "Whose?"

"I don't know. I didn't really hear them as much as sense them. I was afraid." Turning away, she wrapped her arms around her body. "I was afraid and I couldn't wake up and stop the dream."

"Dream," he murmured. "Or memory?"

She whirled around, her eyes passionate again, her hands balled into fists inside her pockets. "I don't know. How can I? Do you think I can snap my fingers and say, ah, of course, I remember now?" She kicked at the little white stones along the edge of the path. "I walked with Bennett in the garden and all I could think was what a charming man. Damn! Is that the way I should think of my own brother?"

"He is a charming man, Gabriella."

"Don't patronize me," she said between her teeth. "Don't you dare patronize me."

He smiled at that, because whether she knew it or not at that moment, she was all princess. Royalty flowed through her—somehow admirable and amusing to a man who'd seen his share of aristocrats. Still, he rose and spoke gently. "Who thinks you should snap your fingers, Brie? No one's pressuring you but yourself."

"I'm pressured by kindness."

"Don't worry," he said with a shrug. "I won't be kind to you."

"I can depend on it." She paused a moment, frowning at him. "You said once before that I was selfish. Why?"

Without thinking, he ran a finger between her brow where the line of temper formed. "Perhaps the word should be 'self-absorbed.' You may have a right to be at the moment."

"I'm not sure I like that any better. You also said spoiled."

"Yes." He let his hand fall away so that they faced each other without touching.

"I refuse to accept that."

"Sorry."

Her eyes narrowed. "You're sorry because you said it?"

"No, because you refuse to accept what you are."

"You're a rude man, Reeve MacGee. Rude and opinionated."

"True enough," he agreed, and rocked back on his heels. "I also said you were willful."

Her chin came up. "That I accept," she told him coolly. "But you haven't the right to say it to me."

He gave her a very slow, very arrogant bow. It wasn't difficult when she chose to play the princess for him to play the pauper. "I beg your pardon, Your Highness."

Fire flared, in her blood, in her eyes. She found the fingers in her pockets itched to make solid contact with his face. Breeding hampered her, and she found she didn't care for the restriction. "Now you're mocking me."

"We'll add 'astute' to the list."

Amazed at how quickly the anger rose, she took another step toward him. "You seem to be going out of your way to insult me. Why?"

There was something irresistible about her when she was haughty, angry, icy. Reeve took her face in one hand, holding it firmly when her mouth dropped open in surprise. "Because it makes you think of me. I don't give a damn how you think of me, Gabriella, as long as you do."

"Then you have your wish," she said evenly. "I do think of you, but I don't think well of you."

He smiled slowly. She found this made her throat dry and her skin hot. "Just think of me," he repeated. "I won't strew roses on the floor when I lead you to bed. There won't be any violins, and satin sheets. What there'll be is you and me."

She didn't step back. Whether it was shock or excitement that kept her still she didn't know. Perhaps it was pride. That's what she hoped. "You seem to be the one in need of the analyst now.

I may not remember, Reeve, but I feel certain I choose my own lovers.''

"So do I."

She felt light-headed. Frightened? No—yes. When he spoke she felt the decision had already been made. Another lack of choice. "Take your hands off me." She said it quietly, with a hint of arrogance that hid the fear.

He drew her closer, just a little closer. "Is that a royal command?"

She might have been wearing a robe and a crown. "Take it however you choose. You need my permission to touch me, Reeve. A man of your background knows the rules."

"Americans aren't as subject to protocol as Europeans, Brie." His lips hovered over hers, but didn't quite touch. "I want to touch you, so I touch. I want you, so I'll take—when the time's right for both of us." As he said this, his fingers tightened.

Her vision blurred, her knees shook. It was dark again, and the face close to hers was indistinct. She smelled wine, strong and stale. Fear tripled, pulsing through her like a drug. Abruptly she struck out at him, swaying as she did. "Don't touch me! Don't! *Relâchez-moi, salaud—*"

Because her voice was more desperate than angry, he let her go, then almost immediately grabbed her again when she swayed forward. "Brie." He had her back in the chair, her head between her knees, before she could think. Silently cursing himself, his voice was gentle, calming. "Breathe deep and relax. I'm sorry. I've no intention of taking any more than you want to give."

He wouldn't. No, he wouldn't. Her eyes shut, she tried to clear her mind, clear the dizziness.

"No." When she struggled against his hand, he released her. Her face was still pale when she looked up at him, but her eyes were dark and intense. Terrified. "It wasn't you," she managed. "It wasn't you at all. I remembered—I think…" On a frustrated breath, she closed her eyes again and fought for composure. "It was someone else. Just for a minute I was somewhere else. A man was holding me. I can't see him—it's dark or my mind just won't let me get through to his face. But he's holding me and I know, I know he'll rape me. He's drunk."

Her hand reached out for Reeve's and held it. "I could smell the wine on him. Just now I could smell it. His hands are rough. He's very strong, but he's had too much wine." She swallowed. Reeve saw her shudder just before she took her hand from him and straightened in her chair. "I had a knife. I don't know how. I had a knife and its handle was in my hand. I think I killed him."

She looked down at her hand. It was steady. Turning it over, she stared down at her palm. It was white and smooth. "I think I stabbed him with the knife," she said calmly. "And his blood was on my hands."

"Brie." Reeve started to reach out for her, then thought better of it. "Tell me what else you remember."

She looked at him then and her face was as it had been in the hospital. Colorless and strained. "Nothing. I only remember struggling and the smells. I can't be sure if I killed him. There's nothing after the struggle, nothing before." She folded her hands in her lap and looked beyond him. "If the man raped me, I don't remember it."

He wanted to swear again, and barely controlled the impulse. Everything she said made his little power play of a few moments before seem hard and crude. "You weren't sexually assaulted," he told her in brisk, practical tones. "The doctors were very thorough."

Relief threatened to come in tears. She held them back. "But they can't tell me if I killed a man or not."

"No. Only you can—when you're ready."

She merely nodded, then forced herself to look at him again. "You've killed before."

He took another cigarette and lit it with a barely restrained violence. "Yeah."

"You—in your work. It was necessary for defense, protection?"

"That's right."

"When it's necessary, it doesn't leave any scars, does it?"

He could lie, make it easy for her. He was tempted to. When he looked at her, her eyes were so troubled. Inadvertently he'd forced a memory out of her. A dark, horrible memory. Did that make him responsible? Hadn't he already chosen to be responsible?

He could lie, but when she learned the truth, it would be that much worse. Yes, he'd chosen to be responsible. "It leaves scars," he said briefly, and rose, taking her hand as he did. "You can live with scars, Brie."

She'd known it. Even before she'd asked, before he'd answered, she'd known it. "Do you have many?"

"Enough. I decided I couldn't live with any more."

"So you bought a farm."

"Yeah." He tossed down the cigarette. "I bought a farm. Maybe next year I'll even plant something."

"I'd like to see it." She saw his quick, half-amused look, and felt foolish. "Sometime, perhaps."

He wanted her to, and felt foolish. "Sure, sometime."

Brie let her hand stay in his as they walked through the gardens, back toward the white, white walls of the palace.

Chapter 6

Barefoot, wrapped only in a thin silk robe, Brie sat dutifully on the bed while Dr. Franco took her blood pressure. His hands were deft, his manner kind, almost fatherly. Still, she wasn't entirely accepting of the weekly examinations by her family's doctor. Nor was she resigned to the biweekly sessions with his associate, Dr. Kijinsky, the eminent and scholarly psychiatrist. She wasn't an invalid, and she wasn't ill.

True, she tired more easily than she might have liked, but her strength was coming back. And her sessions with the renowned analyst, Dr. Kijinsky, were no more than conversations. Conversations, she mused, that were really no more than a waste of time. And it was time, after all, that she was so determined to recover.

The plans for the charity ball the first week of June were her priority. Food, wine, music, decorations. Entertainment, acceptances, regrets, requests. Even though she seemed to enjoy the preparations, they weren't easy. When someone paid a good sum of money to attend an affair, charitable or not, he expected and deserved the best. She'd spent three long, testy hours with the florist just that morning to guarantee the finest.

"Your pressure is good." Franco tucked the gauge back into his bag. "And your pulse, your color. Physically, there seem to be no complications. My complaint would be that you're still a bit thin. Five pounds wouldn't hurt you."

"Five pounds would throw my dressmaker into a frenzy," she returned with a half smile. "She's thrilled with me at the moment."

"Bah." Franco rubbed a hand over his trim white beard. "She looks for a coat hanger to drape her material on. You need some flesh, Gabriella. Your family has always tended to be just a bit too slim. Are you taking the vitamins I prescribed?"

"Every morning."

"Good. Good." He pulled off his stethoscope, dropping that into the bag, as well. "Your father tells me you haven't cut back on your schedule."

Her defenses came up immediately. "I like being busy."

"That hasn't changed. My dear..." Setting his bag aside, he sat down on the bed next to her. The informality surprised her only because she'd become accustomed to the rules she was bound by. Yet Franco seemed so at ease she decided they must have sat just this casually dozens of times. "As I said, physically, you're recovering perfectly. I have great respect for Dr. Kijinsky's talents, or I wouldn't have recommended him. Still, I'd like you to tell me how you feel."

Brie folded her hands in her lap. "Dr. Franco—"

"You're weary of doctors," he said with a wave of his hand. "You're annoyed by the prodding, the poking, the sessions. Questions, you think, too many questions. You want to get on with your life."

She smiled, more amused than disconcerted. "It doesn't seem you need me to tell you how I feel. Do you always read your patient's mind, Dr. Franco?"

He didn't smile, but his eyes remained kind, tolerant. All at once, she felt petty and rude. "I'm sorry." She touched him because it was her nature to do so when she apologized, and meant it. "That sounded sarcastic. I didn't mean it to be. The truth is, Dr. Franco, I feel so many things—too many things. Everyone I know seems to understand them before I do."

"Do you feel we're simplifying your amnesia?"

"No..." Unsure, she shook her head. "It just seems as though it's taken for granted that it's a small problem that should resolve itself. Politically, I suppose it's necessary to think that."

The resentment, ever so slightly, was there. Franco, who knew what her father was going through, refrained from commenting directly. "No one, especially your doctor, makes light of what you're going through. Yet it's difficult for those around you, those close to you, to fully understand and accept. It's because of this that I'd like you to talk to me."

"I'm not sure what I should say—even what I want to say."

"Gabriella, I brought you into the world. I ministered to your sniffles, treated you through chicken pox and took out your tonsils. Your body is no stranger to me, nor is your mind." He paused while she took this in. "You have difficulty talking to your father for fear of hurting him."

"Yes." She looked at him then, the pleasant face, the white beard. "Him most of all. Before Bennett left—he went grumbling back to Oxford yesterday."

"He'd prefer to stay here with his dogs and horses."

"Yes." She laughed, shaking back her hair. "With Bennett here, it was easier somehow. He's so relaxed and open. With him I didn't always feel compelled to say the right things—the kind thing. Alexander's different. I feel I should be very careful around him. He's so, well, proper."

"'Prince Perfect.'" Franco smiled at her expression. The vague disapproval was a good sign. "No disrespect, Gabriella. You and Bennett dubbed him so when you were children."

She nearly smiled herself. "How nasty."

"Oh, he can handle himself. Bennett's called 'Lord Sloth.'"

She made a sound suspiciously like a giggle and folded her legs under her. "Natural enough. I volunteered to help him pack. It wasn't easy to believe anyone could live in such a sty. And me?" She lifted a brow. "Did my brothers give me a title?"

"'Her Obstinacy.'"

"Oh." Brie sat for a moment, then chuckled. "I take it I deserved it."

"Then and now, it suits."

"I think—I feel," Brie amended, "that we're a close family. Is this true?"

A simple yes would mean nothing, Franco thought. A simple yes was too easy. "Once a year you go to Zurich, *en famille*. For two weeks there are no servants, no outsiders. You told me once that this was what helped you cope with the other fifty weeks."

She nodded, accepting. And, gratefully, understanding. "Tell me how my mother died, Dr. Franco."

"She was delicate," he said carefully. "She was speaking for the Red Cross in Paris and contracted pneumonia. There were complications. She never recovered."

She wanted to feel. It would be a blessing to feel grief, pain, but there was nothing. Folding her hands again, she looked down at them. "Did I love her?"

Compassion wasn't something a doctor carried in his bag, but something he carried with him. "She was the center of your family. The anchor, the heart. You loved her, Gabriella, very much."

Believing it was almost, almost as comforting as feeling it. "How long was she ill?"

"Six months."

The family would have drawn together, knotted together. Of that she was certain. "We don't accept outsiders easily."

Franco smiled again. "No."

"Reeve MacGee, you know him?"

"The American?" Franco moved his shoulders in a gesture Brie recognized as French and pragmatic. "Only slightly. Your father thinks highly of him."

"Alexander resents him."

"Naturally enough." Franco spoke slowly, intrigued by the turn of the conversation. Perhaps she didn't know her family yet, but they were still, as they had always been, her chief concern. "Prince Alexander feels protective of you, and doesn't welcome the assistance of anyone outside the family. The pretense of your engagement..." He paused at Brie's narrowed look, but misinterpreted it. "I don't gossip. As physician to the royal family, I'm in your father's confidence."

She unfolded her legs and rose, no longer content to sit. "And do you agree with his opinion?"

Franco lifted one bushy white brow. "I wouldn't presume to agree or disagree with Prince Armand, except on medical matters. However, the engagement is bound to annoy your brother, who feels personally responsible for your welfare."

"And my feelings?" Abruptly her calm vanished. She turned to where the doctor now stood beside her bed, his hands locked comfortably behind his back. "Are they considered? This—this pretense that all is well, this farce that I've had a whirlwind romance with the son of my father's friend. They infuriate me.''

She snatched up a mother-of-pearl comb from her dresser and began to tap it against her palm. ''The announcement of my engagement was made only yesterday, and already the papers are full of it. Crammed with their speculation, their opinions, their chatty little stories. Everywhere I go there are questions and flutters and sighs.''

The impatience was obvious and, to the doctor, familiar. With his fingers still linked behind his back, he remained silent and waited for it to run its course.

''Just this morning while I'm trying to organize for the ball, I'm asked about my wedding dress. Will it be white or ivory? Will I use my dressmaker, or go to Paris as my mother did? My wedding dress,'' she repeated tossing up her hands. ''When I have to finalize a menu for fifteen hundred people. Will I have the ceremony in the palace chapel or the cathedral? Will my good friends from college be in the wedding party? Will I choose the English princess or the French countess as my maid of honor—neither of whom I remember in the slightest. The more we try to gloss over and hide what's real, what's true, the more absurd it becomes.''

''Your father is protecting your welfare, Gabriella, and his people's.''

''Are they never two separate things?'' she demanded, then tossed the comb back on the dresser. ''I'm sorry.'' Her voice calmed. ''That was unfair. Deception is difficult. It seems I'm involved in it on so many levels. And Reeve—'' Brie broke off, annoyed with herself for permitting her thoughts to travel in his direction.

''Is attractive,'' Franco finished.

With a slow cautious smile, she studied her doctor. ''You're an excellent physician, Dr. Franco.''

He gave her a quick, dapper bow. ''I know my patients, Your Highness.''

''Attractive,'' she agreed. ''But not in all ways likable. I don't find his consistent dominance particularly appealing, especially in the role of fiancé. However, I'll play my part. When my memory returns, the American can go back to his farm, I can go back to my life. That's how I feel, Dr. Franco.'' She put both hands on the back of a chair. "That, simply stated, is how I feel. I want to remember. I want to understand. And I want to get back to my life."

"You'll remember, Gabriella."

"You can be sure?"

"As a doctor, nothing is ever sure." Bending, wheezing a bit with the movement, he picked up his bag again. "As someone who's known you from the cradle, I'm sure."

"That's the opinion I prefer." She stepped forward toward the door.

"No need to see me out." He brushed her back with the habitual pat on the hand. "I'll give your father my assurances before I go."

"Thank you, Dr. Franco."

"Gabriella." He paused with the door just opened. "We all have our pretenses to keep up."

The inclination of her head was cool and regal. "So I understand."

Discreetly she waited until the door closed behind him before she whirled away, fuming. Pretenses. Yes, she'd play them, she'd accept them. But she detested them. With her temper unsteady, she pulled out of the trash the paper she'd wadded up and discarded that morning.

PRINCESS GABRIELLA TO WED

Brie swore as princesses are only allowed to do in private. There was a picture of her and one of Reeve. With her head tilted and the sun streaming in on the newsprint, she studied him.

Attractive, yes, she decided. In that just-on-the-edge-of-rough, just-on-the-edge-of-sleek sort of way. Like a big predatory cat, she mused, who could swagger away or pounce as the mood struck. He'd make his own choices. A man like that caused mixed feelings. Not only in her, she noted with some satisfaction. The press was of two minds, as well.

There was obvious excitement and a proprietory sort of satisfaction that one of the royal children was to wed. It was pointed out, she noted, that she, of all the princesses in the history of Cordina, had waited the longest to take the plunge. About time, the paper seemed to say with a brisk nod.

The family tie between the Bissets and MacGees counted in

Reeve's favor, as did his father's reputation. But he was, after all, an American, and not precisely the ideal choice according to the citizens of Cordina.

Whatever satisfaction Brie might have gained from that was offset by the mention of several more eligible options. It was disconcerting to find herself matched, if only in the press, with a half a dozen eligible bachelors. Princes, lords, marquesses, tycoons. Obviously from the brief stories attached to the pictures, she'd met and spent time with them all. One of them might have meant something to her, but she had no way of being sure. She could study their names and faces for five minutes, an hour, but there'd be no change. She turned back to Reeve. At least with him, she knew where she stood.

Apparently the press was prepared to reserve final judgment on the American ex-policeman—son of a well-known and respected diplomat. Instead it chose to speculate on the wedding date.

She tossed the paper on the bed so that it fell with the photos up. Her father had accomplished his purpose, she reflected. The focus was on the engagement rather than the kidnapping. No one would question Reeve's presence in the palace, or his place at her side.

No one would question him—no one would question her. Slowly Brie turned her hands over and stared down at them. There was something she'd been unable to speak of to either of her doctors. Something she'd been unable to put into words to anyone other than Reeve.

Had she killed a man? Had she taken a knife and... Good God, when would she know?

Trying to force herself to remember brought nothing but frustration. Concentration on this would cause her head to pound until she couldn't concentrate on anything at all. What snatches came, came in dreams. And like dreams, when she awoke the images were vague and distorted. But the images, rather than easing the pressure, only increased it. Every morning she lay quietly, hoping the memories would come naturally. Every day there was only the dregs of dreams.

She could work, Brie reminded herself. Filling the hours each day was anything but a problem. The work was enjoyable, fulfilling—but for the fact that she now had this foolish engagement to contend with. The sooner she could brush that aside and go on, the better. She'd view it as one more goal to reach—or one more obstacle to overcome.

"Come in." She answered the knock at the door, but she was frowning. The frown didn't diminish when Reeve walked in.

"Surely I'm considered safe in my own bedroom."

The room smelled subtly of flowers. They were there in a vase on a table by the window, on a stand beside the bed. Through the open window, the breeze traveled in and tossed the scent everywhere. "Dr. Franco says you're recovering nicely."

Brie deliberately took her time settling on the long, cushioned window seat. It gave her the opportunity to control her temper. "Does the doctor report to you, as well?"

"I was with your father." He saw the newspaper on the bed, the photos, but said nothing. It wouldn't do to admit that the front-page splash had given him quite a jolt that morning. It was one thing to agree to a mock engagement, and another to see evidence of it in black and white.

Instead he wandered over to her dresser and idly picked up a small glass jar. He'd concentrate on that for a moment until he could forget just the way she looked in that thin ivory robe. "So you're feeling better?"

"I'm quite well, thank you."

The icily formal reply had his lips twitching. She wouldn't give an inch, Reeve mused. So much the better. "How's your schedule for tomorrow?" he asked, though he'd already made it his business to know.

"I'm not free until after noon. Then there's nothing until dinner with the Duke and Duchess of Marlborough and Monsieur Loubet and his wife."

If Reeve read her tone correctly, she wasn't looking forward to the dinner any more than he was. It would be their first as an officially engaged couple. "Then perhaps you'd like to go sailing for a few hours in the afternoon."

"Sailing?" He watched her eyes light up just before she swept her lashes down and spoke coolly. "Is this an invitation or a way to keep me supervised?"

"Both." He opened the jar, dipped a finger into the cream and rubbed it between his thumb and forefinger. It smelled like her skin—soft and sexy. At night, he imagined, and in the mornings, she'd smooth on the cream until its fragrance was part of her.

He was here to protect her, he thought ruefully as he closed the jar again, but who was going to protect him? As she sat in silence, he put down the jar and crossed to her.

"If you want to weigh the pros and cons, Brie, consider that you'll be away from the palace and responsibility for a few hours."

"With you."

"Engaged couples are expected to spend some time together," he said easily, then put a firm hand on her arm before she could jump up. "You agreed," he said with the steel just below the calm tone. "Now you have to follow through."

"Only in public."

"A woman in your position has little private life. And," he continued, moving his hand down to hers, "I've put mine under the microscope, as well."

"You want gratitude? I find it difficult right at the moment."

"Keep it." Annoyed, he tightened his grip until her eyes met his. "Cooperation's enough."

Her chin was up, her eyes level. "Yours or mine?"

He inclined his head slightly. "The answer seems to be both again. Officially, we're engaged. In love," he added, testing the words.

The words worried her. "Officially," she agreed. "It's simply a trapping."

"Trappings can be convenient. And since we're on the subject..." Reaching into his pocket, Reeve brought out a small velvet box. With his thumb he flipped up the top. The sun shot down and seemed to explode within the white, square-cut diamond.

Brie felt her heart begin to thud in her breast, then her throat. "No."

"Too traditional?" Reeve drew the ring out of the box and twisted it in the sunlight. The white stone was suddenly alive with color. "It suits you. Clean, cool, elegant. Ready to give off passion at the right touch." He was no longer looking at the diamond, but at her. "Give me your hand, Gabriella."

She didn't move. Perhaps foolishly, she felt she didn't have to. "I won't wear your ring."

He took her left wrist and felt the pulse thud under his fingers.

The sun poured through the window, showering on her hair, into her eyes. The fury was there—he could feel it. And the passion. Hardly romantic, he thought as he pushed the ring onto her finger. But, then, romance wasn't the order of the day.

"Yes, you will." He closed his hand over hers, sealing the bond. He didn't allow himself to think just yet of how difficult it might be to break.

"I'll just take it off again," she told him furiously.

He spoke in a tone she didn't trust. "That wouldn't be wise."

"Still following my father's orders?" she said between her teeth.

"It seems we both are. But the ring was my idea." He cupped the back of her neck with his free hand. It was long and slender and smooth. "So's this."

When he kissed her, he gave her no choice. She stiffened; he stroked. She shuddered; he soothed. The moment he felt her respond, he took her deep and fast.

His fingers were in her hair, his hand on hers, yet her body throbbed as though he touched everywhere. She would have welcomed that. The mouth didn't seem to be enough to give, to take, to demand. Whole worlds opened up and spun at the touch of mouth to mouth. She could taste what he offered—passion, wild, ripe, free. Fulfillment was there, churning within her if she chose to let go.

She came alive when he held her. Reeve hadn't known a woman could be so electric while remaining so soft. He could feel pulse beats, tempting him to touch them, one by one. He started with her throat, just a skim of a fingertip. Her moan rippled into his mouth. The inside of her elbow—the blood pounded there. At her wrist it jumped frantically.

He drew her bottom lip into his mouth to suck, to nibble. Her body trembled, arousing him beyond belief as he took his hand slowly up from her waist to find her breast. The thin robe she wore could have been pulled away with one hand, leaving her naked, but Reeve kept the barrier knowing his sanity would be pulled away with it.

When he made love with her, fully, completely, there wouldn't be servants or staff or family. When he made love with her the first time, there'd be nothing, no one but the two of them. She'd never forget it. Or him.

He ran his hand down her once, one long, firm stroke. Possession, threat, promise. Neither of them could be sure which. When he let her go, neither of them was steady.

Brie saw something in his eyes that had her skin heating. Desire, but more. Knowledge. His eyes were blue, dark, not quite calm. In them she saw the knowledge that she wouldn't walk away from him easily. Not today. Not tomorrow.

She drew back against the window seat, as far away from him as she could. "You have no right."

He looked at her until she had to hold back the tremble. "I don't need any." When he reached up to cup her face she went still. It was a habit of his she hadn't quite fathomed. It might be gentleness; it might be arrogance. "I don't want any."

Her strength was nothing to be underestimated. She was still, yes, but she wasn't weak. "I'll tell you when I want to be touched, Reeve."

He didn't remove his hand. "So you have."

Try a different tactic, she decided. Something had to work. "I think you're taking this charade too seriously. You overstep yourself."

"If you want bows and protocol, you'll have to look elsewhere. Remember, you told me not to be kind."

"A request that isn't difficult for you."

"Not at all." He smiled, then lifted her hand where the diamond flashed. "You and I know this is no more than a pretty rock, Brie. Another trapping." On impulse, he turned her hand over, held it, then pressed his lips to her palm. "No one else will."

This time she jerked her hand away and rose. "I told you I won't wear it."

Before she could pull the ring off he was beside her. "And I told you you would. Think." When she paused, the ring half off her finger, he continued. The tone he used was precisely the tone he used to draw the answer he wanted out of reluctant suspects. Deals, he thought ruefully, were deals. "Would you rather swallow your pride and wear it, or explain every time you go out why you don't have an engagement ring?"

"I could say I don't care for jewelry."

He grinned, touching the sapphires on her right hand, then the deep-blue stones she wore at her ears. "Could you? Some lies are more easily believed than others."

Brie pushed the ring back on. "Damn you."

"Better," he said with a nod of approval. "Curse me as much as you like, just cooperate. It might occur to you, Your Highness, that I'm just as inconvenienced by all this as you."

Trapped, she turned away. "Inconvenienced? You seem to be enjoying it."

"I'm making the best of a bargain. You could do the same, or you can stomp your feet."

She whirled back around, eyes flashing. "I don't make a habit of temper tantrums."

"Could have fooled me."

She calmed, only because to have let loose would have gratified him. "I don't like it when you make me feel like a child, Reeve."

His voice was equally calm. "Then don't object when I make you feel like a woman."

"Have you an answer for everything?"

He thought of her, of what was growing inside him. Briefly he touched her cheek. "No. A truce for the moment, Brie. Before this business of the engagement came up we got along well enough. Look at it as a simplification."

She frowned, but discovered she was willing to call a truce. Until she had her full strength back. "A simplification of what?"

"Of everything. With this—" he lifted her left hand again "—you won't have to explain why we spend time together, what I'm doing here. As an engaged couple we can get out a bit, get away. People are tolerant of lovers escaping. You won't be as tied to the palace."

"I never said I felt tied."

"I've seen you looking out the window. Any window."

Her gaze came back to him and held. Abruptly she surrendered and, with a sigh, sat back on the window seat. "All right, yes, sometimes I feel closed in. None of this is familiar to me, and yet it isn't altogether strange. It isn't a comfortable feeling, Reeve, to feel as though you belong, but never being quite sure you won't make a wrong turn and find yourself lost again. And the dreams—" She broke off, cursing herself. It was too easy to say more to him than was comfortable.

"You've had more dreams?"

"Nothing I remember very well."

"Brie." The patience wasn't there as it had been with Franco, but the knowledge was.

"It's true, I don't." Frustrated, she pulled her fingers through her hair. He saw his ring throw out fire against the fire. His fire, he thought. And hers. "It's always basically the same—the dark, the smells, the fear. I don't have anything tangible, Reeve." For a moment she closed her eyes tight. Weakness was so easy. Tears were so simple. She wouldn't allow them for herself. "There's nothing for me to hold on to. Every morning I tell myself this could be the day the curtain lifts. And every night..." She shrugged.

He wanted to go to her, hold her. Passion he could offer safely. Comfort was dangerous. He kept his distance. "Tomorrow you won't have to think about it. We'll go out on the water. Just sail. Sun and sea, that's all. There won't be anyone there you have to play a role for."

A few hours without pretenses, she thought. He was offering her a gift. Perhaps he was taking one for himself, but he was entitled. Brie looked down at her ring, then up at him. "Nor you."

He smiled. She thought it was almost friendly. "Agreed."

Chapter 7

Like too many other things, Brie had forgotten what it was to really relax. Learning how was a discovery in pleasure, and one that was blissfully easy. She hoped that when other memories came back to her, they'd be as sweet.

Still, she'd found one more thing she could be certain of. She was as at home on the sea as she was on land. It was a simple pleasure—as relaxing was—and therefore an important one, to find that she knew her way around canvas and rope. If she'd been alone on the pretty little sloop, Brie could have sailed her. She'd have had the control, the knowledge and the strength. Of that she was certain.

She could listen to the noise of the water against the hull as the boat gathered speed and know she'd heard the sound before. It didn't matter where or how.

She loved to sail. Everyone Reeve had spoken to had confirmed it. The idea for a day on the water had come to him when he'd noticed that the finely strung nerves, the strain and the depression hadn't eased. Not as much as she pretended. She'd told him not to be kind, but it wasn't always possible to follow even the orders of a princess.

Relying on his instincts, he'd let her take the tiller when they'd cast off. Now he watched her turn it slightly, away from the wind. In accord, he pulled in on the mainsheet to quiet and stretch the flapping canvas. As the boat sped across the wind, it gathered more speed. He heard Brie laugh as the sails filled.

"It's wonderful," she called. "The best. So free, so simple."

The wind exhilarated her. Speed, on this first run, seemed to be imperative. Power, after being for so long under the power of others, was intoxicating. Control—at last she'd found something she could control. Her hand was light on the tiller, adjusting, as Reeve did, whenever it was necessary to keep the pace at maximum.

Walls, obligations, responsibilities disappeared. All that was left was water and wind. Time wasn't important here. She could push it aside, as perhaps she'd done before. As she now knew she'd do again. The sun was as it should be on a holiday. Bright, full, warm—gold in the sky, white on the sea. Holding the tiller steady with her knee, Brie slipped out of the oversized cotton shirt. Her brief bikini made a shrug at modesty. She wanted the sun on her skin, the wind on it. Skillfully she navigated so that she avoided any other boats. Privacy she wouldn't sacrifice.

For a few hours she'd be selfish. For a few hours she didn't have to be a princess, but only a woman, stroked by the wind, soothed by the sun. With another laugh she shook back her hair, only to have the wind swirl through it again.

"I've done this before."

Reeve relaxed; the wind was doing the work for the moment. "It's your boat," he said easily. "According to your father, Bennett can outride anyone, Alexander can outfence the masters, but you're the best sailor in the family."

Thoughtful, Brie ran a hand along the glossy mahogany rail. "*Liberté*," she mused, thinking of the name on the stern. "It would seem that like the little farm, I use this for an escape."

Reeve turned to look at her. Through his amber-tinted glasses she looked gold and lush. Primitive, desirable, but still somehow lost. Whatever his inclinations, it wouldn't do to be too kind. "I'd say you were entitled. Wouldn't you?"

She made a little sound, noncommittal, unsure. "It only makes me wonder if I was happy before. I find myself thinking sometimes that when I remember, I'll wish I'd let things stand as they are now. Everything's new, you understand?"

"A fresh start?" He thought of his own farm, his own fresh start. But, then, he'd known where he'd ended, where he'd begun.

"I'm not saying I don't want to remember." She watched Reeve pull his T-shirt over his head and discard it. He looked so natural, she thought, so at ease with himself. His trunks were brief, but she felt no self-consciousness. She'd been held against that body. Brie let herself remember it. He was lean, hard. Little drops of spray glistened on his skin. A dangerous man. But wasn't danger something she'd have to face sooner or later?

Yes, she remembered his embrace. Should she be ashamed to discover she wanted to be held against him, by him, again? She wasn't ashamed, she realized, whether she should be or not. But she was cautious. "I know so little," she murmured. "Of myself. Of you."

Reeve took a cigarette from the shirt he'd tossed on the bench. He cupped his hands, flicked his lighter, the movements economical. As he blew out smoke, he looked at her again. "What do you want to know?"

She didn't answer for a moment, but studied him. This was a man who could take care of himself, and others when he chose. This was a man, she was all but certain, who made his own rules. And yet...unless she was very mistaken, he was a man who'd lived by rules already set for most of his life. Which was he doing now? "My father trusts you."

Reeve nodded, making the adjustments as the sail began luffing. "He has no reason not to."

"Still, it's your father he knows well, not you."

His lips curved. The arrogance was there again, she thought, no matter how elegant, how well groomed he was. It was, unfortunately, one of the most attractive things about him.

"Don't you trust me, Gabriella?" He made his voice deliberately low, deliberately challenging. He was baiting her; they both knew it. So her answer, when she gave it, left him speechless.

"With my life," she said simply. She turned into the wind again and let the boat race.

What could he say to her? There'd been no guile in her words, no irony. She meant exactly what she'd said, not merely the phrase but the intent. He should have been pleased. Her trust, theoretically, would simplify his job. So why did he feel uncomfortable with it, wary of it? Of it, he asked himself, or of her?

It came back to him now what he'd realized from the first moment he'd seen her again in the hospital bed. Nothing between them would ever be casual. In the same way, he was all but sure nothing between them could ever be serious. So he was caught, very much as Brie was, in an odd sort of limbo.

They were both, in their own ways, beginning a new life. Neither of them had any reason to want the other complicating it. The truth was that Reeve had made himself a promise to simplify his life. Almost as soon as he'd begun, there had been the call from Cordina, and things had become tangled again.

He could have said no, Reeve reminded himself. He hadn't wanted to. Why? Because Brie, as she'd been at sixteen, had stayed in his mind for too many years.

Since he'd come to Cordina, things had only become more involved. The bogus engagement had the international press kicking up their heels. A royal wedding was always good copy. Already three of the top American magazines were begging for interviews. The paparazzi were there like eager little terriers every time he or Brie stepped out of the palace.

He could have refused Prince Armand's request that he pretend to be engaged to Brie. The fact that it was a logical solution to a delicate problem was outweighed by the nuisance value. But he hadn't wanted to. Why? Because Brie, the woman he was coming to know, was threatening to stay in his mind for a lifetime.

Being with her, and not being with her, was like taking a long, slow walk a few inches over very hot coals. The steam was there, the sizzle—but it wasn't possible to cool off or take the fatal plunge into the heat.

"That little cove." Brie lifted her hand to point. "It looks quiet."

Without fuss, they began to tack toward the small shelter. She worked with the wind, coaxing it, bowing to it. Once the lines were secure, Brie merely sat, staring across the narrow strip of water.

"From here Cordina looks so fanciful. So pink and white and lovely. It seems as though nothing bad would ever happen there."

He looked with her. "Fairy tales are traditionally violent, aren't they?"

"Yes." She smiled a little, looking up at the palace. How bold it looked, she thought. How bold and elegant. "But, then, no matter how much it looks like one, Cordina isn't a fairy tale. Does your practical, democratic American mind find it foolish—our castles, our pomp and protocol?"

This time he smiled. Perhaps she didn't remember her roots, but they were there, dug in. "I find it intelligently run. Lebarre is one of the best ports in the world, regardless of size. Culturally, Cordina bows to no one. Economically, it's sound."

"True. I, too, have been doing my homework. Still..." Brie ran her tongue over her teeth before she leaned back and circled her knee with her arms. "Did you know that women weren't granted the right to vote in Cordina until after World War II? Granted, as though it were a favor, not a right. Family life is still very Mediterranean, with the wife subservient and the husband dominant."

"In theory, or in practice?" Reeve countered.

"From what I've seen, very much in practice. Constitutionally, the title my father holds can pass only to a male."

Reeve listened, looking across the water as she did. "Does that annoy you?"

Brie gave him an odd, searching look. "Yes, of course. Just because I have no desire to rule doesn't mean the law itself isn't wrong. My grandfather was instrumental in bringing women's suffrage to Cordina. My own father has gone further by appointing women to positions of importance, but change is slow."

"Invariably."

"You're practical and patient by nature." She gave a quick shrug. "I'm not. When change is for the better, I see no reason for it to creep along."

"You can't overlook the human element."

"Especially when some humans are too steeped in tradition to see the advantage of progress."

"Loubet."

Brie sent him an appreciative look. "I can see why my father enjoys having you around, Reeve."

"How much do you know about Loubet?"

"I can read," she said simply. "I can listen. The picture I gain is one of a very conservative man. Stuffy." She rose, stretching so that the bikini briefs went taut over her hips. "True, he's an excellent minister in his way, but so very, very cautious. I read in my diary where he tried to discourage me from my tour of Africa last year. He didn't feel it proper for a woman. Nor does he feel it proper for me to meet with the National Council over budget matters." Frustration showed briefly. She was, Reeve noted, learning fast. "If men like Loubet had their way, women would do no more than make coffee and babies."

"I've always been of the opinion that such things should be joint efforts."

She smiled down at him, obviously amused and relaxed. "But then, you're not such a traditionalist. Your mother was a circuit-court judge." At Reeve's steady look, her smile widened. "I did my homework," she reminded him. "You weren't a subject I overlooked. You graduated from American University summa cum laude. Under the current circumstances, I find it interesting that you have a degree in psychology."

"A tool," he said easily, "in the career I chose."

"True enough. After two and half years on the police force and three citations for bravery, you went undercover. The facts become vague there, but rumor has it that you were on the team responsible for breaking one of the major crime rings operating in and around the District of Columbia. There's also a rumor that at the request of a certain United States senator, you served on his security force. With your reputation, your intelligence and your record you could easily have made the rank of captain, despite your age. Instead you chose to resign from the force altogether."

"For someone who said they knew little about me, you certainly have enough data."

"That tells me nothing about you." She walked to starboard. "I want to cool off. Will you come?" Before he could answer, she was over the side and in the water.

She was unbelievably provocative, but he'd yet to determine if this was deliberate. Thoughtful, Reeve rose. Finding out might be an education in itself. As smoothly as Brie, he slipped into the water.

"Soft," she said as she treaded water lazily. She'd already been under and her hair was wet, sleeked back from her face. Dripping, struck by the sun, it was nearly copper. Without makeup, in the strong light her face was exquisite. She had the bone structure, the complexion, photographers strove to immortalize. As an image, Reeve mused while he floated in the cool water near her, she was flawless. And as an image, she intrigued him—as images intrigue any man.

It was the woman he hungered for. He had yet to resolve whether he could separate one from the other and have what he wanted. He'd worked in law enforcement too long not to understand that every act had consequences. For everything taken, certain payments had to be made. It was far from clear as yet what his payment would be.

"I'm told you use the pool every day," she began, tipping back to drench her hair again. "You're a strong swimmer?"

He put just enough power into his kick to keep afloat. "Yes."

"Perhaps I'll join you one morning. I'm beginning to catch up with my work enough to lose an hour or so a day. Reeve…" She cupped water in her hand, then let it fall back into the sea. "You know the AHC ball is only a few weeks away."

"I'd have to be deaf not to. There's hammering and confusion in the Grand Ballroom almost every day."

"Just a few necessities," she told him offhandedly. "I only mention it because I feel you should know as my…" Her gaze went automatically to the ring on her left hand. Though he watched her, Reeve couldn't read her expression. "As my fiancé," she continued, "you'll be expected to open the ball with me and, in a very real sense, host it."

He watched her hair float and spread on the surface of the water. "And?"

"You see, until then we can keep social engagements to a minimum. The kidnapping, though we're playing it down, is an excellent excuse to keep a low profile, as well as the engagement itself. The ball, however, will be a full scale event with a great deal of press, and many people. I wonder if my father took into consideration the social pressure you'd be under when he asked you to take this—position."

Reeve dipped lower in the water, moving closer to her, but not close enough to touch. "You don't think I can handle it?"

She blinked, then focused on him with a laugh. "I've no doubt you'll handle it beautifully. After all, Alexander admires your mind and Bennett your tailoring. You couldn't have a better endorsement.''

It amused him. "And so?"

"It's simply that the longer this goes on, the larger the favor becomes. Even after the engagement's broken, you'll have to deal with the repercussions, perhaps for years.''

He turned to float on his back, and closed his eyes. "Don't worry about it, Brie. I'm not.''

"Perhaps that's why I do,'' she persisted. "After all, I'm the cause of it.''

"No.'' His disagreement was mild. "Your kidnapper's the cause of it.''

For a moment, she said nothing. After all, he'd given her the opening she'd been angling for. Though she wasn't sure if she should take it, she went ahead. "Reeve, I won't ask if you were a good policeman. Or if you're good as a private detective. Your record speaks for itself. But are you happy in your work?''

This time he fell silent. His eyes closed, he could feel the sun beat down on his face while the water lapped cool over his body. He was still hovering over those coals.

No one had ever asked him if he'd been happy in his work. In fact, he hadn't asked himself until recently. The answer had been yes. And no.

"Yeah. I get a certain satisfaction from my work. I believed in what I was doing on the force. Now I only take a case if I believe in it.''

"Then why aren't you investigating the kidnapping, instead of guarding me?''

He shifted positions until the water lapped up to his shoulders and he could see her. He'd wondered when she would ask. "I'm a private investigator, not a cop anymore. Either way, I wouldn't have any jurisdiction here.''

"I'm not talking about rules and laws, but of inclinations.''

"One of the most admirable—and annoying—things about you is your perception.'' He wondered how her hair would feel now, wet from the sea, and gave in to the urge to reach out to it. He wondered how she would react if she knew he'd been doing some quiet probing, some peering behind the curtain of protocol and drawing his own conclusions without filling her in. In chess, even a queen could be used as a pawn.

"Yeah, I've thought about it." He answered easily, as easily as he treaded water. "But until your father asks, I'm officially security. Just security."

She felt the slight tug where his fingers tangled in her hair. Barely, just barely, their legs brushed under the water. "And if I asked? Would you consider it then?"

He kept his hand on her hair, but her question distracted him. "What do you want, Brie?"

"Help. Between my father and Loubet, I know next to nothing about the status of the investigation. I'm being protected, Reeve. Both of them want to cocoon me, and I don't like it."

"So you want me to do some digging and fill you in?"

"I thought of doing it on my own, but, then, you have more experience. And..." She smiled at him then. "It isn't possible for me to make a move without your being there in any case."

"Found another use for me, Your Highness?"

With a brow lifted, she managed to look dignified while she was soaking wet. "It wasn't meant to be an insult."

"No, probably not." He let her go. Perhaps it was time to use her and be used by her in a more active sense. "I'll give it some thought."

She decided it would be more strategic to retreat than advance. "I'll have to be content with that." In three smooth strokes she was back at the boat and pulling herself over the side. "Shall we try some of the wine and cold chicken Nanny packed for us?"

Nimbly he dropped onto the deck and stood a moment as the water drained from him. "Does Nanny always take on kitchen duty for you?"

"She likes to. We're all still children to her."

"Okay, then. No use letting the food go to waste."

"Ah, practicality again." She picked up a towel, rubbing it briefly over her hair before she tossed it aside again. "Well, then, come down into the cabin and help me. I heard that we have apple tarts, as well." With water still beaded on her skin, she ducked down into the small cabin. "You seem very at home on a boat," she commented when he joined her.

"I used to do a lot of sailing with my father."

"Used to?" Brie drew the bottle of wine from the cooler and gave the label a nod of approval.

"There hasn't been as much time for it the past few years."

"But you're close to him?"

After a quick look, Reeve found a corkscrew and took the bottle from her. "Yes, I'm close to him."

"Is he like my father. I mean—" She heard the quiet pop of the cork and began to look for glasses. "Is he very dignified and brilliant?"

"Is that how you see your father?"

"I suppose." She was frowning a bit as he poured the wine. "And kind, yes, but controlled." She knew she had her father's love, but his country and his power came first. "Men like that must be, after all. So are you."

He grinned as he touched his glass to hers. "Dignified, brilliant or kind?"

"Controlled," she returned, giving him an even look as she sipped. "You make me wonder what you're thinking when you look at me."

The wine was cool and dry on his tongue. "I think you know."

"Not entirely." She took another sip, but hoped he wouldn't know it was for courage. "I do know that you want to make love with me."

The sun slanted in the open cabin door and framed her. "Yes."

"I ask myself why." Brie lowered her glass but held it with both hands. "Do you want to make love with every woman you meet?"

Under different circumstances, he'd have thought she was teasing, but her question was as simple as it sounded. So was his answer. "No."

She managed a smile, though her nerves were beginning to jump. Was this how the game was played? she wondered. And was it a game she was trying to play? "Every other one, then?"

"Only if they meet certain requirements."

"Which are?"

He cupped her face with his hand again. "If they make me think of them first thing in the morning, even before I know what day it is."

"I see." She twisted the glass between her fingers. They were damp from nerves but still steady. "Do you think of me first thing in the morning?"

"Are you looking for flattery, Gabriella?"

"No."

He tilted her head up just a little more. She didn't stiffen, didn't move away, but again he sensed she was braced—not so much wary as waiting. "What, then?"

"To understand. Not knowing myself or my past, I want to understand if I'm attracted to you or simply to the idea of being with a man."

That was blunt enough, he mused. Not particularly flattering, but blunt. He'd asked for it. When he took the wineglass from her to set it aside, he noticed her fingers were tense. It gave him some satisfaction. "And are you attracted to me?"

"Are you looking for flattery?"

Humor came into his eyes. Reeve saw her smile in response. "No." Lightly, briefly, he touched his lips to hers while they watched each other. "Apparently we're both looking for the same thing."

"Perhaps." She hesitated only a moment before she brought her hands to his shoulders. "Perhaps it's time we discover if we've found it."

It was the way he'd wanted it—away from the palace, away from the walls. There was only the lap of water against the boat, so quiet, so rhythmic it was barely there at all. The cabin was small and low. There were shadows; there was sunlight. They were alone.

It was the way he'd wanted it—yet Reeve found himself hesitating. She looked so delicate in this light. Delicate, and he'd agreed to protect her. What sort of objectivitity would he have left after they became lovers? Brie rose on her toes to touch her mouth to his again. Reeve felt the pleasure, the sweetness, the need ease through him and settle.

What sort of objectivity did he have now? he admitted. It had been no less than the truth when he'd spoken of thinking of her every morning.

"You're not so sure," Brie murmured as she brushed his cheek. Excitement was rising in her, quicker, freer than she'd anticipated. He had doubts, she realized. He had second thoughts. It relieved her, aroused her. How inadequate she would have felt if he'd been so sure and she'd been the only one with nerves. "I come to you without any past. For now, for this moment, let's forget either of us has a future. Just today, Reeve. Just an hour—or a moment."

He could give her that. He would give her that. Take just that. This time when their lips came together it wasn't lightly, wasn't briefly. When it's only for the moment, needs intensify. They drive; they compel. Passion pent up; passion held back. Passion set free.

It was only for the moment. They'd both agreed; they'd both decided. They'd both forgotten.

Bodies pressed, flesh to flesh. Mouths tasted. Hungry, so hungry. He felt her hands skim up his back, small and smooth with the nails oval and tidy again. First they brushed, then they gripped and held. Strength—it poured from her making it easy to forget the delicacy. Needs—hers throbbed against him, making it easy to forget logic, plans, decisions. Longings had no logic; there was no plan to passion. The scent of the sea was mild. Her perfume was heady. Swimming in both of them, Reeve drew her with him onto the neat, narrow bunk.

Brie felt the tiny ridges of the woven spread as her back pressed against it. He'd told her there would be no roses, no satin sheets for them. Nor did she want them. Illusions weren't important. Reality was what she'd been searching for. With him she'd find it.

Legs tangled, arms tight, they drove each other. Some journeys are fast, furious and uncontrollable. She no longer thought, have I felt this before? Now was all they had. Opening her eyes, she looked up at him. His face was close, shadowed. It filled her vision. Now was all she wanted.

She reached up to bring his mouth back to hers.

Sweetness. Perhaps rose petals growing hot and ripe in the sun would taste like this. Pungent, like wine mulled over an open fire. Intoxicating, like champagne just uncorked. The more he tasted, the more he understood the meaning of true greed. And when he touched, he understood obsession.

She was like a statue, finely crafted, lovingly polished. But she was flesh and blood. Under his hand she moved, she pulsed. A statue might be admired, revered, studied. He could do that as his gaze roamed, as his hands stroked. But it was the woman he wanted. And the woman, he realized, had little more patience than he.

On a moan of pleasure she rolled, pinning him beneath her so that she could touch as freely as he. Pounding inside her was a need so wild it had no form, no beginning. Perhaps that's why she didn't fight it. Neither did she have a beginning.

She wanted to draw in that rich, deep male taste. And she did. She wanted to see her hand, pale and feminine, against his tanned skin. And she did. The sensations it brought her were something she'd never be able to describe with cool, clear reason, but she recognized happiness.

When she felt the top of her bikini loosen there wasn't any self-consciousness, only pleasure. *Touch me.* Her mind hummed the words only an instant before they were obeyed.

Lost in each other, they twisted on the bunk, demanding as much as they gave, offering as quickly as taking. As his mouth followed after his hands, she arched, crying out in astonished delight. If there was more, she'd have more. But if this was everything, she'd need nothing else.

Had she known her body was so sensitive? Had he? Incredibly, he seemed to know just where she craved to be touched, where she longed to have his lips brush or linger. There would be no less for him.

Bold, confident, she yanked at his brief trunks until there was nothing between him and her hands. Excitement careened through her when he groaned, when he shuddered. When she felt the last dregs of civilization desert him.

He'd made love before. He could remember what it was to feel a woman's body, to bury himself in one. Why was it he couldn't remember anything like this? If needs had ever clawed at him this sharply before, he had no knowledge of it. She was filling him, overwhelming him. All at once, there was nothing else—no sea lapping, no sun streaming through a door, no subtle movement of a boat beneath. There was only Gabriella, strong, sleek and seductive. There was only Gabriella, and a desire so tangled with emotion he couldn't fight it. He couldn't fight what he didn't understand. Instead he gave himself to it, and to her.

She arched, with her fingers digging into him like spurs. He heard her gasp, felt her stiffen. Then she was going with him, racing with him. Neither knew nor cared who set the pace.

Perhaps only moments had passed. It seemed like only moments. They were still tangled together, damp flesh against damp flesh, fast heart against fast heart. She wasn't relaxed, but stunned. Perhaps, she thought as Reeve's breathing continued to come unsteadily against her ear, she'd never relax again. Certainly she'd never be the same again.

She looked at the sun coming into the cabin. The same sun. She heard and felt the motion of the sea. The same sea. But not the same Gabriella. Never the same, from this moment. Innocence was gone. It was only now that she could be certain she'd had it to lose. And it was only now, she realized, that she was sure she'd wanted to.

"So there was no one else," she murmured, thinking aloud.

He felt something twist inside him. Lying still, he closed his eyes until it eased. When he lifted his head, he saw that her eyes were heavy, but her skin had that glow that spoke of the aftermath of passion. And he saw, when he looked down at her, that he'd lost a great deal more than his objectivity.

His heart, which he'd always believed was very firmly in his possession, was hers. At that moment, he knew, she could break him in half with a careless word. So it was he who spoke almost carelessly.

"No, there was no one else. Do you want an apology?"

She wasn't sure how to react or how to respond. Did a man feel responsible when he'd taken a woman's innocence? How would she know? Maybe not responsible, she thought, but uncomfortable. She couldn't afford the luxury of showing just how that idea hurt. Instead she kept her eyes level and her voice calm. "No, I don't look for apologies. Do you?"

His tone didn't change, nor his expression. She could read nothing in either one. "Why would I?"

"I started this, Reeve. I'm well aware of that." She started to rise, but he held her in place.

"Regrets?"

Her chin came up, just a bit, but enough to show him her mood. "No. Have you?"

The first time she'd been with a man, he thought, and he'd started a stilted, foolish conversation for his own defense. She was entitled to some tenderness, some sweetness and some truth. He touched her face, just a fingertip along her cheek.

"How could I regret being given something beautiful?" He kissed her then, softly, lengthily. "How can I regret having made love to you when it's something I'm already thinking about doing again?"

Reeve saw her lips curve just before he shifted so that he could cradle her against him. When they started back to Cordina, he knew he'd have to begin thinking again, planning. If he was to help her…but not now. Not just yet.

Content, and finding she could indeed relax, Brie rested a hand over his heart. It put her engagement ring directly in her line of vision. In the shadowed light it didn't seem so stunning, so demanding. It seemed—almost—as if it belonged there. But it wasn't real, she told herself quickly. It wasn't anything more than a prop in a complicated game. Not real. She closed her eyes, settling her body against Reeve's.

No, the ring wasn't real, but this was, she thought as she let herself drift. This was real—for as long as it lasted.

Chapter 8

Nothing seemed to become easier, Brie thought as she walked down the wide, window-lined corridor toward the Grand Ballroom. There were paintings that any artist with a soul might have wept over. There was furniture that had been lovingly polished for centuries. She passed by without a glance.

Rather than simplifying with each day, life became more complicated. Hadn't Reeve told her life was never simple? It wasn't any use wishing he'd been wrong.

Nearly a week before, she'd lain beside him on a narrow little bunk, half dozing until they'd turned to each other again. And made love again. Didn't that make them lovers? she asked herself as she stopped by one of the windows. Weren't lovers supposed to be at ease with each other—continue to desire each other? Yet a week had passed. In that week, Reeve had been faultlessly polite, outwardly attentive. He'd even in his own way been kind. And he'd gone out of his way to avoid touching her.

Putting her hands on the sill, Brie looked down. The guards were changing. As she watched the quiet, rather charming procedure, she wondered if Reeve felt it was time her guard also changed. And what she'd do if he left.

Of course, she'd known all along she'd have to face the gossip. Their engagement was still top news, not only in Cordina and

Europe, but in the United States, as well. It wasn't possible to leaf through a magazine without finding herself.

That was nothing, Brie told herself with a little shrug. Gossip came and went. Unconsciously she twisted the diamond on her finger. Yes, gossip wasn't important. But Reeve was—perhaps too important.

If she understood herself better, her life better, would she know how to deal with what was happening? Or should she be dealing with what wasn't happening? No, life wasn't simple.

Falling in love must be difficult enough when everything was normal, but when there were so many blank pages, so many responsibilities to be learned, it was more frightening than exhilarating.

He'd go back to his farm, she reminded herself. To his farm, to his country, to his life. She, her family and a handful of people who had to be trusted were already aware of that. Even if Reeve asked her, could she go? He wouldn't ask, she told herself, trying to accept it. After all, she was just one lover in his life, one woman, one incident. It couldn't be for him as it was for her, where he was the only one.

Responsibility. She closed her eyes a moment as she forced the word into her head. She had to think of her responsibilities and stop dreaming. There'd be no splashy wedding, no lovely white dress and veil that every designer in the world was hoping to make. There'd be no huge cake, no crossed swords. There'd be an end, and a polite goodbye. She had no right to wish differently. But she hadn't the strength not to.

When she turned, the figure across the wide corridor had her jolting back toward the windows.

"Alexander." Brie dropped the hand she'd pressed instinctively to her heart. "You frightened me."

"I didn't want to disturb you. You looked…" Unhappy, he wanted to say. Lost. "Thoughtful."

"I was watching the guards." The smile she gave him was the same polite one she gave to everyone. Everyone but Reeve. But unlike Alexander, she didn't notice. "They look so trim and handsome in their uniforms. I was on my way to the ballroom to make sure everything was in order. It's hard to believe there's so little time left before the ball and yet so much to be done. Nearly all the responses are in, so—''

''Brie, must you talk to me as if I were someone you had to be polite to?''

She opened her mouth, then shut it again. He'd described it perfectly. She couldn't deny it. ''I'm sorry. It's still so awkward.''

''I'd rather you didn't put on that well-rehearsed front with me.'' He was young, tall and unquestionably annoyed. ''You don't seem to find it necessary with Reeve.''

Brie's voice chilled. ''I apologized once. I've no intention of giving you another apology.''

''I didn't want the first one.'' He crossed over to her with the quick measured steps of a man who had to know where he was going. One day he'd rule; the path was already worn. Though he was taller, they met now, as they always had, on level ground. ''What I want is for you to give your family the same consideration you do a stranger.''

She was tired of guilt, smothered by it. Her voice held no apology, only a challenge. ''Is that advice or an order?''

''No one's ever been able to give you an order,'' he snapped as the temper he'd been clinging to for weeks broke free. ''No one's ever been able to give you advice, for that matter. If you could be trusted to behave, it wouldn't be necessary for us to call in outsiders.''

''I don't think it's necessary to bring Reeve into this conversation.''

''No?'' He took her arm as he spoke, an old habit. ''Just what's between the two of you?''

Her voice had chilled before. Now her eyes followed suit. ''None of your business.''

''Damn it, Brie, I'm your brother.''

''So I'm told,'' she said slowly, forgetting in temper any hurt she might cause. ''And my younger brother by a few years. I don't find it necessary to be accountable to you, or to anyone, for my personal life.''

''I might be younger,'' Alexander said between his teeth, ''but I'm a man, and I know what's in a man's mind when he looks at a woman the way the American looks at you.''

''Alexander, you should stop referring to him as 'the American,' as though he were an inferior breed. And," she continued before he could respond, "if I didn't like the way Reeve looked at me, I'd put a stop to it. I'm capable of taking care of myself."

"If you were, none of us would have gone through that agony a few weeks ago." He saw her pale, but anger carried him further. "You were abducted, held, hospitalized. For days we waited, prayed, sat helpless. Doesn't it occur to you that the rest of us went through hell? Maybe you don't remember us, maybe we mean nothing to you right now. But that doesn't change the way we feel."

"Do you think I like it?" Unexpectedly tears started. If she'd had any warning, she might have stopped them. "Don't you know how hard I'm trying to get back? Now you push me into a corner, criticizing, demanding, insulting."

Temper faded, to be replaced by guilt. He'd forgotten just how lost she'd looked when she'd stood by the window. "It's what I've always done," he said gently. "You used to say that I'd practice ruling Cordina by trying to rule you and Bennett. I'm sorry, Brie. I love you. I can't stop loving you until you're ready for it."

"Oh, Alex." She went to him, for the first time holding him against her. He was so tall, so straight, so driven. But this time she felt a certain pride in knowing this. It wasn't easy for her to wait until things were clear, nor would it be easy for a man like her brother. "Did we always argue a great deal?"

"Always." He tightened his hold for a moment, then kissed the top of her head. "Father used to say it was because we both thought we knew everything."

"Well, at least I can't claim that anymore." With a quick, cleansing breath, she drew away. "Please don't resent Reeve, Alex. I can't say I didn't in the beginning, but the point is he's making quite a sacrifice staying here, going through all these maneuvers, when he'd rather be in his own country."

"It's difficult." Alex put his hands in his pockets and looked out the window. "I know he's under no obligation and what he's doing is done as a favor. I like him, actually."

Brie smiled, remembering that Bennett had used the same phrase. "I thought you did."

"It's just that I don't think things like this should go out of the family. Loubet's bad enough, but unavoidable."

"Would you get angry if I said I'd rather have Reeve hovering around me than Loubet?"

For the first time she saw Alexander grin. It was fast and endearing. "I'd think you'd lost your mind if you said otherwise."

"Your Highness."

Both Alexander and Brie turned. Janet Smithers gave them each a faultless curtsy. "I beg your pardon, Prince Alexander, Princess Gabriella."

She was, as usual, flawlessly groomed, with her dark hair tidy in a chignon and her rather thin face touched by only the most discreet of cosmetics. Her diction was perfect, unaccented, clear. Her suit was classicly and cleanly cut. And, to Brie's eyes, boring. Janet Smithers was efficient, intelligent, quick and quiet. If she were in a room with more than four people, no one would notice her. Perhaps for that reason alone, Brie was driven to be kind to her.

"Did you need me for something, Janet?"

"You've had a phone call, Your Highness, from Miss Christina Hamilton."

"Miss..." Brie trailed off a moment as she struggled to put details with the name.

"You went to college with her," Alexander supplied, dropping a hand on Brie's shoulder. It struck him that he was explaining to her about her closest friend. His touch was gentle. "She's an American, the daughter of a builder."

"Yes, I've visited her in—Houston. The press is sure she'll be in my wedding party, if not the maid of honor." Brie thought back on the newspaper clipping she'd been provided. A tall, stunning woman with a mane of dark hair and wicked smile. "You said she phoned, Janet. Did she leave a message?"

"She requested that I locate you, Your Highness." Not by the slightest expression did Janet reveal her thoughts on the request. "I'm to tell you that she'll phone back at exactly eleven o'clock."

"I see." Amused, Brie looked at her watch. That gave her fifteen minutes. "Well, then, I'd best go down to my rooms. Janet, if you don't mind, could you check the ballroom for me and make notes on anything left undone? I'm afraid I won't have time now."

"Of course, Your Highness." She gave the same lifeless curtsy before she continued on down the corridor.

"What an extraordinarily uninteresting woman," Alexander commented when she was out of earshot.

"Alex," Brie murmured, reprimanding him automatically even while she agreed.

"I know her credentials are impeccable and her efficiency's unquestionable, but God, it must be a bore to have to deal with her every morning."

Brie made a little movement, half shrug. "It doesn't start the day with any stimulation. Still, I must have had a reason for hiring her."

"You said you wanted a single woman you wouldn't get so attached to. When Alice left—Janet's predecessor—you moped around for days."

"I certainly chose wisely, then." When Alex gave her another quick grin, she shrugged again. "I'd best go down before this phone call comes through." She didn't add that she wanted to take a quick look through the notes and refresh her memory on Christina Hamilton. But before she left, she held out her hand. "Friends?"

Alexander took her hand, but gave a mock bow over it. "Friends, but I'm still keeping an eye on the American."

"As you please," she said carelessly, and turned to walk down the corridor. Alex watched her until she turned the corner toward the staircase. Perhaps he'd have a little talk with Reeve MacGee, as well.

Once in her sitting room, Brie sat down on the love seat with a stack of notes. She'd taken them in detail from instructions given by Reeve and her secretary. They were alphabetized, neat and thorough. They had to be thorough. The words on paper were her only reference to the people she'd once known so well. If her amnesia was to remain a closely guarded secret, she couldn't make a foolish mistake.

Christina Hamilton, she mused as she found the two pages that would comprise her knowledge of a woman who'd once been her friend. They'd spent four years together at the Sorbonne in Paris. When Brie closed her eyes, she thought she could almost see Paris—rain-washed streets, mad traffic and lovely old buildings, dusty little shops and gardens that could break your heart with color. But she couldn't see Christina Hamilton.

Chris, Brie corrected, noticing the nickname. Chris had studied art and now owned a gallery in Houston. There was a younger sister, Eve, whom Chris had alternately praised and despaired of. There had been romances. Brie's brows lifted as she ticked off the names of men Chris had been involved with. But not involved enough to marry. At twenty-five, she remained single, a successful, independent artist and businesswoman. Brie felt a dull twinge of envy that came and went so quickly it nearly went unnoticed.

Interesting, she reflected. Had there been rivalry between them? She could be given facts, data, information, but no one could list feelings to her.

When her private line rang, Brie kept her notes in one hand while she reached for the phone with the other. "Hello."

"The least you can do when an old friend calls you from across the Atlantic is to be available."

She liked the voice instantly. It was warm, dry and somewhat lazy. This time the twinge Brie felt was one of regret for not being able to recognize her emotions. "Chris..." She hesitated, then went with instinct. "Don't you know royalty keeps busy hours?"

The laugh rewarded her, but Brie didn't relax. "You know that whenever your crown gets too heavy you can take a break in Houston. God knows I can always use an extra pair of hands at the gallery. How are you, Brie, really?"

"I..." Oddly she found herself wanting to pour out everything, anything. There was something so comforting in the faceless voice. Duty, she remembered. Obligation. "I'm fine."

"It's Chris, remember? Oh, God, Brie, when I read about the kidnapping, I nearly—" She broke off, and Brie barely heard the quiet oath. "I spoke with your father, you know. I wanted to come. He didn't think it would be the best thing for you."

"Probably not. I've needed time, but I'm glad you wanted to."

"I'm not going to ask you questions about it, love. I'm sure the best thing to do is forget it entirely."

Brie gave a quick, uncontrollable laugh. "That seems to be what I'm doing."

Chris waited a moment, not quite satisfied with Brie's reaction.

Ultimately she let it pass. "I will ask you what the hell's going on over there in Camelot."

"Going on?"

"This secret, whirlwind romance that's now at the engagement point. Brie, I know you've always been discreet, but I can't believe you didn't say a word to me, not a word about Reeve MacGee."

"Well, I suppose I really didn't know what to say." That had the ring of truth, Brie thought bitterly. "Everything's happened so fast. The engagement wasn't set or even discussed until Reeve came out here last month."

"How does your father feel?"

Brie gave a wry smile, grateful she didn't have to guard her expression. "You could say he nearly arranged it himself."

"I can't say I disapprove. An American ex-cop—you always said you'd never marry anyone too suitable."

Brie smiled a little. "Apparently I meant it."

"Actually, I was beginning to think you'd never take the plunge. You've always been too clever about men for your own good. Remember that model in Professor Debare's class?"

"The male model?" Brie hazarded, and was rewarded by another long laugh.

"Of course. You took one look at that magnificent study in masculine perfection and dubbed him a shallow, vain opportunist. The rest of us were drooling over his pectoral muscles—then he took Sylvia for fifty thousand francs."

"Poor Sylvia," Brie murmured, lost.

"Ah, well, she could afford it. Anyway, Brie, I know you're busy. I've called to invite myself, and Eve, for a few days."

"You know you're always welcome," Brie said automatically while her mind raced. "You're coming for the ball. Can you stay over then?"

"That's the plan. I hope you don't mind me dragging Eve along, but the girl's driving Daddy mad. Brie, the child wants to be an actress."

"Oh?"

"You know Daddy, all business. He just can't see one of his darling girls wearing greasepaint and costumes. Now if she wanted to be an agent... Anyway, I thought it might do them both good to be a few thousand miles apart for a week or so. So if you can find an extra couple of beds in that palace of yours..."

"We've always got the folding cots."

"I knew I could count on you. We'll fly in the day before the ball, then. I can give you a hand—and meet your betrothed. By the way, Brie, how does it feel to be in love?"

"It—" She looked down at the ring on her hand, remembered what could sweep through her at a touch, at a look. "It's not very comfortable, actually."

Chris laughed again. "Did you think it was going to be? Take care of yourself, darling. I'll see you soon."

"Goodbye, Chris."

After she'd hung up, Brie sat still for a moment. She'd pulled it off. Christina Hamilton hadn't suspected anything. Brie had been bright, cheerful—deceitful. On a surge of temper, Brie tossed her notes so that they scattered, floated, then fell. She continued to frown at them after she'd heard the discreet knock at her door.

No, she wouldn't pick them up, Brie decided. She'd leave them just where they were, just where they belonged. "Yes, come in."

"Excuse me, Your Highness." Janet entered the sitting room with her usual lack of fuss. "I thought you'd like to know that the ballroom is in order. The drapes are being rehung." Though she glanced down to the papers lying on the floor, she made no comment. "Did your call come through?"

"Yes. Yes, I spoke with Miss Hamilton. And you're welcome to relay to my father that she suspects nothing."

Janet kept her hands folded neatly in front of her. "I beg your pardon, Your Highness?"

"Are you actually going to try to tell me you don't report to him?" Brie demanded. She rose, guilt and despair pushing at her. "I'm well aware of how closely you watch me, Janet."

"Your welfare is our only concern, Your Highness." Janet's voice remained colorless; her hands remained folded. "If I've offended you—"

"The subterfuge offends me," Brie tossed back. "All of it."

"I know Your Highness must feel—"

"You don't know how I feel," Brie interrupted as she whirled around the room. "How can you? Do you remember your father, your brother, your closest friend?"

"Your Highness…" After a moment, Janet took a step closer. That kind of temper, that kind of emotion had to be handled gently. "Perhaps none of us really understands, but that doesn't mean we don't care. If there were anything I could do to help…"

"No." Calmer, Brie turned back. "No, nothing. I'm sorry, Janet. I've no business shouting at you."

The smile was slight and did little to change her expression. "But you had to shout at someone. I'd hoped—that is, I'd thought that perhaps after you'd talked to an old friend you might begin to remember something."

"Nothing. Sometimes I wonder if I ever will."

"But the doctors are hopeful, Your Highness."

"Doctors. I've had my fill of them, I'm afraid. They tell me to be patient." With a sigh, she began to rearrange a vase of gardenias. "How can I be patient when I have nothing more than flashes of who I am, of what happened to me?"

"But you have flashes?" Again Janet stepped closer, and after a brief hesitation laid a hand on Brie's. "You do remember bits and pieces?"

"No—impressions. Nothing as solid as pieces." The image of the knife was solid, and too ugly to dwell on. She needed something her mind could accept, something that eased it. "Pieces could be put together, couldn't they, Janet?"

"I'm not a doctor, Your Highness, but perhaps you should accept what you have now."

"That my life began less than a month ago?" Brie shook her head. "No, I can't. I won't. I'll find the first piece."

A floor above, Alexander sat in his cool-colored, spacious office and watched Reeve. He'd planned the interview carefully, and felt fully justified.

"I appreciate your giving me some time, Reeve."

"I'm sure you feel it's important, Alex."

"Gabriella's important."

Reeve nodded slowly. "To all of us."

It wasn't precisely the response he'd expected. Then again, he knew the value of having alternate moves. "While I appreciate what you're doing, Reeve, I feel my father leaned too heavily on an old friendship. Your position becomes more delicate every day."

Reeve sat back. Though there were nearly ten years between them, he didn't consider that he was facing a boy. Alexander had become a man earlier than most. Reeve debated his next move, and decided on an aggressive one. "Are you concerned about the possibility of my becoming your brother-in-law, Alex?"

If there was anger, the prince concealed it. "We both know what games are being played. My concern is Gabriella. She's very vulnerable now, too vulnerable. Since, through my father's wishes, you remain closer to Gabriella than her family, you're in a position to observe and advise."

"And you're worried that I might observe what's none of my business and advise what's inappropriate."

Alexander spread his hands on his desk. "I can see why my father admires you, Reeve. And I think I can understand why Brie trusts you."

"But you don't."

"No, actually, I think I do." He wasn't unsure of himself. A man in Alexander's position couldn't afford to be. But he took a moment, anyway. He wanted to be certain he used the right words, the right tone. "I'm confident that as far as Brie's safety goes, she's in good hands. Otherwise…" He brought his gaze to Reeve's. They held level. "Otherwise, I'd see that you were either sent on your way or carefully watched."

"Fair enough." Reeve took out a cigarette. Alex shook his head at the offer. "So you're satisfied with my position as bodyguard, but you're concerned about a more personal relationship."

"You're aware that I objected—no, let's be candid—that I fought the business of your becoming engaged to my sister."

"I'm aware that both you and Loubet expressed doubts."

"I don't like my opinion coinciding with Loubet's," Alexander muttered, then gave Reeve a quick, completely open smile. "My father considers Loubet's talents and experience as minister of state compensation for his outdated views on a great number of things."

"Then there's the matter of the limp." At Alexander's expression, Reeve blew out a stream of smoke. "A great deal of our families' histories are known to each other, Alex. My father happened to be in the car along with Loubet and the prince when they had the accident some thirty-five years ago. Your father broke his

arm, mine suffered a mild concussion. Loubet, unfortunately, had
more serious injuries.''

"The accident has nothing to do with Loubet's position now.''

"No, I'm quite sure it doesn't. Your father doesn't handle things
that way. But perhaps he's more tolerant because of it. He was
driving. A certain amount of remorse is only human. In any
case—'' Reeve brushed the subject aside ''—it merely serves to
show that our families are tied in certain ways. Old friendships,
old bonds. My engagement to your sister was easily accepted because of that.''

"Do you easily accept it?''

This time it was Reeve who hesitated. "Alex, do you want a
comfortable answer or the truth?''

"The truth.''

"It wasn't a simple matter for me to agree to a mock engagement to Gabriella. It isn't a simple matter for me to go through
the motions of being her fiancé, or to see my ring on her finger.
It isn't simple,'' Reeve said slowly, "because I'm in love with
her.''

Alexander didn't speak, nor did he give any sign of surprise.
After a moment, he reached out and ran a fingertip down a silver
picture frame. His sister looked back out at him, smiling and
lovely. "What do you intend to do about it?''

Reeve lifted a brow. "Isn't it your father's place to ask, Alex?''

"It isn't my father you've told.''

"No.'' Reeve crushed out his cigarette slowly, deliberately. "I
don't intend to do anything about it. I'm well aware what my
responsibilities and my limitations are as concerns your sister.''

"I see.'' Alexander picked up a pen and ran it absently through
his fingers. It seemed he didn't know Reeve MacGee as well as
he'd thought. "And Brie's feelings?''

"Are Brie's feelings. She doesn't need any more complications
at this point. Once she remembers, she'll no longer need me.''

"Just like that?''

"I'm a realist. Whatever develops between Brie and me now is
very likely to change once her memory returns.''

"And yet you want to help her get to that point.''

"She needs to remember,'' Reeve said evenly. "She suffers.''

Alex looked at the picture again, was drawn to it. "I know that."

"Do you? Do you know how guilty she feels that she can't remember the people who want her love? Do you know how frightened she is when she has one of the dreams that take her to the edge of remembering, then leave her lost?"

"No." Alexander dropped the pen. "She doesn't confide in me—I think I see why. And I think I see why my father trusts you completely." Looking down at his hands, he felt helpless, frustrated. "She has dreams?"

"She remembers the dark, hearing voices, being afraid." He thought of her dream about the knife, but kept his silence there. That was for Brie to tell. "It seems to be little more than that."

"I see. I understand a great deal more now." Again Alexander's gaze locked on his. "You've a right to resent my questions, Reeve, but I've the right to ask them."

"We'll agree to both of those." Rising, Reeve put an end to the interview himself. "Just remember, I'll do everything I'm capable of doing to keep your sister safe."

Alex stood to face him. "We can both agree to that, as well."

It was late when Reeve stood under a hot, soothing shower. He needed it more than he needed an empty bed. His evening had been spent escorting Brie to a dinner party, where they'd both been deluged with questions on the wedding. When, who, where? How much? How soon? How many?

If things didn't begin to turn around for Brie after the ball, they'd no longer be able to use preparations for that as an excuse for the lack of plans.

All they needed now was a fictitious wedding date, Reeve thought, letting water pour over his head and beat on his neck. If things didn't begin to jell soon, they'd find themselves standing at the altar just to keep the tongues from wagging.

That would be the ultimate in fantasy and foolishness, wouldn't it? he asked himself. Married to prevent rumors from generating. Yet how much more difficult could that be than what was going on now?

He'd had to sit through dinner, watching her, being congratulated on his good fortune. He'd had to sit within a few feet of her and remember what it had been like for them when they'd just been two people on a narrow bunk in a tiny cabin.

Trouble was, he remembered too well, needed too much. Since then he'd been very careful to avoid any opportunity for them to be quite that alone. When they weren't in the palace or in the car, they were at a party or one of her charity functions. He took her to the AHC headquarters or the Red Cross. He accompanied her to the museum, but he never suggested another sail.

Neither of them could afford it, he decided as he stepped from the shower. Certainly neither of them had planned on his forgetting the rules and falling in love with her. He still had a job to do. She still had a life to rediscover. Once both were accomplished, the ties would be broken.

As they should be, Reeve thought. With a towel hooked around his waist, he rubbed a fresh one over his hair. Brie didn't belong in a ramshackle farmhouse in the mountains. He didn't belong in a palace. It was as simple as that.

Then he stepped through to the bedroom and nothing was simple.

Brie sat in an armchair, a low light shining over her shoulder as she thumbed through a book. The nerves were there, but so was determination. She managed to hide the first as she looked up.

"I think I've always loved Steinbeck," she said as she set the book aside. "He makes me feel as though I've been to Monterey." She rose, and though she'd been too nervous to plan it, she looked like a bride. The simple white robe fell to her ankles and covered her arms to the wrist. Her hair fell over her shoulders, where lace gave a glimpse of the skin beneath.

Reeve stood where he was, as stunned by the ache as he'd ever been stunned by anything. "Did you want to borrow a book?"

"No." She stepped toward him as though she were confident. "You wouldn't come to me, Reeve. I thought it was time I came to you." Needing the contact, she took his hands. Somehow it made the confidence genuine. "You can't send me away," she murmured. "I won't go."

No, he couldn't send her away. Common sense might tell him to, but common sense hadn't a chance. "Pulling rank again, Gabriella?"

"Only if I must." She lifted his hand to her face a moment.

"Tell me you don't want me. I might hate you for it, but I won't make a fool of myself again."

He knew he could lie, and that the lie might be best for her. But the lie wouldn't come. "I can't tell you I don't want you. I doubt I could tell you even if I thought I could make you believe it. And I'm very likely to make a fool of myself."

With a smile, she wrapped her arms around him. "Hold me. Just hold me." She closed her eyes as her cheek pressed against his shoulder. This was where she'd wanted to be. "I've been going crazy waiting, wondering. I nearly lost my nerve tonight coming down the hall."

"It might have been best if you had. It's hardly discreet for you to visit me in my room at midnight."

Laughing, she tossed her head back. "No, it's not. So let's make the best of it."

With her arms flung around his neck, she found his mouth with hers. It was what she wanted, all she wanted, Brie realized as she poured herself into the kiss. Whatever she had to fight to get another day successfully behind her, if she could share the night with him, she could do it.

"Reeve." Slowly she drew away so that she could see him. "For tonight, let's not have any pretenses, any deceptions." She brought his hand to her face again, but this time she pressed her mouth to it. "I need you. Can that be enough?"

"It's enough." He loosened the sash of her robe. "Let me show you."

The light was low, the windows open. She could smell the sweet peas that climbed gleefully on the trellis just below. When he slipped the robe from her shoulders, she shivered. But from excitement, not from the breeze.

"You're lovely, Brie." Now that they were bare, Reeve followed the slope of her shoulders with his hands. "Every time I see you, it's like the first time. The light is different, the angle, but it strikes me just as it did the first time."

He brushed her hair back from her face until only his hand framed it. Then he watched her, only watched, until her heart began to thud. He kissed her, once, twice, slowly but lightly. As her lids fluttered closed, he brushed his lips over them, as well.

Gentleness he hadn't shown before. She'd come to him. Now he could give it.

When he lifted her in his arms, her eyes opened in surprise. She hadn't expected an old-fashioned, romantic gesture from him. There was much more he had to give that she hadn't expected.

They lay together on the bed, naked, needing. But he brought her fingers to his lips, kissing them one by one. When she reached for him he lowered to her, but only for slow kisses, light caresses. Unlike the first time, this fire only smoldered, half tormenting, half delighting.

She'd thought he'd already shown her every point of pleasure her body was capable of. Now he showed her more, exquisitely.

Brie knew there was a restlessness in him. A violence. The first time they'd loved, she'd felt it, sensed it, wanted it. Tonight he brought none of it with him. This night was tender. Tenderness that brought a heavy, misty pleasure she hadn't explored. This excitement was different, drifting, not soothing but sweet. She gave herself to it, willing, for the moment, to be led.

He'd taken her innocence. In some strange way Reeve was aware that she'd given a portion of his back to him. It hadn't been something he'd looked for or wanted, nor was it something he could have prevented. Perhaps one day, when their lives separated and he had to deal with what he'd had and what he'd lost, he'd resent it. Tonight, when she was close, soft, giving, he only treasured it.

So he went slowly, gently. What passed between them this night would be something neither of them would ever be able to forget.

He nibbled, finding the long narrow bone of her hip fascinating. He knew just how strong she was. After all, he'd followed her through days of work and demands and evenings that were social, but equally taxing. Yet just there her skin was so fragile, so sensitive. She had the small, delicate body of a woman who lived her life in luxury. But she had the mind, he knew, of a woman who never took one moment of it for granted.

Is that why he loved her? Did it matter?

She could only sigh as his mouth traced lower, lower down her body. He was taking her places she'd never imagined. This world was dark, but there was no fear. Just anticipation. It drummed through her, to be joined by arousal, pleasure, satisfaction. One layered on top of the other.

There were night birds calling to each other, but the murmur of her name on Reeve's lips seemed sweeter. The breeze whispered across her face, but his breath, skimming across her skin was warmer. The sheets were soft, cool only until they were touched with flesh that quickly warmed them. If she let her eyes open, she could see her own hand stroke over him. And triumph in it.

His tongue traced, teased, lingered, then invaded. Suddenly she was catapulted out of the dark, soothing world and into the light.

She wasn't aware that her fingers gripped her bedsheets as she arched. She wasn't aware that she called out his name mindlessly. But she was aware, all at once, that pleasure could be almost too much to bear. She knew, as he drew from her relentlessly, that he was giving to her, as well. Everything, all things, were there for her to take if only she had the strength. She'd find it.

Quiet thoughts vanished. Turbulent ones tumbled into her. To have him—completely, enduringly. To know that he was rocked by the power even as she was. To feel the shudder that told her he, too, was overwhelmed. That was enough to both ensure survival and to make survival unimportant. Though she trembled, dazed, he didn't give her time to catch her breath before he drove her up and beyond again.

Then, when she thought there could be no more, he took her with all the fierce need he'd kept harnessed.

Chapter 9

Brie knew she shouldn't have stayed with him through the night, but she found she wanted, needed, to sleep with him, even if it were only for a few hours. It had been so easy in the dark, quiet night to forget discretion and to take what lovers are entitled to. It had been so sweet to drift off to sleep with her hand caught in his. If in the morning there were consequences, they'd be worth those few hours.

It was Reeve who awoke first and roused her just before dawn when the light was gray and indistinct. This was the time between, when the night birds began to sleep and the lark awakened. Brie felt the light kiss on her shoulder, and merely sighed and snuggled closer. The nip on her earlobe made her shudder—but lazily, comfortably.

"Brie, the sun's coming up."

"Mmmm. Kiss me again."

He kissed her again, this time on the lips, until he was sure she was awake. "The servants will be up and around soon," he told her as her eyes half opened. "You shouldn't be here."

"Worried about your reputation again?" She yawned and wrapped her arms around his neck.

Reeve grinned and comfortably cupped her breast. She made him feel so...at home. Had he just noticed it? "Naturally."

Pleased with herself, she twined his hair around her finger. "I suppose I've compromised you."

"You did come to my room, after all. How could I risk refusing a princess?"

She arched a brow. "Very wise. So…" She touched her tongue to her top lip. "If I commanded you to make love with me again, right now—"

"I'd tell you to get your buns out of bed." He kissed her before she could object. "Your Serene Highness."

"Very well," she said loftily, and rolled aside. She stood, naked, and shook back her hair. He thought then that she was no Sleeping Beauty just coming to life, but a woman who already knew and accepted her own power. "Since you cast me aside so easily, you'll have to come to me next time." She picked up her discarded robe, but took her time about putting it on. "That is, unless you'd like to be tossed in the dungeons. They are, I'm told, very deep, dank and dark."

He watched her slide one arm in a sleeve. "Blackmail?"

"I've no conscience." She drew on the other sleeve, then slowly crossed and tied the robe.

No, she was no Sleeping Beauty, he thought again. She was a woman who deserved more than promises. "Brie…" Reeve sat up, pulling a hand through his hair. "Alexander and I had a talk yesterday."

Brie kept her hands on the sash, though they were no longer relaxed. "Oh? About me, I assume."

"Yes, about you."

"Well?"

"That royal tone doesn't work on me, Brie. You should know that by now."

As if it were vital, she smoothed out the satin of the sash. "What does?"

"Honesty."

She looked back at him, then sighed. It was an answer she should have expected. "All right, then. Alex and I did our own share of talking—arguing—yesterday. I can't say I appreciate the two of you getting together for a chat about me and my welfare."

"He's concerned. I'm concerned."

"Is that an excuse for everything?"

"It's a reason for everything."

Her breath came out slowly. "I'm sorry, I don't mean to be unfair, Reeve. I don't, though it might appear differently, even mean to be ungrateful. It just seems as though while everyone's so concerned, so worried, everyone continues to make demands." She began to walk as she spoke—to the window and away, to the mirror and back again, as if she weren't quite ready to face herself that morning. "They want me to go along with Loubet's plan about covering up the amnesia so that there's no panic and the investigation can go on quietly. They want you and me to go on with this deception about being engaged. I think—I'm beginning to think that bothers me most of all."

"I see."

She glanced up, unsmiling. "I wonder if you can," she murmured. "On one hand I get sympathy, concern, and on the other, obligations."

"Is there something you'd rather do? Some way you'd rather try?"

"No." She shook her head. "No. What did Alexander conclude, then?"

"He decided to trust me. Have you?"

She looked at him in surprise, then realized how she must have appeared. "You know I trust you. I wouldn't be here with you if I didn't."

He made the decision instantly. Sometimes it was the best way. "Can you clear your schedule today and come with me?"

"Yes."

"No questions?"

She moved her shoulders. "All right, if you want one. Where?"

"To the little farm." He waited for her reaction, but she only watched him. "I think it's time we worked together."

She closed her eyes a moment, then crossed to the bed. "Thank you."

He felt his emotions rise and tangle again. They always would, he realized, with her. "You might not be grateful later."

"Yes, I will." Bending, she kissed him, not in passion, but in friendship. "No matter what."

The corridors were dim when she left Reeve's room to go to her own. But her spirit wasn't. She had hope again. This wouldn't be a day where she just followed the schedule that had been set for her. Today, at last, she'd do something to bring the past and present together. Perhaps the key was at the little farm. Perhaps with Reeve's help she'd find it.

Quietly Brie opened the door to her bedroom, anxious to begin. Humming a little, she walked to the windows and began pushing aside the curtains so light could spill in.

"So."

She jolted, whirled, then swore under her breath. "Nanny."

The old woman straightened in the chair and gave Brie a long, steady look. If her bones were stiff, she gave no sign. Brie felt the patience, the disapproval, and felt the blood creep into her cheeks.

"Well you should blush, young lady, tiptoeing into your room with the sun."

"Have you been here all night?"

"Yes. Which is more than you can say." Nanny tapped a long, curved fingernail against the arm of the chair. She saw the change, but, then, she'd seen it days before when Brie had come back from sailing. When a woman was old, she was still a woman. "So you decided to take a lover. Tell me, are you pleased with yourself?"

Defiant, and amazed that she felt the need to be, Brie lifted her chin. "Yes."

Nanny studied her—the tumbled hair, the flushed cheeks and the eyes where the echo of passion remained. "That's as it should be," she murmured. "You're in love."

She could have denied it. It was on the tip of her tongue to do so, when she realized it would be a lie. Just one more lie. "Yes, I'm in love."

"Then I'll tell you to be careful." Nanny's face looked old and pale in the morning light, but her eyes were ageless. "When a woman's in love with her lover, she risks more than her body, more than her time. You understand?"

"Yes. I think I do." Brie smiled and moved over to kneel at Nanny's feet. "Why did you sleep all night in a chair instead of your bed?"

"Perhaps you've taken a lover, but I still look after you. I brought you warm milk—you don't sleep well."

Brie looked over and saw the thick cup on the table. "And I

worried you because I wasn't here." She brought the woman's hard little hand to her cheek. "I'm sorry, Nanny."

"I suspected you were with the American." She sniffed a little. "A pity his blood isn't as blue as his eyes, but you could do worse."

The diamond weighed heavily on her finger. "It's still just a dream, isn't it?"

"You don't dream enough," Nanny said briskly. "So I brought you milk and found you'd looked for a different kind of comfort."

This time Brie laughed. "Would you scold me if I said I much preferred it?"

"I'd simply advise you to keep your preferences from your father for a while yet." Nanny's voice was dry and amused as Brie grinned up at her. "Perhaps you have no more use for the other comfort I brought you." Reaching beside her, she pulled out a plain, round-faced rag doll in a tattered pinafore. "When you were a child and were restless in the night, you'd reach for this."

"Poor ugly thing," Brie murmured as she took it in her hands. "You called her 'Henrietta Homely.'"

"I hope she didn't mind," Brie began as she ran a hand over the doll's hair. Then she went stiff and very still.

A young girl in a small bed with pink hangings, pink sheets, pink spread. White frills on a vanity table. Rosebuds on the wallpaper. Music drifting up from far away. A waltz, slow and romantic. And there was a woman, the woman from the portrait, smiling, murmuring, laughing a little as she leaned over the bed, so that the emeralds in her ears caught the low light. Her dress was like the emeralds, green and rich. It rustled musically as the best of silks do. She smelled of apple blossoms, of spring, of youth.

"Gabriella." Nanny put a hand to Brie's shoulder and squeezed. Beneath the thin robe, she could feel the skin, icy. "Gabriella."

"My room," Brie whispered as she continued to stare down at the doll. "My room when I was a girl—what color?"

"Pink," Nanny said haltingly. "It was all pink and white, like a pastry."

"And my mother." Brie's fingers dug into the rag doll, but she didn't know it. Sweat pearled on her forehead, but she didn't know that, either. As long as she pushed, as long as she held on, she could see and remember. "Did she have a green silk dress? Emerald green. A ball gown?"

"Strapless." With an effort, the old woman kept her voice calm and quiet. "The waist was very snug. The skirt was very full."

"And her scent was like apple blossoms. She was so beautiful."

"Yes." Nanny's strong fingers held her shoulder firmly. "Do you remember?"

"I—she came to see me. There was music, a waltz playing. She came to tuck me in."

"She would always. First you, then Alexander, then Bennett. Your father would come up if he could slip away, but they'd both come to the nursery before they went to bed. I'll go get your father now."

"No." Brie pressed the doll close. She couldn't hold the image any longer. It left her weak and breathless. "No, not yet. That's all there is. Just that one picture, and I need so much more. Nanny..." Eyes brimming, Brie looked up again. "I did love her. Finally I can feel it. I loved her so much. Now, remembering that, it's like losing her again."

With her old nurse stroking her hair, Brie lay down her head and wept. The bedroom door opened no more than a crack, then shut soundlessly.

"So you're going for a ride in the country."

Brie stood in the main hall, looking at her father. Her face was carefully made up. The signs of weeping were gone. But her nerves weren't as easily concealed. She twisted the strap of the purse she wore over her shoulder.

"Yes. I told Janet to cancel my appointments. There wasn't anything very important—a fitting, some paperwork at the AHC that I can see to just as easily tomorrow."

"Brie, you don't have to justify taking a day off to me." Though he wasn't certain how he'd be received, Armand took her hand. "Have I asked too much of you?"

"No—" She shook her head. "I don't know."

"Never has it been more difficult for me to be both ruler and father. If you asked..." His fingers tightened briefly on her hand. "If you wanted, Gabriella, I'd take you away for a few weeks. A cruise, perhaps, or just a trip to the cottage in Sardina."

She couldn't remind him that she didn't know the cottage in Sardina. Instead she smiled. "There's no need. Dr. Franco must have told you that I'm strong as a horse."

"And Dr. Kijinsky tells me that you're still troubled by images, dreams."

Brie took a breath and tried not to regret that she'd finally told the analyst everything. "Some things take longer to heal."

He couldn't beg her to talk to him as he knew she talked to Reeve. Such things had to come from the heart. Yet neither could he forget how often she'd curl into his lap, her head on his shoulder, as she poured out her feelings.

"You look tired," he murmured. "The country air will do you good. You're going to the little farm?"

She kept her eyes level. She wouldn't be turned away from what she had to do. "Yes."

He saw the determination, respected it. Feared it. "When you come back, will you tell me whatever you remember, whatever you felt?"

For the first time her hand relaxed in his. "Yes, of course." For his sake, for the sake of the woman in the emerald dress who'd tucked her in, Brie stepped forward to brush his cheek with her lips. "Don't worry about me. Reeve will be there."

Struggling not to feel replaced, Armand watched her walk down the long length of the hall. A footman opened the door wide, and she stepped into the sunshine.

For a long time Reeve said nothing. He drove at an easy speed along the winding, climbing, dipping coast road. Turmoil. It was quickly recognized, though the source wasn't. He could wait.

The city of Cordina was left behind, then the port of Lebarre. Now and then they'd pass a cottage where the gardens were carefully tended and the flowers bloomed in profusion. This was the road where she'd run that night, escaping. He wondered if she realized it.

She saw nothing familiar, nothing that should make her tense. But she was tense. The land was lovely in its windswept, rock-tumbled way. It was quiet, colorful, idyllic. Yet she continued to worry the strap of her bag.

"Do you want to stop, Gabriella? Would you rather go somewhere else?"

She turned to him quickly, then just as quickly turned away again. "No. No, of course not. Cordina's a beautiful country, isn't it?"

"Why don't you tell me what's wrong?"

"I'm not sure." She made her hand lie still in her lap. "I feel uneasy, as if I should be looking over my shoulder."

He'd already decided to give her whatever answers she needed without frills or cushions. "You ran along this road a month ago. In a storm."

Her fingers curled. She made them relax. "Was I running toward the city or away?"

He glanced at her again. It hadn't occurred to him to make that particular connection. His respect for her mind went up another notch. "Toward. You were no more than three miles outside of Lebarre when you collapsed."

She nodded. "Then I was lucky, or I still knew enough to go in the right direction. Reeve, this morning…"

Regrets? he wondered as his fingers tightened on the wheel. Were regrets and common sense coming so soon? "What about it?"

"Nanny was waiting for me in my room."

Should he be amused? Whether he should or not, Reeve couldn't prevent the smile at the picture that formed in his mind. "And?"

"We talked. She brings warm milk to me some nights. I suppose I wasn't thinking of such things last night." Brie smiled, too, but only briefly. "She also brought me a doll, something I'd had as a child." Slowly, determined to be very clear on every detail, Brie told him what she'd remembered. "That was all," she said at length. "But this time it wasn't an impression, it wasn't a dream. I remembered."

"Have you told anyone else?"

"No."

"You'll tell Kijinsky when you see him tomorrow." It wasn't a question but more in the line of an order. Brie struggled not to feel resentment but to understand.

"Yes, of course. Do you think it's a beginning for me?"

He'd slowed the car while she'd talked. Now he sped up again. "I think you're getting stronger. That was a memory you could handle, maybe one you needed before you faced the rest."

"And the rest will come."

"The rest will come," he agreed. And when it did, she wouldn't need him any longer. His job would be over. His farm...

He thought of it now, but it seemed as if he'd been away years rather than weeks. It didn't seem merely a quiet, serene spot any longer, but lonely, empty. When he went back, he'd no longer be the same man with the same desires.

Following the directions he'd been given, Reeve turned off the coast road and headed away from the sea. The going wasn't as smooth here. Again he slowed the car, this time because of the uneven road.

Before long, the trees muffled, then silenced the sound of water. The hills were greener, the landscape less dramatic. They heard a dog bark, a cow moo low and deep. He could almost imagine he was going home.

He turned again, doubling back a bit on a road that was no more than dirt and stone. Then a field stretched out on one side, green and overgrown. Trees grew thick on the other.

"This is it?"

"Yes." Reeve turned off the ignition.

"They found my car here?"

"That's right."

She sat for a moment, waiting. "Why do I always expect it to be easy?" she said. "Somehow I think that when I see something, when I know something, it'll be clear. It never really is. But there are times I feel the knife in my hand." She glanced down at her palm. "I can feel it, and when I do, I know I'm capable of killing."

"We all are, under the right circumstances."

"No." Outwardly calm, Brie folded her hands. Agony was kept inside, where she had been taught personal agonies belonged. "I don't believe that. To kill, to take a life, requires an understanding, an acceptance of violence. A dark side. In some, it's strong enough to overpower every other instinct."

"And what would have happened to you if you'd closed your eyes and rejected violence?" He gripped her shoulder harder than was necessary and made her face him. "Blessed are the passive, Brie? You know better."

He pulled out her emotions with a look. She couldn't stop it.

"I don't want violence in my life," she said passionately. "And I don't, I won't, accept the fact that I've killed."

"Then you'll never pull out of this." His voice was harsh as he backed her into the seat. "You'll go on living your fantasy. The princess in the castle—cool, distant and unattainable."

"You speak to me of fantasy?" He was pushing her; it no longer mattered that she'd once asked him to. He was pushing her toward a dark boundary. "You make your own illusions. A man who's spent his life looking for trouble, seeking it out, who pretends he'll be content to sit on the porch and watch his crops grow."

She'd hit the mark. Fury and frustration welled up and poured out in his voice. He had his fantasies, and she'd become one of them. "At least I know what my own reality is and I've faced it. I need the farm for reasons you're not willing to understand. I need it because I know what I'm capable of, what I've done and what I might do yet."

"With no regrets."

"Damn regrets. But tomorrow might be different. I have a choice." He wanted to believe it.

"You do." Suddenly weary, she looked away. "Perhaps that's where we differ. How can I live my life the way I'm obligated to live it knowing that I'm—"

"Human," he interrupted. "Just like the rest of us."

"You simplify."

"Are you going to tell me that a title makes you above the rest of us?"

She started to snap, then let out a long breath. "You've cornered me. No, I'm human, and flawed, and I'm afraid. Accepting my own...shadows seems the most difficult of all."

"Do you want to go on?"

"Yes." She reached for the door handle. "Yes, I want to go on." Stepping from the car, she looked around and wished she knew where to begin. Perhaps she already had. "Have you come out here before?"

"No."

"Good, then it's like the first time for both of us." She shielded her eyes, looking. "It's so quiet. I wonder if I planned to have the fields planted one day."

"You talked of it."

"But did nothing about it." She began to walk.

Wildflowers grew as they pleased, in the field, along the path. Some were yellow, others blue. Fat, businesslike bees hummed around them. She saw a butterfly as big as the palm of her hand land and balance on a petal. The air smelled of grass, rich grass, rich dirt. She walked on without purpose.

A jay swooped by, annoyed by the intrusion. It flew off, complaining, into the trees. No fairy tale here, she mused. It would be hard, hard work to clear, to plant, to harvest. Is that why it remained undone? Had she only been dreaming again?

"Why did I buy this?"

"You wanted a place of your own. You needed a place where you could get away."

"Escape again?"

"Solitude," he corrected. "There's a difference."

"But it needs a house." Suddenly impatient, she turned in a circle. "It needs to live. Look there—if some of those trees were cleared, a house could snuggle in and look out over the fields. There'd be stables there. Yes, and a pasture. A hen house, too." Caught up, she walked farther, quickly. "Right along here. A farm has to have fresh eggs. There should be dogs and children, don't you see? It's nothing without them. Daisies in a windowbox. Laughter through the doorways. The land shouldn't sit unloved this way."

He could see it as she did. After all, he'd seen his own land in precisely the same way. Yet they remained worlds apart. "From what I've been told, it isn't unloved."

"But untended. Nothing alive can go untended."

Annoyed with herself, she turned to walk farther in the high grass. As she did, her foot hit something and set it rattling against rock. Reeve bent down and picked up a red thermos, empty, with the stopper and top missing. His instincts began to hum. He held it by the base, touching no more than was necessary. He'd been a cop too long.

"In your dreams you're sitting someplace quiet, drinking coffee from a red thermos."

Brie stared at it as though it were something vile. "Yes."

"And you were sleepy." Casually he sniffed at the opening,

but his mind was already working ahead. Just how sophisticated was the police lab in Cordina? he wondered. And why hadn't the farm been thoroughly investigated? Why had a piece of evidence so potentially important been left unheeded? He was damn well going to find out.

She'd walked this way on her own, he mused. He'd been very careful not to influence her direction. Then she systematically pointed out where a house, the stables would be. If she'd sat here before... He skimmed until his gaze rested on a big, smooth rock. It was only a few yards away, where the sun would be full and warm in the late morning and early afternoon. A spot for a dreamer.

Yes, if she'd sat there, resting, thinking, drinking coffee—

"What are you thinking?"

He brought his gaze back to her. "I'm thinking you may have sat against that rock there, drinking your coffee, planning. You got sleepy, perhaps even dozed off. But then you tried to shake the sleepiness off. You told me that in your dreams you didn't want to be sleepy. So maybe you managed to get up, stumble in the direction of your car." Turning, he looked back to where his sat. "Then the drug took over. You collapsed and the thermos rolled aside."

"A drug—in the coffee."

"It fits. Whoever kidnapped you was nervous and under enormous pressure. They didn't take the time to look for the thermos. Why should they? They had you."

"Then it would have to be someone who knew my habits, who knew that I was coming here that day. Someone who..." She trailed off as she looked down at the thermos.

"Someone who's close to you," he finished. He lifted the thermos. "This close."

She felt the chill. The urge to look over her shoulder, to run came back in full force. Using all her self-control, she remained still. "What do we do now?"

"Now we find out who fixed your coffee and who might have had the opportunity to add something extra to it."

It wasn't easy to nod, but she did. "Reeve, shouldn't the police have gotten this far?"

He looked past her, into middle distance. "You'd think so, wouldn't you?"

She looked down at the rings on her hand—one a diamond that should have symbolized faith. One of sapphires that should have symbolized love. "My father," she began, but could go no further.

"It's time we talked to him."

It was dangerous for them to meet, but each drove down the long, rough road to the cottage. This was a time it would have been more dangerous not to meet.

The spot was isolated, overgrown, unlovely—a forgotten little cottage on a forgotten plot of land that had never been successfully tilled. That's why it had been perfect. It was close enough to the little farm to have been convenient, far enough away from town to go unnoticed. The windows were boarded, except for one where the boards had been hacked away. They'd already discussed burning the place down, leaving the ashes to rot—like the body they'd buried in the woods behind.

The cars arrived within moments of each other. The two people were too disciplined, too cautious to be late. And both as they approached each other, were strung tight with nerves. Circumstances had made it necessary for them to trust the other with their lives.

"She's beginning to remember."

An oath, pungent and terrified. "You're sure?"

"I wouldn't have contacted you otherwise. I value my life as much as you value yours." They both knew as long as one remained safe, so did the other. And if one made a mistake...

"How much does she know?"

"Not enough to worry yet. Childhood memories, a few images. Nothing of this." A crow cawed frantically overhead, making both of them jolt. "But things are coming back. It's more than just nightmares now. I think if she pushes, really pushes, it's all going to come back."

"We've always known it would come back. All we need is a bit more time."

"Time?" The derisive laugh startled a squirrel. "We've precious little left. And she tells the American everything. They're lovers now—and he's clever. Very clever. I sometimes think he suspects.''

"Don't be a fool." But nerves twisted and tightened. How could the American have been anticipated? "If that idiot Henri hadn't gotten drunk. *Merde!*" They'd seen their carefully executed plans shattered because of wine and lust. Neither of them regretted having to dig a grave.

"There's no use going over that now. Unless we can take her again the exchange is impossible. Deboque remains in prison, the money is out of reach and vengeance is lost."

"So we take her again. Who'd expect a second kidnapping to be attempted so soon?"

"We had her once!" It wasn't so much temper as fear. Both of them had lived on the edge since Brie had been identified at the hospital.

"And we'll have her again. Soon. Very soon."

"What about the American? He's not as trusting as the princess."

"Dispensable—as the princess will be if she remembers too much too soon. Watch her closely. You know what to do if it becomes necessary."

The small silenced gun with its lethal bullets was safely hidden. "If I kill her, her blood's on your hands, as well."

Thoughts of murder weren't troubling. Thoughts of failure, of discovery were. "We both know that. Our luck only has to hold until the night of the ball."

"The plan's mad. Taking her there, right from the palace when it's filled with people."

"The plan can work. Have you a better one?" There was only silence for a moment, but it wasn't a comfortable one.

"I wish to God I'd stayed here with her, instead of that fool Henri."

"Just keep your eyes and ears open. You've gained her trust?"

"As much as anyone."

"Then use it. We've less than two weeks."

Chapter 10

Brie sat with her hands folded in her lap, her back very straight and her eyes level. She waited for her father to speak. Questions, too many of them, had formed in her mind. Answers, too many of them, had yet to be resolved.

Who was she? She'd been told—Her Serene Highness Gabriella de Cordina, daughter, sister. A member of the Bissets, one of the oldest royal families of Europe.

What was she? She'd learned—a responsible woman with an organized mind, a sense of duty and not so quiet wells of passion. But something had happened to take the rest away from her, those vital little details that make a person whole. She was only just beginning to fight for the right to have them back.

Drugged coffee, a dark room, voices. A knife and blood on her hands. She needed those memories, those details to have the rest. She'd just begun to face this.

The room was very quiet. Through the west windows, the light was lovely, serene. It turned the red carpet to blood without violence.

"So you believe the coffee Gabriella carried in this was drugged." Armand spoke without heat as he glanced at the red thermos that sat on his desk.

"It's logical." Reeve didn't sit. He faced Armand, as well,

standing just beside Brie's chair. "It also fits in with the recurring dream Brie has."

"The thermos can be analyzed."

"Yes, and should be." Though his eyes were very calm, he watched Armand's every movement, every expression. Just as he knew Armand watched his. "The question is why it wasn't found before this."

Armand met Reeve's gaze. When he spoke, he spoke with authority, not with friendship. "It would appear the police have been careless."

"It would appear a great many people have been careless." It wasn't as easy as it had once been, Reeve discovered, to hold back temper. He saw nothing on Armand's face but cool, steady calculation. And he didn't like it. "If the coffee was drugged, as I believe it was, the implications are obvious."

Armand drew out one of his long, dark cigarettes and lit it slowly. "Indeed."

"You take it very calmly, Your Highness."

"I take it as I must."

"And I as I must. I'm taking Brie out of Cordina until this business is resolved. She isn't safe in the palace."

Armand's jaw tensed, but only briefly. "If I hadn't been concerned for her safety, I wouldn't have brought you here."

"Without the bond between our families, I never would have come." Reeve's reply was mild and final. "It's not enough anymore. Now I want answers."

Armand was suddenly and completely royal. "You have no right to demand them of me."

Reeve took one step forward. He needed only one. "Your crown won't protect you."

"Enough!" Brie sprang out of the chair to stand between Reeve and her father. If it was a protective move, it wasn't a conscious one. She couldn't have said which of the two she sought to protect. Her anger whipped through her with a force that helped smother other emotions. "How dare the two of you speak around me as if I were incapable of thinking for myself? How dare the two of you *protect* me as though I were incompetent?"

"Gabriella!" Armand was out of his chair before it fully registered how often he'd heard and dealt with that tone before. "Mind your tongue."

"I won't." Infuriated, she turned on him, leaning over the desk with both palms pressed to it. Another time he would have thought her magnificent—as her mother had been. "I won't be polite and inoffensive. I'm not a cotton-candy princess to be displayed, but a woman. It's my life, do you understand? I won't stand here silently while the pair of you bully each other like a couple of arrogant children over the same prize. I want answers."

Armand's eyes were cool and remote. So was his voice. "You want more than I'm free to give."

"I want what's mine by right."

"What's yours is yours only when I give it to you."

Brie straightened, pale but steady. "Is this a father?" Her voice was soft yet cut like a knife. "You rule Cordina well, Your Highness. Can the same be said for your family?"

It struck clean to the bone. Not a muscle on his face moved. "You have to trust me, Gabriella."

"Trust?" Her voice wavered only once. "This," she told him with a gesture toward the thermos. "This shows me I can't trust anyone. Not anyone," she repeated. Turning, she fled from both of them.

"Let her go," Armand ordered when Reeve was halfway across the room. "She's looked after. I tell you she's looked after," he repeated when Reeve continued toward the door. "Let her go."

The words wouldn't have stopped him, but the tone did. There was pain in it, the same vibrant pain Reeve had heard in Armand's voice that day in the hospital waiting room. Because of it, he paused at the doorway and looked back.

"Don't you know her every movement is watched?" Armand said quietly. "So closely that I know where she spent last night." Weariness exposed, he sat.

Reeve stayed where he was, eyes narrowed. He hadn't missed how often servants busied themselves near Brie, but he'd thought it Alexander's doing. "You have her spied on?"

"I have her looked after," Armand said very slowly. "Do you think I'd leave her safety to chance, Reeve? Or even in your very capable hands alone? I needed you for all the reasons I've stated, but with my daughter's life I use everything available to me."

Armand ran his hands over his face briefly, but the gesture was his first outward sign of tension. "Please, close the door and stay. It's time you know more than I've told you."

A man had to trust his instincts. He could live or die by them. Reeve shut the door quietly and came back to the desk. "What game are you playing, Armand?"

"One that will keep my country, my people at peace. One that will, God willing, bring my child back, safe and whole. One that will bring those who wish it differently punished." He picked up the smooth white rock. "Well punished," he whispered as he squeezed his hand tight. He'd vowed it already to the wife he'd loved and lost.

"You know who took her." Reeve's voice was quiet, but the anger still vibrated beneath. "You've known all along."

"Know of one, suspect another." Armand's hand opened and closed on the rock. "You suspect, as well." His eyes, hard and cold, stayed on Reeve's. "I'm not unaware that you've looked into matters, studied the facts, have certain theories. I'd expected no less. However, I hadn't expected you to share your thoughts with Gabriella."

"Who had a better right?"

"I'm her father, but her ruler first. Her rights are mine to give, mine to take." The arrogance was there, the cold, hard power Reeve recognized, even admired.

"You've used her."

"And you," Armand agreed. "And others. The picture's too large, too complex to bring it down to the kidnapping of my daughter. Her Serene Highness Gabriella de Cordina was abducted. My actions are as a result."

"Why did you ask me here?"

"Because I could trust you, as I told you in the beginning. Because I was aware that you'd soon tire of sitting on the sidelines. You'd think, you'd assimilate, and eventually you'd act. I had no intention of allowing you to act until the time was right. It nearly is."

"Why in hell are you leaving her in the dark?" Reeve demanded. "Don't you know how she suffers?"

"You think I don't know how she suffers?" Armand's voice rose, his eyes flared. In his youth he'd been known and feared for his lethal temper. For a moment, the control of twenty years nearly slipped away. "She's my child. My first child. I held her hands as she learned to walk, sat by her bed when she was restless with fever, wept with her by her mother's grave."

Rigid, Armand rose to stride to the window. There he leaned out, his fingers digging into the wood of the sill. "What I do," he said more calmly, "I do because I must. I love her no less."

If he believed nothing else, Reeve believed that. "She needs to know it."

Pride and regret moved through the prince, but above all, was responsibility. "The mind is a delicate thing, Reeve, and we're still so ignorant of it. Gabriella, for all her strength, all her will, isn't able to overcome her mind's decision not to remember. If you thought differently, why haven't you told her what you suspect? Who you suspect?"

"She needs time," Reeve began, and Armand turned back to him.

"Yes. I can do nothing more than give it to her. I'm advised, strongly advised, by Dr. Kijinsky that if Gabriella is told everything before her mind is ready to hear it, understand it, accept it, the shock might cause a breakdown. Her mind might refuse ever to remember."

"She's begun to remember bits and pieces."

"A button's pushed and the mind reacts." Armand continued to move the white rock in his palm. "You've studied enough to know. But if I were to tell her everything I know or suspect, it might be too much, an avalanche. As a father, I have to wait. As ruler of Cordina, I have ways of learning or discovering what I need to know. Yes, I know who took her, and why." Something fierce came into his eyes. The hunter, or the hunted, would understand it. "But the time isn't right. To have them, I need time. As someone who worked closely with—shall we say, governmental intrigue in Washington—you understand. No need to deny," he went on before Reeve could form a response. "I'm well aware of the work you did."

"I was a cop."

"And more," Armand said with a nod. "But we'll leave it at that. You understand that as a ruler I must have absolute proof before I make an accusation. I can't show the weakness of a father in rage over his child; I must be a judge seeking justice. There are some close to me who believe that because of my position I'm not aware of the maneuvers, the bribes, the false loyalties that swim under the surface of my reign. I'm content that they stay unaware. There are some who might think because I have Gabriella back that I wouldn't look further into the motive for her kidnapping. One of the ransom demands was the release of several prisoners. All but one was camouflage. There was only one—Deboque.''

The name struck a chord. It was a name Reeve had heard often in his less publicized work in law enforcement. Deboque was a businessman, a successful one who'd exported drugs, women, guns. He'd dealt in everything from controlled substances to explosives, selling to the highest bidder.

Or he'd been successful, Reeve amended, until a concentrated three-year investigation had unmasked and convicted him. It was widely believed that during the two years Deboque had served so far, he'd continued to pull the strings in his organization.

"So you think Deboque's behind it?"

"Deboque kidnapped Gabriella," Armand said simply. "We have only to prove through whom."

"And you know?" Reeve paused, at last thinking coolly. To accuse anyone close would cause an uproar. Only clear-cut proof would dim it. Only precise proof could tie Deboque in and stop what maneuvers and political machinations he'd already begun. "Can Deboque pull the strings of power in Cordina even from a cell?"

"He believes he's already begun. I think with this—" Armand turned his hand toward the thermos "—it should be a simple matter to twist his string and name one. The other is more difficult." He looked down at his hands a moment, at the ring only he could wear. Some emotion ran quickly over his face. Reeve thought it was regret. "I told you I know where Gabriella spent the night."

"Yes. With me."

Emotion flared again, and was just as quickly controlled. "You're the son of an old friend and a man I respect for himself, but it's difficult to be calm even though I know she went to you. Intellectually, I accept that she's a woman. However..." He trailed off. "Tell me your feelings for Gabriella. This time I ask as her father."

Still standing, Reeve looked down into Armand's face. "I'm in love with her."

Armand felt the break, bittersweet, that a parent feels when a child gives love and loyalty to another. "It's time I told you what has been done. And time I asked for your advice." Armand gestured to a chair and waited. There were no more questions. This time Reeve sat.

They talked quietly, calmly for twenty minutes, though each of them fought his own personal emotional war. Once Armand went to a cabinet and poured two snifters of brandy. The plan was solid. One more of the reasons he'd maneuvered to have Reeve in Cordina was to have the advantage of Reeve's mind, his experience.

The suspects were closely watched. The moment Brie began to remember, the next move would be made. If all went accordingly, Brie would never be in danger.

But things don't always go according to plan.

Brie swept into her office, temper bubbling, to find Janet filing. Immediately, the papers still in her hand, Janet turned and curtsied.

"Your Highness, I didn't expect you back today."

"I need to work." Going straight to her desk, she began to flip through papers. "Do we have the personal menu for the guests who attend the dinner before the ball?"

"The calligrapher sent one for your approval."

"Yes, here." Brie took out the heavy, cream-colored paper and skimmed over the exquisite scroll. Each of the seven courses was complemented by a different wine. She'd selected each herself. Every dish that would be served had been of her choosing. It was a meal even the most rigid or fussy of gourmets would applaud. It wasn't merely flawless, but a work of art, both on paper and in reality. It made her temper boil over.

"I won't tolerate it." She slammed the menu down and sprang up to pace.

"The menu isn't suitable, Your Highness?"

"Not suitable?" With a laugh Brie dug her hands in her pockets. "It's perfection. Call the calligrapher and tell him to go ahead with them. The fifty who dine with us on the evening of the ball will have a dinner they won't forget. I've seen to that, haven't I?'' Passion brimming in her eyes she whirled back. ''I've arranged a lasting memory for a select few.''

Unsure how to respond, Janet remained by the file with the papers still in her hand. ''Yes, Your Highness.''

''Yet even my father denies me the same courtesy.''

''I'm sure you misunderstand,'' Janet began. ''Prince Armand—''

''Has chosen to make decisions for me,'' Brie finished in a rush. ''To play games, to conceal. I know that. I know that though there are hundreds of other things I don't know. But I will know.'' Brie curled her hands into fists. ''And soon.''

''You're upset.'' Janet set the papers aside, neat and orderly, to be dealt with later. ''I'll order you some coffee.''

''Wait.'' Brie took a step forward. ''Who sees to my coffee, Janet?''

Thrown off by the demand in Brie's tone, Janet set the phone down again. ''Why, the kitchen, of course, Your Highness. I'll just ring down and—''

It ran through Brie's mind that she had no idea where the kitchens were. Had she ever? ''Does the kitchen also prepare a thermos for me when I require one?'' Her pulse had begun to beat too fast as she took the next step. ''On an outing, Janet.''

Janet made a flustered little gesture with her hands. ''You prefer your coffee very strong. Habitually the old retainer brews it for you. The old Russian woman.''

''Nanny,'' Brie murmured. It wasn't what she wanted to hear.

''I've often heard you joke that her coffee could stand firm without the thermos.'' Janet gave a little smile as if to lighten the mood. ''She brews it in her room and refuses to give the cook the recipe.''

''So she brings me the thermos before I go out.''

''Traditionally, Your Highness. In the same way, Prince Bennett will take her, rather than his valet, a shirt if the button's loose.''

Nausea came and was forced away. ''A very old and trusted member of the family.''

''She would consider herself more than staff, yes, Your Highness. The Princess Elizabeth would often take her rather than a personal maid when she traveled.''

"Was Nanny with my mother in Paris? Was she with her when my mother become ill?"

"I've been told so, Your Highness. Her devotion toward Princess Elizabeth was complete."

And distorted? Brie wondered. Somehow twisted? How many people would have had the opportunity to doctor that thermos of coffee? Forcing herself to be calm, Brie asked the next question. "Do you know if Nanny brought me a thermos of coffee on the day I went to the little farm? The day I was abducted?"

"Why, yes." Janet hesitated. "She brought it to you here. You were taking care of a few letters before you left. She brought you the coffee, scolding you about taking a jacket. You laughed at her, promised her you wouldn't leave without one and hurried her along. You were impatient to begin, so you told me we'd see to the rest of the correspondence later. You took the thermos and left."

"No one came in?" Brie asked. "There were no interruptions from the time Nanny brought in the thermos to when I left with it?"

"No one came, Your Highness. Your car was waiting out front. I walked down with you myself. Your Highness..." Cautiously Janet held out a hand. "Can it be wise for you to dwell on such things, to pressure yourself with details like this?"

"Perhaps not." Brie accepted the hand briefly before she turned to the window. God, how she needed to talk, to talk to a woman. How she needed to trust. "I won't need you any more today, Janet. Thank you."

"Yes, Your Highness. Should I order your coffee before I go?"

"No." She nearly laughed. "No, I'm not in the mood for it."

But she couldn't stay inside, within the walls. Brie discovered that almost from the moment Janet left her. Thinking only that she wanted air and sun, Brie went out of her office. Though she hadn't realized she'd planned it, she found herself drawn to the terrace where she'd walked with Reeve that first night. Where he'd first kissed her. Where she'd first begun to test the feelings sleeping, not too quietly, inside her.

It was different during the day, she thought as she walked to the stone wall and leaned out. Different, but it wasn't any less lovely. She could see the mountains—stacks of rock, really—that sheltered Cordina from the rest of Europe. They had been a formidable defense in earlier centuries when foreign powers had lusted after the tiny country by the sea.

Then there was the sea itself, banked by sturdy stone walls. Here and there were cannons still at strategic points in the embankment, reminders of pirates and swift-sailing frigates and other threats from the sea.

Closer was the capital city itself, serene in its antiquity, content with its label of "quaint."

She loved it. Brie didn't need facts or details of the past to feel. Cordina was home and a refuge. It was past and future. Every day she lived there, she felt the need to be able to reach out and hold what was hers increase. Every day she lived there, her resentment at the block that prevented her from doing so grew.

"Your Highness." Loubet stepped onto the terrace, favoring his hip only slightly. "I hope I'm not disturbing you."

He was, but her manners were too ingrained. Brie smiled as she held out her hands. In any case, she had discovered over the dinner they'd shared that she liked Loubet's young, pretty wife very much. And she'd found it sweet that the stuffy, practical minister of state should be so obviously in love.

"You look well, Monsieur."

"Merci, Vôtre Altesse." He brought her hand up, giving it an avuncular brush of lips. "I must say, you're blooming. Being home is the best medicine, *oui*?"

"I was thinking—" she turned back to her view of Cordina "—that it feels like home. Not always inside, but out here. Have you come to see my father, Monsieur Loubet?"

"Yes, I have an appointment with him in a moment."

"Tell me, you've worked with my father for many years. Are you also his friend?"

"I've considered myself so, Your Highness."

Always so conservative, Brie thought with a flash of impatience. Always so diplomatic. "Come, Loubet, without the amnesia, this is certainly a question I wouldn't have to ask. And after all," she reminded him with a slow lift of brow, "it is on your advice that my problem remains a discreet one. So tell me, has my father friends, and are you one of them?"

He didn't hesitate, but paused. Loubet was a man who would

always gather his thoughts together, sift through them meticulously, then put them into words. "There are few great men in the world, Your Highness. Some of these are good, as well. Prince Armand is one of these. Great men make enemies, good men draw friends. Your father has the burden of doing both."

"Yes." With a sigh, she rested against the wall. "I think I understand that."

"I'm not Cordinian." Loubet smiled as he looked out over the city with her. "By law, the minister of state is French. I love my own country. I can tell you frankly that I would not serve yours but for my feelings toward your father."

"I wish I were so sure of my feelings," she murmured.

"Your father loves you." He said it gently, so gently Brie had to close her eyes or weep. "Have no doubt there is nothing more important to Prince Armand than your welfare."

"You make me ashamed."

"Your Highness—"

"No, rightly so. I have a great deal to think about." Straightening from the wall, Brie held out her hand again. "Thank you, Loubet."

He bowed formally, making her smile. Then Brie forgot him as she turned back to the view and thought of her father.

Neither of them had paid any attention to the young man arranging pots of flowers farther down the terrace. Or the sturdy maid dusting glass just inside the doors.

Armand was keeping something from her. Of that she was certain. She knew nothing, however, of his reasons. Perhaps they were good ones. Yet even as she conceded this, the resentment didn't fade. Whatever her father or anyone else thought she should or shouldn't do, she'd have to find out.

Reeve found her there—after looking everywhere else he could think of. He had to control both his impatience and his relief as he stepped onto the terrace. Armand had assured him Brie was looked after—and he noticed the two people going about their business not too close to the princess, but close enough. But the prince had been cautious enough to enlist his help from the beginning, as well.

After their conversation, Reeve understood better why Armand had called in the help of an outsider, one whose feelings for Cordina and the royal family were more or less secondhand. Or had been, Reeve thought as he stood looking at Gabriella. Now more than ever he needed his objectivity. And now more than ever he found it all but impossible to find.

"Brie."

She turned slowly, as if she'd known he was there. Her hair was ruffled a bit by the wind, but her eyes were calm. "The first night we walked here I had questions. So many of them. Now, weeks later, too few of them have been answered." She looked down at the rings on her hands—conflicting emotions, conflicting loyalties. "You won't tell me what you spoke of with my father after I left."

It wasn't a question, but Reeve knew he had to answer it. "Your father thinks of you before he thinks of anything else, if that helps."

"And you?"

"I'm here for you." He came to her so that they stood as they had once before, under the moonlight. "There's no other reason."

"For me." She looked at him, searching, fighting not to let her heart lead her mind. "Or to satisfy an old family bond?"

"How much do you want?" he demanded. When he grabbed her hands he wasn't thinking of how small and delicate they were but of how strong, how searing her eyes could be. "My feelings for you have nothing to do with family bonds. And my being here now has everything to do with my feelings for you."

But what were they? she wondered. He seemed so careful not to tell her. Was it so difficult for him to say, "I care"? Brie looked down at their joined hands. Perhaps for him it was, she reflected. Not all fairy tales ended happily ever after. Reeve wasn't a knight galloping to sweep up the princess and carry her off. He was a man. She hadn't given her heart to a knight.

"I want this to be over," she said encapsulating everything from her blank past to the uncertain present. "I want to feel safe again."

The hell with objectivity, with plans. He took her by the shoulders. "I'll take you to America for a while."

Puzzled, she put a hand to his arm, holding on or holding off, she didn't know. "To America?"

"You can stay with me on the farm until this whole business is over."

Until. The word reminded her that some things had to end. Just end. She dropped her hand. "This whole business begins with me. I can't run from it."

"There's no need for you to stay here." Suddenly he saw how simple it could be. She'd be away. He could keep her safe. Armand would simply have to alter his plan.

"There's every need for me to stay. My life is lost here somewhere. How can I find it thousands of miles away?"

"When you're ready to remember, you'll remember. It won't matter where you are."

"It matters to me." She drew away from him then, backing up until she was braced against the wall. Pride came back, as much a part of her inheritance as the color of her eyes. "Do you think I'm a coward? Do you think I'd turn my back and walk away from the people who used me? Has my father asked you to do this so I won't ask any more questions?"

"You know better."

"I know nothing," she retorted. "Nothing except that all the men in my life seem compelled to shield me from what I don't want to be shielded from. This morning you said we'd work together."

"I meant it."

She watched him carefully. "And now?"

"I still mean it." But he didn't tell her what he knew. He didn't tell her what he felt.

"Then we will." But she didn't tell him what she'd learned. She didn't tell him what she needed.

She did step forward, even as he did. She did reach for him as he reached for her. They held each other close, both knowing that so much lay between them.

"I wish we were alone," she murmured. "Really alone, as we were the day on the boat."

"We'll go sailing tomorrow."

She shook her head before she pressed her face harder against him. "I can't. There'll be no time between now and the ball for anything. So many obligations, Reeve."

For both of us, he thought. "After the ball, then."

"After." She kept her eyes closed for only another moment. "Will you make me a promise? A foolish one."

He kissed one temple, then the other. "How foolish?"

"Always practical." Smiling, she tilted her head back. "When the blanks are gone and this is over, really over, will you spend the day with me on the water?"

"That doesn't seem so foolish."

"You say that now." She linked her hands around his neck. She'd hold him there, if only for a moment. "But promise."

"I promise."

With a sigh, she melted against him. "I'll hold you to your word," she warned.

When their mouths met, neither of them wanted to go beyond the moment to that last day alone on the water.

Chapter 11

"So I told Professor Sparks that a man would have to be made of stone to concentrate on Homer when there was a woman who looked like Lisa Barrow in the same classroom."

"Did he sympathize?" Brie asked Bennett absently as she watched the freshly cleaned chandelier being raised back in place.

"Are you kidding? He's got the heart of a prune." Grinning, he stuck his hands in his back pockets. "But I got a date with the divine Miss Barrow."

Brie laughed as she checked the long list of notes she had on a clipboard. "I could tell you that you aren't going to Oxford to thicken your little black book."

"But you won't." Easily he slung an arm over her shoulders. "You never lecture. I got a look at the guest list. It was a pleasure to see that the luscious Lady Lawrence will make it."

That got her attention. Brie lowered the clipboard and scowled at him. "Bennett, Lady Alison Lawrence is nearly thirty and divorced."

He gave her his charming choirboy look that had wickedness just around the edges. "So?"

Brie shook her head. Had he been born precocious? she wondered. "Maybe I should lecture."

"Now leave that to Alex. He's so much better at it."

"So I've discovered," she murmured.

"Has he been giving you a hard time?"

She was frowning again as she watched the next chandelier begin its journey up. "Does he usually?"

"It's just his way." The loyalty was there, too strong to waver. "Prince Perfect."

His face brightened. "Why, you remember—"

"Dr. Franco told me."

"Oh." His arm tightened briefly, both in reassurance and disappointment. "I didn't have much time to talk to you last night when I got in. I've wanted to ask you how you were."

"I wish I could tell you—along the windows, please," she directed as men brought in two twenty-foot tables. They'll be covered with white linen, she thought as she checked her clipboard again, then laden with little delicacies to help the guests get through the long night of the ball. "Physically, I've been given the nod, with reluctance. I think Dr. Franco would like to pamper me a while longer. Everything else is complicated."

He took her hand, turning the diamond so that the facets caught the light. "I guess this is one of those complications."

She tensed, then relaxed. He could feel it. "Only temporarily. Things are bound to fall into place soon." She thought of the dreams, of the thermos. "Bennett, I've been wanting to ask you about Nanny. Do you think she's well?"

"Nanny?" He gave her a quick look of surprise. "Has she been ill? No one told me."

"No, not ill." Brie hesitated because the war of loyalties confused her. Why didn't she simply tell what she suspected about her old nurse? Tell and be done with it? "But she's quite old now, and people often become odd or…"

"Senile? Nanny?" This time he laughed as he squeezed her hand. "She's got a mind like a brick. If she's been fussing around you too much, it's only because she feels entitled."

"Of course." Her doubts didn't fade, but she kept them to herself. She'd watch and wait, as she'd promised herself.

"Brie, there's a rumor running around that you and Reeve are the love match of the decade."

"Oh?" She only raised a brow, but her thumb came around to worry the diamond on her finger. "Apparently we're playing the game well."

"Is it—a game, I mean?"

"Not you, too?" Impatient, she walked away from him toward the terrace doors. "I've done this round with Alexander already."

"It's not a matter of pushing my exalted nose in." Equally impatient, he followed her. Though they were close to an argument, they kept their voices low. Servants were notorious for their excellent hearing. "It's only natural for me to be concerned."

"Would you be so concerned if the engagement were genuine?" Her voice was cool, too cool. That alone gave Bennett the answer to his question. But it didn't tell him whether he should be relieved or disturbed.

"I feel responsible," he said after a moment. "After all, it was more or less my idea, and—"

"Yours?" This time she set her clipboard down on a table with a snap.

Bennett fumbled a bit, wishing he'd kept his mouth shut and his eyes open. If there was one thing he avoided, it was an argument with a woman. He was bound to lose. "Well, I did point out to Father that it would look a little odd for Reeve to be escorting you everywhere, living here, and… Hell." Frustrated by her calm, icy look, he dragged a hand through his hair. "There had been all kinds of talk. *Commérage.*"

"What do I care for gossip?"

"You've never had to deal with that kind before." His voice wasn't bitter, but resigned. "Look, Brie, I might be the youngest of the three of us, but I'm the one with the most experience with the tacky little tabloids."

"Justifiably, it would seem."

He, too, could become very dignified. "Yes, quite justifiably. But while I've chosen to live my life a certain way, you haven't. I couldn't stand seeing your name and picture splashed all over, sneered over. You can be angry if you like. I'd rather have you angry than hurt ever again."

She could have been furious with him. Brie understood it was her right to be. She could have told him, stiffly and finally, to stay out of her affairs. That by interfering, he'd made her more vulnerable than any scandal would. The ring on her hand was a prop—a support. One day she'd look down and it would be gone. It would be over.

She could have been angry, but love poured through her, warm and sweet. He was so young, and so inherently kind. "Damn you, Bennett." But her arms went around him. "I should be furious with you."

He rested his cheek against her temple. "I couldn't know you'd fall in love with him."

She could deny it and save some pride. Instead she shook her head and sighed. "No, neither could I."

Just as Brie drew back, she saw a footman escort two women into the room. She'd left instructions that Christina Hamilton and her sister were to be brought to her as soon as they arrived.

From the photos and newspaper clippings she'd been given, Brie recognized the tall, striking brunette in the St. Laurent suit. She felt nothing but a moment's blank panic.

What should she do? She could rush across the room or smile and wait. Should she be polite or warm, affectionate or amused? God, how she hated not simply knowing.

"She's your closest friend," Bennett murmured in his sister's ear. "You've said you had brothers by birth but a sister by luck. That's Christina."

It was enough to ease the panic. Both women had begun their curtsies, the younger with an eye on the prince, the older with a grin for Brie. Falling back on instinct, Brie crossed the room, both hands outstretched. Christina met her halfway.

"Oh, Brie." Laughing, Christina held her at arm's length. Brie saw that her eyes were soft, but full of irony. The mouth was lovely in a smile, but it was strong. "You look wonderful, wonderful, wonderful!" Then Brie was caught in a hard hug. Christina smelled expensive and feminine and unfamiliar. But the panic didn't return.

"I'm glad you're here." Brie let her cheek rest against Christina's expertly swept-back hair. It wasn't a lie, she discovered. She needed a friend—simply a friend, not family, not a lover. "You must be exhausted."

"Oh, you know flying leaves me wired for hours. You've lost weight. How unkind of you."

Brie was smiling when she drew away. "Only five pounds."

"Only five." Christina rolled her eyes. "I'll have to tell you the horrors of that pricey little spa I went to a few months ago. I gained five. Prince Bennett." Christina held out her hand, casually expecting it to be kissed. "Good God, is it the air in Cordina that makes everyone look so spectacular?"

Bennett didn't disappoint her. But as his lips brushed her knuckles, his gaze shifted to Eve. "The air in Houston must be magic."

Christina hadn't missed the look. Like the kiss, she'd expected it. After all, Eve wasn't a young woman any man could ignore. That's what worried Christina. "Prince Bennett, I don't believe you've met my sister, Eve."

Bennett already had Eve's hand. His lips lingered over it only seconds longer than they had over her sister's. But a few seconds can be a long time. He noted the long fall of rich, dark hair, the dreamy, poetic blue eyes, the wide, full curve of her mouth. His young heart was easily lost.

"I'm happy to meet you, Your Highness."

Her voice wasn't that of a girl, but of a woman, as rich and dark as her hair.

"You look lovely, Eve." Brie took Eve's hands herself to ward off her brother. "I'm so glad you could come."

"It's just the way you described it." Eve sent her a sudden, alarmingly effective smile—alarming because it was as natural as a sunrise. "I haven't been able to look fast enough."

"Then you should take your time." Smoothly Bennett brushed his sister aside. "I'll give you a tour. I'm sure Brie and Chris have lots to talk about." With a half bow to the other women, he led Eve from the room. "What would you like to see first?"

"Well." Not certain if she should frown or laugh, Brie looked after them. "He certainly moves fast."

"Eve doesn't creep along herself." Christina tapped her foot a moment, then dismissed them. After all, she couldn't play chaperon forever. "How busy are you?"

"Not very," Brie told her, mentally rearranging her schedule. "Tomorrow I won't have time to take a breath."

"Then let's take one now." Christina linked an arm through hers. "Can we have tea and cookies in your rooms, the way we used to? I can't believe it's been a year. There's so much to catch up on."

If you only knew, Brie mused as she moved down the corridor with her.

* * *

"Tell me about Reeve," Christina demanded as she plucked an iced pink cookie from the tray.

Brie ran her spoon around and around in her tea, though she'd forgotten to put any sugar in. "I don't know what to tell you."

"Everything," Christina said dramatically. "I'm eaten up with curiosity." She'd tossed off her shoes and had her legs curled under her. The excitement of the flight was beginning to ease into relaxation. But she'd already noticed that Brie wasn't relaxed. She dismissed it—almost—as tension over the ball. "You certainly don't have to tell me what he looks like." She gestured with the half cookie, then nimbly popped it into her mouth. "I see his picture every time I pick up a magazine. Is he fun?"

Brie thought about the day on her boat, about the drives they sometimes took along the coast. She thought of the dinner parties they attended when he would murmur something in her ear that was rude and accurate. "Yes." It made her smile. "Yes, he's fun. And he's strong. He's clever and rather arrogant."

"You've got it bad," Christina murmured, watching her friend's face. "I'm happy for you."

Brie tried to smile, but couldn't quite pull it off. Instead she lifted her cup. "You'll meet him soon and be able to judge for yourself."

"Hmmm." Christina studied the tray of elegant cookies, lectured herself, then chose one, anyway. "That's one of the things that's bothered me."

Instantly alert, Brie set down her tea again. "Bothered you?"

"Well, yes, Brie. Where *did* you meet him? I can't believe you met this wonderful, clever, arrogant man last year when you were in the States, then stayed with me for three days in Houston without breathing a word."

"Royalty's trained to be discreet," Brie said offhandedly, and pretended an interest in the cookies herself.

"Not that discreet," Christina said over a full mouth. "In fact, I remember you telling me specifically that there wasn't anyone in your life, that you weren't interested in men particularly. And I agreed heartily, because I'd just ended a disastrous affair."

Brie felt herself getting in deeper. "I suppose I wasn't entirely sure of my feelings—or his."

"How did you work it out long distance?"

"There's a connection through our fathers, you know." She dug back to something Reeve had said to her once, something she'd nearly forgotten. "Actually, we met years ago, here in Cordina. It was my sixteenth birthday party."

"You're not going to tell me you fell for him then?"

Brie merely moved her shoulders. How could she confirm or deny what she didn't know?

"Well." Christina poured more tea in her cup. Because she found the idea so sweet, she forgot about details. "That certainly explains why you didn't have much interest in all those gorgeous men in Paris. I'm happy for you."

She laid her hand over Brie's lightly, briefly. It was a very simple, very casual touch of friendship. Brie's eyes filled so that she had to fight to clear them.

"I'm glad he was here for you after..." Christina trailed off, no longer interested in her tea. When she set her legs down, she touched Brie's hand again, but the touch was firmer. "Brie, I wish you'd talk to me about it. The press is so vague. I know they haven't caught the people responsible, and I can't stand it."

"The police are investigating."

"But they haven't caught anyone. Can you rest easily until they do? I can't."

"No." Unable to sit, Brie rose, linking her hands. "No, I can't. I've tried to go on with the daily business of life, but it's like waiting, just waiting without knowing."

"Oh, Brie." Chris was at her side, hugging her. "I don't mean to pressure you, but we've always shared everything. I was so frightened for you." A tear brimmed over, but she brushed at it impatiently. "Damn, I told myself I wouldn't do this, but I can't help it. Every time I think about what it was like to pick up the paper and see the headline—"

Brie took a step back from the emotion. "You shouldn't think about it. It's over."

The tears cleared, but now there was puzzlement. "I'm sorry." Hurt, but unsure why, Christina looked down for her bag. "It's too easy to forget sometimes who you are and what rules you have to live by."

"No." Torn between instinct and a promise, Brie hesitated. "Don't go, Chris. I need—oh, God, I do need to talk to someone."

Brie looked at her then and chose. "We're very good friends, aren't we?"

Puzzlement and hurt became confusion. "Brie, you know—"

"No, just tell me."

Christina set her bag back down again. "Eve's my sister," she said calmly. "And I love her. There's nothing in the world I wouldn't do for her. I don't love you any less."

Brie closed her eyes a moment. "Sit down, please." She waited, then sat down beside Christina. Taking one long breath, she told her friend everything.

Perhaps Christina paled a bit, perhaps her eyes widened, but she interrupted Brie only twice to clarify. When the story was finished, she sat in absolute silence for a moment. But, then, volcanoes often sit quietly.

"It stinks."

She said the words in her soft Texas drawl so that Brie blinked. "I beg your pardon?"

"It stinks," Christina repeated. "Politics usually does, and Americans are the first to say so, but this really stinks."

For some reason, Christina's sturdy, inelegant opinion made her comfortable. Brie smiled and reached for a cookie without thinking. "I can't really blame politics. After all, I agreed to everything."

"Well, what else were you going to do, for heaven's sake?" Exasperated, Christina rose and walked over to a small cherry wood commode. She discovered she wanted badly to break something. Anything. "You were weak, disoriented and frightened."

"Yes," Brie murmured. "Yes, I was." She watched Christina rummage and locate an exquisite little decanter.

"I need a brandy." Without ceremony, Christina poured. "You?"

"Mmmm." Brie only nodded an assent. "I didn't even know that was there."

Christina spilled a bit of brandy over the side of a glass, swore and blotted the drop with a finger. "You'll remember." She walked back, and her eyes were bright and strong when she handed Brie a snifter. "You'll remember because you're too stubborn not to."

And for the first time Brie believed it, completely. With something like relief she touched her glass to Christina's. "Thanks."

"If I hadn't let myself get talked out of it, I would have been here weeks ago." With an unintelligible mutter, Christina sat on the arm of the sofa. "Your father, that Loubet and the wonderful Reeve MacGee should all be rounded up, corralled and horsewhipped. I'd like to give all three of them a piece of my mind."

Brie laughed into her brandy. This was what she'd needed, she realized, to counterbalance that fierce protection from the men who cared for her. "I think you could do it."

"Damn right I could. I'm surprised you haven't."

"Actually, I have."

"That's more like it."

"The trouble is, my father does what he thinks best for me and the country. Loubet does what he thinks best for the country. I can't fault either of them."

"And Reeve?"

"And Reeve." Brie looked up from her glass. "I'm in love with him."

"Oh." Christina drew the word out as she studied Brie's face. She'd already made up her mind that she'd stay right there in Cordina until everything was resolved. Now she reaffirmed it. "So that part of it is real."

"No." She didn't let herself look down at her ring. "Only my feelings are real. The rest is just as I told you."

"Ah, well, that's no problem."

Though she didn't want pity, she had been expecting a bit of sympathy. "It's not?"

"Of course not. If you want him, you'll get him."

Both amusement and interest flickered over her face. "Will I? How?"

Christina took a quick swallow of brandy. "If you don't remember all the men you had to brush out from around your feet, I'm not going to tell you. It isn't good for my ego. Anyway, they're not worth it." She touched her glass to Brie's.

"Who isn't?"

"Men." Christina crossed her stockinged feet and examined her toes. "Men aren't worth it. Louses, every single one."

Somehow Brie felt they'd had this conversation before. A laugh bubbled in her throat. "Every one?"

"Every single one, bless 'em."

"Chris." This time Brie reached out. "I'm glad you came."

Chris leaned over and brushed her cheek. "Me, too. Now why don't you come to my room and help me pick out something devastating for dinner tonight?"

When Reeve came to her rooms, she wasn't there. He saw the depleted tray of cookies, the cooling tea. And the empty brandy snifters. Interesting, he thought. He knew Brie drank little, and almost never during the day. He thought she had either been relaxed or upset.

He'd been told Brie was entertaining Christina Hamilton, of the Houston Hamiltons. Rocking back on his heels, he studied the remains of the little tea party. He'd done some careful research on Brie's old college friend. They had passed the point where he'd take any chances. A call to a friend in D.C. who owed him a favor, and Reeve had everything from Christina Hamilton's birthday to her bank balance. He'd turned up nothing that shouldn't have been there. Yet he felt uneasy.

Not uneasy, he admitted as he wandered around Brie's sitting room. Jealous. Jealous because she was spending time with someone else. It was laughable. He hated to think himself so tied to a woman that they couldn't spend an afternoon apart. He hated to think himself that unreasonable—or that sunk.

It was her safety, Reeve reminded himself. His feelings for her were tangled in concern. It was natural—but it wasn't comfortable. When there wasn't any more reason for concern, perhaps his feelings could change. It was logical. It would probably be for the best. It was, he thought ruefully, extremely unlikely.

He could smell her even now, though the room was delicate with the scent of the flowers that were always in vases here and there. It was here, that very feminine, very sexy, very French fragrance that habitually clung to her. He could picture her sitting on the love seat, sipping a cup of tea, nibbling at a cookie, perhaps, but without any real interest. She ate too little.

There had been strain. He knew it—hated it. She would feel dishonest talking with her old friend who was a stranger now.

Is that why he felt so strongly? he wondered. He was, of all the people in her life, the only one who had no strong ties from the past she couldn't remember. There weren't years of memories between them, drawing them together, pulling them apart. There was only now.

And that one night years before when he'd waltzed with her in the moonlight.

Idiot. He dragged a hand through his hair. He was an idiot to think that even without the amnesia she would have remembered a few dances with a man on her sixteenth birthday. Just because he'd never forgotten. Had never been able to forget. Had he been in love with her all this time? With the image of her?

Reeve picked up an earring she'd taken off and set carelessly on a table. It was an elegant design of gold and diamonds. Complex and simple, it changed as he turned it—like a woman. Like the woman. He twisted it in his fingers for a moment and wondered if it was still the image that captivated him.

He knew too much about her, he thought. Too many details that he had no business knowing. She liked her bathwater too hot, collected old pictures of people she didn't know. She'd once had a secret dream to dance with the Ballet Royal. When she'd been fifteen, she'd wondered if she was in love with a young gardener.

He knew before she did those foolish little details of her life. He'd stolen them from her, out of diaries he'd read to do a job. When she remembered all, when she looked at him then, how much would she resent the intrusion?

He knew now the two people who'd kidnapped her, changed her life, stolen her past. He knew who they were and why they'd done so. For her sake, he couldn't tell her yet. He could only watch and protect. And when she knew all, when she looked at him then, how much would she resent the deception?

How could he tell her that two people close to her, two people she trusted, had plotted against her? Used her? It might ease his conscience, but what would it do to Brie?

He'd gone past the point where he'd taken any chances.

He heard the door to the bedroom open and paused with the earring still in his hand.

"Yes, thank you, Bernadette. If you'll just run the bath. I'll see to my own hair. We're dining *en famille* tonight."

"Yes, Your Highness."

He heard the maid move quietly into the bath, then the water striking porcelain. He imagined Brie undressing. Slowly. Unbuttoning the tailored little blouse he'd seen her put on that morning. Odd, he realized. He'd seen her dress in the mornings they'd woken together. But he'd never seen her undress. When he came to her she was already in a robe or nightgown. Or waiting naked in the bed.

Suddenly driven, he set down the earring and crossed into the bedroom.

She was standing in front of the mirror, but she hadn't removed her clothes. There was a small porcelain box on her dresser with the lid off. She took pins from it, one by one, and swept up her hair.

She was thinking, but not, he realized, about what she was doing. Her eyes weren't focused on the reflection. But she was smiling, just a little, as if she were content. It wasn't often she smiled like that.

The maid came out to take a robe out of the closet. If she noticed Reeve in the sitting-room doorway, she gave no sign. As she laid the robe on the bed, Brie fastened the last pin.

"Thank you, Bernadette. I won't need you any more tonight. Tomorrow," she went on with a quick grin, "I'll exhaust you."

The maid curtsied. Reeve waited. The maid shut the door quietly behind her. Still, he waited. Brie put the top back on the box, running her finger over the porcelain when it was in place. With a little sigh, she stepped out of her shoes and stretched, eyes closed. Turning away from the mirror, she went to a small cabinet and switched on the CD player concealed inside. The music that came out was quiet, sultry. Something heard through open windows on summer nights. She unhooked her trim gray trousers, let them fall to the floor, then stepped out of them. While Reeve watched, she bent to pick them up, ran a hand down to smooth them and set them on the bed.

One by one, her mind on the music, she undid the buttons on her blouse. Beneath it she wore pearl-gray silk without frills. The teddy was as smooth as her skin, and very thin. She brushed the first slender strap from her shoulder before Reeve stepped forward.

"Gabriella."

She would have jumped or gasped if she hadn't recognized his voice. She turned slowly because she recognized the need in it, as well. He was standing just inside the room, but she could feel his heat and it immediately aroused her. He made no move, only watched, but she felt his touch slide over every inch of her. The sun was still strong enough to light the room, but her thoughts turned to night. And excitement.

Without a word she held out a hand.

Without a word he went to her.

They spoke with touches, the brush of a fingertip, the press of a palm. *You're mine. I've waited for you. I've ached for you.* Mouth moved over mouth silently, but hundreds of things were said. *This is all I've wanted. You're all I've needed. You.*

She undressed him, not too quickly. Each could feel the ache build to pain. It was exquisite. She drew his shirt from his shoulders, and still the only word that had been spoken between them was her name. In wordless agreement, they lowered themselves onto the bed.

He hadn't known any woman could make him want so badly. He had only to think of her to need. But to touch her…to feel her, soft and strong against him, was enough to make him forget he'd had a life before Gabriella.

He ran his hand over the silk, feeling it warm with the friction, feeling her move beneath. Her skin and the silk slid along his own flesh. Temptation. Her hands roamed over him freely, seeking pleasure, giving it. Desire. A kiss went on endlessly until they both were surrounded by every soft, every sweet sensation. Surrender.

Brie went limp, weakened by a deluge of feeling too strong to measure. He could do no more than go where the kiss led him. Into her.

The silk was brushed away with a stroke of his hand. When he slid inside her, the passion was subtle, timeless. Her breath shuddered. His muscles bunched, then flowed, then bunched again. Together they moved. Neither led, neither followed, because both were lost.

Her hands were firm on his shoulders; his fingers were curled into her hair. Their gazes locked as the rhythm matched the sultry heated music that dripped into the room.

It wasn't a matter of control, his or hers, but of mood. Savor. Prolong. He couldn't have described the sensations that rippled through him, overtook him, enclosed him, but he could have spoken in minute detail of what the sun did to her hair, of how pleasure affected her eyes.

She'd remember this always. If everything else was stripped from her again, Brie knew that this moment would remain perfectly clear.

There was no flash, no sudden storm of speed and desperation. They rose together, sweetly, gently, exquisitely. She could have wept from the beauty of it, but only smiled as his mouth touched hers.

They lay together comfortably, stretching out the moment a bit longer. The early-evening sunlight was quiet. If it hadn't been for obligations, they'd have stayed just so until the morning.

"I missed you."

Surprised, Brie tilted her head on his shoulder so that she could see his profile. "Did you?"

"I've hardly seen you today." He didn't feel as foolish saying it as he had felt thinking it. Smiling a little, he stroked her hair.

"I thought you might come up to the ballroom."

"I came by a couple of times. You were busy." And safe, he added to himself. Three of the workmen had carried guns under their vests.

"Tomorrow will be worse." Content, she snuggled against him. "It'll take hours to set up the flowers alone. Then there's the wine and liquor, the musicians, the food. The people."

She fell silent. Unconsciously he drew her closer. "Nervous."

"A little. There will be so many faces, so many names. I wonder..."

"What?"

"I know just how important this ball is for the AHC and for Cordina. But I wonder if I can pull it off."

"You've done more than anyone can expect already." And he resented it. "Just relax and take it as it comes. Do what feels right for you, Brie."

She didn't speak for a moment, then plunged. "I have already." She shifted so that she could look at him directly. "I told Christina Hamilton everything."

He started to speak, then stopped himself. She was waiting, he could see, for criticism, impatience, even anger. He saw both the apology and the defiance in her eyes. "Why?" But it was a question, not an accusation. He could almost feel the relief from her.

"I couldn't lie to her. Maybe I couldn't remember, but I felt. I really felt something with her, something I needed." She paused only to make a sound of exasperation. "You'll think I'm foolish."

She started to sit up, so he went with her. "No." To emphasize support, he laid a hand over hers. "Tell me what you felt."

"I needed to talk to a woman." She let out a long breath, then looked back at him. Her hair was tumbled, a sensuous mass over creamy shoulders. Her face still held the glow of passion. Yet vulnerability was there. "There are so many men in my life. Kind, concerned, but..." How could she phrase it so he'd understand? She couldn't. "I just needed to talk to a woman."

Of course she did. Reeve brought her hand to his lips. Why hadn't any of them seen it? Father, brother, doctor...lover. But she'd had no one to give her the kind of support, the kind of empathy only those of the same sex can give one another. "Did it help?"

She closed her eyes a moment. "Yes. Chris is special to me— that's what I felt."

"What was her reaction?"

"She said that it stinks." A giggle bubbled in her throat. A sound he'd heard too rarely. "She's of the opinion that you, my father and Loubet should be horsewhipped."

Reeve made a sound that might have been amusement or regret. Basically, it was agreement. "Sounds like a sensible woman."

"She is. I can't tell you what it meant just to talk to her. Reeve, she didn't look at me as though I were ill or odd or...I don't know."

"Is that what we do?"

"Sometimes, yes." She brushed her hair back, looking at him with an eagerness that asked for understanding. "Chris took it all in, stated her opinion, then asked me to help her pick out a dress. It was all so natural, so easy, as if there weren't all these blanks between us. We were simply friends again, or still. I don't know how to explain it."

"You don't have to. But I'll have to talk to her."

Brie's lips curved. "Oh, I think she's planning on it." She kissed him then in the light, friendly manner she could assume so unexpectedly. "Thank you."

"For what?"

"For not telling me all the reasons I shouldn't have done it."

"The decision was always yours, Brie."

"Was it?" She laughed, shaking her head. "I wonder. My bath is cooling," she said, deliberately changing the mood. "You've detained me."

"So I have." Smiling, he ran a fingertip lightly down her breast and felt it tremble.

"The least you can do is wash my back."

"Sounds fair. Trouble is, I've missed my bath, as well."

"That shouldn't be a problem." She drew away from him to rise. "I once wondered if I'd shared the tub with anyone. It's very large." Naked, with the sun filtering in behind her, she began to refasten her pins. "And we have more than an hour before dinner."

Chapter 12

Glitter. Glamour. Fantasy. That was a royal ball in a centuries-old palace. Elegance, sumptuousness, sophistication were what was expected when you brought together the rich, the famous and the royal.

Five Baccarat chandeliers trembled with light. Some of the colors couldn't even be named. A half-acre of floor gleamed, the color of aged honey. There was silver, crystal, white linen and masses and masses of flowers. But even these paled when compared to the glow of silks, the fire of jewels: the beautiful people.

Brie greeted the guests and tried to forget she was tired. For twelve hours she'd worked nonstop to make certain everything was perfect. It was. She had the satisfaction of that to offset her nerves. Cinderella had had her ball, she mused. But Cinderella hadn't had to deal with the florist.

There were gorgeous clothes and luxurious scents, but for her, there was a sea of faces and a mental list of names too long for comfort.

Her father was by her side, dressed in his most formal uniform. It reminded people that he'd been a soldier, a good one. But Brie thought he looked like a god—handsome, powerful. Remote.

She was curtsied to. Her hand was kissed. The conversations, thankfully, were brief and general before each person passed on to Reeve and her brothers.

She'd seen to the details, Brie reminded herself. Successfully. She'd succeed here, as well. She smiled at the man in the black silk jacket with the mane of white hair, recognizing him as one of the great actors of the century, one the British Queen had seen fit to knight. He took her hand, but kissed her cheek. Brie had been told he'd bounced her on his knee when she was a baby.

She was terrified, Reeve thought. And so beautiful. There was nothing he could do but be there. Protect, support—no matter how much she'd resent both. Had anyone told her she'd already pulled off a minor miracle? he wondered. She'd regained her strength, held on to her hope and given herself to her obligations. Princess or not, she was a hell of a woman. For now, she was his.

She looked like a fairy tale tonight. Like the fairy tale he remembered from years before. There were diamonds in her hair, winking fire against fire. She wore them at her ears, subtle and effective, and at her throat in three dripping tiers. And on her hand, he reminded himself, as a symbol.

But while the fire danced around her, she'd chosen ice for her dress. A contrast in fashion? he wondered, or a statement that she had both?

White—stunning, cool, untouchable white—draped her. Slashing low at her throat to frame the fire there, rippling down her arms to meet the light and power on her fingers. Yards and yards of rich, smooth silk flowed down her until it nearly brushed the floor. Aloof, regal? So she was and so she looked. But the fire breathed around her passionately.

Once a man had had such a woman, would he ever, could he ever, turn to another?

"Did you see her?" Bennett mumbled so only Reeve could hear.

He'd only seen one woman, but he knew Bennett. "Who?"

"Eve Hamilton." Bennett gave a low sound of approval. "Just fantastic."

Beside him Alexander scanned the crowd and found her, but there wasn't any approval. She wore a ripe red dress that was cut beautifully, even conservatively. The color said one thing, the style another. "She's a child," he muttered. And he'd found her too precocious and too intelligent a child.

"You need glasses," Bennett told him, then smiled and kissed the hand of a dowager. "Or vitamins."

The line of guests seemed endless. Brie stood it by reminding herself just what the ball would mean to her charity. But when the last black tie and shimmering dress passed her, she almost sighed with relief.

It wasn't over, but with music there was some escape.

The orchestra knew its business. It took only a nod from her for the first waltz to begin. She held out her hand to Reeve. He'd open the ball with her this first and this last time. She let his arms and the music carry her. Sooner or later midnight would strike, and the dream would be over.

"You're beautiful."

They swirled together under the lights. "My dressmaker's a genius."

He did something they both knew was not quite acceptable. He kissed her. "That's not what I meant."

Brie smiled and forgot she was weary.

Prince Armand led out the sister of an exiled king. Alexander chose a distant cousin from England. Bennett swept Eve Hamilton onto the floor. And so the ball began.

It was, as it should be, magical. Caviar, French wine, violins. Oil barons rubbing elbows with lords. Ladies exchanging gossip with celebrities. Brie knew it was her responsibility to be available to dance and to entertain; but it was a relief to discover she could enjoy it.

While she danced with Dr. Franco, she looked up at him and laughed. "You're trying to take my pulse."

"Nonsense," he told her, though he had been. "I don't have to be a doctor to look at you and know you're more than well."

"I'm beginning to believe I'll be completely well very soon."

His fingers tightened only slightly. "Has there been more?"

"These aren't your office hours," she told him with a smile. "And it's nothing you'd find with your little black bag. I simply feel it."

"Then the wait will have been worthwhile."

Her smile only faltered a little. "I hope so."

"Brie looks relaxed," Christina commented as she kept her hand light on Reeve's shoulder through the dance.

"Your being here helps."

She shot him a look. Though she'd seen to it that they'd already had a private talk, Reeve hadn't completely mollified her. "It would have helped if I'd been here sooner."

He liked her, perhaps because of the tongue-lashing she'd delivered. "You still think I should be horsewhipped."

"I'm thinking it over."

"I want what's best for her."

She studied him a moment. "You're a fool if you don't already know what that is."

Brie worked her way expertly through the couples and the groups. Janet Smithers stood discreetly in a corner with her one and only glass of wine.

"Janet." Brie waved the curtsy aside. "I was afraid you'd decided not to come."

"I was late, Your Highness. There was some work I wanted to see to."

"No work tonight." Even as Brie took her hand she was casting around for a suitable dance partner for her secretary. "You look lovely," she added. Janet's dress was both plain and quiet, but it gave her a certain dignity.

"Your Highness." Loubet stepped to her side and bowed. "Miss Smithers."

"Monsieur." Brie smiled, thinking he'd be her solution.

"The ball is a wonderful success, as always."

"Thank you. It's going well. Your wife looks stunning."

"Yes." The smile bespoke pleasure and pride. "But she's deserted me. I'd hope Your Highness would take pity and dance with me."

"Of course." Brie sipped her wine, then found, to her satisfaction, that Alexander was within arm's reach. "But I've promised this dance to my brother." Plucking at his sleeve, she gave him a bland look before she turned back to her secretary. "I'm sure Miss Smithers would love to dance with you, wouldn't you, Janet?"

She'd successfully maneuvered them all. Pleased that she'd given her secretary a nudge onto the dance floor, Brie accepted Alexander's hand.

"That wasn't very subtle," he pointed out.

"But it worked. I don't want to see her huddling in a corner all night. Now someone else is bound to ask her to dance."

He lifted a brow. "Meaning me?"

"If necessary." She smiled up at him. "Duty first."

Alexander cast a look over Brie's shoulder. Loubet's slight limp was less noticeable in a dance. "She doesn't look thrilled to be dancing with Loubet. Maybe she has some taste, after all."

"Alex." But she laughed. "In any case, I haven't told you how handsome you look. You and Bennett—where is Bennett?"

"Monopolizing the little American girl."

"Little—oh, you mean Eve." She lifted a brow, noting the disapproval. "She's not that little. In fact, I believe she's just Bennett's age."

"He should know better than to flirt with her so outrageously."

"From what I've seen, it's hardly one-sided."

He made a restless move with his shoulders. "Her sister should keep a tighter rein on her."

"Alex." Brie rolled her eyes.

"All right, all right." But he skimmed the room until he'd found the slim brunette in the ripe red dress. And he watched her.

She lost track of how many dances she danced, how many glasses of wine she'd sipped at, how many stories and jokes she'd listened to. It had been, she realized, foolish to be nervous. It was all a blur, as such things should be. She enjoyed it.

She enjoyed it more when she found herself waltzing in Reeve's arms again.

"Too many people," he murmured against her ear. Slowly, skillfully, he circled with her toward the terrace doors. Then they were dancing in the moonlight.

"This is lovely." There were flowers here, too, creamy white ones that sent out a delicate vanilla fragrance. She could breathe it in without having it mixed with perfumes or colognes. "Just lovely."

"A princess should always dance under the stars."

She started to laugh as she looked up at him, but something rushed through her. His face seemed to change—recede, blur? She wasn't sure. Was it younger? Were the eyes more candid, less guarded? The scent of the flowers seemed to change. Roses, hot, humid roses.

The world went gray. For a moment there was no music, no fragrance, no light. Then he had her firmly by the arms.

"Brie." He would have swept her up, carried her to a chair, but she held him off.

"No, I'm all right. Just dizzy for a moment. It was..." She trailed off, staring up into his face as if she were seeing it for the first time. "We were here," she whispered. "You and I, right here, on my birthday. We waltzed on the terrace and there were roses in pots lining the wall. It was hot and close. After the dance you kissed me."

And I fell in love with you. But she didn't say it, only stared. She'd fallen in love with him when she was sixteen. Now, so many years later, nothing had changed. Everything had changed.

"You remember." She was trembling, so he held her lightly.

"Yes." Her voice was so quiet he leaned closer to hear. "I remember it. I remember you."

He knew better than to push, so he spoke gently. "Anything else? Do you remember anything else, or only that one night?"

She shook her head and would have drawn away. It hurt, she discovered. Memory hurt. "I can't think. I need—Reeve, I need a few moments. A few moments alone."

"All right." He looked back toward the ballroom, crowded with people. She'd never be able to make it through them now. Thinking quickly, he took her down the terrace, through another set of doors. "I'll get you to your room."

"No, my office is closer." She hung on, pushing herself to take each step. "I just want a moment to sit and think. No one will bother me there."

He took her because it was closer, and it would take him less time to go back for the doctor. It would take him less time to tell Armand that her memory was coming back and the next step had to be taken. The arrests would be made quietly.

The backup guard was well trained, Reeve told himself. He wouldn't have even known he was there if Armand hadn't explained that Brie was watched always, not only by Reeve, but by others.

The office was dark, but when he started to turn on the lights, she stopped him.

"No, please. I don't want the light."

"Come on, I'll sit with you."

Again she resisted. "Reeve, I need to be alone."

It was a struggle not to feel rejected. "All right, but I'm going to get the doctor, Gabriella."

"If you must." Her nails were digging into her palms as she fought for control. "But give me a few moments first."

If her voice hadn't warned him away, he would have held her. "Stay here until I get back. Rest."

She waited until he closed the door. Then she lay down on the little sofa in the corner of the room, not because she was tired, but because she didn't think she had even the strength to sit.

So many emotions. So many memories fighting to get through, and all at once. She'd thought that remembering would be a relief, as if someone released strings around her head that had been tied too tightly. But it hurt, it drained and it frightened.

She could remember her mother now, the funeral. The waves and waves and waves of grief. Devastation—hers, her father's, and how they'd clung to each other. She could remember a Christmas when Bennett had given her a silly pair of slippers with long elephant tusks curling out of them. She could remember fencing with Alexander and fuming when he'd disarmed her.

And her father, holding out his arms for her when she'd curled into his lap to pour out her heart. Her father, so straight, so proud, so firm. A ruler first, but she'd been born to accept that. Perhaps that's why she'd fallen in love with Reeve. He, too, was a ruler first—of his own life, his own choices.

She didn't know she was weeping as one memory slipped into another. The tears came quietly, in the dark. Closing her eyes, she nearly slept.

"Listen to me." The whisper disturbed her. Brie shook her head. If it was a memory, she didn't want it. But the whisper came again. "It has to be tonight."

"And I tell you it feels wrong."

Not a memory, Brie realized dimly, but still a memory. The voices were there, now, coming through the dark. Through the windows, she realized, that opened up onto the terrace. But she'd heard them before. Her tears dried. She'd heard them before in the dark. This time she recognized them.

Had she been so blind? So stupid? Brie sat up slowly, careful not to make a sound. Yes, she remembered, and she recognized. Her memory was back, but it didn't hurt any longer; it didn't frighten. It enraged.

"We'll follow the plan exactly. Once we have her out, you take her back to the cottage. We use a stronger drug and keep her tied. There'll be no guard to make a fatal mistake. At one o'clock exactly, a message will be delivered to the prince. There, in the ballroom, he'll know his daughter's been taken again. And he'll know what he has to pay to get her back."

"Deboque."

"And five million francs."

"You and your money." The voice was low and disgusted and too close. Brie gauged the distance to the door and knew she had to wait. "The money means nothing."

"I'll have the satisfaction of knowing Armand had to pay it. After all these years and all this time, I'll have some restitution."

"Revenge." The correction was mild. "And revenge should never be emotional. You'd have been wiser to assassinate him."

"It's been more satisfying to watch him suffer. Just do your part and do it well, or Deboque remains in prison."

"I'll do my part. We'll both have what we want."

They hate each other, Brie realized. Why hadn't she seen it before? It was so clear now, but even tonight, she'd spoken to both of them and suspected nothing.

She sat very still and listened. But there was nothing more than the sound of footsteps receding along the stone. They'd used her and her father. Used her while pretending concern and even affection. She wouldn't be used any longer.

Still, she moved quietly as she crossed the room. She'd find her father and denounce them both. They wouldn't take her again. She twisted the knob and opened the door. And found she wasn't alone.

"Oh, Your Highness." A bit flustered, Janet stepped back and curtsied. "I had no idea you were here. There were some papers—"

"I thought I told you there'd be no more work tonight."

"Yes, Your Highness, but I—"

"Step aside."

It was the tone that gave her away, cold and clear with passion boiling beneath. Janet didn't hesitate. From her simple black bag, she took out a small, efficient gun. Brie didn't even have time to react.

Without fuss, Janet turned and aimed the gun at the guard who stepped from the shadows, his own weapon raised. She fired first, and though there was only a puff of sound, he fell. Even as she started toward the guard, Brie felt the barrel press into her stomach.

"If I shoot you here, you'll die very slowly, very painfully."

"There are other guards," Brie told her as calmly as she could. "They're all through the palace."

"Then unless you want other deaths on your hands, you'll cooperate." Janet knew only one thing—she had to get the princess out of the corridor and away before anyone else happened along. She couldn't risk taking her in the direction of the ballroom. Instead she gave Brie a quick push.

"You'll never get me off the palace grounds unseen," Brie warned her.

"It doesn't matter if they see us. None of the guards would dare shoot when I have a gun to your head." Her plans were in pieces and it wasn't possible to tell her partner. They wouldn't be able to slip a drugged, unconscious Brie out of the dark side entrance watched by the men on their own payroll. They wouldn't be able to close her quietly into the trunk of a waiting car.

The plan had been daring, but it had been organized. Now Janet had nothing.

"What were you planning to do?"

"I was to give you a message privately that the American needed to speak to you, in your room. He would have already been disposed of. Once there, there would have been a hypodermic for you. The rest would have been simple."

"It's not simple now." Brie didn't shudder at the easy way Janet had spoken of killing Reeve. She wouldn't allow herself to shudder. Instead she made herself think as Janet led her closer to the terrace doors. And the dark.

"It's so beautiful!" Eve had decided to give up being sophisticated and enjoy herself. "It must be fantastic to live in a palace every day."

"It's home." Bennett had his arm around her shoulders as they looked down over the high wall. "You know, I've never been to Houston."

"It's nothing like this." Eve took a deep breath before she turned to look at him. He was so handsome, she thought. So sweet. A perfect companion on a late spring night, and yet...

"I'm glad to be here," she said slowly. "But I don't think Prince Alexander likes me."

"Alex?" Bennett gave a shrug. He wasn't going to waste time on Alex when he had a beautiful girl in the moonlight. "He's just a little stuffy, that's all."

She smiled. "You're not. I've read a lot of...interesting things about you."

"All true." He grinned and kissed her hand. "But it's you who interests me now. Eve—" He broke off with a quiet curse as he heard footsteps. "Damn, it's so hard to find a private place around here." Unwilling to be disturbed, he drew Eve into the shadows just as Janet shoved Brie through the doorway.

"I won't go any farther until I know everything." Brie turned, her white dress a slash of light in the shadows. And Bennett saw the gleam of the gun.

"Oh, my God." He covered Eve's mouth with his hand even as she drew the breath to speak. "Listen to me," he whispered, watching his sister. "Go back to the ballroom and get my father or Alex or Reeve MacGee. Get all three if you can. Don't make a sound, just go."

She didn't have to be told twice. She'd seen the gun, as well. Eve nodded so that Bennett would remove his hand. Thinking quickly, she stepped out of her shoes and ran barefoot and silent along the dark side of the building until she came to a set of doors.

"If I have to kill you here," Janet said coolly, "it'll be unpleasant for both of us."

"I want to know why." Brie braced herself against the wall. She didn't know how she'd escape, but she had escaped before.

"Deboque is my lover. I want him back. For you, your father would exchange the devil himself."

Brie narrowed her eyes. Janet Smithers kept her passion well concealed. "How did you get past the security checks? Anyone who's hired to work for my family is—" She stopped herself. The answer was easy. "Loubet, of course."

For the first time, Janet smiled genuinely. "Of course. Deboque knew of Loubet, of the men Loubet bribed to work for him as well as your father. A little pressure, the threat of exposure, and the eminent minister of state was very cooperative. It helped, too, that he hated your father and looked at the kidnapping as a means of revenge."

"Revenge? Revenge for what?"

"The accident. You remember it now. Your father was driving. He was young, a bit reckless. He and the diplomat suffered only minor injuries, but Loubet…"

"He still limps," Brie murmured.

"Oh, more. Loubet has no children, nor will he ever, even with his young wife. He has yet to tell her, you know. He's afraid she'll leave him. The doctors assure him his problem has nothing to do with the accident. He chooses to believe otherwise."

"So he helped arrange the kidnapping to punish my father? That's mad."

"Hate will make you so. I, on the other hand, hate no one. I simply want my lover back." Janet held the gun so that it caught the moonlight. "I'm quite sane, Your Highness. I'll kill you only if I must."

"And if you do, your lover stays where he is." Brie straightened and called her bluff. "You can't kill me, because I'd be of no use to you dead."

"Quite right." But she aimed the gun again. "Do you know how painful a bullet can be, though it hits no vital organ?"

"No!" Infuriated, terrified, impulsive, Bennett leaped out of the shadows. He caught both Brie and Janet off guard. Both women froze as he lunged toward the gun. He nearly had it before Janet got off the first shot. The young prince fell without a sound.

"Oh, God, Bennett." Brie was on her knees beside him. "Oh, no, no, Bennett." His blood seeped into the white silk of her dress as she gathered him into her arms. Frantically, she checked for a pulse. "Go ahead and shoot," she hurled at Janet. "You can't do any more to me. I'll see you and your lover in hell for this."

"So you will." Reeve spoke quietly as the doorway was filled with light, men, uniforms and guns.

Janet watched Armand go to his children and the guards stand firm. She held her gun out, butt first. "No dramatics," she said as Reeve stepped forward to take it. "I'm a practical woman."

At a signal from Reeve she was flanked and taken away.

"Oh, Papa." Brie reached out. Armand was on his knees beside Bennett. "He tried to get the gun." Brie pressed her cheek to her brother's hair. "The doctor—"

"He's right here."

"Now, now, Gabriella." Dr. Franco's kind, patient voice came from behind her. "Let the boy go and give me room."

"I won't leave him. I won't—"

"Don't argue," Bennett said weakly. "I've got the world's worst headache."

She would have wept then, but her father's arm came around her, trembling lightly. "All right, then," she said as she watched Bennett's eyes flutter open. "I'll let him poke and prod at you. God knows I've had my fill of it."

"Brie…" Bennett held her hand a moment. "Any pretty nurses at the hospital?"

"Dozens," she managed.

He sighed and let his eyes close. "Thank God."

Holding out a hand for Alexander, Brie turned into Reeve's arms. She was home at last.

Epilogue

He'd promised her they'd have one last day on the water. That was all, Reeve told himself as the *Liberté* glided in the early-morning wind. They'd have one last day before the fantasy ended. His fantasy.

It had nearly been tragedy, he thought, and couldn't relax even yet. Though Loubet had already been taken when Eve had rushed into the ballroom, Brie had been alone with Deboque's lover.

"I can't believe it's really over," Brie said quietly.

Looking at her, neither could he. But they weren't thinking of the same thing. "It's over."

"Loubet—I could almost feel sorry for him. An illness." Brie thought of his pretty young wife and the shock on her face. "With Janet, an obsession."

"They were users," he reminded her. "Nearly killers. Both Bennett and that guard were lucky."

"I know." Over the past three days, she'd given thanks countless times. "I've killed."

"Brie—"

"No, I've faced it now. Accepted it. I know I was hiding from that, from those horrid days and nights alone in that dark room."

"You weren't hiding," he corrected. "You needed time."

"Now you sound like my doctors." She adjusted the tiller so that they began to tack toward the little cove. "I think parts of my memory, or my feelings were still there. I never told you about the coffee—about Janet's telling me that Nanny always fixed it for me. I never told you, I think, because I never really believed it of her. I couldn't. The bond was too strong."

"But Janet wouldn't understand that."

"She explained to me how Nanny brought it to the office the day I was kidnapped and scolded me a bit. Then she told me I left directly, that she walked me down to my car so that I'd know there had been no chance for anyone else to have doctored it. What she didn't tell me, what I didn't remember until the night of the ball, was that she'd taken the thermos from me and given me a stack of papers to sign. That gave her enough time to do what she had to do."

"But she hadn't counted on the old woman being sharp enough to go to your father with her suspicions after Loubet and Deboque's cousin Henri had picked you up at the little farm."

"Bless Nanny. To think she was watching over me all those weeks when I thought she was just fussing."

"Your father had you well looked after. He wasn't going to risk Loubet's making another move."

"Loubet's plan would have worked if Henri hadn't had a weakness for wine and I hadn't started pouring my soup on the ground. If I'd kept taking the full dose of the drug, I'd never have managed to hold off Henri or break through the boards over the window." She looked down at her hands. The nails were perfect again. They'd suffered badly when she'd fought to pry her way through the window. "Now it's over. I have my life back."

"You're happy with it. That's what matters."

She smiled at him slowly. "Yes, I'm happy with it. You know Christina and Eve are staying a few more days."

"I know your father would like to erect a statue to Eve."

"We've got a lot to be grateful to her for," Brie told him. "I have to say I enjoy watching her bask in the glory."

"The kid was white as a sheet when she got into the ballroom, but she didn't fumble around. She had the story straight and led us right to you."

"I've never thanked you properly." They glided into the little cove and she dropped sail.

"You don't have to thank me."

"But I want to. You gave me a great deal—me and my family. We won't forget it."

"I said you didn't have to thank me." This time his voice was cool as he walked to the rail.

"Reeve…" Brie rose to join him, wishing she were as sure of herself as she intended to sound. "I realize that you're not a citizen of Cordina and therefore not subject to our laws or customs. However, I have a request." She touched her tongue to her top lip. "Since my birthday is only two weeks away, we can call it a royal request if you like. It's customary for members of the royal family to have a request granted on the anniversary of their birth."

"A request." He pulled out a cigarette and lit it. "Which is?"

She liked him like this, a bit annoyed, a bit aloof. It would make it easier. "Our engagement is very popular, wouldn't you agree?"

He gave a short laugh. "Yeah."

"For myself, I have to confess I'm quite fond of the diamond you gave me."

"Keep it," he said carelessly. "Consider it a gift."

She looked down at it, then at the ring on her right hand. No more conflicting loyalties, she mused. Her emotions were very clear. "I intend to." She smiled as he shot her a cool look. "You know, I have a number of connections. There could be quite a bit of trouble with your passport, your visa, even your flight back to America."

Pitching the cigarette into the sea, he turned completely around. "What are you getting at?"

"I think it would be much simpler all around if you married me. In fact, I'm planning to insist."

He leaned back against the rail and watched her. He couldn't read her now—perhaps his own feelings prevented it. She was speaking as Princess Gabriella, cool, calm and confident. "Is that so?"

"Yes. If you cooperate, I'm sure we can work things out to mutual advantage."

"I'm not interested in advantages."

"Nonsense." She brushed this off, but her palms were damp. "It would be possible for us to spend six months in Cordina and six months in America," she went on. "I believe there must be a certain amount of compromise in any marriage. You agree?"

Negotiations. He'd carried out plenty of them as a cop. "Maybe."

She swallowed quietly, then went on speaking in an easy, practical tone. "Naturally, I have a lot of obligations, but when Alexander marries, his wife will assume some of them. In the meantime, it's hardly more than having a job, really."

Enough, he thought, of details and plans. Enough negotiating. He wanted it plain. "Simplify it." He took a step forward and she took one back.

"I don't know what you mean."

"Tell me what you want and why."

"You," she said keeping her chin up. "Because I love you and I have ever since I was sixteen and you kissed me on the terrace with the roses and moonlight."

He wanted to touch her cheek, but he didn't, not yet. Not just yet. "You're not sixteen anymore, and this isn't a fairy tale."

"No."

Was she smiling? he wondered. Didn't she know how badly he needed her to mean it? "There won't be a palace waiting for you in America."

"There's a house with a big front porch." She took another step back. "Don't make me beg. If you don't want me, say so."

This time she spoke as a woman, not so confident, not so cool. He had what he needed.

"When you were sixteen and I waltzed with you, it was like a dream." He took her hands. "I never forgot it. When I came back and kissed you again, it was real. I've never wanted anything more."

Her hands were firm on his. "And I've never wanted anyone more."

"Marry me, Brie, and sit on the porch with me. If we can have that, I can live with Her Serene Highness Gabriella."

She took both of his hands to her face and kissed them, one at a time. "It isn't a fairy tale, but sometimes life is happy ever after."

* * * * *

COMMAND PERFORMANCE

To Walter Mittermeyer, a true prince,
and his lady, Helen

Chapter 1

She'd been to the palace before. The first time, nearly seven years earlier, she'd thought it was a fairy tale sprung into three dimensions. She was older now, though she wasn't sure about wiser. Cordina was a country. The palace was a building, a beautiful one. Fairy tales were for the very young, the very naive or the very fortunate.

Despite the fact that she knew the palace that housed the royal family of Cordina was stone and mortar rather than wishes and dreams, she had to admire it. It glistened white, almost pristine, atop a jagged jut of land that overlooked both sea and town. Almost pristine, yes, but not detached—and not altogether placid.

Towers speared to the sky, piercing the blue with white. Turrets and buttresses attested to its age-old defensive function. The moat had been filled in, but one could imagine it. In its place were high-tech security systems and surveillance. Windows, some clear, some tinted, gleamed. Like any palace, there had been triumph and tragedy there, intrigue and glamour. It still stunned her that she'd had some part in it.

On her first visit she had walked on a terrace with a prince and, as fate had dictated, had had some part in saving his life. Fate, Eve decided as her limo passed through the high iron gates and beyond the red uniformed guards, was always sticking its fingers into ordinary lives.

Circumstances had led her to the tiny principality of Cordina all those years before, accompanying her sister, Chris, an old friend and schoolmate of the Princess Gabriella. If the circumstances had been different, Prince Bennett might have been with another woman on the terrace that night. She might never have met him or become a part of the closing chapters of the political intrigue that had haunted his sister and the rest of the royal family.

She might never have developed a fondness for the lovely palace in the storybook country. She might never have found herself being drawn back to it time and again. Yet this time she hadn't been drawn back exactly. She'd been called back. Command performance. She wrinkled her nose at the thought. Wasn't it too bad the command had to come from the one member of the royal family who annoyed her.

Prince Alexander, eldest son of the reigning monarch and heir to the throne. She watched trees heavy with pink blossoms bend in the breeze as the car cruised by. His Royal Highness Alexander Robert Armand de Cordina. She couldn't say where she'd learned his full name or why she remembered it. To Eve, it was simply as rigid and humorless a title as the man it pertained to.

A pity he wasn't more like his brother. Just thinking of Bennett made her smile and look forward to the visit. Bennett was charming and approachable. He didn't wear that invisible, but somehow tangible crown every minute of the day. Alexander was like his father—duty, country, family. That didn't leave much time for relaxation.

Well, she wasn't here to relax, either. She was here to talk to Alexander, and to talk business. Times had changed, and she wasn't a young, impressionable girl who could be awed by royalty or hurt by unspoken disapproval. No, Alexander was too well-bred ever to speak his disapproval, but no one Eve had ever known could convey it more clearly. If she hadn't wanted to spend a few days in Cordina again, she would have insisted that he come to Houston. Eve preferred discussing business on her own turf and on her own terms.

With a smile she stepped from the limo. Since she'd given up the first, she'd just have to make sure she won the second. Dueling with Alexander, and winning, would certainly be a pleasure.

The palace doors opened just as she started up the wide stone steps. Eve stopped. Her dark blue eyes took on a wicked light as she dipped into a deep curtsy. "Your Highness."

"Eve." With a quick, pleasant laugh Bennett bounded down the steps to her.

He'd been with the horses again, she thought as his arms went around her. Their scent clung to him, earthy and real. When she'd met him seven years before, he'd been a beautiful young man with an eye for the ladies and a good time. Drawing back to look at him, she saw he was older certainly, but little else had changed.

"It's so good to see you." He kissed her hard, but the passion was friendship and nothing more. "Too long between visits, Eve. It's been two years since you've been in Cordina."

"I'm a working woman, Bennett." She slid her hands down to clasp his. "How are you? If looks mean anything, you're marvelous. And if the scandal sheets mean anything, you're very busy."

"All true." He grinned and his clean-lined, almost poetic face became irresistible. "Come inside, I'll fix you a drink. No one's told me how long you're staying."

"That's because I'm not sure myself. It depends."

Her arm hooked through his, she entered the palace. It was cool, white and wide. Stairs swept up the side of the main hall, curling up and beyond the lofty ceiling. She'd always felt steady here, secure with the flavor of antiquity, continuity. Tapestries stretched over the walls, swords crossed with blades gleaming. A Louis XIV table held a bowl of distressed silver overflowing with jasmine.

"How was your flight?"

"Mmmm. Long." They turned off the main hall into a parlor where the drapes were open wide and the sun spilled in. The rays had long since beaten into the upholstery and faded it comfortably. There were roses here, rising out of porcelain and crystal. Eve dropped onto a sofa and drew in the scent. "Let's say I'm glad to be on the ground, glad to be here. Tell me how everyone is, Ben. Your sister?"

"Brie's wonderful. She'd planned to meet you at the airport, but her youngest has the sniffles." He chose a bottle of dry vermouth and poured it over ice. One of his greatest charms was never forgetting a woman's preferences. "It's still hard, after all these years, to picture my sister as a mother—especially a mother of four."

"I've a letter from Chris and orders to hand-deliver it. She also wants a full report on her goddaughter."

"Let's see which one is that? Ah, Camilla. I can tell you first-hand she's a scamp. Drives her brothers mad."

"That's what sisters are for." Smiling, she accepted the drink. "And Reeve?"

"He's fine, though there's no doubt he'd be more comfortable if they were settled year-round in America on that farm of his. They've done some pretty incredible things with the little farm here, but Brie's still official hostess in Cordina. Reeve would like nothing better than for Alex to marry and shift those duties onto his wife."

"Or you." She sipped, watching him over the rim. "If you took the plunge, some of Brie's responsibilities would shift."

"I love her, but not that much." He sprawled on the sofa, kicking his long, booted legs out.

"No truth to the rumors about Lady Alice Winthrop, then? Or was it the Honorable Jessica Mansfield most recently?"

"Lovely girls," he said easily. "I notice you're tactful enough not to mention the Countess Milano."

"She's ten years older than you." Her tone took on that of a lecturing aunt, but she smiled. "And I'm always tactful."

"So what about you, Eve?" When things came that close to the bone, Bennett was the master of evasion. "How does someone who looks like you manage to keep men at arm's length?"

"Karate. Black belt, seventh degree."

"Yes, I'd forgotten about that."

"You shouldn't have. I decked you twice."

"Oh, no. It was only once." He tossed his arm over the back of the sofa and looked as he was, arrogant, comfortable and sure of himself. "And I let you."

"It was twice." She sipped again. "And you were furious."

"Luck," he said firmly. "Added to the fact that as a gentleman, I couldn't hurt a woman."

"Bull."

"My dear, a hundred years ago you might have lost your head, lovely as it is."

"Your Highness," she said, and smiled with him, "you stop

being a gentleman the moment there's competition. If you could have thrown me first, you would have.''

It was true enough. "Care to try it again?''

A dare was something she could never, would never be able to ignore. Eve took a last sip of vermouth and rose. "At your service.''

Bennett stood and with one foot shoved the table away from the couch. After tossing back his untidy hair with one hand, he narrowed his eyes. "Now as I recall, I was to come up from behind and grab...just here.'' One tightly muscled arm hooked around her midriff. "Then I—''

The rest was cut off as she knocked his foot out from under him and sent him flat on his back. "Yes.'' She brushed her palms together as she looked down at him. "That's precisely as I remember it.''

"I wasn't ready.'' He propped himself on an elbow.

"All's fair, Your Highness.'' With a laugh she knelt beside him. "Did I hurt you?''

"Only my pride,'' he muttered, and gave her hair a tug.

When Alexander walked in, he saw his brother sprawled on the Turkish carpet, his hand intimately twined in Eve's dark fall of hair. Their faces were close, smiling, their bodies just brushing. His jaw set, then tightened.

"I apologize for interrupting.''

At his voice Bennett looked languidly over his shoulder, and Eve's shoulders snapped straight. He looked precisely as she remembered, dark, thick hair curling down his neck and over his ears. He wasn't smiling, though he rarely did that she'd seen, so that his face was rigidly handsome. Royalty suited him. Even as she resented it, she had to acknowledge it. He might have been one of the portraits she remembered from the palace gallery—high cheekbones well defined, the skin tanned and smooth over them. His eyes were dark, almost as dark as his hair, and as disapproving as his full, sculpted mouth, which was drawn now in a tight line. As always, he was militarily straight and impeccably dressed.

She felt mussed and travel stained and foolish.

"Eve's been giving me another lesson in the martial arts.'' Bennett rose, then taking Eve's hand, pulled her up beside him. "I've come out second best. Again.''

"So I see." His bow was formal and just this side of polite. "Miss Hamilton."

She curtsied, but there was no gleam of humor in her eyes this time. "Your Highness."

"I apologize for not being able to meet you at the airport. I trust your flight was pleasant."

"Delightful."

"Perhaps you'd like to freshen up before we discuss the reason I sent for you."

That brought her chin up. He'd hoped it would. Deliberately she reached down and picked up the small envelope bag she'd left on the sofa. "I'd prefer to get our business over with."

"As you wish. We'll go up to my office. Bennett, aren't you speaking at the Equestrian Society today?"

"Not for a couple of hours." He turned and gave Eve a friendly kiss on the nose, sending her a wink only she could see and appreciate. "I'll see you at dinner. Wear something dazzling, will you?"

"Naturally." But her smiled faded as she turned back to Alexander. "Your Highness?"

Inclining his head, he gestured her from the room.

They climbed the staircase in silence. He was angry. Eve was perceptive enough to understand that without understanding the reason for it. Though two years had passed since they'd been face to face, he was as stiffly disapproving of her as he'd always been. Because she was an American? she wondered. No, Reeve MacGee was an American and he had married Alexander's sister. Because she was in the theater?

Eve's lips curled a bit at the thought. It would be just like him. Cordina boasted one of the best theater complexes in the world in the Fine Arts Center, but Alexander could easily be disdainful of people in the theater. Tossing her head back, she entered his office just ahead of him.

"Coffee?"

"No, thank you."

"Please, sit."

She did, but kept her back ramrod straight. His office reflected him, with its elegantly conservative style. There were no frills, no flounces. The only scents were coffee and leather. The furniture was old and glossy, the rug thick and faded with age. Tall glass doors led to a balcony, but they were closed now, as if he had no desire for the sound of the sea or the fragrance of the garden.

The signs of wealth didn't intimidate her. She'd come from wealth and had since earned her own. It was the formality that had her sitting rigidly and waiting for the attack.

"Your sister is well?" Alexander took out a cigarette, then lifted a brow.

Eve nodded and waited as he struck a match. "She's very well. She plans to spend some time with Gabriella's family when they return to America. Bennett told me one of the children is ill."

"Dorian. A head cold." For the first time his features softened. Of all his sister's children, it was the youngest who held the strongest grip on his heart. "He isn't easily kept in bed."

"I'd like to see the children before I leave. I haven't seen any of them since Dorian was christened."

"Two years ago." He remembered, perhaps too well. "I'm sure we can arrange for you to visit the farm." When her lips curved, he drew back. He was no longer indulgent uncle or casual friend, but prince. "My father's away. He sends you his best if he hasn't returned before you leave."

"I read he was in Paris."

"Yes." He closed the door on state business without ever having opened it. "I appreciate your coming here, as it wasn't possible for me to travel at this time. My secretary outlined my proposal?"

"Yes, he did." Business, Eve reminded herself. The amenities, such as they were, were over. "You'd like me to bring my troupe to Cordina for a month's run of performances at the Fine Arts Center. The performances would be for the benefit of The Aid to Handicapped Children."

"That's correct."

"Forgive me, Your Highness, but I was under the impression that Princess Gabriella was in charge of this particular charity."

"She is. I am president of the Fine Arts Center. On this we work together." It was as much explanation as he would give. "Gabriella saw your troupe perform in America and was impressed. She felt that since Cordina has such a strong bond with the United States, using American performers in our country would help bring in desperately needed funds for the AHC."

"So this is her idea."

"One, after long discussions and consideration, I've decided to agree with."

"I see." One rounded nail began to tap on the arm of her chair. "I take that to mean you had reservations."

"I've never seen your troupe perform." He leaned back slightly and blew out a stream of smoke. "We've had American entertainers at the center before, of course, but never for this length of time or as a prelude to the AHC ball."

"Maybe you'd like us to audition."

His lips relaxed slightly, interestingly, into a smile. "It had crossed my mind."

"I think not." She rose, and noted with pleasure that manners forced him to stand, as well. "The Hamilton troupe has, in less than five years, earned both critical and popular approval. We have a reputation for excellence that requires no auditions in your country or any. If I decide to bring my company here, it will be because I respect the AHC and Gabriella."

He watched her as she spoke. She'd changed in seven years from a wide-eyed young girl into a confident woman. Yet somehow, astonishingly, she was even more beautiful. Her skin was flawless, pale, with hints of rose at the crest of her cheekbones. Her face was diamond shaped and just as stunning as the gem, with a full rich mouth and huge poetically blue eyes. Framing it was a mane of luxuriant black hair, a bit mussed now as it tumbled to her shoulders and beyond.

Temper kept her standing straight, but her body was delicate, or so it seemed. He'd wondered, he'd wondered too often, what it would feel like against his.

Even in anger her voice carried the slow, Texas drawl he'd learned to recognize. It breezed soft over his skin until the muscles in his stomach contracted. Carefully, relying on the control he'd fought to develop all his life, Alexander crushed out his cigarette.

"If you've finished, Miss Hamilton?"

"Eve, for Lord's sake. We've known each other for years." Out of patience she stalked over to the balcony doors and shoved them open. Facing the outside, she didn't notice Alexander's brows raise at her breach of protocol, or the slow smile.

"Eve," he said, then let her name hang on the air a moment.

"I think we've misunderstood each other. I'm not criticizing your company. That would be difficult, because, as I said, I've never seen them perform."

"At this rate you never will."

"Then I'd have to deal with Brie's temper. I prefer not to. Sit down." When she merely turned and looked at him, he checked his impulse to command and gestured to her chair. "Please."

She obeyed, but left the doors open. The sea could just be heard. The scent of rose, vanilla and spice wafted up from the gardens. "I'm sitting," she said, and crossed her legs.

He disapproved of her curt, one-to-one manner. He admired her independence. At the moment Alexander wasn't sure how the two could be mixed. He was sure that she stirred, as she always did, something more than polite emotions in him. Slowly he took his seat again and faced her.

"As a member of the royal family and as president of the Fine Arts Center, I must be very discreet and very circumspect in whom I choose to perform. In this case I'm trusting Gabriella's judgment and asking you if we can come to an arrangement."

"Perhaps." Eve was a businesswoman first and last. Personal feelings had never swayed her decisions, and they wouldn't now. "I'll have to see the theater again, check out the facilities. I'll have to be assured contractually that I and my company have artistic freedom—and adequate lodging during the run. Because the performances would be for a charity, I'm willing to negotiate our fee and expenses. Artistically, however, there is no negotiation."

"I'll see to it that you have a tour of the center. The center's lawyers and yours can deal with the contract. Artistically…" He linked his fingers on the desk. "Because you are the artist, I'll respect your judgment, but I'm not willing to toss myself blindly into your hands. The idea is for your company to perform four plays, one week each. The material will have to be approved by the center."

"By you."

It was a negligent, imperial shrug. "As you like."

She didn't like, and didn't bother to pretend otherwise. "What are your qualifications?"

"I beg your pardon?"

"What do you know about the theater? You're a politician."

She said it with a faint, very faint, sneer of contempt. "Why should I bring my company here, thousands of miles from home, for a fraction of what we normally earn so that you can pick and choose the material we perform?"

His temper had never been easily harnessed. Through years of dedication and determination he'd learned how to channel it. He did so now without taking his eyes from hers. "Because performing at the Fine Arts Center in Cordina at the request of the royal family would be a career advantage you would be foolish to ignore." He leaned forward. "I don't believe you're a foolish woman, Eve."

"No, I'm not." She rose again, but slowly, then waited until he stood on the other side of his desk. "I'll see the theater first, and I'll think about it before I ask the members of my troupe."

"You run the company, don't you?"

She tilted her head and a lock of hair fell over one eye. With her fingertips she drew it back. "You forget, America's a democracy, Your Highness. I don't hand down decrees to my people. If I find the facilities adequate and my troupe agrees, we'll talk contracts. Now if you'll excuse me, I'd like to unpack and change before dinner."

"I'll have someone show you to your rooms."

"I know where they are." She stopped at the door, turned and dropped an arrogant curtsy. "Your Highness."

"Eve." He watched her chin jut out. One day, he thought, someone was going to take her up on it. "Welcome to Cordina."

She wasn't a rude person. Eve assured herself of it as she chose a dress for dinner. In fact, she was considered amiable by just about everyone. True, she could get hard-nosed in business dealings, but she'd always considered that in the blood. She wasn't rude. Except with Alexander.

He asked for it, she told herself as she zipped into a snug, strapless dress in vivid blue silk. He was so aloof and condescending. She didn't have to tolerate that, heir to the throne or not. They were hardly playing prince and the pauper here. Her pedigree might not be royal, but it was unimpeachable.

She'd gone to the best schools. Maybe she'd hated them, but she'd gone. She'd entertained and been entertained by the rich, powerful and influential all her life. And she'd made something of herself. Not through her family, but through her own skills.

True, she'd discovered early on that her ambition to be an actress was never going to bear very ripe fruit, but her love of the theater hadn't ebbed. Added to that had been her innate business and organizational skills. The Hamilton Company of Players had been born and had flourished. She didn't appreciate Alexander the Great coming along and acting as though he were doing her a favor letting her troupe perform in his center.

They'd performed at Lincoln Center, the Kennedy Center, the Mark Taper Forum, and to solid reviews.

She'd worked hard to find the best, to develop talent, to stretch her own boundaries, and he came along and nodded graciously. Scowling, she hooked a thick gold collar around her neck. The Hamilton Company of Players didn't need his approval, gracious or otherwise.

She didn't need his approval or his damn royal seal. And she would be unbearably stupid to refuse to perform in Cordina.

Eve picked up a brush and dragged it through her hair. It was then that she noticed she had only one earring on. He was making her crazy, she decided, and found the teardrop sapphire on her dresser.

Why wasn't Ben president of the center? Why wasn't Brie still handling it? With either she could have been easy and relaxed. The job, if she chose to do it, could be done professionally, but without the added headache. What was it about Alexander that set her teeth on edge?

Eve fastened the second earring in place and frowned at her reflection. She could still remember the first time she'd seen him. She'd been twenty, and though he'd been only a few years older, he'd seemed so adult, so dashing. Bennett had led her out for the first dance at the ball, but it had been Alexander she'd watched. She'd been fanciful then, Eve admitted, imagining him as just the sort of prince who rescued damsels in distress and killed dragons. He'd had a sword at his side, for decoration only, but she had seen in her mind how he would wield it.

The crush had come quickly and, thank God, had been gone just as fast. She might have been fanciful, but as Alexander himself had said, she wasn't foolish. No woman pinned her dreams on the unyielding and disapproving. It had been easy to turn her attention to Bennett.

A pity they hadn't fallen in love, she thought now. Princess Eve. Laughing at herself, she dropped the brush. No, that just didn't fit. Luckily for everyone, she and Bennett had become friends before they had become anything else.

And she had the troupe. It was more than an ambition—it was a purpose. She'd watched friends marry and divorce and marry again, or simply drift from one affair to the next. Too often the reason was simple boredom. She'd never had to worry about that. Running the company would take up twenty-four hours a day if she allowed it. At times it came close, whether she wanted it to or not. If she was attracted to a man, her business and her own caution kept things from getting too serious. So she hadn't made a mistake. Yet. She didn't intend to.

Eve picked up her perfume and sprayed it over her bare shoulders before she left the room.

With luck Bennett would be back and lounging in the parlor. Dinner wouldn't be dull with him around, nor would it be strained for very long. He added spark and enjoyment simply by being. She wasn't in love with him, but she loved him for that.

As she walked downstairs she trailed her fingers along the smooth banister. So many fingers had trailed there before. When she was inside the palace, she thought of it only as a place, a sturdy, eternal place. If she understood little about Alexander, she understood his pride.

But when she stepped into the parlor and found him there alone, she tensed. Stopping in the doorway, she scanned the room for Bennett.

Good God, she was beautiful. When Alexander turned, it hit him like a blow. It had nothing to do with the silk, with the jewels. She could have dressed in burlap and still stunned the senses. Dark, sultry, just edging over to hot, there was something primitive, something uncomfortably natural about her sexuality that made a man ache just looking. It had been part of her since she had been hardly more than a child. Alexander decided she'd been born with it and cursed her for it.

His body tightened, his face settled into cool lines, as he saw her gaze sweep the room. He knew she was looking for, hoping for, Bennett.

"My brother's been detained." He stood with his back to a scrubbed hearth. The dark dinner jacket both suited and restrained him. "We dine alone this evening."

Eve stood where she was, as though stepping forward were a commitment she was far from ready to make. "There's no need to trouble for me, Your Highness. I can easily have dinner in my room if you'd like to make other plans."

"You're my guest. My plans are to dine with you." He turned away to pour drinks. "Come in, Eve. I promise you, I won't wrestle with you on the floor."

"I'm sure you won't," she said just as politely. Crossing to him, she held her hand out for the drink. "And we weren't wrestling. I threw him."

Deliberately he swept his gaze down. She was willow slender and barely higher than his shoulder. He wouldn't believe she'd thrown his tall, athletic brother physically. But emotionally was another matter. "Admirable. Then I'll promise I won't give you the opportunity to throw me. Your rooms are agreeable?"

"Perfect, as always. As I recall, you rarely have free evenings at home. No state dinners or official functions tonight?"

He glanced at her again. The lights were dim, so that they gave her skin the sheen of satin. Perhaps it would feel the same. "We could consider dining with you an official function, if you like."

"Perhaps I do." She watched him over the rim as she sipped. "So, Your Highness, do we make polite conversation or discuss world politics?"

"Politics at dinner make for an uneasy appetite. Especially when they're at odds."

"That's true. We never have agreed on many things. Polite conversation, then." She'd been schooled in it, as he had. Strolling to the bowl of roses, she stroked the petals. "I read that you were in Switzerland a few weeks during the winter. How was the skiing?"

"Excellent." He didn't add his real reason for being there, or mention the hours of meetings and discussions. He tried not to look at her long, slender fingers against the deep red roses. "Do you ski?"

"I get to Colorado now and again." The movement of her shoulders was negligent and noncommittal. How could she expect him to understand that she didn't have the time for idle games and casual trips? "I haven't been to Switzerland since I got out of school there. Being from Houston, I prefer summer sports."

"Such as?"

"Swimming."

"Then I should tell you the pool is at your disposal during your stay."

"Thank you." Silence. Eve felt her body tensing as it dragged on. "We seem to be out of polite conversation, and we haven't even had dinner."

"Then perhaps we should." He offered his arm, and though she hesitated, Eve slipped hers through it. "The cook recalled that you were particularly fond of his *poisson bonne femme*."

"Really? How nice." She unbent enough to smile up at him. "As I recall, I was more particularly fond of his *pôts de crème au chocolat*. I drove my father's cook mad until she could come up with a reasonable facsimile."

"Then you should be pleased with tonight's dessert."

"I'll be fat," she corrected, then stopped at the entrance to the dining room. "I've always admired this room," Eve murmured. "It's so ageless, so permanent." She studied it again, the two glistening chandeliers that spilled light onto a massive table and lovingly polished floors. The size didn't intimidate her, though more than a hundred could fit at the table.

As a rule, she might prefer the cozy, the more intimate, but the room had such power. Because she had grown up with it, power was something she expected as well as respected. But it was more the very age of the room that fascinated her. If she were very still, very quiet, she thought she could almost hear the conversations that had gone on there through the centuries.

"The first time I had dinner here, I was shaking like a leaf."

"Were you?" Interested, he didn't usher her in, but stayed at the entrance beside her. "I remember you being remarkably composed."

"Oh, I've always been good at false fronts, but inside I was terrified. Here I was, fresh out of school and having dinner in a palace."

"And this time?"

She wasn't sure why it was necessary, but she slipped her arm from his. "I've been out of school quite a while."

Two places were set at the table with candelabras and fresh flowers. Eve took her place at the side and left the head for Alexander. As they sat, a servant poured wine.

"It seems odd," she said after a moment. "Whenever I've been here before, the palace has been full of people."

"Gabriella and Reeve rarely stay here now that they're settled at the farm. Or farms," he corrected. "They split their time between their countries."

"Are they happy?"

His brow rose as he picked up his glass. "Happy?"

"Yes, you know, happy. It comes somewhere down the list after duty and obligation."

He waited silently as plates of chilled lobster were served. She had been too close to the mark with her talk of lists. He could never put his happiness before his duty, his feelings before his obligations. "My sister doesn't complain. She loves her husband, her children and her country."

"That's not the same thing."

"The family have done their best to lessen some of her duties."

"It's wonderful, isn't it, that after that terrible time she went through, she has everything." She saw his knuckles whiten on his fork, and reached automatically for his hand. "I'm sorry. Even after all this time it must be difficult to think of."

He said nothing a moment, just looked down at her hand, white, slender, covering his. It soothed. He'd never expected that. If it had been possible for him, he would have turned his over to grip hers. "It will always be difficult to think of, and impossible to forget that you were a part of saving both my sister and my brother."

"I only ran for help."

"You kept your head. If you hadn't, we would have lost both of them."

"I'll never forget it, either." Realizing her hand was still on his, Eve drew it away and made a business out of picking up her wine. "I can still see that woman's face."

"Deboque's lover."

He said it with such restrained violence, she shuddered. "Yes. The way she looked when she was holding that gun on Brie. That's when I realized palaces weren't just fairy tales. I'm sure you're all glad she and Loubet and Deboque are in prison."

"And will remain there. But Deboque has pulled strings from behind bars before."

"Has there been more? Bennett and I have spoken of it, but—"

"Bennett needs lessons in discretion."

She flared, swallowing a retort as one course was cleared and another served. "He didn't reveal any state secrets. We were simply remembering once—just as you and I are now—that Deboque had been in prison but had arranged for Brie's kidnapping through her secretary and your father's minister of state. He said he'd be uneasy as long as Deboque was alive. I told him it was nonsense, but maybe I was wrong."

"To be a public figure is to be uneasy." It was simpler to accept that than to remember his own feeling of helplessness, of watching his sister struggle through her trauma and pain. "The Bissets have ruled Cordina for generations. As long as we do, we make enemies. All of them are not, cannot be, in prison."

There was more. She sensed it but knew better than to try to make Alexander open up to her. If she wanted to know, when she wanted to know, she would go to Bennett. "It sounds like commoners have the advantage, Your Highness."

"Yes." With a smile she didn't understand, he picked up his fork.

They dined companionably enough, more companionably than Eve would have imagined. He didn't relax. She wondered about that as they eased through courses toward dessert and coffee. He was pleasant, polite—and on edge. She wanted to help, to ease away the tension so obvious in the set of his shoulders. But he wasn't a man to accept help from an outsider.

He would rule one day, and had been born to do it. Cordina was a small, storybook country, but like a storybook, it has its share of intrigue and unrest. What he'd been destined to do didn't sit on him lightly. Her background and upbringing made it difficult to comprehend, so that often, perhaps too often, she saw only the unbending outer layer.

At least they hadn't argued, Eve thought as she toyed with dessert. Actually, one didn't argue with Alexander; one just fumed and batted against a stone wall.

"That was lovely. Your cook only improves with time."

"He'll be pleased to hear it." He wanted her to stay, just to sit and talk about anything that wasn't important. For the last hour he'd nearly forgotten the pressure he was under. It wasn't like him, but the thought of going up to his rooms, to his work, was unappealing. "If you're not tired—"

"You didn't eat it all, did you?" Bennett bounded in and pulled up the chair beside Eve. "Done?" Without waiting, he took the rest of her dessert. "The food they pushed on me doesn't bear thinking about. I could picture the two of you here while I was eating rubber chicken."

"You don't look deprived," Eve noted, and smiled at him. "The main course was exquisite."

"You always had a nasty streak. Look, after I've finished this, let's go outside. I need the garden and a beautiful woman after hours at that stuffy meeting."

"If you two will excuse me, then." Alexander rose. "I'll leave you alone."

"Take a walk with us, Alex," Bennett invited. "After I finish the rest of your mousse."

"Not tonight. I've work."

"Always does," Bennett murmured. He reached for Alexander's dessert as Eve turned and watched the prince leave. She couldn't have said why, but she had an urge to follow him. Shaking the feeling off, she turned back to laugh at Bennett.

Chapter 2

"When Alexander promised me a tour guide, I didn't expect it to be you."

Her Serene Highness Gabriella de Cordina laughed as she pushed open the stage door. "The center's been a family affair from the beginning. Actually, I think Alex would have liked to take you through himself if his schedule hadn't been so full."

Eve let that pass, thinking Alexander would prefer mounds of paperwork and hours of stuffy meetings to an hour with her. "I hate to repeat myself, Brie, but you look wonderful."

"Repeat yourself," Gabriella told her. "When you've had four children you need all the moral support you can get." Her dark red hair was pinned up in a sleek, simple knot and her white suit was carefully tailored. She was every inch a princess. Still, Eve thought she looked too young and too fragile to have borne four children. "And you," she continued, stopping a moment to study the sister of her closest friend. "I remember the first time I saw you. I thought, what a stunning child. Now you're a stunning woman. Chris has nearly stopped worrying about you."

"I used to hate that." She could smile now, remembering the tug of war with her sister during her long, rebellious youth. "Now that I'm older, I find myself hoping she never stops worrying completely. It's so comforting. Isn't it strange that family comes to mean more to you as an adult?"

"I don't know what I'd do without mine. Those few months that I couldn't remember them, couldn't remember anything..." Gabriella trailed off with a shake of her head. "It's taught me to take nothing for granted. Well." She drew a deep breath and looked around. "What would you like to see first?"

"Let's take the backstage area—dressing rooms, fly. I'll take a look at the light board. If things don't work back here, it doesn't matter how good you are out front."

"You know what you're doing, don't you?"

"Let's hope so."

They spent over an hour backstage. Eve climbed stairs, squeezed into storerooms, examined equipment. It was, as she'd hoped, top rate. The Fine Arts Center was a family affair, built in the name of Gabriella's mother. The Bissets had poured their love for her into making it one of the best theater complexes in the world.

Eve felt the excitement growing. To play here would top anything she or the company had ever done. Already her mind was leaping forward. She would produce four typically American plays for an international audience. The company publicist would have a field day with promotion. Tennessee Williams, Neil Simon, Arthur Miller. She had such a wealth of talent to choose from. And she'd want her own technicians on the lights, on the ropes, on the props.

"I can see the wheels turning," Gabriella murmured.

"I've never been subtle." Eve walked out, stood stage center and let herself feel.

It was incredible, the sensations, the vibrations that hung in the air of an empty theater. This one had been designed for the actor. She could almost smell the greasepaint and the sweat. The seats rolled forward, slashed through by three wide aisles that were carpeted in royal blue. The houselights were enormous chandeliers and the ceilings were frescoed. Box seats tilted out of the walls on either side and straight back was a balcony. Even from the distance she could see the railings were hand carved and gleaming. More important, every seat in the house would have an unobstructed view of the stage.

" 'Tonight, it ends here, miserably. Whatever we've done, whatever we've attempted to do, no longer matters. When tomorrow comes, it begins again, and we—we will never have existed.' "

Her voice flowed out, back to the corners, up to the last row of the balcony, then echoed back. Satisfied, Eve smiled.

"Wonderful." She turned back to Brie. "Whoever your architect was, he deserves a medal."

"I'll suggest it to my father. Eve, what was that from? I don't recognize it."

"You wouldn't. Struggling playwright." She passed it off quickly, not wanting to say the struggling playwright was herself. "Brie, the theater's wonderful. Another time I'd love to do something on that smaller stage downstairs. Something intimate. But for our purposes, this is perfect."

"Oh, I was hoping you'd say that." Gabriella's heels clicked as she crossed the stage to Eve. "Ever since Alex and I kicked the idea around, I've been waiting for that. Eve, we're going to do something important, for your company, for our countries, for the children."

"I'm only going to put on some plays," Eve corrected, squeezing Gabriella's hand. "I'll leave the higher causes to you and Alex. But if we can get the details ironed out, the contracts, and the legalities of it, you're going to see four terrific productions."

"I'm counting on it."

She took one last glance around the stage. She would never perform here, but her company would. One day, maybe one day, one of her own plays would be acted here. She nearly laughed at herself for the fantasy. "Then I'd better get back home and start working."

"Oh, no, we're not letting you go so quickly. I've already planned a family dinner at the farm. Tomorrow night. Now…" She hooked her arm through Eve's. "I want you to go back and be lazy for the rest of the day. Once we put you to work, you won't have another opportunity."

"Is that a royal command?"

"Absolutely."

"Then I'll just have to suffer through it."

It wasn't so hard. Eve discovered that lounging by the pool while a balmy Mediterranean breeze ruffled the palm fronds overhead wasn't such a tough job. In her youth she'd done a lot of lounging. Vegetating, Eve corrected. It amazed her that she had been content to do nothing for such long periods of time. Not that there was anything wrong with doing nothing, she added as she adjusted her chaise one more notch back. It was just a pity to make a career out of it.

She nearly had. Affluence, privilege. It had made it so easy to sit and let others do. She might have continued in just that vein if she hadn't discovered the theater. It had given her something to start at the bottom in, something to work toward. Something Daddy, bless him, couldn't wrangle for her. She could either act or she couldn't. Eve had discovered she could. But it hadn't been stage center where she'd found her niche.

Theater had opened up worlds for her, worlds inside herself. She was competent; she was shrewd; she was blessed with organizational talents she'd never used during her education. Conceiving her own company, bringing it to life, had sharpened all those skills. It had also taught her how to take risks, work hard, and mostly, how to be dependable. There were people relying on her for their art and for their living. The responsibility had turned a spoiled young girl into a dedicated woman.

Now she was being given the opportunity to reap rewards even she hadn't dreamed of. International recognition for her company. All she had to do was select the right material, produce four plays, handle four sets of wardrobe, four sets of props, four sets of scenery. In the meantime she had to deal with lawyers, directors, transportation, seventy-odd actors and technicians. And a prince.

Eve pushed her sunglasses farther up on her nose and sighed. What was life without a few challenges?

He shouldn't have come out. One look at his watch told Alexander he had an appointment in twenty minutes. He had no business going out to the pool when he should have been in his office, preparing for the meeting with the minister of state. He should have known better than to ask, however casually, if Miss Hamilton had returned from the center. He should have known better than to think he could have gone up to his office and concentrated once he knew she was out at the pool.

She looked as though she were sleeping. The brief red bikini stretched low over her hips, rose high at the thighs. She'd untied the straps to the top so that it stayed in place only because of her prone position. He couldn't see her eyes behind the sunglasses, but she made no movement at all when he approached.

He looked his fill. Her skin was glistening with the oil she'd applied to every exposed area. Its scent rose exotically to compete with the flowers. Her hair curled damp and dark around her face, showing him she hadn't sat idly, but had used the pool. Stepping closer, he saw her eyes flutter open beneath the amber-tinted lenses.

"You should take more care. You're not accustomed to our Mediterranean sun."

She lay almost flat on her back, staring up at him. He blocked the sun now, so that it glowed like a nimbus around his head. She blinked, trying to clear her vision and her brain. Damsels in distress and dragons. She thought of them again, though he looked more like a god than a prince.

"I thought you were out." She propped herself up on her elbow before she remembered her bikini. As it slipped, she grabbed for it with one hand and swore. He simply stood there while she struggled with the ties and what was left of her modesty.

"I was out. Your skin's very white, Eve. You'll burn quickly."

It occurred to her that protocol demanded she rise and curtsy. Protocol aside, a curtsy in a bikini wasn't practical. She stayed as she was. "I've slathered on a pint of sunscreen, and I wasn't intending to stay out much longer. Besides, living in Houston toughens the skin."

"It hasn't appeared to." Minister of state or not, Alexander pulled a chair up and sat. "You've been to the center?"

"Yes. You and your family are to be congratulated. It's wonderful."

"Then you'll agree to have your company perform?"

"I'll agree to negotiate a contract." Eve pulled the back of her chaise up so that she could settle into a sitting position. "The facilities are first class. If we can iron out the details, we'll both have what we want."

"Such details are for lawyers and accountants," he said in dismissal. "We need only agree on what is to be done."

Though she thought her father would have been amused by his attitude toward accountants, she folded her hands. "We'll agree after the lawyers and accountants have had their say."

"It appears you've become a businesswoman."

"It doesn't just appear, I have. Don't you approve of women in business, Your Highness?"

"Cordina is a forward-looking country. We don't approve or disapprove on the basis of gender."

"The royal 'we,'" she murmured under her breath. "I'm sure that's very progressive. Aren't you roasting in that jacket?"

"There's a breeze."

"Don't you ever unbutton your collar or take off your shoes?"

"I beg your pardon?"

"Never mind. You're too literal." She lifted a glass filled with citrus punch from the table beside her. The ice had melted, but it was still refreshing. "Do you ever use the pool, Your Highness?"

"When time permits."

"Ever hear the American saying about all work and no play?"

He sat coolly in the baking sun, the gold-and-ruby ring on his finger glinted. His eyes were shadowed. "I believe I have."

"But it doesn't apply to princes?"

"I apologize for not being able to entertain you."

"I don't need entertainment." Frustrated, she rose. When he stood, she spun on him. "Oh sit, will you? It's only the two of us. Don't you think women get tired of having a man pop up everytime they do?"

Alexander settled again, surprised to find himself amused. "No."

"Well, they do. It might do you some good to spend more time in America, learning how to unbend."

"I'm not in a position to unbend," he said quietly and Eve felt her temper ease away.

"All right, though I can't understand why that's true with a friend of the family. You'll have to excuse me, Your Highness. I've little patience with unnecessary formality."

"Then why don't you ever call me by my name?" His question had her turning to face him again, frowning and uncomfortable. "You said yourself, we've known each other for years."

"I was wrong." She said it slowly, sensing something under the surface. "We don't know each other at all."

"You have no trouble addressing the other members of my family by their names rather than their titles."

She wished for her drink again, but found herself unable to cross near him to get it. "No, I don't."

"It causes me to ask myself why." With his eyes on hers, he rose and walked to her. When they were close, face to face, he stopped, but kept his hands at his side. "Or perhaps I should ask you why."

"It never seemed appropriate, that's all."

Nerves? He'd never seen nerves in her before. Intrigued, he stepped closer. "Have I been unfriendly?"

"Yes—no." She caught herself taking a step back.

"Which is it?"

"No." She stood firm and called herself a fool. "You're always polite, Your Highness. I know you've never approved of me, but—"

"I've given that impression?"

He was closer again. She hadn't even seen him move. Eve fell back on the only defense at hand. Belligerence. "Loud and clear."

"Then I should apologize." He took her hand and brought it to his lips. Eve wondered why she should hear thunder when the sky was so clear.

"Don't be charming." She tried to tug her hand away and found it firmly caught.

His smile was as unexpected as the kiss on her fingers, and just as weakening. Yes, she was nervous. He found the unforeseen vulnerability irresistible. "You prefer rudeness?"

"I prefer the expected."

"So do I." Something came and went in his eyes quickly. If it was a challenge, she promised herself it was one she would never answer. "It isn't always there. And from time to time, the unexpected is more interesting."

"Interesting for some, uncomfortable for others."

His smile deepened. She saw for the first time a small dimple at the side of his mouth. For some reason her gaze seemed locked to it. "Do I make you uncomfortable, Eve?"

"I didn't say that." She tore her gaze from his mouth, but found meeting his eyes wasn't any less unnerving.

"Your face is flushed," he murmured, and stroked a thumb along her cheek.

"It's the heat," she managed, then felt her knees tremble when his gaze locked on hers.

"I believe you're right." He felt it, too, sizzling in the air, crackling, like an electric storm over the sea. "The wise thing for both of us is to cool off."

"Yes. I have to change. I told Bennett I'd go down to the stables with him before dinner."

Alexander withdrew immediately. Whatever she thought she had seen in his face, in his eyes, was gone. "I'll let you go, then. The French ambassador and his wife will be joining us for dinner."

"I'll try not to slurp my soup."

Temper, always close to the surface, came into his eyes. "Are you making fun of me, Eve, or yourself?"

"Both."

"Don't stay in the sun much longer." He turned and didn't look back.

Eve watched him stride away in his strong, military gait. She shivered once, then shut her eyes and dove headlong into the pool.

Eve was relieved to find not only Bennett but Brie and Reeve joining them at dinner. Seated between the ambassador and Reeve, she found herself saved from having to make the obligatory dinner conversation with Alexander. As heir, he sat at the head of the table, flanked by his sister on one side and the ambassador's wife on the other.

The dinner was formal but not, as Eve had feared, unbearably boring. The ambassador had a wealth of anecdotes, any of which he would expound on given the least encouragement. Eve laughed with him, urged him on, then delighted him by carrying on a conversation in French. Her years in the Swiss school had stuck, whether she'd wanted them to or not.

"Impressive," Reeve toasted her when she turned to him with a grin. He'd changed little over the years, she thought. There was a touch of gray at the temples, but that was all. No, she corrected, that wasn't all. He was more relaxed now. Happiness, it seemed, was its own fountain of youth.

"How's your French coming?"

"It isn't." He toyed with the rich duck in its delicate sauce and thought how much he would have preferred a steak, rare, cooked over his own grill. Then he glanced over at his wife as she laughed with Bennett. Whatever sacrifices had been made were nothing compared to the rewards. "Gabriella says I'm determined not to learn."

"And?"

"She's right."

Eve laughed and picked up her wine. "I'm looking forward to seeing your farm tomorrow, Reeve. Chris told me the house was lovely, though she got lost when you started in on wheat or oats. And you have horses."

"All the children ride. Even Dorian sits on a pony." He paused as the main course was cleared. "It's amazing how fast they learn."

"How does it feel?" She turned a little more, not certain where the question had come from or why it seemed so important. "Living here, I mean, or living here most of the year, having to sink down another set of roots, learn new customs?"

He could have passed it off as some men would. He could have made a joke as others might. But he had a fondness for the truth. "It was difficult at first, for both of us. Now it's home. Just as Virginia's home. I can't say I won't be happy when Alex marries and Brie has fewer obligations, but I fell in love with the woman. Her rank is part of it, part of her."

"It is more than just a title, isn't it?" she murmured. Before she realized it, before she could prevent it, her gaze drifted to Alexander.

"A great deal more," Reeve agreed, aware of where her interest had shifted. "And more yet for him."

Eve brought her attention back quickly. "Yes, of course. He'll rule one day."

"He's been molded for it from his first breath." Were Gabriella's instincts right? Reeve wondered. Was there a spark between Alexander and Eve that would take very little fanning. He'd never seen it, but tonight he wasn't so sure. If there was, Eve wouldn't find it an easy road. Reeve mulled over his wine a moment, then kept his voice quiet. "If there's one thing I've learned in the past few years, it's that duty and obligation aren't choices for some, or for the people who love them."

He was telling her what she already knew, and more than she wanted to know. "No, I'm sure you're right." To ease the tension that had come so quickly, she turned to the ambassador and made him laugh.

The dinner party moved to the main parlor with coffee and brandy. Calculating that a decent amount of time had elapsed, Bennett took Eve's hand. "Air," he whispered in her ear.

"Rude," she whispered back.

"No, they'll talk for an hour yet. And I'm entitled, even obliged, to entertain you as well as the others. Let's just step out on the terrace."

The invitation was hard to resist. Eve already knew how tempting nights in Cordina were. A quick glance showed her that Alexander had the ambassador engaged in quiet conversation and that Brie and Reeve were dealing with the ambassador's wife.

"All right. For a minute."

Though his flow of words never faltered, Alexander saw Eve move with his brother through the terrace doors.

"Better," Bennett said immediately.

"It was a lovely dinner."

"It was fine, but sometimes I'd prefer pizza and beer with a few friends." He walked to the edge and leaned on a low stone wall. "The older I get, the less time there is for it."

"It isn't easy, is it?"

"What?"

"Being who you are."

He swung an arm around her waist. "It has its moments."

"No, don't shrug it off. You always do that." Eve drew back to study him. He was wonderful to look at and tougher, a great deal tougher, than he allowed himself to seem.

"You want a serious answer." He dipped his hands into his pockets. "It's difficult to give you one. I've always been who I am, what I am. No, it isn't always easy to know that wherever you go there's a bodyguard not far behind or the press not far ahead. I deal with it in my own way. I'm permitted to, as Brie is, to a certain extent. We're not the heir."

"Do you wish you were?"

"God, no."

He said it with such speed and force she had to smile. "There's not a jealous bone in your body, is there?"

"It's hardly a matter of envy. As long as I can remember, Alex has had to work harder, study harder. Be harder. No, I wouldn't step into his shoes. Why do you ask?"

"Oh, I don't know. The American fascination with royalty, I suppose."

"You've known us too long to be fascinated."

"I've known some of you." With a shake of her head, she walked to him. "Do you remember that first night, the night of the ball, when we walked out on one of those high, dark balconies?"

"That's hardly a night I'd forget."

"I was fascinated then. I thought you were going to kiss me."

He grinned and twined a lock of her hair around his finger. "I never got around to it."

"No, you ended up getting shot, instead. I thought you were very heroic."

"I was." He linked his arms loosely around her waist. "You know, if I tried to kiss you now, I'd feel as though I were making a pass at my sister."

"I know." Relaxed, she rested her head on his shoulder. "I'm glad we're friends, Ben."

"You wouldn't happen to have a cousin, a half sister, an aunt, who looks anything like you?"

"Sorry." Smiling, she tilted her head back to look at him.

"Me, too."

"Bennett."

It only took Alexander's voice to have Eve springing back like a child caught in the cookie jar. She cursed herself for it, then balled her hands into fists at her side.

"Excuse me." Coolly regal, he stood just outside the terrace doors where the moonlight didn't reach. "The ambassador is leaving."

"So soon?" Untouched by the biting tone, Bennett squeezed Eve's shoulders. "Well, we should make our good-byes. Thanks for the air."

"Of course." But as he walked through the doors, she stayed where she was, hoping Alexander would follow him.

"If you'd come back in for a moment, the ambassador would like to say good-bye. He was quite charmed by you at dinner."

"All right." She walked to the doors, but found her way blocked. This time she didn't step back, but angled her chin so she could see his face. It was in shadows, and only his eyes were clear. "Was there something else, Your Highness?"

"Yes, it seems there is." He caught her chin in his hand, surprising both of them. It was soft, with the pressure still a threat or a promise. It wasn't a lover's touch. He refused to allow it to be. "Bennett is a generous man, a compassionate one, but a man who has little discretion with women. You should take care."

From someone else, from anyone else, the comment would have made her laugh. Meeting Alexander's eyes, she didn't feel like laughing. "It appears you're warning me I might get burned again. It wasn't necessary this afternoon, and it isn't necessary now." Her voice was slow and sultry, but somehow managed to take on the sheen of ice. "You might have observed, Your Highness, that American women insist on taking care of themselves and making their own choices."

"I have no desire to take care of you." There was a sting in his voice that might have made her shrivel if she hadn't been so angry.

"We can all be grateful for that."

"If you're in love with my brother—"

"What right do you have to ask me that?" Eve demanded. She didn't know why the temper had come or why it was so fierce, but with every word it grew. "My feelings for your brother are *my* feelings and have nothing to do with you."

The words twisted inside him hatefully. "He is my brother."

"You don't rule Bennett and you certainly don't rule me. My feelings for your brother, or for anyone, are my business."

"What happens in my home, in my family, is mine."

"Alex." Brie came to the door, her voice subdued to indicate theirs weren't. "The ambassador's waiting."

Without a word he dropped his hand and strode inside.

"Your brother's an idiot," Eve said under her breath.

"In a great many ways." Sympathetic, Brie took Eve's hand.

"Take a deep breath and come in and speak to the ambassador and his wife a moment. Then you can go up to your room and kick something. That's what I always do."

Eve set her teeth. "Thanks. I believe I will."

Chapter 3

PRINCE BENNETT COURTS AMERICAN HEIRESS.

Eve read the headline with her morning coffee and nearly choked. Once she managed to swallow and take a second look, she began to giggle. Poor Ben, she thought, all he had to do was look at a woman and there was a romance. Ignoring her croissant, Eve read the text:

> Eve Hamilton, daughter of millionaire T. G. Hamilton, is the guest of the royal family during her visit to Cordina. The long and intimate connection between Prince Bennett and Miss Hamilton began seven years ago...

The article went on to describe the events that took place in the palace resulting in the abortive kidnapping of the princess and Bennett's subsequent injuries. She couldn't help but smile when her own part was played up heroically. Amused, she read that she and Bennett had enjoyed periodic rendezvous over the years.

Rendezvous, she thought with a snicker. Well, it was true that Bennett had come to Houston to help her celebrate her twenty-first birthday. One of her closest friends had fallen madly in love with him for about a week. Because of the connection, she'd been asked to accompany him on a tour of Washington a few years before.

And she had visited Cordina a few times with her sister. Then there was the time she and Bennett had hooked up in Paris quite by accident. It was difficult to think of one lunch in a public café as a rendezvous, but the press needed to print something.

"Will another member of the royal family choose an American?"

The article ended with the question. Don't hold your breath, she answered silently, then set the paper aside. What would the press have to talk about when Bennett did meet the right woman and settle? Laughing to herself, she picked up her cooling croissant. By then it was very likely Brie's children would be old enough to marry.

"Interesting reading?"

Eve glanced over at the entrance of the little solarium. She should have known he wouldn't let her have breakfast in peace. "I enjoy a joke, Your Highness." She started to rise, when he waved her back into her seat.

"You consider this funny?"

"I got a laugh out of it, though I imagine Ben gets tired of having every woman he smiles at added to the list of prospective wives."

"He thinks little of it." As, under most circumstances, Alexander did himself. "Ben enjoys a scandal."

Because it was said without heat, she smiled. If he wanted to let the words exchanged the night before be forgotten, she was more than willing. She'd spent long enough stewing about them. "Who doesn't?" At a closer glance he looked tired, and more than a little strained. Sympathetic, she softened. "Have you had breakfast? I can offer you coffee and croissants."

"Yes, a few hours ago. I could use the coffee."

She rose and took another cup and saucer from the server. "It's barely ten, but you look as though you've had a difficult day."

For a moment he said nothing. Such was his training. Then he relented. It would be on the radio and in the papers soon enough. "There was news from Paris this morning. A bomb at the embassy."

Her fingers tightened on the handle of the coffeepot. "Oh, God, your father."

"He's not hurt. His secretary was injured slightly." He paused, but his voice was calm and even when he continued. "Seward, the assistant to the minister, was killed."

"I'm sorry." She set down the pot to put a hand on his arm. "I'm so sorry. Do they know who did it?"

"No one's taken the credit. We have only suspicions."

"Is the prince coming home?"

He looked through the glass to where the sun was bright and the flowers blooming. Life would never be just that simple, he reminded himself. Never just that ordinary. "The business in Paris isn't completed."

"But—"

"He'll come home when it is." He lifted his cup and drank the coffee black and steaming. "Cordina, like many other countries, takes a strong stand against terrorism. They will be found."

"I hope so." She pushed the flaky croissant aside and found the headline no longer amused her. "Why is it so many innocents pay for the politics of others?"

His fingers tightened on the cup, part in fury, part in frustration. "There is no politics in terrorism."

"No." There was a great deal she didn't understand and more she would have liked to close her eyes on. But she knew that burying one's head in the sand did nothing but put grit in one's eyes. "No, you're right, of course."

"Seward leaves a wife and three children."

"Oh, how awful. Have they been told?"

"I have to go tell them now."

"Can I help? I could go with you."

"It's not your affair."

Eve retreated, calling herself a fool for being hurt. When he rose, she stared down into her coffee and said nothing.

Why had he come here? Alexander asked himself. He'd needed to tell her, to share his frustration, his anger, his grief. It wasn't wise for a man who had to rule to need comfort, a soft word, a hand to hold. He'd been taught to rely on himself, yet he'd come to her. And he still needed.

"Eve." It wasn't easy for him. She couldn't know that a simple request set off a violent tug-of-war inside him. "It would help if you went with me. I think she could use a woman."

"I'll get my purse," was all she said.

The Sewards lived in a pretty pink stucco house with a small, neat lawn bordered by white flowers. Eve saw a red bike in the drive. It was that more than anything that clutched at her heart. She knew what it was like to lose a parent, and that the hurt and grief never completely healed over.

Alexander offered his hand after he stepped from the car. Eve accepted it, then let hers remain there.

"If you're uncomfortable—"

"No. No, only sad." She walked with him to the door, aware that the driver watched them, but unaware that members of the security staff were stationed up and down the quiet street.

Alena Seward opened the door herself. She was a dark, plump woman of early middle age with lovely eyes and mussed hair. It was obvious they had caught her in the middle of cleaning. Her mouth dropped open the moment she saw Alexander, but she recovered quickly.

"Your Highness."

"Madame Seward, I apologize for coming to your home unexpectedly. May we come in?"

"Of course." Eve saw her eyes shift to the furniture that had yet to be dusted, to toys that had yet to be tidied. "May I offer you coffee, Your Highness?"

"No, thank you. May I present Miss Eve Hamilton."

"How do you do?" The woman offered a hand. "Please sit down."

Alexander took a chair, knowing the woman would remain standing if he did. "Madame Seward, there was news from Paris this morning."

Seated beside Alena on the sofa, Eve felt the other woman tense. "Yes, Your Highness."

"Two bombs were planted at our embassy. One detonated before it was discovered." He knew from experience that bad news, the worst news, was best given quickly. "Your husband was killed."

"Maurice?" Her fingers tightened on Eve's hand, though she was unaware that it had been offered. "Dead?"

"He was killed instantly, *madame*. My father sends his grief and his condolences, and I and the rest of my family give ours."

"There is a mistake?" There were no tears, but the fingers around Eve's hand were like clamps.

He hated the helplessness more than anything else. He could give her no hope, and sympathy was such an empty gift. "No, *madame*. He was alone in the office when it exploded."

"Brandy." Eve forced Alena's attention to her. "Madame Seward, where is your brandy?"

"Brandy?" Her voice was as blank as her eyes. "There is brandy in the kitchen."

Eve only looked at Alexander. He rose and went to find it himself.

"But I spoke to him just yesterday," Alena murmured. "He was well—tired. The meetings drag on so long. He'd bought a little jeweled pin for our daughter. Her birthday is next month." On this her voice began to quiver. "There's a mistake. *Mademoiselle?*"

Then the tears came. Eve did the only thing she knew how. She held. When Alexander entered the room again Eve had the widow's head on her breast. Her own eyes were overflowing as she stroked Alena's hair. Grief filled the room, replacing disbelief. In a movement that had nothing to do with protocol and everything to do with compassion, he knelt in front of them and urged the brandy on Alena.

"You have a sister, *madame*," he said gently. "Would you like me to phone her now?"

"My children."

"I'll have them brought home."

She took a shaky sip of brandy. "I would like my sister, Your Highness."

"Where is your phone?"

"In the office. Maurice's office, down the hall." She turned back into Eve's shoulder and wept.

"You were very kind," Alexander said when they were back in his car.

Eve shut her eyes, leaning her head back against the seat. "Kindness often doesn't seem to be enough."

He could say nothing to that. He'd felt the same. Why when he carried the burden of power was there so little he could do?

"What will happen to her?"

"She and her children will be provided for. We can do that."
He pulled out a cigarette. The taste in his mouth was already harsh.
"We can't heal the wounds."

She heard it in his voice, the bitterness tinged with frustration.
For the first time, she thought she really understood. "You want
to punish someone."

He lit the cigarette, then turned to see her eyes open and on
him. "I will punish someone."

The way he said it had Eve's mouth going dry. He had the
power, not only in his title, not only in his birthright. If he'd been
born a peasant, he'd have had it still. Maybe it was this above
everything else that kept her drawn toward him even as she inched
away.

"When you were on the phone, Alena asked me who had done
it. I had to tell her I didn't know, but I know she'll ask again,
when the grief eases."

"When the grief passes there comes a hunger for revenge."

"You want that."

"It could have been my father." For the first time, she saw his
control slip. It dangled dangerously a moment, showing in the heat
and fury of his eyes, before he ripped it back. "We are responsible
to our country, to our people. Seward's death will not be ignored."

"You believe the bomb was planted for your father?" She
reached out to take his wrist. "It was meant for him?"

"It was planted in his office. It was only coincidence that he
was called away moments before the explosion. Had he not, he
would have died with Seward."

"Then that's all the more reason he should come home."

"That's all the more reason he must stay. If a ruler is intimidated, his country is intimidated."

"Damn it, he's your father."

"He is Armand of Cordina first."

"You don't believe that. You don't really feel that way." The
intensity was in her voice, in her fingers as they gripped his flesh.
"If your father's in danger, you have to convince him to come
back."

"If he were to ask my advice, I would tell him that to return to
Cordina before his business is completed would be a mistake."

She withdrew slowly until they were no longer touching. "Bennett said you were hard, had to be hard. I wonder if he meant this much." When the car pulled up at the palace steps, she was out before him. "For a moment back at that house, I thought I saw something in you, warmth, humanity. I should have known better. You have no feelings, because you have no heart."

He caught her arm before she reached the door. "You understand nothing. I'm under no obligation to explain myself to you or to anyone." Yet he had a need to. The man inside the title desperately needed her understanding. "A man is dead, a good man, an honest man, a man I hunted with, gambled with. His wife is left with her grief and the grief of her children and I can do nothing. Nothing."

He tossed her arm aside, then strode back down the stairs. Eve watched him disappear into the side garden.

For a moment she stood where she was, breathing hard, close to tears. She took a deep breath, another, then went after him.

This woman, damn her, was making him forget who he was, what he had to be. There was a distance that had to be maintained between his feelings and his obligation, between the man and his title. With his family, in private, it could be different. Even with his closest friends the reserve had to be put into place when necessary. He couldn't afford to allow himself the luxury of being too—what had she said—human, when the responsibility was so great. More now than ever.

He'd lost a valued friend, and for what? Because of some vague and violent statement by a nameless group of terrorists. No, he didn't believe that. He tore a blossom from a bush as he passed. A man was more than a stalk to be broken on a whim. There had been a purpose, and Seward had been a mistake.

His father had been the target. Alexander was as sure of that as he was of his own name. And Deboque, the animal, had been the trigger.

"Your Highness."

He turned and saw Eve. The garden flowered around her, ripe, lush and tropical. It suited her name, he thought, as she did. But with the first Eve it had been the fruit that had been forbidden, not the woman.

"I want to apologize." She said it quickly. For her, apologies, like mistakes, were easier to swallow than to speak. "When I'm wrong, I'm often very wrong. I hope you'll believe that I'm sorry."

"I believe you're sorry, Eve, just as I believe you meant what you said."

She opened her mouth to contradict, then shut it again. "I guess that has to do for both of us."

He studied her a moment, aware she was still angry, and angrier still that her conscience had forced her to apologize. It was something he understood perhaps too well, the frustration of having a temper and being forced to restrain it. "A peace offering," he decided on impulse, and offered her the flower. "It doesn't sit well with me to have been rude to a guest."

She took the blossom, breathing in the light tang of vanilla while she struggled not to be charmed. "It would be all right to be rude if I weren't a guest?"

"You're very blunt."

"Yes." Then she smiled and tucked the flower behind her ear. "Lucky for both of us I'm not one of your subjects."

"That's something we won't argue about." He looked up at the sky, as clear and perfect a blue as could be wished for. She saw the strain, the sorrow, and was moved to reach out one more time.

"Is it only permitted for you to mourn in private, Your Highness?"

He looked at her again. There was compassion there, an offering of friendship. For so long he'd forbidden himself to accept even that much from her. But there was a weight on him, a desperately heavy one. He closed his eyes a moment and made a quick negative move with his head.

"He was closer to my father's age than mine, yet he was one of the few people I could talk with freely. Maurice had no pretensions, none of the sharp edges ambition often gives us."

"He was your friend." She came closer, and before he realized her intention, had wrapped her arms around him. "I hadn't understood he was your friend. I'm so sorry."

She was killing him by inches with her warmth, her understanding. He needed more, too much more. His hands rested lightly on her shoulders when he burned to skim them over her to bring her closer. The scent of her hair, of her skin, raced through his system, but he could do no more than stand and be assaulted.

He'd been trained to fight, to defend, to protect, yet he was defenseless. Flowers spread out, curtaining them from the palace, but there could be no haven for a man who coveted what belonged to his brother.

It hurt. He knew that beneath the title, beyond the position, he was flesh and blood, but it was rare to experience pain this sharp and sweet. It tangled with the grief and the anger until it threatened to explode in a passion he would be helpless to control. Feelings released weren't as easily ignored as feelings restrained.

He drew away abruptly and his eyes were cool and distant.

"I have a great deal to see to." The struggle with desire made his voice curt and his manner stiff. "You'll have to excuse me. I'll see if Bennett is available to join you for lunch."

And he was gone while she could only stand and stare after him.

Didn't he feel anything? Eve demanded. Couldn't he? Was he so empty of normal feelings that he hadn't been affected when her insides had turned to jelly? For a moment she'd thought... She'd been a fool to think, she told herself, but found a small stone bench because her knees had begun to tremble. A fool to think he'd felt that need, that longing, that crystal-clear rightness when their bodies had touched.

She'd meant the gesture for comfort, but the moment it had been made her world had turned upside down. She'd wanted to go on just standing there with her cheek close to his, saying nothing, feeling everything. But that wasn't what *he* had felt, she thought, and closed her eyes. She was letting her reach exceed her grasp.

Alexander of Cordina wasn't for her. She should thank God for that, because it would be terrifying if he were. A sane woman might dream of loving a prince, but that same woman would be wise to remember that her choices would diminish if she did, her privacy would end altogether and her chances for a normal life would be nil. Beyond that, the man himself was frightening enough. He wouldn't be kind unless the mood suited him, and he would never be patient. A man like Alexander expected perfection, while she respected flaws.

Yet she'd wanted him. For one mad moment, she'd forgotten

who and what he was, and had wanted to be held, to be loved by him. Would the world change somehow if she were loved by him? In the garden, with the scent of wisteria floating over her head, she thought it might. Yet she'd wanted to be the one to take that strained, weary look from around his eyes and make him smile again.

It would pass, Eve assured herself. She was too practical to indulge herself in foolish fantasies. And if it didn't pass naturally, she would push it along. She had work to concentrate on, plays to produce, a company to organize.

First thing in the morning, she'd be leaving Cordina. By the time she returned, any momentary insanity would be forgotten, and she'd be too busy to indulge in any more.

Not entirely reassured, she rose. At least her legs were solid again. She'd try to find Bennett. Nothing and no one would clear her head faster.

"I can't believe what you've done with this place, Brie." Eve sat on the wide, shady veranda and looked out at the long, rolling lawn, the paddocks, the acres of turned and tended earth. The youngest child, Dorian, sat at the bottom of the steps and fondled a new kitten.

"There are times I can't, either." Gabriella turned her head to see her elder children kicking a ball through the grass. "I'd always hoped for this without ever really believing it. I was pregnant with Kristian when we broke ground for the house, so it's five years now. When we brought him home, we brought him here."

"Only five," Eve mused. "When I look at the house, it's as though it had been here forever."

"For the children it has." The kitten let out a squeal. "Dorian, be gentle."

He looked up, a miniature of his father, and grinned wickedly, but his small, curious hands petted the kitten's fur easily. "Purrs," he said, pleased with himself.

"Yes, and if you pull his ears, he'll scratch."

"It's wonderful here in the evening." Eve watched the sun hang low over the newly planted fields. There were two servants inside, a fraction of what the palace used. The smells of cooking came through the windows, rich and homey, as suited the country. "Is this like your home in Virginia?"

"The house is older there." Gabriella took her eyes off her son long enough to watch Reeve, Alexander and Bennett circle the barn. She knew what they were talking about. The bomb in Paris was on everyone's mind. She and Reeve would talk of it later. Now she turned back to Eve. "It seems we're always fixing something—the roof, the windows. I'm afraid we don't spend as much time there as Reeve would like."

"Brie, you don't have to make conversation with me. I know you're concerned about your father and what happened this morning."

"These are uneasy times." Brie looked at her children again. They were her heart, her life, her continuing link with the real world. "We have to live each day. I know my father will do what's right for Cordina."

"And for himself?"

Gabriella's eyes, a deep, intriguing topaz, seemed to darken, but she smiled. "My father is Cordina, as Alex is. It's the first thing that has to be understood, and the most difficult. You care for him."

"For Alexander? Of course."

"Of course." Amused, Gabriella rose to pick up her son before he could crawl under the porch after the kitten. "I'm not speaking of 'of course,' Eve." She kissed Dorian on the cheek when he started to squirm, then settled him expertly on her hip. "If you ever allow your feelings for him to come to the surface, you'll find a great many pitfalls. If you need to talk, come to me." Then she laughed when Dorian tugged on her hair. "This one needs a good wash before dinner."

"Go ahead." Eve managed to smile. "I'll get the others."

But she sat there alone a few moments longer, not so sure of herself and no longer relaxed. Her feelings for Alexander were on the surface, she told herself. She cared about him as she cared about all the friends she'd made in Cordina. They were like a second family to her. Naturally, as a woman she found Alexander attractive. What woman wouldn't? And perhaps there were moments, occasionally, when the attraction was a little too intense. That was nothing to lose sleep over.

She didn't want pitfalls. She'd maneuver them if she had to. In her career. Romantically—that was a different area altogether. She wanted no complications there. Wasn't that the reason she had avoided romance for so long? Certainly there'd been men who had interested her, but...

There'd always been a "but," Eve thought. Rather than think it through too deeply, she'd always fallen back on the fact that she simply didn't have time for relationships.

The noise of the children shouting roused her. It wasn't like her to daydream, either, she reminded herself. Jogging down the steps, she headed across the lawn. The children groaned a bit, but, after she promised to help them organize a game after dinner, went in to wash up.

With them gone, the farm was so quiet she almost regretted having to find the others and go inside. She'd like to come back, Eve discovered. To sit on the porch in the evening, close her eyes and listen to nothing. It wouldn't do for every day, even every week, but now and again it would be like healing oneself.

She enjoyed the frantic pace of the life she'd chosen. Eve could go for days with little sleep and no spare time and not feel the strain. But once a year, twice a year, perhaps, to sit in the country and listen to nothing... Laughing at herself, she headed for the barn.

There were high windows to let in the evening light, and the scent of horses was strong. No stranger to barns and stables, Eve headed down the sloping concrete floor. She squinted a bit, trying to adjust her vision to the change in light.

"Bennett, I—"

But it was Alexander who turned. The figure she had seen in front of the stall was darker and slightly broader than Bennett.

"Excuse me, Your Highness." Her manner stiffened automatically. "I thought you were Bennett."

"I'm aware of that. He's with Reeve." Alexander turned back to the horse. "They've gone to look at the new bull."

"Dinner's almost ready. I told your sister—oh, she's lovely, isn't she?" Distracted by the mare, Eve stepped closer to stroke. "By the time Brie took me on a tour of the house, I'd forgotten I'd wanted to see the horses. Yes, you're lovely," Eve murmured, and ran her fingers down the mare's nose. "Does she have a name?"

"Spot," he said, and watched Eve laugh.

"What a name for a horse."

"I gave her to Adrienne as a birthday gift. She thought it was a fine name." He nuzzled the mare's ears. "We didn't have the heart to make her change it."

"She's lovely in any case. I named my first horse Sir Lancelot. I suppose I was more fanciful than Adrienne."

He lifted a hand to stroke the horse alongside hers. Their fingers trailed down but never touched. "Strange, I never saw you as the type for knights in shining armor."

"I was six, and I—" The rest was cut off as the mare gave Eve's shoulder a hard push and sent her tumbling against Alexander. "I beg your pardon, Your Highness."

"'Alex', damn it." She was in his arms as she had been that afternoon. It was too late to prepare, too late to stem the feelings that rose up in him. "My name is Alexander. Must you insist on making me feel like a position instead of a man?"

"I don't mean to. I'm sorry." It was washing over her again, that warm giddy feeling. A storm brewing. Water rising. She didn't pull away. Her intellect told her to pull away and pull away quickly. She had no business being with him like this. Alone. Listening to nothing.

His fingers crept into her hair, tangled there. Trapped. "Is it so difficult to think of me as flesh and blood?"

"No, I—yes." She couldn't get her breath. The air in the barn was suddenly sultry, stifling. "I have to find Bennett."

"Not this time." He pulled her close, damning who he was. "Say my name. Now."

There was gold in his eyes. Flecks of it. She'd never seen it before, never allowed herself to. Now, as the light grew dimmer, she could see nothing else. "Alexander." She only breathed his name. Heat flowed through him like lava.

"Again."

"Alexander," she whispered, then pressed her mouth desperately to his.

It was everything she'd wanted. Everything she'd waited for. She heard the thunder, felt the lightning, tasted the heat finally escaped. With no thought to place, to time, to position, she wrapped her arms around him and let her body absorb.

There was no cool control here, not the kind he coated himself with. She'd known it would be different, somehow she'd always known. His mouth was open, urgent, as if he had waited all of his life for this one moment. She felt his fingers dig into her flesh and trembled at the knowledge that she could be wanted so forcefully.

He forgot everything but that he was tasting her at last. She was hot, spicy, aggressive. She'd been born for the tropics, for steamy days and steamy nights. Her hair flowed down her back, through his fingers. He gripped it as though it were a line to safety, though he knew the woman was danger.

His tongue dove deeper to taste, to tease, to tempt. She was an aphrodisiac, and he was mindless with her flavor. Her hands were running over his back, kneading the muscles. He wanted them on his flesh where he could feel each stroke, each scrape.

The air in the barn carried the scent of animal. Each moment his lips were on hers, he lost a bit more of the civilized. He wanted her there, while the sun went down and the barn became dark and quiet with night.

"Eve?" The barn door creaked open, letting in a thin, dusky stream of light. "Did you get lost in here?"

Head swimming, Eve leaned back against the wall and tried to catch her breath. "No. No, Bennett, we'll be right in." She pressed a hand to her throat.

"Hurry along, will you? I'm starved." The barn door shut and the light was lost.

He'd nearly been lost, Alexander thought. Lost in her, lost to her. What right did she have to make him ache and want and need? She was standing there now, silent, her eyes dark and huge. How could a woman look so innocent when she'd nearly destroyed a man's soul?

"You change allegiance easily, Eve."

Her lips parted, first in confusion, then in surprise. The hurt came quickly, but before it could make her weak, she let in the fury. Her hand swept out and came hard against his face. The slap echoed, then silence remained.

"I'm sure you can have me deported for that at the very least." There was no hitch in her voice because she fought it down. There was only ice. "Just remember, if you decide to have me dragged away in irons, Your Highness, you deserved that. That and one hell of a lot more."

Fighting the need to run away, she turned and walked out of the barn as regally as one born to it.

He didn't go after her. His temper pushed him to, to go for her, to punish her somehow in some way. Not for the slap—that had been a small thing. But her words, the look in her eyes had carried more sting. What right did she have to make him feel remorse, to make him feel guilt, when it was she who had turned from one brother to the next without a qualm?

But he wanted her. He wanted his brother's woman with a desperation that was slowly eating him alive.

He'd always wanted her, Alexander admitted as he rammed the side of his fist into the wall. The horses whinnied nervously, then settled. He'd always fought it. He ran a hand over his face, fighting to recapture the composure that was an essential part of his position.

He would fight it still, he promised himself. Love for his brother left him no choice. But he could damn the woman, he thought grimly as he strode out of the barn. And he did.

Chapter 4

"You come and go so much these days I never get to see you."

Eve folded her oldest and most serviceable sweats in her suitcase before she glanced at her sister. "Things have been crazy. They're going to get crazier."

"You've been back from Cordina for two months, and I've talked to your phone machine more than I have to you." Chris dropped on the edge of the bed and studied the sapphire-colored silk blouse Eve packed beside the sweats. She started to suggest tissue paper, then reminded herself that baby sister had grown up.

Both sisters had dark, thick hair, but Eve's was pulled back in a braid, while Chris wore her hair chin-length and swingy. The family resemblance was there, in the shadowy cheekbones, the milky skin. It wasn't age that separated them so much as style. Chris had a polish that had come from years of dealing with the art world and those wealthy enough to indulge themselves with art. Eve had a sensuality that she wore as casually as another woman wore scent. Once it had given the elder sister a great deal of worry. Now Chris could simply marvel at it.

"Now you're going off again. I guess if I want to see my sister, I'll have to do it in Cordina."

"I was hoping you would." Eve tucked a small leather cosmetic case in the side of her Pullman. "I hate to admit it, but I'm going to need all the moral support I can drum up."

"Nervous?" Chris circled her knee with linked hands. "You?"

"Nervous. Me. I've never taken on anything this big. Four plays." She checked the contents of her briefcase for the third time. "Hauling actors, technicians, assistants, seamstresses to the Mediterranean, dumping them in front of an international audience and claiming that we represent the American theater." She pulled out a notebook, flipped through it, then stuck it back in her briefcase. "That's a hell of a boast."

"Too late for cold feet," Chris said briskly. She brushed dark, feathered bangs back from her forehead. "Besides, the Hamilton Company of Players is an American theater group, isn't it?"

"Yes, but—"

"And you'll be performing American plays, right?"

"Right. Still—"

"No stills, no buts." A trio of rings glinted on Chris's hand as she waved Eve's words away. "You *are* representing American theater. And you're going to be fantastic."

"See." Eve leaned over the suitcase to kiss Chris's cheek. "That's why I need you."

"I'll do my best to work my schedule so I can be there for the first performance. Even though I know you'll be too busy to do more than blink at me."

"I promise to do more than that. Hopefully after the first performance, I'll settle down." She folded a pair of slacks by the pleats, then smoothed them carefully into the case. "It's the preparation and paperwork that has me edgy."

"You've Daddy's knack for handling details, a fact that constantly amazes me." Still, Chris had to restrain herself from asking Eve if she had her passport. "I don't doubt you're going to pull this thing off without a hitch."

Had she packed the red suit? Eve started to check one more time, then forced herself to stop. She'd packed it. She'd packed everything. "I wish you were going with me so you could tell me that at regular intervals."

"The Bissets trust you. This wouldn't be happening otherwise. I might not be there for the next few weeks, but you'll have Brie behind you, and Alex and Bennett."

Eve zipped her case closed in one long move. "I don't think I like the idea of having Alexander behind me."

"Still rub you the wrong way?"

"At least. I never get the urge to curtsy and stick out my tongue with Brie or Ben. With him—"

"With him I wouldn't advise it," Chris said with a laugh. "He takes his position too seriously. He has to."

"I suppose."

"Eve, you can't understand what it's like to be the firstborn. I can sympathize in a way. The Hamiltons don't have a country, but as far as Daddy's concerned, we have an empire." She sighed a bit, knowing her own choices had never quite satisfied him. "Since there was no son to pass the business on to, the pressure fell to me to learn it. When the message finally got across that that wasn't going to work, the pressure changed to my marrying someone who could take over the business. Maybe that's why I've never done either."

"I guess I've never really understood."

"Why should you? It was different for you."

"I know. No pressure here." With a sigh, Eve leaned back against her dresser, taking a last look at the room she wouldn't see for months. "Of course I had to go to school and perform well, and it was expected that I'd restrain myself from doing anything to disgrace the family, but if I'd wanted to sit by the pool for the rest of my life and read magazines, it would have been fine."

"Well, you hid the fact that you had a brain very well."

"I did, didn't I?" She could smile at it now. "From myself, too. In any case, by the time it was discovered, the Hamilton Company of Players was too well established for Daddy to expect me to come into the business. So you're right. I don't really know what it is to be the heir and have little say in my own destiny. Even knowing that, it's difficult for me to feel sorry for Alexander."

"Oh, I don't know if you should. He's meant to rule as much by personality as by circumstances of birth. I just wish the two of you got along better." She took a small white daisy out of a vase on Eve's dresser, broke the stem short, then slipped it into her sister's buttonhole. "You're going to be working closely with him and it isn't going to help if one of you is always making the other snarl."

Eve took the rest of the flowers out of the vase, wrapped the dripping stems in a tissue and handed them to Chris. "I don't think we'll be working that closely."

"Isn't Alex president of the center?"

"Presidents delegate," she said, and opened her purse to make sure the airline tickets were in place. "Believe me, His Highness doesn't want to work shoulder to shoulder with me any more than I do with him." She closed her purse with a snap. "Probably less."

"Did something happen when you were out there before?" Chris rose and put a hand on Eve's hands to keep them still. "You seemed very unnerved when you came back, but I put it down to the project. Now I wonder."

"You wonder too much," Eve told her lightly. "The only thing that happened was that I reaffirmed my belief that Alexander is a pompous, arrogant boor. If this project wasn't so important I'd toss it back in his face and let him sink with it. Just thinking of him makes me angry."

"Yes, I can see that," Chris murmured, and decided to write Gabriella the first chance she had. "Well, if you're lucky, you won't have to deal with him personally."

"I'm counting on it," Eve said with such vehemence that Chris thought it wiser to phone Gabriella the moment her sister was airborne. "It looks like I'm packed. Do I still get that ride to the airport?"

"Absolutely. All we need are three strong men and a pack horse to get your luggage down to the car."

Alexander was used to the photographers and reporters, just as he was used to the bodyguards. They had all been a part of his life from birth. Though he'd forced himself not to pace in front of the observation window, he watched the plane land with a vague sense of relief. It had been twenty minutes late and his nerves had begun to stretch.

He hadn't spoken to Eve in weeks. Whatever correspondence had been necessary, whatever details had to be handled, had been seen to through her secretary to his secretary, through his assistant to her assistant. They'd had no contact at all for nearly three months, yet he remembered their few turbulent moments in Gabriella's barn as though they had happened yesterday. If he awoke in the middle of the night, it was the memory of her scent that woke him. If he caught himself daydreaming in the middle of the afternoon, it was her face that had formed in his mind.

He shouldn't think of her at all; yet it was impossible not to. How could he forget the passion and the power that had run through him when he had finally held her? How could he ignore the needs and longings that had burst through him when his mouth had been on hers? He couldn't dismiss her from his mind when, after months had passed, the sensation of her hair tangled in his fingers was so vivid and real.

Work hadn't helped, though he'd heaped it on himself in defense. Worry hadn't helped, though it was there constantly. His father had returned to Cordina. Seward had been buried. Those responsible remained unknown—or unproved. His father's life, his country's well-being, were very much in jeopardy, but he'd yet to erase one woman from his mind. A woman he had no right to desire.

But he did, and desire flared only more strongly when he saw her.

She looked a bit tired, a bit frazzled and very much in charge. Her hair had been braided and clipped on top of her head and she wore large, light-framed sunglasses. As she walked, she talked to several people around her while slipping on an oversized red jacket. The rich hue gave her a look of confidence and energy. Alexander realized she'd chosen it for exactly that purpose. She had a briefcase in one hand, a flight bag over her shoulder. In the ten, perhaps fifteen seconds since she had walked into the terminal, he'd noticed every detail.

Her lipstick had worn off, but there was a slight hint of color in her cheeks. The red jacket had gold buttons. A tendril of hair had escaped and curled in front of her left ear. There was a white daisy, a little droopy, in the buttonhole nearest her heart. It made him wonder who had given it to her, who had watched her plane leave, as he'd watched it land.

When she saw him, the slight hint of color disappeared and her shoulders tensed.

She hadn't expected him to be there. She knew, of course, that they were to be met officially, but she hadn't thought it would be

Alexander. In her mind she'd planned out the first meeting. She would be rested, refreshed after a long soak in the tub at the hotel. She would have changed into the long, glittery evening gown she'd bought precisely for that purpose. And she would treat him with mild but unmistakable coolness.

Now all she could think was that he was here, looking wonderful. He was so tall, so sturdy. His eyes were so dark, so secretive, they made her want to discover what he hid from everyone else. She wanted to smile, to throw out both hands to him and tell him how good it was to see him. Pride had her sinking into a formal curtsy.

"Your Highness."

He didn't notice the spree of flashbulbs or the crowd of reporters. He was focused on her, on the pout of her lips, on the eyes that met his more in challenge than in greeting.

"Miss Hamilton." He offered his hand. When she hesitated, *because* she hesitated, he brought it deliberately to his lips. Only he was close enough to hear her hiss of breath. "We welcome you and your troupe to Cordina."

Her hand squirmed in his and was held firm. "Thank you, Your Highness."

"Your luggage and transportation are being seen to." He smiled at her, really smiled, with an enjoyment he hadn't felt since she'd left. "Two members of my staff will accompany your troupe to their hotel and see them settled."

Her nails dug into the palms of his hand. "You're very kind."

He wondered that no one else heard the quiet insult behind the words. "It is our wish to make your stay here comfortable. If you will come with me." As the reporters closed in, he brushed them off. "Miss Hamilton will answer all your questions at tomorrow's press conference. Now she needs to rest after the long flight."

A few more persistent newsmen pursued them. Alexander simply took Eve's arm and drew her away.

"Your Highness, it might be best if I stay with the troupe."

"You have an assistant?"

"Yes, of course." She was forced to increase her pace to keep up with him.

"That's what assistants are for." There were muscles in the arm under the jacket, taut and sculpted. He wondered what they would feel like when they were tensed and ready to receive him. "You'd be wiser to get to the palace quickly and avoid being run over by the press."

"I can handle the press," she began, then stopped. "I'm going to the hotel. The dinner at the palace isn't for hours yet."

"You've no reason to go to the hotel." They were out the side entrance of the terminal as arranged by security and moving toward the waiting limo. "Your assistant and the members of my staff will see to the needs of your troupe."

"That's all very well and good," she began as she was forced to climb into the limo. "But I'd like to unpack myself, freshen up. I'm sure whatever we have to discuss can wait a few hours."

"Of course." He settled back and signaled to the driver.

"There's no reason for you to go out of your way to take me to the hotel when I could go with the rest."

"You aren't staying at the hotel. You stay at the palace. It's been arranged."

"Then unarrange it." The formality, as well as the brief moment of weakness, was gone. "I'm staying at the hotel with my people."

"It serves neither you nor me for you to stay at the hotel." Calmly he pushed a button. A compact bar slid out. "Would you like a drink?"

"No, I wouldn't like a drink, I'd like an explanation of why I'm being kidnapped."

He'd forgotten she could amuse him. After pouring himself a glass of mineral water, he smiled at her. "Strong words, Eve. My father would be interested that you find our invitation to the palace tantamount to kidnapping."

"This has nothing to do with your father."

"It is at his request that you stay with us. The security at the hotel has, of course, been strengthened."

"Why?"

"These are uneasy times."

There was a ripple of anxiety, but it was for him, not her, not her company. "So your sister said to me a few months ago. Your Highness, if you or your father feels there's danger, I want to be with my people."

"I understand." He set down his glass. "The hotel is very secure, Eve, and we don't feel your troupe is in any danger. My father feels, and I agree, that you, because of your personal connection with our family, are another matter. We would prefer it if you'd stay in the palace if for no other reason than to avoid the reporters who will clog the hotel lobby for the next few weeks. Or you can simply accept the invitation because my father is fond of you.''

"You put it so that if I do what I choose I'm ungracious.''

"Yes.'' He smiled again and picked up his glass.

"Very well, I accept your invitation. And I'll have some diet soda—something with caffeine. A lot of caffeine.''

"You're tired from the flight.''

"From the flight,'' she agreed as he added ice to a glass. "From the weeks before the flight. I think I've been averaging about five hours a night between preproduction meetings, auditions, dry rehearsing and paperwork. I didn't realize all my people would have to go through the security clearances.'' Absently she fiddled with the daisy. He watched her fingers stroke the white petals. "Then when I hired two more, we had to rush them through. I hope it's worth it.'' She sipped and waited for the caffeine to jolt her system back to life.

"Do you doubt it?''

"Only several times a day.'' Her feet had eased out of the toes of her shoes without her being conscious of it. Her shoulders were relaxed. Heavy, her eyes drooped down to sensuous slits. "I am pleased with the new people. She's an ingenue, straight out of college, with a lot of potential. I'm going to have her understudy the second lead in the Neil Simon play. And Russ Talbot's a real pro. He's done a lot of little theater and off-off-Broadway stuff. We're lucky to have him. He's cast as Brick for *Cat on a Hot Tin Roof*. That's going to be our first production.''

She drank again and hoped she wasn't making a mistake there. It was such a steamy play, such a passionate one. For weeks she'd toyed with doing a comedy first, to give both the audience and the troupe a running start. Instinct had her opting for Tennessee Williams as an opener.

"I sent copies of all the scripts with the staging. I assume your assistant has read them all.''

"They've been read,'' he said simply. By him. There was no

need for her to know now just how closely he intended to work with her. "They've been approved—tentatively."

"Tentatively." That had been something that had had her back up for weeks. "I find it difficult to understand why you feel it necessary to have two alternates. From an artistic angle and a practical one, it's going to be very difficult if we have to switch things around now. We open in three weeks."

"Time enough to replace one of your productions if we find it unsuitable."

"Unsuitable? Just who makes that kind of judgment? You?"

He studied his mineral water and said nothing for a moment. There was no one, no one outside his immediate family, who would have dared use that tone with him. Deciding on patience, Alexander wondered if Americans were audacious as a rule, or if she were simply an exception.

"In my capacity as president of the center, the final judgment would be mine."

"Swell." She chugged down more soda. "Just swell. Prince or president, you don't make my life easy. I selected these four because—"

"I'll listen to your reasons tomorrow. We have a meeting scheduled for—nine, I believe. You'll meet Cornelius Manderson, who manages the center. My sister will also be there."

"I can be grateful to have at least one reasonable person around."

"Eve, you go on the defensive before it's necessary."

"Boy Scout motto."

"Pardon?"

"Be prepared," she said, and was amused enough to smile. "All right, then, I won't pick a fight yet. Tomorrow's another matter. I'm ready to go to the wall on this, Your Highness, and you're going to find I'm not easy to beat."

"I'm aware of that already." And he was already looking forward to it. "Perhaps it would be best if we agreed to keep our personal relationship separate from our work at the center."

She held her glass in her hand and tried to concentrate on the palace as they rode through the gates. It always gave her a sense of peace and security. But not this time. She shifted a bit in her seat. "We haven't got a personal relationship."

"No?"

When she turned her head she was surprised and a bit unnerved to see he was amused. She wasn't going to find his smiles as easy to deal with as his scowls. "No. What happened the last time was..." Finding no definition available, she shrugged the attempt away.

"Was unfortunate," he finished, then took her empty glass and set it down. "Unfortunate that it occurred in that manner and ended poorly. Shall I apologize?"

"No, I'd rather you didn't."

"Why?"

"Because then I'd have to accept your apology." Taking a deep breath, she faced him directly. "If I don't accept it, I'll stay annoyed with you and it won't happen again."

"There's a flaw in your logic, Eve." He continued to sit after the car stopped at the palace steps. Even when the driver opened the door, Alexander stayed where he was, watching her, compelling her to watch him. "You are most often annoyed with me, yet it did happen. But for the sake of your argument, I won't apologize."

He stepped from the car and offered his hand, leaving her no choice but to accept it. "Somehow I think I was outmaneuvered," she muttered.

"You were." Then he smiled, abruptly charming, and led her up the palace steps.

She matched her steps with his, but for the first time found herself hesitating to pass through the large ornate doors of the palace. "I never considered you much of a game player, Your Highness."

"On the contrary, I enjoy games very much."

"Chess, fencing, polo." She moved her shoulders restlessly. "Not people games."

Her scent was the same, the same as it had been the last time he'd seen her, touched her. The same scent that had awoken him in the middle of the night when she'd been thousands of miles away. "You called me a politician. What is politics but a people game?" The heavy door slid open soundlessly. Eve sent him a long, cautious look before she stepped inside.

"My father wishes to see you. I'll take you to him. Your bags should arrive shortly."

"All right." She started up the steps beside him. "The prince is well?"

"Yes." He wouldn't elaborate on her unspoken question. The Paris incident wasn't a closed book, but one he thought best to leave untouched.

Feeling the snub, Eve started the climb from the second to the third floor in silence. "You don't want me to speak of what happened in Paris to your father."

"There's no reason for you to speak of it."

"Of course not." The words came out with the brittleness of hurt. "It was nothing to me, after all." She swung up the last of the stairs and down the hall ahead of him, only to be forced to wait at the closed door that led to Prince Armand's office.

"Your emotions remain too close to the surface," Alexander noted. He'd recognized this, even envied it, as a man who'd been forced year after year to keep his own buried. "That wasn't said to offend you."

"No, you don't have to deliberately try to offend."

"Touché," he said with something close to a sigh.

"I don't want to cross swords with you. I don't expect you to include me in your family feelings." She looked away and didn't see his gaze come back to search her face. "The sad thing is you've never understood that I care very much." She folded her arms as if to distance herself when he stared at her. "Will you knock?"

He didn't. A man in his position could afford few mistakes. When he made one, it was best to admit it quickly. "He'll look strained, a bit thinner. The incident in Paris weighs on him." Alexander looked at the closed door, recognizing it for a barricade, one that someday he would have to use. "He doesn't sleep well."

"What can I do?"

God, could it be so simple for her? The words made him want to rest his brow against hers, only for a moment. Rest, be comforted, be eased. But it could never be so simple for him. "You're doing it," he said briefly, and knocked.

"Entrez."

"Father." Alexander opened the door, then stepped to the side. "I've brought you a gift."

Prince Armand rose from his desk. He was a sternly handsome man, straight and lean. When Eve had first met him, his hair had been threaded with gray. Now it was steely, like his eyes, like his body. Seeing her, he smiled, and the rigid lines softened.

"A lovely one." He came around the desk to her in a gesture of friendship she knew wasn't given to many. As she curtsied, he caught both her hands. His were strong. If age sat lightly on him, responsibility didn't. She saw the signs of strain, of sleeplessness, and forgot protocol. Rising on her toes, she kissed both his cheeks.

"It's good to be back, Your Highness."

"It's you who are good for us. Alexander, you didn't tell me she'd grown more beautiful."

"He doesn't notice," she said with a careless glance over her shoulder.

"On the contrary. I simply didn't think it necessary to explain what my father would see for himself."

"A born diplomat," Armand said, and laughed. "Alex, ring for tea, please. We'll keep Eve to ourselves for a little while before we have to share her with the rest of Cordina. So, the young girl is now an important producer." He led her to a chair. "You've come to entertain us."

"I hope so."

"My son tells me the center is fortunate to have your company. Your reputation in America is growing, and as your first international host, we're honored."

Eve smiled. "Bennett loves to flatter."

"True enough." Armand drew out a cigarette. "But in this case it was Alex."

"Alex?" Caught off guard, she turned her head to stare as Alexander took a chair beside her.

"Eve doesn't expect flattery from me, Father." He drew out his lighter and flicked it at the end of his father's cigarette. "She's more prepared to dodge a blow."

"Well, when you've been doing it for seven years, it gets to be—" She caught herself, bit her tongue smartly, then turned back to the prince. "I beg your pardon, Your Highness."

"There's no need. I'm used to squabbling children. Here's our tea. Will you pour, Eve?"

"Yes, of course."

Allowing himself the luxury of relaxing, Armand sat back as the tray was set beside Eve. "Alexander tells me you've chosen four interesting plays. The first is a rather passionate and—what is the word you used, Alex?"

"Steamy," he said, and smiled at Eve's quick look.

"Yes, a steamy story set in your American South. It deals with a family?"

"Yes, Your Highness." She handed him his tea. "A power struggle within a family, both for money and for love. A rich, dominating father, two brothers, one the black sheep, the other a weakling, and their manipulative wives. It's really a story of needs and disillusionment as much as passion."

"A story that holds true in any culture."

"I'm counting on it." She handed Alexander his tea but avoided looking at him. "The plays I've chosen all lean heavily on emotion, though the two comedies accent the lighter side. My troupe's looking forward to working here. I want to thank you for giving us the opportunity."

"It was Alex who did the work and dealt with the board of directors for the center. From some of his comments, I take it they were not as open-minded as he would have liked."

Alexander's strong fingers curled around the delicate china handle. "They simply needed some persuasion."

She couldn't imagine Alexander going to bat for her. At the first flutter of pleasure, Eve pulled herself back. He'd done it for himself—more accurately, for Cordina. "However it was arranged, I'm grateful. We won't disappoint you."

"I'm sure you won't. I'm looking forward to meeting the rest of your company this evening."

Understanding this to be a gentle dismissal, Eve rose. "If you'll excuse me, then, I'd better get unpacked." Because her nature demanded it, she kissed Armand's cheek again. "It really is good to be back."

Though her bags weren't yet delivered, Eve's room was ready, scented with fresh flowers, windows open to the sea. Slipping out of her shoes, then her jacket, she pushed the billowing curtains aside.

The view took her breath away. It was the same every time— the initial disbelief that anything could be that beautiful, then the dizzying pleasure that it was real. The gardens were far below, vivid, delightful in color. Whoever had planted them, whoever tended them, appreciated the need for flowers to grow as they pleased, rather than in neat, orderly rows. The result was dreamlike rather than perfection.

Beyond the garden was the seawall, worn smooth by centuries of wind and salt. The cliff fell off sharply then, sheerly vertical with juts and mounds of rocks for seabirds to nest in. Then there was the sea itself, dark, deep, radiantly blue. Boats glided across it now.

She saw a boat with red sails racing with the wind, and a pleasure yacht so white it hurt the eyes. Someone was waterskiing. She squinted to see if it was a man or woman, but distance made the figure just a figure skimming along the searing blue surface. Enchanted, she knelt on the window seat, propped her chin on her hands and continued to watch.

The knock at her door meant her bags had arrived. Half dreaming, Eve stayed where she was. *"Entrez, s'il vous plâit."*

"It's been arranged for you to have a maid."

Alexander's voice had her jolting straight and nearly losing her balance on the window seat. "Oh, thank you, but it really isn't necessary."

Alexander murmured to the servant to set her bags down and leave. "She can deal with your unpacking at your convenience. Her name is Collette. She won't disturb you until you ring."

"Thank you."

"You look tired." Without the jacket, she looked more fragile, more approachable, almost as if she were a woman he could sit with, talk with, be only a man with. He wanted to smooth the hair from her brow, gently, even tenderly. His hands curled at his sides. "You might want to rest first."

"No, I'm not tired really. I've just been hypnotizing myself with the view."

She waited for him to leave, but instead he crossed to her, drawing the curtains aside a little more. "I have the same view from my window."

"I suppose you're used to it, then. I don't think I'd ever be."

"Early, just after dawn, the fishing boats go out." He rested his hand on the sill beside hers. Eve's gaze was drawn to it, to the long, tanned fingers, the wide back and the ring that stated who and what he was. "They look so fragile, yet they go out day after day."

His hands fascinated her. They had touched her once, not gently but potently. There was strength in them a woman could rely on, as well as a strength to be feared. She wondered why at the moment she should feel only the first.

"I've never been a terribly good sailor myself, but I like to watch. When I was young, my father had a sailboat. I was forever tangling up the lines or getting bashed by the boom. Eventually he got tired of it and bought a powerboat. I had a shot at water-skiing."

"Did you have better luck?" he asked.

"Some." She turned again and searched for the sexless skier. As she did, he or she took an impressive spill. Laughing, Eve leaned back on her heels. "That was about as good as I got, too."

"So you prefer to swim."

"I prefer to have control. That's why I took up karate. I like making my own moves rather than being at the mercy of the wind or a towline or whatever."

"Not at the mercy of the wind," Alexander corrected. "You work with or outwit the wind."

"Maybe you do."

"I could teach you."

Surprised—no, stunned—she looked up at him. It had been said casually, but she'd never known him to do anything casually. She could imagine herself sailing with him, the sun, the wind, his body gleaming in the shimmering light. She could imagine it too well. "Thank you, but my father already judged me hopeless."

"You were a child." The breeze ruffled her hair against his arm. "You're not a child now."

"No." Unnerved and feeling foolish because of it, she looked out the window again. "But I doubt either of us will have much time for sailing lessons while I'm here. Work starts tomorrow."

"And today?"

Her heart was pounding in her throat. It was ridiculous. She wasn't subject to flights of fancy and wide swings of emotion. Meet it head on, Eve advised herself. Meet it head on and push it aside. She turned again and looked at him. "I don't know what you want. I don't—" When he reached down to brush the hair from her cheek, the words simply slid away.

"I think you do."

"No." She managed to find the strength to shake her head. "That's impossible."

"So I've told myself." His fingers tightened on her hair. His eyes weren't so secretive now. In them she saw need, and felt the longing grow in herself to fulfill it. "It becomes more difficult to accept."

"Your Highness." Her hand flew to his wrist when he framed her face. "Alex, please, this isn't right."

"The hell with right."

He took her then, mouth, soul and heart, as the salt-scented breeze billowed at the curtains. Her hands were still at his wrists, her fingers clamping harder and harder, whether in denial or acceptance neither of them knew.

He'd wanted, needed, yearned for the passion and spirit that were so much a part of her. He'd craved the softness and sweetness that offset the rest. If it was wrong, if it was impossible, he'd fight his way through the obstacles. He'd known, the moment he'd seen her again, that he had no choice.

How could she deny what was happening to her? She wasn't a woman who lied to herself, who refused to see her own flaws. Desire, hot and liquid, ruled her thoughts. And it was Alexander, heir to the throne, whom she wanted. Desperately, she realized. Uncontrollably. Even as she tried to reason it out, her body was pulsing with more needs.

To be his, she thought as she released his wrist to comb her fingers through his hair. To be his would be everything.

He was edging toward madness. She was so smooth, so warm. The fire was licking at him, what was his, what had come from her. If he didn't bank it now, it would overwhelm both of them. He couldn't allow it to happen this way, not now, not here. Alexander drew her away, swore, then kissed her again until she went limp in his arms.

"You'll have to choose." His voice wasn't steady, but he drew her head back and kept his eyes on hers. "And you'll have to choose soon."

She ran a hand that trembled over her face. "I don't understand."

"I don't intend to lose." He had her hair in his hand, holding her still. She wouldn't have moved in any case. His eyes would have held her. "Understand that. I didn't apologize for before, and I won't apologize now."

He released her, then strode to the door and out.

Alone, Eve eased herself down on the seat like a woman who'd had too much sun or wine. Perhaps she'd had both somehow. His kiss had been both hot and potent. She had to think. With a shaky sigh, she pressed her fingers to her eyes. The trouble was, she didn't know where to start.

Chapter 5

Eve felt secure in the theater, satisfied with the office that had been prepared for her and grateful for the hours per day she would have away from the palace. And Alexander.

She was a professional woman. A businesswoman with her career in full swing and the ultimate success just at the tip of her fingers. Her biggest challenge to date was spread out before her. Nearly a hundred people were depending on her to make decisions, give orders and do things right. She couldn't afford to spend her nights tossing and turning, trying to figure out a man. She couldn't daydream about him when there were a million things to be done.

But when he'd kissed her in front of the window with the scent of the sea creeping in around them, it had been no less devastating, no less illuminating than the first time. Need, both sharply physical and deeply emotional, had run through her. Not need for a man, for a lover, for a companion, but for Alexander. She'd wanted him—to make love with her there near the window while the sky and the sea were still a perfect blue.

It wouldn't have been lovemaking, Eve reminded herself as she pressed fingers against her tired eyes. It would have been sex, plain and simple. She didn't want that, didn't need it, and she wasn't going to think of it anymore.

It was barely two on her first full day in Cordina. Her morning meeting had gone well enough. Alexander had been more his familiar self—distant, businesslike and exacting. That was a man she knew how to deal with. The man who had kissed her the afternoon before, the man who had made her feel weak and strong and desperate all at once—she didn't know how to deal with him.

He'd been the perfect host to her company the evening before. His charm was on the formal side, but her people had been impressed. In fact, she mused, more than one of her female players had been overly impressed. She'd have to keep her eyes open. It wouldn't do to have anyone distracted over the next few weeks. Including her. With that in mind she began checking and cross-checking her lists.

The glamour of theater, she thought wryly as she rubbed the back of her neck. Just how many tubes of makeup had they shipped—and where the hell were they? Then there was the crate of cable that had left Houston just fine, but had never made the transfer in New York. If the airport didn't call her back by four, she was going to—

"Yes, come in." Harried, Eve barely glanced up. "Yes, Russ. There can't be a problem already can there? But wait." She held up a hand before he could speak. "You and the rest of the troupe aren't due in until tomorrow, right?"

"Yes to both questions. There is a problem already and I'm not due in—but I couldn't stay away." He was a young-looking thirty with a well-built body and a lantern jaw. Eve had liked his looks from the beginning, but had still put him through three readings before she'd signed him. The wavy blond hair and the blue eyes were a plus, but she looked for substance. She'd never have cast him as Brick if she hadn't found it. When he perched on the edge of her desk, she leaned back and grimaced.

"Tell me the problem first."

"Lighting director's having an artistic difference with a twenty K spotlight. Nobody can put his hands on the crate of extra bulbs."

"I'm surprised anyone can put his hands on anything now. Okay, I'll see to it in a minute. Tell me why you're not out soaking up the sun while you have the chance." She smiled and tucked a pencil behind her ear. "Hasn't anyone warned you what a slave driver I am? You show up at the theater, you go to work."

"That's what I'm counting on." His voice was deep and resonant. Still, she wanted him to practice the lazy drawl of his character until it was second nature. "Look, I don't want to sound green, but this place..." He lifted his palms a bit dramatically and took in more than her office. "It's amazing. Being here's amazing. I can soak up sun anytime. If I can't rehearse, I can unpack crates."

"You don't sound green, you sound psychotic." With a laugh, she stood. "And I know just what you mean. Crates, it is. God knows we've got plenty of them. Now why don't we—"

Her door swung open again, this time without a knock. Bennett grinned at her. "They told me I'd find you locked in here and snarling."

"I'm not snarling. Yet." She got up immediately and opened her arms for a hug. "Prince Bennett, Russ Talbot."

Russ hesitated between offering a hand, bowing or standing still. "I'm never sure how to greet princes."

"We say hello," Bennett told him. "I hated missing the dinner last night and meeting your troupe."

"What you missed was seeing how many pretty actresses you could flirt with." Eve picked up her clipboard.

"There's that." He shot his grin at Russ. "Are there many?"

"Enough."

"I knew I could count on Eve. In any case, I've come to take you away from all this."

"Fine." She looked up from her notations. "Come back in two hours."

"Two hours?"

"Better make it three," she corrected after a glance at her clipboard.

"Eve, you'll wear yourself out."

"Wear myself out?" Laughing, she nudged him out into the hall with her. "I haven't even started yet. I could use the lift, though, if it's not putting you out. Say—" She looked at her watch "—five-thirty?"

"All right if—"

"Unless you'd like to stay. We're about to uncrate boxes."

"I'll be back." He gave her a quick kiss before he started down the corridor. "Nice meeting you, Talbot."

"That's the first time I've ever seen royalty get the bum's rush."

Eve sent Russ a smile. "Much as I love him, he'd be in the way."

"Not much like his brother," Russ commented.

"Ben?" Eve shook her head as they walked in the opposite direction. "No. No, he's not."

"Gets a lot of press."

She couldn't prevent the chuckle. "Bennett would tell you it's all true."

"Is it?"

She glanced at him. Her voice cooled a bit. "Possibly."

"Sorry." Russ dipped his hands into his pockets. "I didn't mean to pry. It's just—well, it's interesting, and I'm as susceptible as anyone. It's weird you being so tight with them. We didn't have many royal highnesses in Montclair, New Jersey."

"They're just people." She stopped at the door to one of the storerooms. "No, of course they're not. But they are people, and nice ones. You'll see that for yourself in the next few weeks."

Then she opened the door, stepped back and moaned. Russ peered in around her shoulder at the stacks of trunks and crates. "Looks like we could use some help."

"You go call out the marines," Eve told him, and pushed up her sleeves. "I'll get started."

Within three hours Eve had the beginnings of order and a long list of things to be done. With the help of Russ and a couple of stagehands, the crates were uncarted or stacked for storage until their contents were needed. She worked methodically, as was her style, and lifted and grunted as much as the men who worked with her. After twenty minutes, Russ had stopped telling her not to lift that, not to shove this. She was, he'd discovered, as strong as the rest of them.

By five she was sweaty, smudged and ruffled, but far from displeased.

"Russ, go home." She leaned against one of the crates and wished fleetingly for something long and cool.

"What about you?"

"I've nearly done all I can for the moment, and I don't want my actors too exhausted to rehearse." She wiped her forehead with the back of her hand. "You've been a big help. The rest of this is really up to me and the crew."

He dried the sweat on his face with a sleeve before giving her a look of amused admiration. "I don't know many producers who get their hands dirty."

Eve turned her palms up and wrinkled her nose at the smears of dust. "Apparently this producer does. Ten o'clock call tomorrow. Be fresh."

"Yes, ma'am. Any messages for the rest of the troupe?"

"The same. Tell them to enjoy the evening, but any hangovers tomorrow morning won't be sympathized with."

"I'll keep that in mind. Don't work too hard."

She glanced around as he left the storeroom. "Tell me about it." Hands on hips, she decided she'd done about all the damage she could do for one day. Putting her back into it, she scooted one last box of bulbs into a corner. At the sound behind her, she dug into the pockets of her sweats and pulled out a set of keys.

"Give these to Gary, will you? He'll need to get in here first thing tomorrow." Without looking, she chucked the keys.

"I'd be happy to oblige if I knew who Gary was and where to find him."

"Oh." Still stooped, she looked up at Alex. His light sweater and slacks were spotless, his hair unruffled and his shoes shined. She felt like a dustrag. "I thought you were one of the stage-hands."

"No." When she straightened, he tossed the keys back to her. "Eve, have you been in here shoving at these crates?"

"I've been unpacking and, uh…" She linked her filthy hands behind her back. "Organizing."

"And moving things entirely too heavy to be moved by a woman."

"Now just a minute—"

"Let's say too heavy to be moved by someone of your size and build."

The rephrasing mollified only because her back ached. "I had help."

"Apparently not enough. If you need more, you've only to ask."

"We can manage, thanks. The worst of it's done." She attempted to clean off her hands on the front of her sweats. "I didn't realize you were coming in today. Was there something we left out this morning?"

He came farther into the room. She stood with her hands behind her back and her back against a crate. "We have no business to discuss."

"Well, then." She caught herself moistening her lips. "I'd better get these keys to Gary and clean up before Bennett gets here." She started forward, but he stood in her way.

"Bennett was detained. I've come to take you home."

"That wasn't necessary." She moved to the side as he stepped forward. "I told Ben I'd take the lift if it was convenient." He moved again, and she evaded. "I don't expect to be driven around while I'm here. Renting a car's simple enough."

She smelled like hot honey baked in the sun and waiting to be sampled. "Do you object to driving with me?"

"No, of course not." She rapped her heel on a crate, then stood her ground. "You're stalking me."

"It would seem so." He ran a fingertip down her cheek, and was pleased to detect the slightest tremor. "You're filthy."

"Yes. I do have to clean up, so if you don't want to wait, I can catch a ride with— A cab. I can take a cab."

"I can wait. It's amazing that you manage to be beautiful even under all that dirt. Beautiful." He rubbed his thumb over her lips. "Desirable."

"Alex. Alexander. I don't know why you're... It's difficult to understand why..."

His hand curled loosely around her neck.

"I wish you wouldn't."

"Wouldn't what?"

"Try to seduce me."

"I don't intend merely to try."

"This is ridiculous." But when she tried to shift away, he blocked her again. "You don't even like me, really, and I—well I've always..." His eyes were so dark, dark, amused and as hypnotic as the view from her window. "That is, I've always thought that..."

"I don't recall that you stuttered before."

"I didn't. I don't." She passed a hand through her hair. "You're making me very nervous."

"I know. It's amazingly rewarding."

"Well, I don't like it. No," she said weakly, when he lowered his mouth to hers. This time it wasn't wild or desperate, but soft and teasing. The hand she had lifted in protest fell limply to her side. She didn't reach for him, didn't touch him, but stood swaying...floating...drowning.

The triumph should have moved through him. She was his now; he could feel it in the way her head fell back, her lips parted. At that moment she was completely open to him, his to fill with whatever needs moved through him. But instead of triumph came an ache, a need to stroke, protect, soothe. Promise. He wanted the thrill, and was left with the thirst.

"Go wash your face," he murmured, and stepped aside.

Eve was out of the room faster than dignity allowed.

Eve took a hard look at herself in the mirror of the rest room backstage. She was making a fool of herself—and it was going to stop. For whatever reason of his own, Alexander had decided to play games. That didn't mean she had to go along with it. He was making her feel foolish. Look foolish. She could tolerate a great deal, but not that. Pride was vital to her, pride in who she was, in what she'd made of and for herself. She wasn't going to turn into a babbling idiot because Alexander had suddenly decided she'd make a good playmate. Or bedmate.

That made her swallow quickly. Years before she'd hoped for his attention, even in her girlish way dreamed of it. She'd been stung by his disinterest, galled by his silent disapproval. She'd gotten over all of that. She scrubbed at her hands for the third time.

Maybe the problem was that she'd begun to think of Alexander as a person again, as a man. Things would be better if she thought of him as His Royal Highness—a title, aloof, lofty and a bit cold.

It didn't come easy when she could still feel the way the warmth had transferred from his lips to hers.

Why was he doing this? Eve stuffed her brush back into her bag. It was so totally out of character. For both of them, she realized. If she had written a play with Alexander as the lead, she

would never have staged a scene like the one that had just occurred. No one would believe it.

So why didn't she ask him? Before she could laugh the idea
off, it began to make sense. She was a blunt, no-nonsense woman;
Alexander was a cautious diplomat. She'd put the question to him
flat out, then watch him dangle for words. Pleased with the plan,
she swung back into the corridor.

"An improvement," Alexander said easily, and took her arm
before she could evade it.

"Thank you. I think we should talk."

"Good idea." He pushed the stage door open and led her outside. "We can take a drive before we go home."

"It's not necessary. It won't take long."

"I'm sure it's more than necessary for you to have some fresh
air after being cooped up all day." When he opened the door of
the steel-gray Mercedes, Eve stopped.

"What's this?"

"My car."

"But there's no driver."

"Would you like to see my license?" When she continued to
hesitate, he smiled. "Eve, you're not afraid of being alone with
me, are you?"

"Of course not." She tried to sound indignant, but looked restlessly over her shoulder. Two bodyguards, blank faced and burly,
stood at the car behind them. "Besides, you're never really
alone."

Alexander followed the direction of her gaze. The quick sensation of restraint didn't reach his eyes. "Unfortunately some
things other than fresh air are necessary."

What he felt didn't reach his eyes, didn't show on his face, but
she thought she caught a trace of it in his voice. "You hate it."

He glanced back, surprised and more than a little wary that
she'd seen what he so carefully tried to hide. "It's a waste of time
to hate the necessary." Alexander gestured her into the car, shut
the door behind her and rounded the hood. He didn't glance at or
acknowledge the guards. "Your seat belt," he murmured as he
started the engine.

"What? Oh." Eve stopped rehearsing her speech and pulled the
harness into place. "I've always enjoyed driving around Cordina,"

she began. Be friendly, she advised herself. Be casual, then zero in when he least expects it. "It's such a lovely city. No skyscrapers, no steel-and-glass boxes."

"We continue to fight certain kinds of progress." He eased into the light traffic. "Several times hotel chains have lobbied to build resorts. The advantages are there, of course, an increase in employment, tourism."

"No." She shook her head as she studied the town. "It could never be worth it."

"This from the daughter of a builder?"

"What Daddy's built and where he's built it has generally been a good thing. Houston's...Houston's different. A city like that needs to be developed."

"There are some on the council who would argue that Cordina needs to be developed."

"They're wrong." She turned to him. "Obviously your father feels the same way. What about you? When your turn comes, will you let them dig into the rock?"

"No." He turned away from the city and toward the sea. "Some things are meant to grow naturally. The palace is the highest building in the country. As long as a Bisset lives there, it will remain so."

"Is that ego?"

"That is heritage."

And she could accept it. "We're so different," she said, half to herself. "You speak of heritage and you mean centuries of responsibility and tradition. When I think of it, I think of my father's business and the headache someone's going to be saddled with one day. Or I think of my mother's Fabergé bowl. Heritage for me, and I suppose for most Americans, is tangible. You can hold it in your hand. For you it's more nebulous, but a hundred times more binding."

For several moments he said nothing. She couldn't know how deeply her words, her empathy had affected him. "You understand better than I expected."

She glanced at him quickly, then as quickly away. She couldn't be moved. She didn't dare allow it. "Why are you doing this?"

"Doing what?"

"Driving me along the beach, coming to the theater? Why did you kiss me that way?"

"Which way?"

She might have laughed if she hadn't felt so adrift. "Any way. Why did you kiss me at all?"

He considered as he looked for a private spot by the seawall. "The most obvious answer is that I wanted to."

"That's not obvious at all. You never wanted to before."

"Women aren't as perceptive as they would like the world to think." He stopped the car, shut off the engine and slipped the keys into his pocket. "I've wanted to since the first time I saw you. Would you like to walk?"

While she sat stunned, he got out and came around to her door. "You have to unhook your seat belt."

"That's not true."

"I'm afraid it's difficult to walk on the beach if you're strapped to a car seat."

Eve fumbled with the lock, then sprang out of the car. "I meant what you just said wasn't true. You hardly even looked at me, and when you did it was to scowl."

"I looked at you a great deal." He took her hand and began to walk toward the sand. Her fingers were stiff in his, resisting. He ignored the feeling. It was easier for him when she held herself back, challenged him to outmaneuver. Her one moment of absolute surrender had terrified him. "I prefer the beach in the evening, when the tourists have gone in to change for dinner."

"That's absurd."

His smile was friendly, and sweeter than she could ever remember seeing it. "It's absurd to prefer a quiet beach?"

"I wish you'd stop twisting things around that way." Eve shook her hand free and stepped back a few paces. "I don't know what kind of game you're playing."

"What kind would you like?" He stood where he was, pleased, even relieved to see her confusion. It made it easier somehow to get closer without taking a step.

"Alexander, you did not spend a great deal of time looking at me. I know because—" She cut herself off, appalled that she'd been about to admit how she'd mooned over him.

"Because?"

"I just know, that's all." She brushed the subject away with the back of her hand and started toward the water. "I don't understand why you've suddenly decided you find me attractive or available or whatever."

"Finding you attractive is not sudden." He put a hand on her shoulder and with the slightest of pressure made her turn. The sun would be setting soon. She could see it behind him, spreading golden light. The sand beneath her feet was white and cool, but she discovered as she stared up at him that it was far from solid. "Whether you are available or not no longer matters. I want you." He paused, letting his hand slide over her shoulder to her nape. "I find that matters a great deal more."

She shuddered and crossed her arms over her chest. Her eyes were as blue as the sea now, but more, much more turbulent. "And because you're a prince you can have whatever you want."

The breeze over the sea blew her hair around his fingers. He forgot the beach, the guards, the sun that had yet to set. "Because I'm a prince it's more difficult for me to have what I want. Particularly when what I want is a woman."

"An American woman." Her breath came quickly, erratically. It would have been so easy not to question, but to accept. She wanted to accept, to move into his arms, maybe into his heart. Discovering that was what she wanted most changed everything and compounded the questions. "An American woman who makes her living in the theater. No rank, no pedigree. Not as suitable for an affair as another aristocrat, another European."

"No." He said it simply and watched the hurt come into her eyes. But he wouldn't lie. "To have my name linked with yours wouldn't be suitable to certain members of the council, certain high officials. It's more agreeable when I socialize with a woman of title or with an ancestry."

"I see." She brought her hand up and removed his from her neck. "So it would be more...tactful if I agreed to a clandestine affair."

Anger transformed his face into hard, unyielding lines. No one seeing him now would believe he could smile so sweetly. "I don't believe I asked you to be tactful."

"No, you hadn't gotten to it yet." She was going to cry. The knowledge stunned her, humiliated her. Humiliation snapped her back straight and kept her eyes dry—so dry they hurt. "Well, thanks for the offer, Your Highness, but I'm not interested. When I sleep with a man, I do so with no shame. When I have a relationship with a man, it's in the open."

"I'm aware of that."

She'd started to storm away, but his words brought her up short. "Just what do you mean?"

"You've been very open about your relationship with my brother." There was no smile now, or any sign of temper. His eyes were flat and dark. "Apparently you've had no shame there, either."

Confusion came first, then a glimmer, then a flash of insight. Because it was safer than being hurt, Eve let her fury take her. "So that's what this is all about. Some sibling rivalry, some curiosity about your brother's taste. What did you think, Alex, he'd had his turn, now you wanted to see what all the fuss was about?"

He stood where he was, knowing he didn't dare step toward her. "Be careful."

She was beyond care, but not yet beyond words. "The hell with you. You may be an aristocrat, a prince, a ruler, but underneath you're as much a fool as any other man and I won't stand here and explain or justify my relationship with Bennett to a fool. You could take lessons from him, Alex. He has a heart and a genuine affection for women. He doesn't consider them trophies to be passed around."

"Are you finished?"

"Oh, more than. I suggest you speak to Bennett, Your Highness, if you want to find out my...pros and cons. I'm sure you'd be fascinated."

"What I was feeling for you had nothing to do with Bennett—and everything to do with him. I'll drive you back."

He started toward the car. The two guards who'd kept at a discreet distance climbed into theirs.

Chapter 6

"Ethel, I want another white slip for *Cat*." Clipboard in hand, Eve was going through the costumes, one item at a time, with her wardrobe mistress.

"White slip. Size thirty-four."

"Not too low cut. I want some subtlety."

"A subtle white slip. Size thirty-four."

Eve chuckled, but continued to go through the wardrobe for the first production. "Let's keep within budget. Make it nylon—as long as it looks like silk."

"She wants a miracle."

"Always. Oh, and let out Big Daddy's jackets, say, an inch and a half. I'm going to want Jared padded a bit more."

Ethel chewed her stick of peppermint gum while she noted down instructions. She'd been in wardrobe for twenty-two years. She could, with forty-five minutes notice, make a silk purse out of a sow's ear. "If the cast keeps eating the way they did the other night, you won't need any padding."

"I intend to keep an eye on that, too."

"Never doubted it." Ethel brought her half glasses down farther on her nose and looked at Eve over the straight edge. "Somebody ought to be keeping an eye on you. You give up sleeping?"

"Looks that way." She fingered two children's costumes.

"These may have to be altered. I audition kids tomorrow. Let's pray we can find two who can play nasty little monsters."

"I have a couple I'm willing to lend out." Gabriella stepped into the wardrobe room.

"Brie, I was hoping you'd make it by." Tucking the clipboard under one arm, Eve embraced her with the other.

"I'd have made it by yesterday, but I had four dentist appointments, two haircuts and a meeting with an impossibly tight-pursed budget committee."

"Just another day of glamour and leisure. Princess Gabriella, may I present Miss Ethel Cohen, my miracle worker with needle and thread."

Ethel dropped into an awkward curtsy. "Your Majesty."

"We settle for 'Your Highness' in Cordina." Smiling, Gabriella offered a hand. "So many costumes." She studied the rack, the trays and boxes full of accessories, then fingered a rope of glass beads until she felt Ethel was more at ease. "How in the world do you keep track of everything?"

"I have a system, Your Highness. As long as I can keep certain people from fouling it up." She cast a narrow-eyed look at Eve.

"I'm just checking off," Eve muttered. "I'm not touching anything."

"So far," Ethel said under her breath.

"Did I hear you say that someone should keep an eye on Eve?"

"Yes, ma'am, Your Highness. Too keyed up and not sleeping right. I'd be obliged to anyone who could get her out of my hair for a while."

"A fat lot of respect the producer gets around here."

"Concern's often more important," Gabriella commented. "I believe I can help you out, Miss Cohen. I have twenty free minutes. Eve, I'd love a cup of coffee."

"Brie, I'm up to my ears—"

"I could pull rank."

Eve let out a windy sigh. "And would, too. All right, but we're going to have to make it fifteen, and in my office."

"Fair enough." Brie linked arms with Eve, then looked over her shoulder, mouthing the word twenty to Ethel.

"And how is it you have twenty free minutes in the middle of the day?"

"Luck. Nanny's with the children at the farm, Reeve's in conference with Papa and Alex, and my afternoon appointment came down with a virus."

"You don't sound sympathetic."

"I'm relieved. You have no idea how tedious it is to sit around eating watercress sandwiches—nasty things—and planning a fundraiser with a woman with more hot air than imagination. If I'm really lucky, the virus will last three or four days and I can have the whole thing planned without her."

"Talk about nasty. Well, here, as we say in the States, is where the buck stops." She opened the door to her office and gestured Gabriella inside.

"Adequate enough," Gabriella decided, turning a circle. "But you need some fresh flowers and something to replace that hideous painting."

"I don't even notice really. It's more important that I've been requisitioned a coffeemaker." Eve hit the switch. "It'll be hot in a minute."

Gabriella set her purse on the desk and casually moved to the window. "A pity you don't have a better view."

"I didn't think there was a bad view in Cordina."

Gabriella let the curtain fall back into place, then turned. "You know, Eve, I stopped by home when I dropped Reeve off. Alexander looks every bit as hollow-eyed as you."

Eve moved away to busy herself with cups and saucers. "I suppose he has a lot on his mind."

"No doubt about that, and a bit more than state affairs. Did you quarrel?"

"We had words. Do you want it black or with some of this awful powdered milk?"

"Black." Gabriella waited until Eve poured and handed her a cup. "Like to talk about it?"

"He's your brother."

"And you're my friend." Without tasting, Gabriella sat and set the cup on the edge of the desk. "I love both of you, enough, I think, to be objective. Has he been difficult?"

"No." Eve took a long drink. "Impossible."

"Sounds like Alex." She couldn't prevent the hint of a smile.

"In his defense I have to say he doesn't try to be impossible, he just is. What did he do?"

Eve finished off her coffee, then rose immediately to pour more. "He kissed me."

Gabriella lifted a brow, pursed her lips and considered. "That doesn't seem like such a terrible thing to me."

"Come on, Brie, I'm talking about Alexander the Proper. And he didn't just kiss me," she added because it sounded so foolish out loud. "He tried to seduce me."

"I can't believe it's taken him so long." At Eve's expression, Gabriella lifted a hand in a negligent wave. "After all, Eve, Alex may be an idiot, but he's far from stupid. It's difficult for me to believe you were shocked."

"I was shocked." Then with a grimace Eve relented. "All right, maybe I wasn't shocked, but I was surprised."

"Did you kiss him back?"

If the "him" had been anyone else, she would have laughed. "Really, Brie, that's hardly the point."

"No, it is the point, but it's also none of my business."

"I didn't mean that."

"If you didn't, you should have," Gabriella told her as she sampled her coffee. "Still, if you're angry with Alex, I think there's more to it than a kiss."

She tried to sit, then stood again to roam the room. Nothing seemed right, she thought. Nothing fit into place. "He only kissed me because of Bennett."

While Eve paced the room, Gabriella set her coffee down again. "I hate being dense, but what does Bennett have to do with Alex and you?"

"Just like a man," Eve muttered as she walked back and forth. Her oversized shirt flapped at the hips with each movement. She'd told herself she wasn't going to give it another thought. She'd promised herself that if she did think of it, she wouldn't be upset. So much for promises. She gestured with her cup and nearly sloshed coffee over the sides. "Like a little boy wanting a shiny red ball because it belongs to another little boy. Well, I'm not a red ball." She slammed her cup into its saucer. "I don't belong to anyone."

Gabriella let the silence hang a moment, then slowly nodded.

"I think I'm following you. Stop me if I'm wrong. You think Alex tried to seduce you because he thinks Bennett already has."

"Bingo."

"Eve, that's absurd."

"You bet it is. I said the same thing in more graphic terms to Alexander."

"No, no, no." More than a little amused, Gabriella laughed off Eve's indignant agreement. "I meant it's absurd to think that Alex and Ben have ever played one-upmanship over anything. It simply isn't in their nature."

It wasn't the sympathy she'd counted on. Families stick together, she reminded herself, but Gabriella was a woman. She wanted a woman's reaction. "How do you explain the fact that he said I'd slept with Ben?"

"Alex said that?"

"Yes, he said it. Do you think I imagined it?"

Amusement became a shadow of concern. "No, of course not. I thought you'd misunderstood something he did or said." The concern hovered a moment, then faded. "I still do."

"It was very plain, Brie. Alex thinks Ben and I..." She left the obvious unstated as she thought it through. "Maybe everyone does."

"Anyone who sees you and Bennett together and knows you understands it's nothing but affection and friendship." She stopped, and her lips twitched a little. "Anyone who's seeing clearly."

"You'll forgive me if I don't find this as amusing as you seem to."

"I can't help but be pleased Alexander is involved with someone I respect and care for."

"We're not involved."

"Hmmm."

"Don't say hmmm—you remind me of Chris."

"Good, that means you'll think of me as a sister and listen to some advice."

It was Eve's turn to be amused. "Chris would be the first to tell you I rarely do."

"Then make an exception. Eve, I know how it is to have feelings for someone who seems totally wrong for you."

"I never said I had feelings," she said slowly. "But suppose, for the sake of argument, I did. Alexander *is* totally wrong for me. Moreover, I'm wrong for him. I have a career, one that's important to me. I have ties to another country. I like to do things when and how I choose to without deliberating how it might look to the press. I've never dealt well with rules, which I proved by doing miserably in school. Alexander lives by rules. He has to."

"True." Gabriella nodded as she sipped her coffee. "You know, Eve, your arguments are perfectly valid."

"They are?" There was a little sinking sensation in her stomach. She braced against it and spoke more firmly. "Yes, they are."

"I said I understood and I do. With the man I had feelings for, the arguments were almost identical and just as valid."

Eve poured more coffee. It seemed as though she were living on caffeine, she thought. "What did you do?"

"I married him."

Eve fought back a smile and plopped on the edge of her desk. "Thanks a lot."

Gabriella set her coffee aside, noting that Eve had drunk three to her one. And coffee, she thought, wasn't going to soothe her friend's nerves. Love made wrecks of people no matter how strong they professed to be. It hadn't been so long ago that she'd been in the turmoil of needing to love and being afraid to.

"Do you love Alex?"

Love. The most potent four-letter word. Denying it would be easy. Honesty took more of an effort. Eve felt Gabriella deserved the truth. "I haven't let myself think of it."

"Thinking has little to do with loving. But I'm not going to pressure you anymore."

Affection coursed through her as she leaned over to touch Gabriella's hand. "Brie, you could never pressure me."

"Yes, I could," Gabriella said briskly. "And it's tempting. Instead I'll tell you to try to remember that Alex has had to work very hard to develop an armor to contain his emotions. A strong, objective ruler is necessary for the country. It isn't always easy for him, or for the people close to him."

"Brie, the bottom line isn't my feelings for Alex."

"For those of us who can choose their own destinies feelings are always the bottom line."

"I wish it were so simple." If it were, she could open the door, even for a moment, and examine her own feelings, her own wants, face to face. She didn't dare. They might be much bigger and much stronger than she was. It was a matter of self-protection, she told herself. Of self-reliance. She didn't want to think it was a matter of survival.

"Brie, as much as I care for your family, I can't afford to get emotionally involved with someone who has to put country and duty ahead of me. That sounds selfish, but—"

"No, it sounds human."

"I appreciate that. You know, if—" She broke off as the phone on her desk rang. "No, don't go," she said as Gabriella started to rise. "Wait just a minute. Hello."

"Eve Hamilton?"

"Yes."

"You're close to the royal family. If you have concern for their welfare, tell them to heed a warning." The voice chilled her as much as the words. It was mechanical, sexless.

"Who is this?"

"A seeker of justice. A warning. There will be only one. François Deboque will be released from prison within forty-eight hours or a member of the royal house of Cordina will die."

With the breath backed up in her lungs, Eve shot Gabriella a look. Her friends, her family. The threat wasn't against some faceless title, but against people she loved. She gripped the phone tighter and forced aside terror. "Only a coward delivers threats anonymously."

"A warning," the voice corrected. "And a promise. Forty-eight hours."

The quiet click echoed over and over in Eve's head even after she deliberately replaced the receiver.

Fear. Because she sensed it, Gabriella rose to put a hand on Eve's. "What is it?"

When she focused on Gabriella again, Eve saw the tautness despite the Princess's attempt at composure. Taking her cue from that, she rose quickly. "Where are your bodyguards?"

"In the hall."

"Your car's outside?"

"Yes."

"A driver?"

"No, I drove myself."

"We need to go to the palace. I think one of your guards should ride with us. I'll explain on the way."

Inside Prince Armand's office, three men sat in tense conversation. Smoke hung in the room, its scent competing with that of fresh flowers and old leather. Often rooms take their mood from the man who occupies it. This one held power, quietly, unarguably. Decisions made here were rarely made in haste and never made with emotion. Decisions made here could not be regretted after the heat of anger or the twists of grief had passed.

Prince Armand sat behind his desk and listened to his son-in-law. Reeve MacGee was a man he respected and trusted. He was friend, he was family, and more, Reeve's background in law enforcement and special services made him invaluable as an adviser. Though he had refused any offer of title or position of state, Reeve had agreed to work, quietly, in the capacity of security adviser for the royal family.

"There's little more you can do to improve the security here at the palace without making a public statement."

"I have no desire to make a public statement." Armand passed a smooth white rock from hand to hand as he spoke. "The embassy?"

"The security's been upgraded there, of course. But it's my feeling that unless you're in Paris, they'll be no trouble there."

Armand accepted this with a slight inclination of his head. He knew he had been the target in Paris, and was still living, always would, with the knowledge that another man had died in his place. "And?"

Reeve needed nothing else to know the prince spoke of Deboque. "The security at the prison is excellent. However, no amount of security can prevent Deboque from issuing orders. His mail can be censored, naturally, but he's much too sharp to put anything incriminating in writing. He has a right to visitors."

"Then we agree that the Paris incident and the smaller, less tragic incidents of the past few years are Deboque's doing."

"He planted the bomb, just as he orchestrated the theft of the Lorimar diamonds from the museum two years ago. He's still running drugs while he sits in his cell. In three years, two if he manages parole, he'll be back on the streets.''

Such was justice. Such was the law. ''Unless we prove that through his orders, Seward was killed.''

''That's right. And proof won't come easily.''

''We sit here and talk about increased security. Defensive measures only.'' Alexander crushed his cigarette into a mass of paper and tobacco, but his voice was calm. ''Where is our offense?''

Armand held the white rock a moment longer, then set it on the desk. He understood Alexander better than anyone, the tightly controlled fury, the constantly blocked emotions. A father can feel regret even as he feels pride. ''You have a suggestion?''

''The longer we sit and do nothing but defend, the longer he has to plan. He has a right to visitors under the law. We know that whoever comes to Deboque is tied to Deboque.'' Each time he said the name it left a bitter taste on his tongue. ''I'm sure Reeve can give us a report on each and every visitor in the past seven years.'' He glanced at his brother-in-law and received a nod. ''We know who they are, what they are and where they are. Isn't it time we used that knowledge more forcibly?''

''They are under surveillance,'' Armand reminded him.

''Surveillance on known members of Deboque's organization did nothing for Seward.'' The pain was still raw and still meticulously controlled by both father and son. Silence hung a moment, broken only by the click and flare of Reeve's lighter. ''We need someone on the inside.''

''Alexander is right.'' Reeve blew out a stream of smoke. ''It's something I've been giving a lot of thought to. The problem would be finding the right operative, then getting him in. Infiltrating Deboque's organization could take months.''

''It took him little time to plant his woman as Gabriella's secretary.'' Alexander's resentment hadn't faded after seven years, only evolved into a simmering need for retribution.

Reeve understood, acknowledged, then shook his head. ''It's easier to fake a security clearance, a background, records, than it is to gain a position of trust with a man like Deboque. He's in jail now only through five years of Interpol's concentrated effort.''

''And still he pulls strings,'' Armand murmured.

''And still he pulls strings.'' Reeve picked up his cooling coffee only to wash the taste of frustration from his mouth. "Even after we've succeeded in putting a man on the inside, it'll take more time for him to establish himself in a position of trust. We need someone who can testify that Deboque himself gave an order."

Alexander rose, needing to pace off the excess energy that came from swallowing his thirst for action instead of talk. Intellectually he knew Reeve was right. To successfully destroy Deboque would take time and patience. But emotionally... He wanted revenge, the grimly sweet satisfaction of it. Now, as always, he had no choice but to put his wants second to necessity.

"You have someone in mind?"

Reeve tapped out his cigarette. "I will have within a week."

"In the meantime?"

"In the meantime I suggest we continue to upgrade our security, keep Deboque's people under surveillance and prepare for his next move. It will come." He spoke first to Alexander, then shifted his gaze, cool and calm, to Armand. "And it will come soon."

Armand nodded. "I will leave it to you to contact Jermaine at the Paris embassy. Perhaps tomorrow you will have a report on your conversation with Linnot on palace security."

"Tomorrow."

"Good. Now, I could be allowed a moment to ask about my grandchildren." Armand smiled, and there was warmth in his eyes. His shoulders never relaxed.

"They're hellions."

The laugh came as both appreciation and relief. "I thank God for it. Perhaps one day our biggest concern will be that Damien has dug up the kitchen garden."

The knock came fast and hard. Armand's brows rose only slightly at the interruption, but his body was braced. Because Alexander was already standing, Armand gestured for him to answer. The moment the door was opened, Eve stepped forward.

He saw it immediately, the ice pale skin, the too large eyes. He heard the breath come quickly through her lips as he stood, half blocking, half shielding her.

"Alexander." She reached for him because the need and the gesture were natural. He was safe. She thanked God for it even as the sickness rose in her stomach at the thought of what might be.

Gabriella put a hand on her arm. "We need to speak with Father. Where's Bennett?"

"In Le Havre until tomorrow." Alexander needed no explanation. The look in Eve's eyes, the tone of his sister's voice were enough. Without a word he stepped back to let them through.

Eve forgot protocol and formal greetings as she hurried forward. She went directly to Armand's desk. He'd risen, but even through her nerves she saw he stood as prince, not as friend.

"Your Highness, I received a phone call at the center only minutes ago. You must release Deboque from prison within forty-eight hours."

The veil fell over his eyes—Eve could have sworn she'd seen it fall. "Is this a demand or advice?"

Before Eve could speak, Gabriella again laid a hand on her arm. "A warning was issued through Eve. She was told that if Deboque wasn't released, a member of the royal family would die."

Where was the emotion? Eve wondered as she watched the prince. Where was the fear for his family, for himself? He watched her calmly, then gestured for her to sit. "Alexander, I think Eve could use a glass of brandy."

"Your Highness, please, I'm not the one you have to worry about. No one's threatening me."

"Please, sit down, Eve. You're very pale."

"I don't—" But the slight increase in the pressure of Gabriella's fingers on her arm stopped the protest. She cleared the frantic words away with a long breath and tried again. "Your Highness, I don't believe this was an empty threat. If Deboque is still in prison two days from now, there will be an assassination attempt on one of you."

Alexander placed a brandy snifter in her hands. She looked up and, for a moment, forgot everyone in the room but him. It could be you, she thought with a sudden wave of terror. If he was killed, her life would end.

As soon as the thought jelled, shock followed. Already pale cheeks blanched. She looked away quickly to stare into her brandy. But she saw the truth. She loved him, had always loved him, however impossibly. Before she'd been able to deny it, block it out. Now that he was in danger, her feelings rushed from her heart to her head.

"Eve?"

She pressed her fingers to her eyes and waited for her head to stop swimming. "I'm sorry, I didn't hear you."

Reeve's voice was patient. "It might help if we had the exact wording of the call, or as close as you can remember."

"All right." It helped, somehow it helped, to strain her mind and back away from the less tangible. She sipped brandy first, hoping it would settle her. "First he asked for me by name."

"You're sure it was a man?"

She started to answer quickly, then stopped. "No. No, I'm not. The voice disturbed me right away because it was so mechanical. Not like a machine, but as though it were being run through one."

"Very possibly was," Reeve murmured. "Go on."

"He said...something like I was close to the royal family and I should tell them to heed a warning. When I asked who it was he said...'a seeker of justice.' I'm sure of that. Then he said there'd be only one warning. François Deboque was to be released from prison within forty-eight hours or a member of the royal house of Cordina would die." She compressed her lips a moment, then drank again. "I told him only a coward delivered a warning anonymously."

She didn't notice the glint of approval in Armand's eyes as he sat watching her, or the hand Alexander laid on the back of her chair. His fingers stroked her hair, and though she didn't feel it, she calmed.

"He only repeated that it was a warning and a promise."

"What was the accent?" Reeve asked her. "American, European?"

As if to force the memory out, she pressed two fingers to her temple. "There wasn't one, not a noticeable one. The voice was very flat and slow."

"Did the call come through the switchboard?"

Eve used the snifter to warm her hands as she looked back at Reeve. "I don't know."

"We should be able to check that. If Eve's been used once, she may be again. I'd like to tap that phone and put a guard on her."

"I don't need a guard." She set the brandy aside with a natural arrogance that had Armand measuring her again. "No one's threatened me. Your Highness, it's you I'm worried about. You and your family. I want to help."

Armand rose again, but this time came around the desk. With his hands light on Eve's shoulders, he kissed both of her cheeks. "Your concern comes from the heart. My dear, we are grateful for it. You must allow us to have the same for you."

"I'll have the guard if it eases your mind."

Her grudging acceptance made his lips twitch even now. She was not a coward or a fool, but as strong blooded—even headed—as his own children. "Thank you."

If she noticed the irony, she ignored it. "What will you do?"

"What needs to be done."

"You won't release Deboque."

"No, we will not."

She could accept that, had expected no less. Capitulation didn't stop threats. "But you will take precautions? All of you?" Her gaze slipped to Alexander and held. For an instant, perhaps only a fraction of an instant, her heart was in her eyes. He thought he saw more than concern, more than simple worry. More than he'd ever wanted anything, he wanted to step into what he believed was there and smother in the warmth. Instead he stood where he was, bound by breeding and necessity.

"It isn't the first time, nor will it be the last, that the House of Cordina has been threatened." The pride was there; she heard it. But below that, simmering just beneath, she heard the hunger for violent and decisive action. She didn't retreat from it, but turned. "Gabriella…"

"Eve, we can't allow threats to rule our lives. We have a responsibility to our people."

"We belong to the people, *petite*." Armand's voice softened as he took both her hands. "The walls of this palace are not for hiding behind, but for defending from."

"But you can't just go out, go on as if nothing has happened."

"All that can be done will be." Armand's tone was firmer now, a ruler's. "I would not risk my family indiscriminately. We will not risk ourselves."

She faced a solid wall. Armand, flanked by Alexander and Gabriella. Even Reeve ranged himself with them. She thought of

Bennett, careless, carefree Ben, and knew he would have stood just as solidly with them. "I have to be satisfied with that."

"You are as one of my own." Armand kissed her hand. "I ask you as a father, as a friend, to trust me."

"As long as I'm still allowed to worry."

"You have my permission."

There was nothing more she could do, nothing more she could say. No matter how close she was, she remained an outsider. "I have to get back to the center." She picked up her bag, struggling against the knowledge that she could do no more than that. She cast a look at Reeve. "Take care of them." With a quick curtsy, she hurried from the room.

Eve was halfway down the stairs, when she remembered she had no car. The small inconvenience had her pressing her fingers against her eyes and fighting back an urge to sob hysterically. Three deep breaths brought her back to order. Swearing, she decided that with the energy she had boiling inside, she could walk it.

"Eve. You don't have a car."

She stopped at the foot of the stairs and looked up at Alexander. Did he realize how solid, how powerful, how completely confident he looked? He stood like a warrior, more ready to attack than to defend. He looked like a king, more ready to punish than forgive. Like a man more ready to take than to ask.

As he came down the steps, closer, still closer, she realized that was what she wanted. The strength, the control, even the arrogance.

"I don't want anything to happen to you." Eve said it quickly, before common sense smothered the words.

He stopped on the step above her, rocked more than she could imagine by the breathless sentence. Her concern was a warmth that reached inside his skin and arrowed its way toward his heart. But he was a warrior, and his first move was always defense.

"My father gave you permission to worry. I did not."

It was fascinating to watch her eyes, eyes so blue, go to ice in a matter of seconds. "Then I promise, I won't offer it again. If you choose to take a dive into hell, I won't even bother to watch."

"You change from honey to vinegar quickly. Part of your charm."

"I won't offer charm any more than I will concern."

"I don't want your worry," he murmured as he descended the final step. "But more. Much more."

"That was all I was willing to give." He had her boxed in neatly between himself and the banister. She wondered how he had managed it.

"I think not." He cupped her face in his hands. This was what he needed, if only for moments at a time. To touch her, to challenge her, to forget there was a world outside the walls. "What you say with your mouth and what you say with your eyes are not always the same."

She wouldn't be obvious. She refused to be easily read. What she had felt that moment upstairs would be hers alone until she fully understood it. Perhaps the fact that she had felt it, and he had not, pushed her. "Have you forgotten Bennett?"

She didn't wince, wouldn't permit herself to, when his fingers tightened on her flesh. "You didn't think of Bennett when you were in my arms. When you're in my bed, you'll think of no one but me."

Was it fear that roped into her stomach or anticipation? She knew already, somehow, that in his bed she would find everything she'd ever wanted and more than she might be able to bear. She wouldn't buckle to him. If she could promise herself nothing else, she could promise herself that.

"I won't be ordered into your bed, Alex." With her eyes cool, her hands steady, she pushed his fingers away. "I won't come to you as long as you think I will be. You want your brother's lover." It hurt her, almost more than she could stand, so her voice was as sharp as shattered glass and just as jagged. "That's an old story, and one that never ends satisfactorily for anyone involved."

The accusation cut into him until the temper he warred against daily threatened to pour out. He stepped closer and found her as strong and straight as any foe a man could face. Desire raced with rapier swiftness through his system.

"You want me. I've seen it. I've felt it."

"Yes." She wouldn't deny it. But her eyes were level and challenged the triumph in his. "But like you, I've learned to put my wants behind what's necessary. One day, Alex, one day you might come to me as a man rather than a symbol. One day you might come to me with needs instead of demands.''

Whirling away, she started down the hall. ''I appreciate the offer—of a ride, Your Highness—but I prefer to go alone.''

Chapter 7

Damn the woman! That was a thought that had leaped into Alexander's mind more than once in a two-day period. She made him feel like a fool. Worse, she made him act like one.

He had never had any respect for men who used physical force to intimidate. Such men had no character and very little intelligence. Now it seemed he had somehow become one of them. No, there was no somehow about it, Alexander corrected viciously. It was the woman who had driven him to it.

When had he started backing women into corners? With Eve. When had he started entertaining thoughts of taking a woman whether she was willing or not? With Eve. When had he wanted a woman so badly she clouded his judgment and dominated his thoughts? With Eve.

It had all begun with Eve; therefore it followed that Eve was to blame for his bouts of irrationality.

Because he was a logical man, Alexander recognized the flaw in that deduction. When a man lost control, publicly or privately, he had no one to blame but himself.

But damn the woman, anyway.

Seeing the quick, ironic smile, Gilchrist, Alexander's longtime valet, let out a small, silent breath of relief. Moodiness was something he expected and accepted from the prince. He could gauge within a heartbeat when to speak and when to remain silent. He'd never have lasted ten years otherwise. The smile meant more temperate weather was due, however briefly. Gilchrist knew enough to cash in on it.

"If I may say so, sir, you've not been eating well the past few weeks. If you don't pay more attention to your diet, we'll have to take your clothes in."

Alexander started to brush this off as fussing until he hooked a thumb experimentally in his waistband. There was a full inch of give.

Damn the woman for making a wreck of him.

No more, he promised himself. The insanity stopped here. "I'll see what I can do, Gilchrist, before you and my tailor lose face."

"I'm only worrying about Your Highness's health, not the fit of your clothes." But, of course, he was almost as concerned about one as the other.

"Then I'll have to promise not to give you cause to worry about either." Preoccupied, he nodded for Gilchrist to answer the knock at his door.

"Your Highness." Henri Blachamt had been Alexander's personal secretary for eight years. Before that time he had served in Armand's retinue. Even with twenty years total in service to the royal family, he remained elaborately formal.

"*Bonjour*, Henri. What impossible schedule have you lined up for me tomorrow?"

"I beg your pardon, Your Highness, your day tomorrow is rather full."

He wouldn't sit, Alexander knew, unless the prince seated himself first. Patient, Alexander settled himself on the arm of a chair. "Please sit, Henri, I'm sure that appointment book is quite heavy."

"Thank you, sir." After seating himself with a few of the fussy little gestures he was prone to, Henri reached in his vest pocket for small, rimless glasses. He settled them on his nose, straightened them, adjusted them, in a time-consuming ceremony Alexander would have tolerated from no one else.

His affection for the older man was very real and hadn't dimmed since that moment twenty years before when Henri had slipped the young prince a piece of hard candy after Alexander had received a particularly grim lecture on decorum from Armand.

"You remember, of course, the dinner party at Monsieur and Madame Cabot's this evening. There will be entertainment provided by Mademoiselle Cabot on the piano."

"It isn't possible to call that entertainment, Henri, but we'll let it pass."

"Just as you say, sir." There might have been a glint of amusement behind the lenses, but Henri's voice remained bland. "Council of the Crown member Trouchet will be attending, sir. I presume he will wish to discuss the matter of the proposed health-care bill."

"Your warning is appreciated," Alexander murmured, and wondered if he would survive the deadly boredom of the evening. Unless he missed his guess, the redoubtable Madame Cabot would have him seated between herself and her reedy-voiced, heavy-handed and unmarried daughter.

If only he could stay home, sit in his own garden at moonrise. With Eve beside him. She'd smell darker, more exotic than the gardens. He'd pick a spray of jasmine for her and her skin would be softer, smoother, than the petals. Her eyes would be the rich, dark blue that tempted a man and her voice would pour, warm and fluid over his skin until he was driven to taste her. She would smile at him, for him, as her arms reached out....

Damn the woman.

Both valet and secretary braced as the prince's brows drew together.

"What of tomorrow?" Alexander demanded, rising to face the window. He saw the gardens and deliberately looked beyond them to the sea.

Henri rose automatically and balanced the appointment book on his open hands. "Eight o'clock breakfast with the President of Dynab Shipping. Ten-fifteen, a personal appearance at the opening of the Le Havre Seaport Museum. One-thirty, you speak at a luncheon for the benefit of St. Alban's Hospital. At three-forty-five..."

Alexander sighed and let the rest of his day pass by him. At least he was home, he reminded himself. Plans were already in the works for his European tour that winter.

One day he would visit the moors of Cornwall and the vineyards of France as he wished, rather than as Cordina's representative. One day he would see the people and places as they were, rather than as they looked for a prince. One day. But not today and not tomorrow.

"Thank you, Henri, that's certainly thorough." His hands linked behind his back, Alexander swore at himself. It was hardly Henri's fault. In fact, the only fault lay within himself and his sudden restless yearning to be free. He turned and smiled as the old man took off his glasses as elaborately as he had put them on. "How is your new granddaughter?"

A hint of color came into Henri's cheeks. All pleasure. "She is beautiful, Your Highness. Thank you for asking."

"Let's see, she must be...three months old now."

"Three months tomorrow," Henri agreed, his pleasure doubling that Alexander remembered.

Alexander recognized it, understood that small things were sometimes the most precious, and cursed himself for being so abrupt with his staff over the past few weeks. He would have liked to lay his mood at Eve's door, as well, but found it firmly lodged at his own.

"Certainly you have a picture of her. Annabella, isn't it?"

"Yes, Your Highness." Almost beet-red now, Henri reached for his billfold, carefully tucked into his breast pocket. Alexander took it and studied the nearly bald, chubby-faced infant. She was no beauty, but Alexander found himself grinning at the wide eyes and toothless smile.

"You're a fortunate man, Henri, to have such a legacy."

"Thank you, sir. She's very precious to all of us. The Princess Gabriella sent my daughter the lace dress, which had belonged to young Princess Louisa. My daughter cherishes it."

"So she should, if anything survives Louisa." He glanced at the white lace around the baby's wide face. How like Brie to have been so generous. "Give my best to your family, Henri."

"I will, sir. Thank you. We all look for the day when you give Cordina a son or daughter. That, Your Highness, will be a day of celebration."

"Yes." Alexander handed back the billfold. Give Cordina. His son would be heir even as he was now. The bond, both exquisite and heavy, would never be broken. And the mother of his children would have to accept the rules that had been carved out centuries before. What he would have to ask of her could be no less than what he asked of himself. If he made a mistake in his choice, he would live with it always. There could be no divorce for the ruler of Cordina.

At thirty, Alexander was the oldest unmarried heir in Cordinian history, a fact that the press reminded him and his country of at regular intervals. Yet marriage was something he still refused to contemplate.

Henri cleared his throat deliberately to bring back Alexander's attention. "Your fencing partner will be here by five-thirty, Your Highness. You must be at the Cabots' by eight-thirty."

"I won't forget."

Ten minutes later, dressed in white trousers and jacket, Alexander walked down the main staircase. The tension he'd carried with him for days hadn't eased. No amount of logical thinking helped. The war remained inside him, raging. Duty against need. Responsibility against desire.

The front door opened as he reached the bottom step. He stopped, muscles taut, thinking of Eve.

But it was Bennett who walked through, with a young, very shapely redhead on his arm.

"I can't believe I'm going to get a tour of the palace." Though her voice was breathy with excitement, the diction was perfect. After a moment's study, Alexander recognized her as one of Eve's troupe.

"Are you sure it's all right?"

"Darling, I live here." Alexander heard the amusement in his brother's voice as Bennett stroked a hand over the woman's shoulder.

"Of course." With a nervous laugh, she looked at Bennett. "It's so hard to think of you as a prince."

"That's fine. Why don't you think of me as— Hello, Alex." Bennett straightened away from the woman and his smile was crooked. "Have you met Doreen? She just joined Eve's troupe before they left the United States."

"Yes, we met at the dinner last week. A pleasure to see you again."

"Thank you, Your Highness." On cue, she curtsied. Bennett had a moment to think wryly that she had no trouble seeing Alexander as a prince. "Your brother, ah, Prince Bennett, offered me a tour of the palace." She sent Bennett a glowing look.

"How delightful." No one but Bennett would have recognized the sarcasm in the dry tone. "Perhaps you'd like to see the parlor first." While Bennett looked on in confusion, Alexander took Doreen's arm and led her a few steps down the hall. "It's quite comfortable and some of the furnishings are seventeenth century. You can amuse yourself, can't you, while I have a word with my brother?"

"Oh, yes, Your Highness. Thank you."

Alexander watched Doreen wander toward the mantel and the Wedgwood before he strode back to his brother.

"Very smooth," Bennett commented. "Now why don't you tell me why you wanted her out of the way?" At Alexander's look, Bennett's heart stopped. "Is something wrong? Father?"

"No." Normally Alexander would have hastened to reassure him. At the moment he had only one focus and one purpose. "How could you bring that woman here?"

"What?" Relief became confusion and confusion amusement. Bennett's deep, infectious laugh rolled down the ancient hallway. "Doreen? Alexander, I promise you, I don't intend to seduce her in the portrait gallery."

"But somewhere else, and at the first opportunity."

Bennett stiffened. He tolerated his reputation in the press and, a fair man, was willing to accept the fact that he deserved the title Playboy Prince to a certain extent. Elder brother or not, he wouldn't tolerate it from Alexander.

"If, when and whom I seduce remains my business, Alex. Try to remember you'll rule Cordina, but not me. Never me."

The fury rippled just under the surface of cool, biting words. "I don't care if you take one of the kitchen maids in the pantry, as long as you're discreet."

Bennett's innate humor didn't surface. "Perhaps I should take that as a compliment, but I find it difficult."

"Don't you care anything for her feelings?" Alexander exploded. "That you'd flaunt one of your—distractions here, in her face? And that you should choose one of her own people. I've never known you to be cruel, Bennett. Careless, even selfish, but never cruel."

"Wait a minute." Bennett ran a hand over his face and through his thick mane of hair. "I feel as though I've walked in on Act Two. Are you talking about Eve? You think she'd be upset that I'm, well, let's say flirting with one of her actors?"

Alexander felt the rage spill over for a man who had the sun and only insisted on courting lesser stars. "If you must continually be unfaithful, can't you limit it while she's under our roof?"

"Unfaithful?" Bennett shook his head. "Now I'm afraid I've missed Act Two altogether. I don't have anyone to be unfaithful to…" The words trailed off as the full meaning struck. He stared at his brother, then collapsed in uproarious laughter. "Eve?" He choked on another fit of chuckles and leaned against the newel, carved three hundred and fifty years before into the head of a cat. "I can't believe that you—" Bennett struggled for breath, pressing a hand to his heart as Alexander's eyes grew darker and darker. "I can take that as a compliment, brother, and a truly inspired joke." He draped an arm around the newel, ankles crossed. There was nothing he liked so much as a good joke. "Alexander, you of all people should know better than to believe what you read in the paper."

Rigid with fury, Alexander remained where he was. "I have eyes of my own."

"But your vision's clouded. You can't seriously believe there's anything… God, how to put this delicately." He ran his hand over his face again, then dropped it. The smile was still in place. "Anything intimate between me and Eve?"

"You can stand there and tell me you're not lovers?"

"Lovers? Sweet Lord, I've never even touched her. How could I?" Though the amusement still colored his tone, sincerity balanced it. "She's part of the family. She's as much sister to me as Brie."

Something twisted open in Alexander's heart, but he remained a cautious man. "I've seen you together, walking in the garden, laughing in corners."

Bennett's smile faded slowly as Alexander spoke. Comprehension came just as slowly. His brother loved, and because their family bond was strong, Bennett understood the torment it would have caused him. "Because she's about the closest friend I have, and one I see so seldom. There's nothing between us, Alex." He stepped closer, wondering how long his proud, stubborn brother had been hurting. "If you'd asked me sooner, I'd have told you."

The weight began to lift from his shoulders, the back of his neck, his heart. And yet… "Perhaps there's no attachment on your side. Can you be so sure of Eve?"

The grin returned, quick, dashing, confident. "Alex, if there's one thing I know, it's what a woman feels about me. But if you don't want to go with that, why don't you just ask her?"

"I have. She didn't deny it."

"To spite you," Bennett said with instant comprehension. "It would be just like her—and I'd also guess it had something to do with the way you asked."

Alexander remembered the way he had approached her, with cutting accusations and anger. No, she hadn't denied it, but had let him dance on his own hot coals. He couldn't damn her for that.

Alexander studied his brother again and saw that his feelings were no longer his alone. In youth they had shared a great deal, secrets, complaints, jokes. Alexander could only thank God they wouldn't share the same woman.

"How could you not want her?"

Bennett leaned back again and looked at his brother. Someone had finally pierced the impenetrable, shaken the unshakable. "I did. The first time I saw her, I thought she was the most delectable creature I'd ever met." At Alexander's narrowed look, Bennett chuckled. "Don't challenge me to a duel yet. Besides, if you challenge, I pick the weapons. I'm a better shot than you are."

"Why is it you seem to find this so amusing?"

"Because I love you." It was said with the simplicity of truth. "It isn't often enough that those who love you see you act human, Alex. If I didn't enjoy seeing Prince Perfect falter a bit, I wouldn't be human. I'd say this round of jealousy's been good for you."

The childhood nickname didn't irk him so much as the reference to jealousy. "I haven't had a decent night's sleep in months."

"Enormously good for you." Bennett picked a rose from a vase at his elbow, thinking it would complement Doreen's skin. "But to get you off this pin you're stuck on, I was attracted to Eve, and I like to think it was mutual. Then before anything could be done about it, I was flat on my back in the hospital. She came in every day."

"I remember."

"Fussing and nagging," Bennett added. "Standing over me until I ate that pap they forced on me, lecturing me. By the time I was on my feet again, we were friends. We've never been anything else." He passed the flower under his nose. "Now if you're satisfied, I have a lady with incredibly long legs waiting for me." He started down the hall, then stopped and turned. "You've never been one for advice, but I'll give it, anyway. If you want Eve, don't circle around it. She's a woman for the direct approach, no pretty lies, no staged seductions. She's gold, Alex, solid gold, with a mind as strong and sharp as a scalpel. A man would have to recognize that unless he wants small pieces sliced out of him."

If any man he knew understood women, it was Bennett. Alexander felt the first smile form. "I'll keep that in mind." He watched his brother disappear into the parlor. Seconds later, there was a delighted feminine laugh.

Alexander stayed where he was a moment, trying to absorb what he knew, what he felt. Not his brother's woman. Never his brother's woman. But his. From this moment. Alexander strode toward the east wing quickly, needing to expend the energy racing through him.

She'd had a hell of a day. Tired and annoyed with the world at large, Eve let herself in the east entrance of the palace. Only friends and family used the small, secluded garden entrance. Normally she would have come straight in the front, but at the moment, she wanted to see and speak to no one.

Her director was edgy, and it showed. Her actors were picking up on it and had been sniping at one another as often as they blew their lines.

As producer, she could dump a lot of the heartache on her stage manager. But, damn it, it was her company. She'd conceived it, nurtured it, and she just wasn't ready to cut the apron strings.

As a result she'd spent the past two hours in a full meeting, cast and crew, letting the gripes and misconceptions be aired.

The members of her company were mollified. She was wired.

Face it, she told herself as she closed the pretty, carved door at her back. You've been wound tight for weeks and it hasn't a thing to do with the company.

He was making her crazy—mind, body, soul. How was it he could go through the motions, day after day, night after night, as though nothing had happened between them? How was it he followed routine, apparently without a ripple, when she spent sleepless nights worrying about an anonymous phone call?

The time was up, she thought, and rubbed at her aching temples. Deboque was still in prison, would remain in prison. How long would it take before the threat she'd received became action?

She remembered vividly the picture of Bennett lying on the stone floor of the terrace, the blood seeping out of him and onto the dark rock. It took little imagination to see Alexander there.

She could lose him. Though she knew he wasn't hers, had never been hers, the threat of losing him clenched the muscles of her stomach. Whether or not he loved her, whether or not he trusted or respected her, she wanted him alive and whole.

And the forty-eight hours were up.

Perhaps it had been only a threat. Giving in to fatigue and nerves, she leaned back against the cool wood of the door and shut her eyes. The Bissets weren't taking it seriously. If they were, wouldn't she have seen extra guards at the gate? Wouldn't security have been tightened around the palace? Because she had checked personally, she knew Armand was in Cordina, meeting with the Council of the Crown. The rest of the royal family were keeping both official and social engagements as usual.

And the forty-eight hours were up.

Nothing was going to happen. Anything could happen. Why did it seem that she was the only one wrapped up in nerves?

Royalty! she thought, and pushed herself away from the door. Did they think that because their blood was blue it couldn't be shed? Did they think that a title worked as an invisible shield against gunfire? Even Bennett refused to listen to her. In fact, he wouldn't even discuss it with her. Trust them to bind themselves together in this. But all she could see was the picture of wagons drawing into a circle as Indians attacked.

Enough, Eve warned herself. She was through losing sleep over them, *all* of them. She had a company to run and plays to produce. She'd leave the Bissets to run their own lives and their own country.

Then she heard footsteps, whispers. And froze.

Her first reaction was quick and primitive. Run. Almost as it formed came another. Protect.

Eve braced herself against the wall, breathing deeply. Her legs spread, knees bent, her body turned slightly, she lifted her arms to complete the fighting stance. Warriors had used it for centuries when facing an enemy with no more than body and wit.

As the footsteps came closer, she drew her right arm back, her shoulders set straight as a ruler. She took one step forward, leading with her stiffened open hand. Her breath came out in a whoosh. She stopped a scant half inch from Bennett's straight, aristocratic nose.

"Damn, Eve, I didn't think you'd be that upset about me dating one of your people."

"Ben!" With muscles gone limp, Eve collapsed against the wall. She'd gone white as a sheet and he could do nothing but grin. "I might have hurt you."

Healthy masculine pride came to the rescue. "I doubt it. But what are you doing lurking around the corridors?"

"I wasn't lurking. I've just come in." Her gaze shifted to the young redhead. She should have known Bennett would have ferreted this one out before long. "Hello, Doreen."

"Hello, Ms. Hamilton."

Eve straightened her shoulders, then worked away embarrassment by brushing a speck of lint from her jeans. "Ben, if I'd followed through, I'd have broken your jaw. Why are you sneaking around?"

"I wasn't—" He caught himself on the edge of justifying his presence in his own home. Bennett shook his head, amazed that Alexander would mistake his relationship with Eve for anything like sexual attraction. "It seems I have to keep explaining that I live here. In any case, my jaw is safe. I'm showing Doreen the palace before dinner."

"That's nice." It was only a murmur as nerves flooded back. The hands that had been stiffened and ready to attack twisted together. "Is everyone else home?"

"Yes." Recognizing her concern, Bennett tugged on her hair. "Everyone's fine. Oh, Alexander is a bit out of sorts, but—"

"What happened?" Instantly her hands were clamped to his shirt. "Was he hurt?"

"He's fine. For heaven's sake, mind the material." If he'd had any doubt about Eve's feelings toward his brother, he had none now. "I saw him an hour ago,"; he continued as he pried her fingers from the freshly laundered silk. "He was a bit annoyed at my, ah, flaunting one flower in front of the other. If you get my drift."

She did, and her eyes narrowed. "Idiot."

"Yes, well..." To keep himself from laughing at his brother in front of Doreen, Bennett coughed into his hand. "I straightened him out on all counts. So the problem's solved." He smiled charmingly, glad to do them both a favor.

"Straightened him out, did you?" Now her eyes were slits, dark, dangerous slits. "You feel you had the right to speak for me?"

"For myself." Bennett held up a soothing, or protecting, hand, palm out. "I simply explained that..." He shot a look at a quiet, but raptly attentive Doreen. "Ah, that nothing had ever been—well, been." Uncomfortable he shifted. "It seemed to satisfy him."

"Oh, did it? Isn't that lovely." Eve jammed restless hands into her pockets. "I'll do my own explaining in the future, thank you." Her voice was honey with a dash of bitters. "Where is he?"

Grateful that the temper in her eyes was about to be pointed in another direction, Bennett smiled. His only regret was that he wouldn't see the results. "Since he was dressed for fencing, I'd say he's in the gym with his partner."

"Thanks." She took three strides down the hall before calling over her shoulder, "Rehearsal's at nine sharp, Doreen. I want you rested."

Eve had always liked the area in the east wing the Bissets had converted to a gym. She was a physical woman, and one who could appreciate the beauty and contrast of a room with lofted, carved ceilings and steel machines and weights. There was no scent of the sea here, no pretty cut flowers in crystal vases, but the stained glass windows were rich and ancient.

She passed through the exercise room. Normally she would have admired the first-rate equipment and setup. Now she did no more than glance around to assure herself the room was empty.

The tang of chlorinated and heated water hit her as she entered the solarium, where a red fiberglass spa dominated. Steam rose up; the sun poured in. Through the clear glass you could see the sky and touches of the sea with its deeper blue. Another time she might have been tempted to relieve her tensed muscles in the soothing water. Again she passed through with only a glance. And when she opened the next door, she heard the clash and scrape of swords.

The tall, windowless room had a floor of dull hardwood, spread now with the *piste*, the fencing mat, of linoleum. Along one wall ran a mirror and dance *barre*. Two men in white were reflected in the glass as they moved together, knees slightly bent, backs straight, left arms curled up and behind.

Both men were tall, both slim and dark headed. The mesh masks hid and protected their faces through the thrusts and parries. Eve had no trouble recognizing Alexander.

It was the way he moved. Regally, she thought with a sniff, and crossed her arms over her chest while fighting to ignore the quick surge of need. It would always be there when she saw him. She had to acknowledge, even accept it, and go on.

The room rang, metal on metal. The men were silent but for their breathing. And well matched, Eve decided as she watched and analyzed styles and movement. Alexander would never have chosen an inferior fencer as his partner. He'd want the challenge. Little thrills ran up her arms. And the triumph.

In another century, another life, he would have defended his country with the sword, wielding it in battle to protect his people, his land, his birthright.

He could use it still, Eve realized as he moved steadily forward, offense rather than defense. More than once Eve saw him drop his guard to attack, parrying his opponent's thrust just before the safety tip made contact.

Would he fight so recklessly, she wondered, if the points were honed sharp? Another thrill passed through her, this time to twist in her stomach as she answered her own question.

In this one-on-one he would indeed be reckless in the way he never allowed himself in matters of state. His outlet would be the physical, which she understood, and the sense of danger, which she did not.

Again and again he challenged his opponent. Swords crossed; metal slid whistling down metal. Then with two subtle movements of his wrist, Alexander was past the guard, pressing the safety button lightly to his partner's heart.

"Well done, sir." The defeated drew off his face mask. Eve saw immediately that the man was older than she had thought and vaguely familiar. He had a rakish face and an interesting one, lined at the eyes, shadowed with dark hair over the lip. His eyes were a pale, pale gray and met Eve's over Alexander's shoulder. "We have an audience, Your Highness."

Alexander turned and through the wire mesh saw Eve standing rigidly inside the door. He saw the temper, glowing in her eyes, stiffening her shoulders. Curious, he lifted the mask. Now his eyes, dark, still lit with the excitement of victory, met hers without obstruction. He saw, mixed with the temper, heightened because of it, the passion. The need. The desire.

Slowly, his gaze still locked on hers, he tucked the mask under his arm. "Thank you for the match, Jermaine."

"My pleasure, Your Highness." Under the mustache, Jermaine's lips curved. He was French by blood and had no trouble recognizing passion when he saw it. He would forgo his usual after-the-match wine with his friend and pupil. "Until next week."

"Yes." It was only a murmur. Alexander's eyes had yet to leave Eve's face.

Smothering a grin, Jermaine replaced his *épée* and mask on the rack before moving to the door. *"Bon soir, mademoiselle."*

"Bon soir." Eve moistened her lips on the words and listened to the door click shut behind her. Folding her hands primly, she inclined her head. "You have excellent form, Your Highness."

The softly spoken words didn't fool him for a moment. She was mad as a hornet and already aroused despite herself. But the words snapped his own tension. With a cocky grin, he lifted his sword in salute. "I can return the compliment, *mademoiselle.*"

She accepted this with another slow nod. "But compliments aren't the reason I'm here."

"I thought not."

"I ran into Bennett." She would hold her temper, Eve promised herself. She would strangle it down and defeat him with cool, carefully chosen words. "Apparently you and he had a discussion." She moved farther into the room, strolling to the rack of fencing gear. "A discussion concerning me."

"A discussion that wouldn't have been necessary if you had been honest with me."

"Honest?" The word nearly choked her. "I've never lied. I have no reason to lie."

"You allowed me to believe, and in believing suffer, that you and my brother were lovers."

"That belief was your own." Suffer? How had he suffered? But she wouldn't ask. Eve studied the slim shiny *épées* and promised herself she would never ask. "I didn't choose to deny it because I didn't and still don't consider it any of your business."

"Not my business, when I've felt you melt and burn in my arms?" He examined the length of his own sword. "Not my business, when I lay awake at night dreaming of filling myself with you and hating myself for coveting what I thought was Ben's?"

"*What* you thought." She rounded on him, the softening his first words had begun, vanishing. "What, not even who. You considered me Ben's property, and now that you don't, do you believe you can make me yours?"

"I will make you mine, Eve." Something in the soft, solid tone ran a quiver down her back.

"The hell you will. I belong to myself and only myself. Now that you perceive your way clear, you think I'll tumble at your feet? I tumble for no one, Alex." She drew an *épée* from the rack. "You consider yourself superior to a woman because you're a man, and one with royal blood."

She remembered the times he'd held her and let her go. Because he'd thought she was his brother's. Not once, she thought grimly, not once, had he asked for her feelings, her wishes.

"In America we've begun to think of people as people, and things like respect, admiration, affection have to be earned." She cut the air with the slender sword, testing its weight. Alexander's brow lifted at the easy way she handled it. "If I wanted to be in your bed I'd be there." She brought the sword down in an arch that whistled with restrained power. "And you wouldn't know what had hit you." Now she saluted him. "Your Highness."

The ripple of desire tightened his muscles. She stood, dressed in black, her hair drawn back to leave her face unframed, a gleaming sword in her right hand. Challenging him.

He'd wanted her before. Now with his mouth drying up, he thirsted for her. Pride stung the air, coming from both of them.

"I have yet to ask you to my bed."

Her eyes were as dark and dangerous as the sea. For the first time since she had come into the room, she smiled. The smile alone could have made a man beg. "I wouldn't need an invitation. If I chose, I could have you on your knees."

His head snapped up at that. Eyes narrowed. The truth was too close to the bone. "If I decided the time had come for you and me, I wouldn't be on my knees." He walked closer, a sword's length away. "And you would tremble."

His truth was as sharp as hers. "The trouble is you've dealt with too many subservient women." On impulse she took down a mask and a padded fencing vest. "And with too few who'd dare to meet you on equal ground." Her smile was cool and determined. "I may not beat you, Alexander, but I'll see that you sweat for any kind of victory." Making up her mind at once, she slipped on the mask and vest. She walked to the *piste*, taking her position behind the *en garde* line. "If you're not afraid you might lose to a woman?"

Fascinated, he joined her on the mat. "Eve, I've been fencing for years."

"And took a Silver in the last Olympic Games," she acknowledged while her adrenaline flowed steadily. "It should be an interesting match, then. *En garde!*"

He didn't smile. She wasn't making a joke or an idle boast. He replaced his own mask, so that faceless, they measured each other. His reach was nearly half again as long as hers. They both knew it.

"What do you hope to prove by this?"

Behind the mask her eyes flashed. "Equal ground, Alex. Here or anywhere."

Extending her arm, she met the tip of his sword with hers. Steel, cold and slender, glinted in the mirrors. They held for a heartbeat. And lunged.

It was a teasing, testing start, with power held back. Each gauged the other's style and strength, but here Eve had the advantage. She had seen him fence before—today and years ago. At the moment, she would have cut out her tongue before admitting that she had taken up the sport because she had never forgotten how he had looked with an *épée* in his hand. Through every lesson, every match, she'd wondered if she would ever cross swords with him. Now the moment was here and her heart beat hard in her chest.

But her mind was cool. He preferred the attack. She'd seen this and contented herself with defense.

She was good. Very good. Pride and pleasure welled up in him as she blocked and parried. Nature prevented him from using his full skill, but even as he held back, he realized she made both a formidable and an exciting partner.

The slim black jeans distracted him with images of what moved so supplely beneath. Her wrists were narrow, but strong and flexible enough to keep him at bay. He moved in, challenging. Swords crossed and clashed between them.

For a moment they held there, close enough to see each other's eyes through the mesh. He saw in hers the same heated passion that ran through his own.

Desire tangled with the taste of competition. Her scent was dark and richly feminine; the fist covered by the bowl of her sword was fragile and he could just make out the glint of gold and sapphire on her finger. He wanted her here and now. The desire ground through him.

She sensed it—the longing, the passion, the fantasy. It called to something deep inside her. She wanted to hurl the sword aside, drag off her mask and his and surrender to the needs whirling in both of them. Would that mean victory for him, surrender for her? She thought not, and yet the suspicion of it drove her on.

Abandoning her steady defensive tactics, she attacked full force. Caught off guard, Alexander took a step back and felt the soft tip push against his shoulder.

Alexander lowered his sword, acknowledging the hit. "You had a good teacher."

"I was a good pupil."

There was something free in the sound of his laughter. It caught at her, tugged a smile from her. Then she realized it was a sound

she heard much too seldom. His lips were curved behind his mask
as he lifted his *épée* again.

"*En garde, chérie.*"

This time he gave her the compliment of his full skill. Eve felt
the change and her own lips curved. She wanted no concessions.

The room echoed with the scrape and clatter of steel. The mirror
reflected them, one in black, the other in white, as they met on
equal ground.

Once he nearly disarmed her. Eve felt her heart pump in her
throat, and set for the next move. Her advantage was in speed and
she came close to slipping through his guard a second time. But
he parried, riposted and sent her scrabbling for defense.

Their breathing came quick and heavy. The desire to win
clouded over with desire of a more intimate kind. One man, one
woman, dueling. With or without swords it was as old as time
itself. The excitement of the thrust, the thrill of the parry, the
grandeur of the challenge.

Their swords met with a clash near the grips and their faces met
through the sharp-edged vee. Breathing fast, blades tensed, each
held their ground.

Then, in a move that left her uncertain, Alexander reached up
to pull off his mask. It clattered as it hit the floor. His face was
sheened with sweat; dark hair curled damply around it. But it was
his eyes that had her bracing. Again he lowered his sword, then
with a hand on her wrist, pushed hers point down. He drew the
mask from her face and let it bounce beside him.

When he snaked his arm around her waist, she stiffened, but
didn't pull back. Without a word he tightened his grip. The challenge was still in his eyes. The dare was still in hers. Her body
met his, and she tilted her face up as he lowered his mouth. As
she had with a sword, Eve met him with equal force.

The excitement that had stirred during combat found its release.
They poured it into each other. She moved her hand to his shoulder, skimmed it over the slope and rested it on his cheek. The
gentle movement was accompanied by a quick, catlike nip at his
lower lip. He responded by dragging her closer. A sound deep in
his throat rolled out and teased her questing tongue.

The sword slipped out of her grip. Free, her hand reached for
him, working its way under his jacket to get closer, just that much

closer, to flesh. The heat from his body radiated through the shirt and onto her palm.

More. She wanted more. More of the taste of him, more of the feel of him. More, much more of the heart of him. And more was too much.

She dragged herself away from him, from her own impossible wishes.

"Eve—"

"No." She lifted a hand to run it over her face. "There can't be a winner here, Alex. And I can't afford to be a loser."

"I'm not asking you to lose, but to accept."

"Accept what?" Torn, she turned away. "That I want you, that I'm nearly willing to give in to that, knowing it begins and ends there?"

He felt the tug, the fear. "What is it you want from me?"

She shut her eyes a moment, then drew a deep breath. "If you were ready to give it, you wouldn't have to ask. Please don't," she said when he started to reach for her. "I need to be alone. I need to decide just how much I can take."

She left him quickly, before she surrendered everything.

Chapter 8

It wasn't a night for sleeping. The big, round moon shot its reflection in Eve's windows, lending silvery edges to the blue-and-white curtains. She had drawn them back, far back, but still the breeze ruffled the hems and sent them dancing.

Work had already been tried and rejected. Papers and files brought from her office littered her sitting room. She could hardly concentrate on costumes or ticket sales or blown bulbs when Alexander was lodged so firmly in her mind.

He was exposed, vulnerable. With Deboque still in prison, Alexander was at a dinner party. The foolishness of it had her dragging a hand through her hair. Disheveled from an evening of pacing and worry, it tumbled onto the shoulders of her short blue robe.

He was exchanging small talk over coffee and brandy while she roamed her rooms after a futile attempt to eat at all.

He'd gone out, she thought, despite the consequences. Despite everything. Hadn't that wild, groping kiss they had shared sent his system churning as it had hers? Perhaps she had been wrong, deeply and completely wrong, when she had thought the need had run rampant in him. If it had, how was it possible, even with his control, to block it out while he sat through a seven-course meal?

What was wrong with her? Weary of herself, Eve rubbed her fingers over her eyes. She'd been angry when she'd thought he had wanted her only to compete with Bennett, furious that he had wanted but held himself back because he'd believed she had slept with his brother. Then she'd been enraged because he no longer believed it and still wanted her. Now she was miserable because he might not want her as much as she'd thought.

What did *she* want? Eve demanded of herself. One minute she admitted it was Alexander, and the next she was drawing back, knowing there could be nothing lasting, nothing real between them. A man like Alexander would have to marry, and marry properly. He had to produce heirs. Royal heirs. Even if he desired her, even if he cared for her at all, he would have to look to the European Aristocracy for a mate.

Amazed that her thoughts were drifting in that direction, she shook her head. When had she started thinking beyond the moment, an affair, and toward permanency?

She knew about men—when they were attracted, when they desired, when they wanted only a toy for an evening or two. And she knew how to deal with them. Why was it she knew so little of this man? All the evenings and hours she had spent trying to find the answers, some key to Alexander, had resulted only in finding a key to herself.

She was in love with him. Even the little jabs of fear and the constant twinges of doubt couldn't diminish the scope of the emotion.

And she did fear. She was a woman who had been sheltered most of her life by an indulgent father, a pampering sister. The choice she had made only a handful of years before to strike out on her own had been made as much by whim as curiosity. There had been no real danger in it. If she had failed, there had always been the net of family and family money beneath her.

Even if Eve had squandered her personal inheritance, she would hardly have been left alone to flounder.

True, once she'd begun she hadn't thought of using her family to soften whatever blows she'd encountered. Her troupe had become the focus of her life and the success or failure of it personal.

She had succeeded, made something of herself through her own skill and sweat. Even knowing that, being fully confident didn't erase the knowledge that the risk had been slight.

With Alexander there would be no net to soften a tumble, and a fall with him would mean a nosedive, no blindfold, from a dangerous height. The risk was there, every bit as frightening as the temptation to take it.

If she stepped off the edge and counted on survival, she was a fool. But something told her that if she played it safe and kept her feet firmly planted, she was an even bigger fool.

Caught between common sense and feelings, she dropped to the window seat and let the sea air cool her skin.

He wasn't sure he could survive another night. His rooms were quiet, in sound, in mood. They had been decorated in greens and ivories, cool against warmth, with paintings of the sea and shore dominating the walls. Calm seas in his bedroom where he came most often to be alone and think. The sitting room beyond had deeper colors, more vivid hues. It was there, rather than his office or the family rooms, that he most often entertained friends. It was large enough for an intimate dinner or a competitive game of cards.

Shirtless and shoeless, Alexander paced the bedroom now in an effort to rein in the emotions that had haunted him throughout the long, tedious dinner and entertainment. His fists strained against the soft linen of his trousers as he shoved them into his pockets.

No, he wasn't sure he could make it through another night.

She was only a matter of rooms away, a dozen walls he'd already passed through countless times in his imagination. Sleeping. He thought she would be sleeping now as the clocks in the palace readied to strike twelve.

Nearly midnight and she slept. She slept and he wanted. He ached. No amount of training, no sacrifices, no studying had ever prepared him for the dull, constant ache this woman could bring to him.

Could she feel it? He prayed that she could so he wouldn't suffer alone. He wanted her to feel the pain. He wanted to protect her from all hurts. But tonight, dear God, tonight he simply wanted.

It was a wanting that had grown with the years, heightened, turned edgy. There had been times when he'd told himself the need would dissipate. Times when he'd believed it. Months would pass when he wouldn't see her—though he would still wake in the early hours alone, her face just at the tip of his consciousness. He could fight that back, smother the longing that seemed so nebulous in the face of obligations, responsibilities and a backbreaking schedule.

But whenever she was here, close enough to touch, the longing was no longer vague and was impossible to fight.

Now that he had touched her, tasted her, teased himself with fractions of his own fantasies, was he supposed to deny himself the rest?

How could he go to her when what he offered would be a lifetime of subterfuge or a lifetime of sacrifice? As his mistress he would never be able to recognize her publicly as more than a family friend. As his wife…

Alexander pressed his thumb and forefinger to his closed eyes. How could he ask marriage of her? He would always be tied to his country, his duty. So would whatever wife he chose. How could Eve, with her independence and strength, ever accept the restrictions that went with his title? He would have to ask her to give up country, privacy, career. He would have to ask her to subject herself to the fishbowl, the sometimes dangerous fishbowl, in which he had been born. How could he expect her to have the same pride, the same love for Cordina as he? How could he ask her for a lifetime at all?

But he could ask her for a night. One night.

If she would give him that, perhaps it would be enough.

Alexander stared out the window, the one that faced the same garden, the same sea, the same sky as Eve's. He would have one night, and then, somehow, he would survive an eternity of others.

He didn't knock. Such was his arrogance. The door opened without sound, but she sensed him before it clicked shut behind him. Such was his presence.

She didn't jolt. Such was her pride. Eve remained on the window seat and turned her head slowly from the night to Alexander. She'd known sometime during her contemplation of the sky that he would come. What had been denied, struggled against, wished for, would be met tonight. Through her own vigil, she had made her peace with that. They stayed with the room between them, while the air hummed, then settled.

"I won't rise and curtsy," she said in a surprisingly strong voice.

His brow lifted, in amusement or surprise, she couldn't be sure. "I won't go to my knees."

She felt a tremor dance up her spine, but her hands were steady when she folded them in her lap. "Equal ground?"

His stomach was knotted with tension, desire, but a strange and novel euphoria swam into his head. "Equal ground."

She looked at her hands a moment, so calm and still in her lap, then lifted her gaze to his. His stance was straight, almost unbending, but his eyes were anything but distant. There was so much she knew, so much she'd yet to understand. "Once I believed you wanted me because you thought Bennett and I were lovers."

"Once I despised myself for wanting you because I thought you and Bennett were lovers."

The cool, matter-of-fact tone had her pressing her lips together. Yes, he would have hated himself. She'd been a fool not to understand that. He had suffered. She no longer had to ask how. "And now?"

"I could say I'm relieved to know it's not so, but it would make no difference. Even honor suffers."

Honor. With him it would be as vital as the blood in his veins. She had the power to make him compromise it. She had enough love to see that he didn't. She rose then, but even with her hands still folded, looked anything but meek. "I can't take that as flattery, Alexander."

"It wasn't meant to flatter. I could tell you that you're beautiful." His gaze roamed over her face. "More beautiful to me than any other woman. I could tell you that your face haunts my dreams and troubles my days, and that yearning for you empties me. None of it would be meant to flatter."

At each word her heartbeat accelerated, until now it echoed in her ears. With an effort she stayed where she was, when her heart urged her to open her arms and offer everything. Equal ground, she reminded herself. Honor for both. There was no talk of love.

''Maybe it's best if you said nothing.'' She managed to smile, and even tilted her head. ''Except to tell me why you've come.''

''I need you.''

The words rocked her no less than they rocked him. There was silence while the air seemed to absorb them. He saw it in her eyes, the astonishment, the softening, the acceptance. Moonlight shot through the glass at her back, so that she looked as though she might be a part of it—and still out of reach.

Then she held out her hand.

Their fingers met, steadied, then curled into one another. Contact was made, and the time for words was over.

Her eyes on his, she lifted his hand and touched her lips where their fingers joined. Silence.

His gaze remained locked on hers as he turned their joined hands over and pressed his lips to her palm. Still no words.

With her fingertips she traced the line of his jaw, touching now what she'd never felt she'd had the right to touch. His skin was warm, warmer than the breeze that stirred at the curtains. There was no need to speak.

He used his knuckles to trace the curve of her cheek to her temple, then his fingers spread to comb through her hair, lingering—lingering over it as he had once dreamed of doing. The clock struck the hour. It was midnight.

No words, but feelings nurtured in secret for so long bloomed at last in the first moments of the new day. Desires, refused, denied, were now accepted in the shadowed moonlight of a day just ended.

There were things he wouldn't ask, and more she couldn't admit. So they came together without questions, emotions only, as the bravest of lovers do.

Her arms opened. Her mouth lifted. His arms encircled. His mouth lowered. Body to body, they drew out and drew on the first kiss of the morning.

The tenderness remained somehow, though the excitement thrummed just beneath. There was more than just desire now—a breath of completion for something started long before. Tonight. At last.

The air sweetened with her sigh as she allowed herself the freedom of a wish. The kiss was deep, thorough, awash with the anticipation that poured from each. Then his lips brushed hers lightly, not teasing but promising of delights and demands yet to come. When she trembled as he'd once predicted she would, he felt not the thrill of victory but a gratitude that her need was as sharp as his own.

He ran his hands over the silk on her shoulders, her arms, her back, tormenting himself with visions of what was concealed beneath. So many times he had imagined her. When he drew the silk aside, letting it slither and whisper and pool at her feet, he discovered his imagination was no match for the reality of her, naked and close with moonlight cloaking her.

A poet would have had the words. A musician could have played the tune that streamed inside his head. But he was a prince who had never felt himself more of a mortal man than now, watching his woman shimmer in moonbeams before him.

She didn't need poems or a song. What she saw in his eyes told her she more than pleased him. He would never give her beautiful, melodious words, but a look from him said so much more. With a smile, she stepped into his arms again and pressed her lips to his heart.

It beat so fast, so strong. For a moment she closed her eyes tightly, as if to capture the feeling inside her. His skin was bronze against her ivory. Fascinated with the contrast, she stroked her fingers over him, then spread her palm wide on the plane of his chest. His fingers closed over her wrist as her touch sent arrows of need through him. He felt the trip-hammer of her pulse before she drew her arm away to lock both hands behind his head.

Flesh heated against flesh; mouth hungered against mouth. Her tongue skimmed over his lips, then dipped inside for the darker, richer tastes.

More. Again the craving for more tore at her. But this time she would have it. She found the clasp of his slacks, delighting in the quiver of his stomach as her fingers brushed his skin. The moment hung, then raced by. And he was naked with her.

She, too, had dreamed of this, and now discovered that dreams would never be enough.

He gathered her up and held her in his arms, just held her as she pressed her face to his throat, wound her arms around his neck.

The wind shivered at the windows as they lowered themselves to the bed.

The mattress gave beneath them with only a whisper. The sheets rustled. He buried his face in her hair and let her scent slice holes in his control. She flowed against him, not just pliant but willing.

A touch and a tremor. A taste and a sigh. Slowly, savoring, shivering, they discovered each other. She was so soft here, so firm there. The strength in someone so small never failed to astonish him. Fragrant. Her skin was a garden of delight to all his senses. If he ran his tongue over it, he could taste both passion and delicacy.

How was it she had never understood the compassion, the gentleness, the goodness in him? Yet she'd loved him, anyway. Discovering it all now, she was swamped by feelings deeper than she had believed herself capable of. Here was a patience she'd never seen. A sweetness she had never dreamed of. He gave it all to her, without her ever having to ask. He gave her touches of romance she thought herself too wise to need.

It wouldn't always be like this. No, she knew that. There would be demands, greed, recklessness. That she could accept when the time came. But this time, this first time, he seemed to know she wanted gentleness. More, much more important, he seemed to want it, too.

So her hands caressed. Her lips lingered. She showed him she could cherish as well as be cherished. Even when their breath began to merge together in shudders, there was no rage to complete. Prolong. Only to prolong.

When he filled her, they moved together without the haste of first passions. This was a hunger that had waited seven years to be sated. Together they burrowed in a beauty that came as quietly and as inevitably as a sunrise.

The moonlight still glowed. The curtains still billowed. Apparently the world had decided to go on with routine though everything had changed. The sheets were rumpled at the base of the bed, untended and unneeded as the man and woman fed off each other's warmth.

Eve lay with her head on Alexander's shoulder, a place that seemed to have been reserved for her. A place she'd never thought she would claim. His heart beat, still far from steadily, under her hand. His arm was around her, holding her close, and though she knew he was as awake and aware as she, there was a peace between them that had never existed before.

Had love done it, or the act of love? She didn't know, and wondered if it should matter. They were together.

"Seven years." Her sigh was long and shimmered through the silence. "I've wanted this for seven years."

He lay still a moment while her words were slowly absorbed. His fingers trailed over her face, then under her chin so that he could lift her face to his. His eyes were so dark, and this time the caution in them made her smile. "All along? From the beginning?"

"You were dressed like a soldier, an officer, and the room was filled with beautiful women, dashing men, just like a dream. But I kept seeing you." She wasn't ashamed of it, nor did she regret not telling him before. They had needed the years between. "There were flowers. The room smelled like springtime. And there were those dazzling lights from the chandeliers. Silver platters, wine in crystal, violins. You had a sword at your side. I wanted so badly for you to ask me to dance. For you to notice me."

"I noticed you," he murmured, and pressed a kiss to her brow.

"You did scowl at me once, now that you mention it." She smiled and shifted so that she ranged just above him. "And you waltzed with that lovely blond woman with the English complexion. I've hated her ever since."

He grinned and traced Eve's smile with his fingertip. How incredible it was to be relaxed, to be alone, to be only a man. "I don't even remember who she was."

"I do. It was—"

"But I remember that you wore a red dress with the back draped low and your arms bare. You wore a bracelet here." He brought her wrist to his lips. "A thick gold band with a smattering of rubies. All I could think was that one of your lovers had given it to you."

"My father," she murmured, stunned to learn he had noticed, had felt something. "In gratitude and relief when I graduated. You do remember." Her breath came out on a laugh as she tossed her hair back. "You did notice."

He no longer felt the weight, the twist of guilt or the denial.

There was only pleasure, with himself, with her. "And from the moment I did, you've never been out of my mind."

She hoped it was true. Reckless, she didn't care if it wasn't. "You never asked me to dance."

"No." He twined a lock of her hair around his finger. "I'd already decided that if I touched you it might be the end of my sanity. I saw you leave the ballroom with Bennett."

"Were you jealous?" She caught her bottom lip between her teeth to try to suppress the smile.

"Jealousy is a very low and common emotion." He slipped a hand down to the curve of her hip. "I was eaten with it."

Her laughter was rich and full. "Oh, Alex, I'm so glad. There was never any need, but I'm so glad."

"I nearly followed you." He said this quietly as his expression turned inward. "I told myself I'd be a fool, but if I had—"

"No." She laid her fingertips on his lips. "You couldn't know what would happen."

He brushed his lips over her fingers, then took them in his. "I saw you come back in, alone, pale. You were trembling. All I could think was that Bennett had upset you. I reached you just as you were telling Reeve and my father what was happening on the terrace upstairs. You were as white as a sheet and trembling, but you led us back to them."

"When we got there and I saw the blood and Ben lying on the ground... I thought he was dead." She closed her eyes a moment, then lowered herself to Alexander. "All I could think was that it wasn't right, wasn't fair. He'd been so much alive." Even with her eyes closed she could see, so she opened them and watched the moonlight. "So long ago, but I've never forgotten any of it. When Janet Smithers and Loubet were arrested, I thought it was over and everyone would be safe. And now—"

"Everyone is safe."

"No." She lifted her head again and shook it fiercely. "Alex, don't shut me out of this. The phone call came to me, and the warning. I was there seven years ago to see what Deboque can do from his prison cell. I'm here now."

"It's not for you to worry about Deboque."

"Now you're treating me like a child, the way you think a woman should be treated."

He couldn't prevent his lips from curving. "You can accuse me of that when I have such a sister as Gabriella? Eve, I learned as a child not to expect a woman to like to be coddled. I only mean that you can do nothing about Deboque and that worrying about him is useless." He ran a fingertip down the side of her face. "If it makes you easier, I can tell you that Reeve is working on a solution."

"It doesn't. Every time you leave the palace to perform some duty I'm afraid."

"*Ma belle*, I can hardly remain in the palace until Deboque is dead." Seeing the expression on her face, he kept his voice quiet. It was best she understood, and understood now before they took another step. "Do you think it will end before that? As long as he lives he'll seek his revenge. It is in Cordina he's imprisoned."

"Then have him transferred to another prison."

"It's not so simple as that. Deboque knows how long and hard my father worked to put him behind bars."

"But Reeve said it was Interpol."

"And it was, but without my father's cooperation, without the information gathered by our own security, Deboque might still be free. My life, my family's lives can't be run on the fear of what one might do."

But hers could. Eve gathered him close again. "I couldn't bear it if anything happened to you."

"Then you'll have to trust me to see that nothing does. *Chérie*, where did you learn to fence?"

He was trying to distract her. And he was right. The night was theirs. It would be wrong to let Deboque spoil even that. "In Houston."

"Fencing masters in Houston?"

She was amused, and looked it. "Even America has room for elegant sports. You don't have to be embarrassed that I beat you."

"You didn't beat me." He rolled her onto her back. "The match was never completed."

"I scored the only hit. But if it tramples on your ego, I won't tell anyone."

"I can see we have to finish what we started."

She smiled slowly. In the moonlight her eyes were dark and lustrous. "I'm counting on it."

* * *

The alarm clock shrilled. Groggy, Eve groped for the button, then shoved it in with enough force to make the clock shudder. She could be late, she decided sleepily. This one morning they could get started without her. She rolled over to cuddle in Alexander's arms.

He wasn't there.

Still groggy, she pushed the hair out of her eyes as she sat up. The top sheet was draped over her, but it was cool, just as the sheet beneath was cool. The breeze still tapped at the hem of the curtains, still smelled of the sea, but now sunlight poured through. And the room was empty.

He'd picked up her robe and had put it at the foot of the bed. The bed they had shared. All traces of him were gone. Just as he was gone.

Without a word, Eve thought as she sat alone. She didn't even know when he had gone. It hardly mattered when. She reached for her robe before she rose, then slipped it on, belting it as she walked to the window.

Boats were already on the water, casting out for the day's catch. The cool white yacht was still anchored, but she could see no one on deck. The beach was deserted but for gulls and the little sand crabs she was too far away to see. The gardener was below her window, watering. The sound of his tuneless whistle reached her and quieted the birds. A trio of pale yellow butterflies rose up, fluttering away from the spray of water, then settling on already dampened bushes. Wet leaves glimmered in the sunlight, while the mixed scent of flowers trailed its way up to her window.

The day was in full bloom. The night was over.

She couldn't be sorry. There was no room in her heart for regrets. What she had shared with Alexander had been magic, a wish come true. She had found him gentle, caring and sweet. The glory of that still remained with her. Briefly he had held her to him as though nothing and no one mattered as much as she. Now that the night was over, there were responsibilities neither of them could ignore.

He would never ignore them, not for her, not for Deboque, not for anyone. She could stand at the window, struggling against the fear of what might be, but he would do whatever his duty demanded. How could she fault him for being what he was, if she loved him?

But, oh, how she wished he could be there with her, watching the morning.

Turning away from the window, Eve prepared to face the day on her own.

Chapter 9

From the fly gallery above the stage, Eve had a bird's-eye view of rehearsal. It was in its sixth hour, and there had only been two bouts of temper. Things had settled down since the meeting she had called the afternoon before, but she continued to make notes on the yellow pad secured to her clipboard.

She'd been right about the casting, she thought smugly as she watched Russ and Linda run through a scene as Brick and Maggie. The spark was there, and the sex. When they were onstage the temperature rose ten degrees. Linda played Maggie the Cat to the hilt, desperate, grasping and hungry. Russ's Brick was just aloof enough without being cold, his needs and turmoils raging under the surface.

They were a constant contrast to the second leads, with the nastiness and rivalry not so much obvious as natural. She couldn't help but be pleased with herself, especially since they were going to bring the production in underbudget.

The director took them back, and Linda repeated the same line for the fifth time that hour. Both she and Russ went through the same moves. The patience of actors, Eve mused, and wondered at herself for ever believing she could have thought to be one. She was much better here, supervising, organizing.

But the set...she tapped her pencil against her lips. The set wasn't quite right. Too shiny, she realized. Too new, too staged.

She narrowed her eyes and tried to see it her way. It needed to be a bit more wilted, used, even decaying under a sheen of beeswax and lemon oil. With a focal point, she realized with growing excitement. Something big and brash and shiny that would show up the rest. A vase, she decided, oversize and ornate in some vivid color. They'd fill it with flowers that Big Momma could fuss with while she was trying to ignore the disintegration of her family.

She scribbled hurriedly as she heard the director call for a break.

Maneuvering over ropes, she started down the winding stairs that would take her to the stage. "Pete." She cornered the property master before he could light his cigarette. "I want a few changes."

"Aw, Ms. Hamilton."

"Nothing major," she assured him, putting a hand on his shoulder and walking out onto the set. "Pete, we need to age things a bit."

He was a small man, hardly taller than she was, so that their eyes were level when he turned and began to scratch at his chin. "How old?"

"Ten years?" She smiled in lieu of an order. "Look, the family's lived here awhile, right? They didn't buy all this stuff yesterday. I think if the couch were faded—"

. A long, suffering sigh. "You want me to fade the couch."

"Upholstery fades, Pete. It's one of those unavoidable facts of life. I think if you took off the cover and had wardrobe wash it a half-dozen times that would do it. And dull the gilt on a couple of the paintings. I don't want any scratches on the furniture, but... Doilies." Inspiration hit and she began to scribble again. "We need some doilies."

"And you want me to find them."

"Didn't you once mention that you were a scavenger when you were in the service?" She said it mildly as she moved to a different angle.

"You'd have made general," he muttered. "Okay, faded couch, dulled gilt and doilies. What else?"

"An urn." She narrowed her eyes as they swept the set. It had to be just the right place, not center stage, not too far downstage, but— "Right there," she decided, pointing to the table beside a wing chair. "A big one, Pete, with some carving or a pattern. And

I don't want anything too tasteful. Red, really red, so it stands out like a beacon."

He scratched his chin again. "You're the boss."

"Trust me."

"Ms. Hamilton, none of us has a choice."

She accepted this without a blink. "Don't spend over thirty for the vase. We're not looking for an heirloom."

He'd been waiting for her to get to the bottom line. "You want cheap, you'll get cheap."

"I knew I could count on you. Now on the bedroom set, I think it would be effective if we had some jewelry, gold and a little tacky, left on Cat's vanity."

"Already got the bottles and that big box of dusting powder."

"Now we'll have the jewelry. If wardrobe doesn't have anything suitable, we can pick up something. Why don't you check with Ethel? I'll be in my office for the next twenty minutes or so."

"Ms. Hamilton."

Eve turned at the leg on stage right. "Yes?"

"I never did care much for extra work." He took out his cigarette again while she waited for him to go on. "Problem here is, I can see you've got a feel for it—the stage, I mean."

"I appreciate that, Pete."

"I'll get your doilies." He struck the match. "But I'm going to send one of the women out for 'em."

"I've always admired a man who can delegate authority." She suppressed the chuckle until she was out of earshot.

She never had been quite able to figure out what a man like Pete was doing in theater. It seemed to her that he'd be more at home roping cattle, but here he was. He guarded his props as though they were treasures, and knew the theater history of each one. There wasn't a doubt in her mind that within twenty-four hours she would have everything she'd asked for.

After pushing open the door of her office, she pulled the pins out of her hair. She'd worn it up for the sake of coolness and efficiency, but the weight of it had begun to pull. Letting it fall free, she stuck the pins in her pocket. Priorities being what they were, she went straight to the coffeemaker and switched it on. Then, because she had a half a dozen calls to make, she drew off her left earring and dropped it in with the pins. Before she could sit and pick up the phone, it began to ring.

"Hello."

"The royal family has made a mistake."

She recognized the voice. The hand still in her pocket closed into a fist that snapped the back from the earring. "The royal family doesn't give in to threats."

The call was being tapped. She knew it and remembered through the first fear that her job was to keep the caller on the line.

"You'll have to tell your boss that he will serve out his term in prison."

"Justice must be served. The royal family and all those close to them will have to pay."

"I told you before, only a coward makes anonymous calls, and it's difficult to fear a coward." But she was afraid.

"You interfered once and your seven years of freedom may be at an end."

"I don't bend to threats, either." But her hands were damp.

"They won't find the bomb, *mademoiselle*. Perhaps they won't find you."

As the phone went dead, Eve stared at it. Bomb? There had been a bomb in Paris. Her hand shook lightly as she replaced the receiver. No, he'd meant another bomb, here, today. *Alexander.*

She had her hand on the doorknob when the full impact of the phone call hit her.

Your seven years of freedom may be at an end. Perhaps they won't find you, either.

The theater, she realized. The bomb was here, in the theater. Her heart in her throat, she pulled the door open and began to run. She saw Doreen first, showing off a bracelet to two other members of the troupe.

"I want you to get out of the theater, go back to the hotel, now, all of you."

"But the break's nearly over and—"

"Rehearsal's over. Get out of the theater and go back to the hotel. Now." Knowing that even a mention of a bomb would send them into panic, she left it at a clipped order. "Gary." She hung on to control as she flagged down her stage manager. "I want you to clear the theater, everyone, actors, stage crew, wardrobe, technicians. Everybody. Get everyone out and back to the hotel.''

''But, Eve—''

''Just move.''

She shoved past him and onto the stage. ''There's been an emergency.'' She lifted her voice so that it filled all corners. ''Everyone is to leave the theater immediately. Go back to the hotel and wait there. If you're in costume, leave as you are and leave now.'' She glanced at her watch. When was it set? Would she hear the explosion? ''I want this theater empty within two minutes.''

She carried the authority. There might have been grumbles, there were certainly questions, but people began to file out. Eve left the stage to check the storerooms, the dressing rooms, anywhere someone might have gone before the announcement was made. She found Pete, locking up his precious props.

''I said out.'' Taking him by the shirtfront, she dragged him to the door. ''Leave everything.''

''I'm responsible for all of this. I'm not having some light-fingered—''

''You're out in ten seconds or you're fired.''

That snapped his mouth closed. Eve Hamilton never made a statement she didn't back up. His chin shot up and a dozen different rejoinders rushed through his mind. Wisely he left them there and started down the hall. ''Anything's stolen, you'll have to make it good,'' he muttered.

''Let's just hope something's left,'' she said to herself, and dashed to the other doors. Each one she slammed behind her echoed more hollowly. She found one actor dozing in a dressing room and routed him in seconds. He was shoeless and groggy, but she shoved him out in the hall and in the direction of the stage door.

Everyone was out, she told herself. They had to be. She thought she could hear the ticking of her watch inside her head. How much more time? Time could already be up. But she had to be sure. She was about to dash up the steps to check the second level, when a hand fell on her shoulder.

Her breath came out in a squeak, and though her knees went weak, she whirled to defend.

"Hold it, hold it." Russ threw up both hands. "I'm just trying to find out what's going on."

"What are you doing here?" Furious, she lowered her hands, but they remained in fists. "I told everyone to get out."

"I know. I was coming back in from the break when everyone else came out. Nobody knew why. What's up, Eve? Is there a fire or something?"

"Just go back to the hotel and wait."

"Look, what gives? If this is your way of saying you didn't like this morning's rehearsal—"

"I'm not playing around here." Her voice rose as the last of her control snapped. There were beads of sweat on her temples and a stream of it down her back. Cold sweat. "I got a bomb threat. Do you understand? I think there's a bomb in the theater."

He stood where he was a moment as she started up the steps, then he was scrambling after her. "A bomb? A bomb in the theater? What in the hell are you doing? Let's get out."

"I have to make certain everyone else did." She shook him off and sprinted up the rest of the stairs.

"Eve, for God's sake." His voice cracked as he raced after her. "There's no one left. Let's get out of here and call the police, the fire department. Whoever."

"We will—as soon as I make sure everyone got out." After she'd checked every room and shouted until she was hoarse, she was satisfied. Terror began to edge its way in. Her heart in her throat, she grabbed him by the arm and raced downstairs again. They were nearly to the stage door when the explosion hit.

"I'm pleased you could meet me here, Monsieur Trouchet."

"I'm always at your disposal, Your Highness." Trouchet took the seat Alexander offered, setting his briefcase neatly on his lap. "It was a pleasure to see you at the Cabots' last night, but as you said, such a gathering is not always appropriate for business discussions."

"And as the health-care bill is, shall we say, a pet project of mine, I prefer to give it the time and place it warrants."

Settled behind his desk, Alexander drew out a cigarette. He was well aware that Trouchet objected to the heart of the bill and that he was in a position to sway many members of the council. Al-

exander intended to see the bill put in force, with very few concessions.

"I know your time is valuable, *monsieur*, so we won't hedge.
Cordina has only two modern hospitals. In the capital and in Le
Havre. There are fishing villages and farms in outlying areas that
rely solely on the clinics set up by medical personnel. These clinics, though never conceived as profitable businesses, have steadily
been losing ground over the past five years."

"I am aware of that, sir, as are other members of the council.
I've brought documentation with me."

"Of course." Alexander allowed him to pass neatly typed
sheets, facts and figures, across the desk.

"Taking into account these documents plus the statements from
several village doctors, it is my belief that the clinics will only
remain in force if they are taken over and run by the state."

Though he knew what he would find, Alexander gave him the
courtesy of looking over the papers. "When the state takes over,
it also takes the pride and the independence of the individuals
involved."

"And greatly increases the efficiency, Your Highness."

"People run the state, as well, *monsieur*," Alexander said
mildly. "The state is not always efficient. But your point is well
taken. Which is why I believe that with a subsidy, an allotment
only, the clinics—medical personnel and patients—can retain both
pride and efficiency."

Trouchet closed his case but didn't latch it. His capable hands
folded on the lid. "Surely you can see that a compromise of this
nature is fraught with pitfalls."

"Oh, indeed." Alexander smiled and blew out smoke. "Which
is why I come to you, *monsieur*, to ask your help in filling those
holes."

Trouchet sat back, knowing he was being offered a challenge,
a position of importance and a request for surrender all at once.
He ran a finger down his nose as he chuckled. "I have no doubt
you could fill the holes yourself, Your Highness."

"But together, *monsieur*, we work for greater efficiency, and
ultimately for the same end. *N'est ce pas?*" Alexander drew out
a file of his own. "If we could go over these—"

He broke off, looking up in annoyance as Bennett burst in.

"Alex." He didn't so much as nod at Trouchet as the other man rose. "Reeve just phoned. There's been an explosion."

Alexander was up from his chair, his muscles rigid. "Father?"

Bennett shook his head. "Alex, it's the theater."

His face went white, so white that Bennett stepped forward, afraid he would crumple. But Alexander held up a hand. When he spoke it was only one word. At that moment his world was only one word. "Eve?"

"He didn't know." Bennett turned to Trouchet. "Please excuse us, *monsieur*, we must leave immediately." He went to his brother's side. "Together."

The council member gathered up his papers and case, but before he could shut the lid, he was alone in the room.

"How? How did it happen?" Alexander demanded as they rushed to the car. When Bennett claimed the driver's seat he started to object, then subsided. Bennett was right to do so. He would probably kill them both on the way to the theater.

"Reeve was only on the phone for a minute." Bennett peeled down the drive, with the royal guards close behind. "She got another call, something was said about a bomb—about them not finding a bomb, and…" But he couldn't say the rest, not when his brother was so white and stiff.

"And?"

"And they realized the caller meant a bomb in the theater. The police were there within minutes, five, ten at the most. They heard it go off."

Alexander pressed his lips together. "Where?"

"In her office. Alexander," he continued quickly, "she wouldn't have been in there. Eve's too smart for that."

"She worried for me, for all of us. But not for herself." He wouldn't let go, though there was a pain burning between his eyes and another eating slowly through his gut. "Why is it we never thought of her?"

"If you want to blame yourself, blame all of us," Bennett said grimly. "None of us ever realized Eve would be drawn into this. There's no purpose in it. Goddamn it, Alex, there's no purpose in it."

"You said yourself she's part of the family." He looked blindly out the window. They were a half block from the theater. His muscles began to tremble. It was fear, stark, raging fear. Before Bennett had fully stopped at the curb he was out.

By the stage door, Reeve stopped talking to two of his men and stepped forward to ward Alexander off. At his signal a handful of police shifted over as a shield. "She's not in there. Alex, she's in the grove around back. She's all right." When the grip of Alexander's fingers on his arms didn't lessen, Reeve repeated. "She's all right, Alex. She wasn't in the office. She was nearly out of the building altogether."

He didn't feel relief. Not until he had seen for himself would he feel relief. Pulling away from Reeve, Alexander rushed around the side of the building. His eyes were drawn to the blown-out window, the blackened bricks. Pieces of jagged glass littered the grass beyond. What might have been a lamp lay in a tangle of bent metal on the path to the grove. Inside was what remained of Eve's office.

If he had looked through the space in the wall where her window had been, he would have seen pieces of her desk. Some of the wood, torn into lethal spears, had arrowed into the walls. He would have seen the soaked ashes of what had been her files and papers, correspondence and notations. He would have seen the hole in the inside wall that was big enough for a man to walk through. But he didn't look.

Then he saw her, sitting at the verge of the grove, leaning forward on a bench with her head in her hands. Guards flanked her and the man who sat beside her, but Alexander saw only Eve. Whole. Safe. Alive.

She heard him, though he'd barely even whispered her name. A shudder of emotion passed over her face, then she was up and running for him.

"Oh, Alex, at first I thought he meant it for you, and then—"

"You're not hurt." He had her face in his hands, framing it, exploring it. "Anywhere, anywhere at all?"

"No. Unless you count knees that tend to buckle and a stomach that tends to turn to jelly."

"I thought you might..." But he couldn't finish the thought. Instead he pulled her close again and kissed her as if his life depended on it. The guards kept the reporters at a distance, but the picture would hit the Cordinian and international papers.

"I'm all right," she murmured over and over, because it was finally sinking in that it was true. "You're shaking as much as I am."

"They could only tell me that there had been an explosion at the theater—in your office."

"Oh, Alex." She held him close, knowing the hell he would have experienced not knowing. "I'm so sorry. We were going out the stage door when it exploded. As it turned out, the bomb squad was sending in men through the main entrance. When it hit we just kept going, and the police didn't find us until they started spreading out."

He held her hands so tightly they ached, but she said nothing. "And your troupe? Everyone is safe?"

"I got them out within minutes of the call. All but Russ, that is," she added, glancing behind her at a very pale and quiet actor. "I was going over the second floor to make certain I hadn't missed anyone, when he—"

"You? You were going over?" Now she did wince at the pressure of his hands.

"Alex, please." She flexed her fingers until his loosened.

"Are you mad? Don't you understand that bomb could have been planted anywhere? There could have been more than one. Searching the building is a job for the police."

"Alex, my people were in that building. I could hardly waltz out not knowing if they were all safe. As a matter of fact, I had to drag Pete by the shirt, and—"

"You could have been killed."

There was such bitterness, such fury in the tone, that her back straightened, though her knees had begun to weaken again. "I'm very much aware of that, Alex. So could any one of my people. Every one of them is my responsibility. You understand about responsibility, don't you?"

"It's entirely different."

"No, it's entirely the same. You ask me to understand, to trust. I'm only asking the same from you."

"Damn it, it's because of my family that—" But he broke off as he gripped her shoulders. "You're shaking again."

"Shock." Reeve's voice came from behind. He had his jacket

off and was draping it over her. "Both Eve and Talbot should go to the hospital."

Alexander swore at himself for not taking proper care of her, but before he could agree Eve was backing off. "I don't need to go to the hospital. All I really need is to sit down for a few minutes." Her teeth began to chatter.

"In this you'll do as you're told." Alex motioned for one of the guards to assist Russ.

"Alexander, if I could have a brandy and a quiet room, I would—"

"You can have a quart of brandy and as many quiet rooms as you wish. After you've seen Dr. Franco." He scooped her up in his arms before she could protest.

"For heaven's sake, I'm strong as a horse." But her head found his shoulder and settled there.

"We'll have the doctor confirm that, and bring in a veterinarian if you like." He paused briefly to look at Reeve. "We'll talk later?"

"I'll be at the palace in an hour or two."

Eve lay on the pristine white examining table and frowned as Dr. Franco shone the pinpoint light in her left eye. "Too much fuss," she muttered.

"Doctors like nothing better than fussing," he told her, then shone the light in her right eye. Flicking the light off, he took her pulse again. His touch was gentle, his eyes kind. Eve had to smile at the smooth white dome of his head.

"Don't you consider it a waste of your time to examine a perfectly healthy patient?"

"I need the practice." His lips curved in the bed of his white beard. "Once I've satisfied myself, I can set the prince's mind at rest. I don't think you'd like to worry him."

"No." She sighed as he attached the blood pressure cuff. "I just don't care for hospitals." Meeting the irony in his eyes, she sighed again. "When I lost my mother, we spent hours in the waiting room. It was a slow, painful process for all of us."

"Death is hardest on those left behind—just as illness is often more difficult for the healthy." He understood her aversion to hospitals, but remembered that when Prince Bennett had been recovering from his wounds, she had come every day to sit with him. "You've had a shock, my dear, but you're strong and resilient. You'd be pleased if I assured the prince you didn't have to remain overnight."

She was already sitting up. "A great deal more than pleased."

"Then a bargain must be struck," he added, gently coaxing her back down.

"Ah, the kicker." She smiled again and tried to ignore the fact that she felt like a bowl of gelatin. "How about free orchestra seats to opening night of each play?"

"I wouldn't refuse." Her pulse was strong, her blood pressure well within the normal range, but there was still a lack of color in her cheeks and a hollow look around the eyes. "But to seal this bargain, I must have your word that you will rest for twenty-four hours."

"Twenty-four? But tomorrow I have to—"

"Twenty-four," he repeated in his mild, implacable tone. "Or I will tell the prince that you require a night of observation here at St. Alban's."

"If I have to stay in bed all day tomorrow, I'll need more than a hospital."

"We could perhaps compromise with a walk in the garden, a drive by the sea. But no work, my dear, and no stress."

She could make calls from her bedroom, she decided. Her office would probably take days to repair in any case. And if agreement got her out, she'd agree. "Twenty-four hours." She sat up again and offered her hand.

"Come, then. I'll take you out before there is a rut in the corridor from the pacing."

Alexander was indeed pacing when Dr. Franco brought her out of the examining room. Bennett was leaning against the wall, watching the door. As soon as they came through, both men started forward. Alexander took Eve's hand, but looked at Franco.

"Doctor?"

"Miss Hamilton is naturally a bit shaken, but has a strong constitution."

"I told you," she said smugly.

"However, I have recommended twenty-four hours of rest."

"Not bed rest," Eve put in.

"No," Franco agreed with a smile. "Not complete bed rest. Though all activity should be relaxing. What she needs now is some quiet and a good meal."

"Medication?" Alexander asked.

"I don't believe she requires anything, Your Highness, but a bit of pampering. Oh, and I would disconnect the phone in her room for the next twenty-four-hour period." When Eve's mouth fell open, he patted her hand. "We can't have you disturbed by phone calls, can we, my dear?" With a final pat he wandered away.

"Sharper than he looks," Eve said under her breath, but was weary enough to accept defeat. "Russ?"

"One of the guards took him back to the hotel." Bennett touched her shoulder. "His nerves are a bit shot, that's all. The doctor gave him some tranquilizers."

"Now we'll take you home." Alexander took her arm. Bennett flanked her other side. "My father and the rest of the family are anxious to see for themselves that you're all right."

She was fussed over, pampered, as per doctor's orders, and put to bed by the Bissets' old nanny. The woman who had cared for Alexander's mother, for him and his brother and sister, and now for the third generation, clucked and muttered and had hands as gentle as a baby's. They were curled with arthritis, yellowed and spotted with age, but she undressed Eve and slipped her into night-clothes effortlessly.

"When your dinner tray comes, you will eat."

"Yes, Nanny," Eve said meekly as her pillows were fluffed and piled behind her.

The old woman settled beside her and picked up a cup of tea. "And now you will drink this. All of this. It's my own mixture and will put the color back in your cheeks. All my children drink it when they are sick."

"Yes, Nanny." Even Prince Armand had never awed her as much as the silver-haired, black-clad old woman with the Slavic accent. Eve sipped at the mixture, expecting the worst, and was surprised by a nutty herbal taste.

"There." Pleased with herself, Nanny nodded. "Children always think medicine will taste nasty and find tricks to keep from taking it. I know tricks of my own." Her stiff skirts rustled as she shifted. "Even little Dorian asks for Nanny's drink when he's feeling poorly. When Alexander was ten, Franco took out his tonsils. He wanted my tea more than the ice cream."

She tried to picture Alexander as a child, and only saw the man, so tall and straight and proud. "What was he like, Nanny, when he was little?"

"Reckless. Thunderous." She smiled and the symphony of wrinkles on her face deepened. "Such a temper. But the responsibility was always there. He learned it in the cradle. He seemed to understand even as a baby that he would always have more than other men. And less." As she spoke, she rose to tidy Eve's clothes. "He was obedient. Though you could see the defiance in his eyes, he was obedient. He studied hard. He learned well. Both he and Bennett were fortunate that their personalities were so markedly different. They fought, of course. Brothers must, after all. But they became fond of each other early as people."

She kept a sharp eye on her patient, and noted the tea was nearly finished. "He has the intensity of his father, sometimes more. But, then, the Prince had my Elizabeth to share with him, to soothe him, to make him laugh at himself. My Alexander needs a wife."

Eve's gaze rose slowly over the rim of her cup. She was warm and growing drowsy, but she recognized the look in Nanny's eyes. "He'll have to decide that for himself."

"For himself. And for Cordina. The woman he chooses will have to be strong, and willing to share the burdens." Nanny took the empty cup. "Most of all, I hope she is capable of making him laugh."

"I love to hear him laugh," Eve murmured as her eyes fluttered closed. "Does it show, Nanny? Does it show that I love him so much?"

"I have such old eyes." Nanny smoothed the sheets before she dimmed the light. "And old eyes see more than young ones. Rest now and dream. He'll come to you before this night is over, or I don't know my children."

She knew them well. Eve stirred and sighed and saw Alexander the moment she opened her eyes. He was sitting on the edge of the bed, her hand in his, watching.

"Nanny gave me a magic potion."

He kissed her knuckles. He wanted to go on kissing her, holding her close and tight against him until the nightmare had faded completely. With an effort he kept his fingers light, as well as his voice.

"It brought the color back to your cheeks. She said you'd be waking soon and would be hungry."

Eve pushed herself up. "She's right. I'm starved."

He rose and walked to a tray at the foot of the bed. "She ordered your menu herself." He began to remove covers. "Chicken broth, a small lean steak, fresh greens, potatoes mixed with grated cheese."

"Enough torture." Eve laid a hand on her stomach. "I haven't eaten since breakfast. I'll start anywhere."

"The broth, I think." He placed it on a tray.

"Oh, it smells wonderful." Eve picked up the spoon and began to recharge her system. He sat in silence while she worked her way through the soup. He could remember every word of Reeve's report.

Though tests had still to be run, it was almost certain that the bomb had been the same type as the one planted in the Paris embassy. If anyone had been in the office, or even within twenty feet of the door, it would have been fatal.

Eve's office—where he had once seen her sitting so competently behind her desk.

Security believed that Eve had not been meant to be harmed. Hence the warning. The bomb had been used to terrorize, to confuse, to undermine. But if she hadn't been quick enough…

He wouldn't think beyond that. She was here now, unharmed. Whatever he had to do, she would remain that way. When she'd finished the broth, he removed the bowl and replaced it with the main course.

"I suppose I could get used to the pampering." The meat was pink and tender inside. "It was so sweet of everyone, even your father, to come in and see me, to make sure I was all right."

"My father cares for you. All of us do."

She tried not to make it mean more than it did. He did care. She'd felt it in the way he'd held her when he'd reached the grove. Maybe, just maybe, he even loved her a little. But she couldn't push him, or herself. It was best to deal with other things.

She toyed with her potatoes. "But I really do feel fine now,

Alex. There's no need for you to go to the trouble of disconnecting the phones."

"It's already done." He took a bottle of wine from a bucket and poured two glasses. "There won't be any need for you to speak with anyone outside the palace tomorrow. Brie and her family are moving in temporarily. I'm sure the children can entertain you."

"Alex, be reasonable. I have to talk to my people. They must be frantic. You have no idea how overblown theater people can make things. And getting my office back into shape is going to take days."

"I want you to go back to Houston."

Slowly she set her knife and fork on the tray. "What?"

"I want you to take your troupe back to America. I'm canceling the performances."

She hadn't realized she had the energy for anger. "You try that and I'll sue your royal tail off."

"Eve, this is no time for ego. What happened today—"

"Had nothing to do with the theater and little to do with me. We both know that. If it did, I'd be no safer in Houston than here."

He was through with logic. In this, with her, there were only feelings. "I don't want you here."

The quick slice of pain hit its mark. She let it pass, then picked up her knife and fork again. "It won't do any good to try to hurt me, Alexander. I won't go, and neither will the troupe, not until all four performances are finished. We have a contract."

His French was harsher and a great deal more explicit than his English. He rolled into it as he rose to pace the room. She'd learned enough in her Swiss boarding school, particularly in the dorms, to understand him perfectly.

"Nanny mentioned that you had a filthy temper," she said, and continued to eat. The fact that she'd finally seen it loose pleased her. He wasn't so controlled now, she thought. So she would be. "The wine is excellent, Alexander. Why don't you sit down and enjoy it?"

"Merde!" He swung back to her, resisting the urge to fling her tray and its contents on the floor. "This is not a game. Do you know what I went through when I thought you might be dead? That you might have been in that room when the bomb went off?"

She set her utensils down again and lifted her gaze to his. "I think I do. I go through much of the same every time you go out in public. This morning I stood at that window and thought of you. I didn't even know how long you'd been gone."

"I didn't want to wake you."

"I'm not asking for explanations, Alex." Her appetite gone, she pushed the tray away. "I'm trying to make you see what I was feeling. I looked out at the sea, and I knew you were somewhere, tending to Cordina. Somewhere I couldn't be, somewhere I couldn't help you. And I had to get dressed and go out and go on, when in the back of my mind was the fear that today would be the day I'd lose you."

"Eve, I'm so surrounded by guards that sometimes I think they'll smother me. The security on all of us has been doubled since the bomb in Paris."

"Is that supposed to comfort me? Would it comfort you?" He said nothing, but came and removed the tray from her lap. "You want me to run away, Alex. Will you run away with me?"

"You know I can't. This is my country."

"And this is my job. Please don't ask me to go." She held out a hand, watched him hesitate, then come back to take it. "If you want to be angry with me, wait until tomorrow. All through this hideous day I've wanted you to hold me. Please stay with me tonight, Alex."

"You need rest." But he gathered her close.

"I'll rest after," she murmured, and drew him down with her.

Chapter 10

Her office looked as though it had been bombed. Somehow, even living through it, being told about it, reading the story in the paper, Eve hadn't been prepared for the stark reality of it.

She'd kept her word and had stayed away for twenty-four hours—mainly because she'd been given no choice. Now she stood at the doorway, or what was left of the doorway, and looked at what had been her office.

The debris hadn't been hauled away, by order of the police. They had sifted and searched through the ashes and rubble throughout the night of the bombing, the day she'd been kept away, and the night she'd lain restless and anxious to get back to work. If there had been a sense of order to their investigation, Eve couldn't see it.

There was a hole in one wall, taller and wider than she, so that Eve could see that the small, unoccupied room beyond had problems of its own. Shafts of wood were burrowed into the plaster or lay heaped on the floor. Her file cabinet was a mass of twisted metal, the contents ashes. The carpet was gone, simply gone, with the floor beneath scarred and scored. The window had been boarded up so that no light seeped through. The repair crew was coming that morning, but she had wanted to see it for herself, before it was swept clean.

She didn't shudder. She had thought she would when she had

been walking down the hall. The fear she had expected, had been willing to accept, didn't come. In the hole left by fear, anger came, ripe and deep and cleansing.

All her files, her notes, her records—destroyed. She stepped in and kicked aside a lump of ceiling. Weeks, months, even years of work reduced to rubble in a matter of seconds. Some things could be replaced; other things were simply irreplaceable.

The picture she had had on her desk, her favorite one of her and Chris; it was part of the ashes. Gone, too, was the play she had written and the one she'd been working on. The tears that sprang to her eyes weren't of sorrow, but of fury. Her work might have been rough, maybe it had even been foolish, but it had been her work. Lack of confidence and her own self-deprecating humor had caused her to file it away under *F* for Fantasies.

Now that dream was gone, blown apart by someone who didn't even know her. They had taken away pieces of her life, and would have taken her life, as well, without a second thought.

They would pay, she promised herself as she stood among the wreckage. Somehow, someway, she would see to it personally.

"Eve."

With the back of her wrist she swiped at her eyes before turning. "Chris!"

In that instant she was only a younger sister. The emotion and need swamped her as she scrambled over the wreckage and into her sister's arms. "I'm so glad you're here. I'm so glad."

"Of course I'm here. I came the moment I heard." Chris squeezed tightly as relief came and the hours of dread through her traveling eased. "I went to the palace first. I've never seen so much security there before. If it hadn't been for Bennett I might still be arguing with the guards at the gates. Eve, for God's sake, what's going on?"

"It's gone. Everything. The picture of us at the opening of my first play. It was on the desk. The little china cat Mom gave me when I was ten. I always took it with me. There's nothing left of it, nothing at all."

"Oh, baby." Holding tight, Chris surveyed the room over Eve's shoulder. Unlike her sister, she did shudder, for what might have been. "I'm so sorry. But you're safe." Anxiously, she held her at arm's length to study carefully. "You weren't hurt?"

"No, no, I was nearly out of the building. Reeve said it was just a small plastic bomb. Not much range."

"A small bomb," Chris repeated in a whisper, and pulled Eve against her again. "Just a small one." Her own anger surfaced as she gave her sister a quick shake. "Eve, do you know how it felt to hear about it on the news?"

"I'm sorry, Chris. Everything happened so fast, and I guess I wasn't thinking straight. I should have called you."

"Damn right you should have." Then she let it pass, knowing what Eve's state of mind must have been. "Brie did. Prince Armand called Dad personally. He was all for hopping on the first plane and dragging you back to Houston."

"Oh, Chris."

"You're safe—only because I convinced him we'd have better luck getting you to listen to me."

"I'll call him. Honestly, I never thought the news would get to the States so quickly."

"I want the whole story, Eve, not the watered-down, public relations version I got on the six o'clock news." Chris's voice took on the firm maternal tone she had developed when Eve turned fifteen. "You can give it to me while I drive you back to the palace to pack."

"I'm not going back, Chris."

Chris stepped back and pushed her short, thick hair away from her forehead. "Now listen—"

"I love you," Eve interrupted. "And I understand how you must be feeling right now, looking at all this." She paused to take another scan of the room herself. The fury came back full force. "But I'm not running away. I came here to produce four plays, and by God, I'm going to produce four plays."

Chris started to shout, then checked herself. The one way you never got through to Eve was with orders. "Eve, you know how much I respect what you do, what you can do, but it's painfully obvious that Cordina isn't safe right now. This isn't worth risking your life over."

"The bomb wasn't planted for me. They only used me to get to the Bissets." She laid a hand on her sister's arm. "I can't go, Chris. I think once I explain everything, you'll understand."

"Then you'd better explain real good."

"I will." With a smile Eve kissed her cheek. "But not here. We'll use the theater manager's office." Eve urged Chris out into the hall, taking a quick look at her watch as they went. She intended to be back to work within the hour.

Twenty minutes later they were seated on a neat gray-and-rose sofa, working on their second cup of coffee. Chris drank hers black, using the strong, slightly bitter taste to soothe her nerves.

"Deboque." Her cup clattered in the saucer before she set it down. "All these years later and he's still causing such pain."

"From what Alex said, he'll never stop." As long as he lived. Eve pushed the thought away. She had never thought she could ever wish anyone dead. "I don't even know what kind of man he is. Evil, certainly, and I'd guess obsessed. The person who called spoke of justice—he spoke of it both times. Deboque's kind of justice won't be met until Prince Armand is destroyed. Reeve thinks the bomb in the theater was a show of strength. Chris, what's really frightening is that I know—somehow I'm sure—that the next target is going to be one of the Bissets." She thought of Alexander and pressed her lips together. "It could be any one of them, even one of the children. That's why Reeve and Brie have moved back into the palace for now."

Chris was silent while her loyalties warred inside her. "Eve, you know how I feel about the Bissets. They're a second family to me. But no matter how much I care for them, you come first. I want you home, away from this."

"I can't leave. One of the reasons is the troupe and what we're trying to do here. Please hear me out," she continued as Chris started to speak. When she subsided, Eve rose. She had to move. Time seemed to be pressing in on her from all directions. "I have a chance to prove something here, to myself, to you and Dad, to my industry."

"There's nothing you have to prove to me, Eve."

"I do. You took care of me." She turned back, her emotions a little shaky. "You were only five years older, but when Mom died, you did everything you could to fill the void. Maybe I wasn't always aware of what you were doing or what you gave up to do it, but I am now. I guess I need to show you it was worth it."

Chris felt her eyes fill and quickly shook her head. "Do you think I've ever doubted it? Eve, I did nothing more than be your sister.''

"Yes, you did. You were my friend.'' She came back to take both of Chris's hands. "Even when you didn't believe, didn't approve, you stood by me. What I'm doing here is as much for you as it is for me. I've never been able to explain that to you before.''

"Oh, sweetheart.'' Chris's fingers tightened on hers. "I don't know what to say.''

"Don't say anything for a minute. Just listen. A lot of people in the business chuckled behind my back when I first got started. Spoiled heiress out for a fling, that sort of thing. And maybe it was close to the truth at first. I never did anything worthwhile in my life before the troupe.''

"That's not true.''

"That's absolutely true.'' She had no problem accepting the truth, or using it to push herself further. "I skimmed my way through school doing the least amount of work possible. I lounged around during the summer doing nothing at all. I watched Dad wheel and deal, I watched you take your education and turn it into success with your gallery, and I picked up another magazine. With the theater I started to find a goal, without realizing I'd needed one. Chris, when I stood on the stage for the first time, it was like a light going on in my head. Maybe my place was behind it, not on it, but I found the goal. It took a couple years after the troupe was formed for people to stop laughing. Now I have a chance to do something extraordinary. I can't give it up.''

"I never knew you felt this way.'' Chris ran her hand over the back of Eve's. "I do understand, and I'm proud of you. I always have been, but I'm prouder than ever. I believe you can do something extraordinary, but the timing's off. Six months from now, a year from now, when things have settled down—''

"I can't leave, Chris. Even if they tore the theater down, if every one of my troupe went back, I couldn't leave.'' She had to draw a breath to say it, to say it out loud and calmly. "I'm in love with Alexander.''

"Oh.'' Because the wind had just been knocked out of her, Chris said nothing else.

"I have to be with him now, especially now. Once I thought the troupe was everything, but as important as it is, it doesn't come close to how I feel about him.'' She paused a moment, realizing what she was saying had been there all along—she just hadn't known it. ''You don't have to tell me that nothing can come of it—I've already figured that out for myself. But I have to be with him as long as I can.''

''Once I'd thought that maybe you and Bennett...I'd even gotten a kick out of imagining the two of you. But Alexander.''

''I know.'' Eve rose again. ''The heir. I've loved him for years. I managed to do a pretty good job of muddling that fact, even to myself, but there it is.''

''I'd wondered a couple of times if you might have been a bit infatuated.''

''I'm old enough to know the difference,'' Eve said with a smile.

''Yes.'' Sighing, Chris sat back. ''Does he know how you feel?''

''I haven't told him, but he's a very astute man. We've both been very careful not to mention any four-letter word beginning with *l*. Yes, I think he knows.''

''How does he feel, Eve, about you?''

''He cares, perhaps more than he intended, less than I'd like. It's difficult to read Alex. He's had so much practice harnessing his emotions.'' She took a deep breath. ''Besides, it doesn't matter.''

''How can you say that?''

''Because it can't matter.'' She was a practical woman, or so she told herself. A realist. ''I said I knew nothing could come of it, and I can deal with that. I'm a professional. My career takes a great deal of my time and energy. Even if Alex weren't who he is, I doubt if we could come to terms. I don't have time for marriage and a family. I don't need them.''

''I'm going to take more convincing than that—and so are you.''

''I really don't.'' How many times had she given herself this lecture over the past week? ''A great many women don't want marriage. Look at you.''

''Yeah.'' With a low laugh Chris sat up again. ''Eve, the only reason I'm not married and the mother of six is that I never met a man who was more important to me than my work. You've already told me you have."

"It doesn't matter. It can't matter." There was a thread of panic in her voice. "Chris, don't you see that whatever I want, whatever I'd like, I have to deal with the reality. If I don't accept the way things are, I'll lose. More than anything else, I don't want to lose him. I will one day." Restless, she ran her hands through her hair. "He'll have to marry, start a family. It's a duty he'd never shirk. But until then I can share some part of him."

"You love him so much," Chris murmured. "I don't know whether to cry for you or be happy."

"Be happy. There are enough reasons for tears in the world."

"All right, then." She stood and wrapped her arms around her sister. "I am happy for you." And she reserved the right to believe dreams could come true. "I don't suppose you'd take the afternoon off and go shopping with me?"

"Oh, I can't. I have to get on the phone to Houston and have copies of my records shipped over. I should already be at rehearsal making sure everyone's calm. I have to find some office space around here." She paused, though her mind was clicking off the next steps. "Shopping for what?"

"I only brought an overnight bag. Arrogance," she said as she picked up the leather tote. "I was sure we'd be on a plane by dinner. Now, it seems, I have to see if Cordina has something sensational for me to wear to opening night."

"You're staying."

"Of course. Think I can wheedle a room at the palace?"

Eve gave her a bone-crushing squeeze. "I'll put in a good word for you."

Hours later, Eve sat at the laptop computer in her sitting room. The day had gone quickly, filled with problems to be solved, but the evening had dragged. Alexander hadn't come back for dinner.

Bennett had been there, but even with his jokes and easy manner he had obviously been preoccupied. Reeve and Armand had also been absent. It was a family meal, with Gabriella and her children, Bennett, Eve and Chris—and the empty chairs where the rest of the family should have been. The moment the meal had been over

Bennett had excused himself. The tension even his casualness hadn't disguised remained in full force.

When Eve mentioned the work she still had to catch up on, Chris accompanied Gabriella upstairs to tend to the children. Back in her rooms, alone, Eve tried to fill the rest of her evening with work.

Her four scripts for the upcoming productions had been destroyed, but new copies had been secured before noon. There was no reason to look over them. She knew every word, every bit of staging. If it had been necessary, she could have filled in for any of her actors on opening night.

The opening was only days away, and though the cast had been understandably edgy that afternoon, rehearsals had gone well enough. The second production was almost as polished as the first, and rehearsals on the third play would begin the following week. If there were no more incidents.

The house was sold-out for the first three performances, and ticket sales were mounting steadily. Pete had even managed to come up with the props she had asked for.

She'd thought about reviewing her budget, but the idea of tallying figures had been anything but appealing. She had looked at her watch, soaked in the tub and checked the time again. It had been nearly ten when she'd sat down at the computer, telling herself that Alexander was safe and well, probably asleep in his own bed after a difficult day.

She would work. Her own plays had been destroyed. She could only blame herself for not making extra copies. Maybe it was just as well. That's what she told herself. The first one had been too emotional and flowery in any case. The second—well, that had taken her six months and she'd barely gotten out of Act One.

So she'd start fresh. A new idea, a new mood, and in some ways, a new woman. Act One, Scene One, Eve told herself as she clicked on an icon to create a new file.

Time clicked by. She had printed out—and wadded up—countless sheets of paper. But a satisfying pile of working draft sheets lay at her elbow. This time she would do it, she told herself. And when she was finished, she'd produce, maybe even direct the production herself. She chuckled as she stretched her fingers. Isn't that what she'd told herself whenever she'd begun to write?

Alexander found her that way, hunched over the keyboard, working steadily, with her hair piled on top of her head and her legs drawn up under her. The light was burning on the table and fell across her hands as they moved over the keys. She wore the same blue robe he remembered from the first night he had come to her. She'd pushed the sleeves up to her elbows and it fell carelessly open over her thigh.

Every time he saw her he was freshly amazed at how lovely she was. She exploited her looks when she chose, at other times was negligent of them. It never seemed to matter. Competence. Was that what added so much substance to beauty? Something about her told the onlooker she could do what she set out to do, and do it well.

Her hands appeared delicate, yet she was not. Her shoulders appeared fragile, yet she was strong. Her face was young, vulnerable and so sensitive. Though she might have been all those things, she had a strength and a sense of purpose that made her capable of dealing with whatever life handed her.

Is that why he loved her? For her capabilities? Weary, Alexander passed a hand over his face. He'd only begun to realize this fully, only begun to try to analyze and understand. Attraction had become so much more than an appreciation of beauty. Desire had dipped far beyond the physical.

He'd told her once he'd needed her. It had been true, before that moment and now past it. But he hadn't told her, or fully understood himself, the scope of the need.

When he'd thought he might have lost her, his heart seemed to have stopped beating. He seemed to have stopped seeing, stopped hearing, stopped feeling. Is that what it meant to love?

He wished he could be sure. He'd never allowed himself to love beyond his family and his country. With Eve he hadn't allowed, but had fallen victim to. Perhaps that was love. To be vulnerable, to be dependent, to be needful. Such a tremendous risk, a risk his practicality told him he couldn't afford. Not now, perhaps not ever. Yet it was done.

If he could have one wish at that moment, it would be to take her away somewhere where they could be ordinary people in ordinary times. Maybe tonight, for a few hours, they could pretend it was true.

He watched her straighten, then press her splayed hand against the small of her back.

"You promised you wouldn't overwork yourself."

Her hand stayed where it was, but her head shot around. He saw and recognized the relief, then the pleasure that came into her eyes. "This is what we term the pot calling the kettle black." Her gaze swept over him with a greediness that had his fatigue vanishing. "You look tired, Alex. I thought you'd be in bed."

"Meetings." He stepped into the room. "I'm sorry I couldn't be with you this evening."

"I missed you." Their hands met and held. "And I wasn't going to say it, but I worried."

"There was no need." His other hand came up to cover hers. "I've been in the palace since five."

"I wanted to ask, but..." She smiled a little and shook her head. "I guess I didn't feel as if I should."

"Either Bennett or Gabriella could have told you."

"You're here now. Have you eaten?"

"We had something in my father's office." He couldn't have told her what. He couldn't remember any taste, just the reports. "I'm told your sister is here."

"She got in late this morning." Uncurling herself, Eve rose to go to a small rococo cabinet. There she unearthed brandy and two snifters. "She could use some reassurance, which I hope Brie is giving her. She worried herself into a frazzle before she got here."

"Perhaps with her help you could be convinced to go back to America."

Eve handed him a glass, then tapped hers to it. "Not a chance."

"We could reschedule your performances, wait a few months, a year."

Eve sipped with one brow lifted. "Have you spoken to Chris already?"

"No, why?"

"Nothing." She smiled, then walked over to the CD player. With a few flicks she had music whispering into the room. When you intended to seduce a prince, she decided, you should pull out all the stops. "I'm not leaving, Alex, so it's a waste of time for us to argue about it." She touched her tongue to the rim of her glass. "I hate to waste time."

"You're a stubborn woman." Just looking at her, just hearing her voice made his pulse race. "Perhaps if I didn't want you with me so badly I could pressure you into leaving."

"No. No, you couldn't. But you don't know how much I've wanted you to say you want me with you." She came to him, so that they stood in front of her desk with the light burning beside them.

"Haven't I told you?"

"No." She took his hand again. "You don't tell me a great deal with words."

"I'm sorry." He brought her hand to his lips.

"I don't want you to be sorry." She set down her snifter. "I don't want you to be anything but what you are."

"Strange." He kept her hand close to his cheek. "There have been so many times recently when I've wished to be anything but what I am."

"Don't." Her strength was what he needed at that moment. Somehow she knew it. "No regrets. There should never be any regrets from either of us for being what we are. Instead let's enjoy." Her thumb ran light and caressing under his jawline. "Just enjoy."

"Eve." He didn't know what he could say to her, what should be said, what was best kept inside for a while longer. Her hand still in his, he started to set down his glass. "I nearly spoiled your papers." He put the glass down beside them. "You work too hard."

"There's that pot and kettle again."

He laughed. It was always easy to laugh when he was with her. "What is this? Another play?"

"It's nothing." She started to gather the papers up, but he put his finger down on them. "I don't know this one. What is this title, *Marking Time?* This isn't one of the alternates."

"No." Embarrassed, she tried to draw his attention away. "It's nothing."

"You're already thinking of producing something else?" He thought about her leaving, going on with her life, her career. With an effort he tried to show interest rather than regret. "What sort of play is it?"

"It's going to be—it's a family drama of sorts. Why don't we—"

"There's so little of it here." With his thumb he flipped through and estimated no more than twelve pages. Then it clicked, the way she'd been hunched over her computer, the matted balls of paper. With a quiet smile he looked back at her. "You're writing it."

Caught, she moved her shoulders and tried to draw away. "It's just a hobby."

"You're blushing."

"Of course I'm not. That's ridiculous." She picked up her brandy again and struggled to sound careless. "It's just something I do in my spare time." She swirled the brandy, then drank, and he thought how much he regretted never seeing her on stage.

"*Chérie*, in the past few weeks, I've seen firsthand how little spare time you have." He tucked her hair behind her ear. "You never told me you wanted to write."

"When you're only mediocre you don't broadcast it."

"Mediocre. I'd have to judge that myself." He reached for the pages again, but she was quicker.

"It's very rough. I haven't done any polishing."

"I can respect an artist's temperament about her work not being seen until it's finished." But he intended to see it, and soon. "Is it your first?"

"No." She slipped the papers into a drawer and closed it. "I'd finished one and done part of another."

"Then I'll see the one that's finished."

"It's gone." Again she struggled to keep her voice neutral. "It was in the office."

"Your work was lost." He took a step to her, then framed her face in his hands. "I'm sorry, so sorry, Eve. I would think that whatever one writes is a part of one. Alive. To lose it would be devastating."

She hadn't expected him to understand. Writing, as any art, was emotion as much as skill or technique. Her heart, always open to him, absorbed. "It wasn't a very interesting play," she murmured. "More of a learning tool, really. I just hope I learned enough to make this one better."

"I've wanted to ask you something."

"What?"

"You once wanted to be an actress. Why aren't you acting?"

"Because an actor has to do what he's told. A producer calls the shots."

He had to smile. "As simple as that."

"Added to the fact that I'm a better producer than I ever was an actor."

"And the writing?"

"Sort of a dare to myself." How easy it was to tell him now that she had begun. There was no need for secrets or embarrassment. Not with him. "If I claim to know so much about the theater, what pleases the audience, how to stage and produce a play, why couldn't I write one? A successful one," she added before she drained the brandy. "The first attempt was so miserable I decided I could only get better."

"You enjoy challenging yourself. The theater, fencing, your martial arts."

"I learned, later than most, that challenging yourself means you're alive, not just existing." With a shake of her head she set down her empty glass. "And you're spoiling things."

"I?"

"Yes. You've got me philosophizing, when I was set to seduce you."

"I beg your pardon." His lips curved as he leaned back on the table.

"I suppose you've been seduced before." Eve walked to the door, clicked the lock, then turned back.

"Countless times."

"Really." Her brow lifted as she leaned back against the door. "By whom?"

His smile only widened. "*Mademoiselle*, I was raised a gentleman."

"It doesn't matter," she decided with a wave of her hand. "As long as it wasn't that British blonde you danced with instead of me."

He remained discreet.

"Hmmm. Let's see. I've plied you with brandy. I've added the music. Now I think..." A gleam came into her eyes. "Yes, I believe I have just the thing. If you'd excuse me for just a moment."

"Of course."

She swept by him into the adjoining bedroom. Without a qualm, Alexander drew open her drawer and began to read her play. It caught him immediately, the dialogue between a woman no longer young and her reflection in her dressing room table mirror.

"Your Highness."

He slipped the drawer closed before he turned. He wanted to tell her he thought it was wonderful. Even with feelings prejudicing him he knew there was something special in her words. But when he saw her he could say nothing at all.

She wore a teddy skimmed with lace and a long, open robe, both the color of lake water. Her hair was down now, freshly brushed so that it pooled over her shoulders. Behind her light flickered, shifting and swaying. Her eyes were dark. He wondered how it was he could see his own desire reflected in them. Then, as she had the first time, she held out a hand.

He walked to her and his head began to swim from the scent of candle wax and women's secrets. Saying nothing, she drew him into the bedroom.

"I've waited all day to be with you." Standing close, she began to unbutton his shirt slowly. "To touch you." She ran a hand down his flesh before she pushed the shirt over his shoulders. "To be touched by you."

"When I'm away from you, I think of you when I should be thinking of other things." He slipped the robe from her and let it drift to the floor. "When I'm with you, I can think of nothing but you."

The words thrilled her. He said such things so rarely. "Then think of me."

The room was alight with a dozen candles. The bed was already turned down and waiting. Through the doorway came the quiet music, Debussy now, and nothing else. Wordlessly she drew him with her to the bed and began to love him as every man dreams of being loved.

Her first kiss was tender, reassuring, giving, while her hands stroked easily over him. She brushed her lips over his face, his throat, lingering long enough to arouse, not long enough to satisfy. The lace, the silk, the flesh that was her rubbed and shifted over his body until the flame burned hot inside him.

She undressed him, murmuring and brushing away the hands that sought to help her. Her tongue toyed with the back of his knee, drawing a groan from him. Her eyes half-closed, she looked at the body she brought such delight to. He looked gold in the candlelight. Gold and gleaming. She set out to destroy all semblance of control.

He thought his heart would burst through his chest. No woman had ever aroused him so outrageously. Whenever he reached for her, she evaded, then weakened him with a nip of her teeth or a featherlight caress. Agonizing. Magnificent. The breath backed up in his lungs or he might have begged for her to stop. To go on.

Helpless. She was the first ever to have made him helpless. It was a feeling that skittered through his stomach, rippled through his muscles, smoked through his brain. His skin grew damp, hot, sensitized. Wherever she touched brought a myriad of thrills. A moan wrenched out of him and he heard her low, answering laugh.

How incredible to learn that making a man shudder could be so exciting. How satisfying to discover a power that brought only pleasures. Her mind buzzed with the sense of it until she heard nothing else.

Here he belonged to her. If only here. There was no country, no duty, no traditions.

On the edge of reason, he pulled himself up. Hooking an arm around her waist, he dragged her to him, under him. Ranged above her, breath heaving, he stared down. Her chin was lifted. The dare was in her eyes.

"You're my insanity," he murmured, and crushed his mouth to hers.

They were sucked into the whirlwind, each not fighting to be free, but for more velocity. Once they had fenced and struck power against power. Now it was the same.

They rolled over the bed, mouth to mouth, body to body. He stripped her, but not with the care she'd come to expect. His fingers shook as he pulled the brief barrier from between them. They shook, then pressed and gripped, leaving tiny aches behind.

She moaned not from pain, but from the knowledge that his control had snapped. She'd wanted it, dreamed of what she would find behind that firmly locked door. It was on her now, like a beast breaking chains. Violent, desperate, with a primitive kind of relish.

He drove her beyond the reasonable into a desire so dark, so thick, she was blind from it.

Shuddering, she crested, and while she was still breathless he pushed her up and over the peak again.

"Alexander." She thought she'd shouted his name, but it was only a gasp. "I want you." Her hands traveled down, grasping, and found him. "I want you inside me."

He knew what madness was, true madness, the moment he felt her close around him. Her hips arched, setting the rhythm. He wanted to watch her face, to know when she had reached as high as it was possible to reach. But his vision was clouded.

The power took them both. When it did, he called out in French. It was the language of his heart.

Chapter 11

It was the first time she'd awoken in his arms. The predawn light was smoky gray with a mist that would clear as soon as the sun rose. The sound of the sea was just a whisper through the windows. Candles had gutted themselves out long since, but their scent still hung lightly in the room. He brushed a kiss at her temple and she awoke.

"Alexander." She murmured his name and cuddled closer.

"Go back to sleep. It's early."

She felt him shift away. "You're going."

"Yes, I must."

She wrapped her arms around him and held on to the warmth. "Why? It's early."

He gave a low chuckle, finding her slurred words and sleepy movements endearing. After lifting the arm that held him down, he kissed her hand. "I have early appointments."

"Not this early." She struggled to wake fully. Opening her eyes, she looked at him. His hair was mussed, from the pillow, from her hands, from a night of loving. But in the indistinct light his eyes were alert. "Couldn't you stay an hour more with me?"

He wanted to, wanted to tell her he would spend all the hours of that day and the next with her. But he couldn't. "It wouldn't be wise."

"Wise." She understood, and some of the pleasure faded from

her sleep-drugged eyes. "You don't want to be in my room when the servants wake up."

"It's best."

"For whom?"

His brow lifted, part amusement, part arrogance. It was rare for anyone to question him or his motives. "What's between us is between us. I wouldn't care to have you gossiped about or to see your name splashed in the papers."

"As it was with Bennett." There was a touch of anger in her voice as she pushed herself up, leaned back against the headboard and crossed her arms. "I prefer to worry about my reputation myself."

"And you're free to do so." He ran a finger over her bare shoulder. "But I shall worry about it, as well."

"About mine or yours?"

He wasn't a patient man by nature. It was something he'd had to work on step by frustrating step over the years. Now he put as much as he could into practice. "Eve, there's already talk since that picture of the two of us was in the paper."

"I'm glad." She tossed back her hair and watched him steadily. There was hurt. She wasn't sure where it had come from or why it was so acute, but it was there. Hurt could so easily lead to being unreasonable. "I'm not ashamed of being your lover."

"Is that what you think? That I'm ashamed?"

"You come to me late and leave early, before the sun's up, as if you were ashamed of where you spent the night and with whom."

His hand went to her throat, holding there firmly enough for her to feel the strength and the fury behind it. She kept her eyes level, though emotion burned hot and dark in his. "Don't ever say that. How can you even think it?"

"What do I have to make me think differently?"

His fingers tightened on her throat, making her eyes widen in shock before his mouth came down, hard and furious, on hers. She struggled, wanting words, whatever words he would give her, but his hands were quick and desperate. Ruthless, he took them over her, exploiting every weakness he had discovered in more gentle ways.

Her body was a mass of throbbing, pulsing nerves. Any and all coherent thought had fled, to be replaced by sensation after rioting sensation. Her arms locked tight around him, she accepted what he would give. Her body answered his with the same fire and fury.

The edge of temper met the edge of passion. They scraped, grated, then with a merger that was anything but placid, became one.

He lay looking up at the ceiling. She was curled beside him, but they no longer touched. The sun was burning off the mist.

"I don't want to hurt you."

She let out a shaky breath, but her voice was strong and clear when she spoke. "I'm not easily hurt, Alexander."

"Aren't you?" He wanted to reach out, to take her hand in his, but wasn't sure she would accept it. "We need to find a time, a place to talk. It isn't now."

"No, it isn't now."

When he got out of bed, she stayed where she was. She heard him dress, and waited for the sound of the door opening and closing again. Instead she felt a hand light on her shoulder.

"I feel many things for you, but not shame. Will you wait for me at the theater? I'll find a way to be there by six."

She didn't look at him, knowing that if she did she'd beg him to stay, and perhaps beg for a great deal more than he could give. "Yes, I'll wait."

"Sleep awhile longer."

She said nothing. The door opened and closed.

Eve squeezed her eyes tight, fighting a sense of despair and loss. He'd given her passion, but no answers. Once she'd promised herself his passion would be enough. It was a hard blow to learn now that it couldn't be. She wanted his heart, without the restrictions he placed on it. She wanted to be loved, cherished, accepted. What she wanted was more than she could have, and she couldn't live with less.

Understanding this, Eve rose. It was time to begin her life again. There would be no regrets for the dream that had flickered briefly into life.

Alexander walked into his father's library and acknowledged the men already present. His father sat in a wing chair, just crushing out a cigarette. Reeve, with papers on his lap and spread on the table before him, sat on the sofa with Bennett. Malori, the chief of intelligence, sat on the edge of a chair, lighting his pipe.

The men had met the evening before, and would meet again for however long it took to crush the threat Deboque held over them. They began on familiar ground, starting with the security Reeve had implemented at the palace, at the theater, at The Aid to Handicapped Children Center and at his own home. There was additional information regarding the airport and the docks.

"You've assigned an extra detective to each of us," Bennett put in.

"For as long as it's necessary."

He shifted restlessly against the restraint, but accepted it. "Do you really think they'll go through Eve again? They have to know we'd tap the phones and keep her watched."

Malori puffed on his pipe. "Deboque's greatest flaw, Your Highness, is arrogance. I believe his next move will come through Mademoiselle Hamilton, and soon."

"I repeat what I said last evening," Alexander began. "Eve should be sent back to America."

Malori tapped the bowl of his pipe. "That would not stop Deboque, Your Highness."

"It would ensure her safety."

"Alexander." Reeve watched the prince light a cigarette. "If what the investigation has turned up is fact, we need Eve. If she would go," he continued before Alexander could speak. "I'd put her on a plane myself. Since she insists on staying, the solution is to guard her and wait."

"Wait." Alexander blew out a stream of smoke. "Wait for her to be put in jeopardy again. If, as you believe, someone inside the theater placed the calls, planted the bomb, she's in danger even now from one of her own people."

"Deboque isn't concerned with her," Malori said quietly. "She's only a pawn."

"And pawns are expendable."

"Alexander." Armand spoke for the first time. His voice was as quiet as Malori's but held the unmistakable ring of authority. It was a cool voice, often bordering on the cold, but it was rarely harsh. His arms rested on the chair as he paused and looked over his steepled fingers. "We must deal with this calmly, as calmly as Deboque. You understand that I care for Eve as I care for my own children. Everything that can be done to protect her will be done."

"She is not Cordinian." Alexander struggled with emotion, intellect. "She is a guest in our country. We are responsible for her."

"We don't forget our responsibilities." The authority was there. Mixed with it was a compassion that couldn't be given full sway. "If one of Eve's people is an agent of Deboque's, we will learn the identity. Logically Deboque will not order her harmed, or his agent will no longer have a reason to remain in Cordina."

"And if Deboque is not logical?"

"Such men are always logical. There is no passion in them."

"Mistakes can be made."

"Yes." Armand thought of Seward. The grief remained inside. "Mistakes can be made. We must see we don't make any." His gaze shifted to Reeve. "I leave this to you."

"Everything that can be done on the short term is being done. As to the long term, Malori and I have agreed on an operative who will infiltrate Deboque's organization."

"I agreed with reservations," Malori mumbled.

"No need for them." Reeve's lips curved, then he handed Armand a folder. "Malori and I do agree that the identity of this operative should be known only to the three of us."

"It concerns us all," Bennett interrupted.

"Yes." Reeve nodded. "And the life of this operative depends on secrecy. The fewer people who know who is working for us, the better chance we have of succeeding. It may take months, more likely years. You have to understand we're only planting a seed here. It needs time to grow."

"I wish only to see an end to Deboque in my lifetime." Armand kept the file closed. He would look at it later, then lock it in his personal safe. "I want regular reports on the operative's progress."

"Of course." Reeve gathered the rest of his papers. "If we can capture Deboque's agent and interrogate him, perhaps the rest won't be necessary."

As the group of men rose, Alexander addressed his father. "If you have a few minutes, I need to speak with you."

Understanding his brother's need for privacy, Bennett dropped a hand on his arm. "I'm going to go to the theater this morning. I'll keep an eye on her."

Alexander placed a hand over his brother's. There was no need for gratitude to be spoken. "Don't let her know that's what you're doing. She'll kick you out."

"I'll make a nuisance of myself and she'll tolerate me." Then he walked over and kissed his father's cheek. "We are together in this, Papa."

Armand sat where he was, watching until the door closed at his son's back. None of the reports, the files, the plots that had been discussed, had eased his mind. But the simple words, the simple kiss, had done much more than that.

"Of all my children, Bennett is the only one I cannot predict."

"He'd be flattered to hear it."

"As a boy he found every broken bird, every injured kitten, always believing he could make them well again. Sometimes he did. At times I worry that he feels too deeply. He's so like your mother." Armand shook his head and rose. "Should I order coffee, Alexander?"

"No, not for me. I have to go to Le Havre. Welcome a ship."

"Such enthusiasm."

"I'll show it when the time comes."

"I don't doubt it. This concerns Eve."

"Yes."

With a nod Armand walked to the window to throw it open. Maybe the breeze from the sea would air out some of the tension still in the room. "Alex, I have eyes. I think I understand what you're feeling."

"Perhaps you do. But I've just begun to understand what I'm feeling myself."

"When I was a young man, younger than you, I found myself ruling a country. I had been prepared for it, of course, from the moment of birth. But no one, especially not I, had expected it to come so soon. Your grandfather became ill and died in less than three days. It was a difficult time. I was twenty-four. Many members of the council worried about my age and my temperament." He turned then, smiling a little. "I wasn't always as discreet as you have been."

"Bennett was bound to inherit something from your side."

For the first time in days Armand laughed. "I was not quite that indiscreet. In any case, I'd ruled less than a year, when I took an official trip to England. I saw Elizabeth, and all the stray pieces of my life came together. To love like that, Alex, is painful, and more beautiful than anything you can see or touch."

"I know."

Armand turned fully. His breath came out on a long sigh. "I thought perhaps you did. Have you considered what you would be asking of her?"

"Again and again. And again and again I've told myself I can't do it. She'll make all the sacrifices, all the adjustments. I don't even know if I can make her understand just how much her life would change if she accepted me."

"Does she love you?"

"Yes." Then he paused and pressed his fingers to his eyes. "God, I hope she does. It's difficult for me to be certain of her feelings when I've been fighting my own for so long."

This, too, he understood. When he had fallen in love, he had had no father to speak to. "Do you want my approval or my advice?"

Alexander dropped his hand. "Both."

"Your choice pleases me." Armand smiled and walked toward his son. "She will make a princess Cordina can be proud of."

"Thank you." They clasped hands. "But I think being a princess is something that won't please Eve nearly as much as Cordina."

"Americans." Now Armand grinned. "Like your *beau-frère*, she would prefer to avoid such things as titles and positions of state."

"But unlike Reeve, she'd have no choice."

"If she loves you, the crown she'll wear won't be so heavy. Nor will yours, when your day comes."

"If." Alexander let the word hang. "I appreciate your approval, Father. Now your advice."

"There are few people you can open your heart to, open it fully. When you find a woman to share your life, hold nothing back from her. A woman's shoulders are strong. Use them."

"I want to protect her."

"Of course. Doing one doesn't mean not doing the other. I have something for you." He left the library through the connecting door to his office. Moments later he was back with a small black velvet box. He held it tightly in his hand as he went to his son.

"I wondered what I would feel when I gave this to you." He stared down at the box in his hand. "There's regret that it's mine to give again, pride that I have a son to give it to." His emotions, always so well controlled, swirled to the surface and were battled down. "There's pleasure that my son is a man I can respect, not only a boy I love."

He passed it over, hesitating a moment before his fingers broke contact with the box. "Time passes," he murmured. "This is the ring I gave your mother on the night I asked her to marry me. It would please me, when you ask Eve, if you would give her this."

"There's nothing I would be prouder to give her." He couldn't open the box, but his hand gripped it as tightly as his father's had. "Thank you, Papa."

Armand looked at his son, as tall as he. He remembered the boy and all the years in between. He smiled and embraced the man. "Bring her to me when she wears it."

Eve watched two stagehands, armed with spray cans, painting pipe. She stifled a yawn and made a notation. She was definitely going to have to invest in some new equipment once they were back in the States, which was in less than five weeks. In two days the first production would open; four weeks later the last production would close. They'd take a couple of days to break down the last set, then that would be that.

The company was already booked on a road tour through the fall. She was negotiating a three-week run in L.A. for January. And if she didn't miss her guess, her desk would be piled with offers and inquiries after her return from Cordina.

Her return.

Eve walked to the stage manager's desk at stage right and tried to concentrate on the rehearsal. The actors were in full costume and makeup. She couldn't see a flaw. The big red urn she'd commissioned Pete to buy stood out like the beacon she'd imagined. The upholstery on the sofa was faded. The doilies were bright and stiffly starched.

It was perfect. She had organized it, and it was perfect. She wished she could find the pleasure in it that she'd always felt before.

"It looks great."

The whisper at her ear had her jolting. "Ben." She pressed her clipboard against her heart. "What are you doing here? This is supposed to be a closed rehearsal."

"Of course that didn't include me. I explained that to the doorman. Tell me, do you call him 'Pops' like in the American movies?"

"I wouldn't dare." She glanced behind him and saw his guards hovering at a safe and discreet distance. "Shouldn't you be out doing something official?"

"Don't lecture. I've been slaving away for weeks. I stole a couple of hours." The two precious hours he would have spent with his horses. "I just thought I'd stop by and see how things were going."

"If you're looking for Doreen," Eve began dryly, "she's upstairs in Rehearsal Hall B. We do have three other plays to deal with, you know."

"Okay, I can take a hint. I won't distract Doreen while she's rehearsing." The truth was, he hadn't given her a thought. He scanned the stage as the play unfolded. "Most of your people have been with you quite a while, I suppose."

"Some have, some haven't. Look, let's move down to the audience. I haven't had a chance to watch from that angle today."

Bennett went with her, settling in the center aisle, midtheater. The guards moved in three rows behind. Eve didn't notice there were two more. They had been assigned to her.

"It looks good," she murmured. "I've sat all the way up in the back balcony and it still looks good. The acoustics in this place are simply incredible."

"I guess you get to know your people pretty well," Bennett ventured. "Socially, I mean, not just on a professional level."

"When you take a play on tour you usually do. But, then, actors and theater people are just like everyone else." She smiled as she looked at him. "Some are more sociable than others. Thinking of joining up?"

"Can I get an audition?"

"You might do better applying for a job as a stagehand. They have more opportunity to flirt with the ladies."

"I'll keep that in mind. Just how many people work for you?"

"It varies with the production."

"How about now?"

Brows drawn together, she turned to him again. "Why?"

"Just curious."

"All of a sudden?" she countered. "You're asking a lot of questions you never bothered to ask before."

"Maybe I just thought of them. Ever hear of passing the time?"

"Ben, I know you, and since Reeve asked me some very similar questions yesterday, I have to figure there's a purpose to them. What do my people have to do with the investigation?"

He stretched out his legs, insolently resting them on the seat back in front of him. "Hard for me to say, since I'm not investigating. Eve, I don't believe I've been introduced to the lady onstage in her slip."

"Bennett, don't play games with me. I thought we were friends."

"You know we are."

"Then level with me."

He hesitated only a moment. Because he was her friend, because he respected her, he'd already made up his mind. "Eve, don't you think we should consider all the possibilities?"

"I don't know. You tell me."

"The second call was made from inside the complex." He watched her eyes widen. "I didn't think they had told you. I thought they should."

"You mean here, from the theater?"

"They can't pin it down that specifically. They just know it wasn't made from outside the building. There were guards on every door, every entrance. There was no sign of any break-in. The bomb had to be planted by someone inside. Someone who belongs inside the complex."

"And you're narrowing in on my people." Her protective instinct came first. "Damn it, Ben, there are three other theaters in this complex. How many other actors, technicians, maintenance people?"

"I know, I know." He placed a hand over hers to cut her off.

"The point is, it's very likely the person was someone who wouldn't be questioned for being in this theater, backstage, even in your office. Who'd question one of your own, Eve? It's unlikely even you would."

"And why would one of my people threaten your family?"

"I'm told Deboque pays very well."

"I don't believe it, Ben." She turned back to stare at the stage. Her actors, her troupe. Her family. "If I did, I'd scrub this production right now and send everyone home. These people are actors, technicians, seamstresses, for heaven's sake. They're not assassins."

"I'm not saying it has to be—I'm just saying it could be. I only want you to think about it, Eve." His hand pressed down on hers. "And watch yourself. I love you."

All the anger drained. "Ben, if I thought I'd been responsible for bringing someone here who would—"

"Wait, don't even finish. Whatever the answer is, you aren't responsible. Deboque is."

Deboque. It was always Deboque. "I've never even seen him. I don't know what he looks like, and he's pushing into every part of my life. He has to be stopped."

"He will be." Bennett's voice was mild, but she did know him well. The thread of violence ran through it. "Reeve's already started something. It's going to take time, more time than any of us would like, but he's going to be stopped. I just hope I can have a hand in it."

"Keep your hands in your pockets. I don't want anything to happen to you, either."

The touch of violence was gone as he grinned at her. "You don't have to worry about me. I'm more interested in women and horses than I am in glory."

"Just keep it that way." She rose, dragging her hair back with her hand as she did so. "I should go up and check on the other rehearsal."

"You're working too hard, Eve. It's starting to show."

"Gallant. Always gallant."

"You've got to stop worrying about Alex."

"How?"

"All right, so you don't have to stop worrying about him. Try to trust the fates a bit.'' He rose with her, then reached out to toy with her hair. "He's destined to rule Cordina. I'm not, thank God. Nothing's going to happen to him.''

"I always believe that when I see him. I have a harder time when I can't.'' She kissed him, then decided it wasn't enough and hugged him, too. "I'll see you tonight.''

"Play some gin rummy?''

"You already owe me fifty-three dollars from the last time.''

"Who's counting?''

"I am.'' She managed to smile.

He watched her walk down the aisle and back behind the stage. The two guards trailed after her.

Gabriella and Chris came by and tried to convince her to take the afternoon with them at a seaside café. Her assistant brought her coffee and sugar cookies and clucked her tongue. One of the actors offered his dressing room for a nap and one of the staff from makeup suggested a cream to help with the shadows under her eyes.

Eve was steaming by the time rehearsals were wrapped for the day.

"If one more person, just one more, tells me I should get some rest, I'm punching him right in the mouth,'' Eve muttered to herself as she strode down the backstage corridor.

"You won't hear it from me.''

Her heels skidded a bit as she stopped. Pete was crouched over one of his cases, locking up props. "I thought just about everyone had cleared out.''

"Just about have.'' Keys jingled at his waist as he stood. "I've got a couple of more things to store. Couldn't find a box big enough for that vase or whatever it is.''

"Leave it on the set. It's too ugly for anyone to steal.''

"You said you didn't want class.''

"And you delivered.'' She rubbed at the tension gnawing at the back of her neck. "It's perfect—really, Pete. So are the doilies. I know you're conscientious, but the theater's going to be locked up tight. With security the way it is around here, I don't think you have to worry about anyone making off with the props. Why don't you go get some dinner?''

"Thinking about it." Still he hesitated, toying with his keys.

"Is there a problem?"

"Nope. Got something to say."

Amused, Eve nodded. "Go ahead, then."

"You got my dander up the other day when you ordered me out of here. Yanked on me, too, and threatened to fire me."

"I didn't think you were pleased."

"Guess I'd have moved a lot faster if I'd known what was going on." He scratched his chin and looked at his shoes. "Talbot told us how you were running around the place, making sure everybody got out, when you knew there was a bomb. Seems pretty heroic to me. Stupid," he added, looking back at her. "But heroic."

"It wasn't stupid or heroic. It was necessary. But thanks for the thought."

"Like to buy you a drink."

For a moment she was speechless. It was the closest Pete had come to a sociable concession in all the time she'd known him. "I'd like that, too. I have someone meeting me here tonight. How about tomorrow, right after rehearsals?"

"Sounds all right." Pete scratched his chin, shifted his belt, then started down the hall. "You're okay, Ms. Hamilton."

"You, too," she murmured, and felt better than she'd felt all day.

She started down the opposite way, bypassing her old office for her temporary one. Six-fifteen, she thought with a look at her watch. Alexander was late. She'd waited throughout the day, edgy and short of temper, for six o'clock. She'd just have to wait a little longer.

Why did he want to talk to her? To break things off as cleanly as possible. He had to know how deeply in love with him she was. He didn't want to hurt her. Hadn't he said so? He'd want to break things off now, before things became even more difficult for her.

He still wanted her. She had no doubt about that. But there was his sense of honor. He could only offer her a few hours in the night in secret. His sense of right, of fairness, wouldn't allow him to continue for long. Wasn't that one of the reasons she loved him?

No regrets, Eve reminded herself. She'd known things couldn't last and had accepted that from the outset. Princes and palaces—they had no place in her life.

With a sigh she opened the small book she'd put in her briefcase that morning. Inside was the flower she'd pressed, the one Alexander had tucked behind her ear. Two weeks ago? A lifetime ago. She closed the book, telling herself not all women had even that much to comfort them.

You're okay, Ms. Hamilton. Well, that was exactly right. She was okay, and she was going to go on being okay. Life was meant to be faced for what it was.

She would wait, but she wouldn't brood. Going behind her desk, Eve took out one of the new files she'd started to compile.

The theater was quiet. Then she heard the bang.

Chapter 12

Eve was halfway out of her seat by the time she heard the footsteps race past her door. Her only thought was to lecture whoever among her troupe was still in the theater, making a commotion, when they were supposed to be at dinner. The moment she reached the doorway she saw the body.

Everything froze. Then she was running down the hall, crouching over the unidentifiable man. There was blood already seeping through his shirt. A tray holding a water pitcher and some glasses had been knocked over. Shards of glass were everywhere. Thinking fast, she tore off the long cardigan she wore and draped it over him.

The phone. She had to get to the phone. Fighting for calm, she ran down the hall again and into her office. Her fingers were damp and trembling when she picked up the receiver and dialed.

"This is Eve Hamilton at the Fine Arts Center, the Grand Theater. A man's been shot. I need an ambulance. The police." Her breath caught as she heard footsteps coming softly toward her door. "Hurry," she whispered. "Please hurry."

She set the receiver on the desk and looked frantically around. There was no way out, no way but the door. The footsteps had stopped, but where? How close? Trembling, she edged around the desk. Whoever it was would kill her, kill her and...

Six-twenty. The face of her watch seemed blurred, but she remembered. Alexander. They were waiting for Alexander.

Moisture pearled on her forehead, but she inched closer to the door. She had to warn him somehow. She had to find a way. Even as she reached to pull the door the rest of the way open, it swung slowly toward her.

She saw the gun first. Black, deadly. Then the hand that held it. Biting back a scream, she looked at the face.

The man who had fenced with Alexander. The man who had smiled at her, whose face had seemed vaguely familiar. Now she remembered. He'd been at the theater before.

He wasn't smiling now. His face was grim, set. She looked in his eyes, and knew he was a man who could kill.

"Mademoiselle," he began, and she acted.

She swung, using the back of her fist to connect forcefully with the side of his throat. As the gun clattered out of his hand, she brought her stiffened open hand down on the back of his neck. Panting, she looked down at him, crumpled half in and half out of her office. She wanted to run, just run, but forced herself to think clearly.

Hooking her hands under his arms, she dragged him inside. After a quick fumble through her top desk drawer, she found the key. The room was hardly as long as he was, sprawled on the floor. She stepped over him, shut the door and locked him in.

She shook her head to clear the buzzing that filled it and gave herself a moment, leaning back against the wall and catching her breath. The wounded man a few steps away groaned, and she was beside him instantly.

"Help's coming," she murmured. "You're going to be all right."

"Jermaine..."

"Yes, yes, I know. It's taken care of. You mustn't try to talk." Pressure, she thought. She had to stop the bleeding. She dragged a hand through her hair and tried to think. Towels. "Try not to move," she told him. "I'm going to get something to stop the bleeding."

"Was waiting—was hiding."

"He's locked up," she assured him. "Don't talk anymore. I won't be gone long."

She rose, intending to run to the nearest bathroom for towels, when she heard a noise behind her. She spun around, but the hall was empty. Moistening her dry lips, she stared at her office door. Was he conscious again already? It hit her then, coldly, that she hadn't taken the gun. It was locked in with him. If he woke up and found it...

Then she heard voices out front and ran toward them.

The stage was dark. She hit the main switch, flooding the stage with light. Her chest heaved with a sob at the sound of Alexander's voice. As he climbed the steps to the stage she was racing across it. His apology for being later than he'd promised never materialized. He had her by the arms, holding firmly.

"What is it?"

"The man, Deboque's agent—he's locked in my office. He shot a man, one of your guards, I think. I've already called an ambulance and the police."

"Did he hurt you?" Even as he took the first quick look, his hands moved to her shoulder. "There's blood."

"Not mine, the guard's. Alex, he needs attention. And in my office—"

"It's all right." His arm circled her as he turned to his own bodyguards. "See to it. I'll stay here with her."

"He has a gun," she began.

"So do they. Sit." He lowered her to the sofa she had insisted be faded. "Tell me." He took his gaze from hers only long enough to watch his guards go backstage.

"Everyone went home—I thought everyone went home. Of course I know there's been a guard on me. I heard a bang, then footsteps. There was the body in the hall. I went back to the phone, then I heard someone again. Alex, it was the man you fenced with, that Jermaine."

"Jermaine was shot?"

"No, no!" Dragging her hands through her hair, she tried to be clear. "He was the one. He had a gun. I knocked him out, then—"

"You knocked out Jermaine?"

"I'm trying to tell you," she snapped. "He must have shot the other man, and he was coming back."

"Eve." He shook her gently. "Jermaine is the head of my personal security. I assigned him to you to protect you."

"But he…" She trailed off, struggling to clear her mind. "Then who…?"

"I'm sorry to interrupt." Russ stepped out of the shadows at stage left. In his hand was a revolver, lengthened by a slim silencer.

"Oh, my God." Before the words were out, Alexander was up, placing Eve behind him.

"I have to thank you for sending your guards away, even so briefly, Your Highness. I promise to be quick. I am, after all, a professional."

"No." Eve stepped from behind Alexander to grip his arm. "You can't."

"You, I regret." There was a touch of sincerity in his tone as he smiled at Eve. "You know the business, Eve. I want you to know you're the best producer I've ever worked for."

"You won't get away with it." Alex spoke quietly, knowing his guards would be back in a matter of seconds.

"I've been given the opportunity to learn this theater very well. I can disappear in ten seconds. It should be all I need. If I don't make it…" He shrugged. All of them heard the high, distant sound of sirens. "Well, that's business." He leveled the gun at Alexander's heart. "Nothing personal."

They were standing on the set. The red urn with its bunch of bright paper flowers stood out like a joke. The heat of the spotlights warmed them as though the play had already begun. But the gun was real.

She screamed. It was torn out of her. Without a second thought, with no regrets, she stepped in front of Alexander and took the bullet.

She couldn't die. Alexander sat with his head in his hands as the phrase repeated over and over in his head like a litany. He knew how to pray, but those were the only words that would come to him.

He knew there were others in the waiting room, but they might have been ghosts. Phantoms of his own imagination. His father stood by the window. Bennett sat on the small lounge with Chris's hand in his. Gabriella sat beside Alexander, letting her support come through without words. Reeve was there, then gone, then back again, as he dealt with the police.

If he'd had only a second more, one second, he could have pushed her aside, thrown her aside. Anything to keep the bullet from going into her. She'd jerked against him. As long as he lived, he'd never forget the way her body had jerked in shock and pain before it had gone limp.

And her blood had been on his hands. Literally and figuratively.

"Take some tea, Alex." Gabriella urged the cup on him, but he shook his head. She watched as he lit yet another cigarette. "Don't do this to yourself," she murmured. "Eve is going to need you to be strong, not riddled with guilt."

"I should have protected her. I should have kept her safe." He closed his eyes but could still see that horrifying moment she had swung herself in front of him. Throwing her arms around his body as a shield. "It was me he wanted."

"You or any of us." She put a hand on his knee. "If there's guilt we share it equally. Alex, through the worst days of my life, you were there for me and I wouldn't let you help. Let me help now."

His hand covered hers. It was all he could give.

Reeve came back into the waiting room. He looked at his wife, touched her briefly on the shoulder, then went to Armand, by the window. Armand only nodded, then went back to his silent vigil. He, too, knew how to pray.

Unable to sit any longer, Chris rose and walked to the corridor, then back again. There were tears she hadn't been able to stem drying on her cheeks. She felt Gabriella's arm go around her, and leaned against it.

"We can't lose her."

"No." Gabriella kept her hold tight. "We won't lose her." Gently she drew Chris back toward a chair. "Do you remember when we were in school together, the stories you would tell me about Eve? I had wondered what it was like to have a sister."

"Yes, I remember." Chris took a deep breath and tried to make the effort. "You thought having one would be delightful."

"It seemed I was always surrounded by men and boys." Gabriella smiled and, with Chris's hand in hers, looked around at her family. "You showed me a picture of Eve. She was twelve, thirteen, I think, and beautiful, even as a child. I loved the idea of having someone like that to share things with.''

"And I told you how I'd found her in my room with all my makeup lined up on the vanity, experimenting with my best eye shadow. Her eyes looked like garage doors.'' Chris ran her fingertips under her eyes to dry them. "She thought she looked gorgeous.''

Chris sniffed and took the tissue Gabriella handed her. "She hated being sent away to school.'' Her breath was shaky as she let it out and drew more in. "Dad thought it best, and he was right, really, but she hated it so. We all thought Eve was a lovely girl, a sweet girl, but not too bright. Lord, did she prove us wrong. She just refused to waste her time doing things that held no interest, so she wasted it with magazines or the latest CDs, instead.''

"She used to write you those funny letters. You'd read them to me sometimes.''

"The ones where she described the girls in the dorm or her history teacher. We should have seen then that she had a knack for the theater. Oh, God, Brie, how much longer?''

"Just a little while,'' she murmured. "We used to think that she and Bennett... They seemed to suit so well.'' She looked over at Alexander as he stared down at his own hands. "Isn't it odd that the people we care for should have come together?''

"She loves him so much.'' Chris, too, looked at Alexander, and her heart rose into her throat. "I wanted her to come back to Houston with me. She couldn't leave him. It was almost as if she knew the time would come when she would protect him.'' Her voice broke, and she shook her head before going on. "She said it didn't matter how he felt, she only wanted whatever time with him she could have.''

Brie sighed. "Alexander closes himself in, so often even from himself. But I don't think there can be any doubt now about his feelings. He blames himself. Not circumstances, not Deboque or fate, but himself totally.''

"Eve wouldn't.''

"No, she wouldn't.''

Understanding, Chris rubbed her hands over her eyes and rose. It wasn't easy to cross the room to him. There was resentment. She couldn't avoid it. There was blame and an anger wedged in her heart that had found no room for escape. The step she took was for Eve. When she sat beside him, he didn't reach out to her, but looked over with eyes that were shadowed and red from the scrubbing of his own hands.

"You must hate me." He said it in a voice that was both quiet and dull. "It is small comfort to know that you can't hate me as much as I hate myself."

She wanted to take his hand for Eve's sake, but couldn't. "That doesn't do Eve any good. She needs us to pull together now."

"I could have found a way to make her leave, to make her go."

"Do you think so?" It made her smile just a little. "I can't imagine that. Since she got out of school Eve hasn't allowed anyone to make her do anything."

"I didn't protect her." He covered his face with his hands again, fighting the pressing need to break down. "She matters more than anything in my life and I didn't protect her."

Chris found her hand groping for his, for Eve, yes, but also for herself and for Alexander. "She stepped in front of you." The pain shot into his eyes again. As her own rose to meet it, their fingers linked. "If you have to blame yourself, Alex, blame yourself for being the man she loves. We have to believe she's going to be all right. I need you to believe that with me, or I don't think I can handle any more."

They sat and waited. Coffee was brought and grew cold. Ashtrays overflowed. The scent of hospital—antiseptic, detergent and nerves—grew familiar. They no longer noticed the guards posted in the corridors.

When Dr. Franco entered the room, they all got to their feet. His surgical cap was soaked with sweat, as was the front of his pale green scrubs. He came forward and, with the compassion natural to him, took Chris's hand.

"The surgeon is still with her. They'll be bringing her to recovery very soon. You have a strong sister, Miss Hamilton. She doesn't choose to give in."

"She's all right?" Chris's hand gripped the doctor's like a vise.

"She came through the surgery better than anyone could have expected. As I explained, Dr. Thorette is the best in his field. The operation was tricky because the bullet was lodged very near her spine."

"She's not..." Alexander felt his father's hand on his arm and made himself say it. "She won't be paralyzed?"

"It's too early for guarantees, Your Highness. But Dr. Thorette feels there is no permanent damage. I agree with him."

"Your judgment has always been excellent," Armand told him. His voice was rough from cigarettes and relief. "I don't have to tell you that Eve will continue to get the very best care available."

"No, Your Highness, you don't. Alexander." He used the first name, taking the privilege of an old family friend, one he had taken rarely in over thirty years. "She is young, healthy, strong. I give you my word that I can see no reason she won't recover fully. Still, there is only so much we can do. The rest is up to her."

"When can we see her?"

"I'll check recovery and let you know. It's unlikely she'll wake until morning. No, there is no need to argue," he continued, holding up his hand. "I don't intend to tell you that you can't sit with her. I believe it will only help her recovery if you're there when she awakes. I'll go to her now."

There was a low light on as he kept his vigil. Franco had had a tray of food sent up, but Alexander had only toyed with it and pushed it aside.

She lay so still.

He'd been told she would, that the sedation had been heavy, but he watched her for a movement, for a flicker.

She lay so quietly.

An IV fed into her wrist; the white bandage holding the needle in place stood out in the dark. A line of machines kept up a steady click and beep as they monitored her. From time to time he stared at the fluorescent green lights. But almost always he stared at her.

Sometimes he spoke, holding her hand in his as he talked of walking together on the beach, of taking her to the family retreat in Zurich or sitting in the gardens. Other times he would simply sit, watching her face, waiting.

He thought how much she would dislike the dull hospital gown they had put her in. And he thought of the lace and silk she had worn the last time they had made love. Only one night ago. He pressed her hand against his cheek as his breathing grew jerky and painful. The touch helped soothe.

"Don't let go," he murmured. "Stay with me, Eve. I need you, and the chance to show you how much. Don't let go."

He sat through the hours of the night fully awake. Just as the slats in the window shade let in the first slivers of light, she stirred.

"Eve." He gripped her hand in both of his. The safety bar on the side of the bed was down so that he could lean toward her. "Eve, you're all right. I'm here with you. Please, open your eyes. Can you hear me? Open your eyes, Eve."

She heard him, though his voice sounded hollow and distant. Something was wrong. She felt as though she had been floating, and the dreams... Her eyelids fluttered, came up. She saw only gray, then blinking, began to make out form.

"I'm here with you," Alexander repeated. "You're going to be fine. Can you hear me?"

"Alex?" She saw his face. It was very close, but she couldn't seem to reach up and touch. It was shadowed with beard. It made her smile a little. "You haven't shaved."

Then she went under again.

Though it seemed like hours to him, it was only minutes later when she stirred again. He was sitting on the bed beside her. This time her eyes focused long enough for understanding to come into them.

"You're not hurt?" Her voice was weak and wavery.

"No, no."

"Russ..."

Involuntarily his fingers tightened on hers. "He's been taken care of. You're not to worry."

But she'd turned her head, seen the machine, realized the rest of it. "Not the hospital." At the panic in her voice he brought her hand to his lips.

"Just for a little while, *ma belle*. Just until you're well."

"I don't want to stay here."

"I'll stay with you."

"You won't go?"

"No."

"Alex, you won't lie to me?"

"No." He pressed kisses to her wrist, comforting himself with the feel of her pulse.

"Am I going to die?"

"No." Now he put a hand to her face and bent closer. "No, you're not going to die. Dr. Franco says you're—" he remembered Eve's own phrase "—healthy as a horse."

"I don't think he put it that way."

"That's what he meant."

She smiled, but he saw the quick wince.

"You have pain."

"It feels like—I don't know. My back, under the shoulder."

Where the bullet had been. It had lodged there instead of in his heart. He kissed her cheek and rose. "I'll call the nurse."

"Alex, don't leave."

"Just to call the nurse. I promise." But he found Franco coming down the hall. "She's awake. She's having some pain."

"All of it can't be avoided, Your Highness. Let me examine her, then we can give her something." He signaled to a nurse.

"She's afraid to be here."

"I understand she has a phobia about hospitals. I'm afraid we can't have her moved just yet."

"Then I'll stay with her."

"I can't permit that, Your Highness."

Even without sleep, with fatigue and worry dragging at him, Alexander was royal. "I beg your pardon?"

"I can't permit you to remain twenty-four hours a day. I will, however, permit you to take shifts with Miss Hamilton's sister or anyone else who gives her comfort. Now I must examine my patient."

Alexander watched him walk into Eve's room, then he sank down on a chair outside the door. God, he needed to be alone for just a few minutes, to find some dark, quiet room where he could finally let go of the rage, the pain, the fear.

She'd spoken to him. She'd looked at him. Her fingers had moved in his. He had that now. Leaning back against the wall, he closed his eyes for the first time in more than twenty-four hours.

He opened them again the moment Franco stepped into the hall.

"You can go in, Your Highness. I've explained to Eve about her condition. I've also assured her that she can have someone with her as long as she likes. I'm going to call her sister now. When Miss Hamilton arrives, I insist you go home, eat a decent meal and sleep. If not, I will bar you from her room."

Alexander passed a hand over the back of his neck. "Dr. Franco, if I didn't know that you had Eve's welfare in mind, I'd simply ignore you."

"It wouldn't be the first time I've gone head to head with a member of your family, Your Highness."

"I'm well aware of that, too. Tell me how she is this morning."

"Weak, of course. But her vital signs are good. She feels her legs and can move them."

"Then there's no—"

"No paralysis. She needs, rest, care and support. I hope to have her out of the ICU by tomorrow, but Dr. Thorette will want to examine her first."

"Dr. Franco, I don't have the words to tell you how grateful I am."

"Your Highness, I've always considered it an honor to treat members of the royal family."

Alexander looked back at Eve's door. The ring box made the slightest of weights in his pocket. "You've always been perceptive."

"Thank you, Your Highness. And I have your word that you will leave soon after Miss Hamilton arrives?"

"You have it."

Alexander went back into the room and found Eve awake and staring at the ceiling.

"I thought you'd gone."

"I promised I wouldn't. Chris will be coming. I'll have to leave then for a little while." He sat beside her again, taking her hand. "But I'll be back. You won't be alone."

"I feel like such a fool—like a little girl, afraid of the dark."

"I'm only relieved to learn you're afraid of something."

"Alex, the guard who was shot. Is he—"

"He's still alive. Everything that can be done is being done to keep him that way. I intend to look in on him when I leave you."

"He might have saved my life," she murmured. "And yours. I don't know his name."

"Craden."

She nodded, wanting to remember it. "And Jermaine?"

He hadn't known how good it would feel to smile again. "Recovered, except for his pride."

"There's no reason for him to be ashamed. I didn't earn my black belt by batting my eyes."

"No, *chérie*, it's obvious you didn't. When you're better, you can explain that to Jermaine." He brushed at her hair, just needing to touch. "What kind of flowers shall I bring you? Something from the garden? I've never asked what your favorite is."

Tears welled up in her eyes and began to spill over.

"Don't." He kissed her fingers, one by one. "Don't cry, my love."

"I brought him here." She closed her eyes, but the tears squeezed through. "I brought Russ to Cordina, to you."

"No." He kept his fingers gentle as he stroked her tears away. "Deboque brought him. We can't prove it, but we know it. You have to know it."

"How could he have deceived me so completely? I auditioned him. Alex, I'd seen his work onstage. I'd talked to people who'd worked with him. I don't understand."

"He was a professional. An excellent actor, Eve, who used that to cover his real vocation. He killed for money. Not for passion, not for a cause, but for money. Even our security check showed nothing. Reeve's working with Interpol right now, hoping to learn more."

"It all happened so fast it doesn't even seem real."

"You aren't to think of it now. It's over."

"Where is he?"

He debated only a moment, then decided she deserved the truth. "He's dead. Jermaine shot him only seconds after…" But he wasn't quite ready to speak of the way her body had jerked and crumpled against his. "He regained consciousness briefly, long enough for Reeve to get some information. We can talk of all of this later, when you're stronger."

"I thought he would kill you." The new medication was taking effect. Her eyes drooped.

"You saw that he didn't. How should I repay you for saving my life?"

Drifting under, she smiled. "I like bluebells. Bluebells are my favorite."

He brought them every day. When she was permitted to leave the hospital in the care of a private nurse, he brought them to her room. As the first week passed, she began to fret about her troupe. When she did, the little ball of fear that had remained lodged inside him loosened. She was getting well.

The press hailed her as a heroine. Bennett brought the articles up and read them to her, rolling his eyes at the praise and calling her a glory hound.

Eve insisted that the first play open, then worried that something would go wrong without her being there to fix it.

She read the reviews, dissecting each word. It thrilled her that the play was well received, relieved her that Russ's understudy had turned in a sterling performance. It depressed her that she hadn't seen for herself.

She submitted to the examinations with less and less grace as they went on.

"Dr. Franco, when is all this poking and prodding and fussing going to stop? I feel fine."

She was lying on her stomach while he changed the dressing on her wound. The sutures had come out the day before and the healing was clean.

"I'm told you're not sleeping well at night."

"It's because I'm bored to death. A walk in the garden becomes an event. I want to go to the theater, Doctor. I've missed the first production altogether. Damn it, I don't want to miss the opening of the second one."

"Mmmm-hmmm. I'm told you've been refusing your medication."

"I don't need it." She pillowed her head on her hands and scowled. "I told you I feel fine."

"I've always considered grumpiness a sign of recovery," he said mildly as he helped her to turn over.

"I'm sorry if I'm not behaving very well." She drew together the bed jacket her father had brought her.

"No, I don't believe you are."

She had to smile. "Maybe not, but with everyone hovering around me. Dr. Franco, you can't imagine what it's like to be scrutinized. If Chris hadn't convinced my father to go back to Houston, I'd have gone crazy. He was wonderful, of course. Everyone has been. The children have been drawing me pictures.

Dorian smuggled in a kitten. You're not supposed to know about that.''

"I will consider it privileged information."

"Prince Armand has come in every day. He brought me this music box." She reached over to touch the small hammered silver case on her nightstand. "It was his wife's. He gave it to her when Alex was born, and he said she would want me to have it."

"Because each of you gave him his son."

"Dr. Franco, I don't feel like a hero." The tears started up again, as they had so often in the past few days. She hated them, hated being so prone to them. "I feel like a mess. I need to get on with my life, let other people get on with theirs. I have too much time to think lying here."

"Your thoughts trouble you?"

"Some of them. I need to be busy again."

"Why don't we try an experiment?"

"As long as it doesn't involve another needle."

"No. You will sleep this afternoon."

"Doctor—"

"Ah, wait until you hear the bargain before you complain. You will sleep this afternoon," he repeated. "Then this evening, you will get up and put on your most elegant dress. I suggest a high back for a little while yet. You will go to the theater—" He paused as the light came into her eyes. "As an observer only. You will come directly back to the palace after the play. Perhaps we could allow a light supper. Then, like Cinderella, you will be back in bed by midnight."

"Deal." She stuck out her hand. As they sealed the bargain, she promised herself she would be back to work before the week was out.

Both Chris and Gabriella helped her dress. Eve conducted her own experiment and asked herself if the process tired her. It didn't. She felt exhilarated. After studying the result with the white tube dress and beaded jacket, she decided she looked better than she had before the incident. She was rested, her color was up, her eyes were clear. She drew her hair back with silver combs, added a cloud of scent and felt like a woman again.

"You're beautiful." Alexander took both of her hands as he

came to lead her downstairs. He was dressed in formal black and carried a small spray of bluebells.

"I wanted you to think so." With a smile she took the flowers and drew in the scent. Whenever she did so in the future, she knew she would think of him. "This is the first time in days you haven't looked at me as though I were under a microscope. No, don't say anything. I feel like a prisoner making good her escape."

"Then you should make it in style."

He drew her hand through his arm and led her downstairs. There was a limo waiting outside, its motor already purring. Eve shot Alexander a brilliant smile as she stepped in.

Champagne was chilling. Beethoven was playing softly.

"The perfect getaway car," she murmured as he released the cork from the bottle.

"I intend for everything to be perfect tonight."

She touched her glass against his, then her lips against his. "It doesn't get any better than this."

"We'll see." He reached in a small compartment and drew out a long, slender box. "I wanted to wait until you were recovered to give you this."

"Alex, I don't need presents."

"I need to give you one." He opened her hand and placed the box in it. "Don't disappoint me."

How could she refuse him? Eve opened the lid and stared down at the necklace of diamonds and sapphires. They seemed to hang on threads of silver and dripped down in two layers of teardrops. It was something for a princess, a queen, not an ordinary woman, she thought. Unable to resist, she lifted it up, and the gems glistened in her fingers. Lights from streetlamps rushed over them and caught fire.

"Oh, Alex, it's wonderful. It takes my breath away."

"You've often had that effect on me. Will you wear it tonight?"

"I—" It almost frightened her, the sheer beauty of it, the elegance. But he'd asked almost as if he'd expected her to refuse. "I'd love to. Help me?"

He unclasped the gold filigree collar she wore and replaced it with his gift. Instinctively Eve brought a hand up to touch the necklace as he draped her neck. It was cool, but already drawing on the warmth of her flesh.

"I'm probably going to pay more attention to this than the play." She leaned over to kiss him, a kiss he returned with a surprising delicacy. "Thank you, Alexander."

"Thank me only when the evening is finished."

She was nervous when she entered the theater. Then she was stunned when she entered the royal box and the crowd below rose to its feet to cheer her.

She found her hand caught in Alexander's. There was a smile in his eyes as he bent over and kissed it. Though she felt the emotion swirling, she managed to smile in return, and taking his lead, acknowledged the crowd with a curtsy.

Alexander held her chair with great satisfaction. She had yet to realize it, but she had just completed her first official duty.

"It has to be good." She tried not to squirm as she waited for the curtain to rise. "I wish I could slip backstage for just a minute and see—"

"I have the doctor's orders, *chérie*."

"I know, but— Oh, God, here goes."

She held his hand tightly throughout the first act. Felt her stomach churn time and time again. Mentally she made a list of every small flaw or break in pacing. She thought of half a dozen changes that would improve it.

But there was laughter. Pride in her troupe, in herself, settled firmly as she heard it. The dialogue was sharp, often acerbic and very American, but the theme of a bumpy romance was international.

When it was over, she counted the curtain calls.

"A dozen." She turned, laughing to Alexander. "A dozen of them. It was good. It was really, really good. I want to change the blocking just a bit in the second scene, but—"

"You won't think about blocking tonight." He took her hand and led her out of the box. Three guards stood at attention. She tried not to notice them, to think only of the play.

"I don't know if I can stand to wait until the reviews come in. Alex, couldn't we go backstage for just a minute so that I can—"

"Not this time." With the guards flanking them, he led her down the side steps. There were reporters, and cameras flashed, but security held the media in check. Before Eve had blinked the lights out of her eyes, they were back in the limo.

"It went too quickly." She leaned back, trying to absorb it all. "I wanted it to last and last, yet I was so nervous. It seemed like everyone was looking at us."

"It made you uncomfortable."

"Only a little." That was already past. "I'm going to convince Franco to let me watch from the wings tomorrow."

"You're not tired?"

"No. Honestly." She smiled as she drew in a deep breath. "I feel incredible. I suppose Cinderella felt the same five minutes before midnight."

"You have an hour yet. I'd like you to spend it with me."

"Down to the last minute," she promised.

The palace was quiet when they returned. He led her upstairs, but instead of taking her to her rooms, he turned to his own.

There was a table set for two, with candles flickering in crystal holders. This time the music was violins, as sensuous as it was romantic.

"Now I really do feel like Cinderella."

"I had planned to do this before, on the night—the night I was to meet you at the theater."

She'd walked over to touch the petals of the flowers spread in a low bowl on the table. "You had?" Surprise and nerves mixed together as she turned. Did a man set such a scene to break off an affair? She didn't think so, not even if the man was a prince. "Why?"

"It seems I've given you too little romance, since you are so stunned by it. It's something I intend to make up for." He came to her, gathered her close and kissed her as he had longed to for days. "I thought I might have lost you." His voice roughened with emotion as he took both her hands and buried his face in them. "I've made so many mistakes with you, but that one—"

"Alex, don't. If you wouldn't let me blame myself for bringing Russ here, how can you blame yourself for what he did?"

"And what you did." He moved his hands from hers, to her face. "As long as I live I'll remember that instant you stepped in front of me. I'll relive it, but each time I do, I'll have pushed you aside in time."

There was such suffering in his voice, such bitterness, that the truth came out without a thought to pride. "If he had killed you, do you think I would have wanted to live? You're all that matters. I've loved you since long before I understood what love meant.''

His breath came out like a prayer. No more mistakes, he promised himself. He would do this right. She had not only given him life, but a reason to live it.

''Would you sit?'' he asked her.

''Please, don't thank me again. I just can't bear it.''

''Eve, sit down.'' Impatience shimmered in his voice. Because she was more comfortable with that, she obliged.

''All right, I'm sitting. But I'm not being fed over here.''

''You'll have all the dinner you want after I get through this.'' Nerves were eating at him. He waited a moment until he had them under some kind of control. When he knelt at her feet, Eve's eyes widened.

''I said I wouldn't kneel for you. This one time it seems appropriate.'' When he drew a box out of his pocket, her hand closed into a fist.

''Alex, you've already given me a gift tonight.'' Her voice, usually so rich and smooth, shook.

''This isn't a gift. It's a request, the biggest one I could ask of you. I've wanted to ask you before, but it seemed too much to expect.''

Her heart was thudding, but she kept her fingers curled together. ''You don't know what to expect unless you ask.''

He laughed and, taking her hand, spread her fingers open. ''You always show me something new. Eve, I'm going to ask you for more than I could ever give. I can only tell you that if you agree, I'll do everything in my power to make you happy.''

He placed the box in her hand and waited.

First she had to draw a breath, a long one. She was not an aristocrat; she was not of royal blood. Equal terms. She remembered her own demand and realized she had the chance to make it all real.

She opened it and saw a ring with the same design of sapphires and diamonds as the necklace she was wearing. Not a gift, she thought, but a request.

''It was my mother's. When I told my father I intended to ask you to marry me, he asked that I give you this. It's more than a ring, Eve. I think you know some of the duties, the expectations that go with it, not just to me, but to the country that would have to be yours, as well. Please, don't say anything yet.''

There were nerves in his voice, something she'd never heard before. It made her want to reach out and soothe him, but she stayed still.

''There are so many things I would have to ask you to leave behind. Houston would be only a place to visit. Your troupe— there is the theater here and the opportunity to build a new troupe in Cordina, but the rest would be over. There is your writing— perhaps in some ways that would make up for what you would have to leave behind. Your freedom would be limited in a way you can't imagine. Responsibilities, some of them vital, others incredibly boring. What you do, what you say, will be common knowledge almost before it's done. And as long as Deboque remains alive, there is a very real danger. We've begun something, but it will be a long, long time before Deboque is no longer a threat. These are things you have to know, to consider.''

She looked at him, then at the ring still in its bed of velvet. ''It seems you're trying to convince me to refuse.''

''I only want you to know what I'm asking of you.''

''You're a fair and practical man, Alexander.'' As she took a deep breath, something beyond his shoulder caught her attention and imagination. She didn't smile, not yet. ''Let's consider this then in a fair and practical manner.'' Reaching over, she drew the scales closer. ''Let's see, we have the duties and responsibilities of state.'' There were some glass balls in a jar. She took a handful and placed two on one of the scales. ''Then there's the lack of privacy.'' She added another ball.

''Eve, this is no game.''

''Please, I'm trying to think this through. There's the fact that I would no longer live in my own country.'' Three balls were added. ''And the fact that I would very possibly be bored to tears by some of those functions I know Brie has to attend. There's the press, the paperwork—I believe you left that out—and the traditions I'd have to learn.'' Plus the new ones she'd do her best to begin. ''Then there's Deboque.''

She looked back at Alexander. ''I won't add any pretty colored balls for Deboque. Whether I agree or refuse, he remains who he is. Now, Alex, I have to ask you one question. Why do you want me to take this ring and the responsibilities that go with it? Why are you asking me to marry you?''

''Because I love you.''

Now she did smile. The rest of the weights went in the empty scale and brought it down. ''That seems to more than even things out, doesn't it?''

He looked at them in a kind of wonder. ''I had to say nothing else?''

''That's all you've ever had to say.'' Throwing her arms around him, she brought him to her for a kiss, a bargain sealed, a life begun. She laughed and pressed her lips to his throat. ''Fairy tales,'' she said, half to herself. ''I'd stopped believing in them.''

''And I.'' His lips found hers again. ''But no more. Tonight you've given me even that.''

''Oh, listen.'' The clock in the hall outside began to chime. ''Put the ring on, Alex, before it strikes twelve.''

He slipped it on, then kissed the delicate skin just above the jewels. ''Tomorrow we'll tell the world, but tonight this is only for us.'' He rose then and drew her to her feet. ''I haven't fed you, and it's after midnight.''

''I could eat in bed, Alex.'' She rested her cheek against his chest, holding onto the magic. ''Franco didn't say I had to get into bed alone.''

He laughed as he swept her up. ''Cordina is in for many surprises.''

''So are you,'' she murmured.

* * * * *

THE PLAYBOY PRINCE

For Tara Bell,
with hope that her wishes come true

Chapter 1

The stallion plunged over the crest of the hill, digging hard into the earth and kicking up dust. At the peak, he reared, powerful forelegs pawing the air. For an instant, horse and rider were silhouetted against the bright afternoon sky. One looked as dangerous as the other.

Even as hooves touched earth, the rider's knees pressed to the stallion's side and sent them both recklessly racing down the sheer incline. The track there was smooth, but hardly gentle with a wall of rock on one side and a drop into space on the other. They took it at full speed and gloried in it.

Only a madman rode with such arrogant disregard for life and limb. Only a madman, or a dreamer.

"*Avant*, Dracula." The command was low and challenging as was the laughter that followed. The tone was one of a man who considered fear a banquet and speed the wine.

Birds, startled by the thunderous pounding of hooves on dirt, flew from the trees and bushes on the cliff above to wheel screaming into the sky. Their noise was soon lost in the distance. When the path veered to the left, the stallion took it without a pause. The edge of the road gave way to cliffs that spilled sharply for seventy feet to the white rocks and blue sea. Pebbles danced off the dirt to shower soundlessly into the empty spaces.

The rider glanced down but didn't slow. He never even considered it.

From that height, there was no scent of the sea. Even the sound of waves crashing was indistinct, like thunder far off and still harmless. But from that height, the sea held a danger and mystique all of its own. Every year she claimed her tribute in the lives of men. The rider understood this, accepted this, for so it had been since the beginning of time. So it would continue to be. At times like this he put himself in the hands of fate and backed his bet with his own skill.

The stallion needed no whip, no spur to drive him faster. As always, his master's excitement and confidence were enough. They tore down the twisting path until the sea roared in their ears and the cry of gulls could at last be heard.

To the onlooker, it might seem the horseman was fleeing from devils or racing to a lover. But anyone seeing his face would know it was neither.

If there was a gleam in the dark eyes, it wasn't one of fear or anticipation. It was challenge. For the moment, and the moment only. Speed whipped the man's dark hair as freely as the horse's dark mane.

The stallion was fifteen hands of coal-black energy, wide at the chest, powerful at the neck. The horse's hide glistened with sweat, but his breathing was strong and even. Astride him, the rider sat erect, his tanned, narrow face glowing. His mouth, full and sculpted, was curved in a smile that spoke of both recklessness and pleasure.

As the path leveled, the stallion's stride lengthened. Here, they passed whitewashed cottages where clothes flapped on lines in the sea breeze. Flowers crowded for space in tidy lawns and windows were opened and unscreened. The sun, still high in the sky after noon, flashed its brilliant light. Without slackening, without needing his master's light hands on the reins to guide him, the stallion sprinted for a hedge as high as a man's waist.

Together, they soared over it.

In the distance were the stables. As there were danger and deadly attraction in the cliffs behind, so were there peace and order to the scene ahead. Red and white, and tidy as the lawns surrounding them, the buildings added another touch of charm to a landscape of cliffs and greenery. Fences crisscrossed to form paddocks where horses were being exercised with far less drama than Dracula.

One of the grooms stopped circling a young mare on a lead when he heard the stallion's approach. Crazy as a loon, he thought—but not without grudging respect. This horse and this rider, merged together in a blare of speed, were a common sight. Even so, two grooms waited at attention for the stallion to slow to a halt.

"Your Highness."

His Highness, Prince Bennett of Cordina slid off Dracula's back with a laugh that echoed the recklessness. "I'll cool him down, Pipit."

The old groom with the slight limp stepped forward. His weathered face was passive, but he passed his gaze over both prince and stallion, checking for any sign of harm. "Your pardon, sir, but a message came down from the palace while you were out. Prince Armand wishes to see you."

Not without regret, Bennett handed the reins to the waiting groom. Part of the pleasure of the ride was the hour he normally spent walking and brushing down the stallion. If his father had sent for him, he had no choice but to forgo pleasure for duty.

"Walk him thoroughly, Pipit. We've had a long run."

"Yes, sir," said the groom who'd spent three-quarters of his life with horses. Among his duties had been seating Bennett on his first pony. At sixty, with one leg game from a fall, Pipit remembered the energy of youth. And the passion. He patted Dracula's neck and found it damp. "I'll see to it myself, Your Highness."

"Do that, Pipit." But Bennett loitered long enough to loosen the cinches. "Thanks."

"No thanks necessary, sir." With a quiet grunt, Pipit hefted the saddle from the stallion's back. "Isn't another man here who has the nerve to deal with the devil." He murmured in French as the horse began to dance in place. In moments, Dracula settled again.

"And there isn't another man I'd trust with my best. An extra scoop of grain wouldn't hurt him this evening."

Pipit took the compliment as no less than his due. "As you say, sir."

Still restless, Bennett turned to walk from the stables. He could have used the extra hour to cool himself down as well. Riding fast, riding reckless, satisfied only part of his thirst. He needed the movement, the speed, but most of all, he needed the freedom.

For nearly three months he'd been tied firmly to the palace and protocol, the pomp and procedure. As second in line to Cordina's throne, his duties were sometimes less public than his brother, Alexander's, but rarely less arduous. Duties, obligations, had been a part of his life since birth, and were normally taken as a matter of course. Bennett couldn't explain to himself, much less anyone else, why some time during the last year he'd begun to fret and chafe against them.

Gabriella saw it. Bennett thought perhaps his sister even understood it. She, too, had always had a thirst for freedom and privacy. She'd gained a portion of that two years before when Alexander had married Eve, and the weight of responsibility had shifted.

Still she never shirked, Bennett thought as he passed through the palace's garden doors. If she was needed, she was there. She still gave six months of every year to the Aid for Handicapped Children while keeping her marriage vital and raising her children.

Bennett dug his hands into his pockets as he climbed the stairs that would take him to his father's office. What was wrong with him? What had happened in the last few months that made him want to slip quietly out of the palace some night and run? Anywhere.

He couldn't shake off the mood, but he managed to tame it as he knocked on his father's door.

"Entrez."

The prince wasn't behind his desk as Bennett had expected, but was seated beside a tea tray at the window. Across from him was a woman who rose to her feet at Bennett's entrance.

As a man who appreciated women of any age, of any form, he took an easy survey before turning to his father. "I'm sorry to interrupt. I was told you wished to see me."

"Yes." Armand merely sipped his tea. "Some time ago. Prince Bennett, I would like to introduce Lady Hannah Rothchild."

"Your Highness." Her gaze swept down as she curtsied.

"A pleasure, Lady Hannah." Bennett took her hand, summing her up in seconds. Attractive in a quiet way. He preferred less subtlety in women. British from her accent. He had an affection for the French. Slim and neat. Invariably, the more voluptuous caught his eye. "Welcome to Cordina."

"Thank you, Your Highness." Her voice was indeed British, cultured and quiet. He met her gaze briefly so that he saw her eyes were a deep and glowing shade of green. "Yours is a beautiful country."

"Please, sit, my dear." Armand gestured her back to her chair before he lifted another cup to pour. "Bennett."

Hannah, with her hands folded in her lap, noticed Bennett's quick look of dislike at the teapot. But he sat and accepted the cup.

"Lady Hannah's mother was a distant cousin of yours," Armand began. "Eve became acquainted with her when she and your brother visited England recently. At Eve's invitation, Lady Hannah has agreed to stay with us as Eve's companion."

Bennett could only hope he wouldn't be expected to escort the lady. She was pretty enough, though she dressed like a nun in a gray, high-collared dress that came a discreet two inches below her knees. The color did nothing for her pale, British complexion. Her eyes saved her face from being plain, but with her dark blond hair pulled back so severely from her face, she put him in mind of the old Victorian companions or governesses. Dull. But he remembered his manners and treated her to an easy, companionable smile.

"I hope you enjoy your stay as much as we'll enjoy having you."

Hannah gave him a solemn look in return. She wondered if he was aware, and thought he was, of how dashing he looked in casual riding clothes. "I'm sure I'll enjoy it immensely, sir. I'm flattered the Princess Eve invited me to stay with her while she awaits the birth of her second child. I hope to give her the companionship and help she needs."

Though his mind was on other matters, Armand offered a plate of frosted cookies. "Lady Hannah has been very generous to give us her time. She's quite a scholar and is currently working on a series of essays."

Figures, Bennett thought, and sipped at the hated tea. "Fascinating."

The smallest of smiles touched Hannah's lips. "Do you read Yeats, sir?"

Bennett shifted in his chair and wished himself back to his stables. "Not extensively."

"My books should be here by the end of the week. Please feel free to borrow anything you like." She rose again, keeping her hands folded. "If you would excuse me, Your Highness, I'd like to see to the rest of my unpacking."

"Of course." Armand rose to lead her to the door. "We'll see you at dinner. Be sure to ring if you require anything."

"Thank you, sir." She curtsied, then turned to extend the courtesy to Bennett. "Good afternoon, Your Highness."

"*Bonjour*, Lady Hannah." Bennett waited for the door to close behind her before dropping onto the arm of his chair. "Well, she should bore Eve to tears within a week." Ignoring the tea, he took a handful of the small iced cookies. "What could Eve have been thinking of?"

"Eve became very fond of Hannah during her two weeks in England." Armand walked to a scrolled cabinet and, to Bennett's relief, took out a decanter. "Hannah is a well-bred young woman of excellent family. Her father is a highly respected member of the British Parliament." The brandy was deep and rich. Armand poured it sparingly.

"That's all well and good, but—" Bennett stopped abruptly as he reached for the snifter. "Oh good God, Father, you're not thinking of trying for a match here? She's hardly my type."

Armand's firm mouth softened with a smile. "I think I know that well enough. I can assure you Lady Hannah was not brought here to tempt you."

"She could hardly do that in any case." Bennett swirled the brandy, then sipped. "Yeats?"

"There are some who believe literature extends beyond equestrian handbooks." Armand drew out a cigarette. There was a knot of tension at the base of his neck. He forced it to concentrate there rather than allowing it to spread.

"I prefer the useful rather than poetry about unrequited love or the beauty of a raindrop." When that made him feel small and ungracious, Bennett relented. "But in any case, I'll do whatever I can to make Eve's new friend welcome."

"I never doubted it."

His conscience soothed, Bennett moved on to more important matters. "The Arabian mare should foal by Christmas. I'm betting it's a colt. Dracula will breed strong sons. I have three horses that should be ready to show in the spring, and another I think should be taken to the Olympic trials. I'd like to arrange that within the next few weeks so that the riders will have more time to work with the horse."

Armand gave an absent nod and continued to swirl his brandy. Bennett felt the familiar push of impatience rising and fought it down. He was well aware that the stables weren't high on his father's list of priorities. How could they be with internal affairs, foreign affairs, and the very tricky politics within the Council of the Crown?

Yet, didn't there have to be something more? The horses' not only gave pleasure, but added a certain prestige when the Royal House of Cordina possessed one of the finest stables in Europe. For himself, it was what he considered his only true contribution to his family and country.

He'd worked for the stables as hard and as menially as any groom or stable boy. Over the years, he'd studied everything he could about breeding. To his delight, he'd found within himself a natural skill that had added spark to his education. Within a short time, Bennett had turned a good stable into one of the best. In another decade, he was confident it would have no equal.

There were times when Bennett needed to discuss his horses and his ambitions with someone other than a stable hand or another breeder. Still, he understood, and always had, that that person would rarely be his father.

"I take it this isn't the time to discuss it." Bennett took another small sip of brandy and waited for his father to reveal whatever weighed on his mind.

"I'm sorry, Bennett, I'm afraid it isn't." The father felt regret. The prince could not. "Your schedule this next week. Can you tell me about it?"

"Not really." The restlessness was back. Rising, Bennett began to pace from one window to another. How close the sea seemed and yet how far away. He wished for a moment that he was on a ship again, a hundred miles from any land, with a storm brewing on the horizon. "I know that I have to go into Le Havre at the end of the week. The *Indépendance* is coming in. There's a meeting with the Farmers' Cooperative and a couple of luncheons. Cassell fills me in each morning. If it's important I can have him type up the highlights for you. I'm sure I'm cutting at least one ribbon."

"Feeling closed in, Bennett?"

With a shrug, Bennett tossed off the last of his brandy. Then the easy smile returned. Life, after all, was too short to complain about. "It's the ribbons that do it. The rest, at least, seems worthwhile."

"Our people look to us for more than governing."

Bennett turned from the window. Behind him the sun was high and bright. Whatever he might sometimes wish in his secret heart, the royalty he'd been born with cloaked him. "I know, Papa. The problem is I don't have Alexander's patience, Brie's serenity or your control."

"You might need them all soon." Armand set his glass down and faced his son. "Deboque will be released from prison in two days."

Deboque. Even the name caused fury to churn in Bennett's stomach. François Deboque. The man by whose orders his sister had been kidnapped. The man who had planned assassination attempts on both his father and his brother.

Deboque.

Bennett pressed a finger to the scar just below his left shoulder. He'd taken a bullet there, and the trigger had been pulled by Deboque's lover. For Deboque. By Deboque.

The bomb planted just over two years before in the Paris Embassy had been meant for his father. Instead it had killed Seward, a loyal assistant, leaving a woman widowed and three children fatherless. That, too, had been Deboque's doing.

And in all the years, nearly ten now since Gabriella's kidnapping, no one had proved Deboque's involvement in the kidnapping, the conspiracies or the murders. The best investigators in Europe, including Bennett's brother-in-law, had been brought in, but none of them had proved that Deboque had pulled the strings.

Now, within days, he would be free.

There was no doubt in Bennett's mind that Deboque would continue to seek revenge. The Royal Family was his enemy if for no other reason than he'd been held in a Cordinian prison for over a decade. Neither was there any doubt that during that decade, he'd continued to deal in drugs, weapons and women.

No doubt, and no proof.

Guards would be added. Security would be tightened. Interpol would continue its work, as would the International Security System. But both Interpol and the ISS had been trying to nail Deboque with murder and conspiracy to murder for years. Until he was gotten under control and the strings to his organization severed, Cordina and the rest of Europe were vulnerable.

Hands in pockets, Bennett strode out to the garden. At least they'd dined *en famille* that evening. It had relieved some strain, even though little could be said in front of Eve's new friend. He doubted if anyone that quiet and prim would have picked up on any tension around the table. She had answered when spoken to and nursed one glass of wine throughout the meal.

He would have wished her back to England a dozen times if he hadn't seen how good she actually was for Eve. His sister-in-law was three months pregnant with her second child and didn't need the additional strain of talk of Deboque. Two years before she'd nearly been killed protecting Alexander. If Lady Hannah could keep Eve's mind off Deboque, even for a few hours a day, it would be worth the inconvenience of having her in the palace.

He needed to talk with Reeve. Bennett drove his balled fists into his pockets. Reeve MacGee was more than his sister's husband. As head of security, he would have some answers. And Bennett certainly had the questions—dozens of them. More was being done than the placing of extra guards. Bennett refused to go through the next weeks blindly while others worked to protect him and his family.

Swearing softly, he looked up at the sky. The moon was cloudless and half full. Another time, with the scents of the garden wafting around him, he would have itched for a woman to watch the sky with. Now, filled with frustration, he preferred the solitude.

When he heard the dogs bark, his body stiffened. He'd thought himself alone; he'd even been sure of it. In any case, his aging hounds never barked at family or familiar servants. Half-hoping for a confrontation, Bennett moved quietly toward the sound.

He heard her laugh and the sound surprised him. It wasn't quiet and prim, but rich and delighted. As he watched, Hannah leaned down to stroke the dogs, which pressed against her legs.

"There now, what a lovely pair you are." Smiling she bent farther still to nuzzle. The moonlight slanted over her face and throat.

Instantly, Bennett's eyes narrowed. She hardly looked plain and subdued at the moment. The moonlight accented the hollows and contours of her face, enriching the soft English skin and deepening the already deep green eyes. He would have sworn that he saw both strength and passion there. And he was a man who recognized both in a woman. Her laughter floated out again, as rich as sunlight, as sultry as fog.

"No, you mustn't jump," she cautioned the dogs as they circled her. "You'll have mud all over me and how would I explain that?"

"It's usually best not to explain at all."

She snapped her head up as Bennett spoke. He saw surprise, or thought he did, but it passed quickly. When she straightened, she was the calm, unremarkable Lady Hannah again. He chalked up the passion he'd thought he'd seen to a trick of the light.

"Good evening, Your Highness." Hannah took only a moment to curse herself for being caught unaware.

"I didn't know anyone else was in the garden."

"Nor did I." And she should have. "I beg your pardon."

"Don't." He smiled to put her at ease. "I've always felt the gardens aren't enjoyed nearly enough. Couldn't you sleep?"

"No, sir. I'm always restless when I travel." The dogs had deserted her for Bennett. She stood beside the flowering jasmine and watched him stroke them with strong, capable hands. She was well aware that numerous ladies had enjoyed the same easy touch. "I'd seen the gardens from my window and thought I might walk awhile." In truth, it had been their scent, exotic and alluring, that had urged her to loiter after she'd noted the layout of the space.

"I prefer them at night myself. Things often look different at night," he continued, studying her again. "Don't you think?"

"Naturally." She linked her hands together just below the waist.

He was marvelous to look at, sun or moon. When he'd strode into his father's office that afternoon she'd thought that riding clothes suited him best. The dogs came back to press their noses against her joined hands.

"They like you."

"I've always been fond of animals." She unlinked her hands to stroke. He noticed for the first time that her hands were delicate, long and slender like her body. "What are their names?"

"Boris and Natasha."

"Suitable names for Russian wolfhounds."

"They were given to me as puppies. I named them after characters in an American cartoon show. Spies."

Her hands hesitated only a heartbeat. "Spies, Your Highness?"

"Inept Russian spies who were forever after a moose and squirrel."

He thought he saw it again, the flash of humor that lent something special to her face. "I see. I've never been to America."

"No?" He moved closer, but saw nothing but a young woman with good bones and a quiet manner. "It's a fascinating country. Cordina's become closely linked with it since two members of the Royal Family have married Americans."

"A fact that disappointed a number of hopeful Europeans, I'm sure." Hannah relaxed enough for a cautious smile. "I met Princess Gabriella several years ago. She's a beautiful woman."

"Yes, she is. You know, I've been to England several times. It's strange we never met."

Hannah allowed the smile to linger. "But we did, Your Highness."

"Boris, sit," Bennett commanded as the dog lifted a paw toward Hannah's dress. "Are you sure?"

"Quite sure, sir. Then you'd hardly be expected to remember. It was several years ago at a charity ball hosted by the Prince of Wales. The Queen Mother introduced you to me and my cousin Lady Sara. I believe you and Sara became...friendly."

"Sara?" His mind backtracked and zeroed in. His memory, always good, was faultless when it came to women. "Yes, of course." Though he remembered Hannah only as a vague shadow beside her glamorous and bold cousin. "How is Sara?"

"Very well, sir." If there was sarcasm, it was well coated with manners. "Happily married for the second time. Shall I send her your regards?"

"If you like." He dipped his hands into his pockets again as he continued to study her. "You were wearing blue, a pale blue that was nearly white."

Hannah lifted her brow. She didn't have to be told that he'd barely noticed her. The fact that he hadn't, yet still remembered the color of her gown gave her a moment's pause. A memory like that could be useful—or dangerous.

"You flatter me, Your Highness."

"I make it a policy not to forget a woman."

"Yes, I can believe that."

"My reputation precedes me." The frown was there, then gone, to be replaced by a careless smile. "Does it concern you to be alone in the garden, in the moonlight with—"

"The Royal Rake?" Hannah finished.

"You do read," Bennett murmured.

"Incessantly. And no, Your Highness, I'm quite comfortable, thank you."

He opened his mouth, then laughed and shut it again. "Lady Hannah, I've rarely been put so neatly in my place."

So he was quick—another point she'd have to remember. "I beg your pardon, sir. That certainly wasn't my intention."

"The hell it wasn't, and well done." He took her hand and found it cool and steady. Perhaps she would prove to be a great deal less dull than he'd anticipated. "I should beg your pardon for baiting you, but I won't since you obviously hold your own so well. I'm beginning to see why Eve wanted you here."

Hannah had learned long ago to block off any form of guilt. She did so now. "I became very fond of her in a short time and was delighted with the opportunity to stay in Cordina for a few months. I confess, I've already fallen in love with little Princess Marissa."

"Barely a year old and she's already ruling the palace." Bennett's eyes softened as he thought of his brother's first child. "Maybe it's because she looks like Eve."

Hannah withdrew her hand from his. She'd heard the rumors that Bennett had been half in love, or possibly more than half in love, with his brother's wife. It didn't take even so talented an observer as she to hear the affection in his voice. She told herself to file it away. It may or may not have its uses later.

"If you'll excuse me, sir, I should go back to my room."

"It's still early." He found himself reluctant to let her go. It was unexpected that she would be easy to talk to, or that he would find himself needing to talk to her.

"I'm in the habit of retiring early."

"I'll walk you back."

"Please don't trouble. I know the way. Good night, Your Highness." She merged quickly with the shadows while the dogs whined a bit and thumped their tails against his legs.

What was there about her? Bennett wondered as he bent to soothe his pets. At first glance she seemed almost bland enough to fade into the wallpaper, and yet... He didn't know. But as he walked back toward the palace with the dogs at his heels, he resolved to find out. If nothing else, probing a bit beneath Lady Hannah's quiet breeding would keep his mind off Deboque.

Hannah didn't wait to see if he followed her, but walked quickly through the garden doors. She'd been born with the talent to move quietly, so unobtrusively she could easily be missed in a group of three people. It was a talent she'd honed to a skill and which served her well.

She moved up the stairs without a sound, never looking back. If you had to check whether you were being followed, you were already in trouble. Once inside her own room, she locked the door and slipped out of her practical pumps. Because the woman she professed to be would never leave her clothing scattered, Hannah picked them up, and with only a brief look of distaste, placed them neatly in her closet.

Checking only to see that her curtains were drawn, she peeled off the unflattering cocktail dress.

Although she thought it deserved its day in the garbage, she carefully hung it on a padded hanger.

She stood now, a slimly curved woman with milk-pale skin and long legs in a skimpy lace-edged teddy. Drawing the confining pins from her hair, she let it fall heavily to her waist with a sigh of pure pleasure.

Anyone who knew Lady Hannah Rothchild would have been

stunned by the transformation, so complete, so ingrained was the role she'd played for nearly ten years.

Lady Hannah had a passion for silk and Breton lace, but confined it to nightwear and lingerie. Linens and tweeds were more fitting to the image she'd worked hard to create.

Lady Hannah enjoyed reading a pot-boiling thriller in a steamy bubble bath, but she kept a copy of Chaucer on her nightstand and if asked, could quote and discuss a handful of obscure passages.

It wasn't a matter of split personality, but necessity. If she'd given it any deep thought, Hannah would have been able to state that she was comfortable with both of her selves. In fact, more often than not she thoroughly liked the plain, polite and marginally pretty Hannah. Otherwise, she could never have tolerated the sensible shoes for extended periods.

But there was another part to Lady Hannah Rothchild, only daughter of Lord Rothchild, granddaughter of the Earl of Fenton. That part was not quiet and unassuming, but shrewd and sometimes reckless. More, that part had a taste for danger and a mind that absorbed and stored the most minor detail.

Combined, those parts of Lady Hannah Rothchild equaled an excellent and highly skilled agent.

Ignoring her robe, Hannah opened her top drawer and drew out a long, locked box. Inside was a strand of pearls handed down from her great-grandmother with matching earrings her father had had reset for her twenty-first birthday. In the drawers of the box were several other pieces of jewelry befitting a young woman of her class.

Hannah pulled a notebook out of the false bottom and taking it to the rosewood writing desk, began to write her daily report. She hadn't gone into the garden merely to smell the roses, though she had lingered too long because of them. Now she had the complete layout and no longer had to rely on the information fed her. She took the time to draw a sketch of the palace, including the doors and windows most easily accessible. By the following day, or the day after at most, she would have a schedule of the guards.

It had taken her little time to form a friendship with Eve. Securing an invitation to the palace in Cordina had been as easy as asking for one. Eve missed her sister and the familiarity of her own country. She'd needed a friend, one she could talk to, one who would share her delight in her daughter.

Hannah had obliged.

She felt the quick trickle of guilt again and ignored it. A job was a job, she reminded herself. She couldn't let the fondness she felt for Eve interfere with a goal she'd begun to work toward two years ago.

With a shake of her head, she made her first notes on Bennett. He wasn't completely what she'd expected, Hannah thought now. Oh, he was as charming and as attractive as his dossier had said, but he'd given the dull Lady Hannah his time and attention.

An egotistical womanizer, Hannah reminded herself. That had been her own conclusion after doing her research on him. Perhaps he was a bit bored and entertained thoughts of distracting himself with a vulnerable and accessible woman.

Narrowing her eyes, Hannah looked back on the way he had smiled at her. A man of his looks, position and experience knew how to use that smile or a soft word to enchant a woman of any age and any class. The fact that he'd done so, with astonishing regularity, was well documented. Perhaps he would try to add another jewel to his crown by seducing her.

She remembered the way he'd looked in the moonlight, the way his eyes had warmed when she'd bantered back with him. His hand had been firm and hard when it had taken hers—the hand of a man who did more than wave regally to his people.

With a shake of her head, she brought herself up short. It wouldn't do to consider a dalliance with Bennett for enjoyment, but for its usefulness. Thoughtfully, she tapped her pencil on the pad. No, a romance with Bennett would only lead to complications, no matter how advantageous it might be in the long run. She'd keep her eyes down and her hands folded.

Carefully, Hannah hid the notebook again and replaced the false bottom. The box was locked, but left in full sight if anyone searched her dresser.

She was in, she told herself with a growing sense of anticipation as she looked around the room.

When Deboque walked out of prison in two days' time, he'd be very pleased.

Chapter 2

"Oh, Hannah, I'm so glad you agreed to visit awhile." With her arm hooked with her new friend's, Eve strolled behind the backdrop at the theater. Her body remained slender during the early months of her pregnancy, but her dress was cleverly cut to conceal even the slight weight gain. "Alex doesn't find it as necessary to pamper me to death now that you're here. He finds you so sensible."

"I am sensible."

Eve's low chuckle flowed into her easy Texas drawl. "I know, that's the beauty of it, but you're not always telling me to sit down and put my feet up."

"Men sometimes look at pregnancy and childbirth as a traumatic disease rather than a fact of life."

"That's it exactly." Delighted with Hannah's dry wit, Eve drew her into her office. With Gabriella so often in America and her own sister visiting only rarely, Eve had indeed yearned for another woman to relax with. "Alex keeps expecting me to faint or get overly emotional. I never felt better in my life, except perhaps when I was carrying Marissa."

Tossing back her fall of dark hair, Eve perched on the edge of her desk. Here, at least, she could still claim some measure of the privacy she'd given up when she'd married a prince. Though she never regretted the sacrifice, she always enjoyed stealing a bit of her own back.

"If you hadn't come, I'd have had to fight him tooth and nail to continue working. He only agreed because he felt you'd keep a close eye on me when he's busy."

"Then I won't disappoint him." Hannah took quick stock of the office. No window, no outside access. With a smile, she chose a chair. "You know, Eve, I really admire you. The Fine Arts Center always had a good reputation but since you took over here, this theater has become one of the most important in Europe."

"It's what I've always wanted." Eve looked down at the diamond-encrusted band on her finger. Even after two years it sometimes astonished her to find it there. "You know, Hannah, some mornings I'm almost afraid to wake up; I think that I'll find out it was all a dream. Then I look at Alex and Marissa and think, they're mine. Really mine." Her eyes clouded a moment with both fear and determination. "I won't let anything or anyone hurt them."

"No one will." Eve's thoughts were on Deboque, Hannah surmised. The princess was bound by duty to keep some fears to herself. "Now, not to pamper, but I think we could both use some tea, then you can show me what sort of job I can do around here."

Eve brought herself back with an effort. Nightmares of Deboque, a man she'd never seen, continued to plague her. "Tea's a wonderful idea, but I didn't bring you to the Center to work. I just thought you'd like to see it."

"Eve, you of all people should understand that I need something to do or I'll be bored to death."

"But I'd hoped this could be a vacation for you."

The guilt shimmered a bit. "Some people aren't meant for vacations."

"All right then. Why don't you watch rehearsals with me for an hour or two and give me an honest opinion?"

"I'd love to."

"Great. I'm worried about the opening. We only have a couple of weeks left and I've had nothing but trouble with this playwright."

"Oh, who is it?"

Eve rose and took a deep breath. "Me."

* * *

Hannah drank her tea and stayed in the background. It didn't take long for her to see that Eve was respected not only as the wife of the heir, but for her knowledge of theater. She noted too that guards, unobtrusive but in force, were always close at hand. When the princess was in the theater, every entrance was blocked, every interior door was double guarded. Hannah was also aware that a special unit of security checked the Center daily for explosives.

While seated mid-theater with Eve, Hannah watched the rehearsal. She'd always had an affection and respect for actors, as she understood the effort and skill that went into characterization. Now, while lines were cued and staging set, she matched the members of the troupe with the information she already had compiled on each of them.

They were certainly talented, Hannah thought as she found herself drawn into the rhythm and emotion of Eve's play. The sets were still incomplete, but the players needed no more than Eve's words and their own skill to make a statement. Each one of the actors had a reputation in theater and a complete security check.

But it had been an actor—Russ Talbot—who'd nearly carried out Deboque's revenge two years before. Hannah couldn't forget that it was a strong possibility that someone other than herself had been planted. Deboque was known for covering his bets.

"She's wonderful, isn't she?"

Drawn back, Hannah looked over at Eve. "I beg your pardon?"

"Chantel O'Hurley. She's exquisite." Shifting in her chair, Eve leaned on the seat back in front of her. "She rarely makes a stage performance, so we're lucky to have her. I'm sure you've seen her films in England."

"Yes." Hannah gave her full attention to the curvy blonde center stage.

Chantel O'Hurley. Hannah paused to recollect everything she'd read in the actress's file. Twenty-six. American film star. Residence, Beverly Hills. Daughter of Frances and Margaret O'Hurley, traveling entertainers. Sisters, Abigail and Madelaine. Brother, Trace.

Hannah frowned and continued to watch. She had full background information on the entire O'Hurley family, except the brother. There her sources had closed tight. In any case, Chantel

O'Hurley was a talented actress with an impressive list of screen credits and no known affiliation with any political group. Nonetheless, Hannah would keep an eye on her.

"She's found the heart of it," Eve murmured. "I'd finished the play and was trying to work up the courage to produce it, when I saw her in her last film. I knew immediately she'd be the perfect Julia." On a long breath Eve leaned back again in an unprincesslike slouch. "I can't believe she's here, reciting my lines. There isn't an emotion that voice can't pull out."

"I'm sure she's honored to be performing in a play written and produced by Princess Eve of Cordina."

On a half laugh, Eve shook her head. "If the play had been lousy, I could have been Empress of Europe and Chantel wouldn't have accepted the part. That's what I'm hanging onto."

"A member of the Royal Family doesn't write lousy plays."

At the sound of the voice behind her, Eve was springing up and reaching out. "Alexander! What are you doing here?"

"I, too, have an interest in the Center." He kissed the hand he held before turning to Hannah. "Please, sit, I didn't mean to disturb you."

"No." Eve sighed and glanced back at the stage where rehearsals continued. "You meant to check up on me."

It was, of course, the truth, but Alexander only shrugged. In the dim light, Hannah saw his gaze sweep over his wife's head to the guards placed at several strategic points. "You forget, *ma mie*, that I am still president of the Center. In addition to that, my wife's play is in rehearsal. I have a small interest there as well."

"And you came to be certain I wasn't staying on my feet." Over the frustration came the tug of love. Eve rose to her toes to kiss him. "Thank you. Hannah, tell His Highness I've been taking care of myself in the four hours and forty minutes since he last saw me."

"Your Highness," Hannah began dutifully, "the princess has been taking excellent care of herself."

A smile softened his features, but he continued to stand protectively near his wife. "Thank you, Hannah. I'm sure the credit goes to you."

With a low laugh, Eve tucked her hand through Alexander's arm. "Hannah, you can see that I wasn't joking when I said that

Alex thinks I need a keeper. If you hadn't come I have no doubt he'd have hired a two-hundred-pound wrestler with tattoos.''

"I'm glad I could save you from that." What was this? Hannah wondered. A tug of envy? Ridiculous as it seemed to her, she recognized the emotion as she studied Alexander and Eve. So much in love, she thought. The power of it all but cast an aura around them. Did they realize, could they realize, how rare a thing they'd found?

"Now that I've interrupted," Alexander was saying, "I was hoping to convince you to join me for my luncheon with the American senator."

"The Yankee from Maine."

With a smile, Alexander stroked her cheek. "My dear, it continues to fascinate me how your country divides itself into sections. But yes, the Yankee from Maine. We should be finished by three and be back at the palace when Marissa wakes from her nap."

"But you had a meeting this afternoon."

"I canceled it." He brought her hand to his lips. "I wanted to spend some time with my family."

The glow of pleasure all but lit up the theater. "Give me five minutes to get my things. Hannah, you'll join us?"

"If it wouldn't inconvenience you, I'd really like to stay and watch the rest of the rehearsal." Her mind was already shooting ahead. Alone, she could take a casual tour of the complex. If there were vulnerabilities, she'd find them.

"Of course, stay as long as you like." Eve bent down to kiss her cheek. "We'll have a car wait for you at the stage door. Five minutes," she repeated to Alexander before she dashed off.

"What do you think of the play?" Alexander asked Hannah as he took the seat beside her.

"I'm hardly an expert on the theater, Your Highness."

"In private, please call me Alexander."

"Thank you," she murmured, aware that this gave her an intimacy rewarded to few. "There's an intensity, an immediacy in the dialogue that makes one care deeply about the characters. I don't know the end, but I find myself hoping Julia wins even while I'm afraid she won't."

"Eve would like to hear that. The play—and other things—have her very tense right now."

"You're worried about her." In a gesture that was pure instinct, Hannah placed a hand on his. "She's very strong."

"I know that, better than most." But he'd never been able to block off the memory of how her body had stiffened, then gone limp in his arms when a bullet had struck her. "I haven't told you before how very grateful I am that you came to be with her. She needs friendship. I changed her life, selfishly perhaps because I couldn't live mine without her. Whatever can be done to give her a sense of normalcy, a sense of peace, I'll do. You understand the obligations of royalty. The limitations. Even the risks."

"Yes, I do." Hannah left her hand on his another moment before removing it. "And I understand a happy woman when I see one."

When he turned to her then, Hannah saw the strong resemblance to his father. The lean, almost scholarly face, the aristocratic lines, the mouth that was held firm. "Thank you, Hannah. I think perhaps you'll be good for all of us."

"I hope so." She looked back at the stage, at the players, at the roles. "I do hope so."

Alone, Hannah watched for another half hour. Yes, the play was good, she decided, even gripping, but she had other games to play.

The guards remained, but with no royalty present they were more for the purpose of keeping others out than monitoring those already in. Lady Hannah was already established as the princess's confidante and companion. Trusted by Prince Armand himself, she wasn't followed when she rose and slipped through a side door.

There was a miniature camera concealed in a lipstick case in her handbag, but she didn't use it now. Her training had taught her to rely on her powers of observation first, her equipment second.

A building the size of the sprawling Center wasn't easily secured. Hannah found herself giving Reeve MacGee a nod of respect as she walked through. Heat sensors as well as hidden cameras. But the sensors were activated only when the Center was closed.

Security passes were required at the door for members of the cast and crew. On the night of a performance, however, entrance could be gained for the price of a ticket. Deboque would step from behind bars in a day's time.

As she walked, leaving one corridor for the next, Hannah drew a blueprint in her mind. She'd studied the layout of the Center on paper before, but preferred to walk in it, to focus on it, to touch the walls and floor.

Too many blind corners, she thought. Too many small rooms used for storage. Too many places to hide. Even with Reeve's expertise, the building could be vulnerable with the right plan of attack. But then, Hannah believed any building could be.

She turned into Wardrobe, pretending a casual interest in the costumes. Did the guard at the door know everyone by sight? How easy would it be to replace one of the technicians? A photo was affixed to the pass, but makeup and hairpieces could take care of that. How often had she, or another like her, gained access to a place by faked credentials or a clever disguise?

Once inside, a man could disappear easily. If a man on the security panel could be bribed or replaced, so much the better.

Yes, she'd put that scenario in her report and let her superiors chew on it awhile. She'd add to that the fact that no one had checked her bag. A small plastic explosive could be easily carried and easily planted.

She walked from Wardrobe into a rehearsal hall walled with mirrors. With a little shock, she stared at her reflection on all sides. Then, as she had in the garden, she let out a low, easy laugh.

Oh, Hannah, she thought, how miserably dull you are. Turning to the side, she shook her head. No, maroon did nothing for her, and the high-necked jacket with its bulky belt only made her look unattractively thin. The skirt came well below the knee to hide her legs. She'd braided her hair today, tightly, then had circled the braid at the base of her neck.

Being a part of herself, it was the best cover she could have conceived. She'd been too skinny as a child, with unmanageable hair, and knees that were forever scraped. Her facial bones had been prominent even then, but in the young girl's face had seemed too sharp, too angular.

Then when the other girls had begun to bloom and curve, Hannah's body had remained stubbornly straight. She'd been bright and athletic and cheerful. Boys had patted her on the back and called her a good sport, but they hadn't been interested in taking her to any dances.

She'd learned to ride, swim, shoot skeet and to put an arrow in a bull's-eye from a hundred paces, but she hadn't dated.

She'd learned to speak Russian and French and enough Cantonese to surprise even her father, but she'd gone alone to her own graduation ball.

When she turned twenty, her body changed, but Hannah hid the late blossoming under dull clothes. She'd already chosen her path in life. Beauty turned heads and in her field it was always best to go unnoticed.

Now, she looked at the results in the wall of mirrors and was satisfied. No man would desire her. It was human nature to look at the physical shell and draw emotion from that long before you dipped beneath to the intellect or soul. No woman would envy her. Dull was safe, after all.

No one would suspect a plain, bookish woman of excellent breeding and quiet social manners of deception or violence. Only a select few were aware that the woman beneath was capable of both.

For a reason she couldn't name, that thought made her turn away from her reflection. Deception had been with her all of her adult life, and yet she couldn't quite dismiss the twinges of guilt she felt whenever Eve looked at her as a friend.

It was a job, Hannah reminded herself. No emotional attachments, no emotional involvements were permitted. That was the first and most important rule of the game. She couldn't afford to allow herself to like Eve, to even think of her as anything but a political symbol. If she did, everything she'd worked for could be lost.

The envy had to go as well, Hannah reminded herself. It was a dangerous lapse to let herself look at the love between the prince and Eve and wish something similar for herself. There was no room for love in her profession. There were only goals, commitments and risks.

There would be no prince for her, royal or otherwise.

But before she could prevent it, her thoughts turned to Bennett and the way he'd smiled at her in the moonlight.

Idiot, she told herself and began tightening a few loose pins. He was the last person she should think about in a personal way. If for no other reason, there was his dossier and the astonishing list of women who'd been part of his life already.

Use him, certainly, her mind went on. But don't think about him as anything but a means to an end. Romantic fantasies had ended for her at sixteen. Ten years later, in the middle of her most important job, was hardly the time to begin to weave them again. She would do well to remember that the stiff-lipped, proper Lady Hannah would never see His Royal Highness Prince Bennett de Cordina in a romantic light.

But the woman within dreamed and for a moment strained against the confines she'd built herself.

Hannah turned to look back at the mirrors when she heard the footsteps.

Immediately alert, she cast her eyes down and walked from the room.

"Ah, there you are."

At Bennett's voice, Hannah gave an inward curse, but curtsied. "Your Highness."

"Taking the grand tour?" He walked closer, wondering why she looked as plain as a maiden aunt and continued to intrigue him.

"Yes, sir. I hope it's all right."

"Of course." He took her hand, willing her to look directly at him. There was something about her eyes.... Or perhaps it was her voice, that cool, always composed British tone. "I had some business in town. Alexander suggested I swing by when I'd finished to see if you were ready to go back."

"That's very kind of you." And oh, how she would have preferred a silent, anonymous driver who'd have given her the opportunity to assimilate her report on the drive back.

"I was here." He felt the restlessness layer over him as she drew her hand back to her side. "If you'd like to see more, I'd be happy to take you around the rest of the Center."

Hannah weighed the pros and cons in a matter of seconds. Another quick look might add something, but she'd already gone through the main theater twice, once with Eve and once alone. It might begin to look odd if she went through again with Bennett.

"No, thank you. It is a fascinating place. I've never seen a theater from this side."

"Eve's territory. I confess I prefer front row center myself." He took Hannah's arm and began to lead her down the hall. "If you hang around her for any length of time, she finds something for you to do. With me, it's usually moving boxes. Heavy boxes."

With a laugh, Hannah slanted him a look. "That's one of the best uses a woman can find for a man."

"I can see why Eve took to you." He'd come simply to do his sister-in-law a favor, but now found himself glad. Outward appearance aside, Lady Hannah was anything but dull. For perhaps the first time in his life, Bennett was beginning to look beneath the physical. "Have you seen much of Cordina yet, Hannah?"

She noticed he'd dropped her title, but decided to let it pass. "Only snatches so far, sir. Once I'm a bit more familiar with Eve's routine, I plan to explore a bit. I've heard your museum has some excellent exhibits. The building itself is reported to be a fine example of post-Renaissance architecture."

He wasn't interested in exhibits, but in her. "Do you like the water?"

"Of course. Sea air is very beneficial for the constitution."

With a half laugh, Bennett paused at the top of the stairs. "But do you like it?"

He had a strange talent for looking at a woman as though he were seeing her for the first time. And looking as though it mattered. Despite her training, Hannah felt her pulse rate accelerate. "Yes. My grandmother has a place near Cornwall. I spent several summers there as a girl."

He wondered what she would look like with her hair down and the sea wind teasing it. Would she laugh as he had heard her laugh in the garden? Would he see that light flash in her eyes again? Then he realized it didn't matter how she looked. He went on impulse, knowing he might regret it.

"I have to go into Le Havre in a couple of days. The drive runs along the coast. Come with me."

If he'd asked her to step into the storage room and neck, she would have been no less surprised. Surprise turned quickly to caution and caution to calculation. But beneath it all was the simple pleasure that he wanted her company. It was the pleasure that worried her.

"It's kind of you to ask, Your Highness, but Eve may have plans."

"Then we'll check with her first." He wanted her to go. He found himself already looking forward to spending a few hours with her away from the palace. Perhaps it was for the challenge of it, the challenge of picking away at that prim, proper exterior and finding what, if anything, lay beneath. Whatever the reason was, Bennett didn't question it. "Would you like to go?"

"Yes, I would." Hannah told herself it was because it would give her the opportunity to study him more closely, for professional reasons. She told herself it would give her the chance to see how well security worked away from the palace and the capital. But the truth was as simple as her answer. She wanted to go.

"Fine, then we'll fix it, and you can stand through the long and wordy welcoming ceremony with me."

"Hate to be bored alone, do you?"

Laughing, Bennett took her hand again. "Yes, I can see exactly why Eve brought you to us." Her hand was an inch from his lips when the murmur of voices came from below. Glancing down, more than a little annoyed, Bennett spotted Chantel.

"The anger has to show," she was insisting, walking so quickly the director had to lengthen his stride to keep up. "Julia is not a passive woman. She doesn't hide what she feels no matter what the consequences. Dammit, Maurice, I'll make it subtle. I know my job."

"Of course you do, *chérie*, that I don't question. It is simply that—"

"*Mademoiselle.*" From the top of the stairs, Bennett looked down. Hannah had a firsthand glimpse of how he smiled at a truly beautiful woman. Without thinking, she drew her hand from his and linked her fingers together.

Chantel, reaching one hand up to draw back her pale blond hair, tilted her head back. Even so dispassionate an observer such as Hannah had to concede that few women could claim such a combination of glamour, beauty and sexuality. Her lips curved. Her eyes, a deep, dreamy shade of blue, smiled with them.

"Your Highness," Chantel said in her rich, smoky voice as she dipped into a formal curtsy. She started up the stairs and Bennett started down. In the middle, they stopped, then Chantel reached up to touch his face before bringing him closer for a lengthy kiss. Above them, Hannah felt her teeth snap together. "It's been a long time."

"Too long." Bennett cupped her hand in both of his. "You're lovelier than ever. It's astonishing."

"It's genes," Chantel claimed, and grinned at him. "My God, Bennett, what a beautiful man you are. If I wasn't a cynic, I'd propose."

"If I wasn't terrified of you, I'd accept." They embraced again with the ease of old friends. "Chantel, it's good to see you again. Eve was turning handsprings when you agreed to take the part."

"It's a good play." Chantel gave a matter-of-fact shrug. "Even though I adore you, I wouldn't have come all this way to take a role in a bomb. Your sister-in-law's a talented woman." Chantel cast a look over her shoulder at the director waiting respectfully at the bottom of the stairs. "You might mention to her that I'm fighting to preserve the integrity of her Julia." As she turned back, she spotted Hannah standing on the landing. "Friend of yours?"

Glancing back, Bennett held out a hand. "Hannah, come meet the incomparable Chantel."

The stiffness in her movement only suited her character, Hannah told herself as she started down. All unremarkable women tensed up when slapped in the face with great beauty. She stopped on the step beside Bennett, but kept nearly a foot of space between them.

"Lady Hannah Rothchild, Chantel O'Hurley."

"How do you do?" Formal and proper, Hannah held out a hand. Chantel kept her face passive as she accepted it.

"I do fine, thank you." As a woman, as an actress who understood angles and role-playing, she wondered why someone with such good bone structure and a flawless complexion would deliberately make themselves appear plain.

"Lady Hannah is keeping Eve company for a few months."

"How nice. Cordina's a beautiful country. I'm sure you'll enjoy it."

"Yes, I already am. I also enjoyed watching you rehearse."

"Thanks, but we have a way to go." Chantel tapped a finger on the banister and wondered why she felt such instant distrust.

Dismissing it as overwork, she turned back to Bennett. "I have to run. Try to make some time for me, darling."

"Of course. You're coming to dinner Saturday with the rest of the cast?"

"Wouldn't miss it. I'll see you there, Lady Hannah."

"Goodbye, Miss O'Hurley."

After giving Bennett a quick pat on the cheek, Chantel descended the stairs again and let the director trail behind her.

"She's quite a woman," Bennett murmured.

"Yes, she's very beautiful."

"There's that, too." Without looking at her, Bennett took Hannah's arm again. "I suppose I've always admired her willpower and ambition. She's determined to be the best and isn't afraid to work for it. Every time I see her on the screen, it's breathtaking."

Hannah dug her fingers into her purse and reminded herself she was supposed to be unassuming. "You admire ambition, Your Highness?"

"Nothing's changed for better or worse without it."

"Some men still find ambition in a woman unflattering, or at least, uncomfortable."

"Some men are idiots."

"I couldn't agree more," Hannah said dryly, dryly enough that he lifted his brow as he gazed at her.

"Why am I never quite sure whether or not you're insulting me, Hannah?"

"I beg your pardon, sir, I was simply agreeing with you."

He stopped again. From the stage came the murmur of voices, but the hall was deserted. Bennett took her chin in his hand, ignoring her jolt of shock, and studied her face. "Hannah, why is it when I look at you I'm not convinced I'm seeing all there is?"

Alarm bells went off in her head. Her face paled a bit. She knew it, but thought, hoped, he would take that as natural. Not by another blink did she show concern. "I don't know what you mean."

"I wonder." He moved his thumb over her jawline, then just beneath where the skin was softer yet, and warm. "Yes, I wonder more than I should about you, Hannah. Do you have an answer for that?"

There were amber flecks in his eyes, turning what might have been plain brown into something tawny and compelling. He had the mouth of a poet and the hands of a farmer. Hannah wondered how it was possible to combine the two as her heart, always so steady, began to drum against her ribs.

"Your Highness—" It was both the lady without and the lady within who fumbled.

"Do you, Hannah?"

He saw her lips part. Strange, he hadn't noticed how attractive her mouth was before—soft, just a bit wide and beautifully shaped without cosmetics. He wondered if it would taste as cool as her voice or as rich as her eyes.

She had to stop this, here and now. The yearning building inside her could only be destructive. Even as she longed to reach out, she cast her eyes down. "No, sir, except that many times men are intrigued with a woman simply because she's not what they're accustomed to."

"We'll see." He backed off, though the effort it cost him was a surprise. "I'll take you back now, Hannah, and we'll both give it some thought."

Chapter 3

Hannah was given free run of the palace and the grounds. She had only to ask and her bath would be drawn or her bed turned down. If she developed a craving for hot chocolate at three a.m., she could pick up the phone beside her bed and request it. As a guest of the Royal Family, she was afforded every amenity the palace could offer.

And as a guest of the Royal Family, she was afforded her own guards.

Hannah considered them only a slight nuisance. It was a simple enough matter for someone of her talents to make them think she was tucked safely away in her rooms while she was somewhere else entirely. However, the fact that she was being watched made it difficult to set up a meeting with her contact on the outside.

Using the palace phones was out of the question. Too many extensions made it a risk that even a casual, coded conversation could be overheard. She'd briefly considered smuggling in a transmitter, then had rejected the notion. Transmissions could be traced. She hadn't spent two years of her life to get to this point to see it all wiped away because of some electronic foul-up. In any case, she preferred meetings of such importance to be face-to-face.

Two days after she arrived in Cordina, she mailed a letter. It was addressed to an old family friend in Sussex who didn't exist. Its destination was one of Deboque's many branches throughout

Europe. If for any reason the letter was intercepted and opened, the reader would find nothing more interesting than a chatty note describing Cordina and the weather.

Once the letter reached its destination and was decoded, it would read differently. Hannah had given her name, her rank in the organization and had requested a meeting, detailing the time, date and place. The information would be fed back to the Cordina contact. All she had to do was get there, alone.

One week, Hannah thought once the letter was on its way. In one week she would well and truly begin what had been started so long ago. She had plenty to do to keep her busy in the meantime.

Princess Gabriella and her family were visiting the palace that evening. The staff had been in an uproar for the better part of the day, more, Hannah guessed, because the children were descending than for any other reason. Hannah had heard that the priceless collection of Fabergé eggs was to be put out of reach.

She spent the day quietly enough, visiting Eve and Marissa in the nursery, lunching with several members of the Historical Society, and in the lull of late afternoon, exploring the cellars for vulnerabilities.

Now, she clipped on her pearls and prepared to join the family in the main drawing room. It would be interesting to see them all together, she thought. In that way she could judge the interactions as well as the individuals. Before too much time had passed, she had to know them all as well as she knew herself. One mistake, one bad judgment call, and all could be lost.

"Come back here, you little demon!"

Hannah heard a loud laugh, a thud, then rushing feet. Before she had a chance to open the door to see for herself, it burst open. Barreling through it was a small boy with a thatch of dark hair that may or may not have been combed in the last week. He gave her an amazing grin, showing more than one gap before he scooted under her bed.

"*Cachez-moi, s'il vous plaît!*" His voice was muffled by the skirt of the spread before he disappeared.

Hannah opened her mouth again only to see Bennett filling the doorway.

"Did you see a small, miserably mannered boy?"

"I, ah—no," she decided on the spot and folded her hands. "I did think I heard someone go running past. What are you—"

"Thanks. If you see him, lock him in a closet or something." He started off down the hall. "Dorian, you nasty little thief, you can't hide forever."

Hannah walked to the door and looked out to see Bennett turning the corner before she closed it. Moving back to the bed, she crouched down and lifted the skirt. "I think it's safe now," Hannah told him in French.

The dark hair poked out first, then a sturdy little body dressed in short pants and a white linen shirt that were streaked with dirt. If Hannah hadn't already seen his picture, she would have taken him for one of the servants' offspring. But he was royal.

"You are English. I speak excellent English."

"So you do."

"Thank you for hiding me from my uncle." Young Prince Dorian bowed. Though he wasn't yet five, he executed it perfectly. "He was angry, but he doesn't stay that way long. I'm Prince Dorian."

"Your Highness." Hannah curtsied. "It's a pleasure to meet you. I'm Lady Hannah Rothchild." Then unable to resist, she bent down to his level. "What did you steal?"

Dorian glanced at the closed door, back at Hannah, then grinned. Digging into his back pocket he pulled out a yo-yo. It might once have been blue, but now it was the gray of old wood with a few chips of brighter paint still holding. Hannah studied it with appropriate respect.

"This is Bennett's—His Highness's?" Hannah corrected.

"*Merveilleux, n'est-ce pas?* He's had it since he was five." Dorian turned the toy over in his hand, marveling that it had once been new and shiny when his uncle had been just the age he was now. "He gets angry when I go into his room and play with it, but how else am I going to be able to make it work?"

"Good point." Hannah barely resisted the urge to ruffle the royal head of hair. "And one would doubt he plays with it himself very often."

"He keeps it on a shelf. It isn't that he really minds me looking at it," Dorian explained, loyal to the core. "It's just that when I try to make it work, the string gets all tangled and knotted up."

"It takes a little practice."

"I know." He grinned again. "And I can only practice if I steal it."

"Your logic is flawless, Your Highness. May I see?"

Dorian hesitated only a moment, then graciously handed it over. "Girls usually aren't interested in such things." He made a grimace of masculine disgust. "My sisters play with dolls."

"Everyone has different tastes, I suppose." Hannah slid her finger into the loop, wondering how long it had been since Bennett's had fit there. The string wasn't as old as the toy itself. By her guess, it would have been replaced more than a dozen times over the years. On impulse, she let the yo-yo slide down, dangle, then brought it neatly up.

"Oh, nicely done." Charmed, Dorian watched her with wide eyes.

"Thank you, sir. I used to have one of my own. It was red," she remembered with a half smile. "Until my dog chewed it up."

"Can you do any tricks? I tried Round the World once and broke a lamp. Uncle Bennett scolded me, but then he tossed out the pieces himself so no one would know."

Because she could picture it so well, Hannah smiled. A loud roar, but little bite, she decided and wished she didn't like him the better for it. "A trick?" As she considered she took the yo-yo up and down. Then, with a quick flick of her wrist took it Round the World. When it snapped back in her palm, Dorian laughed and climbed on her bed.

"Do another, please."

Calling on memory, Hannah Walked the Dog and had the young prince bouncing on the bed and calling out for more.

"Well done, Lady Hannah," Bennett said from the doorway. "Obviously you have hidden talents."

Hannah had to bite off an oath as she brought the yo-yo back. "Your Highness." Toy in hand, she curtsied. "I didn't hear you knock."

"I didn't." Bennett pushed away from the doorjamb he was leaning on to walk to the bed. Unrepentant, his nephew grinned up at him.

"Isn't she wonderful, Uncle Bennett?"

"We'll discuss the Lady Hannah's attributes later." He gave

Dorian's ear a twist before turning around. "My property, if you will."

Fighting to keep a straight face, Hannah handed it to him.

"This might seem to be nothing more than a simple child's toy," Bennett began as he slipped it into his pocket. "But in fact, it's an heirloom."

"I see." She cleared her throat on the laugh, but it escaped anyway. Hoping she looked contrite, she stared at the floor. "I beg your pardon, sir."

"The hell you do. And he was in here all along wasn't he?" Bennett pushed his nephew flat on the bed and sent him into a fit of giggles. "You let me go running off all over the palace looking for this petty thief when all the time he was hiding behind your skirts."

"The bed skirts to be honest, sir." She had to clear her throat again, but managed to speak calmly. "When you rushed by with so vague a description, I had no idea you were looking for Prince Dorian."

"I admire a good liar," Bennett murmured as he moved closer. For the second time he caught her chin in his hand. But for the first time, she saw all of the arrogance he was capable of and felt all of its attraction. "And I grow only more intrigued."

"Lady Hannah can do a double Round the World."

"Fascinating." Bennett slid his hand away slowly as he turned back to his nephew. If he'd listened for it, he might have heard Hannah's slow sigh of relief. "I thought we had an agreement, Dorian."

Dorian's head drooped, but Hannah didn't notice that the light in his eyes dimmed in the least. "I only wanted to see it. I'm sorry, Uncle Bennett."

"Sure you are." Bennett hauled him up by the armpits, scowled, then kissed him soundly. "Your mother's downstairs. Don't slide in the halls on the way to the drawing room."

"All right." On his feet again, Dorian bowed to Hannah. "It was a pleasure meeting you, Lady Hannah."

"And you, sir."

He sent her a gap-toothed grin before he dashed off.

"Sweet talker," Bennett muttered. "Oh, you might think he's all charm, but he has a black heart."

"Strangely enough I was reminded of you."

With one brow lifted, Bennett rocked back on his heels. "Indeed, my lady, that is strange."

"He's a scoundrel, without question. And you love him."

"That's beside the point." Bennett stuck his hand in his pocket. "As to the matter of the yo-yo."

"Yes, sir?"

"Try to wait until I'm five feet away before you laugh in my face."

"As you wish, Your Highness."

"It was a gift from my mother when I was ill one summer. I've bought the little devil a dozen of them, but he keeps stealing mine. He knows if I don't get a son of my own by the time he's ten I'll make him a gift of it."

"I have a redheaded doll my mother gave me when I broke my wrist in a fall. I kept it when I outgrew all the others."

It wasn't until he'd taken her hand that she realized she'd told him something he didn't need to know, something she'd never told anyone else. Even as she warned herself such lapses were dangerous, his lips brushed her fingers.

"You, Lady Hannah, have a kind heart as well as a clever tongue. Come, walk downstairs with me and meet the rest of my family."

Reeve MacGee would be a formidable obstacle. Hannah had thought so before, but seeing him with his family, she was sure of it. She knew his background from the time he'd entered the police force as a rookie through his less publicized work for the United States government.

His involvement with Cordina and the Royal Family had the ring of romance, but Reeve was no poet. He'd come out of a self-imposed retirement at Prince Armand's request when Gabriella had been kidnapped. Though she'd escaped, her time in captivity had left its mark. Amnesia had plagued her and Reeve had been enlisted to protect her, and to investigate.

There had been no doubt that Deboque had been pushing the buttons, but though his lover had been captured and imprisoned, she'd never implicated him. Like other powerful men, Deboque inspired loyalty. Or fear.

During the time that Gabriella was struggling to regain her memory, she and Reeve had fallen in love. Although Reeve had refused to accept a title when they married, he'd agreed to head security in Cordina. Even with Reeve's experience and skill, the palace had been infiltrated once again.

Two years ago, Alexander had nearly been assassinated. Since that time, Reeve had managed to block any and all attempts on members of the Royal Family. But Deboque was about to walk out of prison. With freedom would come more power.

Hannah watched Reeve now, seeing a quiet, introspective man who plainly adored his wife and children. He would use everything available to protect them from harm. So much the better.

With her hands folded and her skirts smoothed, Hannah sat and listened.

"We all know your play's going to be a wonderful success." Gabriella, with her hand caught loosely in Reeve's, smiled at Eve. Her rich red hair was styled with casual chic around a face that remained delicate and lovely. "That doesn't mean we don't understand you have to worry about it."

"I'm at the point now where I wish it was over." Eve drew Marissa into her lap.

"But you're feeling well?"

"I'm feeling fine." Eve let Marissa climb down again. "Between Alex's pampering and Hannah's eagle eye, I can hardly lift a finger without a doctor's certificate."

"It's so good of you to come." Gabriella smiled at Hannah before she sipped some sparkling water. "I know firsthand how comforting it is to have a friend nearby. Are we keeping you happy enough so that you're not homesick?"

"I'm very happy in Cordina." Hannah kept her back straight against the sofa.

"I hope you'll come out to the farm while you're here."

"I've heard a great deal about it." Gabriella had been kidnapped there while it had still been an overgrown plot of land. "I'd love to see it for myself."

"Then we'll arrange it." Reeve spoke quietly as he lit a cigarette. "You're enjoying your visit so far?"

"Yes, I am." Their eyes met and held. "Cordina is a fascinating country. It has a fairy-tale aura perhaps, but it's very real. I'm particularly interested in visiting the museum.''

"I think you'll find we have some very unusual exhibits," Armand put in.

"Yes, sir. I did some research before leaving England. I have no doubt that my time in Cordina will be an education.''

Marissa toddled over, still a bit unsteady on her year-old legs, and held her arms up. Hannah placed the child in her lap.

"Your father is well?" Reeve asked her through a haze of smoke.

Hannah jangled her pearls to entertain the baby. "Yes, thank you. It often seems that the older I get, the younger he gets.''

"Families, no matter how large or how small, are often the focus of our lives," Reeve said quietly.

"Yes, that's true," Hannah murmured as she played with the baby. "It's a pity that families, and life, aren't as simple as they seem when we're children.''

Bennett sat relaxed in his chair and wondered why he thought if he could read between the lines, he'd discover a great deal more than small talk.

"I wasn't aware you knew Hannah's father, Reeve.''

"Only casually." When he leaned back, his smile was easy. "I heard that Dorian stole your yo-yo again.''

"I should have locked it in the safe when I heard he was coming." Bennett patted the slight bulge in his pocket. "I'd have given the little devil a run for his money, but he had an accomplice.'' He turned his head to look at Hannah.

"I'll have to apologize for my son," Gabriella's lips curved as she lifted her glass again. "For drawing you into his crime, Lady Hannah.''

"On the contrary, I enjoyed it. Prince Dorian is charming.''

"We call him other things at home," Reeve murmured. The woman was a mystery, he thought. The harder he looked for chinks, the fewer flaws he saw. "With that in mind, I think I'll go out and look for the bunch of them. Adrienne's at the age where you can't be sure she'll mind them or urge them to wade in the fountain.''

Bennett glanced toward the terrace doors. "God knows what havoc they might have wrought in the last twenty minutes.''

"Wait until you have your own." Eve rose to take Marissa from Hannah. "You'll spoil them rotten. If you'll excuse me, I want to go up and feed Marissa."

"I'll go with you." Gabriella set her glass aside. "I thought we might talk over the plans for the Christmas Ball. You know I want to help as much as I can."

"Thank God I don't have to beg. No, Hannah, please, sit and relax," Eve continued as Hannah started to stand. "We won't be long."

"See that you're not." Bennett took out the yo-yo to pass it from hand to hand. "Dinner's in an hour."

"We all know your priorities, Ben." Eve bent to kiss his cheek before she left the room.

"I could use a walk myself." Rising, Alexander nodded to Reeve. "I'll help you round up the children." They were barely out the terrace doors when a servant appeared in the doorway.

"I beg your pardon, Your Highness. A call from Paris."

"Yes, I've been expecting it. I'll take it in my office, Louis. If you'll excuse me, Lady Hannah." Taking her hand, Armand bowed over it. "I'm sure Bennett can entertain you for a few moments. Bennett, perhaps Lady Hannah would enjoy seeing the library."

"If you like to look at walls of books," Bennett said when his father was gone, "you can't do much better."

"I'm very fond of books." Taking him at his word, Hannah rose.

"All right then." Though he could have thought of a dozen better ways to while away an hour, he took her arm and led her through the corridors.

"It's difficult to believe that the museum could have finer paintings than you have here in the palace, Prince Bennett."

"Le Musée d'Art has a hundred and fifty-two examples of Impressionist and Postimpressionist paintings, including two Corots, three Monets and a particularly fine Renoir. We've recently acquired a Childe Hassam from the United States. In return my family has donated six Georges Complainiers, a Cordinian artist who painted on the island in the nineteenth century."

"I see."

Noting her expression, Bennett laughed. "As it happens, I'm on the board of the museum. I may prefer horses, Hannah, but that doesn't preclude an affection for art. What do you think of this?''

He paused in front of a small watercolor. The Royal Palace was beautifully, almost mystically painted. Its white, white walls and turrets rose behind a pink mist that enchanted rather than concealed the building itself. It must have been dawn, she thought. The sky was such a delicate blue in contrast to the deeper sea. She could see the antiquity, the fantasy and the reality. In the foreground were the high iron gates and sturdy stone walls that protected the palace grounds.

''It's beautiful. It shows love as well as a touch of wonder. Who was the artist?''

''My great-great-grandmother.'' Pleased with her reaction, Bennett drew her hand into the crook of his arm. ''She'd done hundreds of watercolors and had tucked them away. In her day, women painted or drew as a hobby, not as a profession.''

''Some things change,'' Hannah murmured, then looked back at the painting. ''Some things don't.''

''A few years ago I found her work in a trunk in one of the attics. So many of them had been damaged. It broke my heart. Then I found this.'' He touched the frame, reverently, Hannah thought. She looked from his hand to his face and found herself caught up in him. ''It was like stepping back in time, generations, and discovering yourself. It could have been painted today, and it would look the same.''

She could feel her heart moving toward him. What woman was immune to pride and sensitivity? In defense, she took a small step back. ''In Europe, we understand that a few generations are only a blink in time. Our history stands before us, centuries of it. It becomes our responsibility to give that same gift to each new generation.''

Bennett looked at her and found her eyes almost impossibly deep. ''We do have that in common, don't we? In America, there's an urgency that can be exciting, even contagious, but here, we know how long it takes to build and secure. Politics change, governments shift, but history stands firm.''

She had to turn away from him. It would only cloud the issue if she thought of him as a caring, sensitive man rather than an assignment. "Are there any others?" she said with a nod toward the painting.

"Only a handful, unfortunately. Most were beyond repair." For reasons he could only be half-sure of, he wanted to share with her things that mattered to him. "There's one in the music room. The rest are in the museum. Here, have a look." With his hand guiding her again, he took her down the hall into the next wing, their footsteps echoing off the mosaic tile.

Leading her through an open door, Bennett took her into a room that seemed to have been fashioned to accent the white grand piano in its center.

There was a harp in the corner that might have been played a hundred years before, or last week. In a glass case were antique wind instruments and a fragile lyre. The flowers were fresh here, as they were in every room in the palace. Trailing blossoms of jasmine spilled out of glossy, Chinese red urns. A small marble fireplace was swept and scrubbed clean with a pile of fresh kindling stacked as though inviting the match.

With Bennett, she walked across an Aubusson carpet to look back in time. This painting was of a ball, festive in bright colors and bold strokes. Women, gloriously feminine in mid-nineteenth-century gowns, were whirled around a gleaming floor by dashing men. There were mirrors that reflected the dancers and doubled them while a trio of chandeliers glistened overhead. As Hannah studied it, she could almost hear the waltz.

"How lovely. Is this room here, in the palace?"

"Yes. It has hardly changed. We'll have the Christmas Ball there next month."

Only a month, she thought. There was so much to be done. In a matter of hours Deboque would be out of prison, and she would soon learn if her groundwork had been clever enough.

"This is a beautiful room." Hannah turned. Keep your conversation light, she warned herself. Keep your mind light, for now. "In our country house there's a small music room. Nothing like this, of course, but I've always found it so relaxing." She wandered to the piano, not so much to examine it as to give herself distance. "Do you play, Your Highness?"

"Hannah, we're alone. It isn't necessary to be so formal."

"I've always considered the use of titles as proper rather than formal.'' She didn't want this, she thought quickly. She didn't want him to close that gap of rank between them.

"I've always considered it annoying between friends." He walked behind her to touch her lightly on the shoulder. "I thought we were."

She could feel his hand right through the neat linen of her dress, through the skinny silk strap beneath and onto her flesh. Fighting her own private war, she kept her back to him. "Were what, sir?"

He laughed, then both hands were on her shoulders, turning her to face him. "Friends, Hannah. I find you good company. That's one of the first requirements of friendship, isn't it?"

She was looking up at him, solemn-eyed, with the faintest blush of color along her cheekbones. Her shoulders seemed so strong under his hands, yet he remembered how soft, how delicate the skin along her jawline had seemed.

Her dress was brown and dull, her face unpainted and unframed. Not a hair was out of place and yet he got a flash of her laughing, her hair unbound and her shoulders bare. And the laughter would be for only him.

"What the devil is it about you?" Bennett muttered.

"I beg your pardon—"

"Wait." Impatient, as annoyed with himself as he was with her, Bennett stepped closer. As she stiffened, he held his hands up, palms out as if to reassure her he meant her no harm. "Just be still a moment, would you?" he asked as he lowered his head and touched his mouth to hers.

No response, show no response. Hannah repeated it over and over in her head like a litany. He didn't press, he didn't coax or demand. He simply tasted, more gently than she'd had known a man could be. And the flavor of him seeped into her until she was all but drunk with it.

His eyes remained open, watching hers. He was close, so close she could catch the scent of soap on his skin. Something that brought images of the sea. Hannah dug her fingers into her palms and fought to keep from showing him the turmoil within.

God, she wanted. How she wanted.

He didn't know what he'd expected. What he found was softness, comfort, sweetness without heat or passion. Yet he saw both in her eyes. He felt no driving need to touch her or to deepen the kiss. Not this first one. Perhaps he already knew there would be others. But this first one showed him an ease, a relaxation that he'd never looked for in a woman before.

He was man enough, experienced enough, to know there was a volcano inside of her. But strangely, he had no desire to push it to the eruption point, yet.

Bennett broke the kiss simply by stepping back. Hannah didn't move a muscle.

"I didn't do that to frighten you." He spoke quietly, for it was the truth. "It was just a test."

"You don't frighten me." He didn't frighten the woman he could see, but the one within was terrified.

It wasn't quite the answer he'd wanted. "Then what do I do to you?"

Slowly, carefully, she unballed her hands. "I'm afraid I don't understand what you mean, Your Highness."

He studied her another moment, then spun away. "Maybe not." He rubbed a hand along the back of his neck wondering why such an unassuming, placid woman should make him so tense. He understood desire. God knows he'd felt it before. But not like this. Never quite like this.

"Dammit, Hannah, isn't anything going on inside of you?"

"Of course, sir, a great number of things."

He had to laugh. He should have known she would put him in his place with logic. "Call me by my name, please."

"As you wish."

He turned back. She was standing in front of the glistening white piano, hands folded, eyes calm and quiet on his. He thought it the most ridiculous thing, but knew he was very close to falling in love. "Hannah—"

He'd taken no more than two steps toward her when Reeve walked into the room. "Bennett, excuse me, but your father would like to see you before dinner."

Duty and desire. Bennett wondered if he would ever find a full merging of the two. "Thank you, Reeve."

"I'll take Lady Hannah back in."

"All right." Still, he paused and looked at her again. "I'd like to talk with you later."

"Of course." She would move heaven and earth to avoid it.

She remained where she was when he left. Reeve glanced over his shoulder before he came closer. "Is there a problem, Lady Hannah?"

"No." She drew a deep breath, but didn't relax. "Why should there be?"

"Bennett can be...distracting."

This time when her eyes met his, she made certain they were slightly amused. A layer, the thinnest of the layers of her outer covering was dismissed. "I'm not easily distracted, particularly when I'm working."

"So I've been told," Reeve said easily enough. He was still looking for flaws and was afraid he might have found the first in the way she had looked at Bennett. "But you've never worked on an assignment quite like this one."

"As a senior agent for the ISS, I'm capable of handling any assignment." Her voice was brisk again, not the voice of a woman who'd been moved, almost unbearably, by a kiss. "You'll have my report by tomorrow. Now I think we'd better join the others."

She started by, but he took her arm and stopped her. "There's a great deal riding on this. On you."

Hannah only nodded. "I'm aware of that. You requested the best, and I am."

"Maybe." But the closer it came, the more he worried. "You've got a hell of a reputation, Hannah, but you've never come up against anyone like Deboque before."

"Nor he anyone like me." She glanced toward the hallway again, then lowered her voice. "I'm an established member of his organization now. It's taken me two years to get this close. I saved him two and a half million by seeing that that munitions deal wasn't botched six months ago. A man like Deboque appreciates initiative. In the last few months, I've been planting the seeds that will discredit his second in command."

"Or get your throat cut."

"That's for me to worry about. In a matter of weeks, I'll be his right hand. Then I'll serve him to you on a platter."

"Confidence is an excellent weapon, if it isn't overdone."

"I don't overdo." She thought of Bennett and strengthened her resolve. "I've never failed with an assignment, Reeve. I don't intend to begin with this one."

"Just make sure you keep in contact. I'm sure you'll understand when I say I don't trust anyone."

"I understand perfectly, because neither do I. Shall we go?"

Chapter 4

Hannah's plans to avoid driving with Bennett to Le Havre were neatly demolished. She'd justified her decision by convincing herself she could detail more useful information by concentrating on the palace. In order to remain behind, she'd come up with the credible, if unoriginal excuse of a headache.

Hannah had deliberately waited until Alexander had finished breakfasting with his family so that she could speak to Eve alone. It took Eve less than ten minutes to turn it on her.

"It's no wonder you're not feeling yourself." Eve sipped tea in the sunny nursery while she looked over her schedule. "I've kept you cooped up ever since you arrived."

"Don't be silly. The palace is the size of a small town. I've hardly been cooped up."

"However big it is, it still has walls. A nice drive along the coast is just what you need. Bernadette." She glanced up at the young nurse who was preparing to take Marissa for her morning walk. "Would you see that Princess Marissa has a hat? It's a bit breezy out."

"Yes, ma'am."

Eve held out her arms for her daughter. "Have a nice time, darling."

"Flowers," Marissa said, and laughed at her own voice.

"Yes, pick some flowers. We'll put them right here in your

room." She kissed both of Marissa's cheeks then let her go. "I hate not being able to take her for a walk this morning, but I have a meeting at the Center in an hour."

"You're a wonderful mother, Eve," Hannah murmured when she saw the concern in Eve's eyes.

"I love her so much." With a long sigh, she picked up her tea again. "I know it's foolish, but when I'm not with her I think of dozens of things that might happen, that could happen."

"I'd say it was normal."

"Maybe. Being who we are, what we are, just magnifies everything." Unconsciously, she rested her hand where even now her second child slept. "I want so badly to give her a sense of normalcy, and yet..." Eve shook her head. "There's a price for everything."

Hannah remembered Alexander saying almost the same thing in referring to his wife.

"Eve, Marissa is a lovely, healthy and happy child. I'm not sure they get any more normal than that."

Eve stared at her a moment, then dropped her chin on her open palm. "Oh, Hannah, I'm not sure how I got through the last two years without you. Which brings me right back to where we were." Briskly, Eve refilled Hannah's cup. "You came here to visit and so far I haven't given you a moment's free time unless you were handcuffed to me. That makes me feel very selfish."

"The reason I'm here is to be with you," Hannah reminded Eve, as she felt herself rapidly losing ground.

"The reason you're here is because we're friends. As a favor, take the day, relax, enjoy the sea air. I promise you Ben can be wonderful company. I guarantee that five minutes after you're in the car, your headache will disappear."

"Someone have a headache?" Ben asked as he strode in. He was wearing the white dress uniform with the red insignia that stated his rank as officer in the Cordinian Navy. On the left breast pocket was the royal seal that proclaimed him prince. Hannah had always considered the opinion that women fell for men in uniform nonsense. Until now.

He looked so...dashing, she admitted, though her practical side searched for a less dramatic word. The snowy-white jacket accented his tan and the dark contrast of his hair. He grinned at her, making Hannah aware that he understood his effect. Automatically she rose to dip into a curtsy.

"Bennett, I'd forgotten what a heartbreaker you are in dress whites." Eve tipped her face up for a kiss. "Maybe I should tell Hannah to take an aspirin and stay behind after all."

"I think Lady Hannah can take care of herself. Can't you, *chérie?*"

Hannah decided then and there that if she had to fence with him, she would wield her foil well. "It's always been the case."

"You are a bit pale." He touched a finger to her cheek. "Are you really not well?"

"It's nothing." She wondered if he could feel her blood stir at the casual contact. "And Eve assures me that a drive along the sea is exactly the right prescription."

"Good. I'll bring her back with roses in her cheeks."

"If you'll give me a moment, I need to get my bag."

"Bennett." Eve stopped him before he could follow Hannah out. "Am I wrong, or did I see something just now?"

He didn't pretend to misunderstand her. "I'm not sure."

"Hannah's lived a very sheltered life. I suppose I don't have to tell you to be…well, careful?"

Though the sunlight streamed in behind him, his eyes cooled. "No, I don't have to be reminded who a man in my position can and can't have an affair with."

"I didn't say that to annoy you." Instantly Eve was on her feet, taking his hands. "We were friends long before we were family, Ben. I only ask because I'm fond of her and I know how irresistible you can be."

He softened, as he always did with Eve. "You always managed to resist."

"You always treated me like a sister." Eve hesitated again, torn between two loyalties. "Would I be pushing if I said she's not your usual type?"

"No, she's not. Perhaps that's what baffles me. Stop worrying." He bent to kiss her brow. "I won't damage your proper British friend."

"It could be I'm just as concerned about you."

"Then don't be." Giving her cheek a careless stroke, he walked to the door. "Tell Marissa I'll bring her some seashells."

Calm and resigned to her decision, Hannah met him at the top of the stairs. "I hope I didn't keep you waiting."

"We've plenty of time. I can promise the drive will be worth the pomp and speeches on the other end."

"I don't object to pomp and speeches."

"Then we're fortunate. Claude." Bennett nodded to the tall, sturdy man who waited beside the main doors.

"Good morning, Your Highness. Lady Hannah. Your car is ready, sir."

"Thank you, Claude." Bennett steered Hannah through the doors knowing the simple statement meant that the road between Cordina and Le Havre had been secured.

Hannah saw the car the moment they stepped outside. The zippy little French convertible sat at the foot of the steps flanked by two solid sedans.

"Do you drive that?"

"Looks like I should wind it up, doesn't it?" Bennett touched the shiny red hood with affection. "Handles like a dream. I've had her up to one-twenty on a straight."

She thought of how it would feel, speeding beside the sea with the wind on her face. Hannah pushed aside such wishes and tried for an uneasy look. "I hope you don't intend to try to break your record today."

With a laugh, he opened the door for her himself. "For you, I'll drive like a grandfather."

Hannah slipped into the seat and nearly sighed with pleasure. "It is rather small."

"Big enough for two." Bennett rounded the hood. Claude already had his door opened.

"But surely you don't travel without your security or an assistant."

"Whenever possible. My secretary will be in the car behind us. Let's give them a run, shall we?" He switched on the ignition. From the rich sound under the hood, Hannah decided it was filled with engine. Before she could draw a breath, Bennett sent the car speeding down the long, sedate drive. He drove the way he rode a stallion. Full speed.

"They're muttering already, I imagine." He gave the guards at the gates an easy salute. "If Claude had his way, I'd never go over thirty kilometers. I'd also be closed up in a bulletproof limo wearing a suit of armor.''

''It's his job to protect you.''

''A pity he has so little humor about it.'' Bennett downshifted, then sent the car squeaking around a curve.

''Did your grandfather live a long and fruitful life?''

''What?''

''Your grandfather,'' Hannah repeated as she folded her hands neatly in her lap. ''I wondered if he lived a long life. It seems unlikely if he drove like this.''

The wind was blowing his hair around his face as he turned his head to grin at her. ''Trust me, *ma belle*, I know the roads.''

She didn't want him to slow down. It was the first time she'd felt true freedom in months. She'd nearly forgotten how sweet it tasted. The sea shimmered blue and white beside the road as they traveled down from the heights of the capital. Palms twisted their way toward the sky, bending and swaying in the stiff breeze. Lush red flowers burst out of bushes that grew helter-skelter along the roadside. The air smelled of sea and perpetual spring.

''Do you ski?'' Bennett asked her as he noticed her watching a man glide over the water behind a low-slung boat.

''I never have.'' It looked wonderful. ''I'm sure you have to be fairly athletic. I'm more at home in libraries.''

''One can't read all the time.''

She watched the skier take a somersaulting tumble into the water. ''I think perhaps I can.''

Bennett grinned and roared though a lazy S-turn. ''Life's hardly worth the trouble without a few spills. Don't you ever have the urge for adventure, Hannah?''

She thought of the last ten years of her life, of the assignments that had taken her from castles to ghettos and everywhere in between. French alleys. Italian waterfronts. She thought of the small-caliber pistol she carried in her bag and the pencil-slim stiletto tucked like a lover against her thigh.

''I suppose I've always preferred my adventures vicariously, through books.''

''No secret dreams?''

''Some of us are exactly what we seem.'' Suddenly uncomfortable, she shifted away from the topic. ''I didn't realize you

were a naval officer.'' Another lie, she thought. But her profession
was built on them.

"I served a couple of years. At this point, it's more of an hon-
orary rank. Second sons are traditionally bound for the military.''

"So you chose the navy.''

"Cordina's surrounded by the sea. Our fleet is smaller than
yours, certainly, but it's strong.''

"And these are uneasy times.''

Something came and went in his eyes. "In Cordina we've
learned that all times are uneasy times. We're a peaceful country,
and because we want to remain so, we're prepared always for
war.''

She thought of the pretty white palace with its exotic gardens
and fairy-tale turrets. Inaccessible by sea, with a cliff-top view that
scanned miles with the naked eye. She sat back as the sea rolled
by. Nothing ever was as simple as it seemed.

Le Havre was charming. Nestled at the base of a long hill, it
clustered together with small white-washed buildings and clap-
board cottages. Fishing and sail boats swayed quietly at neat docks
at one curve of the harbor. Around the seawall of old stone, hardy
blue flowers pushed their way through cracks. There were lobster
traps and nets spread and drying in the sun. The scent of fish was
heady and oddly pleasant in the early morning air.

At a glance, it could have been taken for any tidy fishing town
that survived on and with the sea. But as they rounded the harbor
the docks became more expansive, the buildings larger. Cargo
ships with men hauling freight down gangplanks flanked an ocean
liner. Like much of Cordina, Le Havre was more than it seemed.
Through location and the skill of its people, it was one of the
finest ports of call in the Mediterranean. It was also the center of
Cordina's naval base.

Negotiating the narrow, winding streets, Bennett drove through
a set of gates. He slowed only long enough to be acknowledged
by the guards with snappy salutes. There were bungalows here
painted a faded pink that reminded Hannah of the inside of a
seashell. Palms and flowers grew in profusion, but she recognized
the structure and order of a military facility. Moments later, Bennett drew up in front of a stucco building where seamen in whites
stood at attention.

"For the next few hours," he murmured to Hannah, "we're official." Bennett reached in the back and picked up his hat. Even as he set it on his wind-ruffled hair, one of the seamen reached the door to open it for him. With the brim shading his eyes, Bennett returned the salutes. He knew the sedan had already pulled up behind him, but didn't look back as he guided Hannah into the building.

"First, we have a few formalities," he warned her, tucking his hat under his arm.

The formalities were a group of officers, from admiral down, and their wives and attachés who were waiting to greet and be greeted by His Royal Highness.

Hannah acknowledged the introductions and pretended not to see the looks of speculation. *Not the prince's type.* She could read it easily in every eye that met hers. She fully agreed.

They were given tea and a tour of the building—for her sake. Hannah feigned an ignorance of the equipment shown her, asking the proper questions and looking properly polite at the simplistic answers. She could hardly mention that the radar and communication systems were as familiar to her as they were to the trained operators. In a pinch, she could have rigged the equipment to contact the ISS base outside London or Deboque's headquarters in Athens.

She walked by display cases, listening with apparent fascination as an admiral explained to her the difference between a destroyer and an aircraft carrier.

The pomp and circumstance continued as they were escorted outside to await the docking of the *Indépendance.* The band, their white uniforms blinding in the sun, struck up a rousing march as Bennett stepped onto the dock. Crowds of people cheered from behind the military barricade. Babies and small children were held up so that they could catch a glimpse of the prince.

Hannah counted off a dozen security people mingled with the crowd in addition to the two men who were never more than an arm's span from Bennett's elbow.

Deboque is out, she thought. Everything is a risk.

The battle-gray destroyer maneuvered into position while the crowd applauded and the band continued to play. Seamen on the dock stood at attention as did seamen on deck. After six months at sea, the *Indépendance* was home.

The gangplank came ponderously down. The pipes were sounded. The captain strode down to salute the officers and bow to his prince.

"Welcome home, Captain." Bennett offered his hand, and the crowd cheered again.

There was, as there always was on such occasions, a speech to be made. Hannah kept her face attentive while she slowly scanned the crowd.

It was no surprise to find him there. The small, slightly stoop-shouldered man was on the edge of the crowd holding a small Cordinian flag. In his plain work clothes and quiet face, he would never be noticed or remembered. He was one of Deboque's best.

There would be no move on Prince Bennett today, she thought, though the back of her neck itched. Her successful planting at the palace had been one of her highest contributions to Deboque's organization. The working order now was for care and cleverness rather than a rash assassination attempt.

In any case, she knew Deboque wasn't as interested in Bennett as he was in Alexander, and in Alexander not so much as in Armand. He wouldn't settle for the second in line to the throne after so long a wait.

Still, she closed her hand over the handle of her bag. She shifted, only a matter of inches, but Bennett's body was now more than half shielded by hers.

Had the man been sent with a message for her? Hannah wondered. Or had he simply been ordered to stay close and watch? Instinct told her it was the second. Casually, she swept the crowd again. Her eyes met his and held for only a fraction of a second. There was an acknowledgement, but no signal. Hannah let her gaze move on, knowing they'd meet within a few days at the museum.

The pretty ceremony with its brisk military music and banners continued with a tour of the ship and an inspection of the crew. Hannah walked with the admiral's wife as Bennett was led down the line of officers and seamen. Now and then he stopped to comment or ask a personal question of one of the men. More, she saw that he listened to the answers. Even a casual observer could have seen that he was given more than respect due his rank by the men he greeted. There was love, the kind Hannah was aware only men could give men.

Though she was certain Bennett had seen enough of ships to last a lifetime, he toured the bridge, the officers' quarters and the galleys with apparent fascination. The ship was as neat as a parlor, utilitarian certainly, but freshly scrubbed and without a sign of peeling paint or rust.

Bennett moved quickly through the ship, without seeming to hurry over the decks. There were questions that had to be asked, compliments that were deserved, but he knew duffel bags were packed and waiting. He clasped hands with the captain again, aware that the man had every right to be proud of his ship and his men. As he started down the gangplank, the cheers rose up again. Bennett had to wonder if they were for him or because the ceremonies were finally over and the men could go ashore.

Protocol demanded that he be escorted back through headquarters. It was here that Hannah began to sense his impatience to be off. Still, he was gracious, shaking hands, kissing hands, exchanging a last pleasantry. It wasn't until he was seated in his own car again that he let out a low oath.

"I beg your pardon, sir?"

Bennett merely patted Hannah's hand before he started the engine. "Four hours was a long time to keep you on your feet. Thank you for bearing with me."

"On the contrary, I found it fascinating." Nothing had ever seemed more wonderful than the wind blowing on her face again as the convertible picked up speed. "The tour of the ship was particularly educational. It was clever, wasn't it, for the ship's cook to frame a recipe for crepes where the flour was measured in pounds rather than cups?"

"Food becomes a priority after a few months at sea." He glanced over, surprised she'd been so well entertained by a ship and several pompous speeches. "If I'd known you were really interested I wouldn't have hurried things along quite so much."

"I suppose it becomes all routine and a bit boring for you after a while."

"I was thinking of the men. All they really wanted was to get ashore to their wives or lovers—or both." He was grinning when he turned his head toward her. "You can't imagine what four months at sea is like when the only woman you see is in a glossy photo with staple marks in the middle."

Her lips twitched, but she managed to hold the smile to a bare acknowledgement. "No, I'm sure I can't. But I think you enjoyed your time at sea, Bennett. It showed in the way you spoke with the men and looked at the ship."

He said nothing for a moment, surprised and not displeased that she had understood that so quickly. "I was more of an officer and less of a prince then. I can't say I have the sea in my blood the way Captain Dumont does, but it isn't something I'll forget."

"What is it you remember best?" she asked before she caught herself.

"Watching the sun rise at sea or better, riding out a storm. God, we went through one off Crete. The waves were a fifty-foot wall. The wind was like the wrath of God, so loud, so enormous that you could shout in someone's ear and not be heard. No sky, only water, wall after wall of it. An experience like that changes you."

"How?"

"It makes you realize that no matter who you are, what you are, there's something bigger, greater. Nature's a powerful equalizer, Hannah. Look at her now." With one hand he gestured toward the sea as he negotiated another curve. "Calm, almost impossibly beautiful. A hurricane doesn't make her less beautiful, only more dangerous."

"It sounds as though you prefer the danger." She understood that, perhaps too well.

"At times. Danger's its own seduction."

She could say nothing to that. It was something she had learned herself years before.

With the briefest of signals to the car behind him, Bennett pulled over. "At the moment I prefer the calm." He got out of the convertible, ignoring the guard who stood anxiously by the hood of the trailing car. "Walk with me on the beach, Hannah." He opened her door and held out a hand. "I promised Marissa some shells."

"Your security doesn't look pleased." Nor was she when she noticed how open they were.

"They'd only be pleased if I were sitting in a bulletproof globe.

Come now, Hannah, didn't you tell me sea air was good for the constitution?''

"Yes." She laid her hand in his. He was safe, after all, as long as she played her part and played it well. "You'll have to find shells big enough that they can't be swallowed. At Marissa's age, children tend to eat the oddest things.''

"Always practical." With an easy laugh, he lifted her by the waist over the low seawall. He saw her gaze focus over his shoulder and knew a guard would be following at a discreet distance. "You should take your shoes off, Hannah. You'll only get sand in them.''

It was the practical thing to do, of course. The logical thing. Hannah tried to tell herself she wasn't shedding part of her cover along with the pumps. "You must have some fascinating coral formations in these waters.''

"Do you scuba?"

"No," she lied. "I'm not a very strong swimmer. I went to a marine exhibit in London a few years ago. Until then, I had no idea what an incredible variety of shells there were, or how valuable they can be.''

"Lucky for me Marissa has simple tastes." With his hand on hers, he walked to the sea edge. "A couple of clam shells, and she'll be delighted.''

"It's kind of you to think of her." He *was* kind, she thought. That itself was one of the most difficult things to overlook. "You seem to be a great favorite among your nieces and nephews.''

"Oh, I suppose that's because I don't mind making a fool of myself now and then in a game. How about this one?" Bending, he picked up a long spiral that had broken off a larger shell and been worn smooth by the ebb and flow of the sea. At the top of the curve was a peaked cap that looked almost like a crown.

"Very suitable," Hannah commented when he handed it to her.

"Marissa doesn't care for suitable. She prefers pretty.''

"It is pretty." With a smile, Hannah ran a finger along the curve that went from pale amber to polished pink. "She should have it in her windowsill where the sun would hit it. Oh look." Forgetting herself, she stepped into the surf and pried out an unbroken scallop shell. It was shaped like a fan, bone-white on one side. opalescent pink inside its shallow bowl. "You could tell her that fairies take their biscuits in it when they have tea."

"So Hannah believes in fairies," he murmured.

Caught up short, she handed him the shell. "No, but I think Marissa might."

Bennett slipped the shell into his pocket. "Your feet are wet."

"They'll dry quickly enough." She started to step back. He took her hand again, holding her in the shallow, foaming surf.

"Since we're here, we ought to try for a couple more." Without waiting for a response he began to walk along the shoreline.

The water was warm and soft on her feet and ankles, but no warmer, no softer, than the air that blew in over it. Through the crystal water she could see the bed of white sand and the glittering sparkles of shells that had been crushed by waves. The surf was quiet here, all sighs and whispers.

There was nothing romantic in it, Hannah warned herself. She couldn't allow there to be. The line she walked was thinner and sharper than any she'd walked before. One misstep could mean tragedy at least, war at the worst. Determined to keep her place, she concentrated on the guards a few yards at their back.

"The ceremony today was lovely. I'm grateful you asked me to come."

"My reasons were purely selfish. I wanted your company."

Struggling not to be touched, she tried again. "In England there's often satire and criticism of the Royal Family, but beneath it all is a very real affection. I see that same kind of love and respect for your family here."

"My father would tell you that we serve as well as govern. He gives them solidity and confidence. Alex gives them the hope for the future. A continuation of tradition. In Brie they have glamour and intelligence as well as humanity."

"And in you?"

"Entertainment."

It annoyed her. She couldn't say why but his careless dismissal of himself made her stop and frown at him. "You underestimate yourself."

Surprised, Bennett cocked his head and studied her. It was there again, that something, that indefinable something in her eyes that had attracted him all along. "Not really. I'm well aware that I do my duty. My father raised all of us to understand that we didn't simply inherit a title or position. We had to earn it.'' He drew her back a bit so that the spray from the surf didn't dampen her skirt. "I won't rule. Thank God. That's for Alex and then for the son I continue to hope Eve gives us all this time around. Because I won't, I don't have to take myself as seriously as Alex, but that doesn't mean I take Cordina or my responsibilities to it lightly.''

"I didn't mean to criticize.''

"I didn't think you did. I only meant that above my official duties, my official position, I give the people something—someone to talk about over a glass of wine or an evening meal. I've been haunted by the title of Playboy Prince since I was in my teens.'' He grinned then and tucked a stray hair behind her ear. "I can't say I didn't do everything possible to earn it.''

"I prefer literature to gossip,'' Hannah said primly as she started to walk on.

"Gossip has its place.'' Amused, Bennett stopped her.

"Apparently you enjoy it.''

"No.'' His eyes darkened as he looked beyond her and out to sea. "I'm just accustomed to it. It's difficult, when you're twenty, to know that every time you look more than casually at a woman it's going to be splashed somewhere in bold print, pictures included. I like women.'' This time he smiled and looked back at her. "Since I didn't want to change that aspect of my personality, I decided to live with public speculation. If I've sinned, it was in lack of discretion.''

"Some might say it was the quantity.''

There was only the shortest of hesitations before he threw his head back and roared with laughter. "Oh, Hannah, what a gem you are. So you *have* whiled away some time with something besides Yeats.''

"I may have skimmed a few headlines.''

Laughing again, he swung her in a circle before she could prevent it. "Priceless. Absolutely priceless.'' His eyes were glowing as he set her back down. "I adore how you cut me down to size so skillfully.''

Automatically, Hannah smoothed down her skirt. "I'm sure you've mistaken my intent.''

"The devil I have. That's what delights me about you.''

The frustrated look she gave him had nothing to do with the role she was playing. Delighting him had never been part of the plan. She was there to observe, to cement her position and to carry out a plan that was years in the making. Never before had the proper Lady Hannah had to worry about piquing a man's interest. Even as she calculated how to cancel it out again, he was reaching for her.

"Your hair's falling down." In a casual move he plucked a loose pin that was dangling near her shoulder. "My fault for not putting the top up."

"I must look as though I've been through a hurricane." She reached up to put the practical hairstyle back in place. Pins fell out in her hand, loosened by wind and weight. Even as she swore silently, her hair tumbled free, waterfalling past her shoulders to her waist.

"Mon Dieu." Before she could twist her hair back, Bennett had filled both hands with it. Twined around his fingers it was deep, honey blond and soft as silk. He stared, thunderstruck, by the transformation. It waved wild and free around her face, accenting the slash of cheekbones that only looked hard and angular without the framing. Her face no longer seemed thin and bony, but exotic. *"C'est magnifique. C'est la chevelure d'un ange."*

With her heart pounding, she tried to ignore what she saw in his eyes. It wasn't innocent delight or casual attraction now. Now there was desire, man for woman, basic, strong and as dangerous as the sea in a storm. She couldn't move back from him for his hands were buried in her hair. She couldn't deny the lunge of her own needs as he kept her close.

It wasn't supposed to happen. Even now she could tell herself it couldn't happen. Yet she wanted to be held by him, to be comforted, to be, though the words sounded foolish in her mind, cherished. Desired, needed, loved. All of those things were against the rules, but she found it hard to pull back.

"Angel hair," Bennett repeated in a whisper. "Why does a woman bind beauty up and hide it?"

No, she couldn't deny what was happening inside her, but she could, as she'd been trained, deny herself. "It's more practical worn up." She lifted her hands to scoop it from his and met resistance.

Yes, he'd been right all along. There was more, much more to her than she allowed to show on the surface. Perhaps it was that which continued to draw him in, make him want, make him need in a way he never had before. If it had been possible, he would have pulled her to him then. It wasn't the guards that stopped him, but the trace of anxiety he saw in her eyes.

"If that was true, my most practical Hannah, why haven't you simply cut it off?"

How many times had she nearly done so then pulled back at the last minute? Drawing a deep breath she offered the simple truth because truth was often the best cover of all. "Even I have some vanity."

"It makes you beautiful." He dragged his hands through her hair again, hardly able to believe it had been hidden by a handful of pins.

"Only different." Her smile hid the tension that was pulling her in two directions.

"Any man would approve of such a difference." She was stiff beneath his hands. With reluctance he acknowledged it and released her. "But then, you don't look for a man's approval, do you?"

"I've never found it necessary." With a few expert twists, she had her hair at the base of her neck again. The pins were pushed in until it was secure. She could almost, just almost feel secure herself. "We should be getting back. Eve may need me."

With a nod, Bennett began to walk back to the car with her. There would be another time and another place. He found in himself something he experienced rarely, particularly when it had to do with a woman. Patience.

"You can pin it up, Hannah. But now that I know what it looks like down, I'll see it that way whenever I look at you." When they reached the seawall, he again lifted her over, but this time stood, his hands around her waist and the wall between them. "Knowing this one secret makes me wonder how many others you have, and how soon I'll find them."

Anxiety and desire were a powerful combination. She felt her heart thud with both. "I'm afraid you'll be disappointed, Bennett. I have no interesting secrets."

"We'll see," he said, before he vaulted easily over the seawall.

Chapter 5

It wasn't often Hannah yearned to be beautiful. Her work had given her a fine appreciation for the beauty of being unremarkable, even forgettable. Over the years, she'd experienced a twinge now and then, but only a twinge when she thought of soft colors and filmy dresses. It had always been possible to release the urge when she was off duty and out of the country. Then her appearance could be changed with a more discerning choice of color and cut and a few clever strokes with a makeup brush.

There could be no release now, and no yearning.

Hannah knew everyone would look wonderful for Eve's dinner party. An affair at the palace was meant to be elegant, even extravagant. Hannah had no doubt every woman who attended would strive to live up to the occasion. Every woman, of course, except her.

She'd already seen Eve's glittery black dress with its swirls of material from waist to ankle and its daring draping back. Gabriella would no doubt wear something delicate that would accent her fragile, feminine looks.

Then there was Chantel O'Hurley. Hannah was certain the actress would be stunning whether she chose silk or sackcloth. Remembering how Bennett had looked at her as he'd started down the stairs in the Center took no effort at all.

It shouldn't have mattered.

It mattered too much.

Lecturing herself, Hannah chose the best of the worst in a pale lavender gown with a fussy bodice that played down her curves. With her hair unpinned, it gave her the look of a wanton puritan. An image, she knew, that wouldn't go unnoticed. With only the smallest of sighs, she drew her hair back to begin the laborious job of braiding it into submission.

When it was neatly coiled at her neck, Hannah was satisfied that all traces of sexuality were tamed. She looked presentable, perfectly proper and sexless.

There could be no regrets, Hannah told herself as she slipped her pistol into her evening bag. Duty came above personal desire, and certainly far ahead of vanity.

He'd been waiting for her. The guests were being entertained in the Salle des Miroirs where they were served aperitifs by short-coated waiters. Both the cast and the crew of Eve's production had been invited so that conversation was a babble of noise underlaid with excitement.

Though impatient and distracted, Bennett performed his duty without a ripple. There were always polite questions to be asked, a hand to kiss and a joke to laugh at. Under usual circumstances, the party would have amused and entertained him, but...

Where was she? He found himself straining against the evening clothes he usually wore without a thought. All around him women glittered. Their scents mingled and mixed into one exotic fragrance that did nothing to tempt him. He wanted a moment alone with Hannah. He hadn't the least idea why it was so important, but he wanted it desperately.

He kept one eye on the doorway while he spoke with the wardrobe mistress. His gaze paused briefly on the ormolu clock while he listened to the director expound on the potential of Eve's play.

"Looking for me?" The sultry voice sounded in his ear just ahead of a cloud of scent.

"Chantel." Bennett kissed both her cheeks before drawing her back for a survey. "Stunning, as always."

"I do what I'm best at." Smiling, she accepted a glass from a passing waiter. Shimmering white left her shoulders bare, then dipped low enough to be tantalizing before it closely followed the subtle, feminine curves. "Your home is everything it's rumored to be." She lifted the wine to her lips as her gaze passed over the dozens of antique mirrors that graced the walls. "And how clever of you to choose such a room to entertain a group of narcissistic actors."

"We have our moments." He looked beyond her for a moment, but still saw no sign of Hannah. "I saw your last movie. You were extraordinary."

A woman who was accustomed to absorbing all of a man's attention knew instinctively when she had only a part of it. Still, Chantel only smiled and speculated. "I'm still waiting for you to come back to Hollywood."

"You seem to be keeping busy in the meantime." He reached in his pocket for a box of matches to light her cigarette. "How do you manage to divide your time among tennis stars, oilmen and producers?"

Chantel tilted her head as she blew out a thin stream of smoke. "Oh, much the same way I imagine you divide yours among countesses, marchesas and—was it a barmaid in Chelsea?"

Laughing, Bennett dropped the matches back in his pocket. "*Ma chère amie,* if either of us enjoyed all the incredible and innumerable affairs the press gifts us with, we'd be hospitalized."

With the true affection she felt for few men, Chantel touched a hand to his cheek. "To anyone else, I'd say speak for yourself. However, since we've never been lovers, regardless of the headlines to the contrary, I'll ask you how things are for you, romantically speaking."

"Confusing." At that moment, in the oval glass over Chantel's shoulder, he saw Hannah slip into the room. She looked like a dove lost in a group of peacocks. "Very confusing. Excuse me a moment, will you, love?"

"Of course." She'd seen which direction his attention had taken. "*Bonne chance,* Bennett."

A lifetime of experience allowed him to slip through the groups of people, exchanging a quick word, a smile or a murmured excuse without leaving any offense behind. Less than a minute after Hannah had settled into a corner, he was beside her.

"*Bonsoir,* Lady Hannah."

"Your Highness." She used his title and curtsied as protocol demanded. He caught her hands as she straightened, negating the formality.

"It's usual, when a woman is late, that she makes an entrance rather than slip into a corner."

Damn him for making her pulse skittish. Even as she tried to calm it again, she noted that more than one head was turned in their direction. So much for going unnoticed. "I prefer watching to being watched, sir."

"I prefer watching you." He signaled a waiter, then took a glass from the tray for her himself. "You move well, Hannah, as though you wouldn't make a sound in an empty room."

That had as much to do with her training in tae kwon do as her childhood lessons in ballet. "I was raised not to make disturbances." She accepted the glass because it freed one of her hands. "Thank you. This is a lovely room." She said it casually, as casual as the glance she sent sweeping over the guests. Her reflection was thrown back at her a dozen times. Hers, and Bennett's, close together.

"I've always been partial to it." Now that she was here, he was content. He'd almost heard the click of things falling into their proper place when he'd taken her hand in his. "As it happens it was another Bennett, some generations back, who started the collection. It seems he was miserably vain without much cause and continued to buy mirrors in hopes one would tell him a different story."

She had to laugh. For a moment she felt almost as though she belonged there with the gowns and the glass and the glamour. "I'd say you made that up, but it sounds foolish enough to be true."

"You have the most alluring laugh," he murmured. "It's a laugh that reminds me how you look with your hair down and your eyes dark."

She couldn't allow this. Hannah told herself she was foolish to be moved when she knew how clever he was with women. She was more foolish to be caught off guard when she knew what a dangerous game was being played. This time her voice was cool and formal.

"Shouldn't you see to your guests?"

"I have been." He passed his thumb gently over her knuckles. It was a small gesture and an intimate one that made her wish once again she could have been lovely for him. That she could, very simply, have been for him. "While I was waiting for you." He stepped closer. Because she was already wedged into a corner, there was no place to go. "You smell wonderful."

"Bennett, please." She almost lifted a hand to his chest before she remembered eyes were on them. In defense she lifted her glass instead.

"Hannah, I can't tell you how it pleases me to see you become unnerved. The only time you become at all unsure of yourself is when I'm just a bit too close."

It was true, and a bitter pill to swallow for a woman who survived by being sure of herself. "People are watching."

"Then walk in the gardens with me later, when we can be alone."

"I don't think that would be wise."

"Are you afraid I'd seduce you?"

There was both amusement and arrogance in his tone, but when Hannah looked back at him, she saw desire as well. She sipped again to moisten a throat that had gone bone-dry. "Not afraid. Uncomfortable seems a better word."

"It would give me great pleasure to make you uncomfortable, Hannah." His voice was low, a caress to accompany the brush of his lips over her knuckles. "I want to make love with you in some dark, quiet place. Very slowly and very gently."

The need sprinted inside of her until she had to fight off a shudder of anticipation. It could be like that, with him, it could be. If only...

There could be no "ifs" in her life. They meant uncertainty and uncertainty was lethal. Hannah, pulling herself steady by nerve ends, looked at him. He meant it. There was desire in his eyes—but more a kindness, a sweetness that was almost her undoing. She could marvel at the fact that he felt something real for her, that somehow, he'd looked beyond the surface and cared.

She could want it, but she couldn't accept it. There was only one way to stop what should never have started. She had to hurt him, and she had to do it now.

"I'm sure I should be flattered." Her voice was cool and calm again. "But if you'll forgive me, sir, I'm aware that your tastes are not very selective."

He stiffened his fingers on hers before he released her hand. She saw by his eyes that the arrow had hit its mark. "I'd appreciate an explanation for that, Hannah."

"The explanation seems obvious. Please let me pass, you'll cause a scene."

"I've caused one before." There was something new in his voice now. It was anger, certainly, but a reckless, heedless anger. Hannah knew that if she didn't play her game exactly right now, she'd find her name splashed in headlines for battling with Bennett in public.

"Very well." Setting her glass down on a nearby table, she folded her hands in her usual fashion. "I'm a woman, and therefore of some passing interest. To be blunt, the interest isn't returned."

"That's a lie."

"No." Firmer now, she cut him off. "Though it might be difficult for a man like you to understand, I'm a simple woman with simple values. As you told me yourself, your reputation precedes you." She paused just long enough to see him wince.

Oh, Bennett, I'm sorry. So sorry.

"I didn't come to Cordina to amuse you," she murmured as she took a step to the side.

He suddenly lifted his hand to stop her, and she waited. "You don't amuse me, Hannah."

"Then I must beg your pardon." Knowing it would be more insult than courtesy, she dipped into a curtsy. "If you'll excuse me now, sir, I'd like to speak with Eve."

He held her another moment. Hannah could feel his fury sear through his fingertips and burn her flesh. Then, in an instant, there was ice. "I won't keep you. Enjoy the evening."

"Thank you."

Despising herself, Hannah moved into the crowd. The lights were so brilliant, she told herself. That was why her eyes hurt.

"Lady Hannah, good evening." Reeve stepped beside her and took her arm. "Would you care for some wine?"

"Yes, thank you." Falling into step beside him, she accepted the glass he held out.

"Have you seen this collection of mirrors? I've always found these three particularly impressive. Are you all right?'' he added in an undertone.

"Yes, they are lovely. I'm fine."

He cupped his hand around the end of a cigarette, glancing around casually to be certain no one was within earshot. "It looked as though you were having some trouble with Bennett."

"He's persistent." She sipped her wine, amazed that her nerves had yet to calm. "Surely this is eighteenth-century."

"Hannah." He pointed out another glass as they walked, but his voice softened. "I worked with your father when I first got my feet wet with the ISS. That makes me feel almost like family. Are you all right?"

"I will be." She drew a deep breath and smiled as if he'd said something amusing. "I caused him pain just now. I didn't enjoy it."

Reeve brushed a hand over hers in the most casual of gestures. The touch was as reassuring as a hug. "It's rare to get through an assignment without hurting someone."

"Yes, I know—the end justifies the means. Don't worry, I'll do my job."

"I wasn't worried."

"It would help a great deal if you'd see that Bennett was kept busy over the next week or so. Things should be coming to a head and I don't need him…"

"Distracting you?"

"Interfering," Hannah corrected. She glanced in one of the mirrors and saw him across the room with Chantel. "Though I may very well have taken care of that myself. Excuse me."

He drove the horse hard, but still didn't find the level of release he'd been seeking. Swearing, Bennett plunged down the winding path, but neither joy nor excitement rode with him. Fury left little room.

He ached for her. He damned her to the devil and still ached for her. In the days that had passed since she'd turned him aside, the wanting hadn't eased. Now it was coated with self-derision and anger, but it hadn't eased.

He told himself she was a cold, insensitive prude with no generosity or heart. He saw her as she had been on the beach, with a shell in her hand, her eyes rich with laughter as the wind pulled pins from her hair.

He told himself she was hard as stone and just as unfeeling. Then he remembered how soft, how sweet her lips had been when his own had tasted them.

So he cursed her and rode harder.

The skies threatened rain, but he ignored them. It was the first time in days he'd been able to get away from obligations long enough to take Dracula out for more than cursory exercise. The wind whistled in off the sea and set waves dancing high.

He wanted the storm. By God, he wanted the wind and the rain and the thunder.

He wanted Hannah.

Imbécile! Only a fool wanted a woman when there was nothing returned. Only a madman thought of ways to have what had already been denied. He'd told himself all this before, but still he caught himself dreaming of ways he could gather her up and take her somewhere until he found the right way to show her.... Show her what? Bennett asked himself. Show her that it was different with her?

What woman would believe it?

Dozens, he thought, and his own laughter echoed bitterly behind him. He could certainly attest to that. But now when it was true, when it mattered the most, this woman wouldn't believe.

Because he'd acted like an idiot. Drawing the stallion to a halt, he stopped at a precipice over the sea and looked out. He'd pushed, too hard, too fast. It was humbling to admit he might have done so because he'd never met with a great deal of resistance before.

Women were drawn to him—because of the title and position. He wasn't so vain or so foolish not to know it. But they were also drawn to him because he enjoyed them. He liked their softness, their humor, their vulnerabilities. It was also true that he hadn't been intimate with as many as his reputation allowed, but there'd been enough women in his life for him to understand and appreciate that romance was a two-way street.

Hannah was young, inexperienced, sheltered. The term "Lady" wasn't merely a title, but a way of life. As far as men were concerned, it was doubtful she'd taken herself away from her books long enough to form any strong relationships.

With another oath, Bennett dragged a hand through his wind-tossed hair. And what had he done? He'd tried to seduce her at a dinner party. How could he have expected a woman of her breeding and sensitivity to be anything less than insulted? It had been the clumsiest, and perhaps the crudest of propositions.

Dracula danced impatiently, but Bennett held him steady another moment as he watched the storm roll slowly from the horizon toward the shore.

He hadn't told her, had never attempted to tell her what it was she did to him inside, to his heart. Just talking with her, watching that solemn face and quiet manner excited him in a way the most exotic or flamboyant woman never had. It was something deeper, and so much richer. He'd never said that with her, he was on the edge of finding the love he hadn't been sure would ever be there for him.

He could hardly do all of that now that he'd alienated and insulted her. But he could do something else. His smile began as the first drops of water hit the sea. He could start at the beginning.

Bennett wheeled the horse around. As the first streak of lightning split the sky, they were racing for home.

Within an hour, in dry clothes and dripping hair, Bennett made his way up to the nursery. Bernadette barred him at the door.

"Your pardon, Your Highness, but it's Princess Marissa's nap time. Her Highness is resting with the baby."

"I'm looking for Lady Hannah." He leaned into the room, but Bernadette stood her ground.

"Lady Hannah isn't here, sir. I believe she went to the museum this afternoon."

"The museum." Bennett calculated a moment. "Thank you, Bernadette."

Before she could finish her curtsy, he was gone.

Le Musée d'Art was small and lovely as was the rest of Cordina. It was like a miniature palace itself with its marble floors and carved columns. In the main lobby was a high, domed ceiling of stained glass and a circling balcony that gave the illusion of space.

Rooms ran off this circular hub like spokes of a wheel. On the floor below was a moderately priced restaurant where diners could enjoy a view of the gardens through a wide glass wall.

Hannah had arrived early to take inventory of the entire building. Security was tight but people who rested on the benches near the exhibits were largely ignored. Groups of school children were led by, most of them more impressed with an afternoon away from classes than they were with the paintings and sculptures. Tourists, brochures in hands, muddled through with a weaving of French, Italian, British, and American accents.

On a rainy weekday afternoon, the museum was a pleasant pastime. A healthy number of people flowed in and out. Hannah decided she couldn't have planned it better.

At the time she'd requested in her message, she strolled toward a Monet seascape. She loitered there long enough to read the plaque and study the brushwork. Whoever she was going to meet was probably there, making his own study of the building, and of her. In a leisurely pattern, she moved from painting to painting.

Then she saw the watercolor and both heart and mind raced back to the music room, and Bennett.

The plaque read Her Serene Highness, Princess Louisa de Cordina, but in small letters in the corner of the painting was the signature. Louisa Bisset.

She'd titled it simply *La Mer*. It was indeed the sea, but from a view Hannah had yet to see in Cordina. There was a jagged fall of cliffs that gave way to a sheer incline and ended in a jumble of rocks. From there, the beach spread white to the blue verge of water. But it wasn't peaceful. In this painting, the artist had looked for and captured the power and the danger. The spray rose high, and on the horizon a storm was brewing.

He found this stored in a trunk, Hannah thought and had to resist the urge to touch the frame as he might have done. He'd found it, she thought again, and perhaps had seen part of himself in it.

"An interesting subject."

The voice beside her was French, brusquely accented. Contact was made.

"Yes, the artist is very skillful." Hannah dropped her brochures. As she bent to pick them up she glanced around and was satisfied that no one was close enough to hear or even notice them. "I have information."

"You are to pass it through me."

She turned to smile at him as though they were exchanging a few pleasant remarks about the painting. He was of medium height, dark complexion with no scars. She gauged his age at fifty, though he might have been younger. Certain professions tend to age people quickly. He was not French by birth. The Germanic tone was faint, but she caught it and filed it away.

"There are certain aspects to some of my information that I feel must be given directly to the man who pays me."

"That is against the organization's policy."

"So I was told. However, I'm aware of what nearly happened six months ago because of policy. It wasn't looked on unfavorably when I used my own initiative and saved the organization, shall we say, certain embarrassments."

"*Mademoiselle*, I'm only here to receive your information."

"Then my information is this." Before speaking again, she moved toward another painting. Again, she took her time studying it. She lifted a hand as if to show her companion a certain combination of colors. "I have unlimited access to the palace. Neither my person nor my possessions are searched. I have already compiled the complete statistics on the security system both there, and at the Fine Arts Center."

"That will be most useful."

"And will be given to the man who pays me. That is *my* policy, *monsieur*."

"You are paid by the organization."

"And the organization is run by men. I know who I work for and why." She turned to him then, her smile very cool, very calm. They might have been discussing the weather. "I am not a fool. The...organization has certain goals. So do I. I am more than happy to have them merge to our mutual satisfaction. I will meet and speak with the highest authority. See that it's soon."

"Some people take a step and find themselves falling from a cliff."

"I'm surefooted. Pass this on, *s'il vous plaît*. What I know is worth a great deal. What I can find out is worth even more. You'll find enough to prove it in here." Hannah let her brochure fall to her feet, but this time she left it there. *"Bonjour, monsieur."*

She turned, knowing that such demands would either take her to the next stage, or end in her being summarily disposed of.

Nerves tingling, she began to wander toward the exit. Her heart stopped when Bennett walked in.

A dozen thoughts ran through her mind in a matter of seconds. Had she been set up? Had they used her to get him out in the open at a certain time and place? Had he come for her because Deboque had already struck somewhere else?

It took her only seconds more to dismiss them all as irrational. It was simply coincidence and bad luck that he should show up now on the tail of her meeting.

"I hope you don't mind company," Bennett said before she could think of a plausible opening.

"Of course not." She didn't dare look behind her yet to see if her contact was still there. She smiled, not quite sure how to behave since both she and Bennett had done an excellent job of avoiding each other for days. "The museum is even more beautiful than I'd been told."

"Have you seen everything? I'd be glad to show you around." He took her hand in a casual, friendly way that she realized could only cement her position if Deboque's man was watching.

She let her fingers curl into his, hating herself for using Bennett's generosity against him. "I could spend days looking, but I'm a bit tired."

She saw him then. He'd moved into her peripheral vision. The brochure she'd passed him was in his hand, and though his back was to them, she knew he was listening.

Bennett didn't notice the man, but only her. "Let me give you coffee up in my office. I'd like to talk with you."

She felt the unexpected prick of tears. Everything he said, and the way he said it, only made her claims more plausible. "I'd love some coffee." Hannah let him take her arm and lead her out, knowing every detail would be reported back to Deboque.

With a silent and stone-faced bodyguard, they stepped into an elevator. Bennett used a key to send them up to the third floor.

They crossed pale gray carpet, past uniformed guards to a suite of rooms. Two secretaries, one manning a bank of phones, the other working on a state-of-the-art computer, rose as Bennett entered.

"Janine, could we have some coffee, please?"

"Yes, Your Highness. Right away."

With his hand still on Hannah's arm, Bennett opened a door. The moment it shut behind them, the whispers started. His Highness had never brought a woman to his office before.

It was a room that reflected a man who loved beautiful things. Grays and blues blended softly with ivory walls. Deep-cushioned chairs invited long stays and easy conversation while an ornamental lemon tree thrived in a corner. Glass shelves held small treasures, a china bowl, a T'ang horse, a handful of shells she imagined he'd gathered himself and a chipped demitasse cup that might have been picked up in a flea market.

Though there was a very businesslike antique desk and chair, the essence of the room was relaxation. Hannah wondered if he came here when he needed to escape the palace and his title.

"Sit down, Hannah. If you've gone through the whole museum, you've been on your feet for hours."

"Yes, but I loved it." She chose a chair rather than the cozy lounge and folded her hands over each other on her lap. "I've always loved the Louvre, but this is so much more personal."

"The Board of Directors and the Chamber of Commerce will be delighted to hear it." He remained standing, his hands in his pockets, wondering just how to begin. "If you'd let me know you were coming today, I'd have enjoyed showing you through myself."

"I didn't want to disturb you. In any case, I rather liked just wandering."

Why, he's nervous, she realized. It might have pleased her in some secret place if she hadn't discovered she was nervous herself. It was the meeting, she told herself. No, it was Bennett. It was foolish to deny it.

"Do you work here often?"

"When necessary. It's often more convenient to work out of my office at home." He didn't want to talk about the museum. Bennett dug his hands deeper in his pockets. Since when had he had trouble talking to a woman? Since Hannah, he thought wryly, and tried again. "Hannah—"

The knock on the door had him biting off an oath. Bennett opened the door for Janine and the coffee tray. The pot was silver, Hannah noted, while the cups were violet bone china edged in gold.

"Yes, just set it down there, Janine. I'll see to it."

"Yes, sir." She set it down on the table in front of the lounge then curtsied.

Aware he'd been terse, Bennett smiled at her. "Thank you, Janine. It smells wonderful."

"You're welcome, sir." The door closed behind her with a discreet click.

"Looks like we're in luck." Bennett lifted the pot and poured. "These little pastries are from the restaurant downstairs. They're wonderful. Cream?"

"Yes, thank you. No sugar." How polite we are, she thought as the tension began to spread from her neck to her shoulders. Like two strangers on a blind date.

"Will you come sit over here if I promise to behave?"

Though he said it lightly, Hannah heard the strain. She lowered her gaze to her hands. He couldn't know it was shame and not shyness. "Of course." Rising, she moved over and joined him on the lounge. She lifted her coffee while he left his alone.

"Hannah, I apologize for my behavior the other night. It's no wonder you were offended."

"Oh, please, don't." With a distress even her training couldn't smother, she set her cup down and started to rise. His hand reached for hers and held her still. "I don't want an apology." Fighting for control, she forced herself to look at him. "I wasn't offended, really. I was just—"

"Frightened then? That's just as inexcusable."

"No—yes." Which answer was the right one? In the end, she gave up. "Bennett, the truest thing I can say to you is that no one has ever confused me so well."

"Thank you."

"That wasn't a compliment, but a complaint."

"Hannah, thank God you're back." Laughing, he pulled both her hands to his lips. When she stiffened, he released them but continued to smile.

"Friends?"

Still wary, she nodded. "I'd like to be."

"Then friends it is." Satisfied the first hurdle was successfully negotiated, Bennett sat back. He would wait and be a great deal more cautious before attempting the second. "What did you like best about the museum?"

She didn't trust him. No, Hannah was far too good at game playing not to know when one was afoot. "The airy, unrestricted atmosphere, I think. Too often museums are solemn, serious places. Oh, I did see another of your ancestor's paintings. The one of the sea. It was stunning."

"One of my favorites." He was careful not to touch her again. "I was tempted to keep it locked in my room, all to myself, but..." With a shrug he picked up his cup. "It didn't seem fair."

"And you are fair," she murmured, knowing she'd used him.

"I try to be," he returned, knowing he would use fair means or foul to win her. "Hannah, you ride, don't you?"

"Yes."

"Ride with me tomorrow morning. It has to be early as the rest of my day is full, but it's been a long time since I had any company on a ride."

"I'm not sure I can. Eve—"

"Will be busy with Marissa until ten," Bennett finished.

How she would love a ride. An hour of freedom and movement. "Yes, but I've promised to go with her to the Center. She has appointments there at eleven."

"We'll be back by then if you're willing to start out early." He wasn't willing to lose the opportunity. In her eyes he saw hesitation and pressed his advantage. "Come, Cordina's at its best in the morning on horseback."

"All right then." It was impulse, she knew, but she could use an hour of relaxation.

In a matter of days, she would meet with Deboque. Hannah lifted her coffee again and sipped. Or she would be dead.

Chapter 6

He hadn't lied. Hannah had already thought Cordina beautiful, but in the early morning it was exquisite. With the dawn light, Cordina reminded Hannah of a young girl dressing for her first ball. The colors were soft, shimmering. Pinks and roses and misty blues still gathered to the east as they got mounted.

Settling into her own saddle, Hannah eyed Bennett's Dracula with a mixture of envy and anxiety. Her father's stables included some of the finest horseflesh in Britain, but he had nothing to compare with the black stallion. He looked fast and reckless and just a bit angry. Even as she imagined herself on his back, she could also picture Bennett being thrown.

"A mount like that would have a mind of his own," she commented when the old groom stepped back from the prince.

"Of course." Bennett steadied the stallion as he sidestepped. Then, misunderstanding her, he smiled in reassurance. "Your Quixote's strong, but quite the gentleman. Brie often rides him when she's here."

Hannah only lifted a brow, recognizing the soothing words for what they were. "Thank you, sir. It eases my mind to know you've given me a lady's mount."

He thought he caught a trace of sarcasm, but when he looked at her he saw only calm eyes and a polite smile. "I thought we'd ride to the sea."

"I'd like that."

With a nod, Bennett turned his horse and started off at a gentle trot. "Are you comfortable?"

"Yes, thank you." As she settled into the easy rhythm, Hannah tried not to yearn for a wild gallop. "It was kind of you to invite me. I'm told your morning rides are sacred."

He grinned at her, pleased that she sat the horse well and confidently. "It's often true that I need an hour on horseback before I can be civil. Still, there are times I prefer company."

That hadn't been true lately. Since Deboque's release he felt he could never stretch his arms out without bumping a guard. And still nothing. His eyes clouded, as much with impatience as with anger. He wanted Deboque to move. He relished the thought of being able to deal with him personally, and finally. Instinctively he touched a hand to his shoulder where a bullet had entered. Yes, he would relish it.

The look in his eyes made her uneasy. There was something to watch for and defend against there. The man beside her was not the easygoing, easy loving prince she'd come to expect. Whatever, whoever he thought of seemed to communicate itself to his mount for Dracula shied nervously. She saw how easily he controlled the stallion, only a flexing of muscle. He could be kind or harsh, gentle or rough. Her own palm grew damp on the reins.

"Is something wrong?"

"What?" He glanced over. For an instant the look was still there, hard and dark enough to make her tense. Then it was gone and he was smiling again. There was no Deboque this morning, Bennett told himself. He was sick of having every aspect of his life and his family's lives clouded by one name. "No, nothing. Tell me what you do at home, Hannah. I can't picture you there."

"We live quietly in London." It was partially the truth. She wondered why she thought of it as partially a lie. "I do a great deal of my work at home, which makes it convenient for me to keep house for my father."

"Your work," he repeated. "Your essays?" He was leading her along the easiest route, where the incline was gentle.

"Yes." Again, there was a twinge of discomfort. "I hope to have them ready for publication in a year or two."

"I'd like to read them."

She shot him a look of surprise, then almost immediately felt her muscles tighten. It had nothing to do with fear. Even if he'd demanded to see her work, she had enough that would satisfy him. No, it wasn't fear but a certainty that if she had to continue to lie to him much longer, she would be physically ill.

"You're welcome to, of course, but I don't think my writing would be of great interest to you."

"You're wrong. You're of great interest to me."

She looked down, but not in the shyness he thought he saw. Once again it was shame. "It's lovely here," she managed after a moment. "Do you ride this way often?"

She wouldn't allow him to get too close. Bennett fought back frustration and reminded himself he was in for the long haul. "No, actually I haven't been this way in quite a while." When they reached the top of a rise, he stopped. Her gelding was content to busy himself with the grass alongside the path. Beside her, Dracula nearly shivered with energy. She thought she felt the same impatience from Bennett.

"A little distance changes things," he murmured.

Following his gaze, she looked back at the palace. From here it looked like an exquisite child's toy, a magnificent dollhouse a pampered child might find near the tree on Christmas morning. To the east was the sea, still hidden from view by the cliffs and trees and barely heard. Like the palace, it hardly seemed real.

"Do you need to get away from it so badly?" Hannah asked him quietly.

"Sometimes." It no longer surprised him that she read his moods. With a hand firm on the reins, he controlled the stallion and continued to look at his home. "I had my time at Oxford, and at sea. When I was away, I missed Cordina so badly it was like an ache. In the past six months, past year, I've felt a restlessness, a waiting for something to happen."

They both thought of Deboque.

"Often in England, especially at this time of year, I'll complain about the cold and the damp." She shifted in the saddle then smiled as she thought of her home. "I'll look out the window and think I'd almost sell my soul for a week of warm, sunny days. Then, when I'm away, I begin to miss the fog and the mists and the smells of London."

They began to walk the horses again while she cast her mind back to England. "There's a man who sells roasted chestnuts just around the corner from our house. You can buy a little bag and warm your hands on them and smell them, just smell them long before you ever eat them." Remembering made her smile again, but she had no idea how wistfully. "Sometimes I'd wonder how it could be Christmastime anywhere without roasted chestnuts."

"I didn't know you missed England so much."

Nor had she until that moment. "One always misses home. Our hearts are always there." And what she was, all that she had done, had always been for England first.

"I've often wondered how difficult it was for Reeve," Bennett said. The sounds of the sea became louder as they moved their way east. "Although he and Brie spend nearly six months every year at their farm in America. I know for Brie it's as much home as Cordina is."

"For many, real contentment comes with acclimation." Hadn't it been so for her, all of her adult life?

"It's a great deal harder for Eve. She has only a few weeks with her family in America."

"Some loves are greater than others. Some needs stronger." She was just beginning to truly understand it. "Eve would live anywhere as long as Alexander was with her. And I think the same is true for your brother-in-law."

Yes, it was true. Perhaps that was a part of the restlessness in him. Over the last few years he'd seen how beautiful, how strong, real commitment, real feelings could be. Somehow they always seemed so remote from him, so unattainable. Now there was Hannah.

"For love, could you turn your back on England?"

Hannah caught her first glimpse of the sea as they climbed higher. She concentrated on that, but saw, in her mind's eyes, the twisting charm of the Thames.

Could she? So much of her life, so much of her duty was bound with England. Even her current assignment had been as much to protect her country from Deboque as it had been to insure the safety of the Royal Family of Cordina.

"I don't know. You especially would understand how strong some ties can be."

The trees thinned. Those that remained were bent and battered from the wind that swept in from the sea. The path grew rougher so that Bennett put himself between the edge and Hannah. Her mouth twitched at the move, but she said nothing. He could hardly know that she was capable of riding down the path pell-mell without saddle or reins. Besides, she found herself savoring the unaccustomed feeling of being protected.

Without the trees to break its power, the wind swirled from the sea to the top of the rise, carrying traces of salt. Even Hannah's tightly pinned hair couldn't resist it completely. Wispy tendrils escaped to dance around her cheeks. As she watched, a gull caught the current and glided peacefully up on a stream of air. Another, far below, skimmed the water looking for food.

"It's breathtaking." She relaxed enough to sigh.

He saw what was always in her heart, but which showed so rarely in her eyes. Her love of adventure, of power and of risk. It made her beautiful, arousing, mysterious. The need to reach out for her was so strong, he had to tighten his fingers on the reins to keep them still.

"I wanted to bring you here, but I worried that the height might bother you."

"No, I love it." Her horse shied a bit and she controlled him with the ease of long experience. "There are so many beautiful places in the world, but so few special ones. This is a special one. I think I could…" She trailed off as the full impact struck her. "This is the scene from the painting. There's no storm brewing, but this is it, isn't it?"

"Yes." He had no idea that her recognition of it would mean so much. Nor did he know what to do with the sudden, inescapable realization that he was in love with her. Completely. Unalterably.

He tossed his head back as the wind blew his hair into his eyes. He wanted a clear look at her, at this, perhaps the most important moment in his life.

She sat straight in the saddle, her eyes dark with appreciation of the scene spread out before and below them. Her profile was sharp, sculpted. The plain brown riding shirt and pants did nothing to enhance her pale skin. But when he looked at her, he saw the most beautiful, the most precious thing he'd ever found. And for the first time in his life, he had no words to tell her.

"Hannah." He reached out a hand and waited.

She turned. He was the most magnificent man she'd ever seen. More breathtaking than the view, more dangerous than a plunge to the rocks below. He sat on the huge stallion, straight as a soldier, as heartbreaking as a poet. In his eyes she saw both passion and compassion, both need and generosity.

Her heart betrayed her and was lost to him even before she could tell herself it couldn't be. As duty warred with emotion, she let her hand join with his.

"I know what you think I am."

"Bennett—"

"No." His fingers tightened on hers. "You're not far wrong. I could lie to you and promise to change, but I won't lie or promise."

Before she could stop herself, she softened. Only for this moment, she promised herself. There was magic, if only for the moment.

"Bennett, I don't want you to change."

"I meant what I said, though I said it badly the other night. I do want you, Hannah." Like her, he looked out to sea. "I also understand that it would be difficult for you to believe that I've never said that to another woman and meant it in the same way."

But she did believe him. It was thrilling, terrifying and forbidden, but she did. For one glorious moment, she let herself hope. Then she remembered who she was. Duty was first. Always.

"Please, believe me, if I could give you what you want, I would. It's just not possible." She drew her hand away because the contact was making her weak, making her dream.

"I've always believed anything is possible if you work hard enough for it."

"No, some things remain out of reach." She turned her horse away from the sea. "We should get back."

Before she could move, he'd backed up enough to cover the hands on her reins with his own. His arm brushed her arm, his leg, her leg. His face was close, too close, as their mounts stood in opposite directions.

"Tell me what you feel," he demanded. The patience was gone, dissolved in need and frustration. "Give me that much, dammit."

"Regret." As she spoke, the word shimmered with it.

He released her hands only to cup the back of her neck. "Tell me again how you feel," he murmured, then leaned toward her.

The kiss was like a whisper, soft, seductive, sultry. Hannah tightened her hands on the reins, then let them go limp as emotion swamped her. It wasn't supposed to be like this, so encompassing, so heady, so right. The wind ribboned around them. The sea crashed below. For a moment, just one moment, all rational thought fled, leaving only desires behind.

"Bennett." She only murmured his name as she started to draw away. He held her, firm, insistent.

"Another moment."

He needed it. He needed every scrap she would throw him. Never had he felt the desire to beg for what a woman could give or withhold. It wasn't just the passion he wanted; it was more than the physical. He wanted her heart with a desperation he'd never felt before.

It was that desperation that made him keep the kiss gentle, that made him draw back long before his craving for her was satisfied. If he wanted her heart, he would have to move slowly. His Hannah was delicate and shy.

"No regrets, Hannah," he said quietly, then smiled. "I won't hurt you, or push you further than you're ready for. Trust me. That's really all I want for now."

She wanted to weep. He was giving her a kindness, a sensitivity she didn't deserve. Lies were all she'd given him. Lies were all she would continue to give. To keep him alive, she reminded herself as the tears burned at the back of her eyes. To keep him and the people he loved safe and unharmed.

"No regrets," she told him, letting the words echo through her mind for herself. Tossing her head, she pressed her heels to the gelding's sides and took off in a gallop.

Bennett's first reaction was surprise. He hadn't expected her to ride so well or so forcefully. He took a moment to watch her race down the rise before he grinned and let Dracula have his head. Though she'd taken a good lead, Hannah heard them gaining ground behind her. Delighted, she bent lower over the gelding's neck as she urged him on.

"We can't beat them head-to-head," she called to her mount. "But we might outwit them."

The challenge was enough. Spurred by it, Hannah swung off the track and into the trees. The path here was narrow and rough, but what she sacrificed in speed, she gained in maneuverability. Bennett was hard on her heels, but she kept to the center giving him no room to pass. She burst through the trees and onto a field less than two lengths ahead. Instinct had her veering to the left and pounding up another rise so that Bennett had to check his momentum at the unexpected maneuver. Still, he continued to gain so that when the stables came into view they were nearly neck and neck. Laughing, she veered left again and headed for a hedge.

He felt an instant's panic as he imagined her flying off her mount onto the ground. Then they were sailing over, side by side. Heels down, knees snug, they thundered toward the stables.

Pipit stood with his hands on his hips. He'd watched them since they'd barreled over the rise with the gelding in the lead. Since they'd taken the jump, the stallion had pulled ahead with smooth, easy strides. To be expected, Pipit thought as he rubbed his hands on the thighs of his pants. There wasn't another horse in Cordina—or in Europe as far as he was concerned—that could match the stallion.

But he thought as he watched the woman keep the distance close that Prince Bennett had at last met his match.

Bennett reined in and slid from the horse's back with excitement still drumming in his head. She was only seconds behind him. Her laughter was low and a bit breathless as she started to swing down. Bennett was there to take her by the waist and turn her to him before her feet hit the ground.

"How did you learn to ride like that?"

She lifted her hands to his chest, as much to keep the distance as her balance. "It's the one thing I excel at other than literature. I'd forgotten how much I've missed it these last few months."

He couldn't take his eyes off her. It was pure desire now, basic, vital. The ride they could have together would be as wild, as reckless as the ride they'd just completed. Somehow he knew it, could almost taste it. For reasons he couldn't name, he felt that he was holding two women. One calm, one passionate. He wasn't sure which one drew him more.

"Ride with me tomorrow."

Once had been a risk and a delight. Twice, Hannah knew, would be a foolish mistake. "I don't think that's possible. With Eve's play about to open, there's so much to be done at the theater."

He wouldn't push. He'd promised himself that he would give her the time to become accustomed to having him with her. From the moment on the rise when he'd realized just what that meant to him, he'd been more determined than ever to court her properly.

A first for the Royal Rake, he thought as he stepped back to kiss her hand.

"The stables are at your disposal whenever you find the time to use them."

"I appreciate that." She reached up a hand to her hair to be certain her pins were in place. "I enjoyed this, Bennett, very much."

"So did I."

"Well, Eve will be waiting for me."

"Go ahead. Pipit and I will see to them."

"Thank you." She was stalling. The moment she realized it, Hannah drew herself in. "Goodbye, Bennett."

"Hannah." He nodded, then watched her walk back toward the palace. A smile tugged at his mouth as he patted his horse's neck. "I'm getting to her, *mon ami*," he murmured. "It's just going to take a bit of time."

Time moved so quickly. Locked in her room, Hannah held the letter from Sussex. Inside, she would find Deboque's answer to the demand she'd made only days before in the museum. Her hands were steady as she sat at her desk. With the ivory-handled letter opener provided her, she slit through the envelope. Inside was a casual, even uninspired letter from an acquaintance in England. It took Hannah less than fifteen minutes to decode it.

Request granted. December third, 23:30. Café du Dauphin. Alone. Contact will ask for the time, in English, then comment, in French, on the weather. Be certain your information warrants the exception to procedure.

Tonight. The next step would be taken tonight. Hannah folded the letter back into the envelope, but left it in plain view on her desk. Beside it was a single white rose Bennett had sent to her that morning. Hannah hesitated, then gave herself the pleasure of touching the petals.

If only life were as sweet and as simple.

Moments later, she was knocking on Prince Armand's office door.

It was opened by his secretary who bowed stiffly to her before announcing her to the prince. Armand stood behind his desk as he gave permission to admit her.

"Your Highness." Hannah made a deep curtsy. "I apologize for disturbing you."

"Not at all, Hannah."

"But you're busy." She stood just inside of the door, hands folded. "I only wished to ask your advice on something. If it's convenient, I'll come back later."

"It's convenient now. Please come in and sit. Michel, if you would see to those few matters now, I'll have a private word with Lady Hannah."

"Of course, Your Highness." Michel bowed his way out of the room. When the door was closed, Hannah dropped her hands to her sides. Her stride firm, she walked to the desk. "We've gotten a break. You'll have to call Reeve immediately."

"I'm not easy about this," Armand said some time later when his son-in-law sat across from him. "How can we be sure Deboque will be fooled by the information Hannah will feed him?"

"Because it's so nearly the truth." Reeve downed his second cup of coffee. "Unless Hannah can give him something important, something he has no other way of getting, she'll never get close to him."

"But will he believe her?"

"It's my job to make sure he does," Hannah said quietly. "Your Highness, I know you've had objections to this operation all along, but up to this point it's worked exactly as we've wanted."

"To this point," Armand agreed, and rose. He gestured them both back into their seats so that he could pace in peace. "Now I'm in the position of asking a woman, a woman who both my family and myself have become very fond of, to go alone to meet a man who kills as much for pleasure as for profit."

"She won't be alone."

At Reeve's announcement, Hannah sat straight up. "I have to

be. If Deboque or one of his men have the slightest clue that I'm not, the whole operation goes up in smoke. I won't have it.'' Now, she rose as well. "I've given this two years of my life."

"And I intend to see that you live a bit longer,'' Reeve said mildly. "We suspect that Deboque has his headquarters in a small villa about five miles from here. We'll have men watching it.''

"And they'll have Deboque's men watching them.''

"Leave that part to me, Hannah, and do your job. You have the blueprints and the specs on the security systems?''

"Yes, of course.'' Annoyed, she sat again. "And I know I'm to give them to no one but Deboque.''

"You also know that at the first sign that things are going wrong, you're to pull out.''

She nodded, though she had no intention of doing so. "Yes.''

"There'll be two men stationed at the café.''

"Why don't you just send up a flare?'' Hannah tossed back.

He understood her frustration, but merely poured a third cup of coffee. "It's a choice between that or wiring you.''

"The last agent who attempted to get a wire into Deboque's organization was sent back to the ISS in three boxes.''

Reeve moved his shoulders. "Your choice.''

Again, Hannah rose. "I'm not used to being second-guessed, Reeve.'' When he said nothing, she set her teeth. "I realize that you're my superior on this assignment, so I don't believe I have much of a choice.''

"As long as we understand each other.'' He rose then, and took her hand. "Hannah, I'm aware of your reputation. Why don't we just say I don't want to take any chances on losing one of the best?'' Releasing her, he turned back to the prince. "I have a few things to put into motion. I'll keep in touch.''

Armand waited until the door was closed again. "Another moment, please,'' he said to Hannah. "If you'd sit?''

She wanted to be alone, to plan each detail out carefully. There was only a matter of hours left. Breeding was as strong as training, so she sat. "Would you like me to go over things with you again, sir?''

"No.'' His lips curved, just slightly. "I believe I grasp the situation well enough. I have a personal question, Hannah, and I ask you beforehand not to be offended.'' He sat across from her, militarily straight. "Am I mistaken, or has my son become fond of you?"

She linked her hands together immediately as her whole body went on alert. "If you mean Prince Bennett, sir, he's been very kind."

"Hannah, for my sake, please dispense with the evasions and the manners. Too often duty has interfered with the time I can spend with my family, but that doesn't mean I don't know my children and know them well. I believe Bennett is in love with you."

She went pale instantly. "No." She had to swallow, but the word came out a second time just as strongly. "No, he's not. Perhaps he's a bit intrigued, but only because I'm not the kind of woman he's used to spending time with."

"Hannah." Armand held up a hand before she could continue her rambling denial. "I don't ask in order to upset you. When I began to suspect this, it made me uncomfortable only because Bennett is unaware of your true purpose here."

"I understand."

"I'm not sure you do. Bennett is more like his mother than my other children. So…kindhearted. His temper has more of a lash, but his feelings are more easily reached. I only ask you this because if the answer to my next question is no, I must request that you tread softly. Do you love him, Hannah?"

Everything she felt was in her eyes. She knew it, and lowered her gaze quickly. "Whatever I feel for Bennett, for your family, won't interfere with my job."

"I know enough to recognize a person who will do what has to be done." He felt a stirring for her, a grave kind of pity that twined with empathy. "But you didn't answer me. Do you love my son?"

"I can't." This time her voice wasn't strong and there were tears chasing behind it. "I've lied to him since the first, and I'll go on doing so. You can't love and lie. Please excuse me, Your Highness."

Armand let her go. For a moment, he sat back in the chair and closed his eyes. For the next few hours, he could do nothing more than pray for her.

* * *

The café wasn't one of the pretty little tourist spots in Cordina. It was a local waterfront bar that catered to the crews from the fishing and cargo boats. Inside it was cramped with tables, many empty, and smoke and the smell of liquor. Not as rough as they came, Hannah thought as she slipped inside, but neither was it a place where a woman alone would wander unless she was looking for trouble.

Still, she didn't cause much of a stir as she came in. In her plain gray sweater and slacks, she nearly blended into the walls. The handful of women who were already there were more interesting fare. If she could get this over with quickly, she might not have to discourage any of the locals.

Hannah chose a bar stool and ordered a bourbon, neat. By the time it was served, she had sized up the room. If Reeve had indeed planted two agents here, they were certainly good ones. It was a rare thing when Hannah couldn't spot one of her own.

She'd been drinking silently for ten minutes when one of the men stood from a table and wandered in her direction. Hannah continued to drink while every muscle tensed. When he spoke, it was in French and thickened by whiskey.

"It's a sad thing for a woman to drink alone."

Hannah relaxed only enough to be annoyed. She used her primmest British tones. "It's a sadder thing for a woman not to remain alone when she chooses to."

"When one is so plain, she shouldn't be so picky," he grumbled, but moved away again. Hannah nearly smiled, then another man came through the doors.

He was dressed in seaman's clothes, with his cap pulled low. Beneath it his face was deeply tanned and gaunt. This time she tensed because she was certain.

Still, she idly lifted her drink as he moved to sit beside her at the bar.

"You have the time, *mademoiselle?*"

"Yes, it's quarter to twelve."

"Thank you." He signaled for a drink. Another minute passed as he toyed with it. *"Il fait chaud ce soir."*

"Oui, un peu."

They didn't speak again. Behind them a group began to sing a song, in French and off-key. The wine was flowing freely and the night was still young. He finished his drink and left the bar. Hannah waited only a moment, then got up to follow.

He waited for her at the edge of the dock. There was little lighting here so that he was more shadow than man. Hannah moved toward him, knowing it could be the beginning or the end for her.

"You have the information." Again he spoke in English. It was bland and unaccented, just as his French had been. Deboque chose well, she thought and only nodded.

"We go by boat." He indicated the small open runabout.

Hannah knew she had no choice. She could refuse, or she could go on. Though she knew she would have no backup on the sea, she never even considered the first. Deboque was the destination. That was the bottom line.

Without hesitation, she lowered herself into the boat and took a seat at the stern. In silence, her contact got in beside her, cast off, and started the engine. It sounded like thunder on the open water.

Hannah took a deep breath. She was on her way.

Chapter 7

Reeve would be furious. Hannah rested a hand on the seat for balance as the boat picked up speed. He could afford to be, she thought, but she had to keep her head.

So Deboque wasn't on land in the villa as they'd expected. He was, unless the boat made a sudden and dramatic change in direction, at sea. No, there would be no backup now. Hannah drew another deep breath and watched the water wake behind them. She preferred working alone in any case.

Tonight, she would meet Deboque. She could feel it. Her pulse was slow and steady, her breathing even. The spray the boat kicked up teased her skin as she kept her expression placid. Nerves, what there were of them, couldn't be allowed to show. Her midnight cruise across the Mediterranean was bringing her closer to the goal she'd worked toward for just over twenty-four months.

Excitement, not fear, was building inside of her. Even that had to be controlled. Anything that made the pulse beat too fast or tempted the mind to swing too far ahead was dangerous. She couldn't make a mistake. Over the past two years she'd worked her way up in Deboque's organization, relying for the most part on her own skill. With the backing of the ISS she'd seen several jobs through to completion. Arms sold, diamonds liberated, drugs delivered.

The end justifies the means.

Rungs on the ladder, she thought. If she could continue to climb, it wouldn't be long before Deboque's kingdom of misery would come tumbling down on his own shoulders.

The trickiest rung had been making the well-placed Bouffe look incompetent. Deboque's senior lieutenant wasn't a fool and it'd taken a lot of guile and some risk to see that several of his assignments over the last few months had fallen through, without throwing suspicion back on herself. The biggest of these had been the arms deal with a terrorist group known for their lack of patience.

It had been sticky, but the timing had been perfect. Hannah had managed to make it seem as though Bouffe had nearly botched the deal before she had slipped in to make things right.

The terrorists had their arms—she had to leave the ISS to deal with that. And Deboque had his five million francs. It would be her pleasure to deal with that. And soon.

She saw the sleek white yacht anchored majestically in dark water. A thrill of anticipation moved through her. At the wheel, her contact signaled with an electric lantern. There was an answering flash from the ship. The engine was cut, throwing the night into silence as they drifted alongside the yacht.

Hannah reached out for the ladder and found the metal cool and hard. She knew she would be the same. Without a backward glance, she climbed up, and into the unknown.

"Lady Hannah."

There was a tall, dark-skinned man waiting for her. He took her hand and bowed over it. She recognized him from her last briefing, though she would have placed his accent as Jamaican in any case. He was Ricardo Batemen, a twenty-six-year-old islander, an ivy-league graduate with a degree in medicine. He still used a scalpel, but he preferred to wield it on the healthy and unanesthetized.

He had become a favorite of Deboque's.

"I'm Ricardo." His young, smooth face spread into a smile. "Welcome to the *Invincible*."

"Thank you, Ricardo." She gave a casual look around and counted five more men and one woman on deck. The men were dressed in dark suits and carried machine guns. The woman had a sarong draped over a bikini and looked bored. "Might I have a drink?"

"Of course." His eyes, she noted, were pale, an almost translucent green that never seemed to blink. His voice was like rich cream over hot coffee. "But first, you must excuse our precautions. Your bag, Lady Hannah."

She lifted a brow and met his eyes straight on. "I'll depend on you to see that everything in it is returned to me."

"You have my word." He bowed as she handed it to him. "Now, if you would go with Carmine. She will take you to your cabin. You may like to freshen up after she makes certain no one has planted any electronic devices on you."

A strip search, Hannah thought resignedly. "No one plants anything on me, Ricardo. But I admire a cautious man." Hannah crossed the deck to Carmine as though she was going to tea.

Moments later, Ricardo set Hannah's black alligator bag on a gleaming mahogany desk. "Carmine is seeing to her. She has a small-caliber pistol, her passport and identification and about three thousand francs along with a few cosmetics. There is an envelope, sealed."

"Thank you, Ricardo." The voice was deep and smoky with its traces of France. "You may bring her to me in ten minutes. Then we won't be disturbed."

"Oui, monsieur."

"Ricardo, your impressions?"

"Attractive enough, more so than her photograph. And cool, very cool. Her hand was dry and steady."

"Good." There was a trace of amusement in the voice now. "Ten minutes, Ricardo." He picked up the envelope and broke the seal.

A short time later, Hannah adjusted her sweater. She'd found the search more annoying than humiliating. Carmine had taken her stiletto, but she'd expected that. Ricardo had her pistol. For now, she was alone and unarmed in the middle of the sea. She still had her wits.

Hannah stood in the center of the cabin when Ricardo opened the door. "My apologies again for the inconvenience, Lady Hannah."

"A small annoyance, Ricardo." He hadn't brought back her bag, but she said nothing of it. "I hope there won't be too many more."

"None at all. If you'd just come with me."

Hannah followed him, walking easily as the boat swayed in the current. It was the size of a small hotel, she'd noted. And there were escape routes if it became necessary. The carpet they walked on was rich red. In the cabin where she'd been searched had been an antique mirror with beveled glass and a bedspread in velvet. There had also been a porthole big enough for a child, or a slender woman to work their way through.

Ricardo stopped by a glossy oak door and knocked twice. Without waiting for an answer, he turned the knob and gestured her inside. Hannah stepped through and heard the door click shut at her back.

It was opulent, elegant, even fanciful. Eighteenth-century France seemed to come alive. Now the carpet was the deep shimmering blue of kings and the paneled walls were polished to a mirrorlike gleam. Two delicate, glittering chandeliers sprinkled light over the antique wood and plush upholstery. Brocade had been used lavishly to drape over and around a bed fit for a king. All the colors were vivid, almost shocking.

There was a scent of something floral and something old that merged together into one strangely compelling and oddly uneasy fragrance. With the gentle sway of the ship, a collection of crystal animals shuddered with life.

It only took Hannah seconds to absorb this. As grand and extravagant as the room was, the man who sat behind the Louis XVI desk dominated. She didn't feel the evil she'd expected to. With the truly wicked, Hannah knew you often experienced a chill or a dread. What she saw was a slender and attractive man in his fifties, with steel-gray hair flowing back in a mane from a chiseled, aristocratic face. He wore black. It seemed to accent his almost poetically-pale skin. His eyes were black, too, like a raven's. They studied her now as his full, rather beautiful mouth curved into a smile.

She'd seen pictures of him, of course. She'd studied every scrap of information that had been gathered on him in the last twenty years. And yet... And yet she hadn't been prepared for the shock of sensuality which seemed to emanate from him.

He was a man women had died for. And now she understood it. He was a man who other men had killed for without question.

She understood that, too, as she stood ten feet away and felt the power.

"Lady Hannah." He rose, slowly, gracefully. His body was trim, almost delicate. His hand, as he offered it to her, was narrow and beautiful with a trio of diamonds on long fingers.

She couldn't hesitate, though she felt if her hand touched his she would be pulled out of what she knew into something foreign and frightening.

Hannah smiled and stepped forward. "Monsieur Deboque." She was glad to see his slight surprise at her use of his name. "It's a pleasure."

"Please sit. Will you have brandy?"

"Yes, thank you." She chose a soft high-backed chair that faced the desk. There was music playing through hidden speakers. Chopin. She listened to the notes as Deboque crossed to an enameled cabinet and withdrew a decanter. "Your ship is exquisite, *monsieur*." There was a painting behind his desk. One of six she knew had been stolen from a private collection only the year before. She herself had helped execute the theft.

"I appreciate beauty." He offered the brandy, then instead of going behind the desk again, sat beside her. "To your health, *mademoiselle*."

"And yours." She smiled at him again before she sipped.

"Perhaps you will tell me how you became aware of my name."

"I make it a habit of knowing who I work for, Monsieur Deboque." She shook her head as he drew out a cigarette case and offered her one. "I must congratulate you on your security and your staff. Discovering who, shall we say, reigned, was hardly an easy matter."

He drew in the smoke slowly, as a man who appreciated fine tastes. "Most have found it impossible."

Her eyes were cool and amused on his. "I find little impossible."

"Others have found it fatal." When she only smiled, he let it pass. She was, as Ricardo had said, very cool. "My reports on you are very flattering, Lady Hannah."

"Of course."

It was his turn to smile. "I admire confidence."

"And I."

"It appears I'm in your debt for smoothing over an exchange with our Mediterranean neighbors a few months ago. I would have been, to say the least, annoyed to have lost that contract."

"It was my pleasure. It would seem, *monsieur*, that you have a few weak links in the chain."

"It would seem," he murmured. He'd already debated handing Bouffe over to Ricardo for disposal. A pity, Deboque thought. Bouffe had been a loyal and valued employee for over a decade. "You are enjoying your stay in Cordina?"

Her heart drummed lightly but she sipped again. "The palace is quite lovely." She moved her shoulders as she let her gaze roam around the room. "I, too, appreciate beauty. It helps compensate for the fact that the Bissets are a bit boring."

"You're not impressed with the Royal Family, Lady Hannah?"

"I'm not easily impressed. They are certainly very pretty people, but so…devoted." She tinted her voice with derision, lightly. "I prefer devoting myself to something more tangible than honor and duty."

"And loyalty, Lady Hannah?"

She turned to him again. He was looking deep, trying to see inside, trying to see beyond. "I can be loyal." She touched her tongue to the rim of her snifter. "As long as it's profitable."

It was a chance, she knew. Disloyalty in Deboque's organization was punishable by death. She waited, outwardly cool while a single line of sweat beaded down her back. He studied her a moment, then threw his lion's head back and laughed. Hannah felt each individual muscle in her body sing with relief.

"An honest woman. I admire that. Yes, I admire that a great deal more than sworn oaths." He drew in the rich French smoke then exhaled again. "It would seem to my advantage to continue to make it profitable for someone of your skills and ambitions."

"I was hoping you'd see it that way. I prefer the executive branch, if you comprehend, Monsieur Deboque, but I'm willing to work my way to it. Delegation, organization, is so much more rewarding than execution, don't you think?"

"Indeed, yes." He studied her again, considering. She appeared to be a mild, well-bred young woman of some means. He preferred a quiet, unassuming outer shell in a woman. He thought briefly of

Janet Smithers who he'd used and discarded nearly a decade before. Lady Hannah, he thought, might prove to be a great deal more interesting, and more competent. "You've been with us two years now?"

"Yes."

"And in those two years, you've proven yourself to be very useful." He rose now and retrieved the envelope on his desk. "You brought this to me, I assume?"

"I did." She swirled her brandy. "Though I found the method with which it was delivered irksome."

"My apologies. This information is interesting, Lady Hannah, but I fear, incomplete."

She crossed her legs and relaxed back in the chair. "A woman who writes everything she knows on paper loses her value quickly. What isn't there, is in here." She laid a finger against her temple.

"I see." He admired an employee who knew her own worth, and guarded it. "If we say I'm interested in the security systems of the Royal Palace, the Fine Arts Center, the museum, for the purpose of emulating such systems for my own use, you would be able to fill in the blanks?"

"Of course."

"And if I asked how you came by such information?"

"This was the purpose of my visit to Cordina."

"One of them." Intrigued, he tapped the envelope on his palm. "It was fortunate that you were able to become close to Princess Eve."

"Fortunate, but not difficult. She was lonely for female companionship. I'm accommodating. I fuss over her daughter, listen to her fears and complaints. By easing some of her workload, I also earn the gratitude of Prince Alexander. He worries that his wife will tire herself while carrying his child."

"And you are trusted?"

"Implicitly. And why not?" she added. "My family is well respected, my breeding without mark. Prince Armand sees me as a young cousin of his dead wife. Your pardon, *monsieur,* but aren't these the reasons you enlisted me to find a place at the palace?"

"Yes, they are." He sat back. She pleased him, but he was a long way from giving her his full confidence. "I have word that the young prince is interested in you."

Something inside her froze at that. "Your network of information is admirable." Hannah glanced at her empty snifter, then tilted it in question. Deboque rose immediately to refill her glass. It was just enough time to regain her composure.

"Bennett is, as I'm sure you're aware, invariably interested in the female closest at hand." She gave a low laugh and tried not to hate herself. "He's really only a boy, and spoiled at that. I've found the simplest way to handle him is to act disinterested."

Deboque nodded slowly. "Then he pursues."

"Such men are always more—accommodating under those circumstances."

"I beg your pardon if I seem to be getting too personal, my dear, but how accommodating?"

"He's a bit bored, a bit reckless. His weakness for women should have its uses. I believe with a certain—flair—information can be drawn out of him. It was he, you see, who took me through the Center, and through the naval base at Le Havre." She sipped again, lingering over it. Deboque would already know about her tête-à-tête with Bennett at the museum. So, she would use his knowledge and twist the truth.

"It was a simple matter to ask questions and express interest in how the museum guards its treasures. With that, I was shown the setup, alarms, monitors, sensors." She paused again to let it sink in. "The more a woman pretends ignorance, the more she learns."

Deboque warmed the brandy in his hands. "Hypothetically, you understand, can the security at the palace be broken?"

At last, she thought, they were homing in. "Hypothetically, any security can be broken. I will say that Reeve MacGee has designed an admirable system, but not an invincible one."

"Interesting." He picked up a small china figure of a hawk and began to study it. The room fell into silence long enough for her to be sure he was trying to unnerve her. "And do you have a theory on how this system can be undermined?"

"From inside." She sipped her brandy again. "It's always cleaner from the inside."

"And the Center?"

"Much the same."

"This play the princess wrote, it opens in a few days. It would be amusing to cause a small disturbance."

"Of what nature?"

He only smiled. "Oh, I'm just speaking in theory, you understand. It seems to me that the Royal Family would be uncomfortable if something disrupted the evening. I should hate to miss it. You'll be there?"

"I'm expected." She needed to push him, push him into something definite. "I prefer knowing which door to walk into, *monsieur.*"

"Then you might be wise to remain in the audience. I wouldn't want to lose you now that we've become close."

She acknowledged this, but realizing he would demand the rest of the stats then dismiss her, Hannah changed gears. "As a matter of personal curiosity may I ask why you have such interest in the Royal Family? It intrigues me because I see you much as I see myself, as a person most interested in profit and personal gain."

"Profit is always desirable." He set the hawk down. He had hands that might have played a violin or written sonnets. They rarely killed, only gestured for others to do so. "Personal gain can have a multitude of variables, *n'est-ce pas?*"

"As long as it satisfies," she agreed. "Using the kidnapping of the Princess Gabriella or the threats on the Bissets as a lever to gain your release from prison was one thing. You're no longer in prison." Again she looked with admiration around the room. "I would think you would move on to more profitable waters."

"All business needs a completion." She saw emotion for the first time as his fingers tightened around his glass. "All debts require payment. The interest of ten years is dear, very dear. Do you agree?"

"Yes. Revenge, or retribution if you prefer. This I understand is as sweet as diamonds." And looking at him, she knew he would stop at nothing to collect. "*Monsieur,* you have arranged for me to be in the palace. I intend to continue to remain there until you alter the order, but I prefer to do so with some direction." She gestured casually, palm up. "The revenge, after all, is yours, not mine. I've never worked well blindfolded."

"A man who puts all of his cards on the table loses his edge."

"Agreed. So does a man who doesn't sharpen his tools and use them where they're best suited. I'm in, *monsieur.* Having a map of some sort would be useful."

He intended to use her, and well. Sitting back again, Deboque steepled his hands. His diamonds shot out violent light. He had failed, twice before he had failed to use the Bissets for his own purposes. He had failed to bring Armand to his knees. Whatever had to be done, whomever had to be used, he wouldn't fail this time. In Hannah, he thought he'd found the instrument.

"Let me ask you this. If one man wishes to destroy another, what does he do?"

"The simplest is to end his life."

Deboque smiled, and now Hannah saw the evil. It was coated with class, pampered with elegance, but very real. "I'm not a simple man. Death is so final, and even when it is slow, it's soon over. To destroy a man, the soul, the heart, requires more than a bullet in the brain."

He was speaking of Armand, she knew. It wasn't time to demand he name names and reveal his plan. He would tell her nothing and trust her less. Hannah set down her glass and tried to think as he did. "To truly destroy, you take away what is most valuable." Her heart began to beat in the back of her throat, clogging a wave of nausea. Still, when she spoke it was with cool admiration. "His children?"

"You are intelligent as well as lovely." Leaning over he placed his hand on hers. She felt it from him, the vile, dark movement of death. "To make a man suffer, to destroy his soul, you deprive him of what he loves best and leave him to live with it. His children and grandchildren dead, his country in chaos, a man would have nothing left but misery. And a country without an heir becomes unstable—and profitable—if one is shrewd."

"All of them," Hannah murmured. She thought of little Marissa, so pretty and soft, and Dorian with his smudged face and bright grin. Fear for them was suddenly so strong, so vital, she thought it had to show in her eyes. She kept them down, looking at his hand as it lay over hers and the cold, hard glint of the diamonds.

"All of them, *monsieur?*" When she thought she could trust herself again, she looked back at his face. He was smiling. In the fragile light of the chandeliers he looked wan as a ghost and infinitely more frightening. "Not an easy task, even for someone of your power."

"Nothing worthwhile is simple, my dear. But as you said, nothing is impossible—particularly when one is trusted and close."

Her brow lifted. She didn't shudder or draw away. Business, she told herself. Lady Hannah was all business. She was being offered a job, the most vital one Deboque had to offer.

"You were carefully chosen, Lady Hannah. For more than ten years, I've had one dream. I believe you are the instrument to see it to fruition."

She pursed her lips as if considering while her mind raced ahead. He was giving her a contract, a royal one. As she said nothing, his fingers played lightly over her knuckles. Like a spider, she thought, a handsome and very clever spider.

"Such a responsibility is weighty for someone in my position in your organization."

"That can be seen to. Bouffe is—retiring," he said softly. "I will be looking for a replacement."

She let her hand lie under his as she touched her tongue to her top lip. "A guarantee, *monsieur.*"

"My word."

She smiled a little. *"Monsieur."*

With a nod of acknowledgement, he rose and pressed a button on his desk. Within seconds Ricardo appeared. "Lady Hannah will be replacing Bouffe. See to the arrangements, Ricardo. Discreetly."

"Of course." The pale green eyes half closed as if with pleasure.

Hannah waited for the door to shut again. A man's life was over. "The day may come when you decide to replace me as casually."

"Not if you continue to please me." He lifted her hand again and kissed it. "I have a feeling you will."

"I must tell you, *monsieur,* I have a distaste for killing children." His fingers tightened, very slightly on hers, but she didn't fidget. "I believe it will take five million American dollars to overcome this distaste."

She saw it in his eyes. He would break her fingers as easily as he would kiss them. Hannah kept her gaze steady on his and hoped she hadn't pushed her luck too far.

"Is it money that seduces you, *ma petite?*"

"Not seduces, pleases. I like to be pleased."

"You have two weeks to please me, Lady Hannah. Then I shall return the favor." He kept her hand in his as he drew her to her feet. "Now, as a show of faith, you will tell me what you failed to note down here."

Hannah walked over to the specs and prepared to lie to him.

She was exhausted. In a decade of assignments, nothing had left her feeling so empty and soiled. As she drove through the palace gates, she could only think about a long hot shower where she could scrub off whatever traces remained of Deboque's cologne. Reeve was standing a hundred feet beyond the gates. Hannah stopped the car and waited for him to slide in beside her.

"You were gone a long time." He gave her a long, thorough study. "It wasn't in the plans for you to be out of contact for over an hour."

"It was in the plans for me to get to Deboque."

"And you did?"

She rolled down her window a bit farther. "I met him on a yacht, the *Invincible*. It's anchored about five miles northwest. He has at least six armed guards, double that by a guess. He has the information we wanted him to have. I'm replacing Bouffe."

Reeve's brow lifted. "You must have impressed him."

"That was the idea." She wondered how soon she could wash the taste of his brandy from her mouth. "He's planning something for the opening of Eve's play." When Reeve stiffened beside her, she went on. "I don't believe it's going to be anything directly against the family. He seemed to think it would be entertaining to confuse matters. He's very careful how he phrases things. Nothing too direct. Even if I testified against him, it would be difficult to actually convict him of conspiracy. He hypothesizes, theorizes."

"Did he give you an idea where he intends to make his move?"

She listened for a moment to a bird that was singing its heart out. "He seemed most interested in the palace. It's the biggest challenge. We have two weeks."

"He moves in two weeks?"

"That's how long he gave me to murder your family." She turned to him then and saw his face was pale and set. "All of you but Armand, Reeve. The children, everyone. He wants to destroy

Armand's soul and leave Cordina without an heir. If you trust my judgment, he wants this done as much for personal satisfaction as for the profit he might make when Cordina is thrown into chaos."

Reeve drew out a cigarette but didn't light it. "I trust your judgment."

"We have two weeks to stop him, or to convince him that I've done what he wants."

It was his family, his heart, yet he knew he had to think as coolly as she did. "Is he setting you up?"

She thought for a moment, then shook her head. "I don't think so. It's certainly possible that he'd dispose of me after I've finished the job, but I think it's more likely he'd continue to use me. We did a good job of planting information about me, and over the past two years I've saved him a bit of trouble and money. If he believes I can give him this, he'll sit back and wait."

"Armand will have to be told."

"I know." But not Bennett. Armand and only Armand.

"For now, just go on as usual." He indicated that she should drive ahead. "We'll need some time."

"Eve's opening is in a few days."

"We'll handle it. You get some sleep. As soon as we have a direction, I'll let you know."

Hannah got out of the car, then as Reeve stood on the other side she stopped. "I want him. I want him for myself. I know it's unprofessional and stupid. But if I have the chance, if I find the way, I'm going to take him out myself."

Reeve said nothing as she walked up the steps. He'd already vowed the same thing.

Chapter 8

"I don't want you to go tonight."

"You know I have to." Eve stood, grim and stubborn, facing her husband. "It's my play, my troupe, my production. I don't have a choice, Alex."

"Excuses can be made." He looked at her, dressed in midnight blue that skimmed her shoulders and swirled to her ankles. Her hair was caught up in the back so that it fell over one shoulder like ebony. Even after all the years he'd known her, just looking at her made his pulse race. "You know how dangerous it could be. With the information we have now, we can be sure there'll be an incident tonight. I don't want you involved."

"I am involved." She was frightened. Ever since Reeve had told them that he'd received a tip that there would be trouble at the theater on opening night, her nerves had been stretched tight. Yes, she was frightened, but she was no less determined. She crossed to the beveled mirror above the bureau as if checking the arrangement of her hair was of some importance. "I wrote the play, I produced it, and more important than either of those," she continued before he could interrupt, "I belong at the theater tonight because I'm your wife."

The fact that her arguments were valid meant nothing. He wanted her in the palace, safe, untouchable. His heart would rest easy if he knew she was here, in the suite of rooms she'd decorated, tucked high in the palace that had been his family home for generations. Nothing could happen to her here. Anything could happen outside.

"My love, Reeve is rarely wrong. If he says there'll be trouble tonight, I want you well away from it. The fact that you're carrying a child is a very simple reason for you to be excused. I know the play is important to you, but—"

"Yes, it is," she interrupted. "But you're more important."

"Then do this for me, and stay home tonight."

She tilted her head, holding on to both her nerves and her temper. "Alexander, would you stay behind with me?"

"If it was possible, of course." Impatience had him dragging a hand through his hair. It was a ploy she'd used before, and one there was little argument against. "I can't close myself up every time there's a rumble from Deboque."

"For Cordina," she said quietly. "And Cordina is now my country, too."

"Eve." He thought he loved her as much as it was possible to love. Every day he learned there could be more. "You are the most precious thing in the world to me. I almost lost you once."

She crossed to him then, knowing the first step, the first touch should be hers. When both of his hands were in hers, she looked up into his eyes. "And I you, Alex. I'm going to sit in the Royal Box beside you, where I belong."

From outside the door, Hannah heard the conversation clearly enough. It was moments like this that made it difficult to think of what she was doing, what she had yet to do, as merely another assignment. There were people beyond the door who she'd come to care about. The Bissets were no longer names or symbols, but friends. After ten years of playing dangerous games, she knew how risky it could be to make friends.

She closed her eyes and drew her breath deep before she knocked.

"Entrez." It was Alexander who answered, the impatience in his voice ripe. Hannah opened the door but didn't cross the threshold.

"I'm sorry. I'm disturbing you."

"Of course not." With the warmth that was so much a part of her, Eve smiled and gestured her inside. "I see you're ready for the evening." She felt a little twinge of regret at Hannah's severe beige dress and hairstyle. She'd hoped with a little time she could urge Hannah to soften her image. Tonight, however, there were more immediate matters of concern. "We were just about to come down ourselves."

Hannah saw Eve take Alexander's hand again. "I thought you might need some help."

"No, there's nothing." But the cloud of concern didn't leave Eve's eyes. "Hannah, I don't want you to feel obligated to go with the family. Knowing there's a possibility of an—incident," she began. "Well, it might be more comfortable for you here at home."

"Of course I'm going." With the hated secret tucked inside of her, she shifted the wrap on her arms. "And I really believe everything's going to be fine. If you don't need me then, I'll just go down."

"Please, let's not talk about it anymore," Eve said when Hannah shut the door behind her. "Let's go say good-night to Marissa before we leave."

"Eve." Alexander gathered her close. He could feel the slight swell where another child lay. "I love you."

"Talk's cheap," she murmured, and tried for a laugh. "Promise to show me later, after the play."

He let his cheek rest on her hair. "You have my word."

Bennett was already waiting in the main hall. Even with the distance separating them, Hannah could feel the impatience coming from him. Impatience, she thought, mixed with a recklessness that the elegant evening clothes couldn't disguise. He was looking for trouble, Hannah realized. More, he was hoping for it.

"There you are." Though he smiled up at her, his mind was already on the evening ahead. Instinctively he took her hand, holding it as she reached the bottom of the stairs. "You don't have to go tonight, Hannah. I'd be happier if you didn't."

Guilt came so quickly that she had squeezed his hand in reassurance before she could stop herself. "Now even you sound like Eve," she said lightly. "I want to be there. A vague tip from an anonymous source is a foolish reason to miss a night at the theater."

He touched the pearl cluster at her ear. "Is that what we call British pluck?"

"It's what we call common sense."

"Whatever it's called I want you to stay close. There'll be enough guards to smother us, but I prefer to keep an eye on you myself." Before she could stop him, he was leading her toward the doors.

"Eve and Alexander are nearly ready. I said I'd wait for them."

"Security feels better splitting us up." He acknowledged Claude with a brief nod. "You'll ride with me. Father will come along after Alexander and Eve."

"All right." She walked out into the star-studded night, calmly holding the .22 that lay within her beaded evening bag.

The theater was sold out. Long before the first curtain, the seats were filled so that the babble of conversation rose up to the Royal Box. There was thunderous applause when the Bissets entered. From the background as bows were made, Hannah held her breath and studied the sea of faces.

If Deboque had been there, she knew she would have found him.

"The Center's been swept twice," Reeve murmured in her ear. "There's nothing here."

She nodded and took her seat as the curtain rose.

The play was everything Eve had hoped for, though Hannah doubted anyone in the box had their full attention on the drama and pathos onstage. More than once, she cast a sidelong look at Bennett to find him studying the audience.

Deboque wasn't there. Hannah hadn't expected him. Whatever happened, whenever it happened, he would be far away with an alibi as solid as Cordinian rock.

So they would wait. And watch.

When the lights came up for intermission, Hannah could almost feel Eve relax. A false alarm? No. Though she preferred Eve believing it was so, Hannah knew better. There was an itch between her shoulder blades, vague but persistent. Some called it a hunch. Others called it instinct. Hannah had been in the game long enough to know when to wait and when to go with it.

"Would you like something to drink?"

She turned to Bennett, set to refuse. For personal reasons, she wanted him close at hand. "Yes," she heard herself saying, knowing this would be just one more deception. "I'd love something cool."

The moment he was through the doors behind them, Hannah leaned toward Reeve. "I'm going to look around."

"I'd stay close—I have a feeling." With him it was in the gut. He'd yet to let Gabriella move more than an arm's span away.

"I do too. Deboque said something about me staying in the audience. I want to take a walk backstage."

He started to object, but Gabriella took his hand and gave Hannah the few seconds she needed to slip out. She made her way toward the ladies' lounge until she was certain no one was watching. With the ease of long experience, she slipped into a stairway and began moving down. She had ten minutes, Hannah thought as she checked her watch, before anyone would miss her.

There were costume changes and stretched nerves backstage when Hannah crossed the corridor. Most of the actors were too wound up to spare her a glance. Nothing out of place. Nothing out of synch. And yet, the itch between her shoulder blades persisted.

Chantel's dressing room door was half-open. The actress caught a glimpse of Hannah, hesitated, then called out. "Lady Hannah."

Because she saw no choice, Hannah stopped at the doorway. "Miss O'Hurley. Her Highness wasn't able to come down, but you should know she's delighted with your performance."

"Thank you." Chantel set down the grease pencil she'd been using to touch up her eyes. "And what do you think of the play?"

"It's gripping. Your interpretation of Julia is breathtaking."

With a nod, Chantel moved toward her. The exaggerated stage makeup only made her look more exotic. "You know, I was born into show business. It's in the blood, if you get my drift. And I've always thought one inveterate actor easily recognizes another."

Very cool, almost smiling, Hannah met her eyes. "I suppose that's true."

"Perhaps that's why while I'm still not sure if I like you, I know I don't trust you." Chantel adjusted the cuff of the dress she'd wear in the next scene. "I've always been very fond of

Bennett. A woman like myself has few men she can call real friends.''

There was something strong, something honest in the woman who faced her. Hannah gave as much as she could. ''I can tell you that Bennett is a special man, and one I care for very much.''

Chantel was silent a moment, weighing, considering. ''I'm not sure why, but I believe you.'' She shook her head. ''I can't figure out why you're playing Jane Eyre, but I imagine you have your reasons.''

''Places, Miss O'Hurley.''

Chantel turned to give herself one last check in a full-length mirror. She lifted her chin to a different angle and became Julia. Her voice took on the slightest of drawls, an echo of the American South, as she turned back to walk past Hannah. ''Darling,'' she said in character. ''You must know beige is the worst possible color for you.'' Then she winked and walked to the wings.

Hannah let out a long breath. She'd seen nothing out of place, seen no one who didn't belong and had learned a lesson. Her cover wasn't as foolproof as she'd always thought.

She walked back down the corridor, turned into the stairway and started up. She heard the applause as the curtain came up. Then came the distant sound, the rumble and boom, of an explosion. The lights went out.

There were scattered screams as the theater plunged into darkness. From here, the warning rumble couldn't be heard. In the Royal Box, guards closed in like a wedge. Guns were drawn and held ready.

''Stay where you are,'' Reeve ordered. He gave Gabriella's hand a quick, reassuring squeeze. ''Two of you come with me.'' He moved into the hallway with two guards. ''We'll need a light.'' Swearing, he dug in his pocket for a lighter. ''We'll need someone to go over the PA and keep the audience from panicking.'' Even as he flicked the lighter on, throwing dull and shadowy light off his face, Chantel's voice came cool and clear through the speakers.

''*Mesdames and messieurs,* if you would stay seated for a moment or two. We seem to be having some difficulties with the lights. If you'd like to take advantage of the opportunity by getting to know your neighbor better...''

"Good girl," Reeve murmured as he heard the nervous laughter. "Let's get down to the main breakers."

Hannah hadn't come back. The words kept echoing over in Bennett's mind as he heard Alexander murmuring reassurances to Eve. She was out there somewhere, alone in the dark. Without hesitation, he was moving toward the door.

"Your Highness." The looming figure of a guard inched toward him. "If you would please remain seated."

"Let me pass."

"Bennett." His father's voice cut through the dark. "Please sit. This should be over in moments."

"Hannah's not here."

There was the briefest of silences. "Reeve will handle things."

There was duty, and the honor he'd never questioned. Now there was love. Bennett shoved his way through the door and went to find her.

Hannah had the gun in her hand as she stood in the stairwell. She didn't move, barely breathed, as she debated whether to go up and check on the Bissets, or whether to go down and check the power. If there had been one bomb, there could all too easily be another.

Her head told her that the Bissets were well guarded and her job was to find the source of the trouble. Her heart wanted only to see if Bennett was well and safe. Following it, Hannah started up the stairs. She'd climbed no more than three when she heard the sound of a door closing on the landing below.

With her finger wrapped around the trigger, she pointed the barrel of the gun up and started down again. She saw the beam of the flashlight before she heard the footsteps. Cautious ones. Quiet ones. Like a shadow, Hannah melted into a corner and waited.

She recognized him from the museum. He was dressed now in the dark blue uniform of the maintenance crew and carried a small toolbox. She almost nodded in approval. Anyone seeing him would simply assume he was assigned to fix whatever had gone wrong. The beam skimmed past the toes of her shoes before she stepped out and pressed the gun at his side.

"Be easy," she said in undertones. "I apologize for greeting you this way, but I didn't want a hole in my head before you recognized me."

"*Mademoiselle.*" She heard the tightly controlled fury in his voice. No man liked to be caught unaware. "I was told you would remain out of the way this evening."

Hannah drew the gun back but kept it steady. "I prefer a first-hand look at what's going on. A dramatic distraction," she complimented him. "Are there other plans for tonight?" He was prepared to kill, she was certain. But was he armed? She knew if she detained him too long or pressed too hard, her cover would be in jeopardy.

"Only if the opportunity arises. You will excuse me?"

"Certainly." Her only thought now was to see him out of the theater and away before any opportunity arose. The theater was packed with people, the Royal Family was present. Now wasn't the time for a confrontation. "Can I assist you in making a discreet exit?"

"It's been seen to."

"Very well. Tell our employer that I won't be as dramatic, but I'll be effective." She turned toward the stairs when she heard the door above open.

"Hannah?"

At the sound of Bennett's voice her blood froze. Even as the man beside her made a move, she clamped a hand over his arm. She knew without seeing that he reached for a weapon.

"Don't be a fool," she hissed. "In this light you could too easily miss and ruin everything. Turn off that beam and let me handle it." She felt his resistance, but turned quickly and started up the stairs. "Bennett." She didn't have to fake the fear in her voice. He was hardly more than a shadow at the doorway but she put her arms around him and let her body block his.

"What are you doing down here?" he began.

"I lost my way when the lights went off."

"For God's sake, Hannah. How did you manage to get all the way down here?"

"I—I'm not sure. Please, let's go back."

"You could've broken your neck on these stairs." When he gave her a slight shake and started to draw her back she shifted to block him more thoroughly.

"Kiss me," she ordered in a whisper.

Almost amused now that he'd found her safe, Bennett tilted up her chin. In the dim light he could only make out the vague outline of her face and the glint of her eyes. "If you insist."

Even as he closed his mouth over hers, she gripped the door handle behind him, prepared to shove him through.

Then his fingers spread over her face, gently. His lips coaxed and comforted and asked so little in return. On the handle her fingers tightened as much in response to him as in fear for him. One hand settled at the small of her back, again to soothe. Hannah felt her heart tear. She loved him, yet knew she couldn't. She wanted the kiss to be no more than what it was, a merging of lips, a symbol of caring. But what it was, what it had to be was a tool to give the man below them the time to escape.

Then Bennett would be safe. For seconds only, she put her heart into the kiss. He would be safe, and she could breathe again.

He felt the change and his heart thudded with it. He had imagined her lost in the dark, alone and in need of comfort and physical contact. So thinking, he had buried his own needs and had kissed her as a friend might, with affection and understanding. Her response was thunder and lightning. His fingers tightened on her face as he murmured her name.

The lights came on in a flash.

It happened very quickly then, but Bennett would remember, for a lifetime, each movement, each sound. There was no time for fear, only for surprise, then disillusionment.

When the lights went on, he stiffened. She knew in that moment that Deboque's man had not made his escape as she had hoped, but was waiting to take advantage of the opportunity that had presented itself. Without hesitation she whirled out of Bennett's arms and half shoved him through the door. The man's gun was drawn, but so was hers. And she was very fast.

Bennett had seen the man, and his weapon. He had pushed himself off the door to shield her even as she'd fired. For a moment, he simply stared, stunned at seeing the man fall and lay still. Then he saw the pistol in Hannah's hand. Surprise came and went. His face became very impassive. When he spoke, his voice was neutral.

"What game are you playing, and for whom?"

She'd never killed before. She'd been trained to, of course, but had never actually ended a life by her own hand. As she stood looking down, the gun felt foreign and slimy in her hand. Her face was very pale, her eyes very dark when she turned to Bennett. "I'll have to explain, but there isn't time." She heard the sound of running feet and struggled to pull herself together. "Please trust me."

"That's an interesting request at this point." He started to brush by her to go to the man below.

"Bennett, please." Grabbing his arm, she drew up beside him. "I'll tell you whatever I can later. You can verify it all with Reeve or your father."

She felt his muscles tense. "My father?"

"Please, for his sake, the sake of your family, play this out with me." She pushed the gun into his hand just as Reeve arrived with five guards on his heels. Now she let reaction set it. Again, truth was often the best cover.

"He tried to shoot the prince." Hannah let her voice shake and leaned heavily against Bennett. "He was going to kill him. If Bennett hadn't..." Trailing off, she buried her face against Bennett's shoulder.

He didn't move, though he didn't contradict her, there was no comforting hand now, no murmured reassurances. Reeve bent over the body, then lifted his gaze and met Bennett's. "It's fortunate you were quick—and accurate." The .45 lying beside the body hadn't been fired. His eyes shifted over briefly to rest on Hannah. "We'll handle this quietly."

Bennett's lips curved, but it wasn't a smile. "Of course."

"If you'll go back to your box." Reeve signaled two of the guards to accompany him. "We'll say nothing of this to the family until we can be private." With a pencil, he lifted the .45 automatic by the trigger guard. "The police will come in the back way."

Bennett brushed the guards aside with a gesture. It was the first time Hannah had seen him use true royal arrogance. "I want to talk to you. Alone. Now."

"All right." He'd seen too much, Reeve knew. It had to be handled quickly. "Eve's office then. If you'd give me a few minutes to deal with this first."

"You have ten," Bennett said, and turned his back on all of them.

"I'd like to go back to the palace." Hannah stood on the steps, alone now. Her hands, white at the knuckles, clutched her bag. "I'm not feeling well."

"See to a car and driver," Reeve ordered one of the guards. To another he gave the dead man's weapon before he climbed the stairs to slip an arm around Hannah. "I'll walk you out." The moment they were out of earshot, his voice became curt and professional. "What happened?"

Her knees were shaking, but she schooled her voice to the same tone. Briefly, she gave him her report. "The entire thing couldn't have taken more than five minutes." It had seemed like hours.

"It was just bad luck all around that Bennett found you. Still, the story will hold. He has a reputation for being an excellent shot. All I have to do is calm him down." Reeve let out a long breath at that. He knew his brother-in-law well, just as he knew all the Bissets. Once their temper was lost, it wasn't easily regained. "We'll go over this in the morning so that the story you pass on to Deboque is the most advantageous one."

"He'll never forgive me."

Reeve was intuitive enough to know she wasn't speaking of Deboque now. "Bennett is neither unjust nor hard-hearted. He'll be angry at being kept in the dark, but he won't blame you."

"Won't he?" Hannah walked through the doors and into the night air without looking back.

She sat by the window looking out at the garden. An hour had passed, then two while she watched the moonlight. The palace was quiet. Perhaps the others had come back, but she wouldn't have heard because her rooms faced the back. Guests were always given the loveliest views and the quietest spots.

She could imagine all too well how Bennett would have reacted to Reeve's explanations. But it wouldn't be Reeve he would blame. Hannah knew the blame would be hers and had accepted it. In the morning he would probably demand to speak with her privately.

She wouldn't apologize. Hannah lifted her chin a fraction

higher. She would accept his anger and his coldness, but she wouldn't apologize for being who and what she was.

She loved him. He would hardly believe her now if she had the right to tell him. She would have died for him tonight, not only for duty, not only for honor, but so much more for love. He would never understand or believe that now. Perhaps it was best. If her feelings for him had gotten beyond her control, it was wiser, and safer, if his for her had deadened.

She still had an assignment to complete and two years of work to finish.

Hannah laid her head on the windowsill and wished she were in London where the night would be cold and damp and smell of the river.

He didn't knock. The time for manners, formalities and small kindnesses had passed. She was curled on the window seat with her arms folded on the sill and her head resting on them. She'd loosened her hair so that it fell over the shoulders and down the back of a plain white robe. A man could almost believe she was a woman lost in the night. Bennett no longer believed what he saw and little that he felt. When he shut the door behind him, she was up and standing quickly.

She hadn't expected him that night. Looking at his face, Hannah saw that she should have. Because she knew the worst when she faced it, she braced.

"You spoke with Reeve?"

"Yes."

"And your father?"

His brow lifted. Though he had discarded his formal jacket, he could be very much the prince when he chose. "We talk tomorrow, though that doesn't concern you."

She acknowledged this with a slight nod. "Only inasmuch as it affects my position at the moment."

"Although you're obviously unaware of it, I'm not a fool. Your position remains." He took the small pistol from his pocket. After crossing to the stand beside her bed, he set it down. "Your property."

No, she would not be forgiven. She'd thought she'd been ready to accept it. She'd been wrong. "Thank you." As coolly as he, she walked to the stand, then placed the pistol in the drawer.

"You're an excellent shot, Lady Hannah."

The drawer shut again with the slightest of slams. "I've been well trained."

He caught her chin then, not gently. "Yes, by God, you have. What other talents do you have, I wonder? Deceit is certainly the sharpest. How many women can you be?"

"However many it takes to do my job. If you'd excuse me, I'm very tired."

"Oh, no." With his other hand, he gathered up her hair. He thought of what she'd put him through in one evening. Anxiety, outright terror and betrayal. "I'm afraid I won't fall for that again. With me, at any rate, the quiet, well-bred English lady is quite done. Cards on the table, Hannah."

It was fear, she realized, that had her stomach heaving. Not fear that he would hurt her physically, not fear that he would do something in temper that would jeopardize the operation, but fear, deadly and cold, that he would always look at her the way he was now.

"I doubt there's much I can tell you that Reeve hasn't. The operation was put in effect just over two years ago. The ISS needed an agent on the inside, so—"

"I've been apprised of the basic details." He let her go, dropping his hands to his sides. There, they balled into fists. "A bit late, but the information seems fairly complete. After establishing yourself with Deboque's organization, you pretended an affection for Eve so you could gain access to the palace." He saw the flicker of emotion cross her face at that but wasn't ready to interpret it. "In this way, Deboque would be deceived into believing he had one of his own on the inside. By playing both ends, you would be privy to his plans, and once he makes a move, the authorities would be able to close in and destroy his organization. I'm told I should be grateful you're so good at what you do."

"I don't need gratitude, just cooperation."

"Then perhaps you should have asked for it from the beginning."

She lifted her head. No, there would be no apologies. "I had orders, Bennett. You're no stranger to duty."

"No, but neither am I a stranger to honor. You played me."

Anger broke through the ice so that he held both of her arms. "You used my feelings for you."

"You weren't supposed to have any," she snapped back.

"We can't always choose what we feel. But there are other choices. Did you need to use how I felt for you, Hannah?"

"I had a job to do." Her voice wasn't steady now because she couldn't be sure if she'd done what she'd done coolly or because of her own needs. "I tried to discourage you."

"You knew I cared, that I wanted you."

"I didn't want you to."

"You still lie."

"No." She yanked, but he held her firm. "I did nothing to attract you. Then again, perhaps a woman only has to exist for you to be attracted." She saw the fury bloom but ignored it. "Perhaps by refusing to sleep with you, I became more of a challenge. There are a lot of women who would gladly sleep with royalty."

"Do you believe if all I had wanted was you in bed that you wouldn't have been there a half-a-dozen times already?"

"I go nowhere I don't take myself." She tossed her head back. His voice had been too low, too precise, but she was past caring. "If you're angry because I'm not what you thought I was, it's because your ego's been bruised."

The rest of her words and her breath were knocked away as she fell under him on the bed. Before she could counter the move, her arms were pinned at her sides. She'd been warned about his temper. There had even been some documentation of it in his dossier. But none of that was nearly as awesome as seeing it first hand.

"Ego?" He gritted out with his face only inches from hers. "So to you I'm still only what you've read, only what you've been told." It hurt, how it hurt. He could feel it shimmer inside of him until the only recourse was to turn it into anger. "I won't disappoint you then."

She scissored her legs and nearly succeeded in rocking him off. He shifted until her body was pressed flat against his. One hand rested dangerously on her throat. It gave him grim pleasure to feel her pulse flutter rapidly beneath his fingers.

"This won't prove anything." She managed to free one arm, but he caught it at the wrist. Her pulse beat there as well, fast, uneven. "You'll only demean both of us."

It didn't matter. He'd gone beyond right and wrong, truth and lies. "There was a time when I believed you to be shy and precious. That was a woman I only wanted to show tenderness to. For her I had such patience, such sweet feelings. But for you, we can dispense with such things, can't we?"

"Bennett, don't do this." She said it quietly, knowing it was already too late.

"Why not?" The recklessness was back, in full force, driven by betrayal. "It's a night for lies and passions."

She prepared to do battle, for herself and for him. "You won't rape me."

"No, I won't. But I will have you."

Chapter 9

It would be a battle of wits, a contest for control. Somehow it was easier for Hannah to think of that when Bennett's lips pressed down on hers. He didn't want to make love with her, but to punish, even to conquer. It was anger, not desire that had brought them here. She couldn't afford to forget it, not even for an instant.

Yet the kiss wasn't cruel. Hot and hard he moved his mouth over hers, more taunting than insistent. The hand on her throat didn't so much threaten as control. The callused fingers reminded her of the strength in his hands even as they stroked to arouse and seduce.

She made her body lie still and limp beneath his, waiting not just for a chance to fight back, but for a chance to fight and win.

But her blood was already beginning to stir.

He knew it. He was a man who understood passions, desires, vulnerabilities and how one would feed on the others. He'd used such things before, all in good humor, to give as much as to take. Now he would use them to wound as deeply as he had been wounded.

Women had frustrated him, amused him, baffled him and fascinated him. But no woman had ever hurt him before Hannah. That she'd done so not inadvertently, not in a fit of temper, but coolly, passionlessly, made the sin unforgivable. For the first time in his life he held a woman in his arms with the sole intention of bringing her pain.

Or so he told himself.

There was only flesh beneath the robe. He knew it before he drew the material down her bare shoulder. There was strength there. He'd felt it once before. Now he felt the softness as well. Both moved him, just as, he discovered, his touch moved her. As she began her first struggles, he shifted so that her loosened robe parted for him.

She knew better than to panic, but her heart and her needs betrayed her. The moment he'd stroked his palm down her bare skin the flare of pleasure had opened the door to fear. To excitement. To passion. Her struggles took them rolling over the bed, locked in combat. His lean build and easygoing manner made the steely strength she discovered both a surprise and an arousal. Muscles bunched under his shirt as he countered her moves and took her where he wanted her to go. Hannah found herself trapped beneath him again with her arms pinned by the robe that had slipped down her back.

Breathless, she stared up at him. She was beaten, but far from ready to submit. Moonlight slanted in over her face so that her skin was milky pale, her eyes dark and glowing. The fear in them had turned to condemnation. In a mass of confusion, her hair spread over the bed, making him think of mermaids and witches.

"I'll despise you."

Something ripped quietly inside him. His heart or perhaps his soul. He ignored it and fixed on the need to punish her for making him love an illusion.

He lowered his mouth again, but she turned her head away. A small defense, and an unwise one as his lips found the soft, vulnerable curve of her throat. Her breath caught, then expelled again on a moan. The sound had his heart drumming as he found her taste as unique and as dangerous as his feelings for her.

He wanted to love her, and to hate her. He needed to comfort and to punish. He sought to hurt and to give pleasure. In the midst of his confusion, he forgot everything but Hannah.

Hardened from work, gentle by nature, his hands moved over her. With the tip of his tongue, he traced patterns, tormenting, tempting patterns over her skin. He could feel it heat beneath him so that the flavor and the softness seemed to intensify. She twisted one way under him, then the other so that her agitated movements only served to arouse them both.

All at once her body became very still, almost as if even breathing had stopped. Then the trembling began.

She'd never been more aware of herself, more distanced from rational thought. She wanted to remember why he was with her, why it was wrong for both of them, but could only feel. Reasons no longer mattered, consequences were forgotten. He wanted. She wanted. Right and wrong were for the sane.

When he brought his mouth back to hers again, she was waiting. He didn't find pliancy or panic, but the passion she had ruthlessly strapped down most of her life. For him it was free, and she had a fleeting moment to realize it would never fully be disguised again.

Impatience. Desperation. Together they rolled over the bed again but in a far different kind of combat. Her robe was lost so that her arms were free to capture him. In a move that might have told him everything, she locked him to her.

Stay with me. Love me. Understand me.

Then even that was lost in a torrent of heat that left them both gasping.

Once before he'd sensed a volcano inside of her. Now as it erupted around him, he was rocked by the power, the dark violence of it. The breeze that fluttered the curtains was cool and temperate. In the center of the bed was a furnace each of them stoked higher and higher.

Frantic for more of him, Hannah pulled his shirt open, scattering buttons over the mattress and floor. When her laugh came, it was low and sultry as he'd heard it before, but now it had an edge of something that might have been triumph. Then it was a sigh as she ran her hands up his chest. Her kiss was hot and hungry on his as naked flesh met naked flesh.

Something snapped inside him. As a lover he'd always been clever, considerate, caring. Love had never been a game to him, nor had it been a contest. Always, it had been a result of affection, a natural culmination of needs.

But he'd never needed like this.

Tenderness was forgotten as completely as revenge as he dove his hands into her hair and dragged her against him. His teeth nipped into her lower lip, sending dizzying sparks of pleasure through her. Then he began to move swiftly, leaving her lips unsatisfied while his kisses tortured and tamed wherever they reached.

There was panic again, but so twined with excitement she could recognize neither. Afraid, aroused, she tried to draw him back when with a suddenness that left her gasping, he drove her up and over. Her body contracted, almost in defense, then filled with a rush of heat that had her blood burning. Release came on a flood, on a cry of his name, and with the knowledge that no one would ever take her there but him.

She was weak and shuddering. The hands that had clutched the bed clothes went lax. For a moment, she began to float. Then he fanned the flames again.

This is what he'd wanted for her, from her. Her skin was damp and soft under his hands. Her muscles were limber as she began to move with him again. In the moonlight, he saw her face, dazed with passion, flushed with pleasure. Cupping her hips in his hands, he started a lingering line of kisses up her body. He could feel the moment the strength poured back into her.

Still shuddering, still breathless, she tugged at his slacks. She'd had a sample, a taste, and wanted more. She wanted all. As she pulled his clothes from him, he skimmed his fingertips over her inner thighs, hampering her progress, arousing her unbearably. He watched her eyes fly open with the shock of the fresh climax as her body arched up and strained toward the power. Then even as her muscles went lax, his mouth was on hers again and urging her along the next journey.

He was a drug. Her arms felt like lead as she tried to lift them for him. Her head was spinning from the flood of sensations. The ripe scent of passion covered both of them so that their skin was slick and hot. She could hear her own breath come in sighs and moans as she struggled to focus on his face.

His eyes were tawny, like a cat's before it springs. She remembered how he'd looked on the stallion, daring, dangerous. She shuddered once, then surrendered. With her eyes open and her heart willing, she gathered him close.

She opened. He filled.

The ride was fast and rough. Locked together, they raced. Without slackening pace, they plunged headlong over the cliff.

Silence seemed to last forever. Hannah curled herself into it and waited for him to leave her. Though her mind wasn't cool, some sanity had returned. Covered by the dark, she could admit to herself that she would never be the same. He'd broken through that carefully polished veneer and had conquered the inner woman, the woman he hated. She couldn't tell him that she loved, that she already mourned the loss of what she never really had and would spend the rest of her life wishing for it.

He wanted to reach out to her, to gather her close and stroke her hair in the moonlight. It wouldn't be possible to touch her again. He'd taken in anger what he'd once dreamed of taking in tenderness. The guilt was there, real and ripe even as the sense of betrayal crept back.

The woman he'd fallen in love with didn't exist. She'd been a lie even more than an illusion. Now he'd done what even in his wildest moments he'd avoided. He'd made love with a stranger. And God help him, he'd fallen just as deeply in love with her.

Had he hurt her? He wanted to ask, but held himself back. He couldn't afford to feel remorse or he would end up making a fool of himself over this new Hannah as well. Pride followed honor. Since he'd sacrificed one to temper and pain, he would hold firm to the other.

As he rose, he dragged a hand through his hair. How could he love her when he didn't even know her? How could he still love the woman he knew had never existed?

He dressed in silence while Hannah lay still as a stone on the bed.

"Now it seems we've used each other," he murmured.

She opened her eyes then. There were no tears in them. Thank God she still had the strength for that much. He was standing by the bed, naked from the waist up with the ruined shirt balled in his hand. "We can consider ourselves even."

"Can we?" His fingers went white on his shirt. He'd nearly taken a step toward her before he made himself turn and leave her alone.

Hannah lay and listened to the silence until dawn.

* * *

"You have questions," Armand began as he faced his youngest son. The morning light was strong through the open windows and showed, all too clearly, the marks of a sleepless night on both faces. "I prefer it if you wait to ask them until after I've finished."

He'd been prepared to demand and to rage. The lines of strain and weariness made his father look suddenly old and much too vulnerable. Again, it was love rather than duty that guided him. "All right." Because he needed it, Bennett poured coffee and left it black.

"Will you sit?"

"No."

Armand's gaze sharpened at the tone. Then he, too, let love hold sway. "I shall." Once seated, he set his untouched coffee aside. "Two years ago, I sat in this office with Reeve and Malori. You and Alexander were also present. You remember?"

Bennett paced to the window and looked out. "Yes. We were speaking of Deboque and what could and should be done."

"Then you remember that Reeve, even then, had an operative in mind to infiltrate the organization."

"I remember, too, that it was decided that the name be kept from Alex and me." The trace of resentment he had felt then had grown to true bitterness in one night. "And that Malori was not completely satisfied with Reeve's choice."

"Malori has always been one of the most trusted members of the security staff in Cordina. But he's old-fashioned." Armand saw no need to add that he, too, had had his doubts. "He was concerned with using a woman."

Bennett downed half his coffee. "I felt then, as I feel now, that Alexander and I had a right to know what was being done. More, all of us had the right to know that the woman we accepted as friend was an ISS agent."

"I felt then as I feel now—" Armand's voice, though quiet, held the whip of authority "—that neither of you had a need to know. If I had become ill, Alex, of course, would have been apprised. However—"

"Do you think because I won't rule, Cordina is of less importance to me?" Bennett whirled on his father. The fury on his face was lethal. "All of my life I've been the younger brother. Alex was born to rule Cordina after you. He was molded for it, just as his son will be. Do you think because of that I cared less, loved less or would have offered less?''

Armand said nothing for a moment, knowing the words had to be chosen with care, even as they came from the heart. ''Bennett, I've watched you grow from child to man and have waited for a sign, for a hint that you resented your position. You have been sometimes wild, always reckless and too often indiscreet, but never have I seen anything in you but love and devotion for your country and your family.''

''Then why, when something threatens both, do you keep your plans from me?''

There was a headache drumming behind Armand's temple. He closed his eyes a moment, but didn't lift a hand to soothe it. ''Two years ago, Lady Hannah Rothchild was chosen out of a half dozen highly qualified operatives to infiltrate and destroy Deboque's organization. We were aware, as she was, of the risks involved, and the time and skill it would take to succeed.''

''Why her?'' Bennett found he didn't want to think beyond that for a moment. It was an answer he had to have before he could deal with the others.

''Reeve felt Hannah's talents were uniquely suited to the operation. She's been with the ISS for ten years.''

''Ten years?'' Bennett roamed the room again as he tried to take it in. ''How is that possible? She's so young.''

''She's second generation,'' Armand said mildly. ''Her father trained her himself while she was still in school. Lord Rothchild, though semiretired now, is one of the most valued agents in the ISS. He had some part in Reeve's early training which was another reason Reeve leaned toward Hannah for this assignment.''

''Ten years,'' Bennett repeated. How many women had she been? How many lies had she told?

''Apparently she had a natural aptitude for this kind of work.'' He saw his son's jaw set, but went on. ''After reading Reeve's report on her, I had to agree that she was best suited for what we had in mind.''

''Deboque often uses women,'' Bennett murmured.

''He feels they can be more cunning, even more cruel, than men.'' Armand remembered Janet Smithers and the bullet that had been dug out of his son's flesh. "His preference runs to a certain type, quiet, well-bred, spotless pedigrees."

"Hannah."

"Yes. It was those qualities in her which weighed the decision in her favor. With the cooperation of the ISS a deep background was created for her. The credentials she was given made it possible for her to slip into Deboque's company. In two years, she's moved from messenger to the top of the organization."

"The top?" The fear started then, like something foul in the back of his throat. "What do you mean?"

"She's met with Deboque himself, and by managing to discredit one of his top men, is now filling that position herself. Reeve explained to you that as far as Deboque knows, she's here at the palace as his instrument."

Bitterness was more palatable than fear. He concentrated on it. "She plays the game very well."

"An agent in her position plays the game well or loses her life. You know firsthand that Deboque doesn't hesitate to kill. Her name and the operation itself were kept in strictest confidence not to protect you or the rest of the family, Bennett, but to protect her."

Bennett set his cup down and stopped pacing. "In what way?"

"Three other agents have been killed trying to do what Hannah has nearly succeeded in doing. The last was butchered." He watched Bennett's face pale. He would have spared his son this, as a father. Now, as prince, he could spare him nothing. "By bringing her here in this way, letting you, all of you, believe what Deboque wanted you to believe, Hannah had the only protection we could offer. If she's discovered, even the ISS can't protect her. Now that you know all that you know, her risk is greater than ever."

In silence, Bennett crossed the room to sit across from his father. Though the turmoil was building all too quickly inside, his face was calm. "I'm in love with her."

"Yes." Armand sat back. "I was afraid you were."

"I will not stand still and watch Deboque hurt someone else I love."

"Bennett, there are times, too many times, when our personal feelings can't influence our actions."

"For you." Bennett's voice was still calm, but slightly colder. "Perhaps for Alex as well, but not for me. I prefer to kill him myself."

Armand felt a ripple of fear, a tingle of pride and controlled both. "If you do anything to interfere with the operation at this point, you could be responsible for Hannah's death, not Deboque's."

Pushed to his limit, Bennett leaned forward. "Do you understand, I'm in love with her? If you were in my position, could you do nothing?"

Armand studied his son's face and remembered the only woman he'd ever loved. "I can only say that I would do whatever was necessary to keep her safe. Even if that meant doing nothing." He rose and went to his desk. "Read these." He lifted a small stack of files that carried the stamp of highest security. "These contain background information on Hannah, some of her own reports concerning certain assignments and most recently, her progress with Deboque. I'll leave you so that you can read them here. They mustn't leave this room."

Bennett rose to accept the files. "Where is she now?"

He had hoped the question wouldn't be asked. "She received a message early this morning. She's gone to Deboque."

She had to play this one very carefully. Hannah sat with her hands folded on her lap in the elegant salon of Deboque's rented villa. Though the meeting was on land this time, she knew if her cover hadn't held up, she was just as much alone as she had been on the yacht.

If he had a hint of the part she'd played in the events of the evening before, her throat would be slit before she could voice a denial. A risk every agent takes, she reminded herself. To test herself, she lifted the small china pot on the table in front of her and poured coffee. Her hand was steady.

It was imperative that her mind stay sharp and focused on the assignment.

Every other thought in her mind was of Bennett.

"Lady Hannah." Deboque walked into the salon then shut the double doors at his back. "How delightful to see you again."

She added a careful dollop of cream. "The message I received this morning left little option."

"Ah, I was brusque." He crossed to her, taking her hand and brushing his lips over it. "My apologies. The events of last night caused me some distress."

"And me." She drew her hand away. Instinct told her annoyance was the wisest course. "I find myself wondering if I've chosen wisely."

Deboque chose the seat beside hers, then taking his time, chose a cigarette from a crystal holder. He wore emeralds today. "Meaning?"

"Only months ago, I found myself in the position of having to clean up for another of your employees." She sipped coffee. It was hot and Turkish. "Last night, another of them nearly ruined every carefully laid step I've taken toward the Bissets."

"May I remind you, *mademoiselle,* you were advised to stay out of the way?"

"I'll remind you, *monsieur,* that I haven't reached my current position by not looking toward my own interests. If I hadn't followed Bennett, you and I might even now be sitting in less agreeable quarters."

Deboque blew out smoke. "Explain."

"Bennett was a bit bored with the play and thought to wait in the American actress's dressing room until the curtain. Because I was aware that there were plans of some sort in the works, I decided it best to keep close. When the lights went out, I had to decide whether to go back or keep Bennett within reach. If I'd gone back, *monsieur,* the prince might indeed be dead."

"And for that you wish my gratitude?"

"He might be dead," Hannah repeated, "and a member of your organization would even now be in custody. Shall I pour you some coffee?"

"*Merci.*" He waited patiently while she filled a second cup. At his nod, she added cream.

Hannah sat back again and folded her ringless hands. "MacGee and the guards were already on their way. I spotted your man." She made a look of disgust. "He was bumbling his way around with a flashlight. I managed to distract Bennett by playing the hysterical female, but the idiot didn't take the opportunity to make good his escape. The lights came up again. Bennett saw him and his weapon. You should be flattered that since your release the prince has carried a small-caliber pistol with him. He used it, and for personal reasons, I'm grateful he used it well. Dead men can't name names." Playing up the role, she rose. "I ask you now, was the man under orders to kill one of the Bissets? Do you or do you not trust me to complete the contract?"

Say it! she ordered silently. Say it out loud, say it plainly so that this can be over.

Smoke curled up in a column toward the ceiling as he tapped the cigarette into an ashtray. "Please, my dear, be calm. The man you speak of may have been told to use initiative, but was never given a specific request. I have confidence in you, of course."

"We agreed. I would dispose of the Bissets in return for five million dollars."

He smiled, like a generous uncle. "We agreed that if such a thing were to happen, there would be some compensation."

"I'm tired of playing games." As if to prove it, Hannah picked up her bag. "If you won't speak frankly, if you won't honor our arrangement, there's no reason to go on with this."

"Sit." The order came sharp and clear as she walked to the door. Hannah stopped, turned, but didn't walk back. "You forget yourself. No one who works for me leaves until they are dismissed."

She knew there would be men outside the door, to detain or dispose of her at Deboque's whim. She gambled that he would respect audacity. "Perhaps it's best if I find other employment then. I'm not accustomed to being dealt only half the cards."

"Remember that I hold them. I ask you again, sit."

This time she obeyed. She let the impatience shimmer, but only enough to let him see her control. "Very well."

"Tell me how the Bissets cope this morning."

"With dignity, of course." She pretended to be amused. "Bennett's pleased with himself. Armand is worried. Eve is confined to bed for the day. Gabriella stays with her. MacGee is closeted with Malori—you know the name?"

"Yes."

"I would guess that they are trying to see what purpose the disturbance last night had. Your man did an excellent job on the

main power, though I think the explosive was a bit overstated."
She shrugged as though it had been a hat with one too many
feathers. "In any case, they ran on auxiliary for the rest of the
evening and have a crew in the Center this morning for repairs.
It's their belief that the power was blown so that the assassin could
break his way into the Royal Box."

"A natural assumption," Deboque said as he went back to his
coffee. And exactly the one he'd hoped for. "Though such a move
would have been messy and unstylish. And you, my dear? How
do you cope after witnessing a killing?"

"I've chosen to be shocked and weakened by the events. But
brave, naturally. We British are, you know."

"I've always admired the quality." He smiled at her again. "I
have to congratulate you on the depth of your skill. You look as
though you didn't close your eyes all night."

It was a mistake to remember, to think even for an instant, of
Bennett. "I drank enough coffee to keep me awake until dawn,"
she said easily as her stomach tied itself in knots. "At the moment
I'm supposedly out for a walk to clear my head." To take his
attention from that, she added the last of what she and Reeve had
discussed. "Are you aware that the entire Royal Family will gather
at the palace for the Christmas Ball?"

"So is tradition."

"With Eve being a bit delicate, the Princess Gabriella brings
her family to stay for several days during the preparations. The
MacGees share a wing with Alexander and Eve so that they can
be close to the children."

"Interesting."

"And obliging. I'll require the makings for three plastic explosives."

Deboque only nodded. "The younger prince doesn't reside in
the same wing."

"The younger prince will be fatally injured while trying to save
the rest of his family. Leave it to me. Just make sure the five
million is waiting." She rose again, then inclined her head as if
waiting for his permission to leave. Deboque stood as well, then
surprised her by taking both of her hands.

"I had thought that some time after the holiday I would take a long vacation. I have an urge to sail, to be in the sun. Vacations can be very dull without companionship.''

Her stomach turned over. She prayed the revulsion wouldn't show, even for an instant. ''I've always been fond of the sun.'' She didn't object when he stepped closer, but smiled. ''You have a reputation for discarding women as easily as you collect them.''

''When they bore me.'' He cupped a hand around her neck. His fingers were light, smooth, and still made her think of spiders. ''I have a feeling you won't. I'm not attracted to looks, but brains and ambitions. Together, I believe we could be very comfortable.''

If his lips touched hers, she would retch. Knowing it, Hannah tilted her head back just an inch. ''Perhaps—after our business is completed.''

The fingers on her neck tightened, then released. The marks they had left wouldn't fade for several minutes. ''You're a cautious woman, Hannah.''

''Cautious enough to want the five million before I sleep with you. Now if you'll excuse me, I should get back before I cause any concern.''

''Of course.''

She walked to the door. ''I'll need those supplies by the end of the week.''

''Expect a Christmas present from your aunt in Brighton.''

With a nod, she swung easily through the door.

Deboque took his chair again and decided he'd become quite fond of her. It was a shame she'd have to die.

Chapter 10

It was midafternoon before Bennett went to find her. He'd read every word in the files Armand had given him. Though some had fascinated him, some had frightened him and some had angered him, he still wasn't sure he knew the woman.

Now he, too, was part of the deception, he thought as he made his way up to Eve's rooms. Nothing he'd read, nothing he'd been told could be confided to his brother. He couldn't comfort his sister or Eve with the fact that every move Deboque made was being monitored. He had, as he was coming to understand Hannah had, no choice but to play the game through. So he went to find her, knowing it was long past time they talked calmly.

He found Eve and Gabriella together at a table with piles of lists and a pot of tea.

"Bennett." Gabriella reached a hand out. "Just in time. We need a man's viewpoint on the Christmas Ball."

"Make sure there's plenty of wine." He bent to kiss both of her cheeks. Though she'd smiled at him, he'd recognized the signs of strain, just as he recognized them in Eve. "Hannah's not with you?"

"No." Eve set her pencil down as she lifted her face for Bennett's kiss. "I told her I wanted her to rest today. Last night..." She tightened her fingers on his. "Last night must have been dreadful for her. And you."

He shrugged, remembering too clearly the way he'd left her—curled into a silent ball on the bed. "It wasn't a dull evening in any case."

"Don't joke, Ben. You could have been killed. All I can think is that it's the second time in the theater. The second time one of my plays—"

Keeping Eve's hand in his, he crouched down. "I wasn't hurt, and I don't want you letting that fertile imagination go. I'd be very annoyed if my nephew were born with worry lines. Where's Marissa?"

"Napping."

He rubbed a thumb under her eyes. "You should do the same."

Annoyance replaced the strain, as he'd hoped. "Now you sound like Alex."

"God forbid. Where is he, anyway?"

"Meetings." She nervously traced her fingers over the papers. "Most of the day. Everything's been switched to his offices here because of—because security prefers it."

"Then you should relax." He covered her hand with his. "You should know by now the Bissets are indestructible. At the least you should be grateful he's tied up for a while, otherwise he'd be in here hovering over you."

She managed to smile. "You do have a point."

Rising, he grinned down at Gabriella. "I suppose we can trust you to keep her in line—though you're not looking your best, either."

"Chivalry is never dead with you around."

"What are brothers for?" He wanted to gather them both close and tell them that nothing and no one would ever hurt them again. Instead, he gave his sister's hair a tug. "Now I'll let you two get back to what I'm sure is fascinating work." He'd gotten no farther than the head of the stairs when Gabriella caught up with him. "Ben."

He turned, and though he was ready with a smile, her expression stopped it.

Gabriella looked back over her shoulder to be certain they were far enough away from Eve's office, then laid a hand over his on the banister. "Reeve tells me little about certain matters." A trace of temper came into her eyes, then was dismissed. "That's something I have to live with. But particularly since I once lost everything, I have very good instincts when it comes to my family.''

"I know you're worried," he began. "All of us are."

"It's more than that, though everything comes back to Deboque and his obsession with destroying us. I still have dreams, even after all these years." She could remember a cabin, and the dark, and the fear.

"Brie." He laid a hand on her cheek. "Nothing like that is ever going to happen again."

She closed her fingers lightly over his wrist. "And I remember seeing you shot and bleeding on the terrace floor. I remember sitting in the hospital while Eve hung between life and death. Deboque." Her face was very pale, but there was strength in it and in the hand that lay on his. "It's all been Deboque. And he isn't finished."

"He will be." Something dangerous came into his voice, into his eyes. "That I promise you."

"I want you to be careful, Bennett."

He smiled, so that the look vanished. "How can I be otherwise with a dozen guards smothering me?"

"Very careful," she repeated. "I've never known you to carry a pistol to the theater."

She knew it was a lie. He didn't have to hear her say it, only to look in her eyes. She knew, but didn't understand. And because she was Gabriella, she wouldn't stop until she did.

"Leave it for now."

"So Reeve told me," she said with an impatient gesture. "It's my family. How can I?"

"I only know it's going to be over soon. In the meantime we have to stand together. Something's being done, Brie. Hold on to that."

"I have been." She knew it was unfair to push, so released him. "I want you to promise you won't do anything rash."

"What is this reputation I carry with me?"

"Ben, please."

"All right, you have it." He kissed her again. "I adore you, even if you did bring Dorian into the world to pester me." He gave her hand a final pat before he started down the stairs. *"A bientôt."*

She watched him go, but the worry stayed with her. *"A bien-tôt."*

Hannah wasn't in her rooms. Bennett found himself frustrated yet again when he entered and found them empty. Had she gone out again? he wondered. Was she even now putting herself in danger to protect his family?

He hated it. The thought of her risking her life, of blocking his body with her own as she had done last night was impossible to accept. Whether it was family, friend or country, he protected. How could he do less for the woman he loved?

Wandering in her rooms, he moved to her dresser. There was a small enameled box with a peacock on the lid. He ran a finger over it, wondering where she had come by it. A gift? From whom? A purchase in some little shop in London? He needed to know even those inconsequential details about her. Couldn't she understand that in order to resolve his feelings he had to know the woman he'd given them to?

He looked up, and reflected in the mirror was the bed where they'd fought, and loved, the night before. If he stood very still, he could almost feel the echoes of passion and discovery in the air. Would she hate him for that? Even though the loving had been as intense and as stunning for her as for him, would she forgive him for forcing her to set the barriers aside?

He'd been rough.... Bennett looked down at his own hands, turning them over, spreading his fingers. And he hadn't cared. All of his life he'd taken such pains never to hurt a woman. Now, when he'd found the only woman, he'd set out to do just so.

Walking to the window he stared out and tried to sort out his feelings. He still resented her. No matter what his brain told him, his heart was still bruised by the deception. More, he couldn't shake off the feeling that he'd fallen in love with two women and could trust neither.

Then he saw her in the gardens below.

She needed some time, Hannah told herself. Just an hour alone to clear her mind and calm her nerves. She knew she'd handled Deboque as smoothly as possible that morning. If nothing went wrong, they would close the trap on him in a week. Then she would have succeeded. In her file would go another favorable report. A two-year assignment successfully tied up could very well mean a promotion. She was, she knew, only inches away from a captaincy. Why didn't it excite her as it once had?

Time, Hannah told herself again. She just needed some time.

She would take a much needed and well earned vacation. Perhaps at last she would go to America—New York, San Francisco. Wouldn't it be possible to lose herself in such places for a while?

Or perhaps she would go back to England. She could spend time in Cornwall walking the moors or riding by the sea. In England she couldn't lose herself, but perhaps she could find herself again.

Wherever she went, she would be leaving Cordina. And Bennett.

Wisteria rose up in an arch, sheltering a bench and inviting long, lazy contemplations. She sat, and closing her eyes, tried to bring her troubled mind to rest.

Who was she? For the first time in years she was forced to ask herself and admit she didn't know the answer. A part of her was the quiet woman who enjoyed a long afternoon with a book, who liked to talk of literature and art. A part of her was the woman who kept a weapon within reach and listened to footsteps behind her.

The fact that she could be both had always been a benefit before, never, as it was now, a painful puzzle to solve. She wished she could talk with her father, even for an hour. He understood what it was to live two lives and find contentment and challenge in each.

But she couldn't risk even that. In this, as in the assignment that had brought her here, she was alone.

He detested her. It was Bennett who had caused the ache and the doubts. It was Bennett who had forced her to question what she'd always taken for granted. Last night he'd taken her mind and heart and body, only because he'd wanted to humiliate her. And he had. No one, no one had ever shown her how much there could be, how much she could give. No one had ever left her so empty and alone.

He wouldn't know how much he'd hurt her. He couldn't know, she thought as the tears she'd held off throughout the night began to fall. Because he would never know how strong her feelings were for him, and how hopeless.

She had chosen her path, Hannah reminded herself, and she would live with it. In a matter of days it would no longer cross his.

He would be safe. His family would be safe. And she would be gone.

He found her sitting on the bench, her hands folded neatly in her lap, her eyes closed and her face wet with tears. So many feelings tumbled into him that he couldn't separate them. Regret, confusion, love, guilt.

She'd want to be left alone. He thought he understood her that well. There was still enough bitterness in him to want to leave her alone. He could no more have left her there than he could have left a wounded dog on the side of the road.

As he went closer, Hannah sprang up from the bench. He saw the shock and humiliation run across her face. For a moment, he thought she would turn and run. But she held her ground.

"I thought I was alone." Her voice was cold as she fought anger and embarrassment.

He took out a handkerchief and offered it. At the moment it was the only comfort he could give, or she accept. "I'm sorry I disturbed you." His voice was as stiff as hers. "I think we need to talk."

"Haven't we?" She dried her face then crumpled the linen in her hands.

"Would you like to sit?"

"No, thank you."

He slipped his hands into his pockets. She hadn't slept, he thought as he saw the shadows under her eyes. Neither had he. So perhaps there they were even. "I spoke with my father this morning. You've met with Deboque already today."

She started to cut him off, but relented. The garden was as secure as the palace—for the moment. "I don't report to you on those matters, Your Highness."

Temper narrowed his eyes and balled his hands into fists, but he spoke evenly. "No, but I'm now fully aware of the situation. I read your files."

Her breath came out on a huff of air. Was nothing she was or had done hers alone any longer? "Very well then, your questions have been answered, your curiosity satisfied. You know everything there is to know about me—I hope you were entertained.''

''I didn't read it to be entertained,'' he tossed back. ''Dammit, Hannah, I have a right to know.''

''You have no rights where I'm concerned. I'm neither servant or subject.''

''You're the woman I took to bed last night.''

''That's best forgotten. Don't.'' Her body went rigid as he started forward. ''Don't you ever touch me again.''

''Very well.'' He stiffened even as she did. ''But we both know certain things can't be forgotten.''

''Mistakes can,'' she countered. ''I'm here as an agent of the ISS to protect you and your family, to stop Deboque's plans to ruin Cordina and avoid the repercussions in Europe. Whatever has to be done to assure that, I'll do, but I will *not* let you humiliate me again.'' The tears started again, blinding her. ''Oh, damn you, can't you leave me alone? Wasn't last night enough retribution for you?''

That snapped the very tenuous control he had on his own temper. He grabbed her arm, closing his fingers over the firm muscle. ''Is that all it meant to you? Retribution? Can you stand here now and tell me you felt nothing, feel nothing? How accomplished a liar are you?''

''It doesn't matter what I felt. You wanted to punish me, and you did.''

''I wanted to love you, and I did.''

''Stop.'' That hurt, more than she was able to stand. She pushed him away only to be caught closer. The movement sent wisteria blossoms raining. ''Do you think I couldn't see how much you hated me? You looked at me and made me feel vile. For ten years I've been proud of what I do, and you took even that away from me.''

''And what of you?'' He kept his voice low, but the anger was just as potent. ''Can you tell me you didn't know I was in love with you?'' She started to shake her head in denial, but he tightened his fingers. ''You knew I was in love with a woman who didn't even exist. A quiet, shy and honest woman to whom I only wanted to show tenderness and patience. For the first time in my life there was a woman I could give my heart and my trust to, and she was nothing but a mirage.''

''I don't believe you.'' But she wanted to and her heart began to race. ''You were restless, even bored. I entertained you.''

''I loved you.'' He lifted his hand and held her face very still, very close. She saw his eyes as she had the night before, tawny with passion. ''You'll have to live with that.''

''Bennett—''

''And when I came to your room last night, I found another woman, one who had lied and used me.'' He dragged the hand up, raking through her hair so that pins scattered. ''One who looked like a witch,'' he murmured as her hair fell heavily over his hands. ''And I wanted her just as badly, but without those tender, those sweet feelings. God help me, I still want her.''

When his mouth came down on hers, she didn't protest. She'd also seen the truth in his eyes. He had loved her. Or he had loved the pretense of her. If desire was all he could give her now, she would take it. For duty she had sacrificed love, but even for duty, she wouldn't sacrifice the crumbs she had left.

She wrapped her arms around him. Perhaps if she could give him the passion, some day he would forgive her the rest.

How easily he could lose himself in her. The passion was edgy and achy but it didn't seem to matter. Her mouth was warm, her body slender and straining. If it wasn't love she felt for him, at least there was need. He'd settled for no more than that before.

''Tell me you want me,'' he demanded as he moved his mouth desperately over her face.

''Yes, I want you.'' She hadn't known it possible to feel triumph and defeat at the same time.

''Come with me now.''

''Bennett, I have no right to this.'' She turned her face into his throat, wanting to draw just a little more of him into her. ''I'm here only because—''

With his hands on her shoulders he drew her away before she could finish the denial. ''For today, for one day, we'll put your duty and mine aside.''

''And tomorrow?''

''Tomorrow comes whether we want it to or not. Give me a few hours, Hannah.''

She would have given him her life, and somehow knew that would be easier than what he was asking now. Still, she put her hand in his.

They went on horseback. As Hannah cantered beside him, she could see that Bennett knew the route to their destination well. They turned into the woods where they'd raced once before, and he took the lead. Each time doubts rose up to plague her, she beat them back. She would take the few hours she was being offered.

She heard the stream before she saw it. It was a simple, musical sound that suited the leafy shade and towering trees. When Bennett came to it, he turned his horse south. For a quarter of a mile they rode along the bank in silence.

The stream curved and twisted, then widened at a point where a trio of willows draped over it. Bennett stopped there and swung from the saddle.

"What a lovely spot." Hannah reined in, but found herself not quite courageous enough to dismount. "Every time I think I've seen the most beautiful place in Cordina, I find another. Do you often come here?"

"Not often enough." He'd secured his horse and now walked to her. Saying nothing, he held up a hand.

Here was the choice he'd refused to give her the night before. Perhaps he gave it to her now because he knew the decision had already been made. Hannah curled her fingers into his, held a moment, then dismounted. The silence continued while she tethered her horse beside his.

"I came here when my mother died." He didn't know why it seemed important that he tell her. "Not to grieve really, but because she always loved places like this. See the little white flowers along the bank?" His hand was on hers again as they moved closer to the stream. "She called them angel wings. They're sure to have a complicated Latin name, but angel wings seemed right."

Bending, he plucked one. It was no bigger than his thumb with thin petals cupped around a tiny blue center. "Every summer, before I'd have to go back to Oxford, I'd come here. For some reason it made leaving easier." He tucked the flower into her hair. "When I was a child, I thought the fairies lived here. I used to look for them in the clover and under toadstools."

She smiled and touched a hand to his cheek. "Did you ever find one?"

"No." With his hand on her wrist, he turned his head to press his lips to her palm. "But I think they're still here. That's why this place is magic. That's why I want to make love with you here."

Their lips were still an inch apart as they lowered to the grass. They remained a breath apart as they began to undress each other. Kneeling, gazes locked, they unfastened buttons. Sunlight dappled over skin as material was pushed aside. Their lips brushed, then clung.

He couldn't stop the rush of power, the flood of need. In seconds they were rolling over the grass. He caressed her everywhere, seeking, finding, exploiting until her moans shuddered into his mouth. The need to take her quickly, fiercely, couldn't be fought down, especially when her fingers were already tugging at the clasp of his jeans.

They waited only until all barriers were removed, then joined in a rocketing, furious journey that left them both sated.

Naked, with the grass tickling her back, Hannah looked up at the sunlight filtering through the leaves overhead. It had been moonlight before and she'd experienced a range of feelings from anger, shame, ecstasy and back to shame again. Today, in the sunlight, she no longer felt the shame.

What was between them could be, for this short time, between the man and the woman. Tomorrow they would be prince and agent again.

"What are you thinking?"

She was able to smile and turn her head toward him. "That this is a beautiful spot."

He'd wanted to bring her there before. He'd imagined it. How he would slowly, patiently, show her the pleasures of loving. Shaking off the mood, he drew her closer. This was a different day, and a different woman. "Are you warm enough?"

"Hmmm. But I..." she trailed off, knowing she'd sound foolish.

"But?"

"Well, I've never—" How to phrase it? "I've never lain naked in the grass under the sun before."

He laughed, not even realizing that the tone and the feeling behind it had come from the woman he'd first known. "Life should always include new experiences."

"I'm sure you've found yourself naked in all manner of unusual places."

The dry voice delighted him. Rolling over, he pressed a kiss to her mouth then drew back just to look at her. Her hair was fanned out over the dark grass. The tiny white flower was tangled in it as though it had grown there. Bruising shadows under her eyes made her look both wanton and delicate, as though she were a virgin who'd just spent a night being initiated into womanhood.

This was how he had once imagined her, how he had once wanted, how he had once loved.

"You're so beautiful."

She smiled, relaxed enough to be amused. "Now *that* I've never been."

He traced a fingertip along her cheekbone. "How unobservant of you, Hannah. Or how foolish. Making yourself look less attractive doesn't change the truth. Flawless skin." He traced his lips over it as if to taste. "These elegant bones that make a man wonder if you're made of flesh and bone or glass. Those calm, intelligent eyes that drove me mad wondering how they might darken and cloud if I could find the right way to touch you. And this." He rubbed a finger over her lips. "So soft, so generous." He lowered his head but only traced the shape with his tongue. "Do you remember the first time I kissed you?"

Her breath was already shaking, her eyes already closing. "Yes. I remember."

"I wondered how it was that such a quiet woman could make my knees weak with just a taste."

"Kiss me now," she demanded and drew him down to her.

It wasn't what she expected. There was tenderness instead of passion, patience rather than urgency. She murmured against his mouth in confusion. Bennett only stroked his fingers over her face and waited for her to relax. More, he waited for her to accept. Even when he deepened the kiss it remained gentle. The fire was there but smoldering rather than blazing.

He was making love to the Hannah he'd understood, she realized and wanted to weep. There was lust for one, affection for the other. How could she fight another woman when the woman was herself?

On a trembling sigh, she let her mind empty. She would give him whatever it was he needed today.

He felt the change—the slow, almost fluid surrender. With a murmured approval, he pressed his lips to her throat. He wanted to show her there could be more than flash and speed. If they only had a few hours, then he would use them to give her whatever sweetness she would accept from him.

Lightly he stroked the smoothness of her body. What he'd demanded from her the night before, he now requested, coaxed, offered. He took the time to watch her arousal grow as the sun filtered down on her face and the stream rushed by beside them. He murmured to her as he kissed her throat. There were promises, endearments, reassurances. She answered him in words so fragile they almost dissolved in the air.

She'd never been loved like this before—as though she was precious, as though she was special. Even with her mind fogging over she could hear the gentle hiss of water running over rock. She could smell the grass and the wild sweet flowers scattered through it. With her eyes half-opened, the sunlight seemed gold and bountiful over her lover's skin. She ran her hand over it, finding it smooth and taut and warm.

Her lover. Hannah brought his mouth back to hers and gave him everything that was in her heart. If the place was magic, then so was the moment. Dreams hadn't been a part of her life for too long to remember, but she opened herself to them now.

She was so giving, so pliant. He'd wanted too badly to feel this kind of emotion from her. It went far beyond heat, far above desire. She touched him as though she'd been waiting for him all of her life. She kissed him as though he were her first and only lover. The more she gave, the more he found in himself to give back. The shadows shifted and lengthened over them as they stroked and offered and discovered.

Even when he slipped into her, it was slow and easy. The passion that had built was still harnessed by stronger emotions. They moved together in a harmony that seemed almost painful in its perfection while she framed his face with her hands and his lips met hers.

They glided over the top and settled softly.

* * *

"You wanted to see me, Monsieur Deboque?"

"Yes, Ricardo." Deboque lifted his teapot and poured. He admired the British habit of tea in the late afternoon. It was so civilized. "I have a little shopping list for you." With one hand he gestured toward the desk by the window. "I'd like you to supervise it personally."

"Of course." Always pleased to be given trust, Ricardo picked up the list written on heavy cream-colored paper. His brow lifted only a fraction. "Shall I requisition this from within the company?"

"Please." Deboque added cream to his tea. "I prefer to keep this at home, so to speak. The delivery should be set up with Lady Hannah on…Thursday, I'd say. It's no use passing the merchandise along to her too soon."

"She risks much, smuggling such a—volatile package into the palace."

"I have implicit trust in our British friend, Ricardo." He remembered the way she'd sat across from him that morning. Trim, tidy and cultured. It gave his plans such a pleasant touch when they were carried out by delicate hands. "She has a certain style, wouldn't you say?"

"Class, even when so quietly cloaked, is still class, *monsieur.*"

"Precisely." Deboque smiled and sipped at his tea. "I have no doubt she will carry out her objective with class." He sipped his tea again and sighed. "I do admire the British, Ricardo. So traditional, so resilient. Not as passionate as the French, but so wonderfully pragmatic. In any case, see that the merchandise is shipped from the address on that list. I don't wish it to come through my hands."

"Of course."

"I'm preparing an itinerary, Ricardo. We'll be sailing the end of next week. I'll see Lady Hannah once more. You'll see to the details?"

"As you wish."

"Thank you, Ricardo. Oh, by the way, did you see that a wreath was sent to Bouffe's funeral?"

"Roses as you requested, *monsieur.*"

"Excellent." Deboque chose one of the little sugared biscuits from the Wedgwood plate. "You're very dependable."

"I try, *monsieur*."

"Have a pleasant evening then, Ricardo. Do let me know if we get any further word on the accident at the theater. I'm very uncomfortable with the current report."

"I will. Good evening, *monsieur*."

Deboque sat back, nibbling on the cookie. Ricardo continued to please him a great deal. An intelligent man with sociopathic tendencies was an excellent addition to his staff. Deboque was certain Ricardo would be very grateful to have the assignment of dealing with Hannah when her job was completed. It was tempting, but Deboque discarded it.

He would deal with Hannah himself. After all, the least he could do after she'd given him his fondest wish was to see she died as painlessly as possible.

Chapter 11

Hannah appeared very calm as she sipped tea in the library. She listened to Reeve give an updated report to Malori, filling in occasionally when requested to, then lapsing back into silence.

Bennett had started to show her the library once. Then they'd detoured into the music room. And he'd kissed her. Was that when her life had really begun to change? she wondered. Had it been then, or the day on the beach when he'd given her a shell? Perhaps it had been that first night in the gardens.

"Do you agree, Hannah?"

She snapped back, cursing herself for letting her mind wander at such a crucial time. They had only thirty minutes for the briefing, half of which was already gone. Even within the walls of the palace it was dangerous for them to meet.

"I'm sorry. Could you repeat that?"

Armand had been watching her, wondering if her shoulders were strong enough to hold the fate of so much. "The last few days have been a strain." There wasn't criticism in his voice but concern. Hannah would have preferred the first.

"The last two years have been a strain, Your Highness." Then she lifted her shoulders in a gesture that was more acceptance than dismissal.

"If you're beginning to wear under it," Malori said in his clipped, no-nonsense voice, "it's best we know now."

"I don't wear." Her eyes met his without wavering. "I believe my record shows that."

Before Malori could speak again, Reeve cut in. She was wearing, he knew, but he had to gamble she'd hold out for a few more days. "If we could backtrack? We can assume that Deboque has already ordered the supplies you requested. An educated guess on where he'd procure them?"

"Athens," she said immediately. "I feel strongly that he'd draw from within his own organization. He feels totally secure, invulnerable if it comes to that. He wouldn't want to risk ordering from outside sources. From my other reports, we know that he keeps a warehouse in Athens. He has others, of course, but I think he'd go there because of its proximity to Cordina."

"We'll check our contact there and see if there's news of any explosives being moved." Malori noted it down. "With luck we'll close down his Athens branch once we have him here."

"The ISS won't move on Athens, Paris, London or Bonn until we have an airtight case on Deboque here." Hannah set down her tea. "That's a button I push, *monsieur*."

"*Bien.*" Malori obviously didn't like it, but nodded.

"Will the case be strong enough when Hannah receives the explosives?" Armand glanced at Hannah, then at Reeve. "Hannah has taken the contract, requested the supplies. Once they are delivered, can that be the end of it?"

Hannah started to speak, then subsided. She would let Reeve explain. He was family. "We would have enough for an arrest, possibly for an arraignment. Even with the supplies being traced back to Athens or another of Deboque's companies, it wouldn't be enough for a conspiracy conviction. He's careful enough to divorce himself from business dealings of this kind."

Business dealings, Armand thought as he drummed his fingers on the arm of the chair. "And his request that Hannah assassinate my family?"

"His hypothetical theory of what might happen if such a thing occurred," Reeve corrected. "Your Highness, I'm aware, very aware, of the frustration of not being able to close in on the evidence we have now. We had him once for over a decade, and it didn't stop him. If we want to crush Deboque once and for all, sever all these strings and hack away his control in Europe, we

have to have solid and indisputable evidence of murder and conspiracy. Hannah will give us that in a matter of days.''

Armand drew out a cigarette and shifted his gaze to Hannah.
''How?''

''The payoff.'' She felt herself on solid ground again. It helped
to have Malori there, sharp-eyed and just a bit disapproving.
''When Deboque is convinced I've completed the job, he'll pay
me off. As soon as money changes hands, we've got him.''

''He's not a fool. You agree?''

''No, Your Highness, he's not a fool.''

''But you will convince him you have murdered my family.''

''Yes. If you would look at this diagram, sir?'' She rose and
waited for him to accompany her to a table. With Reeve's help,
she stretched out a long roll of paper. ''The blueprints I smuggled
to Deboque show this wing as occupied by Prince Alexander and
his family. I gave Deboque the information that Princess Gabriella
and her family would also be staying here during the days before
the Christmas Ball.''

''I see. In truth, my son's family's wing is here.'' He skimmed
his finger to the opposite side of the drawing.

''The night before the ball, I'll set some charges here, and
here.'' She laid a fingertip on the areas. ''They'll be much smaller
than what Deboque assumes, but with Reeve's special effects
added, it should be quite a show. There will be some damage, sir,
but it will appear much worse, particularly from the outside, than
it really is. You'll need to do some replastering and painting.''

He lifted a brow, but she couldn't tell if he was amused. ''There
are areas of the palace that could do with some redecorating.''

''It will be imperative, of course, to clear this wing. Discreetly.''

''Of course.''

''Ten minutes before the explosion, I will leave to meet with
Deboque or his agent. The payment will be made after he considers the job done.''

''Have you considered that he would want to have the deaths
verified before he pays you?''

''Yes.'' Hannah straightened away from the diagram. ''To some
extent we'll use the press. In addition, I'm making it clear that
payment must be made that night, as well as arrangements for my
passage out of the country. Deboque has invited me to sail with

him. I shall accept.'' She pressed her lips together as Malori grumbled. ''The money will change hands because he'll believe I'll be easily accessible if anything has gone wrong.''

''And will you be?''

''I'll be with him.''

''The ISS will be covering both Deboque's villa and his yacht,'' Reeve cut in. ''The moment we have Hannah's signal, we move.''

''There is no other way?''

Again there was concern. This time Hannah found herself laying a hand on the prince's arm. On the arm of Bennett's father. ''We could perhaps tie him to other crimes. With the information I've been able to dig up in the last two years, we would have something, but it would take months, even years and we would have no guarantee. This is the only way, Your Highness, to stop him once and for all.''

With a nod, the prince looked over at Reeve. ''You agree?''

''Yes.''

''Malori?''

''It is more dramatic, and certainly more risky than one would like, but yes, Your Highness.''

''Then I will presume that you two will see to whatever details have yet to be seen to. I will expect reports every four hours.''

Recognizing dismissal Malori bowed. Even as Reeve rolled up the diagram again, Hannah was preparing to curtsy.

''Hannah, I'd like another moment, please.''

''Yes, Your Highness.'' She stood by the table, stiff and tense as the two other men left them alone. He would know of her feelings for Bennett, Hannah thought. Even in the brief time she'd been in Cordina, she'd learned that Armand was both astute and observant. He didn't merely rule from a throne, but behind a desk and in boardrooms. If his country was at peace and prosperous, it was largely because he knew how to govern, how to make choices and how to remain objective.

Yes, he would know, she thought again. And he would not approve. She was European. She was an aristocrat. But she was by choice and by profession a spy.

''You're uncomfortable,'' Armand began. ''Sit, please.''

In silence she took a seat and waited.

She looked like a dove, he thought. A small gray dove who

expected and accepted the fact that she was about to be mauled by a fox. Studying her, he had difficulty believing she would be the one to end the turmoil that had haunted his family for more than a decade.

"Reeve has confidence in you."

"I can promise it's not misplaced, Your Highness." She nearly relaxed. It wasn't about Bennett, but Deboque.

"Why did you agree to take this assignment?"

Her brow lifted because it seemed such a simple question with such a simple answer. "I was asked."

"And had the right to refuse?"

"Yes, sir. In such matters an agent always has a choice."

A prince didn't. He understood the difference, yet still didn't envy her. "You took the assignment because your superiors requested it."

"Yes, and because what Deboque does here has affected and could continue to affect my country and the rest of Europe. A terrorist, in whatever garb he chooses, remains a terrorist. England wants Deboque's hands tied, tightly."

"Your first consideration is country."

"It always has been."

He nodded again, knowing this could bring both joy and misery. "Did you choose your profession because you looked for adventure?"

Now she relaxed completely and laughed. The moment she did, Armand saw what had captivated his son. "Pardon, sir, I realize that the word 'spy' conjures up all sorts of glamorous images: foggy docks, Parisian alleyways, nickel-plated revolvers and fast cars. In truth, it's often tedious. In the past two years, I've done more work on telephones and computers than the average secretary."

"You wouldn't deny the danger involved."

"No." She sighed a little. "No. But for every hour of danger, there's a year of legwork and preparation. As for Deboque— Reeve, Malori, the ISS, have taken this plan step-by-step."

"Still, in the end, you'll be alone."

"That's my job. I'm good at it."

"Of that I have no doubt. Under normal circumstances, I would worry less."

"Your Highness, I assure you everything that can be done is being done."

He was aware of the truth of it and that, for the moment, his hands were tied. "And if a mistake is made, how will I comfort my son?"

She locked her fingers together. "I know, I promise you whatever happens, Deboque will be punished. If you—"

"I'm not speaking of Deboque now, but of you, and of Bennett." He held up a hand before she could speak again. "It is a rare thing for me to be able to speak as only a father. I ask you to allow me that luxury now, here in this room."

She drew in a breath and tried to be clear. "I realize Bennett is angry and upset because he wasn't told the reasons for my being here. I believe he feels a certain responsibility toward me because I'm here to protect his family."

"He's in love with you."

"No." The panic set in again, along with the shame and the desperate desire for it to be true. "That is, he thought, before when he believed me to be... At one time he began to feel a certain affection, but when he learned who—what I was, that changed."

Armand settled his hands on the arms of his chair. The ring of his office glinted in the lamplight. "My dear, are you any more clear on your feelings for him?"

She looked up. The dark eyes that watched her were kinder than they had been. Hard yes, he could be hard. But she could see now why his family and his country loved and trusted him. "Your confidence, sir?"

"You have it, of course."

"I love him more than I've ever loved anything or anyone. If I could change things, if I could go back and be what he thought I was, and only that, I swear to you I would." There were no tears. She had shed them once and had sworn not to do so again. Instead she looked down at her hands. "Of course, I can't."

"No, we can't change what we are. When we love, and love deeply, we can accept a great deal. Bennett's heart is very generous."

"I know. I promise you, I won't hurt him again."

His lips curved. She was so young, so valiant. "I have no fear of that. When this is done, I ask that you remain in Cordina for a few more days.''

"Your Highness, I think it would be best if I returned to England immediately.''

"We wish you to remain," he said again, and he no longer spoke as a father. He rose then, extending a hand. "You may want to rest before dinner.''

Left without a choice, Hannah stood and curtsied. "Thank you, Your Highness.''

Dinner was long and formal. Hannah was introduced to the Minister of State and his wife, as well as a German businessman who had interests in shipping and an ancient Frenchwoman who was some vague connection of the Bissets' and was visiting Cordina for the holidays. The Frenchwoman spoke in a husky grumble that kept Hannah straining to hear enough to make polite answers. The German spoke in short, loud blasts and was obviously delighted to have an invitation to the Royal Palace. Hannah was grateful that he was across the table so that she could avoid direct conversation with him.

Bennett wasn't there at all. A late board meeting at the museum had edged into a dinner for the Equestrian Society. Hannah tried to remember that Claude had been joined by two more guards who would keep Bennett annoyed and protected throughout the evening.

As the Frenchwoman hissed in her ear again, Hannah could only think Bennett the fortunate one.

Across the table, Eve sipped sparkling water and listened with apparent fascination as the German regaled her with stories of his business. Only when she turned to pick up her dessert spoon did her eyes meet Hannah's long enough for the humor to come through. Answering a question in low, polite tones, she rolled her eyes once, quickly, in a gesture that said everything. Then she was smiling at the German again and making him feel fascinating.

Hannah had to lift her glass to hide the grin. The royal were human after all. Not the same, not ordinary, but human. The child Eve carried might one day rule, but he would also laugh and cry and feel and dream.

She herself had loved a prince. Hannah picked up her spoon

and began to toy with the elegant chocolate and cream concoction in front of her. She'd given her heart to a man who was second in line to one of the few remaining thrones in Europe. In a few days, she could very likely give her life for him.

For that was the truth of the matter, she thought as the woman beside her droned on. It might have started as duty, to her country and to the organization she had chosen, but when it ended, what she did would be for Bennett.

It would never be possible to tell him, just as it hadn't been possible to say as much to his father earlier that evening. If she admitted what she felt to a superior, even with all the planning, all the time lost, she could very well be pulled out.

So she would say nothing, but she would feel. And feeling as she did, she would see Deboque finished, if she lived.... And then, Hannah admitted, it would be a choice between her captaincy and retirement. Fieldwork would be all but out of the question now. She didn't believe that she could ever maintain the pose of quiet, unassuming Lady Hannah again. Not now that she had loved and been loved by a prince.

It was nearly midnight before escape could be politely made. Hannah deliberated over a hot bath or quick oblivion in bed as she stepped into her room. Eve was insistent about returning to the Center the next day, so she would have no choice but to go along. Would the message come the next day, or would Deboque take her right down to the wire?

She'd walked into the center of the bedroom when the warning signals began to throb at the base of her neck. There was no one in the room. A quick glance showed her nothing had been disturbed. But...

Hannah took a cautious step back and opened the drawer of the bedside table. She took out her weapon. The light was low and at her back as she began to move toward the adjoining room. The door was slightly ajar, but that could have been done by one of the maids. Her feet were silent on the carpet as she crossed to it. With one hand she pressed on the panel so that it opened slowly and without sound.

There was nothing in the room beyond—nothing except the neat sitting room that smelled of the gardenias that lay moist and lovely in a bowl.

So it had been a maid, she thought, relaxing gradually. One of them had set fresh flowers in the sitting room, and—

It was then she heard a sound, material against material, and tensed again. Keeping the gun secure in her hand, she slid against the wall and into the room.

The little settee faced away from the door so she didn't see him until she was fully inside. Bennett lay sprawled on it, his tie unknotted and hanging, his shoes off and his face buried in a blue velvet pillow.

Hannah swore, but softly, as she lowered the pistol. He looked exhausted, and very much at home, she thought as she lifted a brow. Her first instinct was to tuck a cover around him, but there was still enough of the proper Lady Hannah in her to know that it would never do for Bennett of Cordina to be found snoozing in her sitting room. She started to bend down to him, then remembered the gun in her hand.

Almost curiously, she turned it over in her hand. It looked like a toy, but had already proven itself lethal. A part of her job, she thought. A part of her life. Yet she knew it was a part Bennett would find unpalatable. Moving back into her bedroom she secured it. She had to wake him and send him on his way, but she didn't have to keep a physical reminder of their differences close at hand.

She went back to him, and kneeling by the settee put a hand to his shoulder. "Bennett." She shook gently and received a mumbled response. Her lips curved. She had to resist the urge to brush at the hair tumbling over his forehead. In sleep, the energy, the amusement and the temper were put to rest. He looked as though he would be perfectly content to cuddle there, half on, half off the little sofa for days. Hannah bent closer and raising her voice gave him a quick, brisk shove. "Bennett, wake up."

He half opened his eyes, but Hannah noted that they focused quickly. Reaching up, he grabbed her earlobe. "Haven't you any respect for a dead man?"

"Ow!" She grabbed his wrist in defense, but she was already several inches closer. "If it's respect you want, I'll call a couple of the servants and have them carry you out, in state. Meanwhile, let go or I'll have to show you how easy it is to cause unconsciousness by applying pressure to certain nerves.''

''Hannah, you've got to learn not to be so flighty and romantic.''

''It's in the blood.'' She sat back on her heels to massage her ear. ''Bennett, why are you sleeping on my settee instead of in your own bed?''

''I don't know who designed this thing. Another foot longer and a man could be comfortable.'' He dragged himself up a bit so that his feet dangled over the arm. ''I wanted to talk to you.'' He rubbed both hands over his face. ''When I got in, I saw that we still had guests. I took the coward's way and used the back stairs.''

''I see. And Madame Beaulieu spoke so highly of you.''

''Madame Beaulieu doesn't speak, she hisses.''

''I know. I sat next to her at dinner.''

''Better you than me.''

''How gallant.''

''You want gallant?'' With one swing, he had her off the floor and stretched on top of him. He cupped the back of her neck with his hand, pressing as his mouth took hers quickly, completely.

''What does that have to do with gallantry?'' she managed after a moment.

He smiled and ran a finger down her nose. ''All the other women I've known have been impressed by it.''

Hannah drew back another inch. Smiling, she ran a finger down his throat, then up again. ''About those nerves I mentioned.''

He caught one wrist, then the other. ''All right then, tomorrow I'll look for a puddle to toss a cape over.''

''A safe enough promise since it hasn't rained in days.'' She started to shift, but he brought her close again.

''Stay. I haven't seen you at all today.'' His lips were warm and coaxing against her cheek. ''Do you know, Hannah, a man has to have you in his arms, has to have his lips against your skin before he catches your scent. Do you do that on purpose?''

She wore no perfume. It had to do with leaving no traces behind. ''You said you…'' He moved his lips to her ear. ''You wanted to talk to me.''

''I lied.'' His teeth closed gently over her earlobe. ''I wanted to make love with you. In fact, I had a devil of a time keeping my mind off that thought throughout a long and frustrating board meeting and a noisy dinner." He drew down the zipper at the back of her dress. "I had to give a speech." He found silk, thin, fragile silk, beneath the linen. "It was difficult not to babble when I kept imagining myself here, with you."

"I don't want to interfere with your official duties." With her eyes closed, she pressed her lips to his neck and let herself enjoy the gentle stroking of his hands.

"But you do, *ma mie*. I sat listening to the huffing and puffing of ten stuffy men who are more interested in paintings than people, and I imagined you sitting there with your hands neatly folded and your eyes solemn. And you were wearing nothing but your hair."

She'd slipped off his tie, but paused now on the third button of his shirt. "In the boardroom?"

"In the boardroom." Would he ever stop being fascinated by that dry, serious tone and those dark eyes? "You can see why I had such a problem concentrating." He didn't tell her he'd also dealt with unexpected tingles of fear as he'd pictured her with Deboque, at his mercy, helpless, alone. It was an image he hadn't been able to drown out in innumerable cups of coffee or glasses of wine. "So I came in here to wait for you."

"And fell asleep."

"I'd hoped you'd see the irony and reverse the fairy tale. Wake the sleeping prince with a kiss. Instead I got a shove."

With her hands framing his face, she drew his head up. "Let me make up for it now then."

She touched her lips to his, brushed, retreated, teased then touched again. She felt him tense his fingers at her back as she toyed with his mouth. Her tongue traced, her teeth nipped as heat built to a flash point. She didn't object when he pressed her head closer, when his mouth closed hungrily over hers. If he had longed for her through the day, his need had been no sharper than her own. They would take the night hours together.

She had his shirt unbuttoned and open. Her dress had slipped down, revealing the shimmer of honey-colored lace beneath. Bennett let his fingertips play over it while he absorbed the contrasts and delights that were his Hannah. He drew the pins out of her hair so that it flowed over her shoulders and his. The scent of it was as light and elusive as the scent of her skin. What witchery she had was an innate part of her rather than something that came from bottles and pots.

Fresh, real, his. Delirious from her, he tugged the dress down her body and let it fall to the rug.

And his fingers slid over the stiletto strapped to her thigh.

She stiffened, remembering the weapon the instant he discovered it. Passion cooled so swiftly, she shivered. When she drew away he didn't stop her.

"Bennett, I'm sorry." She'd forgotten there could be no apologies, no regret. His eyes were on hers, blank and flat, as he sat up. Because there was nothing for her to say, no way for her to remove the barrier, she lapsed into silence.

Her hair was a riot of honey-toned waves that fell over her shoulders and the silk that echoed the color. Her eyes, darkly, richly green, were solemn now as she waited for him to speak. Or to leave.

Fighting the first stirrings of anger, he let his gaze pass over her, the milk-pale skin, the slender curves, the delicate silk. She was what she'd convinced herself she was not—beautiful, stunning, desirable. On one long slim thigh strapped by thin strong leather, was a knife associated with dark alleys and smoky bars. Saying nothing, Bennett reached for it. She automatically caught his wrist.

"Bennett—"

"Be quiet." His voice was as flat and cool as his eyes. Hannah let her fingers fall away. Slowly, he drew the weapon from its sheath. It was warmed from her skin, small enough to fit into the palm of his hand. Until he pushed the button and the thin blade slid silently, lethally out. It caught the lamplight and glistened silver.

She wore it intimately, he thought. He wanted to ask her if she'd used it, but a part of him knew it was best to keep the question to himself for now. It weighed nothing, but sat heavy as lead in his hand.

"Why do you need this in the palace?"

She pushed a strap back onto her shoulder, then rubbed the skin there that was growing colder and colder. "I'm expecting word from Deboque. I can't be sure when or where it will come from.

Because I may have to respond to it immediately, it's best to be prepared.''

"What kind of word?"

"I think you should ask—"

"I'm asking you." His voice carried a lash he used rarely, but effectively. "What kind of word, Hannah?"

Hannah drew her knees up to her chest, wrapped her arms around them and told him everything. There could be no objection now, she reminded herself. He already knew too much.

"So we sacrifice a part of the east wing. Camouflage." He twisted the blade under the light. He knew, without doubt, he could have plunged it into Deboque's heart.

"The more genuine things seem, the more easily Deboque will be convinced. He won't part with five million dollars until he's sure Cordina is left without an heir."

"He would kill the children," Bennett murmured. "Even Alexander's unborn child. All for what? Revenge, power, money?"

"For all three. He would have his revenge on your father, his own power would grow from the chaos, and money would follow. It's his greed that will topple him this time, Bennett. I promise you."

It was the passion in her voice that had him looking at her again. Her eyes were wide and dry, but the emotion almost leapt from them. To protect his family, he thought as he tightened his hand on the handle of the stiletto. To protect herself. As suddenly as he'd fallen in love, he realized the full truth. Whatever she did, whatever she used didn't matter, as long as she kept herself safe.

He pressed the release and sent the blade back home. And he would see to that himself. After setting the knife aside, he reached over to unsnap the strap from her thigh. Her skin had gone cold, he discovered, though the room was warm. It stirred something in him that he recognized again as a need to protect. She didn't move, didn't speak and flinched only slightly when he rose. She was waiting for him to reject her, to dismiss her, to leave her.

He felt both her surprise and her doubt as he gathered her up into his arms. "You should trust me more, Hannah," he said quietly.

When she relaxed against him, when she let her head rest on his shoulder, he carried her to bed.

Chapter 12

The package was delivered in the most pedestrian of ways. It was carried by Dartmouth Shippers, one of Deboque's less profitable but most useful tentacles. It was marked with the return address of Hannah's aunt in England and stamped FRAGILE.

The only difficulty came from the fact that Eve was present when it was delivered.

"Oh, what fun!" Eve hovered around the package. "It's a Christmas present, isn't it? Why don't you open it?"

"It isn't Christmas," Hannah said mildly, and set the package on the shelf in her closet. She would turn it over to Reeve at the first opportunity.

"Hannah, how can you be so casual about it?" With nerves just below the surface, Eve poked around the room. "Didn't you ever search under beds and in closets for packages at this time of year?"

"No." Hannah smiled and went back to arranging the flowers Eve had brought her. "I never wanted to spoil Christmas morning."

"It doesn't spoil it, it only adds to the excitement." Eve glanced back at the closet. "Couldn't we just peek?"

"Absolutely not, though I can tell you the package probably contains five dozen homemade cookies—as hard as bricks. Aunt Honoria is nothing if not predictable."

"It doesn't feel like Christmas." Moody, Eve wandered to the window. She laid one hand protectively over the swell of her belly and fidgeted nervously at the curtain with the other. "The ballroom's being scrubbed and polished for the holiday, the tree's already trimmed. If I walk by the kitchens there are the most glorious scents, but it just doesn't feel like Christmas."

"Are you homesick, Eve?"

"Homesick?" Puzzled for a moment, she turned around, then smiled. "Oh, no. Alex and Marissa are here. I do hope my sister manages to get away from her art gallery for a week or two, but I don't miss the States really. It's just that everyone tries to pamper me, protect me by hiding things." Sighing, she moved to Hannah's dresser to toy with the little enameled box Bennett had admired. "I know how tense and worried Alex is, no matter how hard he tries to pretend everything's fine. Even when I talk to Bennett, his mind only seems to be half with me. It has to stop, Hannah. I can't bear to see the people I love torn apart this way."

She too would pamper, and protect by hiding things, but it was the only comfort Hannah could allow herself to give. "It's this Deboque, isn't it?"

Eve set the box down again. "How can one man bear so much hate? How can one man cause so much pain? I know, though after years I still can't really understand, I know that he won't be satisfied until he's destroyed us."

"It isn't possible for most of us to understand real evil," Hannah began, though she could and did understand it. "But I think we only add to it when we let our lives be affected so strongly."

"You're right, of course." Eve held out both hands. "Do you know how grateful I am that you're here? Without you I'm afraid I'd be moody and brooding all of the time. Brie's coming later today with all the children. We still have florists and musicians to deal with." She squeezed Hannah's hands as she drew a deep breath. "I hate being helpless. What I'd like to do is to go up and spit in Deboque's eye, but if all I can do is make things easier here, then I'll have to be content with that."

Hannah vowed, at the first opportunity, to spit in Deboque's eye for her. "Why don't you take me up to the ballroom and show me what's been done? I'd like to help." She wanted to help—and she wanted Eve away from the package that sat on the shelf in the closet.

"All right, but I want you to come to my room first. I have a present for you."

"Presents are for Christmas," Hannah reminded her as they walked to the door.

"This one can't wait." She had to get her mind off the undercurrents that were pressing on them all. Dr. Franco had already warned her that her tension could affect the child. "Pregnant princesses must be indulged."

"How clever of you to use that to your advantage when it suits you." They climbed a short flight of stairs and crossed to the next wing. "You said Gabriella would be here soon. Is the whole family coming today?"

"In force, this afternoon."

Hannah relaxed a little. It would be easy to transfer the package to Reeve and continue on with the plan. "Has Bennett put his treasure in the vault?"

"Treasure? Oh, his yo-yo." With her first easy laugh of the day, Eve entered her bedroom. "He adores that child, you know. I've never known anyone quite as good with children as Bennett. He puts an enormous amount of time into the Aid for Handicapped Children even though it takes away from his free days with his horses." She walked into the adjoining dressing room as she spoke. "Another reason I suppose I've been moody is that I know Bennett should be on top of the world right now, and he looks as though he rarely closes his eyes."

"On top of the world?"

"It's taken him six months and a lot of frustration to get approval for the children's wing in the museum. He finally pushed it over the top at the board meeting the other night, but not without a lot of work and fast talking. He didn't mention it to you?"

"No," she said slowly. "No, he didn't mention it."

"It's been his pet project for a couple of years. It took him months to find the right architect, one who'd mesh practicality with the essence of what Bennett wanted to do. Then, because the board wouldn't give an inch, he had the plans drawn up at his own expense. They're wonderful." Eve came back into the room carrying a long box. "You should ask him to see them sometime. He wanted it open, lots of windows so that the kids wouldn't feel closed in. The board mumbled and grumbled when he talked of sculptures the children could make contact with and illustrations from storybooks instead of Rubenses and Renoirs and Rodins under glass.''

"I didn't realize he was so...involved.''

"Whatever Bennett does he does with total involvement. His idea was to introduce children to art through media they could understand and enjoy. Then there's a section that's reserved for paintings and models the children make themselves.''

Eve set the box on the bed and smiled. "I'm surprised he didn't tell you about it. Usually no one's safe. It's taken him two years of planning and six months of fighting to get this project off the ground.''

"It sounds lovely.'' She felt her heart twist and expand and fill with more love. "One often thinks of him as a man only interested in horses and the next party.''

"He enjoys the image, but there's more to Bennett than that. I thought that the two of you had gotten quite close.''

"Bennett's very kind.''

"Hannah, don't disappoint me.'' A little tired, Eve sat on the edge of the bed. "He watches you walk out of a room and waits for you to come into one.''

"He does?''

"Yes.'' Now she grinned. "He does. With all the anxiety and all the tension of the last weeks, at least I've had the pleasure of seeing Bennett fall in love. You do care, don't you?''

"Yes.'' It was almost over. Some deceptions were no longer necessary. "I've never known anyone like him.''

"There isn't anyone like him.''

"Eve, I don't want you to think, or to hope, for something that isn't going to happen.''

"I'm entitled to think and hope as I choose.'' She lay a hand on the box beside her and patted the lid. "But for now, open your present.''

"Is this a royal command or a request?''

"Whatever it takes to get you to open it. Please, I'm dying to see if you like it.''

"Well, it's against my principles to open a present before

Christmas, but..." Giving in, Hannah lifted the lid. She pushed aside the layers of tissue paper, then stood staring.

It glittered like a jewel and shimmered like fire. The dress was the rich, luscious green of emeralds with thousands and thousands of tiny beads that caught the afternoon light.

"Take it out," Eve insisted, then too impatient for Hannah, drew it out of the box herself.

The silk swayed, whispered and settled. It was cut straight, with a high neck that glistened with its beaded band at the throat. The arms would be bare well onto the shoulders as would the back before the material draped again and followed a long line to the floor. It was a dress made to glitter under chandeliers and shimmer under moonlight.

"Tell me you like it. I've driven the dressmaker crazy for a month."

"It's beautiful." Tentatively Hannah reached out. The dress shivered with life at the barest touch. "Eve, it's the most beautiful thing I've ever seen. I don't know what to say."

"Say you'll wear it to the Christmas Ball." Delighted with herself Eve turned Hannah toward the mirror and held the dress in front of her. "Look what it does to your eyes! I knew it." Laughing, she pushed the dress into Hannah's hands so she could step back and take it in. "Yes, I was sure of it. With that skin of yours... Oh yes," she said as she tapped a finger to her lips. "Bennett's going to take one look and babble like an idiot. I can't wait to see it."

"I don't think I should—"

"Of course you should, and you will because I refuse to take no for an answer." She stepped forward, eyes narrowed to pull free a lock of Hannah's hair. "My hairdresser's going to have a whack at you, too."

"That sounds a little ominous." As much as she longed to, she couldn't let herself go. The plain and proper Lady Hannah Rothchild wouldn't have had the nerve to wear such a dress. "Eve, it's lovely, you're lovely, but I don't think I'm made for a dress like this."

"I'm never wrong." Eve brushed off denials with a careless flick of her wrist. She may have been a princess for only two years, but she'd always been determined. "I've spent too long in the theater not to know what suits and what doesn't. Trust me, and if that's too much, do me a favor as a friend.''

They *had* become friends, no matter what the initial reasons were or the ultimate goal. What harm would it do to accept? It was very possible that she wouldn't even be in Cordina for the ball. "I'll feel like Cinderella," she murmured, and wished it could be so.

"Good. And you should remember the clock doesn't always strike twelve."

But it did. Hannah remembered Eve's words as she and Reeve moved silently through the palace. The game was almost up, and so was her time.

The package had contained the explosives she'd requested and a coded message. She was to make her move that night and meet Deboque's agent at the docks at one a.m. The payoff would come then.

"This has to work," Hannah muttered as she carefully set the first charge. The equipment she used now was ISS-approved. The package she'd received was already being traced. Deboque would soon lose Athens and very much more.

"From outside the walls, it'll look as though the fire's burning out of control," Reeve said, working as quickly and competently as she. "The blasts are rigged for more noise than power. We'll blow out a few windows and put on a hell of a show while Malori and his men will remain here to bank it if necessary."

"Is the prince with them now?"

"Yes, Armand is filling the rest of the family in. Malori objects, but I think you're right. No harm can come from them knowing what's under way at this point, and a lot of anxiety can be relieved." He thought of Gabriella. After tonight, perhaps even the nightmares would fade.

"I couldn't bear to think of Eve waking up to the explosion and thinking it Deboque's doing. And Bennett? He's safe in the family wing?"

"Bennett's safe," he said, and left it at that. "I'm giving you ten minutes. That's enough time for you to get off the grounds. The dock's secure, so that if anything goes down there, we'll be on top of you. I'll be on the boat that has Deboque's yacht under surveillance. We'll move in the moment we have your signal. Hannah, I know the wire's risky. If you're searched—"

"If I'm searched, I'll deal with it." The mike was an ISS masterpiece that resembled an intricately worked locket that rested inches below the pulse in Hannah's throat.

"If he sees through this, he'll move fast."

"I'll move faster." She laid a hand on his when he started to speak again. "Reeve, I have a stake in this too. I don't want to die."

He looked at her for a moment as a woman. "I have a reputation for keeping my partners alive."

She was grateful he could make her smile. "I'm counting on it. But if something goes wrong, would you give Bennett a message for me?"

"Of course."

"Tell him…" She hesitated, unused to trusting her feelings to anyone. The clock struck the hour, midnight, and she prayed the magic would hold. "Tell him I loved him, both parts of me loved him. And there are no regrets."

She left through the main door and drove slowly toward the gates. In minutes, the guards who'd not been informed of the camouflage would react in precisely the way it was expected. Anyone watching the palace would see the shock and the action. For now, she passed through the gates with only the briefest of checks.

She kept an eye on her watch as she drove, hearing the minutes tick off and thinking of Bennett. He would be safe now. Whatever happened that night, he and his family would be safe. If Deboque paid her, he would be arrested for conspiracy. If he killed her, he would be arrested for the murder of an ISS agent. The end justified the means.

Hannah stopped the car, waited and heard the explosion. Malori had promised loud, and had delivered. She opened the door and stood beside the car a moment. The palace was a dim white blur against the night sky, but the east wing was lit like day. The fire was impressive from here, and knowing that none of Deboque's men could get much closer, she was satisfied. Within twenty minutes one of Malori's men would leak word that the Royal Family, save Armand, had perished in the explosion.

By the time she arrived, the docks were deserted. Word of trouble had already spread this far. Hannah parked her car in the shadows, then left it behind to wait in the light. She made an excellent target.

The boat anchored off the coast appeared to be a small, expensive pleasure yacht. Several times during the day, a dark-haired woman had appeared on deck, to sun, to read. From time to time, she'd been joined by a man, bare chested, young, bronzed. They'd sipped wine, cuddled, slept. The watch on the *Invincible* had kept it under surveillance, and had taken bets as to whether the two lovers would have sex under the sun. They'd been disappointed.

Belowdeck, the ISS had everything from television monitors to grenade launchers. Eight men and three women crowded into the hulled-out cabin and waited.

Bennett had been confined to the cabin since an hour after dawn. For the past three hours, he'd swallowed nothing but coffee and impatience. He'd watched the monitor until his eyes had blurred. Not once had Deboque appeared in the focus of the long-range camera. He wanted to see him. By God, he wanted to look into his eyes as the trap snapped shut. But more, so much more, he wanted to hear over the transmitter that it was done, and Hannah was safe.

"MacGee's boarding." The man with the headphones spoke, and continued to smoke. Seconds later, Reeve slipped into the already crowded cabin. He was dressed in black from head to foot. Even his face and hands were smeared with it. He took off his sailor's cap and tossed it aside.

"First stage is finished." He nodded toward Bennett. "From beyond the gates, it looks as though the east wing is devastated. The ISS is theatrical."

"The family?" Bennett asked as he looked back to the monitor.

"Safe."

He reached for the bitter, cooling coffee beside him. "Hannah?"

"Word should be coming in within minutes. Some of our best men are on the docks as backup."

Bennett shot him a look that held for a long moment. He'd wanted to be at the docks, as close by as possible. He'd run into the stone wall of his father, Reeve and Malori on that, and eventually had had to concede. If he'd been spotted, the entire operation would have been put in jeopardy.

Now it was only Hannah, he thought, only Hannah who risked it all.

"Deboque hasn't been seen all day."

"He's there." Reeve lit a cigarette and prepared to wait. "He wouldn't want to be too far away tonight."

"Contact." An agent on the port side of the cabin lifted a hand to his headphones. "She's made contact."

The breeze off the water was cool and the night was clear. Hannah recognized the man who approached her as the one who had come into the smoky little bar. He came alone and empty-handed.

"Mademoiselle."

"My part of the bargain is met, *monsieur*. You have the compensation?"

"It's a nice night for a ride on the water."

The yacht. She felt a ripple that was both unease and excitement. "You understand I'm no longer in a position to return to Cordina?"

"This is understood." He gestured toward a small motorboat. "Your needs will be seen to."

As before, she had a choice. She could draw her weapon now and take him in. If luck was with them, he would trade his own freedom for Deboque's. She couldn't risk Bennett's safety to luck. Without a word, she stepped into the boat and sat.

Her life was in her own hands now, Hannah thought, and folded them. However the night turned out, Deboque would be ruined.

Her contact didn't speak again, but his gaze shifted back and forth over the dark water. They were all waiting and watching now. Because the night was clear, Deboque's yacht stood out white and stark on the sea. She could see three men on deck, Ricardo and two others. It was Ricardo who assisted her onto the yacht.

"Lady Hannah, it's a pleasure to see you again."

There was something in his eyes, something smirking and self-satisfied. She knew then, as surely as if he'd held a knife to her throat, that she wasn't meant to leave the *Invincible*. Her voice was cool and calm when she spoke, and she hoped, clearly received across the span of water.

"Thank you, Ricardo. I hope this won't take long. I'm forced to admit I'm uneasy in Cordinian waters."

"We sail in an hour."

"For?"

"A more comfortable climate. The radio has announced the tragic deaths of several members of the Royal Family. Prince Armand is grieving in seclusion."

"Of course. Cordina is left without its heart, and without its heir. Monsieur Deboque has been informed?"

"He waits for you in his cabin." Ricardo reached out a hand for Hannah's bag.

"Are employees always searched, Ricardo?"

"We can dispense with that, Lady Hannah, if you will allow me to hold your weapons." He drew out her pistol and pocketed it. "And your knife?"

With a shrug, Hannah lifted her skirt to her thigh. She watched Ricardo's gaze dip and hold there as she drew out the knife. She pushed the release. On either side of her guns clicked.

"An admirable weapon," she said mildly as she held the blade up to the light. "Quiet, stylish, utilitarian." She smiled and sent the blade sliding back into place. "And one I would hardly use on the man who is about to give me five million American dollars." She dropped the knife into Ricardo's palm, knowing she had only her wits as defense now. "Shall we go? I enjoy the smell of money when it's still warm."

He took her arm in his surgeon's hand and with considerable panache, led her belowdeck to Deboque's cabin.

"Lady Hannah." The cabin was lit with a dozen candles. It was a Beethoven sonata this time that poured gently through the speakers. He wore a burgundy jacket and rubies. Blood colors. A magnum of champagne sat nestled in a silver bucket. "How prompt you are. You may leave us, Ricardo."

Hannah heard the door shut behind her. She didn't have to be told Ricardo would be stationed outside it.

"A pleasant ambience," she stated. "Most business isn't transacted in candlelight."

"There's no need for formalities between us now, Hannah." He was smiling as he moved to the champagne. "The announcements from Cordina are a bit hysterical and tragic." The cork rushed out. Wine bubbled to the lip. "I felt a small, tasteful celebration was in order."

"I rarely refuse champagne, *monsieur,* but its taste goes down so much more smoothly when I have money in my hand."

"Patience, my dear." He filled two tulip glasses and offered one. His face was marble pale in the dim light, his eyes almost black and full of pleasure. "To a job well done and a rich, rich future."

She touched her glass to his then sipped. "An excellent vintage."

"I've come to understand you prefer the excellent, and the expensive."

"Precisely. *Monsieur,* I hope you won't be offended if I say while I appreciate the wine and soft light, I would appreciate them more after our business is completed."

"So mercenary." He ran his fingers down her cheek. The candlelight flattered her, he thought. In time she would bloom under his hands. A pity he couldn't take the risk and keep her with him for a few months. He had only an hour for her. But much could be accomplished in an hour. "You'll forgive me, but my mood is very light. I find myself wanting to celebrate your success, our success."

His hand roamed down her throat, within inches of the microphone. She caught it at the wrist and smiled. "You set the mood, *monsieur,* first by taking my weapons. Do you prefer defenseless women?"

"I prefer amenable women." He lifted his hand to her hair, digging his fingers into its richness. Hannah steeled herself for the kiss. She could show resistance, but not revulsion. "You're strong," he murmured and brought his mouth to hers again. "I prefer that as well. When I take you to bed, you'll give me a fight."

"I'll give you more than that. After I've seen the money."

He tightened his fingers, bringing pain quickly enough so that she gasped. Then they relaxed with his laugh. "Very well, *mon amie cupide.* You will see your money, and then you'll give me something in return."

When he turned his back to reveal a hidden safe, Hannah scrubbed her lips with the back of her hand. "I've already given payment for payment."

"The lives of the Royal Family." He spun the dial as Hannah's heart began to drum. "Five million dollars to assassinate the Bissets. Five million dollars to give me a full plate of revenge and the sweet dessert of power. Do you think it so much?" His eyes glittered as he turned back to her with a large case. "My dear child, you could have asked ten times as much. For over ten years I've plotted, and twice very nearly succeeded in killing a member of the Royal Family. Now, for the paltry sum of five million dollars, you have disposed of them all for me."

"That's it," Reeve announced as Deboque's voice came over the receiver. "Move in. Slowly."

Bennett's hand closed over his brother-in-law's. "I board with you."

"It's out of the question."

"I board with you," Bennett repeated in a hard, icy voice. Moment by moment, he had listened and sweated as Hannah stood alone with Deboque. As Deboque put his hands on her. As Deboque prepared to pay her for the murder of everything and everyone he loved. "Give me a weapon, Reeve, or I go unarmed."

"My orders are to keep you here."

"If it were Brie?" Bennett's eyes were hot and reckless. "If it were Brie, would you stay behind and let others protect her?"

Reeve looked down at the hand closed over his. It was strong and capable. And young. Then he looked into the eyes that were darker than his wife's but that held the same passions. Rising, he took a .45 automatic from the arsenal.

They would move now, Hannah thought and struggled to keep her voice impassive. "Do you tell me this now so I can regret?" She laughed and walked to the desk. "Five million will do me nicely. I plan to invest and to live quietly in Rio for the next few years."

He kept his eyes on hers as he unlocked the case. The money was there, but would be for his own uses. "You have no desire to continue in my employment?"

"Unfortunately, that would be risky for both of us after the events of tonight."

"Yes." His thoughts exactly. But he opened the lid so that she would at least have the pleasure of seeing the money before he killed her.

"Lovely." Clinging to the role, Hannah stepped forward and lifted a thick stack of crisp hundreds. "Do you know how sensual new money smells?" She fanned the stack.

"Indeed." He slid the top drawer of his desk open. Inside was an elegant pearl-handled revolver. He thought it just to kill her with style. He closed his fingers over it when the first shots were heard from above.

Hannah swung toward the door, hoping he would take excitement for alarm. "What game is this?" she demanded. She slammed the lid on the case, and taking the money headed for the door. Her hand closed over the knob.

"Remain still." Deboque warned. The gun was in his hand now and pointed at her heart. A fine film of sweat pearled over his brow as the sound of running feet pounded over their heads. He held the trigger lightly, but didn't press home. Whatever trouble was on deck, he didn't want to draw it down to him. "The case, Hannah."

"A double cross?" Her eyes narrowed as she calculated how much time she dared stall him. "Yes, you would easily have paid me ten times this if you never intended to pay me at all."

"The case." He started toward her, slowly. Fear was blossoming inside him, not of death, not of defeat, but of prison. He would never survive behind bars again.

Hannah waited until he was two feet away, then with both hands on the handle, swung the heavy case at his gun arm.

Deboque's men, whether in loyalty or fear, fought madly. Gunfire exploded back and forth from the two boats. A spray of bullets from a machine gun smashed in the wood above Bennett's head and sent splinters raining down his back. He watched a man fall over the rail of the yacht and into the water below.

Already the firing from Deboque's side was coming more sporadically, but time was speeding by. And Hannah was still with Deboque. Alive, Bennett told himself as he aimed and fired. She was alive. He'd know if it was otherwise because his heart would have stopped. But there was an urgency churning in him, more than the wild night and the scent of blood. Moving with it, he worked his way to stern and slipped into the water.

The night was rent with shooting and the shouts of men. He saw a man dive from Deboque's yacht and swim frantically toward a shore that was ten miles off. His hand brushed a body that floated facedown. ISS or the enemy, he didn't know. While the fighting raged, he swam silently around the yacht.

Because it was nearly over, Reeve signaled for his men to close in. It was then he noticed that Bennett was no longer beside him.

"The prince." His throat went dry with panic. "Where is Prince Bennett?"

"There." One of the men spotted Bennett just before he disappeared around the stern of Deboque's yacht.

"In the name of God," Reeve breathed. "Move in fast. Prepare to board."

There was no one on the starboard side as Bennett dragged himself on deck. There was the occasional blast and rip of bullets, but the shouting had died. He'd spent an hour during that long, endless day belowdeck studying Hannah's diagram of Deboque's yacht. He went to find her.

She'd managed to knock the gun across the room, but he was faster and stronger than he appeared. Even as she dove after it, Deboque was on top of her. One hand closed over her throat, shutting off her air. Hannah freed one arm and brought her fist into his windpipe. Then both of them were gasping. She reached forward and her fingers scrabbled over the handle of the gun. She swore in both pain and fury as he dragged her back by the hair. For thirty grim and exhausting seconds, they struggled on the cabin floor. Her blouse tore at the seam. Beneath, bruises were already forming. She bloodied his mouth but was frustrated, unable to land a disabling injury.

Wrapped like lovers they rolled toward the gun again. She reached again, nearly grasping it. Out of the corner of her eye, she saw the fist coming and dodged. The blow was glancing, but strong enough to send her reeling. Then she was looking into the barrel of his gun.

She'd prepared herself to die. Struggling for breath, she braced. If she could do nothing else, she could fulfill her vow to spit in his eyes. "I'm an ISS agent. The Bissets are safe, and you've nowhere to run."

She saw the fury come into his eyes. She smiled at him and waited for the bullet.

When Bennett broke into the room, he saw Deboque crouched over Hannah, pointing a gun at her head. It happened in flashes, so quick that immediately afterward he couldn't be sure who had fired first.

Deboque's head swung around. Their eyes met. As the gun swiveled from Hannah's head toward Bennett's, she screamed and swung out. Two triggers were pressed. Two bullets exploded.

Bennett felt one whiz by him, so close that his skin shuddered and heated from it. He saw the blood bloom on Deboque's chest an instant before he crumpled onto Hannah.

She started shaking then. All the years of training dissolved as she lay trembling under the dead man. She'd prepared for her own death. That was duty. But she'd seen the bullet smash into the wood less than an inch from Bennett's face.

Even when he came to her, pushing what had been Deboque aside and gathering her close, the trembling didn't pass. "It's over, Hannah." He cradled her, rocked her, pressed kisses to her hair. "It's over now." Instead of the satisfaction, even the glory he'd expected to feel there was only relief. She was safe. And he was going to see that she stayed that way.

"You might have been killed. Damn you, Bennett, you were supposed to be home."

"Yes." He glanced up as Reeve rushed into the room. "We'll both go there soon."

There were tears on her cheeks. Brushing them aside, Hannah struggled to stand. She faced Reeve, but had to draw several breaths. "I'm ready to make my report."

"The hell with that." Bennett swept her into his arms. "I'm taking her home."

Epilogue

She'd slept around the clock. It wasn't until over twenty-four hours had passed that Hannah realized that Dr. Franco, the Bissets' personal physician, had given her a sedative.

She'd woken rested and resentful. And though she'd hated to admit it, aching.

The doctor had fussed for another full day, murmuring over her bumps and bruises in his kind but implacable tones. Because his orders to keep her in bed had come from His Royal Highness, neither doctor nor patient had a choice but to obey.

She complained. Even though visitors came often, she fidgeted at the inactivity. Word was delivered through Reeve from ISS headquarters, word that should have delighted her. Deboque's operation had crumbled. She'd been given her promotion. Hannah sulked in bed and wished for escape.

It was Eve who ultimately provided it on the night of the Christmas Ball.

"You're awake. Wonderful."

"Of course I'm awake." Cranky from two days in bed, Hannah shifted. The fact that her ribs were still sore to the touch only made it worse. "I'm going crazy."

"I'm sure you are." Smiling, Eve sat on the edge of the bed. "And I'm not going to embarrass you by going on again about how grateful we all are for everything you did. What I'm going to do is give you Dr. Franco's latest orders.''

''Oh, spare me.''

''Which are, to get up, get dressed and dance until dawn.''

''What?'' Hannah pushed herself up, wincing only a little. ''I can get up? Do you mean it?''

''Absolutely. Now here.'' Rising, she lifted Hannah's robe. ''Put this on. My hairdresser's expected any minute and she's going to do her magic on you first.''

''Magic.'' With a sigh, Hannah lifted a hand to her hair. ''More like a miracle at this point. Eve, as much as I want to get up and be doing, I don't think the ball is the best idea.''

''It's the perfect idea.'' After helping Hannah into her robe, she leaned over to smell the clutch of gardenias by the bedside. ''From Bennett?''

''Yes.'' Hannah gave in enough to touch the waxy leaves with her fingertips. ''He brought them this morning. I haven't seen a great deal of him.'' Shaking off the mood, she tied the belt of the robe. ''I know how busy you've all been, with the press conferences and public statements to clear up the entire mess.''

Eve lifted a brow. She decided against telling Hannah that Bennett hadn't moved from her bedside throughout the first night. There was enough romance in her for her to want them to discover each other for themselves.

''Speaking of messes, you should see the east wing. Mostly glass. It'll take the maids weeks to get it all. Hannah.'' On a long breath, Eve took both her shoulders. ''I'm going to embarrass you. I know it was an assignment, but whatever reasons brought you to us, you've given us peace. There's nothing I can say or do that can repay that. My child...'' She smiled a little. ''Marissa and this one are safe. I know what Deboque had planned to do.''

''It's over now, Eve.''

''Yes.'' Solemn, Eve kissed both of Hannah's cheeks. ''I owe you my life, and the lives of all of my loved ones. If there's anything I can ever do, and I speak as your friend and as the wife of the heir of Cordina, you have only to ask.''

''Put it behind you, and me. Eve, I've never been able to make and keep friends. I'd like to feel that's changed.''

Eve studied the woman she was just beginning to know. "I have two sisters, the one I was born with and the one I was given by Alexander." She held out a hand. "I'd like to have three."

"Your Highness." One of the young maids hovered at the doorway. "I beg your pardon, but Madame Frissoutte is here."

"Wonderful." Eve hooked her arm through Hannah's. "Prepare to be transformed."

It was a transformation, Hannah thought as she studied herself in the glass. Her hair, curled wild as a gypsy's down her back, was caught away from her face with two glittering combs. The dress sparkled and shimmered as it draped from her throat to her ankles. She was clever enough with makeup to have covered the bruises on her arms and face.

All she needed were glass slippers, she thought with a half laugh. More illusion. But if this was to be her last night with Bennett, she would take it. There would be no regret when the clock struck twelve.

There was already music in the ballroom. Hannah slipped in, as was her habit, and absorbed the brilliance. Mirrors were polished to reflect the glitter and glamour of gowns and jewels. Chandeliers shone like stars. It was all shimmering silver and icy blue with draping garlands and shiny balls. On a tree that towered to twenty feet were a thousand crystal angels that caught the light.

He'd been watching for her. Waiting. When he saw her the breath simply left his body. The couple he'd been chatting with fell silent, brows lifting as he walked away without a word.

He caught both her hands even as she dipped into a curtsy. "My God, Hannah." For the first time in his life his tongue tied itself into knots. "You're exquisite."

"It's Eve's doing." He wore dress whites, with the insignia of his rank and a sword at his side. However many ways she remembered him, and she knew there would be many, she would never forget how he looked just now. "Everything is so beautiful."

"It is now." His hand slipped around her waist as he swirled her into the waltz.

It was magic, she thought. The music, the lights, the mirrors. For hours they danced together, spinning around and around the room, leaving the food and the wine for others. When he circled her out to the terrace, she didn't object. There were still a few minutes until midnight.

Drawing away, she went to the rail to look out at Cordina. Lights glowed in festive colors for the holiday. The breeze held a springtime warmth and scent.

"Do you ever tire of looking at it?"

"No." He stood beside her. "I think it means even more now."

She understood, but wanted to keep even Deboque's ghost at bay. "In England, it would be cold, sleeting. There might be snow by morning, or we'd have gray, heavy skies. All the fires would be lit and the rum warmed. The cooks would have all the puddings and turkeys cooking so that you'd smell Christmas everywhere."

"We can't give you snow." He lifted her hand and kissed it. "But we could offer the fire and warm rum."

"It doesn't matter." She drew a deep breath. "When I'm home, I'll remember standing here with Christmas almost upon us. I'll remember it smelled like roses and jasmine."

"Would you wait here a moment?"

"All right."

"Just here," he said, and kissed her hand again. "I'll only be a minute."

When he was gone, she turned back to look out again at the lights and the sea. She would be home in a few days, and in time, perhaps Cordina would seem like a dream. Cordina, she thought, but never Bennett. She lifted her face to a star but didn't dare wish.

"I have something for you."

With a half smile, she turned, then caught the scent. "Oh, chestnuts!" With a laugh, she took the bag he offered. "And they're warm."

"I wanted to give you something from home."

She looked up. There was so much to say, and nothing that could be said. Instead, she rose on her toes to kiss him. "Thank you."

He brushed his fingers over her cheek. "I'd thought you'd share."

Hannah opened the bag and with her eyes closed, drew in the scent. "Isn't it wonderful? Now it feels like Christmas."

"If Cordina can be enough like home, perhaps you'll stay."

She opened her eyes, then lowered them quickly to the bag. "I have orders to return at the end of the week."

"Orders." He started to reach for her, but held himself back. "Your position in the ISS is important to you." He couldn't prevent the trace of resentment. "I'm told you received a promotion."

"A captaincy." She bit her bottom lip. "I'll be working behind a desk for a good while. Giving orders." She managed to smile.

"Have you ever considered giving it up?"

"Giving it up?"

It was the blank, puzzled look that worried him. Was it possible she could think of nothing else but her duty to her organization? "If you had something to replace it. Is it the excitement that pulls you?" He cupped her face in his hand, turning it toward the light so that the bruise Deboque had put there showed in a shadow.

"It's simply what I do." She drew a breath. "Bennett, we never talked about what happened on the yacht. I never thanked you for saving my life. I suppose it's because I've been used to taking care of myself."

"I would have killed him for this alone," he murmured as he traced the bruise on her cheek. She started to step back, but a look from him stopped her. "Don't back away from me. I haven't spoken before this because Franco was concerned with keeping you quiet and undisturbed. But dammit, I'll speak of it now."

He stepped closer so she could feel it, the recklessness, the barely controlled fury. "I had to sit and wait and listen to you deal with that man. I had to stay where I was, helpless while you were alone with him. And when I broke into that cabin and saw him holding a gun at your head, I had one hideous flash of what life would be like if you weren't in it. So don't back away from me now, Hannah."

"I won't." She steadied her breathing then lay a calming hand on his. "It's over, Bennett. The best thing for everyone is to put it aside. Cordina is safe. Your family is safe. And so am I."

"I won't accept your risking your life again for anyone."

"Bennett—"

"I won't." He caught her hair in his hands and kissed her, but this time with a force and power that left her breathless. He dragged himself away, reminding himself he had a plan and meant to see it through. "Are you going to try those chestnuts or just stand there smelling them?"

"What?" She had the bag locked in a viselike grip. She swallowed and opened it again. "I'm sure they're wonderful," she began, knowing she was going to babble. "It was so thoughtful of you to..." She broke off when she reached in and touched a small box. Puzzled, she drew it out.

"There's an American tradition. A box of candied popcorn with a prize in it. I had an urge to give you your Christmas present early."

"I've always been very strict about waiting until Christmas morning."

"I could make it a command, Hannah." He touched her cheek again. "I'd rather not."

"Well, since it *is* the Christmas Ball." She opened the lid and for the first time in her life felt faint.

"It was my grandmother's. I had it reset but it meant more to me to give you this than to choose another from a jeweler." He touched her hair, just the ends of it with his fingertips. "She was British, like you."

It was an emerald, fiery, stunning, made only more brilliant by the symphony of diamonds that circled it. Just looking at it made her light-headed. "Bennett, I couldn't take something like this. It belongs in your family."

"Don't be thick-headed." He took the bag from her to set it on the wall. The scent of chestnuts mixed with the summer fragrance of roses. "You know very well I'm asking you to marry me."

"You—you're carried away," she began, and this time did step back from him. "It's everything that's happened. You're not thinking clearly."

"My mind's never been more clear." He took the box from her, slipped the ring out and tossed the container aside. "We'll do it my way then." Taking her hand, he pushed the ring on. "Now, I can drag you back inside and announce our engagement—or we can talk about it reasonably first."

"Reasonably." How was it she needed to laugh and cry at the same time? "Bennett, you're being anything but reasonable."

"I love you—unreasonably then." He pulled her into his arms and covered her mouth with his. He could feel her heart thud, hear her breath shudder, taste both need and fear. "I'm not letting you go, Hannah, not now, not tomorrow, not ever. You'll have to exchange captain for princess. Believe me, it can be every bit as wearing."

Was it magic, or was it a dream come true? Her head was still spinning as she tried to get a grip on common sense. "You know I'm not the woman you cared for. Please, Bennett, listen to me."

"Do you think I'm a fool?" He spoke so mildly she was deceived into thinking him calm.

"Of course I don't. I only mean that—"

"Shut up." He caught her face in his hands, and she saw by his eyes he was anything but calm. "I thought the woman I first fell in love with was an illusion." He gentled as he brushed his lips over her cheeks. "I was wrong, because she's right here. There was another woman who made my mouth dry every time I looked." His kisses were more urgent now, more possessive. "She's here as well. It's not every man who can love two women and have them both. And I will have you, Hannah."

"You already have me." She was almost ready to believe it could be real, and true and lasting. "But even you can't command a marriage."

He lifted his brow, arrogant, confident. "Don't be too sure. You told me once you wanted me. Was it a lie?"

"No." She steadied herself with two hands on his chest. She was crossing a line in her life, one that allowed for no deceptions. He was offering her a chance to be herself, to love openly and honestly. "No, it wasn't a lie."

"I ask you now if you love me."

She couldn't speak. From deep within the palace the clock began to strike. Midnight. She counted off the gongs and waited for the illusion to fade. Then there was silence and she was still in his arms. Looking down, she saw the ring glow against her finger. A promise. A lifetime.

"I love you, and nothing's ever been more true."

"Share my home." He caught her ring hand in his and pressed his lips to the palm.

"Yes."

"And my family."

She twined her fingers with his. "Yes."

"And my duty."

"From this moment."

She wrapped her arms around him. She lifted her face for his kiss. Below and as far as eyes could see, Cordina spread out before them and prepared to sleep.

*　*　*　*　*

In the morning the bright, bold sunlight slanted directly across Del's eyes. He shifted, seeking the dark and rather amazing dream involving a lanky redhead with a sexy voice and gilded eyes. And rolled on his bad side.

He woke cursing.

His mind cleared, and he remembered the lanky redhead was real. The fact that she was real, and sleeping under the same roof, made him a little uneasy about the dream. He also remembered the reason the classy dish was in the spare bed was that her car was in a ditch, and the power and the phones were out.

That meant, rather than a hot shower, he was going to take a dip in a cold pond. He gathered what he needed and started downstairs. He stopped when he heard her singing.

The pretty voice with its faintly exotic accent seemed out of place in his cabin. But he couldn't fault the aroma of fresh coffee.

The coffee was heating on the fire, and she was in the kitchen, rooting around in the pantry.

He saw that the floor had been washed. He had no idea it had any shine left in it, but she'd managed to draw it out. There were wildflowers stuck in a tumbler on the kitchen table.

She'd opened the kitchen window, the door to the mudroom and the door beyond that so the fresh and balmy air circled through.

She stepped back, a small can of mushrooms in her hand—and muffled a short scream when she saw him behind her.

He hadn't clomped in this time. He was barefoot and bare chested, clad only in a pair of sweatpants and his sling.

His shoulders were broad, and his skin—apparently all of it— was tanned a dusky gold. The sweatpants hung loose over narrow hips, revealing a hard, defined abdomen. There were fascinating ropy muscles on his uninjured arm.

She felt the instinctive female approval purr through her an instant before she saw the sunburst of bruises over his right rib cage.

"My God." She wanted to touch, to soothe, and barely stopped herself. "That must be very painful."

"It's not so bad. What're you doing?"

"Planning breakfast. I've been up a couple of hours, so I'm ready for it."

"Why?"

"Because I'm hungry."

"No." He turned away to find a mug. If he didn't have caffeine immediately, he was going to disintegrate. "Why have you been up a couple of hours?"

"Habit."

She knew most people's fantasies of a princess were dramatically different from the reality of the life. In official mode, it was rare for her to sleep beyond 6:00 a.m. Not that Delaney Caine knew she *had* an official mode.

"Bad habit," he muttered, and strode back to the coffeepot.

She got her own mug and went back with him. "I took a walk earlier," she began. "It's a gorgeous day and a beautiful spot. The forest is lovely, simply lovely. And there's a pond. I saw deer watering, and there's foxglove and wild columbine in bloom. It answered the question for me why anyone would live here. Now I wonder how you can bear to leave it."

"It's still here whenever I get back." He drank the first mug of coffee the way a man wandering in the desert drank water. Then closing his eyes, he breathed again. "Thank you, God."

"The power's still out. We have three eggs—which we'll have scrambled with cheese and mushrooms."

"Whatever. I've got to wash up." He picked up his travel kit again, then just stopped and stared at her.

"What is it?"

Del shook his head. "You've got some looks, sister. Some looks," he repeated with a mutter, and strode out.

It hadn't sounded like a compliment, she thought. Regardless, her stomach fluttered, and kept fluttering when she went back to the kitchen to mix the eggs.

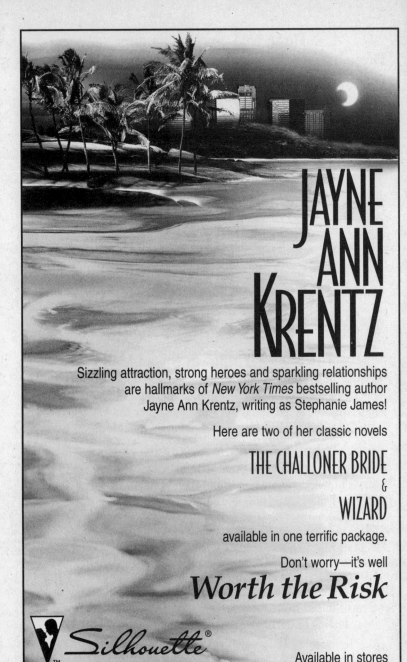